DON + B.A. Lester

Ride With Me

THOMAS B. COSTAIN

Ride With Me

DOUBLEDAY & COMPANY, INC.

Garden City, New York

To
MOLLY

CONTENTS

INTRODUCTION

I BEGAN THIS STORY with the sole intent of relating in fiction form the exploits of an unusual soldier who has been allowed to drop out of sight. As the work progressed, however, the glamour and excitement of the Napoleonic period took possession of me and I found myself obsessed with a desire to get down on paper a detailed picture of those exciting days, particularly as I began to realize that the situation which existed then has been reproduced today with amazing faithfulness in even the smallest matters. That I yielded to the impulse is evident in the size of this volume; for which I apologize, being completely aware that I have succeeded in capturing no more than a fleeting glimpse of those most colorful and prophetic times.

Despite the liberties I have taken with my readers, carrying them from England to the Iberian Peninsula, then back again to England, only to pick them up bodily and transport them to Russia for a view of the tragic business of the Moscow retreat, finally setting them down in France after the Hundred Days to watch the closing scenes of the Bonapartist saga, I have not succeeded in telling the whole story of Sir Robert Wilson. That extraordinary fellow had many adventures which I have had to pass over. It was particularly hard to refrain from telling of the part he played in the feud between George IV and his frowzy German queen but that episode, one of the most spectacular of all, lies far outside the bounds of my story.

I am sure that all who ride with Robert Thomas Wilson in these pages will agree that he was born in the wrong period. He had so many qualities, counted faults at the start of the nineteenth century, which would have been virtues in the days when knights obeyed only the dictates of honor and followed unquestioningly when the finger of adventure beckoned. Lack of discipline accounted for all the black marks on his record; but it may be recalled that it was against Charlemagne's orders that the stout Roland turned at bay in the valley of Roncesvalles to provide chivalry with its brightest annal. Had Wilson lived in the Middle Ages, he also would have inspired great legends. Instead he was born into the England of the last Georges where he was most completely out of place. He was treated, with some justice no doubt, like a disobedient schoolboy. It may very well be, however, that it was not Wilson who was at fault so much as the times in which he lived.

The story I have set down is, of course, a compound of fact and fiction. Wilson did all the remarkable things with which he is credited, although it has been necessary to summon imagination for the fictional embroidery of them. Many other real characters appear at intervals in the pages which follow: Wellington, Dumouriez, Horne Tooke, Kutuzov, the Lavalettes, Michael Bruce, Captain Hely-Hutcheson, La Bellilote. The main characters are all purely fictional as are the situations of the story except as they concern the participation of the historical characters.

I hasten to explain that the newspaper called the *Tablet* never existed. I have taken the liberty of borrowing some details from the history of the London *Times* (particularly in the sending out of the first war correspondent and the introduction of power presses) but the troubles and bickerings of the Ellerys are purely imaginary and in no single respect a reflection of the lives of the members of the Walter family who owned the *Times*.

Many books were read or consulted for the background of the story, between four and five hundred to be more exact, and so a complete bibliography would serve no purpose save to use up valuable space. Instead I wish to put on record my debt to a few writers whose skillful winnowing of pure gold from the dross of the period has been particularly helpful to me:

Giovanni Costigan, *Sir Robert Wilson, a Soldier of Fortune*. Carola Oman, *Napoleon at the Channel*. Comtesse de Boigne, *Memoirs*. August Ludolf Friedrich Schaumann, *On the Road with Wellington*. Robert Blakeney, *A Boy in the Peninsular War*. Marianne Baillie, *Lisbon*. Sir Robert Wilson, *The French Invasion of Russia*.

Ride With Me

BOOK I

England

FRANCIS ELLERY leaned against the side of a bus which apparently had abandoned the idea of going any further in the fog. He was tired and his stiff knee was hurting him abominably. It was with a deep sense of relief that he heard the sharp voice of Sergeant Cripps far ahead give the order for them to break up and get home as best they could.

Borcher the hatter, who had marched with him at the end of the squad, adjusted his scratch wig with blue fingers and then buttoned his tunic tightly over the yellow waistcoat which proclaimed his Liberal tendencies. "What are ye down for tonight, Ellery?" he asked.

"Committee for London defense. And you, Borcher?"

The hatter snorted as he hobbled off aggrievedly into the dense mist. "Waterworks patrol. But I'll never get there in this fog. A lot of blasted nonsense anyway. This damned Corsican certainly plays hob with our lives."

"M'sieur," said a pleasant feminine voice from above, "is it possible you can tell us where we are?"

Ellery looked up and was able to make out that all the upper seats on the bus were occupied by people in evening clothes. "French," he thought. Many times he had seen *émigrés* starting off like this for dinner and unconcernedly taking the cheapest way of getting there.

A male voice said in French, "Allow me to attend to this, Gabrielle, if you please," adding in slow and halting English, "You in blue coat, where is Can-non Square?"

Looking up at the row of expectant heads, Frank answered: "Cannon Square is a good quarter mile from here. I'm afraid you'll have to chance the rest of the way on foot. The bus will never get you there now."

The masculine voice lapsed into French again. "This filthy London! These stupid English! Tonight there will be a soft haze over Paris and people will be riding in open carriages to dinner or the opera. I can't

stand to live among these savages any longer. I think I shall cut my
throat tonight and be done with it." He leaned over the rail and called
down brusquely in English, "A shilling, my man, to show the way."

Frank laughed. "As it happens, I'm going in your direction and I'll be
glad to guide you without any fee, handsome though your offer is." He
paused and then added in French: "I forgive you, m'sieur, for not finding
London to your liking on a night like this. But may I point out that many
thousands of exiles from your gentle France have found it a safe and
friendly sanctuary?"

He heard the pleasant feminine voice expostulating in a low tone.
"Jules, will you *never* learn? Must you always say such things? One can
tell from his voice that he's a gentleman."

"I mean it," said the man impatiently. "I shall cut my throat tonight."

Through the open door of a tavern a hoarse voice said, "Ye won't see a
'and afore yer 'umping face in 'arf a 'our." This was no exaggeration.
Already the fog was settling down like a damp blanket, with blinding,
choking insistence, blotting out the buildings, filling every crevice, turning the lights from shopwindows into faint yellow smudges against the
pervading gray. Voices heard at a distance of more than a dozen feet
seemed to issue from the air with a suggestion of ventriloquism. It was
a lucky thing, Frank said to himself, that he knew every foot of this
part of London.

The French party was climbing down the steps of the bus with much
talk and laughter. He wondered that they could be so gay. It was the
talk of London that most of them had been forced to accept any form
of menial work which offered and that they subsisted on almost nothing.
This was largely hearsay, however, for the refugee colony kept exclusively to themselves and had little to do with their English neighbors.

The owner of the pleasant voice proved to be a young girl with a worn
cashmere shawl around her shoulders. The rest were shadowy figures to
him, even when they had reached the ground and stood about in an expectant group, but somehow he could see her as clearly as though she
were on a floor of a ballroom with candles by the hundred. She was
wearing a Mary Queen of Scots cap, and under its tartan band her
reddish-brown hair curled closely. Her face was a slender oval in which
her dark and lively eyes seemed unusually large. He could see that her
feet (skirts were being worn much shorter than ever before this season)
were very trim in a fragile pair of velvet slippers and that the hand
clasping the shawl around her neck was small and white. She was so
lovely, in fact, that he had a tendency to stammer when he addressed
her.

"If you can spare the time, mademoiselle, I will try to find sedan chairs for you and your friends."

The man who had offered him the shilling, and who had followed immediately after her down the steps, did not favor this idea. Frank saw that he was tall and quite handsomely attired in lavender coat with a flowing cravat and a well-powdered wig.

"We're late as it is, Gaby," said the dandy. "The Comtesse will think we're not coming and will be having a perfect tantrum."

The girl nodded and then said to the Englishman: "I think we shall have to walk, m'sieur. Will you be so very kind as to show us the way, then?"

Frank bowed. "I know this section quite well, but it will be necessary to proceed with the greatest caution. I'm going to walk close to the buildings so I can feel my way along. You had better follow in single file, and I suggest you join hands. It's very easy to become separated in a fog like this."

The dandy muttered to himself in French, "What an abominable situation!" But the girl said in gay tones: "I'll follow after you, m'sieur, and I shall hold on to your coattails. I hope you won't think it too undignified, but we can't afford to lose *you*. Jules, take this end of my shawl. It will be like a game."

Frank thought, "I'm going to play follow-my-leader with the court of Versailles." The disgruntled Jules was saying, "But, Gaby, I would rather you held *my* coattails and I took his." The rest of the party fell into line with more talk and laughter than before. Some of them were elaborately dressed, and all of the women had jewels sparkling on their necks.

"Thieves are sure to be out on a night like this," said Frank. "You must all hold tight to your purses and other valuables."

Behind him the girl whispered with a suggestion of a laugh: "Don't worry about that. I'm quite sure we haven't a sovereign between us. As for the jewels, they're all copies. The good *uncle* got the originals long ago."

He led the way slowly, with a quite perceptible limp, until the corner was reached, conscious every step of the way of the light tug of her hand. Here he turned cautiously to the right. "The way now is narrow and rough," he called. "Step with the greatest care." He dropped his voice. "It's very muddy, mademoiselle. Your shoes will suffer, I'm afraid."

She seemed to be enjoying the adventure. "Then it's all for the best. My shoes are quite old, and if they get very muddy my father will have to allow me another pair."

"Have you been in this country long?"

"Nearly fifteen years. I was so young when we left France that I have no recollection of it at all."

"Then England must seem like home to you."

"No, m'sieur." Her tone was quite decided. "We live to ourselves, you know. We've been taught we must remain French in everything, and most particularly in our thoughts. It's hoped we shall be returning home soon. My father has rented our present place for many years but he refuses to take a lease. He says it would show a lack of faith if he did. Most of the others do the same. Lately, though, it has seemed to some of us that—that it will still be such a very long time."

The impatient voice behind them said, "You're doing a great deal of talking, Gaby."

"It's no concern of yours, Jules. And, if you please, don't tug so hard on my shawl. You'll choke me."

Frank said to himself, "She likes to talk to me." The thought set his heart beating fast. Nothing seemed more important than for this lovely member of the exiled colony to have a good opinion of him. Aloud he said: "I'm afraid you're right, mademoiselle. It will be a long time before you can hope to return to France. Napoleon is more firmly settled than ever. And now that Russia is joining with him against us——"

"But, m'sieur, it's not certain that the Tsar will desert us!"

"I'm very much afraid it is. I'm in a position to know because I publish a newspaper, the *Tablet*." He said this with the deliberate intention of identifying himself in her mind and, perhaps, of impressing her a little. "We've been given official information on the secret clauses in the treaty that the Tsar signed with Napoleon at Tilsit. They call for a declaration of war against Great Britain, and we expect it any day now."

He thought he detected a suggestion of admiration for the Corsican ruler of France when she said: "He has won so many victories! The armies of France are so strong that sometimes we think he can never be beaten."

"Sometimes I think you talk too much," grumbled Jules.

"Was your father in the French Army?" asked Frank.

"No, m'sieur. The aristocracy of France is divided into three classes. We are of the court, not the army. All of us here are of the court."

The unfriendly Jules said, "Gabrielle!" and then lapsed into a torrent of rapid French which Frank could not follow. He caught the name De Salle, however, and immediately jumped to the conclusion that his beautiful companion was none other than Gabrielle de Salle, the acknowledged belle of the colony. She would be a great heiress when Napoleon fell and the estates of the Royalists were restored. He had heard it said that the Duc de Berri, third in line for the throne, always paid her marked attention when he was in London. Frank could still feel the light pressure of her hand, but suddenly she seemed to be thousands of leagues removed from him. A daydream which had been growing rosily in his mind as they moved so carefully through the thick gray mist began to dissolve.

The cellar was being dug for a new building at the next corner, and a torch blazed briskly atop the bastion of planks around it. Pausing to consider the best course to follow, Frank saw that the girl was taking advantage of the illumination to look him over carefully. He became acutely aware of his limp and of the ill-fit of his blue tunic of the St. George Marching Association. "She'll think I'm a regular scarecrow," he said to himself.

What she saw was a thin young man with friendly and alert dark eyes in an angular face. He was not at all handsome, she decided, although there was something pleasant about his face; perhaps it was a suggestion of intelligence in the width of his brow or the straight bridge of his long nose. What she noticed most about him was an air of eagerness, as though he expected much of life and was in a hurry to meet it. This made her feel sorry for him, but she could not have explained why. It may have been a conviction that his spirit would be checked by the lagging gait of his crippled knee.

"M'sieur, why do you carry a broomstick?" she asked as they began to edge around the plank barricade.

"I belong to a London company of Fencibles," he explained in a rather self-conscious tone. "They're being organized all over England again to meet the threat of invasion. This is the third time I've joined. First was in '98 when we were so sure Boney was coming over. Then we got feverishly to work in '04, when he had his army back of Boulogne and was collecting a fleet of barges. This time it's certain that he'll try it. There aren't rifles to go around, so we drill with broomsticks."

There was a hint of a laugh in her voice. "Can you be turned into good soldiers that way?"

"Sergeant Cripps doesn't think so. He gave us such a dressing down this afternoon that I haven't recovered my self-respect since."

This, he realized, was a mild report of what had happened. Looking them over with a blistering eye, the five-foot-two martinet had said: "Ye're a poor lot, gem'men, and that's the sullem truth. Ye come out as a matter o' jooty but atter ye does yer bit o' drill ye goes home and eats yerselves dizzy on mutton and steamed pudding. There isn't one o' ye as has lost a inch abart the tripe line, 'cepting Mr. Ellery, who hasn't none to spare. Let me tell ye this. It's only bloody hard fighting what's going to count, and ye'd better get that through yer heads. We'll be lucky if we're alive three months from now, and our wives and childers as well. This is going to be war, and we're all in it—right up to our bleedin' necks! Nah then, do ye want me to make a fair imitashun o' fighting men outa ye? Or do ye want to go on playin' sojer with broomsticks in yer nice white mawleys?"

It had been Frank himself who answered. "We're with you, Sergeant. Every man here, I'm sure, wants to do everything you think necessary." There had been a reluctant spatter of voices to confirm this.

"Very well." The sergeant had glared along the line. "From now on ye'll be treated like enlisteds. Company! 'Shun!" Forty broomsticks had snapped up to freshly braced shoulders. "Throw yer chests out and pull in those suet puddin's ye call stummicks. When I'm through with ye today, ye'll ache in every muscle o' yer bodies. I won't be satersfied with less than a blister on every blasted heel in the squad."

He had been as good as his word. Frank had blisters on both heels, and only the sudden rise of the fog had saved him from the ignominious necessity of dropping out.

"If Napoleon does come over, will it be very bad for us?" asked the voice behind him.

"The British Navy may be able to hold him off. That's our only hope. If he manages to land his army in anything like full strength, it will be very bad for us, mam'selle."

A few minutes later he said: "This is Cannon Square. What number do you want?"

"Number 16. On the south side."

"It faces the gate in the center garden," added Jules.

"Then here we are." Frank drew his tinder pistol from a coat pocket and pressed down with his thumb. For a wonder it caught fire with the first impact of the trigger. He climbed the steps and held the light to a brass plate on the door. "Yes, this is number 16. But the name seems to be Billings."

"We go to the top floor," said the girl. "Have you much farther to walk, m'sieur?"

"A few squares only, thanks."

One of the other men had mounted the steps and was ringing the doorbell. Jules called to him indignantly. "You know it's my privilege to enter first."

The man on the steps looked down over his shoulder. "Must we stand on ceremony on a night like this, De Vitrelle?" he demanded.

"The rules apply to all conditions of weather," declared Jules emphatically. "And in all places, even this miserable London. You know that as well as I do, Fortier."

The girl brushed past him and walked up the steps. "If you're going to be such a great donkey, Jules, I'll settle the matter by entering first myself. What do your laws of precedence say about that?" She turned and bowed to Frank. "It was very kind of you to help us out of our difficulty, m'sieur."

"I'm happy to have been of service. Good evening, Mademoiselle de Salle."

"Good evening, m'sieur."

So he had been right! She was Gabrielle de Salle, and so far above him that what little was left of his daydream crashed about him now in complete dissolution.

The rest of the company began to press up the steps. Some of them wished him good evening. The door had swung open, projecting a faint ray of yellow light into the pea-soup thickness of the fog. He watched Gabrielle de Salle walk in first, her lovely head thrown back as though in defiance of the ceremonious Jules. The episode was over.

"I'm afraid that I'll never see her again," he said to himself.

As he stumped homeward he thought dispiritedly how right Borcher had been in his parting remark. The Corsican had indeed played hob with the life of Francis Ellery.

Through the nineties the *Tablet* had begun to pay such large profits that Joseph Ellery had purchased Caster Towers. He had been promised a peerage, and the prospects of the family had looked bright indeed. Frank, the eldest son, was going into the army. He had always been keen on the idea of soldiering and had devoted the year that most sons of gentlemen spent on the Grand Tour in making a ground study of the battlefields of Frederick the Great. He could hardly wait to get into a uniform. Caradoc, the second son, was aiming for a political career; he was a born leader, everyone agreed on that. The third son, Humphrey, was not old enough to figure in any definite plans, but in due course a pleasant niche would be provided for him; the church perhaps, or the management of the farms, with a good marriage to consolidate his position. It had been taken for granted that there would always be level-headed fellows to manage the *Tablet* for them and to insure a continuous supply of the golden eggs.

The invasion scare upset all these pleasant plans. Frank had organized a company of Fencibles and had seen to it that fifteen-year-old Caradoc was put in charge of a squad. He knew the rest of the family were secretly quite sure that Carr would make a much better soldier than he; and at the start it had looked as though they might be right. Red was the color chosen for their uniforms, and stalwart young Carr had looked like a Viking at the head of his company. He proved a careless Viking, however, managing to discharge his musket at the wrong moment. Most of the buckshot had lodged in Frank's knee.

Everyone had seemed as sorry for Caradoc as for the victim of the accident. They had patted him on the back and assured him that it wasn't his fault at all. Caradoc himself had been contrite in his bluff way. "Great God, but I'm sorry, old fellow," he had said as he helped carry Frank off the field. "Wouldn't have had this happen for anything in the world. Still, it'll toughen you up for the real thing. We all need a cod of toughening up. I know that I do; someone ought to give me a load of buckshot too." To their father he had explained in a whisper: "Didn't know there was a charge in it, Pater. Well, it'll take more than a few slugs of lead to stop old Frank."

But the slugs of lead did stop old Frank. A bone in his knee had been shattered, and from that time on he used a cane. He had been compelled to resign his command of the Fencibles; and the urge for soldiering which had so completely possessed his mind and soul had to find release in the writing of a book on Frederick's campaigns.

The threat of invasion upset the plans of the Ellery family in other ways as well. With every pair of eyes in the nation fixed on that line of coast behind which lurked the lightning armies of the Corsican ogre, conditions had become very unsettled. Merchants showed a decided disinclination to spend money for advertising. The supply of golden eggs became less certain. Two footmen were dismissed at Caster Towers, and the pocket money of the three sons was cut in half. Joseph Ellery became glummer as the anxious months and years rolled by, and on occasions his sound judgment deserted him. Twice he lashed out in print at the top men in the government. The first time it was intimated to him that the promised peerage would be withheld; the second time he was placed under arrest and actually spent several hours in a sour anteroom at the Old Bailey before the papers arrived for his release. The incident did something to his spirit, and after that his conduct of the paper was both indecisive and unproductive. A week after William Pitt, disheartened by the Napoleonic victories, turned his face to the wall, Joseph Ellery signed his name in an uncertain hand to a complicated and crabbed will and then turned his face to the wall also.

For nearly two years now Frank had been in charge of the newspaper, and, in spite of the fact that everyone disagreed heartily with all his decisions, he had been successful with it. The circulation had come up to five thousand, and the volume of advertising was larger than in the best days of his father's control. The profits were so considerable that his socially ambitious mother kept Caster Towers filled with guests. A seat in the House had been secured for Caradoc, and a commission in a regiment of the line had been purchased for Humphrey. Frank realized, however, that he was getting little thanks for his pains. One of the clauses of the will provided that all points of policy should be settled at the monthly board meetings, and invariably he found opposition to his plans, led by Caradoc, whose ideas ran along arbitrary lines. Only by the exercise of great patience and diplomacy, with the help occasionally of Aunt Francilea, who owned a tenth and had a shrewd brain in her old head, was he able to keep a free hand for himself in the matters that counted.

Not that he cared particularly. He considered what he was doing an interlude and he was not concerned over the loss of money which sometimes resulted from this interference. He was always content to have his mother draw on his personal share of the profits to pay for her lavish entertaining. She was angling to get Lady Mary Murreys, only daughter of their neighbor, the Duke of Westgate, as a wife for Caradoc, and that was bound to prove expensive. Caradoc was making friends fast in political circles. In the family a feeling of certainty existed that another boy premier would soon rise to dispute the fame of Billy Pitt, but in moments of inner candor Frank was not completely sure of this.

As he limped along, sparing his blistered heels as much as possible, he thought how sadly everything had been mixed up. Caradoc should have been the eldest son; he was born to be a landlord, to take a seat in the Peers, to make a brilliant marriage and raise a handsome family. He, Frank, would gladly sell his birthright for a sound pair of legs and a chance to play a man's part in the struggle against Boney. He smiled grimly as he considered that here he was, soldiering at last, as a private in an awkward squad of volunteers, and barely able to keep pace with his overfed companions, carrying a broomstick instead of a sword!

Boney was playing hob with many other lives. He thought of the worn shoes of Gabrielle de Salle, the thinness of her old shawl. If it had not been for the Corsican, the royal line of France would have been restored long before this and she would have been back in Paris, living the luxurious life of a member of the aristocracy of the court. She, and all the unhappy refugees in London, had much more reason for complaint than he had.

2

ALL THE OTHER HOMES on the south side of Dacre Square formed a solid
terrace, and so the Ellery town house took on an air of importance by
standing back in a garden of its own, with a standoffish stone fence and
a forbidding high iron gate. The lights which penetrated the fog from
all the windows on the first two floors warned Frank that his mother had
come to town and was entertaining at dinner. He paused at the gate, so
utterly tired that he dreaded the thought of facing guests. From where he
stood he could see the outline of the Tablet Building on the north of
the square, and he decided that the mist was beginning to thin a little;
at any rate his eye could follow the sharp angle of the spandrel above
the main entrance, and there was a curl of smoke visible from each
chimney.

"I ought to have looked in for a few minutes," he thought. The foreign
newspapers were due from the post office that afternoon, which meant
the whole staff would be kept busy. Oh well, Cope would have things
in hand.

He felt guilty nevertheless. He knew that his desk would be heaped
high with mail and damp proofs marked RUSH, and that old Clayhorn
would be waiting to pounce on him. That ancient pest would be pacing
up and down the corridors, his head full of complaints and suggestions.
It would be a relief to escape this daily inquisition for once. Old Clayhorn had been his father's business manager, and by some quirk in
Joseph Ellery's clouded mind he had been left a tenth interest in the
business. Perhaps the old publisher had foreseen how it would work
out and had planned it that way. No longer capable of serving actively,
old Clayhorn spent his time in furtive observation of everything that
went on, quick to detect any departure from the established way of doing
things. He slunk in and out of the pressroom; he dug into the ledgers
like a clawing terrier after moles; he peered into all the tiny offices with
a cheap round watch cupped in a greasy hand; he jotted down notes
on a cuff rancid from long wear. And each evening at five forty-five to
the second he would come pattering on eager tiptoe into the corner office
which had been Joseph Ellery's and was now occupied by Frank. He
never failed to begin his long recital of error and shortcoming with either
one of two opening salvos: "I feel you ought to know——," or "Now,
Mr. Francis, your father would never have allowed this——"

Fancies will flock into an exhausted mind which would never find lodgment there at any other time. It seemed to Frank there was something symbolic about the struggle the lights of the *Tablet* were making to show through the fog. In much the same hesitant way the press of the country was moving toward the right of free opinion and expression. There were times when he felt bitterly concerned about it, as his father had been before the paper began to pay so handsomely that its revenues were worth conserving at any price. Most publishers, he knew, were unhappy under the restrictions imposed on them, although they did nothing much about it. Perhaps they were waiting for someone to take the lead. Despite the depth of his feelings in the matter, Frank was quite sure he would never be the one. He was no Jack Wilkes and he had no taste for notoriety; and in any event his interest in publishing was limited to performing for the time being the work which circumstances had forced on him. As soon as he could, he intended to relinquish the control of the *Tablet*.

They had not waited dinner for him. When he made his belated appearance in the long and narrow dining room, Caradoc was seated at the head of the table with their mother on one side and a rather nice-looking girl with honey-colored hair on the other. Frank was surprised to see Lady Mary here, for the old Duke of Westgate had been showing some exasperation lately over her open infatuation for Caradoc. Her cheeks, he noticed, were flushed (sitting beside his handsome brother would account for that), and she was dressed rather better than usual in something pink. She was the first to notice him, and called out in a happy voice: "Well, Frank, you *are* late. I don't think it very nice of you when you knew I was coming up with your mother."

"But I didn't know it. I had every expectation of dining alone tonight on a grilled bone and a bit of cheese."

"Francis, I sent you a note." His mother's voice carried a definite suggestion of annoyance, and her blue eyes were frowning at him under her fringe of reddish hair. She was still a very pretty woman.

"I'm sorry but it never reached me, Mother." There was only one chair left, at the foot of the table, and he slipped into it, happy to find that Aunt Francilea was his neighbor. She patted his hand under the table and whispered, "Watch your step, young man. The Queen of Sheba is very angry with you."

"Francis!" When his mother used that tone all talk was certain to stop. She had a way of accenting her words, as though she thought in capital letters. "The note was sent this afternoon. I must say, you show little Pride of Family. Didn't you remember what an important Occasion this was?"

"You mean because Carr was making his maiden speech in the House today? I didn't forget." He added, smiling at his brother: "I was sorry to miss it, Carr. I'm sure you gave a fine performance and put Billy Pitt completely in the shade. But a drill was called at the last minute and I considered it my duty to attend. Defense comes ahead of everything now, of course."

Caradoc waved an amused hand. He was looking more striking than usual in a suit of blue broadcloth and a black stock which overflowed the low V of his waistcoat. "You certainly take this invasion scare seriously," he said. "I wish you had been there to hear me, old man. I don't believe in false modesty, you know, and so I don't mind saying I gave a rather good account of myself."

"You were wonderful, Caradoc," declared Mrs. Ellery. "I felt as I listened to you that it was the Start of an Epoch. But that means nothing to Francis, it seems."

"Come, Mater. I'm going to make many speeches, and Frank will have plenty of chances to hear me."

"Of course I will. I'll be listening to him speak from the treasury benches before long." The elder son's smile vanished as he went on. "That is, if Boney doesn't come over and use the House as a printing plant for his invasion medals."

Their mother sniffed impatiently. "There you go again. I declare, you never think of anything else. Your mind seems to run in a perfect groove."

Caradoc said expansively: "I was talking to a group of big men in the government the other day. Perceval wasn't one of them, but it was plain that some were in his confidence. They agreed that the danger of invasion was over. Nelson ended it for all time at Trafalgar. I think with you, of course, that we must take steps to reorganize the Fencibles. We mustn't leave any stones unturned. But—well, I'd put the fear of invasion out of my mind if I were you, Frank."

"There!" said Mrs. Ellery. It was clear she considered the matter settled.

Purdy, the butler, who traveled back and forth between Caster Towers and the town house in the wake of the mistress, whispered in Frank's ear: "The soup's cold, Mr. Francis. And I would hardly recommend what's left of the turbot, sir. Just the head and tail and a scrag of bones. Will you have beef or mutton, sir?"

Aunt Francilea, who was eating mutton with her usual zest, said: "This is fine billy-butter, Frank. Better have some."

"Mutton," said Frank.

He looked around the table with a weary air. There were a dozen guests, all of them friends of the second son. Across the table a pair of young bucks were deep in a discussion of their morning golf. One of them was saying: "That ass of a Winters turned up in a cherry-dery coat instead of the club uniform. Shockin' bad form! He was so angry when I played my ball against his on the green and sent it slapping back into the whins that he wouldn't give up the hole when he couldn't find it. A shockin' bad sportsman, really!"

The other nodded and plunged instantly into his own experiences. "I was in every water track and rabbit scrape on the course," he mourned. "And every time I used a timber club I knocked the leather off a ball. There were feathers all over the place. A dozen balls ruined at a shillin' apiece! But I made two rounds, by Gad! Ten holes in one day!"

Most of them were younger members of the House, and the general conversation was all of politics, of what Castlereagh had done and what Canning, that infernal puppy, had said.

Frank was too tired to eat. It was just as well, for his slice of mutton was cold. He took a few mouthfuls and then laid down his fork. He whispered to Aunt Francilea, "Were you in the House?"

The old lady glinted at him down the length of her long nose. "I was there. As your mother says, it was quite an Occasion."

"Was Carr in his best form?"

There was a moment's hesitation and then Aunt Francilea inclined her head toward his ear. "He looked positively magnificent. You know that way he has of squaring his shoulders and throwing back his head? Whenever he did that I thought every woman in the gallery would swoon with delight. Poor Mary Murreys was in transports."

"But what about the speech?"

"I don't remember a word of it."

"Francie, what are you saying?" demanded Mrs. Ellery suspiciously.

"I'm telling Frank about Caradoc's speech."

"I hope," interjected Lady Mary eagerly, "that you won't forget the passage about the Gracchi."

"I was just coming to it," said Aunt Francilea dryly.

The conversation swung back to politics at once. Someone remarked bitterly on the fact that Canning had worn trousers that afternoon, a clear indication that he was not a gentleman. They went at once into the ten-year-old controversy, most of them fanatically favorable to breeches. To Frank's surprise, however, Caradoc was disposed to hedge.

"Well, now," he said, "I'm beginning to have doubts. You all know I've stood out for the good old way. Breeches show a leg to advantage, and I don't mind acknowledging that I'm rather proud of my shanks. But George Brummell"—by some quirk of mind he always referred to the famous Beau in this manner—"George Brummell has invented a way of buttonholing trousers snugly around the ankles. It's quite neat, I must say; and you all know what will happen if George Brummell really takes to wearing 'em himself."

Frank was surprised that Caradoc, who took the lead himself in practically everything, showed such a tendency to defer to the famous Beau in matters of deportment and dress. As far as he knew, his brother had never met George Bryan Brummell, but he dragged his name into conversation all the time.

He, Frank, was all in favor of trousers because they enabled him to conceal the deformity of his knee; and he was sure there were sounder standards of gentility than what a man wore on his legs.

The dessert proved to be a black currant pudding, which Frank detested. He contented himself with a small piece of cheese, therefore, and a glass of madeira. Slipping back into his chair, he let his thoughts drift to the adventure in the fog. Although he had enjoyed no more than a few glimpses of the French girl, he found that he remembered every line of her face, every expression, every intonation of her voice. Gabrielle de Salle! A beautiful name, he thought; it sounded in his ears like a bar of music.

He finished his glass of madeira and got to his feet. "Will you excuse me, Mother?" he asked. "I'm behind in my work as a result of today's drill."

Caradoc looked up at once to ask, "Who was on the House today?"

"Stemper, of course. He's our best man."

The younger brother nodded. "Stemper's good enough. A little prosy perhaps, but he gets the substance of a thing down. His report will be satisfactory, I think."

"It had better be," said Mrs. Ellery.

The fog was lifting perceptibly, and Frank struck across the square with a rise of spirits. The work ahead of him was congenial; it would be better, certainly, than listening to the talk at home.

A voice whined at his shoulder, "Please, help an old sojer, mister."

He stopped and looked around. The beggar was so bent that he looked like a dwarf, and his eyes had an almost animal-like gleam under his disreputable three-cornered hat. There was nothing about him, certainly, to suggest service in the army.

"Where did you fight?"

"I was with the Juke o' York at Turking, and I rode ahind Bobby Wilson at Willing-an'-Catchit. Yes sir, I've seen my share o' fighting, I has indeed, sir."

"Then you were a dragoon." It seemed impossible that this bent gnome of a man could once have had the stature for the cavalry, and yet Frank's doubts were beginning to dissolve. He knew that only among the men in the ranks was the famous charge at Villers-en-Cauchies called Willing-and-Catchit.

"Yes sir, I was in the old Fifteent'. Ye may think as it's not possible, but I stood me full five foot eleven then. That I did, sir; but I got a blue plum on the retreat and they kep' me a full three days in a bleeding wagon afore anythin' was done about it. I've had on'y half a back since, sir."

Frank was convinced now that the man was telling the truth. He began to calculate. "It's fourteen years since that campaign. What have you been doing since?"

The old soldier looked bewildered. "I don't rightly know, sir. I ain't good for much and I never can hold a job. I've just kep' body and sould t'gether one way an' t'other. The Old Poger'll be gettin' me soon, I expects."

Frank's hand was in his pocket. "How much were you going to ask me for?"

The man said eagerly: "Tuppence, sir, or even a bender. But seeing as how ye're so kind, perhaps ye might run to a full slat."

"Half a crown?" Frank's tone was compassionate. "You haven't been very well treated, and I'd like to make it up to you as far as I can. I might do better than a slat. And I can arrange to get you steady work if you don't drink too hard."

There was a long silence, and then the old soldier shook his head. "It 'ud only mean trouble for ye, sir. I'm too far gone for that. Better give me the money and let me go."

"Here you are, then." The man let out a hoarse whistle of surprise at the size of the coin. Frank added: "Can I depend on you to use it with some sense? It will keep you going for a while if you do."

"I will, sir, I will!" The husky voice was trembling with excitement. "Ye can't tell, sir, what it'll mean to have some o' the ready in my pocket. I'll make it last a long time, that I will."

"You won't change your mind about the work?"

"It 'ud do no good, sir." The man began to walk away in the fog but came back into sight again almost immediately. "I must ask ye, sir. I wouldn't feel right about it if I didn't. Would ye think me ungrateful, sir, if I laid out a bender of it on max? I'd like to forget things for oncet and get bloody well bubbed."

Frank was realizing that there was a sharper nip in the air. Turning up the collar of his coat, he looked at the twisted back of the beggar in its ragged covering. "Go to that house across the square where you see all the lights. Ask for Purdy and tell him I sent you. Tell him to give you the mulberry coat I handed him this morning to be cleaned. After that"— shaking his head with a smile—"you might as well have whatever comfort you can find in getting well bubbed."

Frank never entered the red brick building where the *Tablet* was published without a certain sense of excitement. The smell of ink and paper made him feel as though he were in a different world at once. Perhaps there would be a letter on his desk announcing a great battle fought, the death of a king, an exciting turn in the diplomatic struggle that was engaging all Europe. The leader writer would drop in on him immediately to discuss the article for the day. There were always questions to be settled. Would it be advisable to speak sharply of Mr. Wordsworth because of his persistent Jacobinism? Would there be objections if Horne Tooke were quoted on this or that? Was not a sharp reprimand due these pushing Wellesleys? Cope also would be waiting to talk over the selection of the flash article for the day. It was all interesting and exciting. The truth of the matter was that either he was unaware of the grip the work had taken on him or still unwilling to admit it.

On his desk was a neat slip of paper containing the daily balance—the revenue from the advertising booked for the day, the amount of money paid out, the amount received. This was one of the many systems that Joseph Ellery, who had a passion for detail, had devised. Frank looked at the figures and felt a certain degree of elation. Things were going very well indeed under his control.

Cope came in at once and dropped into a chair beside the desk. He was a small man with a rather belligerent air, which could be credited in part to the waxed fierceness of his mustache. His clothes were always chosen with an astonishing predilection for color combinations. On this occasion he wore a pink stock (even the most daring of the Macaronis never aspired to anything but black and white) and a waistcoat of the kind known as a Charlie Present. Accustomed as he was to the Cope magnificences, Frank gazed at this last with awe. It had been tailored out of sunset yellow and was embroidered in Chinese red; what's more, the pockets were elaborately frilled and the buttons were the latest thing, made of porcelain and inlaid with brightly colored representations of playing cards.

"Frank," said the assistant editor in a voice surprisingly deep for so small a frame, "you might as well have stayed home. The translations from the foreign papers came over from the post office and they're the poorest catch yet. There's a bit about Humboldt and his plans for a complete mapping of the world; that's the only thing that interested me at all. Even the Vienna papers are saying gentle things about the Man of Destiny. I tell you, Frank, the little beggar has all Europe licking his boots, and it's going to take a longer time than any of us estimated to undermine him."

"Fifteen years," ventured Frank. "Unless he undermines us first."

Cope did not agree with this reckoning. "No, not more than ten. It would take a century if it depended on our efforts, but Boney himself will make mistakes. Things have gone to his head; you can see it in everything he does now. This determination of his to gobble Spain is the first of his mistakes. I know something about that country and the people. It's pretty bare land, and if the French move in they won't live off it the way they've been able to do on the fat German countryside. As for the Spanish, they'll lose every battle they fight and their armies will run like Johnny-be-damned, but the people themselves will take a hand. They'll pick off stragglers and skin them alive or nail them up to doors. They'll show Boney a universal kind of war he's never had to contend with before, and he'll have to keep armies there if he wants to hold the country." He bobbed his head solemnly. "If he goes into Spain it will be his first major mistake."

"You're the only man in London who believes that."

Cope sat forward on the edge of his chair, his slightly myopic eyes boring intently into those of his chief. "Frank, the people of England must be made to see the light! We must be ready from now on to take advantage of the mistakes Napoleon is going to make. Our army must be ready. We must get rid of that zany of a Duke of York and have brisk young generals in command, men like the marshals of France. We must be in a position to take the initiative when the chances come." The deep voice boomed on. "Let me preach this in the *Tab*. The people must be made to see how badly they're being led in this crisis. It won't do to mince words." He took off his glasses and gestured with them. "On the other side of the channel there's a keen, bitter, intuitive mind plotting our destruction. Can we leave the countermoves to old Nobs and his silly ministers? Frank, do you realize what this means? Our homes, our lives, our liberty—they're all at stake."

Frank protested, "The government would put us both in the stocks if we printed one line like that."

"Very well. Let them make Babes in the Wood of us. Would it be any worse than having French bayonets in our throats? I'm willing to be locked in the harmans every day if it will help to waken England up to her peril."

Frank regarded his fiery lieutenant with a trace of envy. "I wish it were as easy as that, Copey," he said. "The departments would cut off our printing contracts. How long could we publish profitably if that happened?"

"Profits be damned, Frank! Anyway, we would sell so many copies we wouldn't miss the contracts."

"It's easy to say that. Can you guarantee it? And has it occurred to you that my hands are tied by Father's will? I hold two tenths only, you know. The others would vote against me solidly if I proposed this suicidal course to them."

"There are more ways than one of committing suicide. The worst way is to sit still and let Boney come over. Oh, he will in time. If not now, when he gets the Peninsula under his thumb." The belligerent note was oozing out of Cope's voice, however. "I see your difficulties, Frank. If you could only get around that will! Otherwise we must continue our policy of masterly silence. My first article must stay locked up in my desk. It's ready, Frank, whenever you are. I've written it and rewritten it and polished it until it's got the roll of kettledrums in it. It glitters like a line of bayonets at the charge. Is it no good for anything but to gather dust in a drawer?"

"I'm afraid not, Copey."

There was a moment's silence, and then Cope said: "A man named Frederick Koenig was in to see me this afternoon. I had a long talk with him."

Frank's hand was straying among the papers on his desk, and his voice had taken on a note of preoccupation. "Who is he?"

"Frederick Koenig is a German printer with a shop on Castle Street, Finsbury Square. He's making a power press. When he gets it right, it will print—now don't shake your head and say it's impossible—one thousand sheets an hour."

"I certainly do say it's impossible. Does he want to sell us one of these miraculous presses?"

"Not yet. He isn't ready. But he did want us to go and see his model."

Frank slit the seal of a letter with a rip of his steel cutter. "How can we spare the time, Copey? And just what do you mean by a power press? I don't understand anything about machinery, as you know."

Cope answered eagerly. "One that operates by steam. All the printer will have to do is to feed in the sheets; a turning shaft will do the rest. When we have one of those presses working for us, Frank, you'll hear a sound all through this building like the distant rumble of cannon. And it will be music to my ears, a symphony of human progress, the promise in booming chords of a free press and a free world. When we have that instrument for universal education running every day, no government will dare tell us what we may print and what we may not."

The assistant editor got to his feet, revealing the fact that his knee breeches were sky-blue and his stockings white. "So much for these dreams of the future. Stemper sent me in his copy on Caradoc's speech." He winked. "He seemed to think it might call for some editorial consideration."

Frank dropped the letter he had been holding and looked uneasily at Cope. "What's the tone of the report?"

"Well, mildly laudatory. Stemper's too honest to drape laurels on an undeserving brow even if it belongs to a member of the Ellery family. Still, I think I see a way of satisfying Master Caradoc without creating any—any guffaws, shall we say?—on the outside. He got into the question of the French *émigrés* and the need for watching them through the present crisis. It's the kind of thing to stir up talk, so I'm taking the speech right out of the parliamentary report and putting it on the front page under a heading of its own: 'Can We Trust Our Honored Guests?' I've written an introduction on this danger from Napoleonic agents and I'm inclined to think we'll skirt Charybdis with it and still not fall into Scylla—or is it the other way around?"

Frank smiled. "Thanks, Copey. You've taken a great weight off my mind."

As Cope walked out of the room, Frank's eye lighted on an item in the proofs on his desk. With a startled exclamation he picked up the long sheet and read the story through. "Copey!" he called. "This report of the trials at the Old Bailey! Who's this Benjamin Fuller, sentenced to be hanged for stealing a gold ring?"

Cope came back at once. "I intended to mention it. It's a simple fellow from down your way. He wanted to marry some pretty little slut of a girl and hadn't the brass to buy a ring. So he stole one. The jury, according to reports, tried to estimate its value under the hanging limit, but the judge would have none of that. So the poor fellow has to swing for it."

"Great God, I know him well!" Frank stared at the other with a deep horror in his eyes. "Benjie Fuller was in my company of Fencibles. A fine young chap. He can't be hanged for a thing like this!"

"Plenty are. The only way he can be saved is to persuade the Home Secretary to do something about it. Or, failing that, to go to old Nobs himself."

"We'll have to save him! I tell you, Copey, he's a thoroughly decent fellow. Surely the *Tablet* has enough influence to prevent such a miscarriage of justice!"

"It won't be a miscarriage of justice, Frank. Not as long as the present law stands. It says that theft of any article over a certain value is punishable by death. Fuller's guilt was established clearly enough. It's practically impossible to do anything under the circumstances."

Frank's brow had become damp with the intensity of his feelings. He mopped it with an unsteady hand. "We must do everything we can. It's a rotten law. Copey, I've played cricket with him. We used to let him fish at Willars Bend. I haven't seen him for a couple of years because he had to hire out as a footman with some rich family in town. I'll never forgive myself if I fail to get him off! Forget everything else and we'll talk over what we must do."

"Very well," said Cope. "But remember, the majesty of the law is exceeded only by its stubbornness. I doubt if we'll be able to save your young friend."

3

FRANK WAKENED at an early hour in the morning with a feeling that something momentous had happened. This was not unusual with him; often he would experience a brief mood in which he knew that a crisis of some kind was impending. There was nothing physically disturbing about it; other newspapermen, in fact, had told him that they were subject at times to similar reactions; but it never failed to prove the forerunner of important developments.

He got out of bed and walked to the window. The fog had disappeared, and there was the first bare suggestion of gray light in the sky. The new day would be clear and cold. Silence lay over the great city, although he could hear at a distance an occasional sound: the turn of a wheel, the beat of a horse's hoof, the unpleasant interruption of a human voice.

Well, whatever had happened, he would know about it in due course. Certainly no intimation of the nature of the event could be gleaned by contemplation of the heavy drabness of the sleeping city. He went back to bed.

It was several hours later when he was wakened a second time by the sound of Tinker stirring about in the next room. Tinker was Caradoc's man, and it was apparent that he was filling a tub for his master's morning bath. Caradoc was a great hand for cold baths. In a moment, Frank knew, his brother would bound out of bed and immerse himself without any hesitation in the icy water that filled the wooden biddy. He would slosh it gustily over the muscular whiteness of his magnificent body, talking as he did so in his forthright way to the admiring Tinker. Yes, there it started; a splash, an involuntary gasp from the bather, not entirely of pleasure, and then an assured: "Ha, Tinker, this is the way to start off the day. This is what puts life in a man, I tell you!"

Frank had never allowed himself the luxury of a personal servant. He had not been able to afford one, in fact, because of the strain imposed on him by the purchase of his second tenth interest in the *Tablet*. Probably he would never have a man. He had a sense of restraint which made the care of his body a purely personal matter. There could be no enjoyment for him in having anyone scrub his back or hold up the trousers into which he was to step. While in the next room Caradoc splashed and threw scraps of talk to Tinker, Frank gave himself a scrubbing from the water in his pitcher. It had turned ice-cold, and he enjoyed it so little that he hurried the operation through. He pulled on his loose trousers and buttoned over his shoulders a new contrivance he had been persuaded into buying by his tailor—a crossed pair of felt straps called braces. He decided that he liked them; they held up the trousers evenly and securely.

Frank smiled when he saw that Purdy had put his plate of kedgeree and a folded copy of the *Tablet* at the head of the table. He glanced over the paper as he applied himself to the food and frowned when he realized that the printers had been at fault again. The sheets were "monks"; that is, they had been given a weak impression. He wondered if the power press that Cope had been talking about would overcome this continual difficulty of proper inking.

Twisty, the second man, took his empty plate away and said: "Topp's outside, sir. Says he must see you at once."

Frank looked up from the paper in surprise. Topp was the office runner. He had served with the army in India and had the reputation around the office of being even more worthless than most ex-soldiers. It was hard to conceive of any matter in which he was concerned being of sufficient importance to warrant this early appearance.

Framed in the rear door, Topp was wearing a long yellow garment which reached to his heels and seemed to combine the functions of great-coat, coat, and "weskit" all in one. He bobbed his head and spread out his arms in an oriental salutation, saying, "Salaam, sahib," in a voice which owed nothing to any part of the world but East London.

"What is it, Windy?"

The runner looked up and winked. "Something odd, sahib," he said. "Something *very* odd. I was busy as a gravedigger last night, what with messages to be took by hand and a note to the Peers and another to the Commings. It wur clost to four in the small uns when I gets through and starts for my p'lashull quatters. I'm close to White'll when I sees a gent hobbling along and leading his prad by the bridle. I wonders what he's up to, and then I sees he's studying the houses."

"Come to the point, Windy. I'm in a hurry this morning."

Topp made the same gesture with his arms. "So be it, sahib. Well, I follows along. I 'spects to see him took up by a night dubber or get a oliver skull emptied over him from one o' the bedroom winders. And then I gets close enough to see his face and, sahib, it gives me a start. It wur Riding Bobby hisself."

"Do you mean Sir Robert Wilson?"

"Yes, sahib. Bobby Wilson. I knows he left Frog-and-Toe* for Roosha just two months ago, and by rights he ought to be up to his armpits in snow this very minute. He couldn't get back so soon, and yet there he wur."

Frank was thinking: "If he's correct about this, it means Wilson has turned right around and come back. Only one thing could cause that. Russia has declared war on us." Aloud he asked, "Are you sure you would know Sir Robert Wilson if you saw him?"

The runner laughed. "Know him if I see him? Sahib, I'd pick Riding Bobby out of a millyun. I cheered myself black in the face the day old Nobs knighted all the ossifers what rode in the charge, and I see Bobby as close as I am to ye now. And I see him once atter he mizzles to Gretner Green with the young ledy from the chanc'ry and gets hisself hitched. I knew him in a brace o' snaps, sahib, and make no mistake about it."

"Where did he go?"

"That's the point, sahib. I follows atter him, and he stops at one o' the houses and knocks loud enough to waken the comp'ny on a cold-turkey slab.† It takes a lot of it to waken anybody, but fin'lly a rainbow in a red nightcap comes to the door. He says, 'What the banging hell and brim-

---

* Frog-and-Toe was the cant name of the moment for London.
† The morgue.

stone do ye mean, ye cup-shot, getting honest men outa their beds at this bloody something hour?' Riding Bobby says something to him in a whisper and the rainbow straightens hisself up and says respeckfull like, 'I'll waken the master at once, sir.' Riding Bobby hitches his prad and goes inside, and I waits half an hour and he don't come out. So I gets home and goes to Ruggins for a few hours. Then I gets up and comes here."

Frank said, "You were right to let me know, Windy." He was thinking it had been four o'clock when he wakened the first time; this, then, was what it had meant. War with Russia! He asked, "Can you take me to the house?"

The runner winked joyously with a sense of his own importance in the matter. "I can that, sahib. And I knows who lives there. The Hunrubble George Canning hisself. What's more, I knows where Bobby stays when he's in London if ye should want to go there."

There could be no doubt about the meaning of Wilson's sudden return. Frank said: "Twisty will get you something to drink. I'll be with you in a minute."

He hurried back into the house, part of his mind busy with the importance of the information he had received, the other part running on the exploits of Sir Robert Wilson, the one hero that the disastrous campaign in Flanders had produced for a victory-hungry country. He began to sing in an undertone:

> "The French were five to England's one;
> 'Ride 'em down!' cried Bobby.
> Their thunder spoke from every gun;
> 'Ride with me,' said Bobby."

In the central foyer he encountered an excited and chattering group with linked arms, his mother (who seldom appeared before noon) in the center between Caradoc and Lady Mary. They wheeled around to face him, all three beaming with the promise of good news. The two ladies were in white muslin with their morning muffs of black fur dangling from their wrists. Frank was always surprised to see how young his mother could look. She appeared to much better advantage in the girlish round skirt, which the fashion of the day made incumbent for early wear, than Lady Mary, who lacked this happy gift of always looking right. Mary, he reflected, appeared at her best on the back of a horse; and then she was quite superb.

"Francis, my boy," trilled Mrs. Ellery, "we have news for you. *Such* good news!"

"I don't think it's going to surprise him," said Caradoc, throwing back his head with one of his hearty laughs. "Frank has guessed what it is. He knows a thing or two."

Frank looked at Mary. Her eyes were flushed and happy, and there was a suggestion of breathlessness about her; also, alas, a slight shine on the tip of her nose.

"Dear Frank!" she said. "I know he's going to be glad."

"These two children are going to be married," announced Mrs. Ellery. "It's too Romantic for Words. Caradoc proposed to Mary before we came to town. It was just after she heard him rehearse his speech. It was so fitting that way."

"I'm delighted to hear it." Frank gave his brother a hearty slap on the back and then shook hands with him. "Congratulations, you lucky dog. You're both going to be very happy, I'm sure. You know how I feel about you, Mary, and about this."

Lady Mary said, "You might kiss me, then." Her cheek was warm, and the hand she placed on his shoulder trembled a little. "Yes, we're going to be very happy. But I can never be happier than I am right now."

Mrs. Ellery took Frank by the arm. "They're going to have breakfast together now. I had my cup of chocolate before I got up. We'll leave them to themselves."

Caradoc's eyes were fixed on the newspaper under his brother's arm. He reached out an eager hand for it. "I'll read that at the same time," he said. "Of course, I'm not seriously concerned about the report. You've got to disregard such things when you're in public life."

Mrs. Ellery led her oldest son to the small sitting room on the ground floor which she had dedicated to her own use. It had come to reflect her personality; a pretty room in which one person, and one only, could be completely comfortable. The raised stone hearth was spotless in spite of the ample fire crackling in it, the hinged fall-front escritoire was tidy even though it catered quite obviously to a voluminous correspondence, the chairs were placed just right. Frank always held his breath here for fear of causing some upset to its perfect order.

She seated herself in the exact center of the walnut day bed, which left him the choice of standing or trusting himself to one of the two delicate chairs. He elected to stand. A fluffy yellow poodle, which had pranced ahead of them into the room, sprang up beside his mistress and fixed the intruder with a supercilious eye as though to say: "You see? I can sit here but you can't."

"I want to talk to you about Caradoc," she began. "You realize now, I'm sure, what a future he has. It was very clear to me yesterday—and to everyone who cared enough to be there to hear him—that he's going to become a Great Man."

"You don't have to tell me that, Mother. Have you read the notice in the paper?"

"Yes." There was the slightest trace of reserve in her voice, as though she suspected something had been done about it but could not be sure what it was. "I had Elsie read it to me before I got up. It was—it was Good." She shook her head and sighed. "It will be unfortunate, Francis, if Caradoc doesn't have the right kind of influence behind him. Even with his great talents, he needs influence."

"I'm not sure that he does." Frank drew up one of the chairs and seated himself after all. This, he knew from experience, was going to be long and perhaps a little tedious.

"That just shows you haven't given any real thought at all to your brother's problems." There was a suggestion of suppressed resentment in her voice. "You can't be truly concerned or you'd know that offices can be withheld when there isn't pressure from above."

"But, Mother, he's only twenty-four. He needn't worry if he doesn't get into office at once. He'll get there soon enough, never fear."

"William Pitt was Prime Minister at the age of twenty-five," declared Mrs. Ellery. It was clear she had made up her mind that anything less than that would be unworthy of her son's transcendent ability.

There was a moment's silence. Then: "What can we do about it, Mother?"

She sat up straight at that, fixing him intently with her vivid blue eyes. "*You* can do something, Francis. But you must bring yourself first to be sympathetic and—yes, a mite unselfish."

"I'll try to be both. I hope I haven't been too lacking in those qualities in the past."

Her voice quivered. "He's such a wonderful boy, Francis! You must do this for him. You must, Francis!"

"Do what? Tell me what you've got in your mind."

The poodle for no good reason at all raised its head and barked. Mrs. Ellery slapped it impatiently. "Naughty dog! To bother me at a time like this!" She looked at her oldest son with a hint of tears. "It's about his engagement. Francis, I'm sorry to tell you that it's not all plain sailing."

"The Duke is against it?" Knowing His Grace of Westgate, Frank was prepared for opposition in that quarter.

Mrs. Ellery's face flushed with anger. "Yes, the Duke is against it. I can't understand it. I—I'm so upset when I think about it that I don't know what to say. After all, Mary is no beauty. And Caradoc—well, my

Caradoc could pick and choose. They should feel honored that his choice has fallen on her. They should indeed." She swallowed hard. "He's a stubborn old fool!"

"I'm surprised he allowed Mary to come to London with you under the circumstances."

"It's a secret." His mother lowered her voice instinctively. "Mary is supposed to be visiting her cousin, Melisande Courcy, at Great Bayles. The poor child felt she would die if she couldn't hear Caradoc make his speech in the House, so we planned things this way. She's leaving right after breakfast."

"It's too bad the old boy is against it," he said. "Isn't there some way he can be won around?"

"That's the point exactly. It would do Everything for Caradoc." As his mother said this, Frank had an uncomfortable feeling that the obvious advantages of the match had played some part in Caradoc's decision. He hoped he was wrong, for he was fond of Mary and did not want to see her hurt in any way.

"I know he looks on us as climbers," said Frank, thinking back. "There was that trouble also over fishing rights, and then Father bought the old Fenelon farm under his nose. He and Father disagreed about many things. They didn't get along at all."

Mrs. Ellery's eyes hardened. "Your father, Francis, didn't get along with anyone." Frank had always known how things stood between his parents. Joseph Ellery was many years older than the young bride he had found in the crowded home of a West Country vicar. He had a profitable printing business at the time and no doubt had looked a good catch to Amy Lawcey, with her four older sisters and the dreary life she shared with them at Little Vandery. After bearing him three sons, however, she had made it abundantly clear that she had nothing but detestation for her moody, ambitious spouse. The loss of the promised title had been the final blow. It had seemed at times to Frank that she included him in her resentment because of the likeness he bore his father.

"Well," he asked, "what steps do you propose we take to soften the old boy toward us?"

"There would be no difficulty at all if Caradoc had been the first son." She watched him closely as she said this.

"It's a little late to do anything about that."

"Well, not necessarily. There's something we can do. There *is* something, Francis, if you'll only see things in their right light." There was a pause, and then she went on in an almost wheedling tone. "You go to Caster Towers so seldom. I'm sure you've never loved the place the way

Caradoc does. He seems to be—well, growing into it. He rides over the farms every day; and he's *such* a fine horseman, sitting up so straight in his saddle! He loves to fish at Willars Bend. He even likes to direct the help and discuss matters with the tenants. He's quite the squire now."

"And what you want me to do is to transfer the Towers to Carr?" There was a weary note in Frank's voice, as though he were realizing for the first time how exclusively her affections and interests were pledged to his brother.

"No, to sell it to him. To—well, to make a trade." She was speaking rapidly and nodding her head as though to compel his acquiescence. "The place means so little to you——"

"Why are you so sure of that?"

"Well, you come down so seldom."

"Has it occurred to you that I'm so busy making the money to keep the Towers running that I haven't the time? You might be surprised, Mother, if you knew how much we spend these days."

"Francis, you're just saying that. I *know* how little you care for the place. And it would make all the difference if Caradoc had the Towers. I mean as far as the Duke is concerned. Mary sounded him out after she had said yes to Caradoc, and he was quite violent about it. He said—I'm telling you everything frankly—that if it had been *you* she wanted, he wouldn't have minded, but he wouldn't let his daughter marry a landless second son who had suffered reverses."

"Reverses? Just what does that mean?"

"Surely you know about it."

"I know nothing about it at all." Frank's tone had become sharp. "If Carr has been in difficulties, he hasn't seen fit to consult me. He never does, of course. He always makes it clear he doesn't value my opinions."

"You know how he is, Francis. He's so self-reliant. And so proud. He doesn't like to lean on anyone. He said to me, 'Mother, what I've done is my own trouble.'" She looked almost pleadingly at her oldest son. "He saw this coming and he wanted so much to better his position. He put some of his money in colonial ventures which haven't turned out very well. There have been losses."

Frank got up and began to pace about the room. A needlepoint footstool got in the way of his stiff leg and almost tripped him. He resented any mishaps due to his lameness, and he kicked the stool aside angrily. He was finding it hard to control himself. Those so-called colonial ventures had been outright swindles. He had known about them and had warned his brother, had supplied him with proofs of their worthlessness. And there had been no need for Caradoc to better his position. The will had left the two residences to Frank as the oldest son, but it had provided a very considerable sum of money for Caradoc as an equivalent; their mother had seen to that. Each of the three sons had been left his one share in the *Tablet*. Humphrey, now in India with his regiment, had been the one to come off badly; poor little Hump, who had never complained about the small sum of money he had inherited with his tenth interest.

He stopped in front of his mother. "Are the losses heavy?"

She nodded reluctantly. "Heavy enough, I'm afraid. The poor boy has none of his father's capacity for business. Sometimes I'm glad of it." She hastened to add, "That's one of the reasons he must get into office as soon as possible."

"If he has thrown away any considerable part of the money Father left him, he's in no position to make a trade with me."

Her eyes began to show a hostile gleam. "I can almost believe it's your father speaking when you say things like that. And in that Tone."

"Is that anything for me to be ashamed of?" Frank felt a sudden surge of loyalty for the bitter, aloof man who had done so much for all of them. "Father was a remarkable man. He made the *Tablet* the best newspaper in England. I'm proud to be like him."

Perhaps she realized she had gone too far. She did not reply at once but got to her feet and walked behind a dainty screen in one corner of the room, where she applied a dampened towel to her face.

She returned and sat down. "Talk like this always upsets me, as you know. But we must get something settled. A fair arrangement can be made, I'm sure."

"But what kind of an arrangement could be made which would be fair to me? After all, Carr and I shared equally. Would he include in the deal his interest in the *Tab*?"

Mrs. Ellery protested indignantly at this suggestion. "He could never keep up the Towers," she said, "if his income was cut off. Surely you must see that."

Frank laughed. "Yes, I begin to see, Mother. Carr is to have his cake and eat it too. Or rather, having eaten a good part of his own, I'm to hand over the biggest part of mine to him. It's a gift you mean, after all."

"Now you *are* talking like your father, and I don't mind saying, Francis Ellery, that I don't like it. We have a suggestion to make but you won't listen."

Frank seated himself again. He was trying to think of ways to make her see the injustice of what she was proposing. He took no special pride in the ownership of the great old house which had stood for so many centuries, but the land was a different matter. He loved the rolling sweep of its green acres around the many twists and turns of Philips River, the line of its wooded hills against the northern sky; he loved it at least as much as Caradoc. He had had his dreams of the day when he would marry and settle down there. It was an inheritance that gave him eligibility as a suitor, even if his fancy should soar far above his social standing. Even—well, it did not seem completely impossible, after all. Many of the *émigrés* had married to escape the difficulties of their position. As a landed proprietor he might have a chance. His mother was asking him to throw this chance away.

"Has it occurred to you," he asked, "that I may want to marry myself?"

"You'll have the town house. And you'll do well, as your father did. You could buy another place later."

"Must Carr's career be put above everything? Have I no prospect of a career which might be furthered by retaining the place?"

His mother regarded him with a set look. "Surely," she began, "you won't let any feeling of jealousy influence you now that Caradoc has shown us what he is capable of——"

"Well, what is the arrangement you have to propose?"

"A payment of money. One thousand pounds. That's all the poor boy can spare now. Then he'll agree to buy the second tenth he's allowed in the will as soon as he's married. He and Mary could manage that between them, and it would be turned over to you. That would give you a share almost large enough to control the paper. That would be worth *some* sacrifice, wouldn't it? Of course, the transfer of the property would have to be made at once in order to win the Duke over."

Frank indulged in some hasty calculations. "What I would receive would represent a little more than half the value of the property. Do you realize that, Mother?"

"You know the will provides that, when Clayhorn dies, his heirs must offer to sell back his interest. Caradoc would agree to let you assume it all."

He felt that he would not be able to contain himself if the discussion were continued.

"Carr knows, of course, that you're making this suggestion to me?"

She hesitated. "Yes. We've talked it over several times. He's pinning all his hopes on it."

"Does Mary know?"

"No, no. We've said nothing to her."

"I'm glad of that. I'm sure she would be unhappy about it if she knew."

He was silent for a moment. "Well, Mother, the best I can say is that I'll think it over."

In the hall he met Aunt Francilea. She was prepared for the long drive back to her cottage on the Sussex coast. A scarlet pelisse was wrapped voluminously around her, and she wore on her head something fearful and wonderful which resembled in a curious way the dome of St. Paul's. Apparently she sensed that something was wrong from the expression of his face, for she seized him brusquely by the arm and swung him around.

"What has the queen been saying to you, Frank?"

"We've been discussing business matters."

"There's more to it than that. I know you, my boy, and I can see you're all upset." The old lady tightened her lips into an ominous line. "Now you listen to me, Frank. Whatever this is, I won't have it! Don't you give in to her. She's your own mother, so I suppose you're bound to stand up for her; but just the same, I'm going to tell you something for your own good. I've understood Amy Lawcey from the first moment my poor brother brought her to meet me. She's a selfish woman and she's trying to talk you into something. I don't know what it is and I'm sure you won't tell me. But I know one thing. It won't be to your best interests. It's something she wants for herself—or for Caradoc." She smiled reluctantly. "I love Caradoc. No woman could help it, I guess. But he's more Lawcey than Ellery. And you're all Ellery, Frank."

"It concerns Carr's career."

"Damn his career! Oh, I suppose he'll do well enough in politics. He's a glib young rascal. But I still say the best career for him would be to marry some girl with a lot of money. I suppose he's going to marry Mary Murreys because the Westgate connection will help him in the House." She laid a compelling hand on Frank's arm. "You're too easy, young man. I don't know where you get it; certainly it doesn't show in either family. Well, you mustn't be easy this time. Whatever Amy's asking you to do, say no. If you don't, I may change my will."

4

As THEY STARTED OFF, the runner squinted up at his employer. "Is Boney coming over at last, sahib?"

"It looks like it."

Topp shook his head with an air of deep satisfaction. "It'll be the very best thing in the world if he does, sahib. It'll end the suspense, like. For more'n ten years we've been a-worrying and a-palpitaking and a-agitaking, and none on us has settled down to anything. Take the case of my own fambly, sahib. I got four brothers and the i-den-tikal number o' brother-in-laws. Not a one on 'em cares if he has a job or lays by a slat or two for a wet day. Nah, nah, not them. 'What the banging hell,' they says, 'Boney'll be over and take it away from us.' So all they ever does is play voles or they tries on the hook and snivy game with the taverns, or mostly they sits around on their fat double juggs and drinks all the max they can get their hands on." He nodded his head emphatically. "Won't be no one settling down to honest work until it's over and done with, one way or t'other. So I says, let 'im come! Let's have it out with the perishing Frenchie!"

"There's a lot in what you say, Topp. I suspect most of us have been marking time, waiting for the war to be over."

The runner had been correct in his surmise as to where Wilson could be found. Frank pulled the bell above a shiny brass plate with the name Bosville, and a maidservant, with a mop in her hand, answered promptly. "I don't know nothing 'bout Sir Robert," she said in answer to his query, "but her ledyship might see ye, sir."

Frank followed her inside, leaving Topp to loiter by the area steps and exchange pleasantries with a footman who was washing windows on the opposite side of the street. After a wait of several minutes in a small room with a black and fireless grate, a pretty young woman came into the room. She was feeling her way with a cane, and he realized with a sense of shock that she was blind.

"I am Lady Wilson."

"I'm sorry to disturb you, Lady Wilson, but I have an urgent need for a few words with Sir Robert. I'm Francis Ellery, publisher of the *Tablet*."

"The newspaper?" She shook her head helplessly. "Oh dear. I don't know what to say. This is most upsetting."

"I happened to learn by an unusual chance that Sir Robert had arrived back in London."

Lady Wilson seemed completely perplexed. "It's not to get in the newspapers. It would be a very serious matter if anything were printed about it. I don't see how you could have heard, sir. Only one man has seen him."

"Mr. Canning."

"Then you *do* know." She smiled with relief. "Yes, my husband returned last night, or perhaps I should say this morning. He's sleeping now. He hadn't slept for two nights, except for little snatches, and he could barely stand up when he reached here." She stopped, assailed again by doubts. "I don't know. I'm afraid it's wrong to tell you anything about it."

"You have my solemn promise, Lady Wilson, that I'll not repeat anything you tell me until it's proper to do so. I promise that nothing will be printed in the *Tablet* until I have sanction for it."

"In that case I'm sure it's all right. Do you want to see my husband when he wakens?"

"It's my hope he'll give me a few minutes then."

"I'll send for you when he gets up. I hope it won't be for a long time, Mr. Ellery. He needs all the sleep he can get, poor boy."

"It won't be necessary to send for me. I'll leave my man outside, and he can carry the message. It's clear Sir Robert lost no time in getting back home."

Lady Wilson's face lighted up. "He's done a remarkable thing, Mr. Ellery," she said. "I *must* tell you. You know he's here anyway; and I confess I'm fairly bursting to talk about it. But it's too cold in this room. I think we had better go to the library."

She led the way from the room, walking with a light and assured step and making very little use of the cane. After traversing a long and very cold hall they came to a dark apartment with books covering the walls from floor to ceiling and a fire snapping in a marble fireplace. Lady Wilson seated herself in front of the fire and motioned Frank to another chair. "Russia has declared war on us. The Tsar's ministers—it couldn't have been the Tsar himself, he's such a great gentleman—didn't send the notice to our embassy until Russian couriers had been three days on the road with the news. My husband says they did it so all Russian ships would have time to get out of ports where they might be captured. Our Ambassador in Russia asked Sir Robert if he would undertake to bring the word home, and of course he said he would. It had been snowing heavily—he says it was drifted up to the window sills when he and Lord Gower were talking—and it was bitterly cold. He started at once."

"I can imagine what it was like," said Frank. "I spent some time in St. Petersburg one winter."

"I'm sure he never stopped for a moment. He rode across Russia to the Baltic, and there he hired a boat to cross the sea to Sweden. There was a terrible storm, and they had to keep putting in at small islands. The crew didn't want to go on, but Sir Robert forced them to. He had to bully them into it, he says. They reached Stockholm before the Tsar's couriers got there, even with their three days' start."

"He seems to have lived up to his name. You know, of course, that he's sometimes called Riding Bobby."

Lady Wilson smiled. "Yes, and he was certainly Riding Bobby this time. Sweden is still friendly to us, and he persuaded the government to put an embargo on all shipping; so the Russian ships *there* didn't get away. But they let him take an English ship out. They landed at Newcastle to save time, and Sir Robert rode all the way to London. He knew that every hour counted. A meeting of the cabinet was held at five o'clock this morning. And," she added proudly, "I guess the Tsar's messengers are still plodding their way across Europe with the news."

Frank was thinking, "What a story! I must manage to publish it before the rest somehow." He said aloud: "It was a great feat, Lady Wilson. Sir Robert will be more of a hero than ever to the people of England when they hear about it. I hope he'll be disposed to give me all the details so I can tell it in the *Tablet* as it should be told."

"Oh, I hope so!" She leaned forward eagerly. "He needs all the credit he can get. My husband is one of the finest soldiers in the world, but—well, they don't seem to like him at the Horse Guards. He's never given a chance. Do you know why?"

Frank said, "I know he published a pamphlet criticizing the army and that it wasn't very well received."

A smile crinkled around her eyes. "He told them the truth for once. No, they didn't like it. They gave him a terrible wigging and told him he might as well sell his commission. We were snubbed by everyone after that. He didn't sell. That's not Bobby's way. He swallowed all the insults and hung on. That was nine years ago; but they've never forgotten it."

"They'll have to recognize what he's done for us this time."

She was silent for several moments. Then she said, with a doubtful shake of her head: "I'm not sure. Sometimes I think it will always be the same. He has powerful friends, too, and we hear things that make us believe he's to get a good command at last. But something always comes up to block it. Instead they send him off on little missions where they think he'll be out of the way." She broke into a sudden smile. "Every time they do it he finds a chance like this. They can't keep him down, Mr. Ellery."

"I've heard it said that Mr. Canning is well disposed toward him."

She nodded her head eagerly. "Oh yes, he's been a good friend to Bobby. He insisted on sending him to Russia to see if his influence with the Tsar would help. It may sound like boasting, but my husband is one of the Tsar's best friends. They met after Napoleon had beaten the Prussians so badly, and the Tsar seemed to like him very much. They dined together alone several times, and Alexander talked to him as though they were equals. Bobby says the Tsar is a really great man and that he wants peace more than anything else. But he fell under the influence of Napoleon, and our government as usual was very stupid and stiff about it. And so this happens."

Frank got to his feet. "You've been more than kind, and I want to repeat my promise that I'll make no use of what you've told me until I have your husband's consent. My man will remain handy. I'll be more than ever in your debt if you'll send word by him as soon as Sir Robert is ready to see me."

He contented himself with a cold dinner in his office that evening, having no stomach for further discussion with his mother and being anxious as well to act immediately when Topp returned. He dismissed old Clayhorn sharply when the latter tried to unload a two days' accumulation of grievances on him. Even Cope got a brief hearing when he dropped in to go over the news of the day.

"Use your own judgment, Copey," said Frank. "I'm busy tonight."

"You're brimming over with something." The assistant editor eyed him suspiciously. "What's in the wind, Frank?"

"I may have a story this evening which will set the whole country talking. That's all I can say now. I'm under promise to keep a still tongue in the meantime."

Cope said grumblingly: "Whatever it is you've got, I've something to tell you of infinitely greater importance. That man Koenig was in again."

"I've no time to hear about him."

"You're being very blind about this, I must say. He's sure now that he's found the way to print on a flat bed with a revolving cylinder. Do you realize what that means?"

"No, I'm afraid I don't."

"Then I'll tell you. You're not too damned busy to hear this. It means a revolution in the making of newspapers. It means that in time it will be possible to print by the thousands on a single press. It means that everyone in the world will be reading newspapers. This is how it works. The tympan moves the sheet forward, and then it's gripped by a frisket——"

"That's all Greek to me. For God's sake, Copey——"

Cope, who was wearing a bottle-green coat and a large silver tinder plate in place of a watch fob, leaned on the desk. He was unwilling to drop the subject. "Frank, Frank! Have you no sense of perspective? This fabulous story of yours may seem important tonight. I'm trying to tell you something that will play a part in men's lives centuries after Napoleon has become a legend. Can't you see how completely these fast presses will change the whole world?"

Another pressing matter came into Frank's mind. "What about Benjie Fuller? Have you any word?"

"The death warrant hasn't been signed. Old Nobs has gone under a cloud again, and there's a pile of unsigned state papers on his desk. No one can say when he'll get around to it. I've arranged it so we'll hear at once if he should sign."

"Have the facts been laid before the Home Secretary yet?"

"Stemper has talked two good friends of ours in the House into seeing him. The appointment's for Friday."

"That's something. I wrote a dozen letters to men of prominence this afternoon. Do you think we're doing all we can?"

"I can't think of anything else. Trutnall is on the case and will have a story for the paper soon. I told him to pitch in strong and have no regard for the tear ducts of our readers."

"Poor Benjie! I suppose you've arranged to let him know we're doing all we can. Have you sent in food for him?"

"All attended to, Frank."

Topp returned at nine o'clock. It was clear that he had spent his period of waiting in the nearest tavern. "Ye're to go back at oncet, sahib," he said in a thoroughly mellow tone. "The maid said as how Riding Bobby had wakened up and was a-settling into his vittles as though he hadn't had a bite o' food since he left Roosha. He's ready to see ye as soon as ye can get there."

Frank left unfinished the letter he had been writing, not waiting even to replace the pen on its silver frame. On his way out, however, he stopped in the doorway of one of the long row of tiny cubicles where the writers for the paper were ensconced. The fireplace had been smoking, and it was hard to make out the occupant bending over his desk.

"Any word about Russia, Gavin?"

The writer, a lean Scotsman, blinked at him through the smoke. "I was at the Furrin Office not later than two hours gone, Muster Ellery," he said. "They've been buzzing there like angry hornets all day long. They insist nothing has happened, but I'm not disposed to tak' their word on it. There's a Russian ship, the *Specknoi*, in port. I heard it was to be seized, but they deny it at the Furrin Office. It's said, sir, that the vessel carries"—he swallowed hard, as though awed by the magnitude of the sum—"a million pounds in gold specie."

"Better pay the Office another visit before we close, Gavin."

"Aye. But they'll not like it. I've been blowing in and out of the place all day like a williwaw, and they're weary of the sight of me. If you say so, I'll try them once more, Muster Ellery."

Arriving at the Bosville house, Frank was ushered into the library. A moment later there was a sound of quick footsteps on the stairs, followed by a loud thud as the last few steps were taken at one bound. The door flew open and a tall man in a blue dressing gown came briskly into the room.

"Mr. Ellery! You wanted to see me."

Sir Robert Wilson's voice was as brisk as his manner. With his arrival the room seemed, in fact, to vibrate with energy. Frank felt it at once. There never was a time from then on when the appearance of Riding Bobby did not light everything up for him. If it happened to be in the open, the effect was the same as though the sun had come out from behind a cloud; if indoors, as though a bank of candles had been lighted all at once.

"It's good of you to see me, Sir Robert. Particularly in view of what you've just been through."

A keen pair of eyes under a thatch of ginger-colored hair studied him intently. "Jemima talked rather too freely," he said. "Still, I'm not blaming her, not blaming her at all. Now that I've had a look at you, I'm inclined to trust to your discretion too." He motioned his visitor to a chair and took one himself, spreading out his long legs in front of him with an air of great content. "I was well into a bottle of port. We'll have it down and discuss it between us at the same time we discuss this little business I've been through."

A few minutes later, tilting a glass of port to his lips, Sir Robert said: "The announcement that we're at war with Russia won't be made officially until sometime tomorrow afternoon. I'm relying on your promise not to get in ahead of the field."

"You have it, of course."

"They would be furious at the War Office, simply furious, if word got out sooner. I confess I'm tempted to rile the old boys by telling you to jump right into print and be damned to them." He smiled and shook his head. "No, it wouldn't do, wouldn't do at all. Our grand moguls of diplomacy and strategy can't possibly get any angrier at me than they've always been. You may not know it, Mr. Ellery, but a solemn disapproval of me and everything I do pervades those dark, silent catacombs.

Still, I promised Canning and I must stand by it. I'll make it up to you by giving you a story, a story that no one else will have, by Gad. That is, if you want it."

"The hope that you would tell me every detail of that epic ride of yours was what brought me here, Sir Robert."

"Then here goes. Ellery, are you fond of the use of adjectives? Here's a chance for you to trot them out in double harness, in tandem style, and in files of four for artillery. I'm not modest, you know, not modest at all."

Wilson got to his feet and began to pace about the room. He had a habit of turning suddenly and breaking into excited words, advancing toward his listener as he did so. It gave the suggestion that he was charging at his subject. This individual style of narrative suited admirably the story he had to tell. Frank listened spellbound as the tale unwound. He had enough imagination of his own to feel the icy blast of the Russian winds, the drunken slant of sails on a small sloop tossed about in biting gales, the jolt of post horses galloping down the English coast on frozen roads, the intense anxiety in the rider's mind as to the progress of the rival couriers. He made no notes, confident that not a single detail of the dramatic story could possibly desert his mind.

Wilson came to a full stop in front of his listener. "Well, there you have it. I beat them, by Gad, I beat them. But I'm wondering if it did us any good after all. We're in a fix today, Mr. Publisher, in a damnably tough, strangling fix. Have you any idea how serious the situation is? Listen to this. Prussia may go in against us as well as Russia. Spain, Portugal, Sweden even, may be forced into the coalition. Austria doesn't dare make a move, not a move. With his flanks protected, Bonaparte is free for the first time to throw his full power against us. And here we are, standing all alone."

He paused and then plunged into an even more rapid monologue, his habit of repeating words for emphasis becoming more apparent. "I've often criticized Boney. He has his weaknesses—weaknesses of vanity and malice. But he knows how to use his power. God, how he can use his power! I saw him in action in Prussia. He smashed the confident Prussies to ribbons and overran the country in two weeks. In two weeks, Ellery; ripping, tearing, smashing, every minute of the time. I tell you, this scurvy genius has made new rules of warfare. He doesn't slow up his armies by taking along provision and hospital trains. His men live off the land—that is, if they can; and if they're wounded or fall out, they're left to die. It's fast, brutal, and logical war that he fights. And what has there been against him, against this rushing juggernaut? Armies under old generals who must have their grilled bone and port every night of a campaign; armies as slow and cumbersome as a church picnic wagon." He threw out his arms in a gesture of despair. "We never learn! We don't want to learn, that's the dreadful part of it. If he gets over the channel, he'll crush us like eggshells!"

"I'm convinced he's going to try it."

The soldier looked at his visitor with new respect. "Are you? Are you really? Splendid! Splendid! You're one of the very few with the sense to think so. Every man I talk to, every damned one of them, says that Trafalgar settled that danger for all time. Trafalgar! We've got that word on the brain. They smile so contentedly when they point out he hasn't tried to build another fleet. At Downing Street they're ready to wager Pompey's Pillar to a stick of sealing wax that he won't try it. The blind fools, the blind, sleeping fools!" He indulged in more pacing and then came back across the room on tense feet. "I'll make another kind of wager. He's figuring his chances out to the smallest decimal point. If he sends two thousand barges across the water, how many of them can our navy sink in transit? My guess is five hundred. That might mean that we would drown fifty thousand Frenchmen. They lick their chops over figures like that in the War Office. What do they think they could do against the hundred and fifty thousand he could land? How can we be sure that cold, calculating brain won't decide to throw fifty thousand Frenchmen away? He may be saying to himself this very minute, 'It will be worth it if I can capture England and settle this war once and for all.' Remember, he's absolute now. As absolute as Genghis Khan was. He wouldn't have dared risk such a slaughter before. Today he snaps his fingers at public opinion in France."

The strong frame of the man who had ridden from Russia settled down into a chair. "That's the situation, sir. How are we going to meet it?"

"By keeping him busy on the Continent," said Frank. "He's showing so much interest in Spain that he may decide to gobble that country up first. We must see to it he never gets finished in Spain."

"And how would you go about it?"

"By sending armies to help fight him in the Peninsula. Large armies, not little landing parties."

Wilson looked at his guest with a trace of surprise in his eyes. "You've taken the words out of my mouth. It's the only way, the only way. But they don't think so at the War Office. The Peninsula is perfect for a defensive campaign. Broad, bare moors with nothing for an army to live off, and mountain ranges to hide behind. The Creator made Spain for the purpose, made it so we could beat Boney." His voice raised to its former excited pitch. "The government must be forced to see it! And, by Gad, you can help with that newspaper of yours. You have a great opportunity today, Ellery, a great opportunity. A sacred duty to perform. Tell the people of England the truth! Din it into their ears."

Frank felt a tingle of excitement. "I want to do what I can, Sir Robert. But there are difficulties."

"Wait." Wilson settled back into his chair. "This thing goes deeper. Much deeper. We can't send armies to the Peninsula if we're going to let Farmer George put his boggling, guzzling son in command. That must be made clear. We must have a general in command who knows more about this new warfare than a nacky greengrocer. We can't let the Duke of York throw our armies away, not this time. There are two good men in the army: Sir Arthur Wellesley and Sir John Moore. I say Wellesley. He's a cool, steady fellow. His campaigns in India were models in their way. The fellow is cut out for a fight on hot, open country. Yes, I think he would do. Now then, are you prepared to go the whole distance? To tell the King, God bless him, to keep his fumbling fingers out of this pie?"

Frank hesitated. "I'd go the whole distance. But I'm not sure I can even make a start. I said there were difficulties. It's a matter of the control of the paper. My father left the stock in ten parts. My mother was willed two shares. Each of my brothers and I were given one share and the right to purchase another. I've already purchased my second. The other two are held separately, one by an aunt I can depend on, the other by a former business manager. My youngest brother is in India, so only seven shares can be voted. There would be four against me at the start."

Wilson said impatiently: "The matter of a will can't be allowed to stand in the way. Let me talk to your mother about this. I have a way with women, quite a way. I think I could convince her."

"Not my mother," said Frank with a smile. "It would be wasted effort, I assure you."

Wilson frowned abstractedly. "Something might be done about the old fellow. We might even abduct him before the meeting."

"That would leave us in a tie. The will provides that any change in policy must be decided by majority vote."

"Your brother, then?"

"He's in Parliament and committed to the administration. No chance there."

"Come, come, Ellery, we mustn't give in as easy as this." Wilson's eyes began to light up. "We might abduct both men. You don't think I mean it? I assure you I'm ready to carry off your mother as well. I wouldn't boggle at that in a good cause. My young friend, we'll find a way out between us. It was the hand of Providence which directed your man to the spot where he saw me this morning. We were fated to come together —for the good of our country."

The serving maid put her head in the door and said: "A gem'man to see you, Master Sir Robert. A furrin-looking gem'man. I can't get my tongue to his name, master."

Wilson frowned. "What does he look like, Flossie?"

The maid rubbed a hand around her cheeks and said: "All around here and here, Master Sir Robert, he's a sort of funny color. He don't look nat'ral at all."

The soldier laughed. "I think it must be Dumouriez."

Dumouriez! Frank sat up in his chair at this. He had studied the campaigns of Charles François Dumouriez with great care and believed him to be a man of unusual military capacity. It was unfortunate that he was French and, in a sense, a renegade.

"That's it, master. He looks a deal like a h'undertaker."

"Now I wonder how the old war horse heard I was back?" Wilson turned to Frank to ask, "Do you know Dumouriez?"

Frank shook his head. He had never seen the victorious General of the French Revolutionary armies who had turned his coat during the Terror and finally come to England for sanctuary. The motives for the change were easy enough to understand, the Revolutionary leaders having displayed a tendency to send even their most successful captains to the guillotine, but Dumouriez had never been entirely welcome in England. The British Government paid him a pension, in return for which he drew up and submitted to them a succession of detailed plans for the overthrow of Napoleon; all of which were promptly pigeonholed and forgotten.

"Send him in," said Sir Robert.

The squat and aging man in dingy brown, whose face looked almost purple in the dim light of the candles, bowed to Wilson and then blinked at the newspaperman.

"Mr. Ellery, of the *Tablet*," said Wilson. "I'll have in another bottle, my old fire-eater, and we'll drink, hopefully but not at all confidently, to lack of success in a certain quarter."

The Frenchman bowed elaborately to Frank and then slumped down into a chair. He allowed his head to droop slightly and his hands to dangle over the sides of the chair, a perfect picture of dejection.

"I'll drink the toast," he croaked, "but only because it has been a long walk and I am devilish thirsty, Sir Ro-bert. Napoleon will never be beaten now, never! My third plan, drawn up in the fullest detail and offered to your army heads with the strongest letter I could pen, would do it. But has it been opened, even, by those zealous guardians of your country's safety? I doubt it. If you don't mind, Sir Ro-bert, I would prefer to drink your health. After what has happened, it seems more fitting than the other."

Wilson laughed. "Will you tell me, m'sieur, how you happened to hear of my return? It's supposed to be a deep secret still."

"I hear everything." The expatriate sighed. "It does me no good. I have no way of making use of what I hear and what I know. I am, as you say, on the shelves."

The maid returned a second time. "Another gem'man, Master Sir Robert." She seemed very much impressed. "He's in a h'unifoam. Sir Arthur Wess-essley."

Wilson looked amazed. "Wellesley!" he said to his guests. "The news of my return seems to be getting around. Well, I must say it's handsome of Sir Arthur to pay me a visit so soon."

Frank was thinking how fortunate in every respect this visit was turning out to be. Nothing could have pleased him more than a chance to meet the young general who had been performing such military marvels in India. Nevertheless he looked at his host and asked in a whisper, "Do you want me to go?" Wilson shook his head in an emphatic negative. "Stay, by all means. You ought to hear what's said."

The new arrival looked even younger than his bare forty years, in spite of the air of dignity that sat on his plainly cloaked shoulders. He had a bold beak of a nose and an icy blue eye which surveyed the two other guests with doubt and even disapproval.

"Ha, Sir Robert," he said. "They tell me you've been riding again. You seem to have done us a good turn this time. I dropped in to congratulate you."

"Thanks. I appreciate it, Sir Arthur. You know General Dumouriez, of course."

An even frostier gleam showed in the cool eyes of the army's youngest, and most successful, general. "Of course," he said gruffly.

"And this is Mr. Ellery, of the *Tablet*."

"A newspaper writer?" Wellesley looked alarmed. "I trust, Wilson, you've been discreet. It would be damned awkward for us if——"

"Ellery knows what's in the wind, but I have his promise that nothing will be printed before the proper sanction is given."

"I'm glad to hear it, Wilson. I'm very much relieved." He drew his host aside and whispered in his ear. Frank caught one word only, the name of the Russian ship. Wilson nodded his head eagerly and seemed very much pleased with the news, whatever it was. He led the newcomer to a seat by the fire, winking cautiously at Frank over his shoulder.

"A glass of port? I'll send for some biscuits. We seem to be doing things rather better than back in '94 when our paths first crossed, Sir Arthur."

Wellesley sat down in front of the fire, swinging one trim shank over the other. The tilt of his high-arched nose suggested that he found some offense in the presence of Charles François Dumouriez, and he kept his eyes fixed stonily on that morose individual. "Rather," he said. He leaned over and clapped his host on the knee. "That was a damned bad mess, Wilson. We were lucky to get out of it with our lives. I didn't expect to." He threw back his head in a sudden and high-pitched laugh. "I thought once there that I was going to be called on to sit in a court-martial on *you*, young Sir Robert. If that raid you and Calcraft made on Pichegru's headquarters hadn't turned out so damned well, by Gad, the pair of you would have been called to account for moving without orders. You were devilish lucky that none of your men were lost."

There was a moment's silence, and then Wilson said, "I'm sure we all agree on what's necessary to be done now."

"Can there be any question?" demanded Dumouriez.

"There's no doubt in my mind," declared Wilson. "We must land an army in the north of Portugal without a moment's delay. Or at Corunna."

"No, no! Never at Corunna. Junot has dropped back. He's at Lisbon, the great fool."

Wellesley looked as though he had something to say on the subject but was constrained by the presence of a fourth party who happened to be a writer for the press. His caution melted, however, as the talk flowed on. He expressed himself in agreement with the need for an immediate move into the Peninsula and even paid Dumouriez the compliment of listening to his views. The three minds seemed to meet perfectly on most phases of the situation, each of them contributing something particular to the discussion. The daring of Wilson and the ingenuity of the Frenchman supplemented the cold and practical logic of Wellesley. Frank listened with the greatest eagerness.

He stayed as long as he dared and then got to his feet. "I must go now, Sir Robert," he said. He bowed to the two generals, who were deeper still in points of strategy. "I appreciate the great privilege this has been. Good evening, gentlemen."

Wellesley looked up briefly to say, "Ah, yes, good evening, sir," but Dumouriez did not even turn his head. As Frank left the room he heard the former say, "If we can whip the Spaniards into line, which is very doubtful, by Gad——"

Wilson escorted him to the hall. "The *Specknoi* has been taken," he said. "So far we have the Rusky-muskies on the hip. I've done that much, at any rate." His eyes were full of the excitement of great plans. "I hope all this talk has had the effect of strengthening your resolution. Those two in there haven't any idea of the help the press can give us. But I see it so clearly. We can't bring the dull plodders in the cabinet around to this without the pressure of public opinion. That's going to be your share, Ellery. Don't fail us."

"I'd much prefer," said Frank, "to have a share in the fighting at the front. That's impossible, but I'm afraid I would be a poor instrument for what you suggest."

Wilson ran a quick hand through the long lock on his forehead. "I'm a fair judge of men, I think. You can do it. I'm certain of that."

5

FRANK was in a depressed frame of mind. He had spent the previous evening with Sir Robert Wilson, listening to the sweeping arguments of that dynamic dragoon, and the night in making up his mind. He riffled a listless hand through the pile of letters on his desk and had no inclination to open any of them until he encountered an envelope addressed in a stiff foreign hand. He broke the seal, and his mind raced excitedly when he saw the signature: Robert, Comte de Salle.

What could the father of Gabrielle be writing him about? Many wild conjectures occurred to him, only to be dismissed when the purpose of the note became apparent in the first sentence. Robert, Comte de Salle, was registering a complaint. In concise and somewhat stilted French he protested against the charge in the *Tablet* that members of the Royalist colony were working secretly for the usurper and tyrant, Bonaparte. It was inconceivable that any of the devoted nobility who had gone into voluntary exile (Voluntary? thought Frank. Had he forgotten the guillotine?) could lend aid to the despoiler of their homes and the assassin of so many of their number. The *Tablet*, in brief, was requested to do justice in print to the faithful band of patriots it had thus traduced.

Frank leaned back in his chair, the open letter in his hand. He had feared he would never see Gabrielle de Salle again, but here, after all, was the chance to do so. He would call on the Comte to present his regrets and to secure such facts as might be necessary for an article on the true attitude of the French colony. That certainly constituted a reasonable basis for a visit, and if he had luck he might see the beautiful daughter of the family and recall himself to her notice. He looked up at the face of the large astronomical clock on the wall opposite him. The monthly meeting of the shareholders should be over by three o'clock, and he could reach the home of the Comte by four.

He went over in his mind everything that had occurred that evening in the fog, conning each word she had said to him, treasuring his memory of how she had looked. Had she remembered it only as a trifling incident, an encounter of no importance at all? He recalled that Walter Scott, the rhyming border sheriff, had fallen in love at first sight with the pretty daughter of an *émigré* and had succeeded in winning her hand, even though her family had been of noble extraction. The Charpentiers, of course, had not belonged to the nobility of the court, but he need not assume that this difference in grade would prove an insurmountable obstacle. The De Salles must be in severe straits when Gabrielle found it necessary to brave the dampness and the cold of a December evening in such a thin wrap and such inadequate shoes. There was hope for him there perhaps.

He forced himself finally to think of the day's work ahead. He dreaded the meeting because it was going to be necessary to fight for the decision he had reached, to commit himself and the *Tablet* to the policy Wilson had been urging on him. It would inevitably cause a rift in the family, and that was not a pleasant prospect. He would be publicly criticized, his motives would be attacked, he might even be charged with disloyalty. The indignation of the governing classes would descend on him, and there would, without a doubt, be reprisals from the administration. He felt a little weak at the pit of the stomach. There was still time to change his mind, of course. Perhaps he would have done so if he could have forgotten one thing that Wilson had said: "We were fated to come together—for the good of our country."

His mother came into the office, well bundled up in a fur-trimmed pelisse. She was wearing a poke bonnet of yellow straw with brown ribbons. Frank admitted grudgingly to himself that it was extremely becoming, although the fashion of wearing straw hats in cold weather seemed to him the height of absurdity.

"Francis," she said, seating herself beside his desk and applying a wisp of handkerchief briefly and daintily to her nose, "you have been avoiding me. Purposely, I'm sure. Caradoc will be here in a few minutes, and I think we should settle matters before he arrives."

He regarded her steadily, his thoughts busy. The two problems had become tied in together. One decision now depended on the other.

"We've been at the Towers," went on Mrs. Ellery. "Caradoc and I. We lunched at Bilber, and the Duke was really quite affable. I began to hope he had changed his mind because he talked to Caradoc for a long time and praised his speech. But when Caradoc spoke to him later about Mary, he put his foot down. He said he didn't regard him as an eligible husband for a daughter of the house of Murreys. Those were his exact words. You must see now, Francis, that my plan is the only possible way to win him over."

"Why do you think he can be won over? It doesn't seem likely to me after what he said."

"Hughie brought Mary over to see us the next day. He said his father had talked to him about it. It seems he doesn't object to Caradoc at all. It's only because the poor boy has no position. I took Hughie aside and hinted to him—well, that something might be done about *that,* and he said right away it would make a great difference. Hughie is very fond of Caradoc and is all in favor of the match. That's very important because the old man can't live forever, and then Hughie will be the head of the family."

Frank brought himself to a final decision. He would go through with the course he had planned and face the consequences, whatever they might be. Reaching into a drawer of his desk, he brought out two legal-looking documents and spread them in front of him.

"The proposal is completely one-sided as far as values are concerned," he said. "The property on any reckoning is worth double the one share in the newspaper. And, remember, I would have to wait for that until after Carr had married. You said the loss would be made up to me by the prospect of finally getting control of the paper. Very well. Carr would step into the property and enjoy the full benefit of the deal at once. I don't propose to wait indefinitely for the control of the paper. It comes down to this, Mother. If you and Carr will sign these documents I've had prepared, I'll transfer the Towers to him on the terms you propose."

Mrs. Ellery looked at the papers on the desk with a suspicious and reluctant eye. "What are they?" she demanded. Her voice had become sharper. "I don't like signing papers, Francis. You know how I dislike it. I'm sure I would be signing away something."

"I'll be signing away something, Mother, when I give Carr a deed for the Towers—if I do. What I'm proposing is simple enough. These are a form of proxy. They give me the right to vote your shares in the newspaper on all points which come up at our monthly meetings for a period of five years."

Her eyes snapped at him indignantly. "You're asking us to give you our shares? I've never heard of such a thing."

"No, no. The shares remain yours. You'll continue to draw the profits on them, of course. I'll have nothing but the right to vote them. At the end of the five years that right would lapse. In the meantime, if you so desired, you could sell the shares, although they would carry no voting privilege until the end of the five-year period."

At this point Caradoc came into the room with a brisk "Hello, Frank." He settled himself into a chair and smiled cordially at his older brother. "Have you and Mother settled this little matter between you? I suppose we're asking a lot of you, old fellow. For that reason, I've been—well, I've left it in Mother's hands. But don't think that I'm not convinced you stand to benefit by this, Frank. After all, if I go up, the family goes up with me. That's the main consideration, I think."

"Caradoc," said their mother, "a proposal has been made. I'm not sure just what it means. I'm afraid Francis wants too much from us. I'm not at all sure it's Fair."

"Well." Caradoc waved a careless hand. "We can soon get to the bottom of it. Frank and I are intelligent men, I rather think." He turned to Frank and smiled again. "What is this Machiavellian scheme which has put our little mother into a state of mind?"

Frank explained the plan again and then handed over the papers for inspection. Caradoc read them through with a trace of a frown on his handsome brow.

"Well," he remarked finally, "I can't say that I like the idea exactly. After all, old fellow, the *Tablet* is a mutual property now, isn't it? I would be very reluctant to sign away my right to have any part in its direction. I feel that I've been a steadying factor in the conduct of it. I've been—well, shall we say a pole horse?"

"The Towers belong to me," said Frank. "That property is not a mutual concern at all. Yet you're asking me to transfer it to you."

"That's true." Caradoc nodded his head. "We must be broad-minded about this. You have a point there."

Their mother interjected a question which showed she was less at sea about the meaning of the proposal than she had led them to think. "What are you planning to do about the paper, Francis? Is it likely you would do things we wouldn't approve?"

"It's certain I would. I'm sure you wouldn't approve many of my decisions. We must face this issue honestly, and so I'm going to say that I would take steps which would make you very angry."

"What could we do about it?"

"Nothing. Absolutely nothing, Mother. Once you sign these papers you lose any right to interfere."

"I like that! I do indeed." Spots of angry color showed on her cheeks. "How do we know what awful things you'll do? This is absurd. It's beyond all Reason."

Caradoc nodded his head. "That's how I feel about it. You're asking too much."

Frank was keeping himself under a taut rein. "Hasn't it occurred to you, Carr, that you're asking a great deal too much?"

"Frankly, I don't think so. As I said before, it's all for the ultimate good of the family. We must pull together. I must get into office. Once I do, I'll guarantee to move on up. I'll get that title Father let slip through his fingers." His eyes flashed. "Perhaps I'll even get an earldom in time. I don't see why that's too much to aim at. I'm ambitious, Frank. I propose to make our family a great one."

"The title, when it comes, will be yours," said Frank dryly.

There was a silence of several moments' duration. Frank waited for his brother to break it. "Well, old fellow," said Caradoc finally, "just where do we stand? Let's get the issue squarely before us and get it settled."

Frank motioned toward the proxy papers. "I stand on that," he said. "I'll leave you and Mother alone so you can talk it over. Take all the time you want. The meeting can wait."

He walked out into the hall, closing his ears to the sound of his mother's voice. She had gone into what she herself would have spoken of as a Tirade.

Old Clayhorn bore down on him, watch in hand. "Meeting's six minutes late," he said. "We never used to be late, Mr. Francis."

"Calm yourself, Horny. The meeting isn't likely to start for a long time."

The subeditor, a bespectacled little man whose pinched-up nose formed an ill-tempered triangle with his bare cheekbones, popped out at him, carrying a wad of copy in his hands. He was perturbed at the critical tone of a theatrical criticism. "Let it go as it is, Spinnycraw," advised Frank. "I'm sure it's a matter of small consequence." The subeditor was not content to do this. He made it a rule, he said, not to let the writers go too far. He made it a rule to avoid making enemies for the *Tablet*.

"From now on," sighed Frank, "we're going to make nothing but ene-mies. I'm sure the notice can be published safely. It will go practically unnoticed in the issue we put out tomorrow morning."

He had been listening with no more than half his mind. The thought kept recurring: "Perhaps they won't agree after all." He was beginning to hope they would refuse his terms. It would be so easy then to tell the importunate Wilson that the plan had fallen through. He would keep Caster Towers and perhaps—well, his chances of winning a bride might then be less remote than, say, the heavenly bodies embossed on the astronomical clock.

A young man from the obscure offices in the rear where the business department carried on its activities commanded his attention next. He was carrying a sheet of stiff paper, filled with squares and spidery lines. This was an invention of Joseph Ellery's to show the trends in advertising and circulation. The first owner had made them himself, using different colored inks and laboring meticulously with them. He had called them charts, and it was his rule to have one before him whenever he called in his aides for a consultation. Frank, it must be confessed, considered them a great bother.

"The circulation is moving up, Mr. Ellery. See, this shows the whole picture. The red line is ours. It tends steadily up. The black line is the combined figures for the other papers. Observe, sir, that the black line dips down. We're beating them all, sir."

"I may be very much interested in your charts after tomorrow," said Frank.

He spent a quarter of an hour with Nathan Cope, talking over the news of the day. Then he made his reluctant way back to the corner office.

"Well, Carr, what decision have you reached?"

His brother did not look very happy. Mrs. Ellery's mouth was drawn down into severe lines, and she was gripping her handkerchief with tight fingers.

"We'll agree," said the second son. "Candidly, I'm very much dis-turbed about this. You may play ducks and drakes with the publication when you have this free hand. You know, old fellow, I've kept you out of many things in the past."

Frank said to himself that this was quite true. Many ideas which he had every reason to believe were sound and progressive had been blocked by his brother in the monthly meetings.

"But we have no alternative," went on Caradoc. "I must have a better position in the county. I despise snobs, but there's no getting around the fact that in politics your social standing counts."

"I hope, Francis," said their mother, regarding him with a reproachful look, "that you're satisfied."

Caradoc said hastily, "You're not forgetting the matter of the town house, Mother?"

"No." Mrs. Ellery's tone was quite positive. "I'm forgetting nothing. We're making one condition, Francis. It will be Highly Essential for us to entertain more in town. Caradoc says that promotions are won over the dinner table. I want to have a free hand. It will be necessary to make changes."

"Where will the money come from?"

She brushed that question aside. "The dining room and the pantry back of it must be thrown into one so we'll have room to entertain suitably at dinner. I don't think that will be very expensive. I must find a number of linen-fold panels to replace the top of the screens where those cracks can be seen. And something must be done about the furnishings. You may not realize it, Francis, but people who Know are not content any more with all this Chippendale and Hepplewhite. It's just a little *parvenu,* and I wish we didn't have so much of it. It's the latest twig to go to much earlier periods. I wish I could throw everything out and begin all over. Certainly I'm not going to have a single piece of French stuff in the house. I know where I can lay my hands on a dozen James I chairs. They're inlaid oak and beautifully ugly; but I'm afraid they're going to cost us a pretty penny. Then there's a Tudor refectory table with gadroon carving that I saw in an inn out Norwich way. *That* I must have above everything."

"Have you thought of a way of paying for all this?"

"I have some money of my own." Frank was well aware of this fact. Their mother had great tenacity in all matters which concerned her own capital. "I shall pay for this myself. But on that account I'm insisting, Francis, that I have a completely free hand. If you're to have five years to do what you want with the newspaper, I must have five years of a lease on the house. That's only fair."

Frank was puzzled. "A lease? Why, Mother, you know you can have the complete run of the place without that. As long as I have a roof over my head, I'll not complain of anything."

Caradoc broke in. "The mater's right," he declared. "Better to have it all down in black and white. We're being very businesslike about everything."

Well, they had provided him with a loophole. He could refuse to meet them in this last exaction. There was no reason why he should add to the magnificence of their bargain a five-year lease of the town house. But immediately his mind went back to the talks with Sir Robert Wilson. He could not let so small a matter as a lease stand in the way. It was very likely, in any event, he reflected grimly, that he would be spending more time in prison than in the town house.

"We'll have a lease drawn up, Mother," he said.

The meetings were held in a severe room of small proportions at the other end of the corridor. As he took his place at the head of the round table Frank realized that he hated this room. Old Clayhorn and Aunt Francilea were in their usual places, and Evans, the new business manager, was at the other end to take notes of the proceedings. Old Clayhorn's eyes opened in surprise when Frank said that the session would now begin.

"Your mother and brother are not here, Mr. Francis," he said in a tone of reproof.

"They won't attend today." Frank picked up the seal of the business and tapped on the table with it. "I wish to announce that I've decided on a change of editorial policy, beginning at once. Subject to the consent of the board, of course. In view of the national emergency which exists, and the danger that our government may not take sufficiently prompt and aggressive steps to protect the interests of our country—no, the certainty that they're neglecting to do so—it's my desire to abandon our attitude of automatic approval of administration measures and to adopt instead a position of watchful independence. I feel we must be free to demand stronger steps to protect the country from invasion."

A deep silence fell on the room. The pen of Evans stopped scratching. Aunt Francilea watched her nephew with a look of amazement. Old Clayhorn's face had turned red, and he was, literally, gasping for breath.

"The printing contracts!" the latter managed to get out finally. "They may be cut off if we say anything against the government!"

"I think we may take it for granted that we shall lose all government printing."

"But—but——" Old Clayhorn was spluttering with indignation now. "Do you want to ruin us? You—you must have lost your mind, Mr. Francis. This is an unheard-of proposal!"

Frank asked quietly, "Would you expect to get printing contracts from Napoleon, Mr. Clayhorn?"

"I—I see no point in that at all!"

"It's the real point at issue nevertheless. The only thing that counts today is the need of preventing him from getting over. It's my purpose to do what we can to stiffen the resolution of the country to more sound and aggressive measures."

Old Clayhorn suddenly pounded the table in front of him. "I insist," he shouted, "that we postpone any further discussion of this insane, this —this damnable proposal until we have a full meeting!"

"That's not necessary," said Frank. He tossed the proxies across the table to Evans. "I'm voting the shares of my mother and brother from now on. I think, Mr. Evans, you'll find the authorization in proper order."

The old man seized the papers from the hands of the business manager with a clawing motion. He began to read in frantic haste, muttering some of the phrases in a partly audible voice. His hands were trembling.

"Extraordinary!" he gasped. "Most extraordinary! I don't believe it. I won't accept these documents until I've spoken to both Mrs. Ellery and Mr. Caradoc. I don't understand this at all." He dropped the sheets and glared across at Frank. "I suspect, sir, I suspect undue influence!"

Frank answered quietly: "Please return the proxies to Mr. Evans so they may be entered in the minutes. You'll find there's nothing wrong with them, Mr. Clayhorn. And now, if you like, I'll tell you in a little more detail what I propose to do."

He spoke briefly, explaining in general terms the policy that the *Tablet* was to follow. As he talked he could see that his aunt was beginning to understand a little better. She even smiled and nodded her head at one point. Evans was taking no notes. His mouth had fallen open and he was watching his young employer with a stupefied air. Clayhorn was beyond speech for the moment.

"I think now you all understand the nature of my proposal," he concluded. "I shall, therefore, put it to a vote. Mr. Clayhorn?"

The old man gathered himself together. "I demand a discussion. We— we must have time."

"My mind is made up and I have the authority to proceed. Further talk would be useless. How do you vote, sir?"

Clayhorn shouted, "No! I vote no! It's an outrageous scheme."

Frank turned to his aunt. "And you?"

Aunt Francilea swallowed hard. "I must confess I'm a little stunned. It seems like a very dangerous step. Still, I've always had confidence in you, Frank. I'll vote yes."

He smiled at her and said, "Thank you, Aunt Francilea. I hoped you would be with me."

Old Clayhorn exclaimed: "She doesn't know what she's doing!"

"I vote my five shares in favor of the proposal. That makes it six to one." Frank looked around the table and then tapped again with the seal. "The meeting is adjourned."

The old man got to his feet and rushed from the room in an explosion of angry energy, throwing back over his shoulder, "I'll look into this!" Evans gathered up his papers and prepared to follow him. He began to say, "I suppose this is all in order, Mr. Ellery, but I——" then changed his mind and left his doubts unsaid. When he, too, had left, Aunt Francilea walked over behind her nephew and laid a hand on his shoulder.

"Are you sure you know what you're doing, Frank?"

He nodded his head. "Yes, I'm fully aware of what it may lead me into. I've considered all the risks."

"I can get along without any profits from the paper," she said after a moment. "I'm not concerned about that at all. But I am worried about you, Frankie."

"Winning this war is the only thing we should think about. I can't fight, so I must do what I can in this way. I know it's going to be pretty unpleasant." He stopped. There was a long pause. "Will you do something for me, Aunt? Mother and Carr are back in my office, and by this time they'll understand the full enormity of the steps I propose to take. I—I don't seem to have any stomach for further arguments with them today. Go back and talk to them. Tell them for me that there's no backing out now."

"I'll do that, Frank."

"They've got what they wanted. But they've also got something they didn't want at all. They aren't going to be happy about it."

"I hope not!" The old lady's tone had become grim.

Frank went to Nathan Cope's office. It was a foot or two wider than the other cubicles and boasted a chair for the convenience of visitors. Dropping into this, he looked across the desk into the intent eyes of his assistant.

"I'm glad you're wearing your purple waistcoat today, Copey," he said. "It's your very best, isn't it? That makes it quite fitting, because you're going to have something to celebrate. Have you that article of yours handy? The one in which you blast His Majesty's Government? I want to show it to Sir Robert Wilson and get whatever suggestions he may have to make about it." He paused. "I think we'll be publishing it at once."

6

THERE WERE in London many odd little corners which opened off busy streets but were themselves quiet to a suspicious degree in a city so given over to noise. They never boasted of more than one short block, and they came to dead ends against dirty brick walls, over which loomed the blank windows of warehouses or the rusty spires of unimportant churches. The houses always had one thing in common—a tendency to huddle closely together in shabby reticence. They were shaded from the sun in daytime and forbiddingly dark at night. People lived unobtrusively in these stagnant backwaters, and visitors were few, although the sound of footsteps led instantly to much drawing back of shabby curtains and apprehensive peering from upper windows; there being on the part of the inhabitants a constant dread of bill collectors and tipstaffs and even of the police.

Brinsley Place was one of these, and Frank Ellery shook his head uncomfortably at the thought of the family of the once great Comte de Salle living in such sordid surroundings. Number 24 was shabbier if possible than its neighbors. Its area steps showed wide cracks, and the paint was peeling in leprous strips off the plain front door. A small boy with an iron on one leg limped up the steps ahead of him. A bag of books strapped on his back and a small cotton bag clutched in one hand indicated that he was returning from school.

"Can you tell me, my fine kincher, if the Comte de Salle lives here?" asked Frank.

The boy nodded with grave politeness. "Yes, m'sieur. I am the son of Antoine, the butler. The Comte"—with a touch of pride—"occupies the whole of the ground floor."

"Perhaps, then, you'll show me the way in. I've come to see the Comte."

"Yes, m'sieur." The boy hesitated and then pointed to the knocker on the next door, about which was wrapped a pair of once clean white gloves. "If M'sieur will pardon me, I should very much like to know why it has been necessary for the Finnertys to do that."

"It means the stork has paid a visit to the Finnerty home." Seeing that he should be more explicit, Frank added, "A new baby has been left there."

"Indeed! I am afraid, then, that the stork has made a serious mistake. It was wrong to leave the baby at the Finnertys'."

"Why do you think that?"

"But, m'sieur! They have five children now, and it's said M'sieur Finnerty is of limited means. They have only two rooms. And think, m'sieur, how bad it will be for the baby, having to grow up in the same house with Mick Finnerty!"

"You don't admire Mick, I take it."

The boy shook his head. "He is two years older than I am, and very large and strong. I sometimes wonder why the stork thought it necessary to leave him at any home at all."

He opened the door and led the way inside. Frank found himself in a long and dark hall which ended in a flight of stairs. Laying a hand on the knob of the only door opening off the hall, the boy said: "My father will be with the Comte, I think. I shall speak to Margot. What is M'sieur's name?"

"Ellery. I'm from the *Tablet*, a newspaper. I think the Comte will understand the purpose of my visit."

"He sees very few people." The boy hesitated and then nodded his head. "Margot will know what to do, m'sieur. We will leave it to her."

Frank was greatly surprised at the appearance of the room into which they stepped. No candles had yet been lighted, but it was evident that it was of unusual dimensions and that the furnishings were on a scale of considerable grandeur. He could make out that the walls were covered with tapestries and large paintings, and that the chairs scattered about were handsome and old. The carpet under his feet was soft and yielding. The Comte, he decided, had managed to bring some of his finest things with him in his flight from France.

"Margot!" called the boy.

An agitation developed near the top of the heavy curtains which draped the front windows. Frank strained his eyes and saw that someone was perched there on a stepladder and that a duster was being applied briskly to the valances.

"Yes, Jean Baptiste Achille?" answered a preoccupied voice.

"There is a gentleman who asks to see the Comte, Margot."

After a pause the figure of a girl descended the steps. She came forward, duster in hand, and bowed gravely to the visitor. Frank saw that she was quite young; not more than twelve, he decided. A smudge of dust from temple to temple accentuated the width of her brow, and under it her eyes looked enormous in a very thin and pointed face.

"Your name, m'sieur?"

"Francis Ellery. Of the *Tablet* newspaper."

The girl pondered. Then she nodded to him and smiled. "I remember.

Yesterday I mailed a letter to the *Tablet*. Perhaps it is about that, m'sieur?"

"Yes. I'm anxious to discuss it with the Comte."

She bowed. "I shall speak to my uncle. I think he has wakened now and that Antoine is with him. Will M'sieur be seated, please?"

"Thank you, Mlle. Margot. If it's inconvenient for the Comte to see me now, I can return at any time he may care to set."

"No, it would be better now. He has been feeling a little better today." She was seized with a sudden doubt. "M'sieur speaks French, I hope? My uncle has never learned English. He—he has refused to try. He says it would mean he expected to stay in this country. My uncle thinks every mail will bring word that the old order has come back in France. He is a—I'm afraid I have forgotten the word."

"An optimist?"

She bobbed her head. "That is it. My uncle is a very great optimist. Each morning when he wakens he looks at the sky through his window and says to Antoine, 'It will be a good day to start our journey' or 'It will be a bad day to start.' Generally, of course, the weather is bad. He keeps all his papers packed so that he will be ready to go."

"I admire him for it," said Frank in French. "It takes a great heart to remain optimistic in these times. You, mam'selle, are quite adept at English. And so is this young fellow."

The girl looked at Jean Baptiste Achille and nodded proudly. "Ah, yes, he is a fine little scholar, our Jean Baptiste Achille," she said. "You see, he is not very strong, and it is hard for him to go to school with the English boys. They call him 'Froggie' and they tease him a great deal. But our stout Jean does not mind that at all. He is always at the head of his class. And he wins their marbles from the great, strong English boys. Don't you, Jean Baptiste Achille?"

The boy's eyes had a troubled look as he answered, "Yes, Margot."

"See! He has won again today. The bag is quite full."

"He must be a dead shot, a regular demon with the alleys and com-moneys."

"Yes, he is clever, that one. Now I shall speak to my uncle."

The small boy was about to follow her, but Frank said: "Stay with me, Jean. It may be some time before the Comte is ready. I'm very much interested in what you do at school."

"It is not usual, m'sieur, for me to stay in this room." The boy's face had an unhappy look which puzzled Frank in view of all the praise which had been lavished on him. He walked to the hall door but turned when his grubby hand was on the knob. "I must be honest, m'sieur. I cannot let you believe the things Margot has said." He gulped as though on the point of tears. "You see, m'sieur, I am not strong and I will never be a fine big man like my father. He was a soldier once, and I know he does not like it that I can never be a soldier too. I am sure they are all disappointed in me, and so I try to make them proud of me about other things." He gulped again. "M'sieur, I am never head of my class. I am often at the very foot. The teacher says I am a dunce, and all the boys laugh at me. Mick Finnerty calls me a nickin and a nizey. That's the truth, m'sieur."

"You mustn't let that worry you, Jean Baptiste Achille. After all, it's hard for a French boy to do well in an English school. I'm sure this Mick Finnerty would be at the bottom of the class if he had to go to a French school. You would be calling him a—whatever you call nickins in French."

"*Très bête!*" said the boy eagerly.

"Yes, *très bête.* And then, of course, you're the champion at knuckle-down. That makes up for a great deal."

Jean Baptiste Achille shook his head miserably. "No, m'sieur. That also is not the truth. Never once have I won at holy-bang. I am even very poor at ringtaw and bounce-eyes."

"But you still have a good supply in your bag."

"Observe. They are stones, m'sieur. I carry them so no one will know I have lost all I had."

Frank looked down at the small figure. "You're a brave boy, Jean Baptiste Achille. And a very honest one to tell me about this."

He fished half a crown from his pocket and put it in the boy's hand. The small fingers closed over the coin convulsively.

"A slat, m'sieur! A whole slat, and all for me! Or perhaps"—another gulp, full of the agonies of doubt—"M'sieur expects me to get him change."

"No, Jean Baptiste Achille, no change. It's all for you. A reward for a very honest boy."

"All for me! M'sieur, it is riches! Once I was given a bardy, but it was a mistake and I had to give it back. And what is a sixpence to a full slat!" His hand was still on the knob but he did not go. He seemed to be struggling with more doubts. "Does M'sieur know that a bardy would buy all the commoneys I need, and even a blood alley?"

"Yes, I still remember something about prices. Use the rest to buy other things. You must get hungry, on the walk from school. Now you can buy yourself a Banbury Cross bun sometimes, or make a deal with the candy man."

"M'sieur is very generous." The boy still hesitated. "I hope it will not be necessary to tell Margot what I told him."

"No, Jean Baptiste Achille, your secret is safe with me."

The girl Margot came back almost immediately with a silver phos bottle in her hand. "My uncle is feeling well after his afternoon nap. He will be glad to see you." She caught a light at the neck of the bottle and applied it to one of a dozen candles in the sockets of a high torchère. "We will have one only, if M'sieur does not mind. You see, there is to be a large company tonight, and we must be careful of the supply."

Frank saw by the light thus provided that she had washed the dust from her forehead and had donned a cap with a blue ribbon in it. She looked almost pretty now, in spite of the disproportion of her brow and eyes to the rest of her face, and the adult gravity of her manners.

"I'm causing you a great deal of trouble," he said.

"No, no, m'sieur. It's a pleasure. We have so few people here. My uncle is very set about some things. He receives only his old friends. The line is drawn even at the Creoles. I think sometimes it's a pity. The Creoles are very gay, and they're much more prosperous than my uncle's friends. Money is coming through to them now from their estates in the islands, and they're able to live very well. No money comes through from France at all. Sosthène and Gabrielle would like to make friends with some of the Creoles, but my uncle is very firm and won't allow it. He says we must never compromise."

"I can see your uncle is a determined character."

"Yes indeed, m'sieur. There was a German baron who was very much in love with Gabrielle and wanted to marry her. He was quite wealthy, and Sosthène was losing money at the time, but my uncle sent him away. Sosthène—he's my cousin and will inherit the title someday *and* the estates, if we ever get back to France—was rather taken with a Creole heiress just recently, but my uncle said he would disown him." She paused and sighed. "I'm talking too much. Will M'sieur excuse me now? I have other work to do."

The light of the single candle enabled Frank to get a better look at the contents of the room. He inspected the paintings first and was amazed to discover that some of them were the work of the greatest French artists. There was a Poussin, a LeBrun, a Le Sueur, a Vernet, even a Claude Lorrain. The apartment was filled with beautiful and quite obviously costly articles. There were fine cabinets containing porcelains and silver *objets d'art,* and a long table at one end, set out with a silver service and much fine glass. He looked closely at a gold clock on the mantel above the fireplace and saw that a tag was attached to one of its legs; unmistakably a pawnbroker's ticket. The clock, then, had been out, and the tag had been overlooked when it was redeemed and restored to its place. "That's most odd," he thought. "They could live very well for a long time on the sale of one of those pictures."

He had returned to the Claude Lorrain and was studying it with a sense of real pleasure when the door at the far end opened again. A creaking Bath chair, in which was huddled an old and very sick man, was wheeled in by a solemn male servant. The occupant was wrapped up to his yellow chin in a worn pink dressing gown and held on his lap a black cat as ancient and sickly as himself.

"Good day, m'sieur," said the old man. "You are from the *Tablet*, I am told. The proprietor, yes? I take it you have received my letter?"

The servant wheeled the chair over toward the fireplace. He looked first at the wood laid there and then, inquiringly, at his master. The Comte de Salle shook his head in a firm negative and then suggested to Frank that he take a chair beside him. "My hearing is no longer good, M'sieur Ellery. I think it is the continued cold and dampness. You need sunlight and warmth to keep from growing old and useless."

"It's been an uncomfortable autumn," agreed Frank, seating himself.

"You were looking at my pictures, m'sieur, and wondering perhaps why I live in a quarter such as this and yet keep a fortune in pigment on my walls." The Comte's thin cheeks wrinkled in a mirthless smile. "I don't enjoy being thought guilty of inconsistency. These are copies, m'sieur. The originals were in my Paris house. An artist, who had received many good commissions from me and conceived himself in my debt, made these copies after I left. He managed to get them out of the country and to me here. They are remarkably good and they afford me a great deal of pleasure. Where the originals are now I do not know. Probably they have been taken by Bonaparte or some member of his thieving family." He looked up sharply at the servant. "Come, Antoine, I need you no longer here. There are other duties for you."

The cat on his lap opened a rheumy eye and gave a complaining squeak. The heavily veined hand of his master caressed his head. "My old Thibault is not well," said the Comte. "I think it has become a race between us as to who will go first. Probably it will be poor Thibault, for it is ordained I shall see France again before I die. There is little comfort for those as old as Thibault and I. He has only one tooth left, and I—I am somewhat lacking in that respect also."

"I've called on you, sir," said Frank, "because I wanted to make it clear that the item in my paper was no more than a report of what had been said in the House. It occurred to me also that a paper might be published to give the other side of the question. It would be interesting and, perhaps, helpful."

The Comte turned his shoulders painfully in the direction of his visitor and said with a sudden access of energy: "It is incredible, m'sieur, that any of the French people living in this country could be in the pay of that bloody butcher and thief! They would die rather than give any aid to the usurper!"

"I'm sure that applies to all those you know, M'sieur le Comte. It's a fact, however, that three men were caught today who had been sending out information. I'm afraid it must be admitted that greater caution is necessary on the part of our government."

"Three Frenchmen?" The yellow mask showed both scorn and indignation. "I refuse to acknowledge them as countrymen. They were spies, paid informers, m'sieur. That is entirely beyond the point. Scum of the kind is spawned by every race, even the French. I did not refer to them. I spoke only for the members of my own class, the people who have ruled France for many centuries."

"Then what remains to be done is to establish the difference. That I'll be glad to do."

"Exactly, m'sieur. We who represent the real France must not be saddled with the sins of common traitors and Bonapartist spies."

Frank's back was to the door. He heard it open but could not see who had entered. Was it the daughter of the house? A sense of delight flooded over him when he heard her voice say: "Here I am, Father. Have I been selfish in staying away from you so long?"

His stiff leg made rising difficult, and he was bitterly conscious of the awkwardness of his movements. With the first glance he realized that his memory of her had been completely inadequate. Gabrielle de Salle looked radiant in a dark red wraprascal, which muffled her up to the chin, and a small fur turban with a pompon of the same color on top. The sharp bite of the wind had put a flush in her cheeks, and her eyes were sparkling. She was taller than he had thought and infinitely more lovely.

"I have a visitor, Gabrielle," said the Comte. His tone made it clear that no introduction was to be made, but the girl crossed the room toward them, nevertheless, dropping a parcel on a marquetry table as she passed. Her eyes were fixed inquiringly on Frank.

"I'm sure I know you, m'sieur," she said, smiling at him. "But of course! You were the man in the fog!"

"Yes, mademoiselle. I trust you had less difficulty in getting home that night?"

"Oh, it had cleared long before we left. We were very gay that time. We danced until after two o'clock. Do you remember, Father, that I told you of our difficulty and how a very kind Englishman saw to it that we did not have to spend hours on the top of an uncomfortable omnibus?"

"I am glad of the opportunity of thanking M'sieur Ellery," said the old man. His tone was both stiff and reluctant but, as Frank noted with satisfaction, he had compromised to the extent at least of mentioning his name.

"I see now that I got an entirely wrong impression of you that evening," went on the girl, unloosening the neck of the wraprascal. "Of course, I saw little of you but the back of your head while I was holding on to your coattails. Don't frown, please, Father; you have no idea what it's like to be caught in one of those terrible fogs. You're thankful for a coattail to hold, I promise you. I remembered you, m'sieur, as very tall and very dark and with a *very* large nose. Now I see how wrong I was."

Frank's mind was in such a whirl that he found it hard to speak. He managed to say, finally: "A fog will sometimes cause curious illusions, particularly in the matter of size. I remember thinking once that the golem was loose in London and bearing down on me out of the mist. It proved to be a greengrocer with a basket of turnips on his head."

Gabrielle de Salle laughed. Her voice was silvery and with an infectious note to it. Frank joined in. "That accounts, then," she said, "for my mistake in the matter of your nose. Now that I see it more clearly, it's a very creditable nose. Do you still drill with broomsticks?"

"We drill every day. But we have cast-off army muskets now, and that's a very important advance."

"Splendid, m'sieur! Perhaps we shall beat the terrible Bonaparte after all."

The Comte continued to stroke the back of the cat with an unsteady hand. "It's a record of the firmest devotion, that of the exiles of France," he said, as though speaking to himself. "Twelve and more years we have had of it. Poverty, suffering, uncertainty; driven from one refuge to another, never sure where the next day would find us; waiting, hoping, for something which never happened. We have endured under the fogs of London and the snows of the Baltic, thinking always of the warm sun of our lovely France." He looked up suddenly. "Are you aware, young sir, that it would be very easy to return to France now? That it has been so ever since the Corsican assumed the imperial title?"

Frank nodded. "I've heard that Napoleon has been striving to get the old families back and has been offering concessions."

"We would be received with open arms. Our estates would be restored, our titles recognized. The usurper thinks his throne would be secured if he could rally the old nobility back of him. He thinks we will be only too glad to lend him that support after wandering for so many years in the wilderness. But he is wrong, m'sieur! We will continue to suffer, we will die in exile rather than give in to this assassin."

Thinking how many of the *émigrés* were accepting the bait of reinstatement and returning to France to make their peace with the new order, Frank said to himself, "Here's one family which will stand out in spite of everything."

"That is what should be said about the exiles of France," went on the old man. "There should be no doubting of their honor or their good faith, m'sieur. They are a devoted band, and all their hopes are bound up with the cause of this country. You cannot know the extent of our devotion, young sir. One of our group has made a vow never to wear a hat until he sees again the towers of his home in Tours. Another wears a blue ribbon even in his bath, being unwilling to live a single moment without the feel of it around his neck. This may sound comic, m'sieur, but to me it is proof of a great depth of faith." He paused. His train of thought had carried him away from the present, for he looked at his daughter as though he had been unaware of her for the moment. "You are back, Gabrielle. That is good. You will add your persuasions to mine, and between us we may get the consent of M'sieur"—he frowned uncertainly—"M'sieur Ellery to join us at dinner tonight."

This was so much more than he had dared hope for that Frank felt a great surge of elation. He was being offered a whole evening in which to feast his eyes on her warm beauty, to hear her voice! There would be further chances to talk with her, to improve his slim acquaintance. It seemed incredible that such great luck should be his. He wondered why the Comte had suddenly become so cordial.

"We are having a few of our oldest friends with us," continued the Comte. "All of them have been in London for many years. I often wonder how some of these brave people continue to subsist. Their resources are so slender, m'sieur! But they remain constant to their faith in spite of everything. I would like you to see for yourself, young sir, to become convinced of what I have told you."

The girl's eyes smiled to second the invitation. Frank rose and bowed. "I shall be very happy to join you. At what hour do you dine?"

"At six. We are poor, m'sieur, and we dine simply. You must be prepared for plain fare. But the company will be pleasant, the talk good; that much I can promise you." He turned to his daughter. His head was beginning to tremble on the withered stalk of his neck. "Gabrielle, my dear, I think our visitor will forgive me now. I have allowed my emotions to become seriously involved, and it is trying on an old man. Will you summon Antoine?"

When father and daughter were alone, the girl said with a suggestion of a frown: *"Father!* Why did you do that? It was the very last thing in the world I expected of you. And I must say I'm worried about food. We are never lavish in our preparations, you know."

"There will be plenty. I am sure our industrious little Margot has been the good provider as usual. She can stretch our resources to cover another place." His head had fallen against the reclining back of the Bath chair. "It was an impulse. I am not subject to them, as you know, my dear. I have never done such a thing before, but there was something about that young man. I am sure he can help us." He sighed wearily. "It is apparent that he is quite opulent, my dear. He may prove a little more generous than our regular guests. Has Sosthène told you he has been having no luck at all lately? We may soon be at the point of parting with more of our things."

Gabrielle threw off her wraprascal. She was dressed in a very plain dress of a becoming gray, which fell in straight lines from the high waistline of the mode. The tip of a worn slipper showed for a moment when she began to walk toward the door in the rear.

"I hate all this, Father!" she exclaimed. "I'm not sure I can stand it any longer. Why can't we be more honest? Perhaps what I have to tell you will make you see what I mean. There is news. It seems that His Majesty has been gracious enough to extend permission to all his noble subjects, who care to do so, to engage in work without losing caste. None of our privileges will be withdrawn because of it."

There was a moment's silence. "That is indeed gracious of His Majesty," said the old man earnestly. "It is most generous. It will relieve the minds of so many of our friends who have been compelled to take employment."

"Father!" Gabrielle walked beside the chair which Antoine was now wheeling to the rear. She laid a beseeching hand on his arm. "Don't you think you could consent now if Sosthène and I were to find some kind of work to do? Sosthène never seems to win any more. Perhaps his luck has deserted him for good. We lived on it for so long, Father! He's finding it very hard to keep up appearances. I can work in a dress shop if nothing better offers. I'm strong, Father. And then think—we wouldn't have to give more dinners like this!"

The Comte shook his weary head. "Please don't discuss it now, my dear. I am very tired. I lack the resolution to face such a problem at the moment." His voice fell to such a low note that it was hard to follow him. "Why are you away so much? I miss you, Gabrielle."

A visitor would have been shocked at the contrast between the fine drawing room, with its luxurious appointments, and the rest of the apartment. The rear door led to a windowless box of a hall from which three doors opened. Those to right and left were ajar, revealing two miniature bedrooms. One of these was occupied by the Comte, for Antoine halted the Bath chair at the door. It was so completely filled by a four-poster bed that no room was left for either washstand or chair. The other had a cot only and so permitted a washstand in one corner. The fact that a handsome satin coat was draped over the baseboard of the cot, and that a sword was suspended from a nail on the wall, indicated that this bare cubicle was dedicated to the slumbers of Sosthène. The conclusion could easily be drawn that the two male De Salles shared the washstand between them.

While Antoine proceeded to help his master from the creaky vehicle to the bed, Gabrielle walked through the third door into the kitchen. It was a large room, lighted by one economical candle and filled with a tantalizing odor of food. Margot was at the table, engaged in the task of making ice cream. She had set the dish containing the mixture in a huge bowl of ice and salt and was agitating it briskly with a pewter spoon.

Gabrielle almost danced up to her small cousin and opened her purse with an air of intense pride. "See, Margot! I was paid today. Ten whole shillings! Money, Margot, money; and honestly earned. I was so excited when Mme. Lebery handed it to me. Now we can pay a little to Antoine on his back wages, and we can get a piece of muslin for a new curtain—I'm sure the Finnertys can see us dressing through that hole—and a new hat for you, my uncomplaining Margot. It will have to be a cheap one, though."

Margot suspended the movement of her thin arm. "That's splendid, Gabrielle. I'm as proud about it as you are. And Uncle Robert does not suspect anything. At least, I don't believe he does. But about the money now. You mustn't be rash, Gabrielle. Antoine, yes, he must have a little. The bonnet for me will have to wait. I go out so seldom anyway that it's not as necessary as so many other things." She sighed. "I spent the last of the household purse in the marketing."

"How did you do about dinner?"

"Quite well, I think. I've kept the cost down to a shilling a head."

"Then we'll have a good profit tonight. I'm sure I don't see how you manage it, Margot."

"I asked Father Jean to get the fish for us. They're always kind to priests at the fish market. He got all we needed for one shilling. Sole, Gabrielle, and very firm and good. The soup is made. I have everything ready for the ragout. And, see, we are to have ice cream."

"Excellent! Our guests will be very happy tonight. You are a worker of miracles, Margot."

Gabrielle vanished behind an arrangement of screens which closed off one side of the kitchen. The niche thus provided served as a bedroom for the two girls. Wires were stretched from one screen to another, and on them articles of clothing were suspended with clothespins: a few— a very few—dresses, covered with muslin bags, stockings (recently washed and pitifully limited in number), a few more intimate garments of good material but lacking the fine embroidery which ladies of fashion demanded, even a small variety of hats. Loops of cord had been sewn to the back of the screens to serve as holders for half a dozen pairs of shoes of all kinds.

Against the wall were two bunks, one above the other as in the cabin of a ship, made out of plain pine boards. These primitive beds were made comfortable, however, by the finest of mattresses (brought from France with the rest of the furniture, no doubt) and were given a bravely frivolous appearance by richly embroidered coverlets of the finest satin. A close inspection would have revealed the fact that both coverlets had been neatly darned in many places and were wearing dangerously thin.

Her fingers busy with the strings of an apron, Gabrielle called to her cousin: "I'll be with you in a minute, my Margot. And, oh! We have another guest tonight."

"Another!" There was dismay in the voice of the young cousin, and for a brief second the beating of the spoon ceased. "Oh dear, that will make things difficult. The soup is ample, of course, and there will be plenty of the fish. I'm not sure of the ragout. I suppose we'll have to be generous, then, in the helpings of the fish and put another egg in the dressing."

"It's an Englishman who visited Father today. He has just left."

"M'sieur Ellery. I talked to him." The beat of the spoon went briskly again, and in Margot's voice there was a suggestion that she was reconciled to the idea of the additional mouth to be fed. "I'll do the very best I can, Gabrielle. I liked M'sieur Ellery. He's quite nice-looking, I think."

"Not at all handsome, Margot." The daughter of the house was encasing her feet in comfortable slippers of knitted wool. "One gets so tired before the end of the afternoon. I was running all day long, I believe. Upstairs and down! He's pleasant enough. M'sieur Ellery, I mean."

The voices of the cousins went back and forth across the patched screens.

"Is Jules coming?"

"Yes, Gabrielle. He sent a note this morning. You must look your best. The light green muslin, perhaps?"

"I don't know. I was thinking of the white tonight."

"Your very best! Gabrielle! Jules will think you do him great honor. Perhaps he'll speak tomorrow to Uncle Robert."

"I don't know. Margot?"

"Yes, Gabrielle."

"It will be nice to have a new face at dinner tonight. Even if he is an Englishman."

7

GABRIELLE DE SALLE knew that Frank Ellery had fallen in love with her. She had seen the symptoms so often that it was easy to recognize them. She had already begun to think of him as "my Englishman."

She emerged from behind the screens with an apron of a cheerful new material called gingham around her waist and a cap to protect her hair. Margot had finished the ice cream and had placed the bowl on the sill of an open window. Two busy pairs of hands started immediately to work on the all-important ragout. Antoine came through the back door with an armful of silver plate which had been burnished with soldierly thoroughness. His entrance allowed a glimpse of the interior of a low outbuilding which served many purposes—woodshed, drying room, storehouse, and bedroom for Antoine himself and his small son.

"We can't upset the order of the seating," said Gabrielle with a worried frown. "Jules would never recover from it, I'm sure, if we made the smallest change in the arrangements. So. Let me think how it can be done." She pursed up her lips and frowned again. "I'm afraid it will be necessary to place my Englishman between the Abbé Force and the old tartar."

"Mme. de Gaseau?"

"None other. Yes, that's how it must be done. It won't be at all pleasant for my Englishman, but the Abbé will be glad to sit that much further away from her heavy breathing for once. And I must remember to warn Antoine that none of the special dishes are to be placed within his reach.

He would celebrate his release from *la Gaseau* by gobbling everything."

"Is he yours already, Gabrielle?"

"I held on to his coattails for half an hour. And it's possible I tugged at them a little more than was strictly necessary. I think he's rather nice, Margot."

The son of the family returned soon thereafter, for the rumble of a deep masculine voice and the tread of a heavy foot could be heard in the front of the apartment. Sosthène de Salle did not take long to dress, appearing very soon in the kitchen door; a huge figure with sloping shoulders which appeared a little ridiculous in conjunction with the extreme thickness of his trunk and legs. He was many years older than Gabrielle, being the son of a first marriage. The length of his waistcoat, which reached almost to his knees, marked him as a reactionary. He looked, in fact, dull, as well as sluggish physically, and this was completely misleading; for the mind behind his sulky features was sharp and observing.

"A good dinner tonight, I hope," he said.

"The dinner will be of the best," declared Margot. "You will enjoy it, I'm sure, Sossy."

"But with not too great an appetite!" warned his sister. "You'll content yourself with one helping of everything tonight, my greedy one. And Antoine will see to it that we of the family are served light."

"Were you lucky today?" asked Margot.

The heavy young man shook his head morosely. "It was a cocking main. I'm an indifferent judge of the birds. Tonight I've an appointment to play piquet with a fellow who fancies himself a tercel at the cards. It will be different, I promise you, my small Margot. I'm unbeatable at piquet." He turned to Gabrielle. "I shall eat as much as I please tonight."

When the last of the tasks had been completed, Gabrielle ran behind the screen to dress. The apron flew in one direction, the cap in another, both being promptly retrieved and hung on the line by the assiduous Margot. One expert wriggle and Gabrielle was out of the dress, which fell in a billowing mass to the floor, revealing that she wore no more in the way of undergarments than a wisp of chemise, a pair of stockings, and the usual pantalets. The latter, in the style of the moment, were a sham, extending only from instep to knee, where they were bound by black velvet garters.

Gabrielle looked down at the lacy network with a shake of the head. "I'm very much afraid, Margot, that the bottoms are soiled. I wouldn't wear the silly things, but they're the twig now, and so Mme. Lebery insists on them when I'm acting as a *demoiselle d'magasin*. How many have you ironed for me this week?"

"This will make the ninth time."

Gabrielle shook her head again. "It's too bad, my dear child. But what can we do? The sad part of it is that we put them on to interest the men, and then we wear such long skirts that the poor creatures never get as much as a glimpse.

"I'll wear my *calecons* tonight," she added, stripping off the stockings and replacing them with a pair which reached to the hips. "They're so much warmer and more comfortable. Mme. Lebery says we should wear them even if they are so much criticized. Isn't it absurd to call them opera drawers because actresses have been known to give small glimpses of them on the stage? I'm sure it's quite proper for a lady to wear them, because *she*, goodness knows, never shows as much as an inch of them at the ankle."

"You have such a *lovely* figure!" exclaimed the younger cousin, looking enviously at the slim and shapely legs so fully displayed. "Do you suppose, Gabrielle, I'll ever look at all like you?"

An enormous skirt of waxed calico was now laced to the waist, Margot lending her aid in the operation. It had no hoops, for the staid English court had ruled them out, and the French visitors were reluctantly in the position of having to conform to foreign dictates. It was stiffened with long strips of whalebone, however, and so stood out enough to sway gracefully with every move. Over this a second skirt was then draped, a flutter of tulle with a furbelow of old lace.

A third skirt was added. It also was of tulle and was draped over the second to show a V in front. It had a few silver spangles and a touch of silver in each tuck. Margot held up a square mirror, and her cousin pirouetted in front of it, striving to catch glimpses of herself in it. "It's still not bad at all," she sighed, "even if it is two years old. Do you know, Margot, that neither of our mothers ever wore a gown more than three times? How wonderful it must have been!"

The servant bustled in through the back door, saying in a hearty voice, "It's just old Antoine." As he passed by the screens he added: "Ah, the white one, Mam'selle Gabrielle!"

Margot looked after him with a suspicious air. "I wonder if he's been at the wine! I must find a new place to hide it. I've thought of keeping it under the coals, but it would be so hard to get at if I did."

The full company had assembled when Frank arrived at six sharp. He had taken great pains with his toilet for perhaps the first time in his life.

His frilled silk shirt, projecting through a low-cut lavender waistcoat, was impeccable, and his long-tailed black coat was tailored so perfectly that not a single wrinkle showed. The buckles on his shoes and the knee buttons on his satin breeches were of silver; and, despite the flattening of his one kneecap, he filled his white stockings creditably enough.

Antoine, stationed at the door, announced him in a pompous voice, and he made his way to where his host was seated in front of the fireplace. The Comte de Salle extended a shaking hand and said: "I am happy to welcome you, M'sieur Ellery. This is my son." The bulky figure of the heir of the house, looming gloomily over the chair, bowed almost imperceptibly. Other introductions followed, but Frank found it impossible to distinguish any of the names. He saw Gabrielle at the far end of the room, where the long table was set for dinner, talking with animation to a group of middle-aged ladies, all of whom were generously loaded down with paint and jewelry. Her shoulders were white and slender above the precarious line of her gown.

The room was lighted now by dozens of candles and seemed, to the young Englishman, like a glimpse of Versailles. The silver and the old glass on the table shone brilliantly, and the articles behind the glass doors of the cabinets had acquired an added air of rarity. The company was very gay, and a buzz of talk and laughter filled the room. Antoine, his duties on the door at an end, had vanished. A glance at the rear of the apartment, where the servant had gone, would have puzzled Frank much more than the other guests. They had become inured to such contrasts by years of exile.

At table he found himself seated between the most grotesquely bedizened of the middle-aged ladies and a mountainous churchman with beady black eyes like currants in a suet pudding of a face. The conversation flowed along without a break, serving to cover the slowness of the service, which Antoine was managing alone. The churchman said to him in a rumbling voice: "I am the Abbé Force. And you, m'sieur, are a newspaper publisher, I understand. Do you happen to know the devious scoundrels who put out these newspapers in French for the use, if not the delectation, of the French residents of London?"

"No, M'sieur l'Abbé. It seems to me there's a suggestion of blackmail in their operation."

"Rather more than a suggestion." The Abbé was spooning up his soup gustily. "They are filled with the most idle and troublesome of gossip as well. This is excellent soup but, I fear, there will be no second portions."

Frank lowered his voice. "I noticed that some of the guests placed what seemed to me to be coins in a silver dish on a console in one of the front windows. Should I—is there something I've overlooked?"

"It's the custom here," grumbled the churchman. "I am exempt from it but, with the rest, it is expected. Each leaves a small fee. Two shillings, three, as much as he feels free to give, in fact. It's the rule at a few other houses."

"Would I be considered presumptuous if I followed the custom?"

The Abbé did not answer for a moment. His gloomy prognostication about the soup had been borne out; there had been no suggestion of second helpings. He plunged a fork into the slice of fish which had been placed in front of him. "Ah, sole!" he said. "And quite excellent! We are going to fare better than I had expected tonight. Yes, M'sieur Publisher, obey the custom of the house by all means. I think our worthy host would be disappointed if you allowed any scruples of modesty to check your generosity."

The Abbé devoted himself to the food for some time, then, demolishing the better part of a plate of macaroni tartlets which had been placed within his reach in spite of Gabrielle's warning. He would take one, crush in the crusty sides with his fingers, pop it into his mouth, and it was gone with one crunch of the jaws. Finding himself free, therefore, Frank took advantage of the chance to watch Gabrielle. Everything about her delighted him: the close curl of her brown hair, the fact that her nose, although slightly aquiline, still managed to be a little impudent, that her eyes were not black, as he had thought, but a warm brown. She was talking to Jules and managing to bring an occasional smile to the cold features of that convinced olympian. Frank was finding it an easy matter to dislike M. de Vitrelle.

"M'sieur Publisher, do you know Gosfield?" asked the Abbé suddenly.

"I know it only as the present residence of your King."

"There's a difficulty about his presence there. It's too far from London, too far to make consultation possible with his subjects here. A new place of residence must be found for His Majesty, but we cannot discover any way of meeting him to discuss the situation. Obviously we cannot go to Gosfield in sufficient numbers for the purpose. It is equally clear that His Majesty can't come to London."

"Why not, if I may ask?"

"The expense. The King would have to make a proper entry. In addition he would have to pay a number of calls, to show himself in state, to distribute certain gifts. It would be ruinous, quite beyond his present purse, in fact."

"But the British Government allows him an income of six thousand pounds a year. Surely that would make a single visit possible."

The Abbé shook his head. "He has nearly one hundred people with him. They receive no set stipends, naturally, but they must be fed and clothed and provided with a little money for personal expenses. His Majesty finds it a difficult matter to stretch his budget to cover such costs."

The churchman's gravity made it clear that the problem was one of first importance to the members of the London colony. Frank suggested, suppressing a smile, that the solution would seem to be for the two parties to meet each other halfway. The King, he pointed out, might bring his court to some place not too far from London so that his subjects could go out to meet him without encountering any great difficulty.

"An excellent idea," concurred the Abbé. "Has M'sieur any such place in mind? It would require to be of a considerable size."

An idea suddenly flashed into Frank's mind; he was becoming prolific of plans to provide further opportunities for seeing Gabrielle. "I've a country home which might serve," he said, forgetting the transaction of the afternoon. "It's not far from Windsor and, therefore, easy enough of access from London. I would be very glad to loan it for the purpose."

The Abbé suspended a motion of his arm in the direction of the sole remaining macaroni tartlet. He turned around in his chair and regarded his companion with the first show of real interest.

"Indeed, m'sieur! This is most interesting. I would like to hear something about this estate of yours. I must point out that it would have to meet certain pressing requirements."

"Perhaps you will enumerate them, then."

"With pleasure. First, as to size. His Majesty would bring as many as thirty with him." He began to check over lists. "The two Ducs, the Archbishop of Rheims, D'Avaray, all the gentlemen of his immediate household, at least two confessors, a handful of valets and *officiers du gobelet*, the faithful Turgy perhaps. Her Majesty would not be likely to come, being in the very worst of health. The Duchesse d'Angoulême would accompany him, naturally. A few ladies of the household. Yes, there would be thirty."

"Caster Towers could not provide for the fifes and drums of the Hundred Swiss," explained Frank with a smile, "but there would be reasonable accommodation for as many as sixty people."

The Abbé's broad face showed signs of something approaching excitement. "In that case it might serve. It might indeed. We would have to choose our delegation with great care to keep it down to thirty. They would *all* want to go. Could we include any ladies under the circumstances?" The churchman was talking as though to himself. "Well, a few perhaps. His Majesty likes young faces about him whenever possible, and I am sure the Duc de Berri would consider it almost in the nature of an affront if our pretty Gabrielle were not of the party." Frank sighed with relief. "I must ask for more details, m'sieur. Your dining room is large enough for the *Grand Couvert?* His Majesty would feel it incumbent on him to dine alone in view of the full court at least once."

"If my memory serves me right, it's one hundred feet long and fifty wide. There's a gallery at one end."

"Excellent! And the state bedroom—does it contain a bed large enough to provide His Majesty with full comfort? He is—well, quite stout, as you doubtless know. A matter of two hundred and sixty pounds." The Abbé smiled. "At least, m'sieur, he has never acknowledged that he exceeds that weight. The bed must be low because he objects to climbing."

"I'm sure the bed is large enough. And it's quite low."

"And now about the—is it the dunagan that you call it?"

Frank smiled. "It's known as that sometimes. The nearest one is located under the stairs a short distance down the corridor."

"That is most important, m'sieur. It must be close and yet not too close." The Abbé shook his head apologetically. "I'm sure you will pardon me, m'sieur, for asking so many questions when I have explained that, in matters of the court, one cannot be too careful. Every detail must be thought of and every possibility provided for. There are so many people to be pleased that every small move becomes a point for prayerful consideration. But we are progressing, m'sieur. Now we come to the kitchens. They are large, no doubt, and amply equipped for so many discriminating guests? The ladies and gentlemen of the court, although they have had to subsist often on the plainest and the scantiest of fare, are gourmets. No, I should go further. They are quarrelsome gourmets. A sauce which contains a single lump, the wrong wine selected for any one course! M'sieur, the storm that can be raised! His Majesty is not as hard to please as some of the people around him. He has a great liking for boned mutton cutlets. Give him a dish of truffles, cooked *au champagne,* and he is happy; although it must be served piping hot. With His Majesty, the worry would come in the matter of the wines. None of those we have been served tonight would do at all. A single glass of the lightest chambertin and a sup of the heaviest burgundy; after that he must have the rarest only. Have you cypress, pacaret, malaga, tokay?"

"There is a supply of malaga and tokay in the cellars. The others, no."

"Still, it is something. Perhaps Bastange could be sent down in advance with some bottles of the rest, enough for His Majesty. Your cellars, m'sieur, could be made to serve for the ladies and gentlemen of the court."

Frank felt reasonably sure that Caradoc would fall in with the plan. Entertaining the exiled King of France would attract a great deal of attention, the kind of interest that might prove useful to a rising politician of the conservative stripe. Clearly it was going to prove expensive, but that did not worry him. It would provide opportunities of the most golden kind. He leaned back in his chair, paying little attention to the other details which the Abbé brought up. He saw himself escorting Gabrielle through the long gallery (after getting rid of the attentive Jules), taking her to see the unique beauties of the yew walk, even perhaps stealing away with her for an excursion to Willars Bend.

Sosthène de Salle had been regarding Frank from across the table with sullen disapproval, caused no doubt by such Jacobinic experiments as the bringing of newspaper fellows into the homes of gentlemen. The Abbé Force, laying aside the proposal for discussion later with those on whose shoulders rested the making of all such momentous decisions, proceeded to regale the Englishman with whispered comments on the unfriendly Sosthène.

"If the Comte should die," he asserted, "that great mountain of selfishness would return to France at once and make his peace with the usurper. We're all sure of it. He thinks of nothing but himself, that Sossy. Sometimes I'm glad that his luck has not held. Would you believe, m'sieur, that for years he made as much as thirty thousand francs a year at the gaming tables? The family lived well in those days; they had no financial worries as the rest of us did. But of recent years it has been different. They're glad of the shillings and the occasional half crowns which are left in the dish."

The company began to diminish as soon as dinner was over. Sosthène vanished immediately, on the trail, no doubt, of the tercel fellow who was prepared to back his skill at piquet. Frank saw some of the older people shake hands with their host and then retrieve their wraps from the chairs near the entrance where they had been deposited on entering. He gravitated to the window embrasure where the console stood and added a guinea to the pile of coins; having decided, after much earnest thought, that this represented the limit of generosity without verging on ostentation. He then approached the Comte, whose ear in the meantime had been appropriated by the Abbé Force.

"From what the Abbé is telling me," said the old man, who was looking the better for his dinner and the wine which he had imbibed rather generously, "your visit with us, m'sieur, has borne excellent fruit. The plan appears to me an excellent one."

"I'm sure we will be in a position very soon to discuss it with you more definitely," declared the churchman, nodding his great bare dome of a head.

Gabrielle was engaged at the far end of the room but, as Frank donned his greatcoat and gave the customary whisk of a sleeve to the crown of his tall beaver hat, she left the group she was with and joined him at the door.

"You're leaving early, m'sieur," she said reproachfully. "Has the company been so dull, then?"

"I publish a morning newspaper, mademoiselle, and my evenings are always devoted to it."

"I'm very sorry. It was pleasant to have you with us, although this is the first chance we've had to talk. Would you believe it, m'sieur, that we've entertained this same company at least a dozen times? Always the same faces, and some of them so—well, so uninspiring. Always the same order at table; a change would precipitate a terrible crisis! Always the same things talked about! I found it a real pleasure to glance down the table and see a new face for once."

"You didn't glance down the table as often as I would have liked. As for the rest of your guests, I thought they were all quite pleasant."

"Well, I can't agree about some of them. Oh, I'm not criticizing them. They have admirable qualities, m'sieur. Would you believe it that almost all of them here tonight have found it necessary to engage in some employment? There were"—she began to count—"two governesses, a teacher of music, two of languages, one fencing master. And, yes, m'sieur, one cook!"

"A cook! Which one was that?"

"The lady on your left. Mme. de Gaseau. We didn't put her there because of that, m'sieur! She was seated as usual. She's employed in one of the fashionable inns and can get away one evening only during the week."

"I remember now that she spoke to me once only, and it had something to do with the sauce on the ragout."

Gabrielle looked up at him with her eloquent dark eyes. "I've heard something of what you've suggested to the good Abbé. It's most extraordinarily kind of you. I'm so excited about it. I've never seen His Majesty, and so I *must* be one of those to go. I'm already doing what I can to make sure of it."

"It would be an honor and a pleasure to see you at the Towers. In fact, that was my sole reason for making the invitation."

"M'sieur! How very flattering."

"If you are not on the list, mademoiselle, I'll contrive to have a fire or to arrange a convenient outbreak of smallpox among the help. You might drop a hint of that if the need arises."

Her fan brushed his sleeve lightly. "I've already told you how flattered I am. But must you go to such elaborate pretexts? If you want to see me, you can always pay us a call."

Frank's head was in a whirl. "I can't tell you how happy it would make me to come again."

"I'll be much offended if you don't. And soon." She smiled up at him. "Good evening, M'sieur Ellery."

8

CARADOC CAME STRIDING into the dining room with a copy of the morning edition in one hand. He had not waited to dress completely. A frilled shirt with full sleeves was stuffed into the top of his breeches, and he was carrying his shoes in his other hand.

"This is outrageous, positively outrageous!" he exclaimed, holding the paper out at arm's length and shaking it, like a terrier with a rat. "I had no idea yesterday that what you planned was anything so rash, so unheard-of! Why, damn it, this article of Cope's is an open attack on the administration!"

"I thought I made it clear that such was my intention."

Caradoc continued to splutter. "I should have suspected it. You're a damned sly fellow, Frank. You talk us into an agreement and then use it to stab my political friends in the back!" His blue eyes blazed furiously at his brother. "The nation's at war and you have the effrontery to criticize the men at the head of the government. There's going to be a storm about this, mark my words. It may even be considered treason."

"Every Englishman has a right to his opinion," answered Frank. "If he knows the administration is acting in a slow and stupid way, it's his right and his duty to say so."

"But not in print! Not in print, you blind fool!" Caradoc dropped everything and began to stride about the room. "At the dinner table, in your club, on the streets, if you must. But never in print!"

"It's the only way to make criticism count, Carr."

"I suppose it means nothing to you that you've prejudiced my chances for advancement?"

"I'm sure I haven't. You'll know what to do about that. I'm ready to take the full responsibility."

"I wish the damned paper had never been started!"

"If it hadn't, you wouldn't be a member of Parliament today."

Caradoc whisked up a slice of toast and began to munch it savagely. "Great God, I don't know what to say or do. My chance for a career may be damaged beyond repair. It's simply incredible that a thing like this could happen to me at the very time when the eyes of the treasury bench are on me! I think you've gone insane, Frank. It's either that or you're so damned jealous that you're trying to block me. It's one or the other. What will the members of the cabinet say?"

"I consider what they may say a matter of supreme unimportance. Carr, can't you see that the administration is too weak to stay in control of the destinies of the nation in this emergency? We must have stronger men at the head of things. Foresighted men to meet Bonaparte with something of his own energy."

"What men? The Whigs? A fine lot they are!"

"Not the Whigs necessarily. There must be men in England strong enough to lead us well. We can find another Chatham. If you would only see it, Carr, this is your great chance. Forget politics, stop playing the stale old game of the Ins versus the Outs. Stand up in the House and demand a vigorous prosecution of the war. The country needs men to-day with the courage to do that." Frank got to his feet and dropped a hand on his brother's shoulder. "Carr, I mean it. This *is* your great chance. Instead of standing around and waiting for whatever they may condescend to give you, you can make yourself a leader overnight. If enough of the members would show the right kind of courage, this senile and incompetent crowd could be forced out."

Caradoc shook off his hand impatiently. "What do you think I am, a damned turncoat?"

"I was hoping you were a patriot."

"By God, I am a patriot! I believe the only way we can win this war is to back up our government in everything. To stand by our guns. To do our duty."

"We have so few guns to stand by, Carr. And such antiquated ones! Do you know anything about the artillery Napoleon used to blast the Prussians at Jena and the Russians at Friedland? If you do, you know that much more than the honorable gentlemen at the head of our government."

"That's just quibbling. Playing on words."

"I agree with you that we must do our duty. But what is our duty at this moment?"

Caradoc snorted. "To work for King and country. I know no other duty." He threw back his shoulders. "I'm going to support the King's ministers to the best of my ability. And as soon as I can get into my clothes, I'm going to see a lawyer. That agreement you talked us into signing is going to be broken before you can do any more harm."

"It can be broken in one way only. By mutual consent. And get this through your head, Carr: I'm not going to have it broken. I've started this campaign and I'm going to see it through."

"You'll ruin the newspaper if you do. And you'll land in jail yourself." Caradoc laughed scornfully. "I don't know what's got into you, Frank. You ought to have enough sense to see that it won't do any good. I'm going to tell you the truth for once. You haven't got it in you to do this kind of thing. It takes—well, you know yourself what it takes. More ability and more determination than you've got, my boy. And more courage."

There was a moment's silence. "You're probably right," said Frank finally. "I know my own shortcomings even better than you do. But in spite of all the things I lack, I'm going on."

"Very well, then, go on with it. I've warned you. You're a fool, Frank, a jealous fool!"

Frank walked from the house, his mind full of what his brother had said. Ability, determination, courage! Did he lack these qualities so conspicuously? He had always known that the other members of the family had a poor opinion of him, even little Hump, who worshiped Caradoc and had tried to model himself in every way on the masterful second son; but no one had voiced that feeling so openly before. He was not concerned about the first point of the indictment; he *had* ability of a kind, for he had managed to do well with the paper. But he could not be sure about his courage. He had never been put to a test. Perhaps he did lack it, as his brother had said; the fact that his natural inclination had been toward soldiering did not prove anything.

He walked slowly, unaware that his feet were getting wet. Once he looked up and blinked in the light of the sun. "If I'm a coward," he thought, "I'll soon find myself out." His eyes were so dazzled that he did not see a tall man in a military cloak who waved to him from the other side of the square.

"Hallo! I was on my way to see you, my bold crusading editor."

It was Sir Robert Wilson. They met at the entrance of the Tablet

Building, and the soldier clapped Frank heartily on the back. "I got up early to read the article," he boomed. "It was splendid, splendid! I said to myself, 'There it is, the first shot in a campaign to drive these blockheads out of office!' You've done a great thing for the country, Ellery, a great thing. And, by the way, I've never thanked you for the account of my ride from Russia. It was a spirited bit of writing, my boy. You couldn't have done better if you'd made the ride yourself."

"I'm not feeling too happy about things at this moment."

"A natural reaction. Let me tell you, Ellery, all London's talking about what you've done. Just now I heard a man say to another on the street, 'The *Tablet's* giving the guv-ment bloody fits this morning.' It's a safe wager every office in the city is buzzing with it. I'd give a lot to see Perceval's face when he reads it. Canning, of course, will be secretly in agreement with you."

"I've been hearing from my brother about it. He—he took me down a peg or two."

"Don't give anything he says a second thought," declared Wilson, with a wave of his hand which dismissed the lordly Caradoc from all further consideration. "I've been sitting in the House the last few days and I've kept an eye on that young man. He's a born politician. He'll play his cards the way most of them do: sit around and make speeches only when he gets the nod from the great men on the bench; vote right on everything and never be guilty of a thought of his own. Oh, he'll get on. They'll use him when they need him and shove some profitable things his way. But never make the mistake, my friend, of letting anything he says affect your feelings or your course."

"He said I lacked the courage to go through with this." Frank got it out with considerable difficulty. "It disturbed me. I can't be sure he isn't right."

"Courage? What gives that young rooster the right to lecture you about courage?" He seized both lapels of Frank's coat and proceeded to talk with intense earnestness. "There are two kinds of courage, Ellery. One is much rarer than the other and harder to find. The first is the physical kind. Most men have it. There've been times when I've looked over a squad under me and decided they were the poorest kind of human misfits, and then I've seen them stand up under fire without a single man of them flinching. I've led a charge or two and gained some sort of reputation because of it. That's an easy thing to do. The trumpets sound and there's a wild cheer and you see the banners going forward. Your horse begins to gallop and then you hear that mad thunder of hoof-beats, and the excitement of it carries you away. It's easy to be brave then. But the other kind of courage is different. It's having the mettle to stand up to adversity, to go on with something when it's hard and unpleasant. I think you have that kind, Ellery, as well as the other."

"It makes me feel better to hear you say it."

Frank was beginning to notice the cold, but Wilson made no move to go inside with him. His whole face seemed to have lighted up. "When I was knighted by old Nobs," he said, "I made a vow. You see, I was pretty young, and it rather went to my head that I was getting the honor so early. I was sure I was destined for great things. When I felt the sword on my shoulder, I said to myself: 'Sir Robert Wilson, you're going to be from now on the kind of man the order of knighthood was intended for. You're always going to do what you think is right and just. The ideas of other men are never going to sway you from that course, and you're not going to let the hope of favors change your mind.' That's what I said to myself, Ellery, and I've tried honestly ever since to live up to my vow. It hasn't helped me much. I guess you know all about that. I've never been given much of a chance, and I begin to think I never shall. But it doesn't matter. I'm going to continue on my course just the same.

"The point I'm trying to make in this long speech," he went on, "is that you and I are going to be in the same boat, from the present look of things. You're doing what you see is your duty in this crisis. It isn't going to be easy, and I've a strong conviction that you're not going to get anything out of it but hard knocks. At first, I mean. In the long run you're certain of the finest of all rewards: the knowledge that you did your country a great service and, perhaps, some belated recognition of that fact. Keep your mind on the future and you won't feel the knocks you get in the present quite so much."

A caller was waiting inside the entrance. Windy Topp, who had let him in, was staring down at him with a sort of dubious wonder.

"Here's a boy, sahib," he said, shaking his head. "Here's a joov'nile C'lumbus, a globe-trottin', Gulliver-travelin' sort of a boy. He's been all over Lunnon in the snow, he says, looking for a Mouser Ellery, and now as he's found the place at last he shuts up like a urster and not a word'll he say as to what he wants. He speaks English as good as you or me, sahib, but he lets the cat out of the bag with that 'mouser.' He's a French furriner."

It was Jean Baptiste Achille, and he was looking very cold and tired. His feet were wet, and there was still some snow on the bag of books over his back.

"M'sieur," he said with a deep sigh of relief, "I thought I would never find you. I wanted to see you before going to school, but London seems a very large city. A very difficult city to find one's way in, m'sieur."

"Well, Jean Baptiste Achille," said Frank. He took the small boy by the hand. "We'll go into this office here where there's a fine fire and we'll be nice and warm. And then you can tell me what it's all about. Both the young ladies are well, I trust?"

"Quite well, m'sieur. Mam'selle Gabrielle went to her employment, of course, this morning——" He stopped with a stricken look. "That is a secret, and no one was to be told. It was wrong of me to speak without thinking. But perhaps"—hopefully—"M'sieur already knew?"

"No, I didn't, but you mustn't let that worry you. I'll see it's kept a deep secret. And Mlle. Margot?"

"Margot was scrubbing when I left. She is a very good scrubber."

The office into which they turned was occupied by a clerk who had kept his muffler on for extra warmth and was pretending to be very busy at some task which involved the use of a ruler, a paste pot, and a pair of shears longer than the iron on the French boy's leg. The poker lay on the desk beside him, for greater facility, no doubt, in jabbing frequently at the fire. It was not as fine a fire as Frank had promised, so he pulled a chair up in front of it for Jean Baptiste Achille. The boy held his hands before the blaze at once.

"I think I was getting the hot-ache in my fingers, m'sieur," he said. "That is what Mick Finnerty calls it, and sometimes it is very painful."

"Toby," said Frank, addressing the clerk, who was now wielding the ruler as though his continued employment depended on it, "can you find something else to do for a few minutes? This young gentleman and I have some weighty matters to discuss."

"I'll be glad to, Mr. Ellery," said the clerk, dropping the ruler and blowing on his hands. "I don't want to register a complaint, sir, far from it, but this chimbley, sir, it draws the worst of any in the whole place."

"And now, Jean Baptiste Achille," said Frank, when they had the room to themselves, "what took you all over London on such a cold morning?"

"It's about the money, m'sieur," said the boy. "Did you know how much would be left over after I bought the marbles? Indeed, m'sieur, I can buy them for two dace or half a gob at most. That will leave me with a great deal of money."

"I told you to spend the rest for other things."

"But, m'sieur." The boy's face took on an even more serious expression. "This morning quite early I was helping to clear the table, and I was not feeling so very well, and Margot said I should lie down on a couch until I felt better. It was dark in the room, and while I was there the Abbé Force came in to talk to the master, and they did not see me because I was not feeling well at all and was lying very still. They were talking about His Majesty, and then they talked about money. I could not help hearing what they said, m'sieur, though it was wrong of me to listen. The Abbé was saying that His Majesty was finding it hard to live because—I think he said it was because money was losing its value. I did not know what that meant, but it frightened me because now I have money too and I don't want it to lose its value. I thought I should find out what he meant."

"Well," said Frank, finding it hard to keep from smiling, "it's quite a serious matter about money today. You see, Jean Baptiste Achille, this country has been at war with Napoleon so long that we're running into very heavy debts. That's bad for a country because prices go up and people don't have more money to buy things with, and so money loses some of its purchasing power. If the government should start to remedy it by putting out paper money, then it gets very bad. Savings become of very little value. That's what the Abbé meant."

The boy frowned as though such things were hard to believe. "Do you mean, m'sieur, that I could save the rest of my money and then, if I wanted to spend it later, I could not buy as much with it as I can now?"

"That's exactly it."

"You mean, m'sieur, that it might not be worth more than one hog instead of two?"

"It might even be worth nothing at all."

The boy's face went white on learning of such infamous possibilities. "I know this must be true, m'sieur, because it is you who say it. But it is hard to believe there could be such wickedness. Who would be punished for it?"

"No one would be punished for it. It would be too hard to decide who had been responsible. You see, things like that just seem to happen."

"No one!" Jean Baptiste Achille's universe was tumbling about him. "But, m'sieur, it is foolish then to save! I have always been told that to save is the most important thing of all. What am I to do?"

"I'll tell you what we had better do about this, young man. Here you have some capital that you're in danger of losing if we should run into trouble. And here I am with a business where I can always make use of more capital. Suppose you turn it over to me, and I'll make you a solemn promise that, whenever you want it back, I'll pay you enough to equal the purchasing value of a double shilling today. In addition to that, I'll give you a nice return on your money. Shall we say one penny a month?"

The boy indulged in some earnest calculations. "That would be a very fine return on the capital, m'sieur. Your business must be a very good one to pay so much interest."

"It's a very good business. Well, what do you say? Would you like to invest your money that way?"

Jean Baptiste Achille gulped but managed to produce the money in a reluctant hand. "Yes, m'sieur, I think it will be wise to invest my money. It isn't easy to part with it. It is very pleasant to keep it to yourself so you can look at it and know it is all there. But it will be pleasant too, I think, to feel it is safe. Am I to call here each month for the interest?"

"No, no. The essence of the bargain," said Frank with a smile, "is that I am to call on you each month and deliver the money myself. I won't mind doing that at all. I don't want you to say anything about this, but it will be very pleasant for me that way."

"I hope M'sieur doesn't think it is wrong for me to ask him about money. You see"—he hesitated—"my father does not understand much about saving. He earns very little money, and mostly it is in arrears. When he does get some, he is very likely to spend it all on drink. When he gets old, m'sieur, he will have nothing laid away at all. It will be very hard for my father if I don't save something for him." He looked up at Frank and added in a hurry, as though fearful that he had given a wrong impression, "I hope you won't think badly of my father, m'sieur, because of what I have said. Lots of fathers drink. Mick Finnerty says his father drinks more than any man for ten squares in every direction. Mick is proud because his father drinks so much."

"I understand how it is," answered Frank gravely. "You and I, Jean Baptiste Achille, must do something about this between us. We'll see that money is laid away for your father. It's a good thing that we both understand something about saving, isn't it?"

Another visitor was waiting in the hall above, a plump individual who had thrown open his greatcoat and was irritably twirling his watch chain on an extended finger.

"Mr. Ellery?" he demanded when Frank appeared at the top of the stairs. "I'm from the customs, sir. I fancy you know what I'm here about."

"I'm afraid I shall have to ask you to state your business."

"You should know, sir. After publishing that infamous article in this morning's edition. Well, sir, the head told me to come personally and hand you this letter. He couldn't wait for the mails, sir. Not the head, sir. When he wants a little matter like this attended to, he wants it attended to without delay. Here, sir, take it. It's a notification that we're cutting off the printing contracts. We want nothing more to do with you, sir.

The head authorized me to add anything that I felt called on to say. In fact, he said I could Pitch it Strong. I want to tell you, young man, that in cutting off the contracts we're cutting them off for good. In other words, sir, you've cooked your goose."

"In that case," said Frank, "we shall have to do without the printing contracts. You might tell the head that I'm sorry he felt it necessary to act in such a hurry. It hardly seems possible that he's given the matter due consideration. He'll find we acted in the best interests of the country in publishing the article. And that applies equally to the other articles we plan to use."

"More articles?" The eyes of the customs official seemed ready to pop out of his head with indignation. "More attacks on the gov'ment! You amaze me, sir. They're very angry with you now. I'm sure they won't be disposed to forgive more articles like this one."

"They?"

"They, sir, they! The Prime Minister of Great Britain, sir, the Chancellor of the Exchequer, sir, the Home Secr't'ry, sir, the lords of the Admiralty, sir, the Paymaster General, sir. All the responsible heads of the gov'ment, sir."

"It must be gratifying to you to be in the confidence of so many of the great men of the country."

"What's that, sir? I don't like the tone of it. I may report to you further, sir, what the head said to me. He said, 'Higgs, I'll see that young firebrand in the pillory one of these days.'"

"Perhaps he will," declared Frank.

The visitor having departed, Frank walked into his office. The fire had not been laid long, for the room was very cold. He could see his breath as he seated himself at his desk.

It was piled high with notes. He did not need to open one to know what they were. They had all been delivered by messenger, and it seemed to him that indignation showed itself in the sharp lettering of the addresses. *They* were venting their feelings over the stand the *Tablet* had taken; and he was sure they were Pitching it Strong.

Frank sighed and reached for a letter cutter.

9

FRANK ELLERY'S DAYS were so full of work that he saw little of his mother and brother for the next fortnight. It was just as well, perhaps. Mrs. Ellery never spoke to him on the rare occasions when he sat down to a meal at home. The sight of him was enough, in fact, to bring her lips down into what Aunt Francilea called the Lawcey pout. Caradoc, who prided himself on being broad-minded, tried to argue with him at times, slapping him on the back and saying, "Now really, old fellow, this sort of thing's got to be stopped"; but he would lose his control almost immediately and lapse into lordly rages. On all such occasions the talk would then be continued over the head of the older son. Mrs. Ellery would say something like, "Well, Caradoc, we'll never sign any tricky papers again, now we know what he's Really like," or "To think I have a Scamp and a Traitor for a son!" Caradoc would talk about the need to think of himself and his career, and there would be dark hints of conferences in the offices of solicitors and of legal action pending.

On the day before Christmas Frank found himself completely alone. Mrs. Ellery had departed for the Towers, taking all the servants with her. Caradoc was remaining for the final session of the House but would post down to the country immediately after. There had been an unvoiced understanding that the disturbing element in the family would not appear there for the festivities, an arrangement which he accepted willingly enough, although he could think of no other way of spending the holiday.

When he appeared at the office Gavin McSwain had returned from his first rounds with a longer face than usual.

"Well, Gavin, what is it now? Bad news, I'm sure."

It was bad news. The post office had refused with brusque finality to give the *Tablet* any translations from the foreign newspapers. Frank was seriously disturbed. It had never occurred to him that he could be barred from this essential source of news.

"But we pay them three hundred guineas a year for the service," he protested. "Why, the quarterly payment was made less than a week ago. We must demand the translations, Gavin."

"A Scotsman is always good at demanding, Muster Ellery," said the writer, "and I think I gave a convincing performance. But it had no effect on the post office laddies. They laughed at me. They said that a rascally sheet—I'm quoting them literally, Muster Ellery—like the *Tab* could whustle for its translations."

Frank pondered a moment and then said: "I think, then, we'll leave them in undisputed possession of the field. They have the whip hand and we won't give them the satisfaction of refusing us again. We must find some other way of getting foreign news."

"The *Times* laddie whuspered to me, Muster Ellery, that we would never miss the news given out today." Mr. McSwain added this reluctantly, as though temperamentally unwilling to brighten the picture.

Frank said briskly: "Cope and I will work out a plan to engage an agent in Brussels or Amsterdam. He can secure the foreign newspapers for us and send them over direct in a fishing ketch. We might even hire a cutter for the purpose." He nodded his head in a more cheerful mood. "It will cost us considerably more than the three hundred guineas, but we may be able to get the papers over ahead of the post office copies. You can never tell, Gavin. This may be a blessing in disguise after all."

Cope was wearing his Charlie Present waistcoat, and when he heard what had happened his face turned an excited red, which matched the hues of that garment.

"We've got to expect that they'll fight us at every turn," he said, giving a still more militant twist to the ends of his mustache. "Now we'll have to get on with something we should have done long ago. We must stand on our own legs, Frank, and build up an exclusive news organization. What's the sense of depending on the post office and having exactly the same items from abroad that all the other papers print? There's never any grape seed in their translations anyway. They're a dull lot, and I'm sure they miss all the livelier bits."

"We'll have to do it as cheaply as possible. You know what's happening to our revenue, Copey."

"How's the mail today?"

"It sets a new record." Frank shook his head dolefully. "Seventy-three letters of protest. I—I get kind of sick when I look at them. It isn't pleasant to have everyone in the country calling me a scribbling rat and a presumptuous puppy. The batch today is the worst yet."

Cope proceeded to light his pipe with a cheerful air. A piece of flint was attached to the initialed silver plate he wore at his belt. He struck it against the plate and secured a spark which he applied to the braided cotton in a small silver cylinder on a chain of delicate links. Sucking in his cheeks and emitting clouds of smoke, he said:

"I wouldn't bother to read them if I were you, Frank. They all come from cranks and cakeys."

"But they don't. Today's mail includes a score of letters from members of the House and the Peers. There's one from an admiral and half a dozen from army officers. They all say the same thing: that Nelson put a fiddlestick's end to the possibility of invasion and that all we're doing is lending comfort and aid to the enemy." He shook his head with an air of even deeper despondency. "The worst of it is that we're quite as unpopular with the public as well."

Cope grinned. "They're howling for the government to put the 'banging stach' on us. But what of it? We knew in advance that all this would happen." He continued to smoke with complete ease. "You're taking it too hard. Why do you bother to answer all the letters?"

"It's got to be done. I try to be cool and reasonable in my answers, but it's getting harder all the time."

"When did you get through last night? Close to dawn, I'll lay a wager."

Frank nodded. "It was quite late. Barshley had squeezed out the last ink ball when I left and the run on the press was over. The run gets shorter every day, Copey!"

"We're near the turn. Depend on it, public opinion is bound to veer our way soon."

"The turn will have to come soon. Our funds are running damned low."

What Frank himself knew on that score was supplemented a few minutes later when Evans came up from the business offices to show the balance sheets. He wore a dismal air and he placed the sheets in front of his employer with a gesture which said, "I told you so," more clearly than any words. Frank looked the figures over with a worried eye.

"It isn't favorable, is it, Evans?"

"Favorable! Francis, if we go on at this rate we'll be in bankruptcy in no time at all. Do you realize how much we've lost in the last two weeks? There's got to be a change. All our ready money will soon be exhausted in meeting our bills. I would hesitate to sell any of the consols in the reserve fund. Consols have dropped off since the news about Russia. We would take a big loss on any we sold today." He shook his head. "And there was a time when we had a profit of twelve thousand pounds a year!"

"Is advertising still falling off?"

"Advertising!" The business manager's manner suggested that he had no right to bring the point up after creating such difficulties for them. "It's become a non-existent commodity. The merchants of London declare, Francis, that they'll never chant in the columns of the *Tab* again. The truth of the matter is that they're afraid. They say it would reflect on their loyalty if they appeared with us. There you have it, Francis. I hesitate to speak so bluntly, but it's the truth."

"They'll come back to us." Frank tried to speak cheerfully, although inside himself he had no feeling of confidence whatever.

"Yes? I'm glad you think so, Francis." There was an ominous pause. "Four more of the printers left us today."

"Well, we can hire others to take their places."

"We cannot hire others, Francis. The men we have left are finding it hard. People are telling them they should quit us. There's a—may I say, a stigma?—in working for us under these circumstances. At least, that's what the men are being told."

"What do *you* think about it, Evans?"

The business manager hesitated, then looked up with a feeble pretense of a smile. "I'll stay with you to the bitter end. But I'm thinking, Francis, that it's likely to be quite a bitter end for all of us."

Frank smiled at him. "Good! That makes me feel a little better. I'm going to need you. Don't take all this too hard, Evans. We'll weather the storm."

On the desk lay a note from Stemper. There was no question in Frank's mind that the purpose of the note was to warn him of further aggression on the part of the administration. He hesitated before running a finger under the flap.

DEAR FRANK:

There is talk of throwing me out of here, neck and crop. The Liberal Opposition (which is so pitifully weak!) may raise a protest if the exclusion move comes to a head, but we can't count too much on them. They're a pusillanimous lot since Fox is no longer alive to lead them. Of course, there will be other ways of covering the debates if I'm driven like a modern Adam from this parliamentary Garden of Eden.

STEMP

P.S. Caradoc Ellery, M.P., has just risen and said in a resounding voice: "Mr. Speaker, honorable gentlemen of the House of Commons: I find myself in a painful position. . . ." Frank, he's going to wash his hands of us! I've been expecting it. He has refused to speak to me for a week. I advise we publish his speech in full. I'm going to turn my knowledge of good old John Byrom to account and take it all down in shorthand.

Well, he had been expecting it too, Frank said to himself. He tried to think that Caradoc was not to be blamed, but a deep sense of hurt pride blotted out everything else. He had retained a flicker of hope that his brother would come to see the light finally and line up beside him in the struggle. Well, it was not to be that way; Caradoc was setting his feet instead in the safe road to political preferment.

He dropped the note from Stemper and took up the first page proof to come through. Generally three quarters full of advertising, the page now carried no more than a few inches of paid matter in one corner. There was a notice of "good seats at reasonable prices for the Monday hangings," a dressmaker's announcement of low prices on "Spanish lamb's-wool drawers, warranted not to shrink in washing," a hint from a moneylender named McClan that funds could be obtained "on easy, brotherly terms." Frank's eye ran nervously over the news on the page and fastened on the Old Bailey items. Four names were down for the Monday hangings, but that of Benjamin Fuller did not appear. Thank God for that!

Sir Robert Wilson dropped in after dinner for a consultation. He had been attending a regimental gathering and was in full uniform, looking very impressive in the scarlet tunic of the dragoons, with its black and gold facings. They talked over the details of an article to be written on the Martello towers which were being shoved up hurriedly along the whole southern coast of the island and in which the public had been taught to place faith as a second line of defense after the "wooden walls" of the navy. "Boney's guns will topple 'em over like cow byres," was Wilson's verdict. "He'll bypass them," was Cope's opinion. As usual Cope displayed a thorough knowledge of defense tactics. When he had left them together, Wilson said to Frank with a puzzled shake of the head: "You know, Ellery, this country is full of armchair Napoleons, but our friend Charlie Present is the only one of 'em who knows what he's talking about. The fellow amazes me."

"I hear there's talk of barring the *Tab* from the gallery of the House," said Frank, getting back to the matter which had been on his mind ever since receiving the note from Stemper.

Wilson threw one gray-clad leg, with the scarlet dragoon stripe, over the other. "I don't think they'll go through with it. Since the Almon case, they've been a little shy of stirring up the hornets of the press."

"We mustn't be too confident of that. The House has never granted the right to report proceedings. The threat of ejection or libel hangs over us all the time. Were you in the House today?"

"Yes. I heard that cub of a brother of yours speak his little mind. He made it clear that you're acting in the face of his complete disapproval. Well, as I've said before, I don't believe that anything our ranting Ralph Spooner says or does is of any real consequence. He got a round of applause when he sat down and only a few boos from the Opposition side. Don't let it worry you, my dear boy."

"Has the House risen?"

"At seven. Only the fact that the country faces an emergency could keep them deliberating on the day before Christmas. What a mad scramble there was to get away! Half of the seats were empty at that."

"I'm much more worried about financial matters," confessed Frank. "Our revenue has fallen away to practically nothing. The business manager is afraid we'll have to draw on our reserve fund soon. That's a painful prospect."

Wilson said easily: "It's a situation which can be remedied. The Opposition isn't doing anything openly to support you yet, but they see eye to eye with you—in a discreet way. Let me speak to Grey. He's a very good friend of mine. I'm sure something could be arranged. There's a lot of real wealth in the Whig party, you know."

Frank shook his head. "I'd rather not. After all, these difficulties have risen because I elected to take the *Tab* into an independent position. I'm not going to change masters even if enough Whig money were offered to see me through."

"A good general takes whatever he needs to carry on his campaign without a thought of where it comes from. The country's at war, Ellery. Nothing matters but the need to rouse the administration to action."

Frank did not answer until after a long pause. "I haven't come yet to the point where a decision must be made. I think, Sir Robert, I shall carry on in my own way as long as I can."

A clamor suddenly broke out in the square below. Sir Robert sprang up and ran to a window. He turned back at once and looked at Frank with real concern.

"A mob is gathering down there. I'm afraid there's going to be trouble."

Frank joined him at the window. The square was in darkness, but from the sounds they could tell that a large number had gathered in front of the building. A torch was lighted and almost immediately similar blobs of light sprang up in all directions. They could see now that more men were coming. They were crowding into the square from all the streets that ran into it, shouting and singing tavern songs.

"This isn't a spontaneous demonstration." Wilson shook his head. "It's been carefully organized. Someone has been rounding up all the hoodlums in London and leading them down here."

A hoarse voice shouted below: "Traitor! We'll teach ye to print a pack of lies!" Others joined in. "Come out and show yerself! Come out, liar and traitor!" They could hear an authoritative voice saying: "Spread out! Spread out! Keep your torches up, fools, so we can see what we're about!"

A stone crashed through the window next to the one where they stood. The sound of splintering glass was followed by a sustained bedlam of triumph from the mob. Wilson motioned vigorously to Frank. "This is going to be a riot. Get every light out at once, man! Quick! They mustn't have any marks to shoot at." His voice had become almost exultant, as though he welcomed the opportunity for action. "I'm going down, Ellery. I'll talk to them."

"No, no!" shouted Frank. "They're in an ugly mood. You can't tell what they might do."

"I have a way with mobs," laughed Wilson.

Stones were rattling against the sides of the building, and they heard the crash of glass in other rooms. Another smashed through the window beside them, striking the face of the astronomical clock. They could hear men running in the corridors and shouting in panic to each other. Wilson was already at the door.

"Get the lights out!" he called over his shoulder. "I'm going down! But, for God's sake, don't show yourself yet. They'll get completely out of hand if you do."

Frank went into action. He reached the corridor, shouting orders as he ran. "Every man back to his own room! Put out your lights! Then collect downstairs in the hall. Keep cool, all of you."

He negotiated the stairs in the dark and almost capsized the foreman, who had just emerged from the pressroom. "Take half a dozen of your men, Barshley, and collect whatever you can find in the way of clubs," he ordered. "We may have to defend ourselves. Be quick about it! Green, see the side doors are locked. Stevens, take the back door!"

Wilson's voice said from the darkness: "That's good. Station a man at each window on the ground floor as well. Have them armed. If a head shows, bash it in! Remember, they mustn't get a foothold inside under any circumstance." He added impatiently: "Isn't there a room where a light won't show on the outside? You can't all go milling around in the dark like this."

"Light candles in the circulation room," called Frank. "Is every man here?"

Windy Topp came tumbling into the hall. By the faint gleam now showing from the business offices in the rear, Frank saw that he had armed himself with an iron rule which he was brandishing above his head. "Bring 'em on!" he was shouting. "Bring 'em on, the swilltubs!"

Some of the men were not armed yet. Frank remembered that his father had experimented with a system of wires strung along all the halls in the hope of creating a quick means of distributing mail and copy among the various departments. It had never worked, but the equipment, which had not been removed from the walls, included a number of long hardwood arms.

"Tear down the carrier," he ordered. "The supports can be used as clubs. And, Topp, control yourself. We must keep cool."

In a few minutes Barshley reported that all the doors and windows were guarded. A few members of the mob had found their way to the yard in the rear but had been chased off the premises, one at least with a broken head. The noise from outside seemed to be increasing each minute, and the rain of stones against the front walls was incessant. The men in the front hall were keeping commendably cool, however.

"Don't lose your heads if they get in," admonished Frank. "We're strong enough to hold them. If we give way they'll wreck the place."

Barshley, who had been on the rolls since the paper was established, answered him. "Depend on us, sir, to give 'em more than they're counting on. It'll take more than a drunken mob to wreck the *Tab*."

Frank went to a window on the ground floor. All the glass had been broken, and a strong draft of cold air was pouring through. A paving stone missed him by an inch, breaking a picture on the opposite wall. He stationed himself close enough to the aperture, however, to get a view of what was going on outside. Sir Robert, he saw, had already reached the street and was climbing up on the marble mounting post. A strong desire to be out there with him took possession of Frank, and only the sure knowledge that his appearance would precipitate matters held him back. With a sudden sense of elation he realized that he felt no fear whatever.

"Listen to me!" shouted Wilson. His voice was drowned out immediately. Jeers and catcalls came from every corner of the square.

"A bleeding sojer!" roared a drunken fellow who had succeeded in climbing to the top of the front gate and was waving a torch above his head. "Knock the dirty redcoat off his perch!"

"I've got something to say to you." Sir Robert's voice could be heard faintly above the din now. "My name is Wilson. You all know who I am."

The leader tried to climb up on the mounting post also. "We didn't come here to listen to a lot of talk!" he shouted. "We came here to do our duty as honest citizens. We're going to see to it that no more treason is printed——" He was not able to finish the sentence because Wilson shoved him back off the post. The mob, still pressing forward, broke his fall.

The drunken man on the gate had recognized the figure in uniform. He let out a wild screech and waved the torch with still more frantic zeal. "It's Riding Bobby!" he shouted. "Boys, it's Riding Bobby Wilson!"

The men nearest caught the words and stopped pressing forward. "Wilson! Wilson! Riding Bobby!" they began to shout in chorus. The man on the gate called: "We can't go back on *him*. He brought the news from Roosha." "No, let him speak," contributed another voice. "Good for Riding Bobby. Let's hear what he's got to say."

Sir Robert was quick to seize his opportunity. "I want to tell you that

I believe every word that's been printed in the *Tablet!*" he called. "I believe our country is in grave danger. I'm sure Boney's going to come over if we give him half a chance. We're leaving things wide open for him."

"That's fine talk!" cried the leader. "That's not the kind of thing we ought to hear from an officer of the King!"

"It's what you're going to hear from me." More fires had been started, and the square was as light as at midday. Wilson raised an arm above his head. "How many of you have fought against Boney? How many of you have seen what happens to a country when his armies have passed through? I've done both. I tell you, it isn't a pretty thing to see men hanging by the neck from every tree! I've been in villages where half the men had been lined up as hostages and shot. It hasn't happened in England but, by God, it will, if all of us don't start to give thought to what this newspaper has been saying."

The leader of the mob interrupted with his former plea. "We didn't come here to listen to speeches! We came here to act, men!"

Wilson leaned over. "You, my friend, might be one of his first victims. He has a pleasant little way of silencing noisy customers like you. And the same thing might happen to any of you. Get this through your heads. You've been having it very easy in England. You don't know what war is like since Boney started in to conquer the world. He hates England and he hates Englishmen. He won't feel safe until he's wiped us out." He straightened up and raised his voice until it could be heard all over the square. "Free speech is the right of every Englishman. A brave editor has spoken up to save us all from the greatest danger in which the people of England have ever stood. Do you want to reward him by smashing his presses and making it impossible for him to speak any longer in your defense?"

"Yes!" shouted the leader.

"No!" screeched the drunken man on the gate. "Riding Bobby's right, boys. Listen to Riding Bobby Wilson."

"Of course I'm right! I tell you I've seen it with my own eyes. I've seen what happened in Egypt, in Italy, in Austria, in Germany. I know what will happen in England." He paused for a moment. "Why did you come here? Who got you all started? Think that over a minute and you'll see that there's a purpose behind this that not one of you would support if you were in your right senses."

"I know why I came," contributed the drunk. "I came because everyone was coming. That's why."

"That's it!" cried Wilson. "That's why most of you came. I don't need to say another word. I can leave the matter now in your hands, men of London. I know you'll see what the truth is at this time when England stands alone against the whole world."

The mob had quieted down. Voices rose from all quarters. "He's right. Perhaps the paper's been telling the truth after all."

Wilson raised a hand above his head. "I've just one thing more to say. If you don't break up now and go home like decent Englishmen, I hope Boney comes over and hangs every one of you!"

When the crowd had dispersed, Wilson came back into the front hall of the building. "Well, it's over," he said. "Gad, Ellery, it was touch and go out there. They were in an ugly mood at first. But you can depend on it now that they won't come back. I rather think they may give the ringleaders a bad time of it."

"You saved the day for us, Sir Robert," said Frank gratefully.

"I got you into this." The soldier smiled at the earnest knot of printers standing there with clubs still in their hands. "I see you were ready to give them a warm reception. That's the spirit. You can get back to your work now, I think." He shivered. Every window had been smashed, and the sharp December wind was whistling through the corridors. "You'll be well advised, Ellery, to see that no candles are left untended tonight. You won't want a fire on top of all this." His eyes met Frank's with a satisfied smile. "Didn't I tell you I had a way with mobs?"

It was several hours later when Frank dropped his pen. The broken windows had been hastily stuffed with papers, but this did little to keep out the cold. His hands were blue, and he shivered as he straightened up in his chair. Barshley came to the door with a printed sheet in his hand and asked if he could "let 'er go." Frank nodded, and in a few minutes the first thumping of a press in action could be heard. At the same time a party of waits invaded the square and raised their voices in a Christmas carol. They sang well in spite of the lateness of the hour and the consumption of liquid rewards which unquestionably had kept them on their rounds; Frank, remembering all that he had been through this day, could not check a grim smile when the first bars came beautifully clear through the half-filled windows:

> "*God rest you, merry gentlemen,*
> *Let nothing you dismay. . . .*"

10

SNOW HAD CONTINUED to fall most unseasonably, and now it lay like a solid white blanket over the countryside. Frank had hired half a dozen sleighs to convey his guests from London, and he watched them come jingling up the oak-lined drive with a feeling of mounting excitement. Gabrielle, he kept saying to himself, would now see him in a new light. She could not fail to think of him henceforth as in some degree an equal and not as the obscure guide who had helped her through a London fog. But supposing they had changed their minds about including her in the party? It was a disturbing thought. The men in charge of the arrangements, he knew, were quite capable of arbitrary decisions. They had been completely matter-of-fact about everything, even making it clear that he must not expect to greet the King in the capacity of host. He had agreed to all conditions.

No, they had not excluded her from the list. He recognized her at once among the thirty-odd figures, muffled in shawls, which emerged slowly and painfully from under the high-piled robes in the sleighs. She waved gaily to him from her position near the foot of the line. From that moment he was barely conscious of the file of notabilities who brushed by him on their carefully ordered procession to the front entrance.

"It seems to take an upheaval of nature to bring us together, m'sieur," she said when she came up the steps. "First a terrible fog and now all this snow. But I love the snow. I've never seen so much of it. I'm tempted to try to skate."

Frank, who had stationed himself on the raised stone bridge which crossed the moat, looked down and nodded. "It's frozen solid. I'm sure I could find you skates, but I'm afraid I can't volunteer to act as teacher. I haven't skated since the accident to my knee. I'm happy to welcome you to Caster Towers, mademoiselle."

"It's going to be wonderful! I hope it snows so hard that we won't be able to leave for a long time."

"I hope so too. I didn't see your father, mademoiselle. Wasn't he well enough to come?"

She shook her head regretfully. "No. Poor Father isn't well at all. He hoped they would allow Sosthène to come in his place, but it seems they had too many other claims to consider. Sosthène was furious. You'll have to be content with one member of the family, m'sieur."

"I'm sorry the others couldn't come. But"—smiling at her—"I'm more than content."

She looked up at the huge oak door. "Your place is very old. And very impressive, m'sieur."

Frank wished he could claim as his own the escutcheon on the stone over the entrance with its cross and triple fusils. He said: "Yes, this part is very old. In fact, it's supposed to date back to the time of King John. Someone discovered that the number nine doesn't occur in any of the detail, and the belief comes from that. King John had a superstitious dread of the number. Isn't the Comte de Vitrelle of the party?"

The girl laughed. "Jules is furious too. He was on two of the lists they made, but they left him off the final one. He swore he would return to France, but he was reported to be on his way to his club when we left. He'll get over it."

"I mustn't keep you out here in the cold any longer." As they passed in under the high stone arch he felt compelled to make an explanation. "We bought this place, mademoiselle. And it isn't all as old as this. The left wing is frankly George I, and the general effect, I'm afraid, is rather mixed."

They found, on joining the rest of the party in the stone-flagged entrance hall, that the valets had already carried in the boxes. The numbed gentlemen of France were grumblingly hunting out their wigs and at the same time shedding their hats and shawls. As the wigs were adjusted, each man lowered his head while one of the servants sprayed fresh powder on him from an open container, using a bellows for the purpose. Not until the last of them had been properly dusted did the line form again for entrance to the great hall.

Standing just inside the oak screens, Frank felt a deep sense of pride. This was not entirely due to the age of the hall, so authentically indicated by the masonry of the great fireplace (the logs blazing on the hearth were a dozen feet long) and the high vault of the roof. He was thinking that the tenure of the Ellery family had done something for the place, achieving a note of comfort without detracting from the Norman austerities. The mullioned windows had been skillfully repaired, and yet they looked exactly as they had done in the days when the domestics of Hugh le Fitzguy le Masters, the first owner, had dusted and tended them (assuming that dusting and tending were done in those days). The gleaming copper utensils in the buttery promised good cheer to all who shared the comfort of being indoors on this very cold day in the year of our Lord 1808, and yet it would have seemed completely fitting if servingmen in green jerkins had been leaning their elbows on the hatch.

He was proud of the tapestry on the west wall, which was tattered about the edges and very ugly and, on both counts, old and valuable. He heard the Abbé Force say in a tone of surprise, "Humph, thirteenth-century, I do believe!" while he struggled with both hands to adjust a wig which looked greasy and moth-eaten in spite of the attentions of the powder blower.

There was some delay about the seating in front of the fire, for again a proper order of precedence had to be observed. The bearers of the oldest titles were careful to insist on the chairs nearest the blaze and on the first of the steaming bowls of soup which Purdy and his staff were handing in through the buttery hatch. Gabrielle was placed out at one side, and almost directly under the portrait of Lady Morna, which was quite far from the fire. Observing that she seemed interested in the sallow sadness of that long-deceased lady's features, Frank joined her to point out the lines carved on the oak panel under the painting:

> You gave me sons, O Lord, then took them all away:
> Take me too, dear Lord, I do not care to stay.

"How very sad!" She studied the portrait with renewed interest. "How many sons did the poor lady have?"

"Fourteen."

"Fourteen!" Gabrielle's laughter bubbled out without restraint. "But that spoils the story. Two would have been a desolating loss, three a calamity. But fourteen! M'sieur, she should have despaired so much sooner!"

"The allotment of rooms is out of my hands," explained Frank, "and I have no idea where you're to be placed. As soon as I find out, I'll see that a very special fire is built for you. And I've picked one of the servants to act as your personal maid: the red-haired girl standing on the other side of the hatch. Her name's Daisy and she'll be on hand to serve you as soon as you're ready."

"How very thoughtful of you!" Gabrielle smiled at him gratefully. "I've never had a maid, not even in the days when Sossy was doing better. It will be a great pleasure, m'sieur. The girl looks very neat and pretty. She's smiling at me."

"I told her," said Frank, "that she was going to have the honor of serving the loveliest lady that ever lived. I'm sure she's thinking that I didn't exaggerate at all."

"You seem determined to spoil me, M'sieur Ellery. After so much luxury, how am I to go back to Mme. Lebery's?" She paused. "Did you know I was employed now?"

"Yes. I'm finding out everything I can about you."

"Please! You mustn't find out too much."

After the soup had been disposed of and glasses of mulled wine had been handed around, there was a movement among the older, and presumably more important, members of the party. The Abbé Force motioned to Frank to join them. "If you will be good enough to have us shown to the library or some other suitable room," he said, "we shall proceed with the allotting of the rooms."

At dinner Frank sat at the end of the long table with the gluttonous Abbé across the board from him. He had planned an excellent meal. There was a rich soup, followed by baked fish with a yellow sauce, a haunch of venison, and a dozen roasted capons. On the sideboard were cold dishes: a loin of veal, a goose, a round of beef. He had decided to introduce his guests to some typically English sweets: a deep-dish apple tart, a roly-poly pudding, and foaming pitchers of syllabub. They accepted them, when the time came, with a degree of reserve which amounted almost to distrust, but, after the first few spoonfuls, seemed to find them worthy of consumption. The Abbé, for one, wallowed in roly-poly until his face became red and blotchy. The wines were good enough to win nods of grudging approval from the rest.

Almost before the servants had shoved the table and the refectory benches against the wall, the guests were gathering in the center of the room with zestful impatience. One of them, a withered old buck whose lavender waistcoat covered his knees, began to stamp his feet and snap his fingers, chanting: "The dance! The dance! Let us begin."

Frank saw with satisfaction that the musicians he had brought from the nearest town were already ensconced in the gallery. They were tightening their fiddle-strings and emitting preliminary toots on their horns. He had instructed them to begin with *Vive Henri Quatre,* the favorite song of the French Royalists, and was a little worried over the rendition they might give it; they ran more, he knew, to hunting airs and such light trifles of the moment as *Lovely Fan and Manly Ben.*

If he had known of the curious conditions under which the De Salle family lived, he would have been surprised at the splendor and the newness of the dress in which Gabrielle had appeared for dinner. It was a delicate blue, trimmed with exquisitely fine old point lace and with the smallest of water-lily edging in a darker shade. If he had realized how very poor they were, he would no doubt have concluded that her employer had loaned her the dress or that Sosthène had been unusually lucky in his encounter with the tercel gentlemen at the piquet table. She was no different from the rest in this respect, however. All of them had managed, by scrimping and saving and by devious methods which were strictly their own business, to achieve new clothes for this most important occasion. The air was filled with the rustle of silk and the sharp pat of new heels on the oak floor.

"I'm being most completely spoiled," said Gabrielle when he sought her out. "My little Daisy is so willing. I can't thank you too much, m'sieur, for your thought in giving her to me. How shall I ever do without her after this?" She sighed. "Life must have been very pleasant at home in the old days. I've never realized before what it must have been like. You brave English must defeat Napoleon for us soon!"

"Victory would have one serious drawback, mademoiselle. It would take you back to France."

"I have been hoping that our host would ask me to dance with him. And after such a very fine compliment——" She left the sentence unfinished.

Frank's face fell. "I'm sorry, mademoiselle. I never dance. My knee!"

"Of course. It was thoughtless of me not to realize. I hope M'sieur regrets it as much as I do." She smiled and nodded her head at him. "You see? I have no regard for the conventions at all. I say exactly what I think. It is a very bad habit, I am afraid, for everyone criticizes me because of it."

"I'll have the consolation of watching you every second of the dance which should have been mine." Frank added, in a sudden burst of courage, "And of every other dance also, mademoiselle."

"That too is a very pretty compliment." She hesitated. "I know it's wishing for the impossible but—if only we could have some of the tonish new dances tonight! One gets so tired of these very proper minuets. Sometimes"—in a confidential whisper—"when none of the older ones are with us, we dance to much faster airs. Even the rigadoon. Even—but you must never repeat it, for we would be disgraced and disowned forever and ever if they found out—even La Carmagnole!"

"The musicians know La Carmagnole. They asked me about it."

"If as much as one bar of it were played," she warned, "we would have to walk out of your house, m'sieur. And that would be most painful on a night like this."

She began to hum under her breath one of the latest London favorites.

> "He'll get a wife as fast as he can,
> With a haily, gaily, gal-go-raily."

Frank smiled. "That's a sentiment I can understand. I should like to get a wife as fast as I can. But, mademoiselle, I'm wondering how you happened to learn that song."

"Oh, you would be very greatly surprised if you knew us in our—I think you call it 'off moments.' You see, we keep so much to ourselves that the only English people we seem to meet or talk to are bus drivers and hairdressers and waiters——"

"And newspaper publishers."

"It's a rare thing for us to meet anyone as nice as a newspaper publisher. But what I meant was that all the talk we learn is of the shops and the streets. You would be shocked at the slang some of us use."

"This may be the last time I'll see you for quite a while. You see, mademoiselle, I think they'll send me to prison at any time now."

Her mood changed at once. "It's a wonderfully brave thing you're doing. We seem to talk of nothing else. Father demands that your paper be brought in every day. I tell him what you've printed and he gets more pleased and excited than I've ever seen him. He says you're right about everything, that there's no other way to defeat Napoleon. He has a high esteem for you, M'sieur Ellery."

"I'm very happy to hear it. If you felt the same way, I would need no other encouragement to go on."

"I don't think you need to be told that I feel the same way. Margot also talks about you all the time. Even Sosthène has been pleased about it."

The leader of the musicians stood up and sounded a warning note on his flute. There was a moment's pause and then the band crashed into the opening bars of *Vive Henri Quatre*. The company stood stiffly to attention. The dancing began immediately after that, and Frank withdrew to a seat in the gallery where he could command a view of the whole floor. He lived up to his promise by never taking his eyes off the animated figure of Gabrielle during the three hours that the dancing continued. She was on the floor continuously, being in very great demand as a partner, and she seemed to be having a good time. On several occasions when the movement of the stately measures brought her near the gallery, she looked up and smiled at him. When this happened he felt completely rewarded for everything.

He left at an early hour the next morning and so did not have a chance to speak to her again. Mrs. Ellery and Caradoc were coming up from London and would remain in the house for the two additional days of the visit. The property transfer had not yet been completed, but it had seemed proper to let them share in whatever honor went with the entertainment of an exiled monarch.

It had turned colder, and he realized as soon as he got into the saddle that it was going to be an uncomfortable jaunt back to town. Riding was the only form of exercise which was easy for him, however, and he decided to brave the elements further by dropping in at Bilber Castle on the way. There was no trace of sun, and the wind was from the west. He wrapped his cloak tightly about his neck and kicked at the ribs of old Solomon to force him into a livelier pace. A few discouraged birds flew after them from tree to tree, with a monotonous piping. At the top of Halter Hill he reined his mount in and looked back at the Towers. Snow had continued to fall during the night, covering the ice in the moat and settling in uneven mounds on the sloping roofs. Except for the smoke which rose sluggishly from the rear chimneys, there was no suggestion of life about the place. His glance progressed slowly over the horizon from the white-topped trees in Grovers Spinney to the weir at Willars, the farthest point of the property. It was a gloomy day to make his farewells, and his spirits were lower than the mercury in the thermometer he had glanced at as he walked to the stables.

It was farewell. He had no illusions on that score; he would not likely set eyes again on these broad acres for a long time, if ever. He would not be welcome after today.

Bilber Castle, in spite of its far from romantic-sounding name, is one of the most fascinating of the great homes of England. One comes across it suddenly; for the road leading there inclines steeply upward through a tangle of wood. When the top of the slope is reached, there lies spread before the eyes a broad valley with low hills against the sky and the white towers of Bilber standing gracefully in the green of the forest background.

As he rode across the valley this morning he saw that the snow had banked on its roofs and turrets, blotting out all other shades of color and giving it more than a suggestion of unreality. He was able to forget his own troubles and fears and hopes as he reflected on the strange and bloody history of Bilber and the family of Murreys which had clung tenaciously to their ownership through seven centuries. Stories clustered about every dark corner of the interior.

The Duke of Westgate was having his breakfast. He had been a famous athlete in his day, but lack of the accustomed exercise through his middle years had upholstered his immense frame with an almost incredible structure of flesh. He was so heavy now that his life had become a labored progress from one reinforced chair to another.

"I want to apologize for the earliness of my call, Your Grace," said Frank. "I'm riding back to London today and I thought you would forgive me if I dropped in to pay my respects."

The Duke made no reply at once. It was clear that he was having trouble again with his teeth, for he was breakfasting on beef hash, and a pyramid of bread crusts had accumulated beside his plate. He scowled at Frank as he plied an active fork. "I can't make up my mind about you, young man," he said finally. "It's not clear to me whether you're some new variety of quixotic idiot or just a plain damn fool."

"It's sometimes hard to define the border line between those two states of imbecility," answered Frank with a smile. "I hope you'll concede me the justification of a quixotic intent at any rate. I'm convinced that what I'm doing is in the best interests of the country."

The Duke suspended a loaded fork halfway between plate and mouth. "I don't mean that," he grumbled. "I mean what you're up to about the property. You've put me in a bad fix, by Gad!"

"I don't follow you, Your Grace."

"Of course you do. You know exactly what I mean; it's as plain as that long bowsprit of yours. You're making it hard for me to find a reason for refusing to let my little Mary take on that blasted brother of yours. That's what I mean. What have you got to say for yourself?"

"I can see no reason why it isn't a proper match," declared Frank stoutly. "Caradoc has a fine future ahead of him. I'm sure he'll provide you with plenty of grounds for pride in him as a son-in-law if you'll give him the chance. And I'm sure you know the state of Mary's feelings. She's as much in love with Carr as he is with her. Their happiness depends on the match."

"Your brother Caradoc, if you'll forgive my saying so and I don't give a damn whether you do or not, is like those fine houses you see in London nowadays. He's all façade. A handsome façade, I grant you; but what's behind it?" A huge hand raised a tankard of ale to the ducal mouth, and the summation of Caradoc's character was suspended for a moment. "He's too damned handsome. Chuckleheaded women run after him all the time. They'll run after him as long as he lives. What kind of a prospect is that for my little Mary? I don't credit your precious brother with the decency to remain faithful to a fine wife such as my gal would be. There you have it in a nutshell."

"I admit that he's not good enough for Mary. But you'll wait a long time for a man who will be."

A somewhat less antagonistic light began to show in the sharp blue eyes of the peer. "My little Mary's happiness is my chief interest in life. Hughie's all right. He'll manage here after I'm gone, in some kind of a decent imitation of the Murreys tradition. But that gal of mine . . ." He paused and shoved his plate away from him. "Frank, my boy, to me she's nothing short of perfection. There was a time I was afraid she took too much after me. She had a grand hand on the reins and she could drive a ball out of the whins or the fog grass better than that fellow Hughie. She was the only woman in the country playing golf, and it worried me. I didn't want to see her turn into a rantipole.

"She got over that nicely," he went on. "She's still a fine horsewoman, but in every way she's now as gentle and womanly as her mother was. Yes, by Gad, there's no one like her, and I won't see her throwing herself away on a fellow who'll bring her nothing but unhappiness."

"Have you considered how unhappy she might be if you stood in her way now? Sometimes that kind of unhappiness continues through a lifetime."

"Of course I've considered it." This was said with renewed fury. "I've thought of nothing else for the last fortnight—since you spiked my guns by turning the fellow into a landed country gentleman, you rascal! It was a smart trick, Frank. None of the objections I had been raising held good after that." He turned in his creaking chair to glower at Frank. "If it had been you, I might have given in with a little better grace. But not Caradoc! I get so angry at this worship of the fellow! Caradoc says this, Caradoc says that; you would think he was another Billy Pitt; and that soft lummox of a Hughie is as bad as Mary. I'm standing out alone but I'll tell you this, young Mr. Frank—I'm not giving in until I'm a lot surer of the thing than I am now. I've told Mary she must go away for a while. I'm packing her off to her aunt Jerusha in Shropshire for a few months. She must think it over carefully. I'm hoping, of course, that she'll be cured of it by the time she comes back."

"I doubt if she will, Your Grace."

The Duke reached back of him and tugged impatiently at the embroidered bellpull which hung beside a marquetry hanging cupboard on the wall. A footman answered the summons, to be greeted with: "The mail, Simmons, the mail. And the morning papers, in God's name!"

"There's no mail, Your Grace," said the footman, who had the longest and handsomest legs and the smallest head Frank had ever seen. "And no papers. Parker's coach didn't arrive this morning, Your Grace."

"The country's coming to a pretty pass when a little snow holds up the mails." The old peer grinned suddenly at his visitor. "I wanted to read what you were saying about the government this morning, Frank. I'm with you in *that*. What this country needs is a blasted good shaking up, and you're giving it plenty of the right medicine. Keep it up, my boy. We've got to lick Boney this time."

11

THE BRASS PLATE with the name MME. LEBERY was freshly polished, and there was a general air of prosperity about the establishment in contrast with the other shops on the street, which were shabby and down-at-heel. Frank was admitted by a footman with a long black beard who said dubiously: "Mam'selle de Salle? It's unusual, m'sieur. I shall have to consult Mme. Lebery."

Apparently the proprietor of the dress shop gave the necessary permission, for the owner of the black whiskers returned almost immediately and led the way through a front salon, which had several expensive plateglass mirrors and a dozen or more handsome gowns displayed on wire forms, and from there by way of a cold and drafty passage to a still darker flight of stairs. Descending the stairs, they found themselves in an uncomfortably cold lower hall.

"In here, m'sieur," said Black Whiskers.

It was a small room with a pitiful excuse for a fire, in front of which Gabrielle was crouching with a shawl wrapped around her shoulders. She sprang up at once when she perceived who it was.

"I'm so glad to see you," she said with a smile. "If I had another chair, I would ask you to sit down. But, as you see, there's only one."

"I was passing by and, when I spied the name on the plate outside, I thought I would drop in to see you." A lame excuse if she had known how many times he had walked by before getting his courage up to the point of ringing the bell! "I was curious to know what form your employment here took."

"I keep busy most of the time, very busy," said Gabrielle. "Just now there are no customers in, and all the tidying upstairs has been done—I do that, too, although I'm not very good at it, being a most untidy person —and so I was enjoying a rest."

She looked pale and a little tired, Frank thought. He was disturbed to note that there were violet shadows under her eyes.

"You aren't too comfortable here, I'm afraid. It's cold and very damp."

"Oh no. I'm quite all right." She shivered nevertheless. "It's always rather cold downstairs. It's hard to believe when you're inside that spring is really starting. I think I'm a true Frenchwoman. I don't enjoy cold weather at all." She looked up at him and smiled again. "At first I thought it was someone who had come to make a purchase. Gentlemen do come in, you know. In fact, a large part of our trade is with them;

and I'm not sure, although I really shouldn't mention it, that what they order is always for their wives. When we're sure it isn't, Mme. Lebery sees to it that a little extra is added to the bill."

"I didn't come in with any such idea. It was just that I—I hadn't been lucky enough to see you for quite a long time."

"You've been neglecting me and I've felt quite hurt about it."

Frank's dismay at finding her in such surroundings became more apparent in the tone of his voice. "I think it should be possible for you to find some less trying employment. I'm distressed at finding you here."

"It's the same everywhere. I'm really very much favored. There are six seamstresses in the next room, and it's no larger than this. Mme. Lebery tries to be most considerate to me."

"Have you long hours?" He knew when she left at night, as he often hovered about in the neighborhood for a glimpse of her when she started home.

"No, not long. She favors me there too. Eight to four, and a very good lunch at noon. The rest of them, poor little creatures, work much longer than I do. Their hours are six to seven. Sometimes, when there's a rush, they work right on through the evening. And they're not paid as well as I am. Mme. Lebery spoils me shamefully."

Frank felt like saying, "You're being brave about it," but realized she would not welcome any such expression of sympathy. At this point a bell on the wall began to ring. "Customers," said Gabrielle. The ringing continued, and she counted the strokes attentively. "Three short, two long. Oh dear, that means *L'Enchanteresse!* I'm afraid it will be taken this time. It's so lovely, I don't want anyone else to have it." She smiled with a trace of embarrassment. "I'm afraid it will be necessary for you to leave now. No, I want you to see me in it. It's the loveliest thing I've ever worn. Do you care to step out into the hall again and wait there until I tell you to come back?"

He walked back into the damp passage from which he could see into another cubicle where a number of women were seated at work. They continued to stitch with nimble fingers, but it was apparent that they managed at the same time to look him over with close curiosity. His knowledge of French was just enough to follow some of the chatter which was going on. They were discussing him, of course.

"English," he heard one of them say. "But not nearly as handsome as the other one."

The other one? What had she meant by that?

In a very few minutes Gabrielle called to him to return. She had changed into a black gown of flowing lines with touches of red in the skirt and sleeves, which lived up fully to the praise she had lavished on it. She looked very lovely as she made him a curtsy and then pirouetted so that he could inspect it from every angle; so lovely that he caught his breath and was not able to make any comment at all.

"Well, how do you like it?" she demanded gaily. "Or rather, how do you like me in it?"

"I can't find words to tell you how beautiful you look in it." Frank hesitated for a moment. "I wish—there was some way I could purchase it for you. It would be a sacrilege for anyone else to have it. It's so obviously intended for you and for no one else."

She laughed. "I'm afraid that isn't possible, though I thank you, sir, for the very kind thought. Some dumpy little Englishwoman will have it, and she'll look—well, I like to believe it won't become her quite as much as it does me. I'll have that much satisfaction, at any rate. Now I must hurry upstairs. Mme. Lebery will be getting impatient."

She vanished up the stairs in a flutter of black skirts, turning at the top to wave farewell to him. The footman ushered him out by a side door, accepting with surly surprise the shilling he tendered.

The other one? The pleasure he had found in seeing her could not banish the uneasy speculations roused by the chance remark he had overheard.

He saw her again a few days later. It was full spring now. Cattle drovers and horse dealers were loitering again in the yards of inns, and a potted daffodil was displayed behind a flyspecked window in Brinsley Place. Frank noticed it as he turned in at number 24.

The Comte was glad to see him. The long winter had not been kind to the old man, but he summoned up enough energy to discuss the situation on the Continent and to point out certain straws in the wind which to him were indications of the breaking up of the Napoleonic hegemony. Frank listened with a hopeful eye fixed on the front door. When a diversion came, however, it was from the rear.

"I didn't know you were here," said Gabrielle in a dismayed tone.

Frank rose and bowed, thinking how lucky it was that he had found her at home.

"Well, you've caught me. I stayed in today because I have a cold. I haven't done anything to my hair and I'm terribly afraid that my nose is red." It *was* a little red, and yet she managed to look, in the eyes of the infatuated visitor at least, completely charming. She was a little untidy in dress also; but no one can quarrel with an untidiness which displays a little more than usual of a very white throat and a pleasantly rounded pair of elbows. "I was finding things very dull, m'sieur, and so I'm glad you've come, even though I do look a fright."

Frank's eyes must have conveyed his complete satisfaction, not only with her appearance, but with her intention to remain. She sat down and asked if he had been recently to the Towers. Were there any flowers yet in that lovely bit of woods she had been able to see from her bedroom window? Frank said no, he had not been to the country yet, but the woods, he was sure, would be full of flowers: hepaticas, adder's-tongue, bloodroot. The names did not seem to mean anything to her, for she did not pursue the point. Her father was nodding sleepily in his chair, so she proposed, with quite a little eagerness, a game of piquet. Frank agreed and she brought out a small table, setting it down in the front window.

"But not piquet," she amended in a whisper, glancing over her shoulder. "Father would be angry if he heard me, but what I want to play is voles. Piquet is a dull game."

Voles was a popular diversion with people of a lower station than those devoted to the other. Frank was surprised that she knew anything about it, but he agreed at once that it was much the livelier of the two.

"The girls at the dress shop taught me how to play," said Gabrielle, riffling the cards with nimble fingers. "It's so much fun, isn't it? A shilling a game, m'sieur?"

"A shilling a game," said Frank.

It soon became apparent that she had some, at least, of her brother's facility at cards. Frank, perhaps, was not sufficiently attentive, being more interested in the delicate arch of her brows and the amazing length of the lashes shading her lively brown eyes. He made many mistakes which she took advantage of promptly, snapping up his cards with deft fingers. The first game was over in no time at all. He drew a shilling from his pocket and laid it on the board beside her.

"Thank you, m'sieur. You'll have to pay more attention to the game or I'll get all your shillings."

"I'm finding it hard to pay attention to the game."

Her lashes lifted in a smile. "Perhaps, then, you would rather not play more?"

Frank protested that there was nothing he wanted to do more than play another game. He would very much like, he declared, to go on playing forever. His hand touched hers as he reached for the cards, and he thought how wonderful it would be if he could brush aside the obstacle of the table and gather her slender form into his arms.

"Really," said Gabrielle, "it will be more advantageous for you if you watch the cards a little more closely."

In the middle of the second game, which was going as badly for him as the first, Frank got up his courage to ask a question which had been on the tip of his tongue since she entered the room. "Did you see my brother at the Towers?"

She glanced up at him and then lowered her eyes to the cards again. "Yes. He came after you left." There was a pause. "I thought him remarkably handsome, m'sieur."

Nothing more was said on the point. The second game was finished and another shilling deposited beside the first. A third went the same way, and Frank rose reluctantly to his feet.

"I must get back to my work," he said. "Although I haven't won a game I feel that I've been very lucky today, mademoiselle."

She accompanied him to the door, and it was apparent to his observing eyes that she had something to say to him. There was a reluctance in her manner, however. "M'sieur Ellery," she asked finally, "who is Fouché?"

He did not know what he had expected but it was not this. "Fouché?" he answered. "He's Bonaparte's Minister of Police. A sly and dangerous individual from all reports. A spider, spinning his webs all over France, and in many parts of Europe as well. It's said his operations extend even to this country."

"His name was mentioned last night." Her tone had become casual again. "I had never heard it before and so I wondered about him. Thanks, m'sieur. You will come again soon?"

Ensconced in his office, with the warm spring sun pouring over his shoulder, Frank settled down unwillingly to his work. His mind was filled with questions. Why had she asked about Fouché? Had he been right in assuming that she had been reluctant to discuss Caradoc? Absent-mindedly he picked up the proofs of the leader for the next day, but with the first sentence his attention focused sharply on the matter in hand.

Three months have passed [Cope had written] since Junot, commander of the French Army in Portugal, dissolved the Regency and proclaimed himself Governor of the kingdom. Three months of inactivity on our part; three months of planning on the part of Bonaparte for the blow he is aiming at the security of this country. We have made no move to fulfill our obligations to our downtrodden ally. . . .

Cope had written with even more than his usual vigor, telling of the massacre of innocent Portuguese peasants, of executions by firing squad in every town and hamlet, of the spoliation of a once prosperous and contented little country. "He's making it too strong," Frank thought. "I'm afraid it will have to be toned down this time."

Then his glance fell on a report from the business office which lay on his desk beside the proof, and all interest in the matter of the leader left him. It was impossible to remain cool in the face of the figures the report contained. A crisis had been reached. For over four months Evans had been dipping into the reserves which Joseph Ellery had so carefully built up. It had seemed like an impregnable base on which the *Tablet* could stand for all time; but it takes a great deal of money to operate a newspaper when the revenue is reduced practically to nothing, and so the funds had been melting away like the snows of March. Publication could still continue but, as the tables Evans had set down demonstrated with a grim finality, the last stage was being reached. A few more months would find the treasury bare.

The maddening part of it was that public opinion had been swinging around to the view the *Tablet* advocated. It was clear now that Napoleon did not intend to enter at once on the bloody gamble of an invasion of England but was proceeding instead with his plans to gobble up the Peninsula first. He had sent an army under his rattlebrained favorite, Junot, into Portugal and now was assembling large forces along the Pyrenees with the avowed purpose of "protecting" Spain. Men were beginning to say that Britain's turn would come next, that as soon as the two Latin countries were engulfed the usurper would make his final effort to end the long war by the subjugation of the islands. They were even repeating what the *Tablet* had contended: that the best way to fend him away from the white cliffs was to keep him engaged in the Peninsula. Clubs and coffeehouses buzzed with excited talk as to how this could best be done, and there was plenty of support for the *Tablet* argument that a large enough army must be sent into Portugal to drive the French out, that, moreover, the command must be entrusted, not to a prince of the blood or a veteran general, but to the best man available. The public choice was divided between two comparatively young men: Sir Arthur Wellesley and Sir John Moore; again, the two candidates the paper had been putting forward.

Under the circumstances it had not been too much to expect that the favor of the public would swing back to the newspaper which had guided opinion to this vigorous and aroused stand. But it had not done so. Accepting the truth of what the *Tablet* had preached, men still retained their dislike for the medium of their conversion, still spoke of it as "that contemptible sheet." The circulation had come back to some extent, but the advertising columns were still as bare as in the strenuous days when the campaign was first launched. And the attitude of the governmental departments continued to develop a deeper bitterness as though in resentment of the policy into which the administration was being forced.

Frank realized that he must now choose between two courses. With victory in sight, he could drop the campaign and try to appease the administration by taking up again the old policy of unquestioning support; or he could fall back on the silent financial backing which Sir Robert Wilson had said would be available. He disliked the first as much as he feared the latter.

He was pondering the decision which lay ahead of him when Aunt Francilea came in. Despite the warmth of the day she had wrapped herself up in a long pelisse and she wore a woolen imitation of the very popular Patmos hat pulled down almost to her eyes, thus making herself into a rather absurd imitation of a stage driver. When she sat down beside his desk, Frank saw that she was wearing the serviceable variety of ankle boots which laced up the back.

"Young man," she announced, "I've come for a serious talk with you. I want the truth."

"Then you shall have it." He handed her the business office report and watched while she digested the figures it contained. Her lips drew tight as she pondered them.

"Just as I thought. You're getting to the end of things." She handed back the summary. "What do *they* say about it?"

"They've said nothing recently. As a matter of fact, I'm not on speaking terms with Mother. Carr has been away on some mysterious political errand for the past few weeks. But of course they don't like the way things are going. Carr is beginning to believe I talked him into accepting the Towers so I could get my hands on the paper. Mother has been saying to friends that she wishes I would leave the town house."

"She has, has she! Indeed!" Aunt Francilea threw back her head and snorted scornfully. "That's just like her. I hope you won't be foolish enough to do it, Frank."

"I've been considering it. You see, Aunt, it isn't very comfortable for me at home any longer."

"And what would you do?"

"Take rooms, I suppose. It would be the sensible thing. I don't enjoy being treated like a—well, like a pariah dog."

The old lady produced an umbrella from somewhere underneath her capacious cloak and hammered it down on the floor with angry emphasis. "Amy Lawcey! Acting that way to her own son. Well, she made no bones of her feeling for my poor brother, so I suppose it's easy for her to treat a son the same way." She snorted again and began to indulge in a disjointed reflection of the angry thoughts trooping through her mind. "That tuppenny-ha'penny vicarage and her gluepot father with his two hundred a year! . . . Four of them, and every dress turned twice and *then* handed down. I must say! Fine prospects *she* had. . . . Very high and mighty she is now. . . . *She* has enough to keep you going for as long as you need. You can trust her to hang on to every penny—Amy Lawcey, indeed!"

"There's no point in getting angry about it. After all, they have their side. I'm running the paper into the ground, and it's a sorry prospect for Carr. He's going to be married before very long, and he'll have the Towers on his hands and no income to keep the place running. We've got to be fair about this."

"Fair, fiddlesticks! Nothing would do them but he must get the place away from you. I'm not going to waste any sympathy on Master Caradoc. He made the bargain himself, and I'm almost glad it's turning out bad for him."

"Things wouldn't be so bad if the government hadn't pressed down so hard on us." He stopped for a moment, thinking back over the events of the last few months. "First, they refused us our copies of the translations from foreign newspapers. Cope and I set up a new system. We got in touch with an ex-royal officer in Brest who was willing to work with us. He had all the papers sent on to him from Paris and put them on a small packet which was making night trips across the channel. At first we were beating the other London papers because we got them before the government did. They soon discovered what we were up to and set a watch in every port. The captain of the packet was smuggling, of course; so they seized on that as an excuse to search him every time he came in. Anything addressed to the *Tab* was thrown overboard. Well, we had no recourse. We had to swallow our medicine. Naturally, this did us a lot of harm, for there were times when we carried no foreign news at all.

"Right now we have them on the hip," he went on, with a trace of a smile. "We're still bringing the papers in, but they're concealed in packages consigned to a firm in Gravesend: Staples & Wellwine. They come on to us from our papermakers, who make a rule never to deliver before eleven o'clock at night. I don't think the government officers have wakened up yet to what we're doing; although they must wonder how we get the foreign news we print. I know they have men watching the building; I run into them every time I go out. They'll find out in time, of course, and come down on us. What we'll do then I don't know."

Aunt Francilea, whose face had become fiery red as she listened to this recital of injustices, checked him at this point. "Frank, I don't want you to say another word. If I hear anything more, I'm likely to go down to Whitehall and break this umbrella over somebody's head. Not another word before I've had *my* say. I've made up my mind about this. Now you just listen while I tell you what we've got to do." She began to speak with deliberation, shaking an admonishing finger in the air. "First, you just move out of that house! I've changed my mind about *that*. I'm not going to let the Queen of Sheba have the satisfaction of telling you to leave. What a donkey you were to give her that lease! I know her; she'll tell you to go one of these days. Second, we must find some way of keeping on here. We're not going to quit now, not us! It will break my heart if you don't win out in spite of all of them. I have ten thousand pounds laid away that I don't need. Does that surprise you, my boy? I'm pretty well to do, if you must know. Don't ask me how or why I have this bit handy; I guess everybody has been keeping something ready just *in case*. Well, it's yours. I'll have no hemming and hawing about it, if you please, Francis Ellery. Into the business it goes, every shilling of it."

Frank shook his head. "Aunt Francie, you've got the biggest heart in the whole world but I—I can't do that. I know what you're up to. You're going to sell some of your bonds to get me this money. I won't have it. I'm not going to ruin you on top of everything."

"You're as stubborn as your mule of a father. I tell you, Frank, this is money I'm not getting any good out of at all. It's safely tucked away in the attic at home. It's in gold, mind you. It's wrapped up in stockings in the hollowed-out legs of an old highboy. If you must know, I had it ready in case we had to run to America to keep out of Boney's clutches. Your father was the one who advised me to do it. Well, I've got along without it all these years, and Boney *hasn't* come over, and perhaps now he never will. So you just think of one good reason why it shouldn't be used in the business. I dare you to find one."

A lump had come into Frank's throat. He said, finding it very hard to keep his voice steady: "I don't want to find any reasons. It would save the day. I was making up my mind as you came in to give up the fight. But I would never forgive myself if——"

"It's settled, then. I don't want another word out of you. This matter is of my arranging, and I think I'm entitled to my own way about it. The money will be here as soon as I can post down to get it and come back. And do you know what I'm going to do right now? I'm going out to find rooms for you. I wouldn't trust you to pick them. You would end up in some dark pigsty over a smelly stable, that's what you would."

Windy Topp came into the room with a letter in his hand. "Salaam, sahib," he said. "Respects to you, ma'am. Letter just arrived. Handed in by a rainbow in red and gold. Gorjus was the word for it, sahib; made me want to get into service myself. Must of been a juke's man, no less."

Frank looked at the crest and, after skimming the note, said to Aunt Francilea: "It's from Bilber Castle. His Grace wants to see me at once. I wonder what has happened?"

"It's something about Caradoc and Mary," predicted the old lady. "Has Caradoc been cutting up? Or perhaps the Duke has changed his mind and agrees to an early wedding."

Frank shook his head. "I don't think the Duke has changed his mind yet. He talked frankly to me the last time I saw him, and he was far from reconciled then. As for Carr, he's been the Sir Galahad of the Commons, I assure you. No, it must be something else. I think I'll ride down tonight and find out what's on the old boy's mind."

Outside they met Nathan Cope, swishing his long coattails down the hall in a state of extreme excitement. "A consignment just in from Staples & Wellwine," he said. He was always a little uneasy when the ladies of the family were around, and he bobbed his head stiffly in the general direction of Aunt Francilea. "Boney's on the move! Five million biscuits are being baked. Every oven in the south of France has been requisitioned. The Bidassoa swarms with troops. He's going into Spain!"

"Then we'll be too late!" exclaimed Frank. "He'll overrun the country in a few weeks and what chance will we have then to land an army in Portugal? The same old story, always too late!"

"That's not all," declared Cope. "Murat's in Madrid. He got there on March thirteenth with a huge staff. Calls himself 'Lieutenant of the Emperor.' He's paralyzing the Spanish Government with lies, promises, threats. Boney fights with more than armies. He knows how to use guile and treachery just as well as an artillery brigade. The whole damned country—begging your pardon, ma'am—may fall without a blow. It's a catastrophe, Frank."

"Is it bad news?" asked Aunt Francilea, who apparently had not understood a word.

"It may be the beginning of the end," declared Frank. "If the Peninsula collapses, he'll soon be gathering his barges again at Boulogne. We will fight it out here after all. Well, they'll know we were right now."

"We've won the last battle before." Cope's eyes gleamed. "The thing to make sure of is that Freddie doesn't command the army back of Dover!"

They walked down the stairs in complete silence, their minds so filled with the momentous nature of the tidings that the unexpected presence of Caradoc in the lower hall made no impression on them at first. He had come from the business department, and there was a gleam in his eye. It was clear also that he had just arrived in town, for his calfskin boots, fitting close to the leg as far as the knee, were caked with mud, and his handsome broadcloth coat was gray with dust.

"Well!" he said, planting himself in front of them. "I'm very glad to find that this—this absurd and vicious crusade of yours will soon be over, Frank."

"No, Carr." The older brother spoke soberly. "It's not over. I would say, judging from the word we've just received, that it's only beginning."

Caradoc laughed confidently. "I don't give a snap of the fingers for the news you've got. You can't go on! I've just been talking to Evans and looking at some figures. That's all I need to know! There'll have to be a change around here now; and I rather think, old boy, we shall be compelled to throw you out. The only thing that will save the *Tab* now will be for me to assume the direction of the paper."

Aunt Francilea said sharply: "So that's what you propose to do, is it? You would throw your own brother out!"

Caradoc frowned at her. "What else can we do? You must realize that the antagonism of the government will continue as long as Frank remains in charge. I'm convinced myself that the confidence of the public can never be won back unless there's a change. We've got to be sensible about this, you know. I think people consider me sound in my views and that they'll forget what has been happening here once I step in. It's the only thing to do. We'll get in a new editor, a man that the administration will approve, and in no time at all, the *Tab* will be back where it was before."

"You've got it all figured out, I see. Well, let me tell you, young man, you're counting your chickens too soon." The old lady was so indignant that she was speaking in explosive snorts. "Throw Frank out, will you! I think not. He's just told me that he's been able to make some—some financial accommodations, I think it's called. What have you to say to that, Master Caradoc? He'll have plenty of funds. You and your government and your new editor and the silly public, indeed!"

Frank looked at Cope and nodded confirmation of this news. The latter, who had been a perfect picture of gloom before, straightened up and indulged in a whistle of triumphant relief. Caradoc demanded brusquely of his brother: "What's all this mean? Are you taking in new capital?"

"The matter will be explained at the next meeting," said Frank. "I'm getting an unconditional loan."

Caradoc's eyes narrowed. "Then you've made some political deal. I was warned it might come to this." He was silent for a moment, turning over in his mind the possible sources of the new backing. "The Whigs have been mum in the House, but they're only too glad to have you attack the administration. Well, it's just postponing the day. We're going to cut the ground right out from under your feet. I've been on a tour with some other members, getting firsthand information about the defenses of the kingdom. We've done it on our own initiative so it will have twice the effect of a government investigation. What we've found will make a laughingstock of you, Frank."

So that was what had taken him out of town! Frank had hoped that he had absented himself to be near Mary.

"We made a tour of the south coast from the estuary of the Thames to the Scilly Islands. Let me tell you that Boney will get more than he bargains for if he ever tries to invade us."

"Sir Robert Wilson says——" began Frank.

"Sir Robert Wilson is completely in the bad books of the War Office," declared Caradoc. "They consider him an irresponsible agitator. Nothing that he says is of any importance. The figures you've been printing are all wrong. Do you realize that the British Army today is up to a strength of one hundred and sixty thousand men, including twenty-six thousand cavalry? It's stronger than it's ever been."

"I've printed those figures. You overlook the fact that thirty-two regiments are stationed in overseas posts. And do you know that Napoleon could get an army of half a million men together for the invasion? He has the Confederacy of the Rhine and all of Italy to draw on as well as France. And now Russia and Denmark are against us, and perhaps Prussia."

"There are eighty thousand men in the militia," went on Caradoc. "And the volunteer bodies throughout the country number two hundred and ninety thousand."

"You can dismiss the volunteer bodies. They couldn't stand up against the trained battalions of Bonaparte. They would be useful only for guerrilla operations and perhaps the handling of supplies. The militia could be whipped into shape if the necessary steps were taken. But the necessary steps aren't being taken. You must know that."

"I have no intention of arguing the point with you. The spirit we found everywhere was enough to put heart in even the worst croakers like you. What we saw will convince the country that you've been completely wrong. Our findings will be laid before the House at once."

"You'll find you're too late with that kind of talk. The *Tab* may never get any credit for it, but the country has become convinced we must strike in the Peninsula. You're out of touch with public feeling, Carr." Frank paused and then demanded, "Did your travels take you into Shropshire?"

Caradoc shook his head. "I haven't had time. It was my intention to get up there, but it's been strictly impossible. Public obligations come before personal ones, you know." He looked down at the muddy condition of his boots and frowned. "I wonder what George Brummell would say if he saw me like this!"

Aunt Francilea said in grim tones: "Public obligations, fiddlesticks! You may find, Master Caradoc, that your anxiety to curry favor with those stupid donkeys at Whitehall has cost you something much more valuable."

12

IT WAS STILL LIGHT when Frank reached Bilber Castle. He had enjoyed the ride. The air had been warm and he had felt in an exultant frame of mind over the solving of his financial problems. With Aunt Francilea's ten thousand pounds he could weather the storm. He was even able to view the latest news from the Continent with a certain degree of optimism. Napoleon would have to march his armies across the plains and mountains of Spain, and there might still be time to land a British army in Portugal.

A footman escorted him to the library and, as he walked under the fanstone tracery of its wide door, he saw that the Duke was sitting alone beside an open window, bundled up almost to the ears in a heavy robe. The old man turned at his entrance and said in rumbling tones: "Listen to that. They're playing cricket on the south crease. They'll cut up the sod damnably, but Hughie and his friends couldn't wait another day. Gad, I would give anything to have a bat in my hands just once more!"

"You could teach them all a few things still, Your Grace," said Frank. "I never saw you play, but I've been told you were too much for the best bowlers."

The Duke reached for a gun which stood against the back of his chair. He took it up, smoothed and fondled it with an unsteady hand.

"There's nothing like a sound healthy interest in sport," he said. "I like to see them so keen about cricket. As long as that keeps up, we needn't lose faith in ourselves. We'll always give them a run for it. Any word from the Continent?"

"Yes, Your Grace. Bad news, I'm afraid. Boney is going to move his armies into Spain."

"Sit down, man, sit down. You can tell me of this latest catastrophe on a chair as easily as on your feet. So Boney's going to gobble Spain! If we had an army in there now, the Spaniards might feel they could put up some resistance. As it is, they'll probably throw in the towel. Well, I suppose we'll wait to see what they're going to do about it before we make a move."

"I'm afraid so, Your Grace."

The Duke switched the subject abruptly: "Well, the match is off. I'm writing to that blasted brother of yours tonight and telling him he must never see my girl again. I got a note off to her this afternoon. She'll take it hard, my blessed little Mary, but there's nothing else to be done. I thought it only fair to give you an explanation. I like you, Frank, and have enough respect for you to tell you why I'm doing this." He brought a hand down on his knee. "I shall do nothing of the kind as far as *he* is concerned. He's entitled to no explanation at all and that's what he'll get."

"What has Carr done?"

"Just what I expected, the philandering puppy! He's been running around with a Frenchwoman—a painted, powdered Jezebel by the name of—I've forgotten her outlandish name."

By chance Frank's eyes were fixed on the oak roses of Henry VIII which made up the decorations above the window. He traced out each petal and leaf in the dim light, trying not to think, not to speculate. It almost certainly was Gabrielle!

"He met her at your house," went on the Duke. "One of your maids, girl named Daisy, told one of ours about it. She was standing behind the minx when your brother arrived. Must have understood their heathenish lingo, for she says the woman said, 'Who is that gorgeous creature?' They were together all the time after that, and there were a lot of notes passing back and forth, and one of the Frenchmen became so angry he tried to pick a quarrel with Master Caradoc. The servants did a lot of tattling, and finally I got wind of it. A pretty thing to hear about the man who wants to marry my daughter!"

Frank's eyes were still fixed on the carved roses above him. Never afterward could he see one of that variety without a twinge of mental pain.

"He's been seeing her since. I've had him watched. A dirty business; but what would you have me do?" The old man broke off and regarded Frank anxiously. "I say, are you ill? You're as white as a sheet."

Frank dragged his eyes away from the window molding with a physical effort. "No, Your Grace," he said. "I'm quite all right. A twinge in my knee. That's all."

"You look as though you had seen a ghost. Well, as I was telling you, he's had the indecency to be seen with her in the city. She works in a dress shop, it seems; parades the dresses for customers, the brazen hussy. He calls there to see her home. Sends her flowers and gifts. To the shop, mind you. It's been a hole-and-corner business right along. I suppose they are afraid of her father, who undoubtedly would put a stop to such proceedings. He's a man of title, it seems——"

"The Comte de Salle."

"That's the name. Then you knew something of this already?"

"No, Your Grace. I've dined at their house in London and I—I recognized Mlle. de Salle from what you've told me. But," he added with sudden heat, "I fail to see any fairness or truth in your description of her. She's a lady of great beauty and fineness, Your Grace. I'm not saying this to excuse my brother's conduct, which is beyond defense, but to make it clear that no criticism in the matter can be made to include her. I'm certain she's completely blameless."

"By Gad," grumbled the peer, "you speak as though you were in love with her yourself. Well, I haven't seen the girl, and for all I know she may be the paragon you say she is. I'm willing to concede her all the graces and allow that she's the personification of beauty; but, just the same, her merits are in no sense an excuse for the way that rascally cub has behaved." He leaned forward and peered anxiously at his visitor. "I swear, my boy, that you look desperately ill. Perhaps it's the dim light that gives you such a ghastly appearance. Pull that bell again, if you'll be so kind. We must have the candles lighted."

Frank was feeling as ill as he looked, but his sickness was of the mind and not the body. His dream had been completely shattered. He was trying desperately to collect himself, to control his feelings so that nothing more of this would show on the surface. He kept repeating phrases to himself. "I must not blame Carr. It's not his fault. It's the most natural thing in the world. If I hadn't been such a blind and fatuous fool, I would have known it was inevitable. Gabrielle was bound to be attracted to him and, certainly, no man in his right senses could resist her. I've just got to accept it and try to be sensible." But even while he was striving to bring his feelings under control, he had momentary flashes of blind anger in which all reason deserted him and he knew that he was beginning to hate his brother.

"Well, that's what I had to tell you. I'm sorry you had to be dragged into it but I wanted you to know that I'm not acting on prejudice in refusing my consent. It's a filthy business. My little Mary is going to suffer because of it, but your splendid Caradoc won't get off scot-free. There never was an engagement, so my hands are tied and Hughie's too, worse luck. We have no grounds to call him out; we would only make the poor girl look ridiculous if we did. But I'm going to do everything I can to put spokes in his political wheel, and I rather think I'll prove a sound wheelwright at *that* kind of thing."

Frank slept at an inn, making the excuse that he must be in London early the next morning. He was up and away soon after dawn, but it was close to noon nevertheless when he had stabled his horse and found his way to 27 Prater Street.

It was a noisy neighborhood, given over largely to the kind of business concerns which take over unhappy sections of a city when fashionable favor has passed. They ensconce themselves in the ground floors of the tall, shuttered houses: dressmakers and doctors of the shadier sort, moneylenders and fortunetellers, women with no visible means of support but with quite visible charms, who manage somehow to support themselves quite well, chemists and greengrocers and tripe men and the very smug practitioners who cater to the grim affairs of the laystalls, and even frowsy individuals who issue out from back lanes with hand-barrows for the collection of old iron and rags and whatever else they can pick up in more progressive parts. There are always rooms to be let on the floors above. Signs sprout like a rash in all the windows, offering extra special inducements to single lodgers and even to families of limited size. The sheriff and the tipstaff are the most frequent of all visitors, and rickety one-horse vans are continuously engaged at moving in and out the poor sticks of furniture which represent the worldly wealth of the shabby people who accept for brief periods the claims of the aforesaid signs.

Aunt Francilea had found first-floor rooms for Frank in a rather better kept-up house on the more respectable fringe of such a neighborhood. It was apparent at first glance that a dentist had the ground floor, for on one of the front windows appeared the painting of a hand (presumably human) holding up a dripping object which was intended to represent a forcibly extracted tooth, and the words PATCHER PULLS WITHOUT PAIN. It developed at once that Patcher himself was the landlord. Frank had barely set foot in the dark hall at one side of the chamber where the painless extractions were performed than he emerged with the suddenness of a jack-in-the-box and proceeded to bid him welcome.

"Mr. H'Ellery, sir, you are most welcome, you are h'indeed." Mr. Patcher, as his new lodger was soon to learn, was ceaselessly engaged in a genteel effort, but not a successful one, to master his aspirates. "Mrs. Beamish, sir, said you would be in today. I hope, sir, you will find h'everything to your liking."

"I'm sure I will. Have my things arrived, Mr. Patcher? You *are* Mr. Patcher, I presume."

"Yes sir, I h'am. Dentist, sir, and a good one, I make bold to assert. Your things have arrived, Mr. H'Ellery. Mrs. Beamish attended to it herself. The whole first floor, sir, four of the lightest, cleanest, and most desirable rooms to be found. First quarter paid by Mrs. Beamish in advance, quite proper h'and shipshape." He smiled broadly, to display a perfect set of teeth, and indulged in a professional joke. "H'extracted painlessly, sir."

The worthy dentist was holding a curious variety of wrench in his hands, turning it around and around as he talked. Seeing that his new roomer's eyes had been attracted to it, he held the object up with an air of conscious pride. "My pelican," he explained. "Used for purposes of h'extraction, sir. Sometimes it's called a key. The key to relief, sir. If you h'ever need such relief, sir——"

"My teeth are in excellent condition, thank you," said Frank, setting a foot on the stair.

The dentist raised an importunate hand. "You can never be sure, sir. Sometimes trouble stalks without warning. No pain at h'all, sir, but the dread caries is at work. I specialize in nature's helps; a term of my h'own, sir, not holding with such misleading words as 'false' and 'h'imitation.' My nature's helps are not bone, sir. Bone breaks too h'easy, so I favor the Egyptian Pebble, sir."

"I'll remember all this, Mr. Patcher, when I find myself in need of some help that nature can't supply. You won't mind, I trust, if I say that I hope it won't be for a very long time."

The rooms were light enough and even quite neat, he found; with chairs covered in yellow linen and a huge bed with pink dimity curtains hanging limply between its high posts. An artistic note had been attempted by the hanging of miniatures on the walls, which he learned later were the unsold stock of a far from successful portrait painter who labored in a near-by attic.

There was a copy of the morning edition on the table in his new sitting room. In spite of the dreary apathy with which Frank now viewed life in general, he felt a slight tingle of curiosity as to what his fire-eating assistant had elected to say about the latest developments in the war situation. With a deep sigh he settled into a chair and proceeded to run an eye over the flash. The first rounded sentences caused him some uneasy speculation.

"Copey is going too far," he thought. "He shouldn't have put it that way."

Further reading confirmed this impression. Cope *was* going too far and most certainly was putting things in a way that was very far indeed from discreet. In order to lend force to his argument that seniority and precedent should be discarded in finding a suitable commander for such military operations as the government might elect ultimately to undertake, he had reviewed the past performances of Frederick, the favorite son of the King, in a tone of unqualified frankness. One phrase stood out from the column of cold print. "His Grace," the daring Cope had written, "may be a good administrator of army affairs from the ease of his chair at the War Office but it is impossible to conceive of a more inept leader in the field."

Frank let the paper fall to the floor. The Throne had never tolerated any form of criticism in print. He could recall the exact wording of the brief note which had resulted a few years before in the owner of the *Times* going to prison. It had been little more than a hint that His Majesty was displeased with the conduct of his two oldest sons. If the royal wrath had kindled so fiercely over a mild innuendo of that kind, what repercussions might be expected from the bold phrasing of Cope's attack?

Frank felt a strange hollowness at the pit of his stomach. For several moments he stared blankly out of the nearest window, unable to focus his mind on the course he should now follow. "There's nothing to be done," he thought finally. "This will bring matters to a head. We may even be suppressed permanently." His next thought was, "Well, I have nothing to lose now." He did not mind the prospect of quick and drastic punishment which faced him, but he had the keenest dread of the publicity which would go with it, the need to appear and be stared at in open court, the bitter harangues he would have to face, the hostility of the crowds. "If they would just take me away and leave me in jail, I wouldn't mind it," he said to himself.

He could not get his resolution up to the point of going to the office. Things would be in a turmoil there, he knew. Perhaps the law had already acted to put padlocks on the presses; perhaps also the warrant had been issued for his arrest. He wanted it done in the easiest way; let them come and get him here.

He found in a very few minutes that his last surmise was well founded. There was a clatter of footsteps on the stair and Windy Topp broke into the room without the formality of knocking. The runner was completely winded and for the first time made no attempt at his customary obeisance.

"They're coming, sahib!" he gasped. "Mr. Cope's been took and they've got him over at the Old Bailey this very minute. They were at the office for you and they'll be getting here in a brace of snaps. Quick, sahib, there's not a second to be lost if you don't want 'em landing you in Lob's Pound too!"

Now that the expected blow had fallen, Frank found to his surprise that he had become cool again. "There's nothing to be done about it, Windy," he said. "It's kind of you to warn me but, if there's a warrant out, I'll wait here until it's served."

"Sahib!" Topp's voice had a resentful tone. "That's no way for us to take it. We got to give 'em a run for their brass. I've thought how to do it, sahib. Listen. There's a h'undertaker's in this same block and you can get there through the back. We'll put you in a 'ternity box and deliver you alive and kicking to some safe place out of voil. We'll give 'em the slip that way. They'll never look in a wooden habeas, I'll take an oath on that."

Frank shook his head at his voluble helper. "It wouldn't do. The law has to be faced sooner or later. We'll face it now, Windy, and take our medicine."

Topp ran to the front window. "Medicine, is it!" he said bitterly. "Well, here's your first dose of it, sahib. And it ain't done up in a 'arf-crown bottle. It's coming on two legs with the bracelets out and all ready for use!"

13

FRANK TURNED his head slowly and painfully to look at his companion in distress. An egg had splattered on Cope's head and was draining down into his eyes. The spiked ends of his mustache were red with the juice of a squashed tomato. All about them there was a roar of sound, laughter, jeers, catcalls. A hoarse voice shouted, "How d'ye like it in stretchneck, ye dirty traitors?" and the crowded square took up the question with obscene amendments.

In a desperate effort to keep his mind detached from their predicament, Frank kept his thoughts on the trial which had resulted in their being here. They had stood for hours in the frame prisoner's enclosure at the Old Bailey and he had been in a state of dread that his bad leg would give out before the end of the hearing. Leaning heavily on the railing, he had prayed for the strength to see it through. He had noticed that the face of his companion wore an almost ecstatic look. "I believe he's glad to be here," he had said to himself.

It had been for Frank the worst imaginable ordeal. The large square mirror, suspended over them on a decided slant, had made them clearly visible in every part of the crowded room. He had kept in one corner to escape the feeling of being under dissection. Seldom had he allowed his eyes to wander in the direction of the committee gallery, knowing that as high as three guineas had been paid for seats there, and that the purchasers were eying him avidly. The continual uproar which came through the open windows testified that the streets outside were filled.

The jury had not found it necessary to adjourn from their seats, and it had been with a feeling almost of relief that he had heard the rasping voice of justice pronouncing sentence. ". . . You have been found guilty of the most despicable offense, disloyalty to our beloved sovereign, His Majesty, King George III. . . . You shall stand for the space of one hour in the public pillory. . . . A month's imprisonment . . ." Cope had moved over and whispered in his ear, "I got you into this, Frank," and he had whispered back, "No, we did it together, Copey." There had been a moment of complete silence then, the stern face of the judge glowering about him as though daring anyone to disturb the sacred calm of the court. Cope had spoken up in a loud voice, "This is the proudest day of my life."

Cope did not seem to be taking the first stage of their punishment with the same high resolve. Perspiration was beading out on his mild round face. He said to Frank now in a desperate whisper: "Someone's trying to dislodge the bar from under my feet. I can't see who it is and I can't do anything about it!"

He was four inches shorter than Frank and, before closing down and locking the oak beam over their heads, the official in charge had placed him on a slab of wood so that they could stand on the same level. "Great God!" thought Frank, knowing that his companion would be left hanging by the neck and arms if the wood were knocked out from under him. "His neck may be broken!"

They were confined so closely in the pillory that neither could see more than the section of spectators immediately in front. Frank asked, "Can you see where the officers are?"

"No, I can't. I can only turn my head a little way. It's someone at the side. He's striking at the wood with a club, I think."

"Press down hard with your feet."

"I am. But it doesn't do much good. I can just touch the bar with my toes as it is."

"Officer! Watch what's going on here!" shouted Frank in renewed panic.

His cry was drowned out in the loud roars of the crowd. They seemed to take it for granted that he was appealing for relief from his own discomfort, and the idea afforded them intense satisfaction. More eggs and vegetables were hurled at him, and something hard struck him on the forehead. A rotten egg smashed on the frame beside his head. Even a few stones were thrown this time, and one caught him on the left hand, flattening his fingers against the palm. He felt a sharp pain and saw that blood had been drawn. "Traitor!" "Liar!" "Agitator!" rose from every side. Someone with an ingenious turn of mind started to chant: "Treasonmonger Ellery is locked up in the pillory."

The crowd liked the jingling sound of it and began to repeat, "Ellery's in the pillory! Ellery's in the pillory!"

"Serves him right for printing a pack of dirty lies!" screamed an old beldame whose gin-sodden face was directly in his line of vision. She brandished a bottle in the air and continued to assail him with insulting epithets.

He could see now that carriages were drawn up around the sides of the square and that smartly dressed ladies and gentlemen were standing on the seats to get a better view. "I suppose they've brought lunches with them so they won't miss anything," he thought. One of the fashionable onlookers, a tall young buck in a green surtout, waved his beaver hat above his head and shouted something. It must have been particularly offensive, for the figure of a woman rose suddenly from the carriage back of him and drew a whip from its socket. The sweep of the lash tore the hat from the head of a lady beside the man in green before descending around his shoulders. The hat-waver tried to grapple with his assailant, almost falling off the seat in doing so. The crowd turned to this new source of amusement and loudly cheered the angry woman on, not caring that they were changing sides in doing so. "Give it to him, missus!" they shouted. "Give it to him hot, the banging dandy!"

Frank saw with a catch of his breath that his champion was Aunt Francilea. She freed himself and brandished the whip vigorously, inviting anyone who cared to repeat the offense to share in her mode of answer. "God bless her!" he thought. "There's one stout heart in the family after all."

His thoughts went back immediately, however, to the dangerous plight of his companion. Cope's face still reflected the most intense anxiety. "He keeps pounding at it," he panted. "Can't we do something, Frank? I don't want to be strangled."

Relief came in the nick of time. Frank saw a coat of scarlet in the press directly in front of him. The wearer was Sir Robert Wilson and he was pushing and struggling vigorously to get closer. As soon as he reached the front files he grinned up at the two smeared heads wedged so tightly in the oak frame and called: "Only fifteen more minutes of it. Keep a stout heart, Frank."

"Look to Cope!" cried Frank. "Do something about it quick! He's in danger."

Apparently the soldier realized what was happening, for he plunged through the single line of spectators still in front of him and disappeared out of sight at the side. Sounds of altercation could be heard for a few seconds and then Sir Robert came into view again. "I've put a stop to *that!* The dirty dog has something to remember you by that he didn't expect." He smiled up at Frank again and called out in a loud tone: "I asked permission to stand up there with you today but they refused me that great honor. Well, I'm here to announce my hearty concurrence in everything you've done. I want to say that this is a disgrace to English justice——"

An official voice interrupted gruffly: "No speeches allowed. That's orders, Mr. Officer."

Wilson tried to go on but was drowned out by loud shouts of angry disapproval. He gave up the effort finally and contented himself with holding his watch up over the heads of the mob so that the two prisoners could see the dial. Frank watched his lips move and made out that he was trying to say, "Only ten minutes more."

Nothing else happened for the remainder of the specified time. Frank felt a hand fumble at the padlock beside his arm and heard a screech of rusty springs as the heavy oak beam was raised in the grooved stone pillars. A gruff voice said in his ear, "Come on now, sharp! Ye've done yer hour, ye lousy scribblers. Follow me in before the crowd turns ugly on us." He caught another glimpse of Wilson and of his courageous old relative, who had torn off her bonnet and was waving it at him, then he turned and ran on the heels of the keepers through a narrow and jostling lane of hissing spectators.

Cope paused on the stone steps of the prison to ask, "Are you hurt, Frank?" Receiving a negative nod, the little editor said ruefully, "Two perfectly good suits of clothes ruined!" Inside the heavy doors, he stopped and shook himself with an air of disgust. "Whew! All those eggs were pretty bad. There's been an uneven distribution of rewards today, Frank.

Did you know it's been given out that Caradoc will be on the next honor list for the little job of investigation he undertook? Rotten eggs for us, a knighthood for him! Sir Caradoc Ellery! Well, that's the way things go."

The turnkey who received them was a little fellow who carried his head on one side and wore a perpetual smile. He had worn it so long, in fact, that deep wrinkles had been etched around his eyes as though announcing to the world, "Here's a pleasant fellow, one to be trusted and looked to, and you can depend on *that*." The funny part of it was, however, that a closer inspection left no promise of kindliness or jollity in him at all. To complete this reversal in impressions, he was jingling a bunch of keys on a large iron ring with an eagerness that suggested he could hardly wait for the pleasure of locking them up.

"Harry Daunce, at yer service, guv," he said, looking at Frank. "Ye're the two perlitical prisoners, I takes it, from the looks of ye. They *did* make proper cockshies of ye, didn't they? Ye'll both be wanting State Side, in course."

"Perhaps you'll be good enough to explain what you mean by State Side."

Mr. Daunce proceeded to count off on his fingers. "We has eight in all, guv. Male Debtors, Female Ditto, Chapel Yard, Middle Gate, Male Felons, Female Ditto, State and Press Yard. Press Yard is for them as is set for the Paddington frisk." Reading lack of comprehension in their eyes, he added with proper scorn: "Collar day, guv. Ye can't go *there*. The rest is common and dirty and *very* crowded, so it's State Side ye want. It costs a little mint. Twenty-eight shillings a week gets a room for the pair of ye, as snug as bugs under a log. I'd advise offering thirty, guv, if I was you, because that allows"—he winked broadly—"for certain little extras."

"I've no intention of buying any form of special privilege," declared Frank. "There's no reason why we should be treated any better than the rest of the poor unfortunates here."

"Fust time I ever heard 'em called that. They're a rough *and* ready lot, guv." The turnkey winked at Cope. "So ye wants to be treated like the rest? Well, ye'll soon get over *that* idea and make no mistake."

"We won't get over it."

The turnkey said in a testy voice: "Come, come, guv, ye mustn't be stubborn about this. Ye've no idea how bad it is. One hour with the lot in Male Felons and ye'll be sending word to Harry Daunce to get ye out." He continued to smile, but it was clear he was rapidly gaining an unfavorable opinion of his new charges. "Ye'll find it pays to side in with authority. And we've got to live, ain't we? We depends on our little extras, guv, so ye'll be wise to give in now."

"Lock us up and be done with it."

Daunce spat vigorously. "Locked up it is, then. But first ye'll hand over the garnish."

"Garnish?"

"Half a guinea each. It goes to the prisoners' fund and ev'ry man Jack as comes in pays it or parts with his clothes. It's pay or strip and, if ye was to ask me, I'd say pay."

"I've heard of the custom now that I come to think of it. The prisoners elect someone to collect and handle the funds for them."

Daunce nodded. "The prison steward. Elected by all the wards. He has his little priv'leges. A slice of the chummage and the best of ev'thing for hisself. Mostly, though, he looks after the garnish. Well, guvs, post the cole."

Frank handed over a guinea without further discussion. As he proceeded to wash himself in a rusty basin in one corner, he heard the turnkey say in a tone of deep disgust to another keeper, a fellow with long and spindly legs: "They're set on Sheepie-run. Got to be showed, Gander." When both of the prisoners had succeeded in removing the proofs of public disfavor, Daunce led the way down a flight of stone steps and along a dark passage in which a faintly acid odor struggled feebly against a heavy wave of human smells. It became apparent as they progressed further that the smells came through a barred door at the far end.

"All the yards closed today," explained the turnkey over his shoulder. "Repairs. Makes it kind o' bad inside."

When the door closed on the trio they were confronted with a scene straight out of the *Inferno*, except that the actors in it wore everyday clothes and had faces faintly recognizable as English in type. It was a long room with a greasy stone floor and no more than three small windows high up on the walls. A swearing, shouting, fighting mob filled it to overflowing. At first they could see nothing but faces: evil faces, diseased faces, sunken faces which bore the mark of unbearable suffering, massed together as tightly as caterpillars in a tent. A closer inspection revealed the fact that some of the inmates of the crowded ward were keeping themselves as busy as the limited space allowed. Some were playing profanely at crebs in corners, and in another spot a noisy game of bumble-puppy was in progress to the accompaniment of much scuffling and quarreling. A few were sitting along the walls in hopeless apathy, with their knees drawn up close to keep clear of the feet of the more active.

All were shabby and dirty and all had the unhealthy pallor of the prison on their unshaved cheeks.

The odor of the place assailed the newcomers like the breath of pestilence.

Daunce turned his twisted neck in their direction. "Like it here, guvs? Can ye stand a month of this?"

"We'll stand it," said Frank shortly.

The noise of the ward had increased with their arrival. A concerted shout was kept up. "Harry Daunce! Old Harry! Harry All-of-a-Sweat! Dirty Daunce! Dirty Daunce!"

The smile never left the turnkey's face but he kept swiveling his head around and muttering in malevolent tone: "Dirty Daunce, is it! I'll make these thieving barstards pay for this!"

The fact that he had new prisoners in tow became apparent to the mob and the cries changed to: "Garnish! Garnish! Pay or strip! Here, Steward, here's garnish for ye."

Daunce waved them back and announced: "The garnish has been forked over and'll be paid in at once. Pipe down, ye active citizens,* while we takes a good look at yer dirty fronts."

All the activities in the place had ceased, and a hundred pairs of eyes were fixed on the visitors; watchful, crafty, vicious eyes, although in some of them could be read a trace of better feeling, and in a few the dregs of tragedy. A voice from the rear broke the brief silence. "That's them. Ell'ry an' Cope. Babes just outa the wood for a-slangin' o' old Nobs." Loud jeers followed this news, and Frank could see that the eyes riveted on him had turned unfriendly and threatening. Some of the prisoners began to press forward toward them. "We'd better get out, guv," said the turnkey. "They're a-turning nasty. They're going to need a good going-over."

Before anything could happen a tall fellow in shirt sleeves, with huge red arms bare to the elbow, shoved himself to the front and waved the rest of them back.

"Zads and moshers we may be," he orated. "And bulks and files. And even pushers of whistlers. But we're Englishmen, ain't we? We got rights, ain't we? Why should we turn agin a pair of coves what's stood right up to old Nobs and told 'im 'ow to lick Boney? We want Boney licked, don't we? We don't want 'im coming over 'ere and taking away our rights and priv'leges and telling us what we can do and what we can't do. A nice sort o' place this 'ud be if 'e did get over."

_____
* Active citizen = a louse.

"He'd break open the prisons if he did," called a dissenting voice. "That's what he'd do. I say, let him come!"

"And that's where ye're wrong, my knee-cuffed friend," declared the first speaker. "He might crack the jails but he'd only do it to shove us into uny-forms and put muskets in our 'ands——"

"Come along, guv," said the turnkey, leading the way back into the corridor. "We'll let them settle that one by theirselves. Jack Griffey'll talk 'em down. He's the steward. And a good un. He's tough with 'em, Jack is."

The door clanged to and Daunce said sourly: "We're full up over here anyway. Can't put ye in any o' the wards, so I guess it's a case of chumming in with the last batch we got. They ain't much, guv. A mosher from up Newmarket way and a burn-crust what used a kneading iron in a argument with a customer. They're heavy smokers and drinkers, both of 'em. Still, they're a fair average. Ye might do better but ye might do a lot worse. Ye'll get used to their ways and there won't be trouble if ye watches yer step with the burn-crust. He's touchy."

Frank could not believe his eyes at first when he saw the room to which they were assigned. By the light filtering in through a narrow slit of window he made out that there were four occupants and two of them were stretched out stark naked on stone slabs against the wall. Their flesh had a purplish tint which did away with any need of explanation. The horror he felt was so great that he scarcely noticed the mosher and the burn-crust, who were huddled together in one corner and living up to their reputation as heavy smokers.

Daunce nodded. "Yes, guv. It's the cold turkey. We don't like to put any'un in here; but what can we do when we're full up and more o' ye coming in every day? It ain't so bad in some ways. There's a good window and the walls is dry. Sometimes ye'll have the place to yerselves. These two"—indicating the still bodies on the stone slabs—"goes out tonight. I don't think as they died of anythin' infechus. Durkin there, the one with the beard—and a tough un he was—drank hisself to death, in my opinion. The t'other had trouble with his lungs." He rattled his keys. "On the whole, guv, ye'll have more real comfort here than in any o' the wards."

The two new prisoners looked at each other and there was a grudging decision in each pair of eyes. "We'll pay to live on the other side," said Frank shortly. "It goes against the grain but we—we can't stomach the thought of this."

Harry All-of-a-Sweat nodded with approval. "That's the kind o' talk. That's sense! I knew ye'd come to it. They all does. Three guineas down for the priv'lege o' getting changed, and a week's rent on top o' that. Thanks, guv. And now we'll get along to where ye belongs."

The two prisoners followed thoughtfully in the wake of the turnkey. Cope said in a tense whisper: "I'm glad this happened to us. We'll have to print something about what we've seen when we get out of this. It's unbelievable!"

"I'm beginning to think it's more important than what we've been trying to do," answered Frank in an equally low tone. "The invasion scare has been hanging over us for ten years only, but this has been going on for centuries. We'll beat Boney now, or he'll beat us; but these horrible dens will be kept on for centuries more, if something isn't done about them. I thought John Howard got the jails cleaned up but he barely touched the edge of things. We've let ourselves forget everything he told us. Copey, do you realize that there are many innocent men back in that hole? Men who haven't even been brought to trial yet?"

Thinking of the innocence of some of the unfortunates they had seen reminded him of a matter which had been at the back of his mind since the moment they entered. He tapped the turnkey on the shoulder.

"Daunce," he said, "there's a man in here I'd like to see. His name is Fuller. Benjamin Fuller."

"Fuller?" Daunce squinted at them thoughtfully. "Oh, *him*. He's in Morning-drop Row. Why do you want to see the likes of him?"

"I know him. He's a decent young fellow and I'm hoping we can get him out of it before it's too late."

The turnkey laughed. "Anything *you* can do won't help him any now. There's no chance for them anyway when once they goes to Morning-drop Row. Sometimes they stays around for quite a while but they dances at Bielby's ball in the end. It's agin the rules but, in course, something could be arranged if ye wanted it bad enough."

"Half a crown?"

"Half a guinea," said the turnkey emphatically. "Couldn't take the risk for less, guv."

"Very well. If you'll lead us there now."

The condemned cells were reached at the end of another long stone hall and at the top of a curving flight of clammy stairs. They would have known where they were if they had stumbled on it by chance. There is a hush, a hint of deadly expectancy, in the atmosphere of all places where men wait the arrival of the fatal day. Jailers will tell you that the condemned have ways which cannot be explained of learning what is in the wind. They seldom have to be told when the paper arrives, fixing the day and hour; they have already sensed it from something in the air, from the sound of footfalls, from the tone of voices heard at a distance. Certainly the atmosphere of the short corridor into which they turned through a heavy iron door was different from that in any other part of this grim, teeming institution. The perturbation aroused by this unexpected visit was evident in the sound of feet hurrying to the gratings, in the desperate tone of the question asked almost in whispers, "What is it, Daunce, what is it?"

"We're a bit crowded," explained Harry All-of-a-Sweat. "Hasn't been a working-off in some weeks."

He called "Fuller!" and a tall young fellow came to the barred door of one of the cells and looked out inquiringly. Frank remembered him at once; he had a pleasant face, with a good forehead and a pair of mild gray eyes. The dampness and confinement of prison life had not yet given his cheeks the usual gray tinge. Fuller rested his arms on the bars to carry the weight of his chains.

Frank walked to the bars and shook hands with him. "How are you feeling, Benjie?" he asked.

"Quite well, Mr. Ellery, sir," said the condemned man. "I'm glad of the chance to thank ye for the food ye send in. It's most welcome, Mr. Ellery, sir. The food here"—he hesitated—"well, it isn't good."

"What's wrong with the food?" demanded Daunce sharply.

"Well, Mr. Daunce, there's not enough of it for one thing."

Frank drew closer to the bars. He said in a whisper: "We've been trying to do something for you, Benjie. I'm not now in a position to exert any influence, as you can see, but others are doing their best. Men of some position. I spoke to the Duke of Westgate the last time I saw him and he promised to act in your behalf."

"It's most kind of you, Mr. Ellery, sir." The pleasant gray eyes lighted up. "I think it's going to be all right for me. You see, sir, I've been here a long time. Four months, three weeks, and six days. That must mean something. All of us here think it means something. We think it means transportation. I wouldn't mind transportation, Mr. Ellery, sir. They say the country isn't bad. A little warm perhaps, but you can get land when you've worked out your time, and raise sheep, sir. I'd be good at that. We talk about transportation here a lot and we all think it wouldn't be bad."

"It's the best you can hope for, Benjie. You mustn't count on it too much, of course, but everything that can be done is being done. Do you get the food regularly?"

"Like clockwork, sir. Four o'clock regular. One day it's beef and the next mutton. Once it was chicken. What a time we had that day! I hope you don't mind, Mr. Ellery, sir, that I divides some of it around. You see, none of the rest of us has friends like you."

"I'll have the quantity increased, Benjie. But you must keep enough for yourself, you know."

The condemned man dropped his hands to a lower bar to relieve his arms of strain. "I wonder what's happening to Becky, sir. She can't write, so I never hear from her. None of us has friends who can write and it makes it—well, kind of dull and hopeless at times. Don't think I'm complaining. I've much to be thankful for, Mr. Ellery, sir. But I must get word to her when the news about the transportation comes. She'll want to hear about it. I'm very hopeful, sir, that she'll wait for me. I shouldn't say it that way, sir; I *know* she will."

"I'm sure she will."

"She's a fine girl. I hope I didn't make it too hard for her in her position by what I did. She's a maid, sir."

"I'll have someone go to see her at once, and tell her what you've said."

"Would you do that, Mr. Ellery, sir? It will make me very happy. I think about her all the time, sir."

Frank became increasingly aware of the eyes staring at him from all sides. There was something disturbing about the intentness with which they watched every move he made. It was not curiosity, he felt, but a hungry desire to take advantage of every small contact with the world from which they were cut off, the world they would never see again except for one brief and tragic half hour. He marveled at the stillness they maintained.

"Your—your companions seem to take this very well," he whispered.

Fuller nodded. "Yes sir. We take things easy in the main. We talk and sometimes we joke and laugh, and sometimes a few of us sing. Not very often though. They're not a bad lot, Mr. Ellery, sir. It's mostly theft with us. Petty theft, sir. There's Freedy for holdup and a stagecoach robber in number 8. I've never seen *him*, but he sings a lot and sometimes he curses by the hour. He's a thorough bad un, I guess."

"Are you allowed visitors?"

"Not often, sir. None's been here for me. My old mother has no way of getting to London, and I'm sure Lady Wasser would dismiss Becky if she as much as mentioned coming. Some days the warden comes through and looks us over. There was a man in a big wig came in with him one day, and they stood out there and whispered. We were all fair frightened *that* time, Mr. Ellery, sir."

"Guess you've talked enough to him, guv," said Daunce suddenly. "There's rules to be thought on, ye know."

They shook hands again and the condemned man said in an almost cheerful tone: "I'm feeling sure about it. The transportation, I mean. And it's meant such a lot to talk to you. Do you suppose they'll let you come again, Mr. Ellery, sir?"

"I hope so, Benjie."

"Don't think I'm ungrateful because I haven't said anything about what's happened to you, sir. I—I hope it wasn't too hard today, sir."

"No, it wasn't too hard. And now it's all over. Good-by, Benjie."

14

DAUNCE POKED his head through the bars of the door and grinned like a facetious cat at a pair of mice. Shifting a frayed cigar from one corner of his mouth to the other, he said, "Sun's out, guv. Nice day for outsiders. Church bells are ringing and people are pouring lively into the cackletub down the street. And there's two visitors for ye."

"Visitors? Who are they?"

"Well, I can't put a tongue around their names, guv. An odd pair. Furriners; and kinchers to boot."

Cope, who was lathering his face in front of a broken piece of glass, heard only the word "visitors." He seized his razor and began to shave with furious haste.

"Here they are, guv."

Margot and Jean Baptiste Achille came into the room. The girl looked thinner and more peaked even than Frank had remembered her to be and, as she was wearing a Patmos cap which obviously had been discarded by her cousin and was several sizes too large for her, she lived up to the term the turnkey had used. Jean Baptiste Achille, in a jacket which had been cut down in length but left completely undisturbed in point of width, looked even odder.

"M'sieur," said Margot in a hesitant tone, "we thought, as it was Sunday and such a very nice day, you might like to have some flowers."

She held out to him a bunch of daffodils tied with white ribbon. They were not exactly fresh—in fact, to say they were wilted would hardly have fallen into the category of exaggeration—but they were as cheerfully yellow as only daffodils can be and they brought with them the suggestion that summer was just around the corner.

"I must have the ribbons back," said Margot. "You see, m'sieur, we had one of our dinners last night and the daffodils were used to decorate the table. I'm sure no one will miss the flowers, but we always use the same ribbon."

Frank accepted the bunch after she had untied the white strands and tucked them away in a pocket of her voluminous skirt. "I hope you won't be scolded, Mlle. Margot," he said. "They're very pretty and I think it was most thoughtful of you and Jean Baptiste Achille to bring them. I must see if we can find a jug and some water. Was the dinner a pleasant one?"

"It was a *very* fine dinner, m'sieur. The Duc de Berri was with us. It was a great honor, and Uncle Robert was happy about it. The Duc insisted that Gabrielle sit beside him. Jules de Vitrelle was very angry."

"I'm glad," said Frank. "I mean that I'm glad the dinner was a fine one and that the Duc came as a guest; not because Jules de Vitrelle was angry."

"He's terribly jealous, m'sieur. He didn't say a single word all through the meal. Gabrielle gave him a talking-to afterward. I heard her. And I saw the Duc de Berri. I peeked through the door while Antoine was serving." She added proudly: "We had a helper for Antoine. Mr. Finnerty from next door. He's a waiter. We had to watch him because he was a little drunk when he came."

Frank insisted that his young visitors must use the only seating capacity the room offered, which happened to be his unmade bed.

"I'm sorry I have no refreshment to offer you," he said. "We don't quite run to that sort of thing here. I'm very glad Jean Baptiste Achille came along, as I realize I'm in his debt and I—well, I'll hardly be in a position to deliver the money in person for a while."

"We all feel terribly about you being here, m'sieur," said Margot. "Uncle Robert says things must be getting as bad in this country as during the worst days in France. He was so upset when he heard about you that he could eat nothing. Gabrielle——"

"Yes," eagerly. "What did your cousin have to say?"

"She said she knew you were a brave man as soon as she saw you."

"That was more than kind of her." He hesitated. "She has many admirers, of course. There are new ones all the time, I'm sure. Even some Englishmen."

Margot shook her head. "I have heard of no English admirers. Unless—unless M'sieur means himself. It is quite true that Gabrielle has great success with all men. His Majesty paid her many compliments when he was at M'sieur's house."

Frank was thinking that the old Duke had been right, then, in saying that Caradoc's acquaintance with Gabrielle was a hole-and-corner affair.

His brother obviously had not put in an appearance at Brinsley Place; Margot could not have overlooked him if he had been there. He was realizing also that it was no longer possible for him to think of his brother's latest infringement without a sense of furious frustration. That he must remain locked up for several more weeks while his handsome rival escorted Gabrielle to and from the dress shop, loading her with flowers and gifts and ingratiating himself more securely all the time in her favor, was more than he could bear. "If I must lose her," he said to himself, "let it be to Jules de Vitrelle. Even to the Duc de Berri. But not to Carr."

"You spoke of a payment, m'sieur," piped up Jean Baptiste Achille.

Frank smiled down at the boy, whose legs, dangling over the side of the bed, were not nearly long enough to reach the floor. "Yes, my keen young business friend," he said, handing over a penny. "The monthly dividend is three days overdue. The first time it has occurred, I think."

"Yes, m'sieur. The payments have always been prompt."

"Were you worried, Jean Baptiste Achille?"

The boy gulped with embarrassment. "Yes, m'sieur, a little," he confessed. "It did not seem to me that a business could be doing very well when the head of it was in prison. I did not expect any more payments."

"The business is not doing very well. I hope it's going to do much better a little later, however. And that doesn't concern your investment with me, young man. You see, the loan you made me is secured in a very special way. It carries a personal guarantee. The capital will always be safe and I'm obligated to see to it personally that the dividends are paid. It's a sort of personal mortgage, you might say."

The boy's face lighted up. "That is very good news, m'sieur." He added, as though one piece of good news had taken his thoughts to another, "Mick Finnerty has been sick."

"And what's wrong with the doughty Mick?"

Jean Baptiste Achille struggled with the name of the disease which had laid his enemy by the heels, finally arriving somewhere near it. "The numps, m'sieur. He is very sick, they say, and his face is all swollen up and red."

Frank was studying the thin face of the girl. "Margot," he asked, "were you born in England?"

"No, m'sieur." She seemed a little reluctant to talk about it. "My father and mother and my brother went to Italy when the Revolution began. I was born there. In Naples, m'sieur. My parents were so poor then that I'm afraid I was a very great problem. My father was employed at a fish market. It was only after they all died—all of them at once, of the smallpox—that I was sent to England. I was no more than a year old and so I can't remember any of them." She sighed. "They say my mother was just as lovely as Gabrielle's. They were sisters, you know. It doesn't seem possible that both mothers could be beautiful, does it, m'sieur, when you think how different I am from Gabrielle? I wish I had seen my mother; I would have memories to keep if I had. Not to know any of your own family is a little hard."

"I presume they belonged also to the aristocracy of the court."

She shook her head. "My father was Raoul March. He was of the lesser nobility, but he had quite considerable estates. If it hadn't been for the estates they wouldn't have allowed my mother to marry him. I think from what I've heard said that everyone considered she married beneath her. But"—hastily—"they all speak well of him. He was an extremely tall man, nearly six feet, m'sieur! I have a miniature of him. He was quite dark and—well, I'm sure he must have been a kind man. I don't like to think of him working in a fish market. There is no miniature of my mother."

Daunce appeared at the door. "Time's up," he said. "Can't wait here all day. Not visiting hours anyway."

When they had gone, Cope rubbed the last of the lather from his face and asked, "Who might that pair be?"

"Very good friends of mine. French émigrés. I'm fond of both of them."

"The boy," declared Cope, who apparently had been keeping his eyes and ears open, "has the acquisitive sense of the French people. I didn't know he was a shareholder of ours but he seems disposed to check up on us like old Clayhorn. I liked the girl very much. She looks a little like a plucked chicken but she'll improve with time."

Daunce put his head back in the door. "Better go to chapel today, guvs," he said. "Not compulsory. Ye can go to chapel, or ye can play skittles, or ye can stay easy and comfortable on yer double juggs. But if ye ask me, I'd say go. It's a collar-day service."

Frank walked over to the door. "What does that mean?" he asked in anxious tones.

"There's to be a working-off tomorrow. Murderer came in to us what had heard the black-cap lecture on Friday. Murderers allus goes the next Monday. It seems old Nobs was persuaded to put his hand at the same time to some of the other warrants piled up on his desk. Eight of them this time, guv. Seats outside selling like sixty already. Prices going sky-high; two, three, four guineas for front winders, ten shillings for the roofs, two and six for area railings. Prices was never better."

Frank was almost afraid to ask the question, "Is Benjamin Fuller one of them?" He finally managed to get it out.

"Don't know, guv. It's not my beat and I ain't seen the list. I know one of the wimmen is down. Milly Corbin, a redheaded mab. Been quite a gal of the town, Milly has; as accommodating as a barber chair, ev'ybody served. Light-fingered too, but the dubbers wink at a little of that sort of thing. Then she stole a watch and *that* was going a bit too far. She's a rough one, Milly, and it's my idea she won't be worked off easy."

Frank asked slowly, "Is there always a special service for those who must die the next day?"

"Is there!" The turnkey winked. "Better go, guv."

Frank had no stomach for the spectacle so enthusiastically recommended to him, but he realized he would have no peace of mind until he knew whether or not Fuller was one of the unhappy eight. Cope at once expressed his intention of going. It was his duty as a newspaperman to see everything that went on, he declared. When the sound of a loud bell boomed down the corridors, accordingly, they got to their feet and joined the procession of prisoners pouring out from the wards and the private cells on all sides. It was clear that word had spread through the prison of what was afoot; there was an expectant look on all the faces bobbing and weaving about them.

The chapel had high white walls and a vaulted roof, and it had much more the appearance of a court of justice than of a house of God; which is a very different thing, or at least it was in these days. The pulpit was covered with bay leaves and sweet herbs in profusion, and Frank had not been there a moment before he realized why. The prisoners brought the odor of the wards with them, and the air had already become so thick that he wondered if he would be able to stay for the full service. He found he was to have no option on that score. As soon as the last seat had been filled, the doors were banged to and closed. Frank felt he had never heard a sound which depressed him more—the locking of doors in a house of divine worship.

His eyes scanned the sullen congregation and came to rest with a start on a pew immediately in front of the pulpit. It had been built up above the level of the rest and seemed to him very similar to the prisoner's box at the Old Bailey, except that it lacked the slanting mirror above. As far as he could see, it contained no bench, but what had attracted his eye there in the first place was the fact that it was swathed elaborately in black. What unnecessary cruelty, he thought, to stamp it so unmistakably as the pew of the condemned! Was the purpose to add to the mental suffering of the wretched men and women who must stand there for an hour or more under the avid eyes of the criminals of London?

"They're coming," whispered Cope.

The condemned prisoners came in one at a time with guards on each side. The woman was first. She had chains dangling from her wrists, and she carried herself with an attempt at bravado.

"Here I am, boys!" she called, tossing her head until the plumes in her hat waved. "Milly Corbin, dragged in here so ye can all stare at her for the last time. Better men have stared at Milly Corbin, I'll have ye know!"

"Good girl, Milly," "They can't get *you* down," and "Ye're worth looking at, Milly," came from different parts of the room. A guard shouted "Order!" in an angry voice and the word was taken up in derision until the chapel resounded with cries of "Order! Order!" The woman flounced into the pew and stood boldly near the front rail, nodding her head to those she recognized. It was clear that she had been well fortified for the ordeal.

Frank's eyes were on the others who were being led in at intervals, his mind filled with the most intense anxiety. The second to arrive was the murderer, he decided; at any rate the guards were handling him roughly, a furtive little specimen whose rodent eyes were never still. Five more men were escorted in, sullen, frightened, white-faced, and then there was a delay of several moments. Frank's hopes had risen with each new arrival but, when the last man came, he turned to Cope with a face as pale as those of the unhappy prisoners.

"It's Benjie!" he whispered. "Cope, he's to die after all. And here we are, prisoners like the rest of them, and unable to do a thing for him!"

Fuller was carrying himself better than the rest, although his face was pale and set. He took his post at the end of the line in the black pew and kept his eyes straight ahead of him, as though he could see something much less grim than the cold whitewashed walls of the chapel; perhaps the pleasant fields and green hedges where he had been raised as a boy, and the wooded stretch of Philips River. He was much younger than the rest, and in comparison with them he appeared clean and untouched by the grim experience through which he was passing.

The chapel organ began to play. Cope nudged Frank's elbow. "Must be a funeral service as well," he whispered. "There's the coffin now."

The door, through which the condemned prisoners had been brought in, opened again to admit two of the prison staff, carrying a long black box between them. It was surprising that they could handle it so easily, but the reason became apparent at once. The casket was empty!

The two guards carried it to the center of the chapel and there deposited it on a table directly in front of the pew occupied by the seven men and the one woman who were to die the next day. Frank saw that the face of Milly Corbin went blank and then turned white as she looked down into the empty space in the black box. Several of the men gasped, and even Benjie Fuller seemed on the verge of losing control of himself.

The man directly in front of them was whispering excitedly. "This is the third time I've seen that eternity box lugged in, and it always throws 'em into a proper fit. What I hope is I never has to sit and look down into it while the gluepot preaches hell-fire at me!"

Cope turned a white face toward his companion. "Frank! I can't believe it. This must be an ugly dream. This is England, not Africa or China or some other heathen country! Things like this don't happen here!"

Frank whispered back: "This is a church service, so it must have been a servant of God who thought of this form of torture! Such cruelty is hard to believe."

"What must those poor devils be thinking! That tomorrow they'll fill coffins of their own! But that's wrong; they won't be given coffins. Their bodies will be buried in quicklime. The earth must not be polluted with the bodies of those who stole a little something from their betters!"

The service was under way, but at first Frank did not hear a word, his mind being full of desperate speculation as to how a last-minute reprieve might be obtained. It was not until the sermon began that he was able to bring himself back to the present. He regretted it immediately, for the clergyman was taking advantage of the opportunity to lay stress on the wickedness which had brought the unfortunate group to this last pass. There was no hint of compassion in the dry staccato voice in which he spoke of regard for the laws of the land, no promise of a more lenient hearing before the final Judge they would meet when earthly justice had had its way with them.

"I don't believe Benjie's hearing a word of it," thought Frank, watching the young face at the end of the line. There was some comfort in the belief that at least one of the eight was not suffering under the clerical lash.

"I don't think I could have stood another minute of it," said Cope as they inched their way out to the corridor.

Frank was looking for Daunce. He saw the turnkey as soon as they emerged from the door of the chapel, standing in line with several other jail officers. Daunce winked at him as though to say, "Well, what did I tell you?"

"I must have a table," said Frank in hurried tones. "And ink and paper. Plenty of paper. And I want to send a message at once to a man named Topp, an employee of the *Tablet*. I don't care what the cost may be as long as this can all be done without any delay whatever."

"Right, guv," said Daunce cheerfully. "We'll talk about the little matter of costs later. I'll have ye fixed up in something less than no time at all." He winked again. "Reverend was a-pitching of it on, wasn't he?"

The table had been brought, a rickety affair for the use of which he knew he would pay as much as the value of the article itself. When the ink and paper and two quill pens had been spread out on it, Frank said to the expectant turnkey: "And now get Topp here. Please see that he brings with him half a dozen runners who will put themselves under his orders for the rest of the day."

"Copey," he said when they had the cell to themselves, "we're going to write letters to everyone we know who may have any kind of influence whatever. That boy must be saved!"

They sat down on opposite sides of the table and for a long time there was no sound in the stone-walled cell save the hurried scratch of the quill points on paper.

Hour after hour the two pens scratched over the dwindling piles of paper. Topp came and went, reporting that many of the letters had failed to reach those to whom they were addressed ("Oh, that long week end," thought Frank, "so pleasant when nothing is at stake, so damnably cramping in times of crisis!") but that the rest had been delivered safely. The runner was enjoying his chance to direct the efforts of his crew and was urging the preparation of more. "You write 'em, sahib," he would say with a cheerful grin, "and I'll see as how they're taken. I'm a-making their coattails crackle, sahib, ye can be sure o' that. They're going it on the run."

At ten that night Frank threw down his pen and flexed his cramped and aching fingers. "I can't think of anyone else who might conceivably be of use," he said reluctantly. "And yet I hesitate to stop. Perhaps we're overlooking the one man in a position to apply the needed pressure. It's a terrifying thought, Copey."

"I can't write another line," confessed Cope with a guilty air. "I've only one writing hand and it's serving notice that it's through. How many have we done between us?"

"At least fifty letters," answered Frank, after a brief calculation. "Do you think we've done him any good at all? I shudder when I think that some word of this will reach ears higher up. We may have ruined whatever hope he had otherwise."

"He had none at all. *That* we can be sure of. Well, we've done one thing at any rate. We've become tired enough to sleep in spite of that savage and uncivilized ceremony we sat through today."

"I'm afraid Benjie will get no sleep. He'll hear the hammers going all night out in the street. They'll start to set up the scaffolds after midnight." Frank shook his head wearily. "Copey, I'm thinking we'll have another crusade on our hands when we get out of here. A long one and perhaps a fruitless one."

"One?" Cope laughed mirthlessly. "When the press of this country is allowed the freedom to speak out, we'll find ourselves with hundreds of evils to be righted. Slavery. And the bedlam houses. And unemployment and the filthy little bits of wages paid to workingmen. It's going to be one long crusade, I'm thinking. Don't you realize, Frank, that this world we live in needs to be turned completely inside out and made over from top to bottom before it will be fit for human beings to live in? That almost everything we do, or the way we do it, is wrong and cruel and wasteful? And that nothing can be done about it until we have a free and enlightened press?" He yawned in spite of the vehemence of the mood which had taken possession of him. "I'm proud to think that I may live to see a start made on all this and perhaps have a share in the doing of it."

As he fumbled with aching fingers at his stock, Cope said suddenly: "Frank! Did you notice the two men who carried in the coffin? Our friends, the mosher and the burn-crust, so called! We've been nicely taken in, Frank. Those two guards were planted in the morgue for our special benefit. They knew we would cave in when we saw that."

15

FRANK WAKENED at seven o'clock. The grim job of construction had been finished; at any rate no sound of hammering was to be heard. There were plenty of other sounds, however, all loud enough to penetrate the thick walls of the prison, and to seep through the foul corridors, and into the wards where gloomy prisoners sat about and waited. On execution days there is a curious stillness in prisons, perhaps to compensate for the noise and excitement on the outside. It was clear that the public was very much excited about what was to happen this day. The noises indicated that the streets and the rooftops were already filled.

Frank demanded of the first keeper to pass their door, "Has word come yet of a reprieve for any of them?"

The man shook his head. "Nuh. And take my word for it, there ain't a-goin' to be any. Not for this lot." A gossipy mood took possession of the man. "Milly's havin' tantrums. Screamin' and carryin' on fit to wake the dead. Most o' the others is too sunk to eat their breakfus'. Extrys served to 'em too—soup and bread and a morsel o' meat."

Frank looked at his watch and then turned back toward Cope, who was struggling into his clothes in a mood of deep dejection. "There's plenty of time still, of course. I hardly expected any results as early as this."

"Don't get your hopes up, Frank. There's a dislike among the heads of English Government to any interruption in the solemn march of justice. And I suppose the King's at Windsor. That's a long way off and the roads will be bad."

At nine o'clock Frank asked another passing official, "Any word of reprieves or pardons?"

"No word, mister. We're havin' our troubles with this crew. The matrons can't do a thing with Milly. The gluepot's with the men, but only one on 'em will listen to him."

"That will be Fuller, I know."

The keeper nodded. "Yes. The young un. Don't ye wish ye could be out front to see it, mister?"

At ten o'clock he got the same answer. And at eleven as well. He turned back from their barred door then and said to his companion: "I'm afraid there's no hope now. If anything was going to be done . . ." He could not finish the sentence.

"We did our best. Don't take it too hard."

Frank began to pace up and down the room. "It will be a crime if he dies. I'm sure now that every hanging—except in the most desperate cases—is a crime against nature and against God. The state itself is the worst criminal we have. Think of that!" He continued his nervous march, making the turns with furious energy and stamping hard on his heels. "Is there anything we can do still? Surely there's something! Think, Copey, think!"

"There's nothing we can do and you know it. Sit down, man, you'll work yourself into a fever if you keep on this way."

"How do you suppose that poor fellow is feeling? He's so decent and fine, Copey!"

Daunce came by and stopped at the door to grin in at them. Frank went over to him at once. "Could it be arranged for me to see Fuller?"

he demanded. "I'll make it well worth your while, Daunce. I can't bear to think there's no one to say a friendly word to him."

Daunce appeared very skeptical. "It's never allowed, guv. It might cost me my sit, and I can't have *that*, no sir! I'd have to split with the lot to make it any way safe at all to try it on."

"I told you I don't care what it costs." Frank was feeling in his pockets. He produced three sovereigns. "Here. Will this be enough?"

"I'll take ye down to the yard where they waits afore they goes in to get their irons struck off. There'll be plenty about then and ye may not be noticed." The turnkey held out his hand for the sovereigns. "Post the cole, guv."

Sunlight struck down into the yard over the high stone walls which surrounded it on all four sides. It did not succeed, however, in warming the shrinking flesh of the eight condemned who had been marched down in file and lined up along one wall. They trembled visibly, even Milly Corbin, who had passed the violent stage and was now weeping copiously. The parson in attendance was reading from a Bible, holding it spread out on both hands, but no one seemed to be paying any attention to him.

"You might as well go orderly," the warden was saying in a patient voice. "We don't want to use violence. We don't want to take measures of any kind."

Frank was aware that all the barred windows and doors opening on the yard were filled with the faces of prisoners. At first he wondered why they had not been confined elsewhere, and then it occurred to him that this partial freedom was allowed them so that the lesson of what was taking place could strike home. Capital punishment can be defended only on the ground of the effect it has on the criminal-minded. The spectacle was having its effect, as a glance at the grim faces made abundantly clear; but Frank was conscious of a doubt as to whether it was quite what stern justice expected.

Having in mind the injunction which Daunce had laid upon him, he tried to keep out of the range of the warden's vision as he edged over to the end of the line where Benjie Fuller stood. The purloiner of a wedding ring was the only one of the unhappy eight who appeared in any way calm. He even managed to smile; a rather wan effort, but a smile nevertheless.

"They told me what ye were doing yesterday, Mr. Ellery, sir," he said in a whisper. "It was kind of ye; but I haven't been thinking that anything could come of it. I've been resigned to it since the word was read to us on Sat'day. Nothing can stop it once that happens."

"There's still time," said Frank, although he had lost hope completely. "Word may come yet. You see, they would have to refer it to the King, and he's at Windsor."

"I'm ready to go, Mr. Ellery, sir. The parson has been with me and I've made my peace with God. I believe there'll be forgiveness for me, and that's a great comfort." He looked directly at Frank for the first time. "Please, sir, would you do something for me? I can't write a single word and I'd like a message taken to Becky."

"I'll be glad to do anything I can. You know that, Benjie."

The tall young man blinked back the first suggestion of tears that Frank had yet seen in his eyes. "Tell her, Mr. Ellery, sir, that I thought of her. That I thought of her right up to the end. Tell her I'm sorry for what I did because it brought so much trouble and sorrow on her. And tell her, please"—he hesitated, but for no more than a moment—"she must forget about me now. She must put me out of her mind and go right on as though I'd never been in her life at all. She's so pretty and sweet that other men will want her, sir. She must marry one of them and make a new and happy life for herself. Make it very clear to her, sir, that I want it to be that way."

"Yes, Benjie. I'll make that clear to her."

"And about my mother, sir. Would it be asking too much for you to see her too?"

"Of course not."

"I've tried to think of some message to comfort her. But I can't, sir. She's all alone and she'll be taking this very hard. Please, Mr. Ellery, sir, try to think of something that might ease it for her a little."

"I'll think of something, Benjie. And I'll do whatever I can to look after her. I promise you that."

"Thank you, sir. I knew you would. You've been so kind to me."

The warden called out in a tone of sharp authority. "Now then, the irons must come off. You'll go in order—in the same order you'll go out *there*." He consulted a paper in his hand. "Fuller, you're first."

The head which had been held so high drooped for a moment. The lips quivered. Then he straightened up and smiled at Frank a second time. "You see, sir, I'm to have a bit of luck at the last," he said.

He walked firmly between two of the keepers through a door in front, and in a few moments they could hear the sound of a hammer ringing on iron. The chains which he had worn for so many months were being removed at last.

Frank thought desperately: "The last chance has gone! Why did he have to be the first?" He dropped back to an inconspicuous post by the wall.

The silence hanging over the place had been complete, none of the staring prisoners betraying the emotions they felt by so much as a word. The clang of the hammer, however, seemed to release their pent-up feelings. One of them let out a cry and, as though it had been a signal, the rest took it up. The shouts rose in volume until they filled the yard and rang in the ears of the somber group assembled there like the cry of doom. The faces in all the apertures of the four walls became congested with anguish, fury, desperation. They were shouting threats, imprecations, appeals for their unfortunate fellows.

"I won't have it!" cried the warden. "I won't have this every time on collar day. Shut them up, you men, send them back to their dens, the raving maniacs!"

A keeper ran to one of the doors, waving frantically for order. The din increased instead. It carried a distinct note of menace now, of defiance to all order. The keeper ventured too close and was seized by savage hands. They held him against the bars and rained furious blows on his head and shoulders.

"Help!" he shrieked. "They'll kill me! Get me away from them!"

One of the four armed men ran over from his post. "Back there, ye scum," he ordered. "Leave him go or I'll riddle ye with buckshot!"

The threat went unheeded. Blows continued to descend on the limp form of the keeper, and the noise, if possible, became more deafening than before. The armed man looked about him uncertainly. He saw the warden gesturing at him and, taking it for an order, raised the gun to his shoulder.

Frank heard himself shouting to stop, that murder would be done, but realized that his voice could not be heard over the din.

The gun went off and a figure at the barred door crumpled up and disappeared. The hands holding the keeper released him and he stumbled back, shaking his head in a dazed way. The gun was discharged again, this time at point-blank range. A third shot! A frenzy seemed to have taken hold of the man and he would have continued firing if he had not been seized from behind and dragged away.

"The bloody idiot lost his head!" cried the warden. "There'll be trouble over this! Remember, all of you, I gave no orders. I call on you now to remember that."

A white-faced turnkey emerged from the door which had swallowed up Benjie Fuller, and Frank heard him say to the warden: "It's a riot inside! They're tearing up everything to use as weapons, sir! Send for the sojers or we'll all be murdered!"

Daunce had been near the door where the shots had been fired. For once the set expression of his face could not be classified as a smile. "One on 'em's dead!" he reported. "His head was blown clean off 'is shoulders. There's plenty more hurt."

All Frank could think of, in spite of the excitement, was the fate of Benjie. "Have they been going on with it outside?" he asked himself. "Has he died with this horrible din in his ears?"

Daunce, remembering suddenly that he was there, came over and clutched at him frantically. "Great God, I'd clean forgot *you!*" he croaked. "Get back where ye belong! Get back afore anyone sees ye. They won't want any witnesses to be called up on *this*. I'll lose my sit if they finds out ye've been here all the time."

"What's happening outside?" demanded Frank. "Has—has Fuller gone?"

"How do I know!" The turnkey was shoving at him frantically. "I know what's happened here and that's all as I wants to know. Get outa sight, guv, in God's name!"

Frank allowed himself to be half carried and half shoved back into the corridor. Daunce was prepared to go on, but he held the turnkey forcibly by the flapping tails of his coat.

"What will come of this?" he demanded.

The riot had not diminished, judging from the din which reached their ears. Daunce flinched away.

"There'll be investigashuns. A lot of 'em are hurt and it looks like a earth bath for two more at least. He lost his head complete, the bird-witted fool!"

Frank could still see into the yard. Two new men had arrived and were talking to the warden. Had they brought a pardon? His excitement mounted when one of the newcomers produced a paper. He watched the faces of the trio eagerly, hoping to learn in that way what it was about. He was so concerned that he paid no attention when Milly Corbin was led inside, shrieking and struggling, to have her irons struck off.

"What is it?" he demanded of Daunce. "Has a pardon arrived? Those two men have been on the road."

"I don't know what's up any more than you do, guv. Come, get back now. I'll bring ye the word as soon as I can."

The corridors they followed were strangely quiet after the horrible din of the yard. Frank could think of nothing now but the grim fact that the hour had struck just before the rioting in the prison began. Had Benjie Fuller been taken out and hanged immediately on the stroke of twelve? If it was a pardon from Windsor that the two men had brought, it may have arrived too late! It was a horrifying thought. It had been apparent even at a distance that the warden had been grave, perhaps even frightened, as he studied the paper. Was it fear of consequences? Or was it a reflection only of his disturbed state of mind over what had happened inside? "Was it another proof of the malignant fate which has followed poor Benjie," he thought, "that he was drawn to go out first?"

Cope was standing with his face pressed against the bars, his eyes bright with excitement. "What's been happening?" he demanded. "Has there been a jailbreak? I've nearly gone crazy, back here by myself."

"There's been a riot," said Frank, after the turnkey had locked the door on him. "I think a pardon has been received for Benjie. I can't be sure of it. I can't even be sure the sentence hasn't been carried out. I'm nearly going crazy too. It's all been such a dreadful and bloody mess!"

Cope shook his head. "You think a pardon's been received and yet you say the sentence may have been carried out. There's no sense to that. Just what do you mean?"

"It may have arrived too late. I'm so afraid of it that I can't think at all. I can be sure of one thing only—that I'll go mad if we don't hear soon." He began to pace up and down the cell, his hands pressed to his temples. "A guard fired into one of the wards. A man was killed and several others were injured. I've never seen anything so ugly and terrible in all my life! It's hard to believe the things that happen in this place. They treat men like wild beasts!"

There was silence for several moments and then Cope said: "Better calm down, Frank. This won't do you any good, you know."

The sounds had been renewed in the streets. A continuous murmur reached their ears, punctuated with louder shouts at intervals. Frank shuddered. "That means they're hanging the rest of them now! God, how horrible it is! The look on that poor woman's face! All she did was to steal a watch from some fine gentleman who picked her up on the streets. You can't conceive anything like the terror in her eyes. And it does no good. That's the awful part of it. Crime goes on just the same; it gets worse, in fact. Have our lawmakers gone completely blind? Have they closed their minds and their eyes as well as their hearts?" His brow had become moist, and he brushed a hand across it. "You have to come close to this business of hanging to realize how wrong and cruel and bestial it is!"

"They seem to be enjoying the spectacle out there!" Cope shuddered in turn. "Ladies and gentlemen have paid their guineas for seats, and the mobs in the street have fought for their places. Well, I suppose they're feeling well rewarded for their money and their pains. There seems to be a lot of the wild beast in all of us. It comes out at a time like this, doesn't it? It makes you feel pretty sick and humble."

The noise outside did not stop. The two men looked at each other with stricken faces each time that the sounds gained in volume, for they knew this meant another of the poor wretches had taken the fatal drop, thereby driving the spectators into a frenzy of excitement. Finally it was all over. They could tell that the streets were being cleared, that the crowd was dispersing and that the usual traffic was once more flowing through.

"Justice has had its way!" said Frank bitterly. "The lives of those poor unfortunates have been taken. The majesty of the law has been vindicated!"

"London's great treat is over," muttered Cope. "Until the next time!"

It seemed hours before any word reached them, but it was in reality not more than twenty minutes later when the turnkey returned. He was in a more composed mood as he halted before their door.

He said cheerfully: "Things are going to be hushed up. Another on 'em is dead but the rest of 'em'll pull through. There'll have to be a inquest but it won't come to anything. The attack on Progger fixes everything up nice and proper. They had to be fired on to save him. That's clear enough."

Frank shouted at him in a frenzy of doubt and fear. "But what of Fuller? Did he go with the rest? Speak up, man!"

"You were right about *that*, guv. It wur a pardon for him. It come direct from Windsor."

"But—but was it received in time?"

Daunce nodded. "Just. In the very nick it wur, guv. He wur right out on the scaffold and the gluepot reading to him from the Book like sixty. The hangman was a-fumbling with the rope, getting ready to drop it over his head. Then all hell busts out inside. Everyone stops and listens. It was that as saved him, guv." Daunce was rubbing his hands in appreciation of the dramatic aspects of the case. "Two on 'em was killed 'cause of it but t'other was saved. He'd a been dangling on the end of the rope when the messenger got through if it hadn't been for the trouble inside."

Frank sat down limply on the edge of his bed. "Thank God! Oh, what a relief this is! You look to me like an angel of mercy out there, Daunce, after bringing us this news." His hands were cold and he felt as though his heart had stopped beating. "The King has a kind heart after all. Good old Nobs! I'll always feel grateful and loyal to him."

The turnkey added zestfully: "Don't you wish you'd been out there to see it, guv? There's never been the likes of it afore. Three guineas wasn't too much to pay for *that*."

16

AN ARMY was being assembled for duty overseas. No one talked of anything else. Sir Caradoc Ellery, M.P., made a speech in the House on the subject of supplies, and it was noted that a beautiful woman sat in the gallery. Officers were posting out of London to make their farewells and posting back again, with portmanteaus stuffed to overflowing and Bibles in their pockets, tearfully inscribed by mothers, wives, and sweethearts. Recruiting sergeants, to the shrill piping of fifes, planted their drums at street corners and crossroads, and the public helped them along by singing and whistling:

> *The war drums beat in Frog-and-Toe,*
> *Crowdy, down your grog and go!*

It gradually became understood that Sir Arthur Wellesley was to have the command. His commission was for "a particular service" and, as the Spanish people had risen against the French in spite of the supine attitude of their rulers, it was assumed that it would be somewhere in the Peninsula. His Majesty, it was said, was not at all sure of the wisdom of trusting a young general and was inquiring about the qualifications of veterans like Sir Harry Burrard and Sir Hew Dalrymple. It was feared that he still favored Frederick.

Frank found Sir Robert Wilson and General Dumouriez in his rooms the night it was announced an army would be sent to Portugal. They had located a cut of cheese and a bottle of wine in the larder and were making themselves thoroughly at home. Wilson sprang up and welcomed him exuberantly.

"Well, my brave young jailbird, I'm sure you've heard the news," he shouted, putting down his glass and coming forward to shake hands. "They've come around to us. They've seen the light at last. I'm so delighted with the whole thing that I can't sit still."

Frank nodded. "The army's for Portugal. I've heard that much. It's good news, the very best. Are you to have a hand in it, Sir Robert?"

A shadow crossed Wilson's face. "Yes," he said. "But not with the regular forces. *That* was too much to expect. The Horse Guards have seen to it that my urgent requests for a place have been met with the usual silence. No, they don't want me; but I'm going, in spite of their high and mightinesses. My good friend here has thought of a plan."

"I have thought of several plans," amended Dumouriez, as though unwilling to concede that only one course would suggest itself to him at such a juncture. He was eating cheese with approving nibbles but frowning unhappily at the wine. "One of them, I am bold to assert, is a masterpiece."

Wilson began his usual pacing up and down the room. "Yes, it's a good plan, a damned good plan. London is full of Portuguese, Ellery. They came over in droves when the French moved into their country, and now they ask nothing better than a chance to go back and fight with us. I'm going to organize them into a brigade under my own command, and the War Office has condescended to say that the idea has their august sanction."

"It looks like a great chance for you, Sir Robert."

Wilson's enthusiasm was mounting again. He said in brisk tones: "Yes, in a way it's better than the other. I'll be under no orders; at least, I hope not. I'm to get together some English officers, men like me who've been disappointed in the matter of posts with the army. Funds are promised for the equipment. I've a name already—the Loyal Lusitanian Legion."

"I thought I had the name," amended Dumouriez with an injured air.

"We worked it out together. No offense meant, my good friend. The word 'Legion' was yours, the rest of it mine. The uniforms will be green——"

"No, no, not green!" protested the Frenchman. "Blue. A lighter blue than we use in France. Or even a gray. But green, never! It is a completely unmilitary color, Sir Ro-bert. Has there ever been an army garbed in such a poisonous shade?"

"There's going to be one. The finest little fighting brigade since Cromwell's Ironsides. Green with facings of a darker shade. My fine Portuguese are so pleased with the idea that I wouldn't disappoint them. No, General, green it must be."

While they argued, the young publisher's mind had gone off on a different tangent. An idea had taken possession of him, a wild and perhaps impossible one; one so completely new that he wondered if it could be put into practice. And yet, why not? There would be difficulties, but if they could be overcome he would have a sure instrument in his hands for reviving the fortunes of the *Tablet*.

In a pause of the discussion he said: "I know there are always plenty of civilians in the train of an army—commissioners, sutlers, and such. Is there any reason why a newspaper shouldn't send a man to write accounts of what he sees?"

Wilson gave the idea some thought. "I don't see why it couldn't be arranged. There would be no danger of military secrets getting out that way. By the time the articles appeared the whole campaign would have entered on another phase. It would be different if the army happened to be in a tight spot and the enemy could cut off the outriders; but even then, he would know already what the articles contained. On the whole I fail to see any serious objection from a military standpoint."

"A commander," declared Frank, "should be glad of the chance to have the movements of his army and the battles he fights reported at firsthand. His successes would be given to the public in a manner to help his reputation. A clearer picture of everything that happened could be preserved for posterity."

"Ellery, it's an excellent idea, excellent," declared Wilson. "I wonder why it has never been done before?"

Frank's enthusiasm for the plan was growing by the moment. "I've an ax to grind, of course. I need something to put the *Tablet* back on its feet, and I'm sure now this would do it. We could arrange for a system of fast relays to carry the letters. I suppose there will be a steady flow of ships back and forth from Portugal?"

"With thirty thousand men there? Yes, there will be ships arriving and leaving every day. You would have to make a deal with someone on board to handle the packets for you. That wouldn't be at all hard."

"They could be dropped off at Portsmouth and carried on from there by riders." Frank began to calculate. "Let's see now. A month at the worst from the front lines to the offices of the *Tab*. Why, we would have firsthand information and impressions days before the bare hint of news got out through official channels! Our dispatches would be published weeks before any regular letters from the front were received. Do you realize, Sir Robert, that most of the news from the Continent that we publish today is dated April, or even March?"

Dumouriez was shaking his head. "I am not in favor. No writer would have been tolerated with the armies I commanded. That I can tell you."

Wilson laughed. "The whole face of warfare is being changed. We have Boney to thank for that. Why shouldn't the public be told in detail of the progress of campaigns on which their whole future depends? I see this as a means of stimulating patriotism, in addition to everything else."

"Sir Robert," asked Frank, "would you allow me to send a man with your brigade? To report the exploits of the Loyal Lusitanian Legion?"

Wilson nodded emphatically. "You have my promise. The idea appeals to me as something that would do both of us a great deal of good. But, Ellery, I won't be able to get my men into Portugal for some months yet. We haven't begun to organize. You mustn't wait for us. My advice would be to send a man over at once. The French haven't occupied the north of Portugal yet. Your man should be there to witness the landing of Wellesley's army. He could join my forces later. Better still, have two men."

"I think you're right. It will cost money, but I'm in a position where heavy chances must be taken." Frank's mind was traveling fast. "We can't hope to keep the advantages of such an idea to ourselves very long. After one campaign of it, the other newspapers will be sending out men too. But in the meantime I might win back the public to the *Tab*. I'm going to do it. And I've thought of a name for my man. A war correspondent. Does that seem a good one to you?"

Dumouriez was helping himself to another slice of the cheese and a fresh glass of the despised wine. Wilson drew the young publisher to a corner of the room.

"I'm sure, Ellery," he whispered, "that I'm going to make history with my fine little brigade and that you'll be doing the same thing with this idea of yours. You'll probably think me completely crazy, but I want to tell you how I feel about this. I'm sure, Ellery, that I'm destined to be the man who beats Boney in the end. I must sound like an egotistical idiot to say such a thing. I wouldn't blame you if you laughed in my face! He's the master of Europe and I'm a discredited officer of minor rank. But there's something inside me that tells me all the time that it's the truth. It's going to happen! Somehow, sometime, I'll get my chance; and, by Gad, I'll know how to take advantage of it!" He looked sharply at his companion. "Does it sound amusing to you?"

"On the contrary, I'm quite ready to believe you. Nothing would gratify me more than to see things work out that way."

"Thanks." Wilson nodded his head with sudden gravity. "Wellesley has his chance now. Mine will come later. I'm so certain of it that I can accept any disappointments with perfect equanimity. That may be an exaggeration; I do champ at the bit at times. But in the main, I'm willing to wait."

Two weeks passed. The country seethed with war enthusiasm, and cheering mobs followed the military bands in the streets. It became known that Sir Arthur Wellesley was in Ireland and would sail from there. Swarthy-skinned foreigners poured in and out of the headquarters which Sir Robert Wilson had set up, and samples of green cloth hung over the backs of chairs in his office. The troops were said to be ready, but recruiting still went on. Rough-tongued sergeants stopped Frank on the street to say, "Why ain't *you* in uny-form, ye banging hulks?" and they even invaded the portals of Prater Street to say to the deft Patcher that he had better "get hisself into a red chunic and take a pull at Boney's teeth."

At the *Tablet* entrance one morning Frank encountered Benjamin Fuller in the scarlet regimentals of the dragoons. He had been given a fine fit and was openly proud of the smartness of his appearance.

"I've took the shilling as ye see, Mr. Ellery, sir," he said. "I thought as I owed it to my country after—after what happened."

"I envy you, Benjie," declared Frank. "I'd like to be going along with you to fight the French. You make a fine-looking soldier. Your Becky must be proud of you."

The face of the new recruit fell. "She's married, sir. It was a blow to me but—it wur no way her fault. I'm sure of that. The others kept picking at her when I was in prison. A lot of old fussocks they wur, sir, and she couldn't stand it. She was sure I was done for anyway, and so she said yes to the butler in a neighboring house and moved over there. I took it hard at first, sir, but I guess now as I'm going to get over it."

"You'll find someone better, Benjie, so you mustn't take it to heart. I'm not completely over what happened to you that day myself; my heart nearly stops when I think how close it was."

"It was all due to you, Mr. Ellery, sir. I wouldn't be dressed up in this fine chunic today but for what you did. I know that." His face became almost moist with gratitude. "I like sojering, sir. You see, I've a knack with the prads so I'm in the right spot with the dragoons. I'm hoping to get a stripe soon. The serg'nt says I'm being talked of for it next." He dropped his voice. "Would you believe it, sir, that eleven men in my company has been in Newgate? It's the same all through the army."

The Tablet Building was not an inspiring sight. The glass in the front windows had been replaced, but economy had dictated the use of paper in repairing those on the sides. The remnants of the overhead carrier still clung drunkenly to the walls. A subdued atmosphere pervaded the place, and even old Clayhorn's vigilance yielded small fruits in an establishment where every penny had to be so closely watched. To Frank he seemed like an unhappy ghost brooding aimlessly over a dismantled castle.

Cope wore the only cheerful face in the place. The idea of sending

writers to describe the campaign had appealed to him so completely that
he talked of little else. Already he had worked out a system for the for-
warding of the dispatches, and he spent hours discussing the making of
waterproof envelopes with the paper men, the hiring of strings of post
horses between Portsmouth and London, and the selection of special riders. He smacked his lips over the term "war correspondent" and boasted
that the circulation of the *Tablet* would rise to record heights as soon
as the dispatches began to appear in print.

Aunt Francilea paid a flying visit to say that she was ready to find
more funds if the "little bit" she had advanced was not enough to see
them through their difficulties. "I'm proud to have a nephew who's been
in prison in such a cause, Frankie," she said. "I boast about it all the
time. Old George and Marg't Callery talk about their son who's been
presented at court, but I say, 'That's nothing, my Francis has been in the
pillory, and it takes a great man to get *there* in these days.'" She drew
her lips in tightly. "Do you think the queen suspects I'm helping you?
I got a nasty little note from her which makes me think she does. She's
one person I'm *not* going to see this trip. And what's this I hear about
Caradoc's engagement being broken?"

The broken engagement had not been mentioned on the fleeting occasions when Frank had seen the members of his immediate family. It
became one of the main topics of conversation, however, when he paid
a visit to the town house in response to a brief and peremptory note from
his mother.

He found Mrs. Ellery in her special sitting room with sheets of paper
all around her and a worried frown on her face. She looked up without
any change of expression and plunged at once into the matters which
had prompted the summons.

"I'm making inventories," she announced. "It's a very trying matter,
but I'll get through it somehow. It may interest you to know that we're
finding it necessary to lease this place."

Frank was too much taken aback to reply immediately. He managed
finally to say: "But, Mother, this place, after all, is mine. I should have
been consulted about such a step."

"You don't consult *us*." Her tone was sharp and she tapped the floor
with an impatient foot encased trimly in a shoe with three bows of velvet
ribbon on the instep, one above the other. "You're impoverishing *us* and
not allowing us to have a word to say about it. And make no mistake,
Francis, I have the full right to lease the place. It's in my full possession
for five years, and the lawyers say to Go Ahead."

"Just what are you planning to do, Mother?"

"I've found a tenant, a Mr. Harvey Sharlett. I don't know much about him except that the bank reports he is Good. He comes from the north. The money he pays us will help to keep the Towers going. We're at our wit's end to do *that*, thanks to you. That's all I'm going to tell you."

"Very well," said Frank quietly. "Mr. Harvey Sharlett may have the house and you may spend the money any way you see fit. I'll raise no objections."

"I think you hadn't better, Francis!" She was dressed to go out, and the flowers in her hat shook with the emphasis of her nod. It was, he noted, an anagram hat, the very latest thing in millinery, trimmed with anemones, mignonette, and a miniature yucca bloom to spell out her name. "You're doing enough harm to us as it is, young man. And now there's another matter. Can you tell me why Caradoc and Mary have broken up?"

Frank hesitated. "Hasn't Carr discussed it with you? After all, Mother, it's his affair."

She seemed reluctant to acknowledge that she was in the dark about the wrecking of the plan which had been closest to her heart. "Caradoc for once has refused to confide in me. I don't understand him at all. He —he is proving stubborn about it. I wondered if you knew the real reason."

"I suspect he became interested in someone else."

His mother looked at him sharply. "And you don't suspect it had something to do with you standing in the pillory and being sent to prison like a common thief or murderer?"

"I'm sure it hadn't. Think back, Mother. Didn't Carr get the word from the Duke before I was arrested?"

"Then you knew it was His Grace who wrote the letter! I thought so."

"Yes. I knew."

"How, may I ask?"

"The Duke told me he was going to do it. He asked me to see him at Bilber."

"Then you know the reason. Was it because of another woman?"

"Yes, Mother. That was what the Duke said to me."

Her tone became almost violent. "It's a very funny thing he would tell *you* and not Caradoc. I don't understand it at all."

"Probably he thought of me as the head of the family. After all, you know, I am. And he seems, peculiarly enough, to have some confidence in me."

A short and scornful laugh was Mrs. Ellery's first reaction to that suggestion. "Confidence in *you* after what has happened! Well, if he had, Francis, I'm sure he hasn't any now. Such disgrace you've brought on us! There are times when I find it hard to hold up my head." She paused for a moment and then threw an abrupt question at him. "Who's the woman?"

"I think you must ask Carr that."

"Do you know who it is?"

"Yes."

"Then you must tell me. It's my right to know."

"I've said, Mother, you must ask Carr."

"So you're going to be stubborn too. Well, I'll find out; I'll get to the bottom of this. If Caradoc isn't to marry Mary—it breaks my heart to think they had to drift apart—he must begin to think of someone else. It's too bad and it's all your fault. Caradoc *must* have his finances in better shape if he's to advance in his career."

"He should have thought of that before."

"You needn't blame it all on him. He's attractive to women and they run after him all the time. I'm sure that's what has happened. Mr. Sharlett has a daughter, and the bank says she'll come in for something handsome. She's a good-looking girl even if she is a little on the heavy side. She'd do if I could get myself reconciled to any wife for Caradoc but my dear Mary."

"Does Carr like this girl?"

"Lisba Sharlett? Enough, I guess. She's Mad about him."

There was a moment's silence. Frank realized that his mother had been leading up to something and that she was on the point of letting him know what it was. He waited.

"He *must* marry Mary. I know everything would come out right if we could only wait. But money matters are pressing us so hard that we can't wait very long. I've discharged four of the staff and I've economized in so many ways; and still we can't make ends meet without our rightful income from the paper." She looked at him with a speculative eye. "You must surely see that you should be ready to do anything in your power to bring them together again after what has happened."

"I want that as much as you do, Mother," said Frank earnestly.

"Then"—eagerly—"you ought to be agreeable to the *only* thing that will bring it about. The *Tablet* must be put back where it will support us all as well as it did before. Let's forget all our quarrels and differences and face this thing honestly. Nothing can be done with the paper as long as you stay in charge. I'm not reflecting on your ability, Francis. We all know you have plenty of that, just as your father had. But the government and the public won't accept the paper as long as you're connected with it. You must give it up."

"And let Carr take it over?"

"Y-yes. But perhaps only nominally. He wouldn't have the time to manage it with all his parliamentary duties. We would have to get an editor to do the work and have Caradoc's name as head. It would mean so much in view of the stand he's taken all along."

"That's what I'm afraid of, Mother."

"What are you afraid of?"

"The stand he's taken all along." He paused and then went on with sudden firmness. "No thanks, Mother. I'll never do that. As a matter of fact I'm going to have the paper on a paying basis again before so very long anyway. It's picking up now, and the plans I'm making will bring it back to greater prosperity than ever."

Mrs. Ellery got to her feet, her face white with anger. "Very well! Then I'll have you know that I'll take steps to make you. I'm going this very minute to the offices of Frazee, Duncan, and McCandless and instruct them to enter suit. Oh, I've taken advice in the matter. I know where I stand. We can sue for an inquiry into your conduct of the property, and I think you know what *that* would show. I'm going there right now and have a writ served on you."

"Is that what you brought me over here to say?"

"I hoped it wouldn't come to that. I hoped you would show some sense and decency. I wanted to give you a chance. Well, are you going to change your mind?"

Frank stood up. "No, I'm not going to change my mind, Mother. It would be painful to me to have our affairs brought out in court but— well, if you insist, that's how it must be."

He walked across the square in a dejected mood. The ledgers would tell an eloquent story in court; he knew how damaging the figures would prove. It seemed to him inevitable that control of the paper would be taken away from him in the interests of the other shareholders. Half-way over, however, he came to an abrupt stop. The thought had occurred that a summons must first be served on him. How long could he hope to escape the attention of the law?

A few moments later he burst into Cope's office and asked to know on whom the latter's choice had fixed for duty abroad. Cope, whose sartorial splendor had been dimming with the decline of the paper and was represented at the moment by a buff coat with brown pockets a little worn at the seams, answered that his nomination was still in doubt. "Trutnall, I think," he said. "He's unmarried and he writes well enough. The best thing about him is his memory. He couldn't report a session of the House without taking a note like the great Henry Woodfall, but he doesn't fall too far short of it. On the whole, I'm disposed to favor Trutnall."

"Well," said Frank, clapping him excitedly on the back, "I've another candidate, Copey. I'm going myself."

"You!" Cope's eyes gleamed at him from behind his glasses with an expression that said he suspected recent troubles had affected his superior's mind. "Great Barnaby, how could you get away at a time like this? We couldn't carry things along without you."

"The point is that I can't afford to stay."

Frank was realizing that all along he had been wanting to go. The thought of following the army in the greatest military effort that Great Britain had yet made had never left him. And now there was a definite reason why he must undertake the mission. He must get away and stay beyond the reach of the law for as long as seemed expedient.

"Put men at both the front and back doors," he ordered gleefully. "If anyone comes along who looks like a process server, I must know at once. Get all the money together that you can, my capable Cope, and see what you can find out about ship sailings for Portugal. I'm not only going myself but—ah, Copey, I can hardly believe my luck!—I'm going today."

He spent two hours in conference with the department heads. Then, with one hundred guineas in gold distributed about his person, and arrangements made for Windy Topp to pick him up in a private coach with all necessary supplies packed inside, he said good-by to the staff and made a stealthy but triumphant exit from the rear of the premises.

He had decided to make one farewell call and, as his feet took him in the direction of Brinsley Place, his enthusiasm began to wane. He feared that he was throwing away whatever small chance he may have had with Gabrielle. He would be gone a long time, long enough at any rate to see whether his special war reports could bring the paper around to an improved financial position and thus make it possible for him to risk a hearing of the suit. His brother, in the meantime, would have an open field.

"Well," he said to himself, "I may as well recognize that I've never had more than the slimmest chance. If I stay, the paper will be taken away from me. It's my duty to go."

To his dismay he found a To Let sign decorating the front window of the house in Brinsley Place. The De Salle family had moved! It had occurred in the last few days because he had wandered regularly through the neighborhood in the hope of seeing Gabrielle, and the familiar curtains had been in the windows the last time he passed. What had happened?

He plied the knocker of the house next door and asked for information from the slatternly woman who answered. Mrs. Finnerty—he knew it must be the mother of the troublesome Mick from her accent—confirmed the fact that the French family had departed, and good riddance to them, the high-and-goramighty furriners! Where had they gone? She puckered up her not too clean brow and came out slowly, and not too positively, with a new address. She could not, she said, take an "affertdavey" on it. Frank thanked her and departed. There would be time, but barely enough, to make a hurried call at the new location before meeting the carriage.

The neighborhood to which Comte de Salle had moved his household was much more genteel than Brinsley Place. At any rate there were no business signs on the austere street and, on the other hand, there were carriages driving sedately over the well-kept-up pavement. Mrs. Finnerty's memory had not been at fault. The number she had provided turned out to be a tall house with no more than two brass plates beside the bell, one of them bearing in unblemished newness the name "De Salle."

"Some luck has come their way," he thought. "Perhaps brother Sosthène has had a turn for the better again."

Margot answered his summons, looking unexpectedly neat and very much more grown-up in a gray dress with lace at the neck and sleeves. It fitted her perfectly, a quality none of her earlier clothes had possessed.

"Come in, M'sieur Frank," she said. "You are our very first visitor here. I am sure you will like our new home."

"You are very grand indeed," said Frank, following her into the drawing room, which was on the ground floor and looked familiar to him because it contained all the furnishings he had seen at Brinsley Place.

"We have two floors all to ourselves. It is really very nice, m'sieur." He found it hard not to smile at the almost naïve quality of her pleasure in the new surroundings. "All of us have our own bedrooms now. There is even a sitting room on the first floor. And quite a tidy pantry. We are very happy about it, m'sieur."

"Is Comte Robert at home?"

The girl shook her head. "Antoine is wheeling Uncle Robert in the park. No one is home, m'sieur. Gabrielle is making a call and won't be back until dinnertime, I'm afraid."

Then he would not see her after all. His face must have shown how disappointed he felt, for Margot hurried to provide him with what com-

fort she could. "Why doesn't M'sieur stay for dinner? I am sure it would
be quite all right. Uncle Robert always speaks so well of what M'sieur
has done. And we—we always have good dinners." She drew his attention to a silver tray on the mantelpiece. "As they say, we are *droit côté*
now."

"The right side? I don't understand."

She explained with some reluctance. "M'sieur must have known that
when we had guests before they were in the habit of leaving us something. It was nothing to be ashamed of. It was the custom, and others
had to do it too. Now when they come they are expected to help themselves if they are in any need." He saw that the tray contained a collection
of coins of various denominations. "It's the way we manage among ourselves. Those who can afford it help the others. This way no one has to
ask."

"I see. It's a very commendable custom; and I can't tell you how glad
I am that you're on the—*droit côté* now. Does Mlle. Gabrielle continue
in her employment?"

"Yes, m'sieur. There have been many discussions about it. Both my
uncle and Sosthène say she must give it up, but she refuses. There is no
reason for her to go on now because Sosthène has been doing very well
again. I—I'm worried about Gabrielle. Something isn't right, but I can't
find out what it is. Twice I've found her in tears and she refused to tell
me why. I can't think what it can be."

"Is she—is she in love, do you think?"

"Somehow I don't think it's that. I believe, M'sieur Frank, she's afraid
of something. Once she was saying to Sosthène——" She stopped herself
abruptly. "But I must not tell about that. No, I don't know what it can
be and I'm very much worried too."

Frank's face showed the concern he was feeling. "I'm glad you told
me, Margot. You see, I—I'm quite fond of Mlle. Gabrielle."

"I know. It's very clear that you like her."

"Is there anything I can do? I can't bear to think of her being in any
kind of trouble."

"I'm sure there's nothing to be done. Not until I can get her to tell
me what it is."

Frank said slowly: "I'm going away. To the Continent. I'll be gone a
long time and it's going to be hard not to know what's happening here.
I'll leave an address with you, Margot, so you could write me if you find
what's wrong with Gabrielle. Would you mind doing it?"

"Indeed, no. I understand how M'sieur feels." She hesitated. "Gabrielle likes you very much. She says so many nice things about you. But

I think perhaps you should know that she's seeing another man quite often. He has been here once only, and I am sure Uncle Robert has no idea she sees him so much. He's an Englishman too."

He got to his feet. "I can't stay for dinner, Margot, although I can think of nothing that would give me more pleasure. I'm leaving in another hour. I hope you will explain to the Comte that I called to pay my respects. Please tell Gabrielle how sorry I am not to have seen her. That's a very mild way of putting it. You see, Margot, I'm terribly in love with her."

She was watching him with the deepest sympathy in her wide-spaced eyes. "Yes, M'sieur Frank. They will both be sorry. I'm sure Jean Baptiste Achille would like to say au revoir. He's been helping me with the silver."

The boy came in immediately, stumping along eagerly on his iron support. Margot was showing signs of growing up, but Jean Baptiste Achille looked smaller and more frail than ever.

"Margot says you are going away, m'sieur. I am sorry to hear it."

"Yes. I thought we had better have an accounting before I went. I won't be here to watch your principal, so I thought it would be better to return it."

The boy looked distressed. "We were hoping to invest more of our funds with you. You see, I have saved all of my dividends and Father has received his wages and so we have a whole sovereign now. I wanted to invest it all before he could spend any of it. A whole sovereign in your hands would have brought us in such a very nice return."

"I'm sorry, Jean Baptiste Achille, but under the circumstances it would be too risky for you. However, your principal has mounted up rather nicely. I'm going to hand it back to you and—it's a full ten shillings now."

"Ten shillings! I think you must be very clever with money, m'sieur. It—it is quite wonderful what you have done for me! Why, I have the start of a fortune!"

Frank shook hands with him gravely. "You must be very glad to be so far away from Mick Finnerty. Keep some of your money so I can invest it for you again when I return. Good-by, Jean Baptiste Achille."

"Good-by, m'sieur."

At the door Margot said: "Do you know this other Englishman?"

"He's my brother."

"Oh, m'sieur!" She looked at him with even more distress. "That makes it very bad, doesn't it!"

BOOK II

The Peninsula

FRANK WAS in a depressed frame of mind and staring out over the black-and-white paving of the O Rocio (later to be called by English soldiers Roly-Poly Square) when Windy Topp came in.

"Hopes ye're feeling livelier, sahib," said the latter cheerfully. It was continually amazing how quickly he had fallen into peninsular ways. After insisting upon accompanying his employer, he had proven himself invaluable at every turn during the six months of their stay. The long yellow coat, which had been the main part of his costume in London, had given way to a curious variety of serape through which his head protruded with something of the effect of a startled turtle. The cloak was a handsome blue and so generously decorated with copper buttons and bits of chain and other odds and ends that Frank often wondered from whom it had been filched, being certain that under no circumstance would his resourceful servant have laid out the sum necessary to purchase it. It covered him to his knees, leaving off just in time to demonstrate that the Topp legs were encased in a dilapidated pair of native gaiters.

"I'm feeling about the same," said Frank listlessly.

"It's always the way with the mullary." Topp began to deposit breakfast dishes on the red-checkered tablecloth. "Bad thing, the mullary, sahib. Gets ye down in speerits. Here's a orange and a bisket. Better have a go at the bisket; it'll stick to yer ribs like nothin' else. And here's a brace o' boiled eggs I garruntees to be fresh, and a pot o' chocklat. Fall to work, sahib. A good meal's what ye need." He fumbled in his pockets. "And here's a letter for ye, as fresh arrived as the eggs."

The letter was from Sir Robert Wilson. Frank recognized the bold, square lettering and broke the seal with an anxious finger. For a fortnight he had received no word from the commander of the Loyal Lusitanian Legion, and he had begun to fear that things were not going well; which would not have been surprising, for things were not going well in any part of the country since Wellesley had won his victory at Vimeiro and then been ordered home to face a military inquiry.

The note was a brief one.

Sorry to hear you're having a bout with the malaria, dear boy. Are you well enough to join me here in Ciudad Rodrigo? Better make it if you can throw a leg over a horse. I'm here with two hundred sabers, two guns, and three hundred of my best infantry, not to mention a couple thousand of the most useless and rascally Spaniards that ever wore a ton of braid. I'm making a *glorious bluff!* I'm going to upset all of Boney's plans with this miserable handful and I want you here to lend a hand. Come as fast as you can. I need you.

W.

Ciudad Rodrigo! So that was where he had led his Legion. It was a strong fortress town across the Spanish frontier, guarding the central approach to Portugal. A month before, a French force of considerable size had been reported to be moving up on it, and Lisbon had been waiting apprehensively, ever since then, for word of its capture. What was Sir Robert doing there of all places? The last news of him had been a rumor that he had left Oporto against the express orders of the bishop commandant of that province and had marched eastward. General Craddock, who had been left in charge of the few British regiments still in Portugal and had a reputation for timidity, had sent orders to the straying Wilson to return at once to his post. No news had reached the city since.

"Windy," said Frank, tearing the note into small bits and dropping them into the pot of thick chocolate, "you've heard, of course, that Marshal Soult has captured Oporto and is ready to march down on us here in Lisbon as soon as the French Army in the center has taken Ciudad Rodrigo?"

"In course, sahib." The runner shook his head affirmatively. "Ev'body in Lisbon's ready to leave. They're loading up ships in a juice of a hurry."

"Marshal Victor is ready to pounce on us from the south," went on Frank. "Between them, I'm afraid, they'll gobble up all of Portugal before Wellesley can get back with his new army."

"No manner o' doubt about that." A cheerful nod of the head. "It's marching orders, I takes it. I'll throw our bits o' things together in a brace o' snaps, sahib. It'll be nice to get back to Frog-and-Toe, but I'm not saying as I'm glad to leave this place. It's lively here. No two ways about *that.*"

"Yes, pack up. Get a couple of good horses. We're leaving at once."

"Horses! Are we going to ride home, sahib?"

Frank laughed. The depressed mood which had gripped him for two weeks past had departed, suddenly and completely. Wilson's letter, with its promise of unpredictable adventure, had done more for him than all the bitter medicines in Lisbon.

"We're not going home, Windy," he said, getting to his feet and clapping his man heartily on the back. "We're going to ride inland. We're going to the border where we'll help give the French a good licking. In fact, Windy, we're going to Ciudad Rodrigo."

Topp's jaw fell open and he stared at his employer as though doubting that he could have heard right. "The border!" he said finally. "D'ye know what that means, sahib? Johnny Craps has a nasty way o' dealing with prisoners. Won't help us any to say we ain't sojering. They'll line us up afore the barking irons, and there'll be open graves ahind us that we've dug ourselves. I've taken my share o' risks in my day, sahib, but I must say as I don't care for the looks o' this at all."

"You don't have to go unless you want to, Windy. But I'm going. That was a note from Sir Robert Wilson, though no one must know it. He's there now and he's up to something. I don't know what exactly. Pack up my things and get me a horse. I'm leaving in an hour."

Topp made a gesture of resignation which agitated the capacious folds of his cloak. "Two prads it'll be then, sahib. And two graves, I'm thinking."

While the packing proceeded, Frank paced about the room with new energy, his mind full of speculation as to what Wilson was doing. A bluff, he had said. The French Army coming up on the center under General Lapisse was officially estimated at ten thousand, although rumors placed it at double that figure; it would take more than a bluff to hold in play a force of such strength.

There would, at any rate, be a great story for his newspaper in what he would witness. The few letters he had received from Cope had indicated that things were going well at home. The last note, dated December 14, had been quite jubilant, in fact.

We've actually turned the corner, Frank [Cope had written]. People scramble for copies when the word gets out that there's a new dispatch from the Peninsula. . . . We're carrying quite a bit of advertising nowadays, enough to make Evans hint that we may resume profit payments with the next quarter. My hat is off to you. . . . You probably won't like it, my most modest employer, but I'm signing your name to them now. . . . There's a whisper in the air that certain parties who had it in mind to start a suit against you have dropped the idea in view of the improved financial position of the *Tab*. Your aunt Francilea looks happy whenever she pays us a visit.

In spite of the cheerful nature of the news from home, Frank felt far from satisfied with his work as a war correspondent. He had to write with such haste that he was sure his dispatches had been hopelessly scrambled. His story of the landing of Wellesley's army had been scrawled on a knapsack on the sands of Mondego Bay. He had indited the account of Wellesley's smashing victory over Junot at Vimeiro in a peasant's hut, surrounded by solemn natives in huge three-cornered hats who chattered about him among themselves and smoked long cigars until the air was blue; with Topp in a corner, picking lice from the clothes he had discarded. When Junot's defeated army marched down to the ships which were to take them to France in accord with the Convention of Cintra (the pusillanimous arrangement made by Sir Hew and Sir Harry after they had arrived to supersede Wellesley), he had found himself with a bare half hour to prepare an account of that historic event before the ship sailed which would carry mail back to England. Well, he would have to do better now that his name was being signed to the stuff.

There had been one letter only from Margot, giving him a few scraps of information about the De Salle household. It had ended with, "Gaby sends her respects to you, monsieur, and says she knows you are having a wonderful time" (Wonderful, when he could not see her!) "but that you must never play cards with the Spaniards or the Portuguese or you will lose *shamefully*." There had been no mention of Caradoc, nothing at all to relieve his mind on that most important of all matters.

"Windy," he said, giving up his pacing, "do you realize how lucky we are not to be going back right now? There will be snow in London and cold fogs for several weeks yet. And just look out of that window, will you? I believe the orange trees are ready to break into bloom."

Topp nodded without any enthusiasm. "Won't be any firing squads in Lunnon," he commented.

They were a happy pair when they caught, beyond the high outline of Great Teson, their first glimpse of the round-domed cathedrals of Ciudad Rodrigo.

Topp squinted at the blaze of pink stucco and whitewashed tile showing above the battlements.

"Food ahead, sahib," he said cheerfully. "And soft beds. And a dash o' hot water in a biddy. Guess we needs all three."

"Worth risking a firing squad for right now, Windy."

The sentinel on the gate had a French musket over his shoulder and, for good measure, a long sword in a red leather scabbard clanking against his skinny calves. Behind him a corpulent fellow in the green of the

Legion called out impatiently: "Are they English? Hail them and find out. Hail them, you *canango!*"

Topp reined in his tired horse and answered, "English we are, cull. From Frog-and-Toe, both on us. And ye might look a lot more nat'ral yerself down Grenitch way, I'm thinking."

The man in green bustled out with a grotesque imitation of a salute. His face was the shape and color of an underbaked bun.

"Is it Mr. Ellery?" he asked in perfect Londonese. "I've a message, if it is."

"My name is Ellery."

The man sighed. "The message is from Sir Robert Wilson, sir. I was to meet you and see that you get settled. He says he'll be back tomorrow. You're to be put up at Waif's Roost. That's just the name we has for it, sir. It's a big castle under the fort. The owner's in Madrid so we took it over, servants and all. The English people what have drifted in are all there now. They're quite an odd lot, they are indeed, sir."

"Where is Sir Robert?"

The man sighed again. "He's up on the Yeltes River, sir. With all his forces, such as they are. And now you've come, I'll have to go back to duty myself. I don't like it very much. You see, sir, I'm not a soldier rightly."

Frank looked at him curiously. "Then how does it happen you're here?"

The green helmet gave a lugubrious shake. "I was traveling with"—his accent slipped momentarily—"with Sir Jimes 'Arkworthy. I was—well, sir, generally it's called a footman, but I liked to think of myself as a sort of donzel, sir. You see I've had education, sir, and I aim to better myself. Sir James was enamored of a Spanish ledy in Madrid and we stayed longer than we should. At the very last minute Sir James got an opportunity to leave in a carriage. There was no room for me, so I had to walk. I was walking, I think, for months, sir. When I got as far as this, and found Sir Robert here, I had to choose between joining up with him or starving." A third, and still deeper, sigh. "I've been through a lot, I have indeed, sir. Name's Daniel Norris, sir."

Topp said in disgusted tones: "I knew it. A banging rainbow, sahib. Well, Dismal Dan, shake yer fat shanks and get us to this Roost ye're talking about."

Waif's Roost was a tall building of dark weathered stone, towering up over the neighboring houses like a highboy on stilts in an April Fool parade. They entered through a gateway with a grilled portcullis suspended on rusty chains above it. Innumerable windows and balconies looked down from the septagon walls surrounding the courtyard. A stout man with a face prickly red with the heat emerged from somewhere and regarded them with open hostility.

"What, more! Good Gad!" he exclaimed.

"It's Mr. Ellery from London, sir," explained Norris.

This did nothing to mollify the stout man. "Well," he snapped, "if Mr. Ellery from London thinks he's going to move in with us and dip into the miserable little food we're able to get—well, all I can say is that Mr. Ellery from London is damned well mistaken, by Gad!"

A feminine voice struck in from one of the balconies. Frank glanced up and saw that its owner was a widow, and a very recent one from the look of things. She was swathed in black from head to foot, with a long veil and mourning badges on each shoulder, and a medallion of the kind known as a "dear-departed" hanging around her neck on a long loop of ebony beads. The face under the veil was archly cheerful in spite of this.

"I'm sure, Mr. Birdsease," she said to the stout man, but smiling directly at Frank, "that we've plenty of room for more companions in misfortune. We must do the best we can, you know. This is war, Mr. Birdsease."

"It's all very well for you, Fanny," declared Mr. Birdsease with rising irritation. "You'll always get *your* share, by Gad, no matter what happens. It's the rest of us as'll have to go short. And"—fiercely—"I'm going as short now as I intend to, and I don't care who knows it!"

Norris whispered to Frank: "Mr. Birdsease was in wine and leather, sir. He had branches in Toledo and Málaga and he was doing very well. Of course it's all gone now. His wife was killed, but I really think, sir, it's the property that sticks in his craw. He's very irritable, as you can see."

Frank addressed himself to the wine and leather merchant. "We have no desire to inflict ourselves on you, sir. It's on orders from Sir Robert Wilson that we've come here."

"Sir Robert Wilson be damned! When Sir Robert Wilson sees to it that we get enough to eat and drink, he'll have the right to shove more people in on us. And not before."

"Now, Mr. Birdsease!" cried the widow. "I'm sure you must have got up on the wrong side of the bed this morning."

The merchant glowered up at her. "Perhaps I did. But my bed was empty at any rate, and I'm not so sure the same can be said for all the beds in this flea-bitten morgue."

"There's plenty of room still, I'm sure," went on the woman in black, passing lightly over the innuendo. "Why, I've three rooms myself and I don't really need them all. I'm quite willing for Mr. Ellery to have one of them if it's necessary."

The wine man shrugged his shoulders. "If you *must* stay," he whispered, "take my advice, by Gad, and get somewhere on the other side of the place."

A short individual, who announced himself as Mr. Tobias Green, from Brighton, appeared on the scene. He seemed to be acting in some kind of official capacity, for he carried a plan in his hand which he consulted with a shortsighted frown. "Sir Robert spoke to me about you, Mr. Ellery," he said. "Let's see now. I'll put you up in the tower, sir. In the owner's room. A great honor, sir. He's a duke or something quite special. A large dry, airy room, Mr. Ellery. Take a good look at the armoire when you get there. They say it has thirty-one secret compartments, but I've only been able to locate eighteen of them. After a most painstaking search, sir."

"Were they all empty?" asked Frank with a smile.

"Quite bare, sir. Now this other one—Mr. Topp, is it?—will have to go on the ground floor. Dinner's in an hour, gentlemen. Our romp boy has done a little better for us today, I'm happy to report. Where he got everything I don't know. The town's bare, sir, as bare—ha-ha—as the armoire, Mr. Ellery. There doesn't seem to be any food coming in from the country at all any more. Well, we're to have mutton and a string of *salchicha* and a very fine mess of *garvanzoes*. There's even an almond cake which *may* go around."

Frank was escorted to his room in the tower by a native in a waistcoat with split sleeves, laced to the wrists, and pantaloons of the usual dun color which also were slit down the front of each leg and buttoned tightly as far as the ankles, where they flared out with dusty abandon. A blazing red sash was wound debonairly around his bulging waist. Frank dropped a coin in his hand and the man spat joyously and said, "Senhora Maria-a-a!"

The room was round with small slits of windows, and the furniture was impressively massive: the armoire, which obviously was very old; a regal bed with satin hangings and decorations on the posts in gold leaf; a gold crucifix on the wall and several gold candle sconces; a half-dozen chairs with high backs embroidered in bewilderingly lavish color. In spite of its high elevation, it was not light, for the windows were all barred and the only candle left was burned right down to the socket.

Dinner was served in a long room with a refectory table capable of seating twoscore guests. It was pretty well filled. The widow was there, still in her full ostentation of mourning, fluttering her reinforced eyelashes at the newcomer; Mr. Birdsease, watching the food with a savagely calculating eye; a squashy individual in a dirty stock who answered to the name of Dr. Perkins; a young couple who, it appeared, had been caught on a walking honeymoon in the Galician mountains and were accepting everything as a great lark; a coarse-voiced woman with three small sons named Dunstan, Wulstan, and Guthrum; a few nondescripts, all of whom looked as though their antecedents might better be left undivulged; and a retiring young woman with intelligent eyes, clothed plainly in mouse-colored dress and hat, who had nothing to say at all. Frank found himself seated between the latter and Mr. Green, of Brighton.

The food did not live up to the happy predictions of Mr. Green. The mutton was strong, the sausage a little on the rancid order, the beans dry; and the almond cake did not go around after all. The guests muttered and complained, and Frank felt that every mouthful he took was bitterly begrudged. The Spanish cook, a large fellow with a villainous mustache, came to the door and stared in at them, as though daring criticism. The three boys vanished and were heard soon after in the courtyard, drawing their mother to the window, where she exploded into an angry admonition, "Guthrum, you keep out of there or I'll break your back!" Frank went to a window himself, glad of any excuse to escape for a moment from such trying company. Darkness had fallen, and the rest of the servants, of both sexes, had built a fire on the cobblestones and were squatted around it, smoking a cigarette; one cigarette quite literally, for they were passing it along, each taking a few puffs before relinquishing it. The outline of Great Teson was still faintly discernible over the top of one wall and the first stars were out. Windy Topp, who had been given a seat at the foot of the board, came over and joined him.

"A bob lot at business, the Spainies," he said in an admiring whisper. "I got it straight from the chuckwalla that there's food in town if ye wants to pay the price. They doles it out and lays on the profit. A full bardy for a seegar and ten shillin's for a dirty mattress."

The squashy individual had begun to pick on a native instrument called a *vihuela*, singing in a nasal voice:

> "*Master I have, and I am his man;*
> *Goll-up in dreary dall.*"

From that he branched off into something Spanish. Frank returned to his seat and slapped wearily at the gnats which circled in clouds around his head. The widow got up and essayed a dance accompaniment to the music. It was not a very successful effort, although she strove to make up for lack of natural grace by overemphasis of the hip movements. Mr. Birdsease, who had at last achieved a slight trace of amiability, clapped his hands and shouted, "Good gal, Fanny!"

A tense voice said in Frank's ear, "That ridiculous creature!" It was the quiet young woman in the mouse-colored dress. She looked up at him with scornful eyes. "Must we let all our standards go because we're caught in a war?"

"It isn't even amusing, is it?" he answered.

"And there's no way of getting out," went on the girl. "Here we are and here we'll stay."

"I suppose all horses and carriages have been requisitioned for the army."

"Yes, a month ago. I've been here several weeks. We'll be taken by the French in the end, of course. I'm reconciled to that."

"I'm not so sure. I've great faith in Sir Robert Wilson."

"He can't perform miracles." She dropped her voice again. "That woman's husband was killed a month ago. I wouldn't mind it so much if she didn't parade her mourning so conspicuously. She might at least take off the medallion. There's something especially indecent about making a show of herself with it on."

Frank looked curiously at her. "How do you happen to be here?"

"I would look much more at home in a country rectory, wouldn't I? I was born in one and I suppose I'll return to my natural environment in time. If I return at all, that is. I'm not sure I care very much one way or the other. You see, Mr. Ellery, I've been a governess for six years and it isn't the kind of life which raises expectations of pleasanter things happening to you."

"But what brought you to Spain?"

"I was governess to the children of a wealthy family in Madrid. It's been the fashion to have English teachers in nearly all continental countries. My employer kept promising to make arrangements for me to leave but he never did. He was attached to Godoy's party, so it was very difficult for him when the French came. He's either dead or in prison now, I'm afraid. I managed to leave finally and got as far as Salamanca. I was there a month, a perfectly dreadful month. Several of the party I was with were shot. Finally I had to leave. Alone. I came here—I can't be quite sure how. It was like a nightmare. I walked all of the way with some clothes strapped on my back."

He was remembering that she had been introduced as Miss Laura Brakespeare. "We'll get back to England somehow, Miss Brakespeare," he said. "Even a country rectory has its advantages, hasn't it?"

"I suppose so. It seems to, at a time like this." She had been speaking in a low voice but her tone regained a note of asperity when she added, "I mind these dreadful people more than anything."

Frank got up and excused himself, saying that he had letters to write. He spent the next three hours preparing a long dispatch on conditions in the Peninsula and the chance of Wellesley's second army landing before the converging armies reached the heart of Portugal. It was a good article, he felt, the best he had written. In the morning he would have to make arrangements with Wilson for the carrying of his dispatches to Lisbon.

When he wakened, after eight hours of luxurious sleep in the bed of the master of the house, the sun was well up in a blue sky laced with tiny white clouds. He went to one of the windows, attracted by familiar voices below, and peered down through the bars.

Topp and Norris were polishing shoes and harness in the courtyard, and the former was in a distinctly critical mood. "Get the elbers into it," he was saying. "I can see ye've been falling into slipshod ways since ye got out o' service."

The sound of a horse's hoofs came to an abrupt stop on the cobbled drive. Norris jumped up and stood to attention. "It's General Wilson," he said in flurried tones. "I suggest you waken your employer, Mr. Topp."

Frank was already on his way down the stairs, regretting that his lameness made it impossible for him to take more than one step at a time.

2

THE FIRST MAN through the gate was not Sir Robert Wilson. A tall fellow, wearing a Spanish cloak of green velvet with a row of silver buttons each as large as a pocket watch, came in under the portcullis and surveyed the courtyard with tired eyes. He had a high white forehead beneath a mop of unruly black curls and, in fact, looked as thoroughly un-English as could be imagined; but his voice, which came rolling out of him like the notes of an organ, was straight from the stage of London.

"Just as I was informed, 'egad! A sanctuary for unfortunate Britishers caught in the backwash of war. A sight for sore eyes indeed; not to mention empty stomachs."

Mr. Green, of Brighton, came running into the courtyard with papers in his hands. He would have brushed by the newcomer if the latter had not reached out and caught him by the shoulder.

"You wear an air of petty authority, my busy friend," said the man in the green cloak, "and so I conclude I should address myself to you. I am English and I understand this haven of peace and, I trust, plenty is dedicated to the use of such as I. For endless days I've been wandering through a country as empty as my own stomach. If you care to assume that I'm offering myself as a candidate for bed and board, you may do so. It would be a correct reading of my purpose in presenting myself here."

"You don't look like an Englishman," said Mr. Green.

"I detect the faintest shade of a compliment in your doubts. A continental air has, undoubtedly, fastened itself upon me. Nevertheless, I hail from the first of all cities, great London no less, and I have documentary proofs of the same which I'll produce if necessary."

Wilson came clanking through the gate at this point. Catching sight of Frank, he let out a hearty shout of welcome.

"Stout lad, Ellery! I was hoping you had arrived. You're just in time."

They shook hands. The commander of the Legion had acquired a lean and bronzed look from the strenuous weeks he had spent in the field. Frank experienced in greater degree than ever the feeling of exhilaration which came over him whenever they met. Wilson, he could see, had changed; he had more of an air of authority about him, of definite purpose.

"I got your note," he said. "And left inside the hour."

"I knew you would. I was sure you would drop everything and come. I've wanted you the worst way, Frank." Wilson nodded his head enthusiastically. "Well, now that you *are* here, I'm going to put you right to work. You're looking fit again, old boy. Nothing like a long hard ride to shake the fever out of you."

Frank smiled, thinking how much that sounded like Caradoc. He was thinking also of the first few days of the journey when he had scarcely been able to remain in the saddle. "The fever's gone, at any rate. I'm ready for anything."

"What news have you been getting from London? I haven't had a scrap for ten weeks myself."

"The Austrians are on the point of breaking with Boney again. They seem to feel that he'll be kept busy here and that they'll take him at a disadvantage."

"The fools!" exclaimed Wilson. "With Russia on his side, they haven't a chance. They can't count on any help from Prussia. That weak fool of a Prussian King can never make up his mind to move in time. Of course it's good news that we may have some help, but I'm very much afraid the Austrians will get a sound thrashing for their pains."

"I've heard from Cope occasionally. He says public opinion on the war is pretty well mixed. The Cintra business was a dampener, as you know. When Moore had to run for it, the public enthusiasm went away down. Still, I judge the people are solidly behind the plan to send Sir Arthur back. And with a real army this time."

"I hope the damned politicians have learned their lesson! Sending pipe-clay experts and three-bottle veterans to fight it out with Boney! It was the stupidest thing ever done by a government with a positive genius for stupidity. But what other news have you? How has the newspaper been going?"

"Much better. This war-correspondent idea seems to have turned the trick. People are reading the *Tab* again, at any rate."

Wilson's eyes began to glow. "Wait until you send them the story of what's happening here! They'll buy your papers then as fast as they can be run off the press. Frank, Frank, I'm doing what I said I would. I'm going to beat all of Boney's men. I'm knocking all his fine plans into a cocked hat. Wait until I tell you what's in the wind."

At this moment the man in the green cloak brushed aside the restraining arm of Mr. Green and walked up to them.

"I think you must be Sir Robert Wilson," he said.

"My name is Wilson. Who are you?"

"My name, sir, is Brown. John Brown. I've been stranded in this country like so many other English people. In fact, I've been having a pretty bad time of it."

Wilson looked at him intently. "I've heard some things about you, I believe. At any rate, you fit the description. Unless I'm very much mistaken, your name isn't Brown. It's Cardyce, isn't it?"

The man bowed. "Yes, my name is Cardyce. Leonard Cardyce, to be exact. You've heard of me, of course."

"Then why did you say it was Brown?"

"I have a reason for anonymity at the moment. A sound and reasonable one. We needn't go into it, however."

"I think we must go into it, sir." Wilson was regarding him with a distinctly hostile air. "I know what your reason is. I've heard a great deal about you, Cardyce, and nothing favorable. You're an actor or a singer——"

"I'm both but I prefer to stand on my reputation as a singer. I'm quite a fine singer, I think."

"You ran away from Madrid with the wife of somebody or other. Somebody of importance. I suppose you find it safer to conceal your identity as long as you're on the Spanish side of the border. From all I heard, you're a pretty shady sort of scoundrel, Mr. Leonard Cardyce."

"I resent your opinion of me, sir. In spite of it, and the unnecessary heat with which you've expressed it, I'm throwing myself on your protection, Sir Robert. As an Englishman, I'm entitled to it."

Wilson was silent for a moment. "Where is the lady?" he asked.

The singer made a resigned gesture with his hands. "I regret to report that I don't know. We found it necessary to part company some months ago. A rumor reached me that she was back in Madrid, but I'm in no position to vouch for it. I trust she's been having a better time than I have."

"Very well, Mr. Singer. If you're determined to put yourself in my hands, I'll find a use for you. I need men badly or I would tell you to go to the devil. You'll be under orders, you know. You'll do what you're told or suffer the consequences."

"I'm prepared for anything, sir. Anything that carries with it the certainty of regular food and, perhaps, a little more security than I've been enjoying."

"Get him something to eat, Mr. Green. And find a spot where Mr. Ellery and I may talk without further interruption."

Seated under a large aloe in a corner of the court, Wilson proceeded to expound his plans. "You know in a general way how much depends on keeping the French out of here," he said, sipping the coffee which a servant, wearing a net over his straight black hair, had brought them in a beautifully chased gold pitcher. "Boney worked out his grand plan before leaving for France, and the marshals are supposed to carry it out to the letter. Soult and Victor are to act in a pincer movement but they won't begin to close in until Lapisse has taken Ciudad Rodrigo and opened the central gate. That's the weak point. Everything depends on the movements of this indolent fellow in front of us. I saw the importance of this sector and that's why I brought the Legion here. So far, Lapisse hasn't done a thing."

"A touch of stage fright perhaps. I understand this is his first important command."

Wilson grinned with delight. "I've got him as nervous as a kitten with fleas in its tail. All he has to do is to move in and shake the plum off the wall. But there he sits, biting his nails and wondering what I'm up to."

"How many men are you using?"

"A miserable handful compared to the ten thousand veteran troops under Lapisse. Less than two thousand in all, and half of them Spaniards at that. My Legionnaires have turned into first-class fighting men, but the Inkies are different. They don't know what discipline means and I can't depend on them at all." His eyes gleamed at his listener over the rim of his gold coffee cup. "I've got my whole force strung out along the line of the Yeltes, which cuts the French off from here. I'm working my fellows hard, Frank. Every man is doing double duty. The buglers sound every call several times, rushing from one post to another. My outriders are in the saddle sixteen hours every day. We're using up horse-flesh at a terrible rate."

"You said you were making a bluff of it. Now I can believe it."

"I'm certain that our stupid M'sieur Lapisse thinks I have three thousand cavalry at the lowest reckoning. You see, I've stationed some *caçadores*—sharpshooters, that is—in the woods on the other side of the river. They pick off the French scouts and make it impossible for them to get close enough to find out the truth about us." He threw back his head and laughed heartily. "There's never been such a bluff, Frank, in the whole history of warfare! If I can keep it up for another month, Wellesley will land his new army and Portugal will be saved! No, that's an understatement; something pretty unusual, coming from me. England will be saved, Frank. That's the stake we're playing for. Boney will be kept busy indefinitely in the Peninsula and he'll have no chance to try an invasion of the islands."

There was a moment's silence. Frank was thinking how lucky he was to have been brought into the middle of this spectacular operation.

"Thermopylae all over again," said Wilson solemnly. "This handful of raw levies may save the world. If we can only hold out long enough!"

"What can I do? I'm a fair shot. You might make a—a *caçadore* of me."

The commander shook his head emphatically. "I've something much more important than that for you, my lad. As a matter of fact, the success of my bluff may depend on you. Don't look so startled. It's a job of organization I want you to undertake for me.

"Here are your orders," he went on briskly. "We must make our front still more impressive. Back of the Yeltes, on this side, there's a high stretch of land which the French outriders can see on a clear day. I want to convince them that considerable reinforcements have moved up and are camped there. As soon as we've finished our talk, I'm off to commandeer every tent in the city. I'll be lucky if I find a dozen, judging from past experience. So I'm going to take every blanket and sheet and tablecloth I can lay my hands on—anything that can be draped over a pole to look like a camp tent in the distance. If necessary I'll have them yank the petticoats off the women. I'm going to commandeer as well every yard of red cloth in the place so you can dress your people up to look like British redcoats. That's to be your share in it, Frank, to set up a phantom camp and keep it in a perfect lather of activity. You must convince Lapisse that you have a couple of fresh divisions camped back of that high bluff. I'll let you have a couple of buglers—they can't be trained in a day, worse luck—but you'll have to manage the rest of it yourself. You'll have to keep a hundred bivouac fires going at night so the sky will blaze with them. Do you see it now?"

Frank's mind was racing with delighted conjectures and speculations. Here was his chance at last. "I see it," he said. "I'll do my best, Sir Robert. But where will I get the men?"

"First, the commandant here will issue a call for volunteers. I doubt if it will net you many. These people take more kindly to the shelter of their stone walls. As a matter of fact, I've already skimmed the cream. In the main, you'll have to depend on our own people."

"You mean these refugees?"

Wilson nodded his head. "A scrubby lot, I grant you. Still, they're all British-born, and I think they can be made to see the crisis we're facing. You must talk them into it. The women as well. A woman can gather wood and keep half a dozen fires going at night as well as a man. Even that singer fellow. That's why I didn't send him packing just now."

The mother of the three boys called suddenly from a balcony above them: "Has anyone seen those little terrors of mine? I'll break their backs for them if they're into any kind of mischief." Frank looked up and saw that the vivacious widow was sitting on another balcony, her veils flowing about her like seaweed. She smiled and waved a hand at them.

"They're a poorer lot than you imagine," he said. "Still, I'll do the best I can. Let me make one suggestion, Sir Robert. You had better talk to them yourself. They'll volunteer for you, but I'll have no influence with them at all."

"I'm sorry but I can't spare the time. Drumming up the supplies will take several hours at least and I should be back at headquarters this very minute. No, Frank, I'm compelled to leave the enlistment problem in your hands." He paused. "I can't spare you a horse. Two or three bullock carts is the best I can do for you. Load the women in them, and the supplies. Pack in every pound of food you can lay your hands on. Things are pretty bare along the Yeltes as it is. You'll be responsible for feeding your own people, so beg, borrow, and steal everything in sight. You'll have to be the boss romp boy from this time on." He dropped his voice.

"The most important point right now is to keep them in the dark. They mustn't know what they're volunteering for until they get to the front; we can see to it there are no leaks then. Keep this to yourself. You can't trust anyone."

"Right, sir. I have my orders. When do you want us there?"

"You must start as soon as the sun goes down. It's a good four *léguas* —twenty English miles. All the men will have to walk. Don't shove them too hard. Ten minutes' rest every half hour. Their feet will blister in no time if you don't. Be sure that you're back of the bluff by daybreak. I want the horizon red with bivouac fires tomorrow night. Lapisse has been showing some signs of activity the last few days. We must shock him back into his coma."

"What happens to these people if the French break through?"

"Nothing pleasant." Wilson got to his feet. "Their plight in that case will be a little more desperate than if they stayed here. They'll have twenty more miles to run."

Frank sprang up also. A mood of intense exhilaration had taken possession of him. "Count on us, sir. Your new division will report for duty tomorrow morning."

The country through which they traveled that night was hilly and rough. The three bullock carts were nothing more than planks nailed on long shafts with low sides. There were no springs, of course, and the ungreased axles screeched like souls in travail. The women, eight in all, rode in one, on a light bedding of straw which did little to protect them from the incessant bumps and jolts. The others were piled high with provisions and supplies. Frank had given his horse to Mr. Green, who suffered from rheumatism, and Topp's was being ridden by one of the other men whose years made walking impossible.

Frank was sure after they had gone a few miles that he would never be able to see it through. The dark was so intense that he stumbled continually, and the effort involved in stumping along on his lame leg soon had him winded and unutterably weary. His knee began to pain him. Many times he decided that he would have to give in and beg a seat in the cart with the women; but somehow his tongue refused the office. Perhaps it was the grumbling tones of Mr. Birdsease as he threshed along ahead or the whining note with which Cardyce cursed the blisters he was raising on his feet. He knew they would jeer at him or, worse still, insist on a similar privilege. That would load the cart down and delay the whole party.

He gritted his teeth and stumped along, perspiration pouring off him in spite of the fact that the night air was cold. The halts which Wilson had recommended began to grow longer. They did him no good, for he was generally so far behind that it took him the whole interval to catch up with the rest. There seemed something malicious about the way the other men sprang to their feet and started off again as soon as he appeared. He thought longingly of the comfort of the jolting cart, the sheer delight he would be able to get out of lying back and resting his aching leg.

Once Topp dropped back beside him and said: "Sahib, I'm as strong as a mule. Let me give you a back-up for a spell."

Frank shook his head. "I'm still quite fresh, Windy. It's just this leg of mine. I have to walk slowly."

There was little consolation now in the thought that he had succeeded in everything Wilson had confided to his care. All of the company had finally volunteered to serve, even the querulous woman with the three boys. He would have preferred not to have Dunstan, Wulstan, and Guthrum along but, clearly, they could not be left behind in a strange and hostile city. Well, they might prove helpful at finding wood. He was well satisfied with the results of his foraging for food. The *corregidor* of the city had invoked his magisterial powers and the result was a cart piled high with sacks of the best bolted flour, haunches of beef and carcasses of mutton, enough *salchichas* to span the circuit of the city fort, not to mention supplies of dried vegetables and half a dozen wild turkeys. He had done very well, he thought.

One of the bullock drivers, hunched down under his enormous hat which made him look in the dark like a puffed-up toadstool, began to sing in a lugubrious voice, *"Munto Santa, munto bonita,"* breaking off after each verse to address his team in a proud attempt at English, "Hup, feelthy brutes! *Arriba!"*

Arriba! Arriba! Go on! Go on! The word beat in Frank's brain with a sickening insistence. He was beginning to feel that every step he took must be the last, that he could not compel his tired muscles to another move. But still he managed to keep it up, stumbling, falling, getting up again somehow, groaning when he was so far behind that no one could hear him. He had lost all track of time, conscious of nothing but the need for keeping on in this dark purgatory of pain and effort. *Arriba! Arriba!*

He became aware finally that the sky ahead of him was no longer completely black. Was it an optical illusion or had they actually marched through the whole of the night? He refused to believe that this could be true until he heard Cardyce somewhere far ahead say in a voice weak with exhaustion, "Behold, fellow pilgrims, we seem at last to have emerged like Christian from the Valley of the Shadow!"

In another half hour they were walking in the full light of a spring sun. The carts stopped on the crest of a sharp grade in a gash between clay walls. The men, their faces as chalky with fatigue as the color of the soil, stood together in a clump, staring straight ahead. When he came up with them, he saw they were pointing to a cold green line which coiled across the receding countryside not more than two miles ahead. Could it be the Yeltes already?

Yes, it was the river. As they watched, a figure in green came riding furiously up the road toward them. The faint boom of a musket shot sounded across the valley. They had arrived at the appointed time!

From the crowded cart with the women he heard the voice of Fanny Parker saying, "Why, the poor man! He's so lame. We should have made a place for him." Laura Brakespeare whispered furiously in reply, "Not so loud, *please!* Do you want to hurt his feelings!"

3

FRANK EYED with repugnance the figure in green swaying slowly at the end of the rope. The face of the hanged man, which was hideously swollen and black, seemed to have acquired a mocking expression in the last few hours. Sir Robert Wilson insisted the body must continue to hang there as a warning to his men that the women in the new camp were to be left alone. The young bride had been the victim in this case, and the commander had been prompt in meting out punishment.

As he turned back in the direction of his shadow camp, Frank reflected that protection was superfluous as far as most of the women were concerned. Only two of the eight were above suspicion: the misused bride and Laura Brakespeare. Even the mother of the three boys was falling into the promiscuous ways of the rest. Back of the camp there was a small village, deserted by its inhabitants, and here his followers had taken up their quarters. There would be plenty of drinking and merrymaking going on there now. Well, he said to himself, they were doing their work at any rate. The fires blazed along the line of the bluff for a half mile in each direction, as they had done each night for the last three weeks; one of the main reasons, without a doubt, for the continued inactivity of the enemy. He remembered with a worried frown that the wood supply was getting low. Parties would have to be sent up into the hills to collect more. There would be plenty of grumbling about it. The food situation was growing acute, and that was the chief of his worries.

A figure came up beside him out of the darkness, and the deep voice of Leonard Cardyce demanded: "How much longer are we going to hang on here, Ellery? We've done everything that was asked of us. Great God, man, we ought to be getting out while there's still time. This fellow Wilson is mad!"

"We've got to keep it up as long as we can. You know that as well as I do, Cardyce."

"They'll be coming down on us. And then what will happen? I don't want to be taken prisoner or strung up alongside that fellow there." He looked at the swaying figure with intense distaste. "He's beginning to smell pretty bad, isn't he?"

"You'll stay here, whether you like it or not, until the order comes to retreat." A sound of loud laughter reached them from one of the huts of the village. "Another drunken party, it seems. I don't know where they get so much stuff to drink."

"My dear Ellery, your disapproval of our efforts to put a good face on the situation is becoming very tiresome. Don't you realize that we're caught in the middle of a war?"

"Is that any excuse for letting down all the barriers?"

"We're made of less heroic clay, it seems, than you are, my puritanical young publisher. Why shouldn't we get drunk while we still have bellies to fill? Why shouldn't we engage in a little gentle dalliance at the same time? You might unbend once in a while. It would do you a lot of good to break down occasionally." He stopped short on seeing a figure approach the nearest fire with an armful of wood. "Well, if it isn't the fair Brakespeare herself. Your devotion to duty, my dear Laura, would be a lesson to all of us, if we were in a frame of mind to benefit by it."

The governess went on with her work of replenishing the fire and made no reply. She was without a hat and her dark hair was hanging in braids over her shoulders. Frank observed with some surprise that this made a decided improvement in her appearance. Cardyce seemed to have reached the same conclusion, for he laughed suddenly and pulled her around by one arm.

"Why, Laura, you look like a different person now that you've chucked that ugly abomination of a hat. You look—Gad, you could be pretty if you tried hard enough. I seem to have been completely mistaken in a woman for the first time in my life. I apologize most humbly, dear lady, for my lack of perception."

She shook off his hand and said angrily, "Let me go!"

"*Dios!* The disposition seems to be the same, hat or no hat. As full of vinegar as ever. Still, I wonder if a few glasses of that sparkling golden wine we managed to find the other day would do anything for it? I believe it might."

"I'll thank you to do your wondering about someone else. Your opinion is of no importance to me at all, Mr. Cardyce."

"This must be looked into, dear lady. I must do what I can to make up for my sad error of judgment. I perceive, however, that the present is not the time to begin. Perhaps I'll have the pleasure of seeing you two slaves to duty a little later in the evening. In the meantime, an affectionate farewell."

He vanished in the darkness and Frank said in an apologetic tone: "I'm very much shamed, Laura, that I can't seem to get things properly organized around here. Too much of the work falls on you. I'm going to see that it's stopped."

"I'm glad to do everything I can, Francis. There's nothing you can do about it. Some of them are shirkers so it falls on a few of us to bear the brunt. It's always the way."

He smiled down at her. "Cardyce was right for once. You look quite different tonight. I'm glad you've gotten rid of that hat. Why did you ever select it?"

She dropped the last stick of wood on the fire and straightened up. "Apparently," she said, "you don't realize what it means to be a governess. Do you suppose a woman would keep you in her house if she thought you might prove attractive to her husband or her sons or to male visitors? For six years I've had to select hats because they were ugly. I've always taken the ugliest I could find. I've had to do my hair in an unattractive way." She was speaking in a casual tone but he could see that her hands were trembling. "I've had to do that because I was sure I would be dismissed if I didn't. Don't laugh at me, please! It hasn't been so very hard after all. I haven't had very much in the way of looks to hide."

"You must have been unfortunate in your choice of employers."

"Not at all. Some of them were nice enough; quite kind and considerate in every other way. But they're all alike in *that* respect."

"Well," said Frank, "there won't be any need for you to go on picking out ugly hats after this. I'm sending dispatches back all the time, and I've taken the liberty of mentioning some of the fine things you've done here. You'll find yourself a heroine of sorts after all this is over."

She shook her head passionately. "I'm sure it's kind of you but it won't make any difference at all. I'll still have to earn a living. And what other way of earning it can I find?"

She unbuttoned the neck of her shapeless scarlet wrap and moved further back from the heat of the fire. They all wore red as part of the deception. From the cut of his own coat, Frank entertained the suspicion that it had once functioned as a petticoat.

"You can marry," he said. "That will be an easy matter if you stop disguising yourself to please women employers."

"Yes, I can marry." She indulged in a short and completely mirthless laugh. "A letter reached me today. How it got to me here is hard to understand because it had been addressed to Madrid. Perhaps it was sent on from Lisbon with the official dispatches. It was from my married sister. I'm being offered a post to raise and teach the children of a widower, a North Country curate with ninety pounds a year. Amelia assures me I can count on an offer of marriage from the Rev. George Leesby within a reasonable time and she earnestly advises me to snap it up. Can't you just see the Rev. George Leesby? I'm sure he has a receding chin and wispy hair and that he snuffles from an incurable cold in the head."

"On the other hand, he may be a fine, handsome fellow. How can you tell?"

"He has six children. Only the kind of man I've described would think of having six children on ninety pounds a year. I'm sure he'll have six more before he's through." She laughed again, this time with a slight suggestion of amusement. "There you have it, Francis. That's the only kind of marriage I can look forward to. So perhaps I'll do better to stick to unbecoming hats after all."

"Well," said Frank, "I'm sure of one thing. You've done all the work you're going to do tonight. I'll rout out someone to take your place. It's high time you turned in."

"I *am* a little tired. Poor little Mrs. O'Mearns was feeling badly today and I looked after her as well as I could." She looked at him with sudden suspicion. "I've talked altogether too much. I'm sure you'll go away now and have a good laugh at my expense."

"On the contrary, I've become convinced you're the only really intelligent person here."

"I'm not so sure. Fanny never turns a hand to anything. There are always half a dozen volunteers to do her share. Perhaps that's the right kind of intelligence for a woman to have." She added, after a moment: "She looks quite dashing in her red jacket, doesn't she? It's the only one that seems to fit."

The village consisted of a score of small adobe huts. As it was no more than a quarter mile back from the ridge, it suited their purpose admirably. Frank shared one with Dr. Perkins and his *vihuela*.

Two horses were tied in front and a light poured through the open door. Wilson's aide was sleeping on the front step, his head against the doorframe, the green plume in his hat falling limply across his cheek and wide-open mouth. Having neglected to remove the aloe leaves which all the natives stuck to their lips to keep them from cracking with the heat, he gave the appearance of having been taken in some kind of epileptic seizure.

"The poor fellow's probably been in the saddle for twenty hours," thought Frank, looking down at him. "Wilson certainly keeps them on the go."

Sir Robert called from inside. "Where have you been, you sluggard? I've been waiting for you exactly nineteen minutes."

He was seated in a rush-bottomed chair, his feet up on the table. He looked worn out and his boots were caked from heel to knee with red clay. Dr. Perkins was sleeping on a mattress in one corner and snoring rhythmically.

"There was wind with the bit of rain we had this afternoon. It took down nearly all the tents." Frank sat down beside his chief, aware for the first time how near he was to the limit of his physical resources. "We've had the devil's own time getting them all rigged up again."

Wilson laughed heartily. "This sham camp of yours! It's a constant delight to me, Frank. Your name should be Potemkin, I swear. Certainly you're taking in the French as thoroughly as that wily Russian did the great Catherine. It's a perfect stage setting, perfect! Sometimes I think myself there must be an army here after all. You can imagine what Lapisse thinks." He stretched out his long legs and groaned with the effort. "I hope you're doing yourself justice in the dispatches you've forwarded."

"I'm telling as much as I dare. The first article should be out now. It ought to give the people some slight comfort after the uninterruptedly bad news I was giving them before."

Wilson looked at him with the familiar gleam in his eye. "I took a big chance today, Frank. I moved my right up beyond the Sierra de Francia. On the other flank I sent Colonel Mayne forward to Puerto de Banos."

Frank whistled. "That *is* taking a chance."

"It had to be done. We've now closed off the main pass between Salamanca and Estremadura, which cuts Lapisse's communications with Victor. Mayne blocks him off from Soult. Do you see what that means? They can't keep in touch unless the riders swing away back into Spanish territory. That makes it a matter of two weeks for any dispatches to get through either way."

"Your line must be very thin now."

"Thin?" Wilson slapped his thigh exultantly. "As thin as paper! As thin as the blood of my whimpering superiors. I got more orders today to pull up instantly and drop back. Don't the idiots realize how important this is?" He indulged in a snort of disgust. "I lighted my pipe with it and told the rider to report he couldn't locate me. He promised but I don't care one way or the other."

"If Lapisse moves up——"

"If Lapisse moves up, he'll drive us out of here like chaff before a north wind. But he won't move, Frank. The sluggish fellow is completely taken in by this time." There was a pause. "I propose very shortly to take another long chance. We cut off a French outrider today. He was carrying word to Lapisse that a convoy with food and supplies was coming on from behind Ledesma."

Frank smiled. "You don't have to explain the next move, Sir Robert. You're going to raid behind their lines and cut the train off."

"Exactly. We're pretty damned short of food ourselves. It will be a touch-and-go business but I think we can manage it."

"I'm going to ask a favor. Let me go along. I'm a little tired of lighting fires and keeping bed sheets suspended on poles. Let me see a bit of action for a change."

Wilson squinted at him in the flickering light. "Are you sure you're up to it, Frank? I'm eternally in your debt and you've never asked any favors; but this will be a hard scramble, you know. We'll have to ride like the wind and there's sure to be a scrimmage on the way back."

"The only place this leg of mine isn't a handicap is on the back of a horse. I can ride well enough. Take me along this once."

The sleeper stirred and then sat up, threshing his arms around to drive off the insects which filled the room. His eyes remained closed. "I'm being eaten alive," he muttered.

They paid no attention to him. Wilson thought for a moment and then nodded his head. "Very well then. You're entitled to it. I'll promise you one thing—there will be something lively for you to describe."

The voice of Windy Topp could be heard at the door. "Come on now, Senhor Tadpole, let two hard-working Englishmen get by. And ye'd best close up that bone box as tight as Pitt's Picture or ye'll be swallerin' all the insects in Spain." Then they heard Norris say in horrified tones, "Great gripe seed, Windy, it's the General's aide!" The pair decamped in a hurry and in a few minutes were stirring about in a lean-to at the rear where Topp had a hammock slung.

Wilson sighed and proceeded to light a pipe. "Well, so much for that. I don't believe I ever told you, Frank, about seeing that French gal of yours in London before I sailed."

"No"—eagerly—"you've said nothing about it. Where did you see her?"

"At a reception. One of those dreadful affairs where all the lovely ladies are monopolized by miserable little tea-swigging nincompoops of men. It was at Andersley House, and the air was full of titles. She was the loveliest one there, and that's a fact."

Frank was thinking of the last time he had seen Gabrielle. It was the afternoon they had played voles and he had lost three shillings in such a very short time. How interested she had been in the game, in spite of her cold, and how lovely she had looked, in spite again of the lucky ailment which had kept her indoors that day!

"Yes," he said fervently. "It doesn't seem possible that there could be anyone else in the world as beautiful as she is. I can sit for hours and do nothing else but think about her."

Wilson sighed. "You should have seen my Jemima when I tucked her under my arm and mizzled to Gretna Green with her. Poor girl, it's pretty awful to lose your sight, especially when you're married to a man who's never home. I won't allow your French gal any margin over my Jemima but—I don't mind saying I took quite a fancy to her at that. She's a high-spirited filly. She was surrounded by men all afternoon so I didn't have the honor of an introduction."

"It's always that way. She's extremely popular. Was the Duc de Berri there?"

"I think so. And, by the way, I saw Sir Caradoc there also."

There was a moment's silence and then Frank said: "I suppose he's getting around a lot these days. A young man in politics has to show himself. Was he by any chance among those dancing attendance on Mlle. de Salle?"

Wilson shook his head. "I don't think so. I seem to remember that our young Sir Galahad was very much in evidence in the circle surrounding Lady Laker, which included the wives of several prominent politicians."

Frank's spirits rose instantly. Perhaps, then, their relationship had not progressed beyond the hole-and-corner stage. Perhaps it had been nothing more than a flirtation and was over and done with already. He found himself wishing fervently that he was back in London. Nothing seemed so important at the moment as a chance to see her again. Nothing else in life, he realized, mattered at all.

"I heard some rumor about that brother of hers," went on Sir Robert. "Do you happen to know him well?"

"No. I saw him several times but he was most aloof. He seemed to me a rather surly fellow." Frank hastened to add: "He's only a stepbrother, you know. They're completely unlike in every way. I believe he's a steady gambler."

"Yes, he's a gambler. From what I heard, he's starting to play for high and dangerous stakes. I hope, for the gal's sake, it isn't true."

Frank was remembering the questions Gabrielle herself had asked him and what Margot had said when he made his farewell call. "Do you feel free to tell what you heard?" he asked.

"Well, it's certain some of the French crowd in London have sold out to Boney. They manage to keep him posted on all military matters. I heard the brother's name mentioned in that connection. It was no more than a rumor, of course. Probably nothing in it."

4

TIME PASSED and the heat became intense. Frank, who had lived the first years of his boyhood in great fear of the eternal punishment so unctuously promised by the minister under whom his father sat, found himself wondering if hell could be any worse than this. Working under the midday sun, certainly, was like having a foretaste of the torments of the damned.

The enemy still had made no move, but otherwise everything was going wrong. Most of the meat he had procured was ruined by the heat. Dysentery had visited the camp, and the medicine chest contained nothing but opium pills, which he distributed doubtfully. Those who were still well enough to get around had to work harder than ever and they complained incessantly. Mr. Birdsease had a finger blown off while hunting with an old Spanish musket. A bullock, brought in for slaughter, broke loose and caught young Wulstan in its path, accomplishing with one angry toss of its horns what the boy's mother had so often threatened. He was the most likable of the three, and the fatality threw the camp into deepest gloom.

Frank returned to the village late one evening in low spirits. He had no idea where the food was coming from to feed his camp and he was very much afraid he would have to acknowledge failure by sending them back to Ciudad Rodrigo. If reports were to be believed, things were not much better there. He had said nothing to Wilson so far about the situation they faced, but it was clear he could no longer keep it to himself.

Windy Topp, trudging along at his heels, said in a far from cheerful voice: "Here's a fixer, sahib. Pockets jingling with dimmock and not able to buy a bite o' food. My father used to say ye ain't really hungry until yer big gut's ready to eat yer little un, or vice versy. From the way I feels inside I expects that very thing to happen any minute now."

"If we can only get our hands on that French provision train, we'll have plenty of food."

"Yes, sahib, and if Boney had kept his men t'other side o' the border we'd be home this minute, tucking into mutton and capers. Right now I'd be willing to trade my share in that train for the tail of a bloater or the slops in a cup of cold tea."

As they passed the one-roomed hut assigned to Laura Brakespeare, she appeared in the doorway with a candle in her hand.

"Is that you, Francis?" she called.

"Yes, Laura. I'm turning in. I'm ashamed to confess that we had no luck today. The whole countryside seems to have been cleaned out of food."

"Could you come in for a minute? I want to talk to you."

"Of course." Frank handed his saddle and shoulder bags to Topp. "Give the room a good looking-over, Windy. Last night I wakened up and found two scorpions under my blanket. Take the bellows and blow everything off the walls and floor."

"Right, sahib."

Laura had walked back inside and, when he followed, she said in a constrained voice, "Close the door, please." She had one candle only, but it lighted the room sufficiently for him to see that she had gone to great pains to make the interior homelike. A curtain had been hung over the one window and there was even a cloth on the small round table. The table, he saw, had been set for a meal.

"Food?" he said. "You must be celebrating."

She was standing with her back to him, arranging the curtains in the window, and she answered without turning her head. "Yes, I think you might call it a celebration. Shall we say I'm doing this to mark my very late arrival at a sane point of view? Perhaps, Francis, we can celebrate together. That is—if you find you agree with what I've come to believe."

"You're being very mysterious."

As she turned to face him Frank received a distinct shock. He had failed to notice before that she was wearing under her scarlet wrap a black silk gown. It was most handsomely trimmed with black velvet and lace and it rustled when she moved. What surprised him still more, however, was the complete change in her appearance. By altering the way of doing her hair, drawing it back in soft waves, she displayed for the first time the full lines of a fine brow. Her eyes seemed larger, darker, very much alive. He refused to believe at first that she had actually applied rouge to her lips and cheeks but closer inspection made it certain that she had done so.

"I hardly know you," he said. "You look—well, very different."

"I hope I look different," she answered in a quiet tone. "I've tried very hard to. I know that I feel different. But don't let's talk yet, Francis. I want you to have some supper first."

"I *am* hungry," he acknowledged, looking at the food on the table and the cracked bowl in the center which she had filled with flowers. "Do I see soup and bread? And a bottle of wine? You're either a witch, Laura, or you've been hoarding your share."

She laid a hand on his arm as they walked to the table but drew it away instantly. "Yes, I've been saving some. I've very little appetite. This will do you a lot more good than it could have done me. You work so hard! The bread was stale and I tried to warm it. I'm afraid the crust is burned. Sit down, Francis. I'll sit opposite you."

There was only one plate and no spoons. He poured out more than half of the soup and offered it to her. She shook her head. "I couldn't possibly eat anything tonight. You must take it all." He drank from the plate. The soup had been made from scraps of meat and vegetables and tasted quite wonderful.

"You make me feel guilty," he said.

"Please don't." After a moment she went on: "I suppose you're wondering about this dress and—and the other things I've done to myself. The dress belonged to Doña Isabella, my employer in Madrid. She couldn't take much with her when she ran away from the French and she was determined to have nothing fall into their hands. She begged me to take some things. I didn't want to but I finally selected this. I'm glad now that I did."

"I'm sure it looks well on you. But I could tell more about it if you would take off your regimental jacket."

"I will," she promised. "Oh yes, I will. But not yet."

There was fruit also on the table, but neither of them touched it. The camp had been subsisting very largely on fruit the last few days.

"Would you believe," she said after a long pause, "that this is the first time in my life I've had supper alone with a man?"

He was thinking that the dingy scarlet went well with her dark hair and eyes. Yes, she was surprisingly attractive.

"It won't be the last time then. I'm rather clumsy at paying compliments but you're looking lovely tonight, Laura."

"I hoped you would think so." She did not raise her eyes. Instead she kept them fixed on her hands, which she held folded together on the edge of the table. The wrap fell away above one elbow and he noticed that her arm was slender and white. "We've talked about the need to keep up our standards through times like these and we've been very scornful of our—our friends here. Francis, we've been wrong! At least we've been very smug and foolish."

"I'm not sure of that. I've admired you for the way you've taken things."

"But is that the kind of admiration a woman wants? I've been thinking a great deal the last few days. What are these standards we're so proud of? Mine—well, I've lived always in strict little schoolrooms, far away from life and all reality. Nothing exciting has ever happened to me before. That's what I'll go back to, if I go back at all. I'll be a governess or a companion all my life; or I'll marry someone like the Rev. George Leesby. Just because my life has been so dull and proper, and will be again after all this is over, must I live through the excitement of a war in the same dull way?" Her voice had risen to a higher note. She raised her eyes now and looked at him intently. "I've decided it's wrong, Francis, and a little silly too. I don't say the rest are right to behave the way they do. But—you and I, Francis, you and I! Surely we don't have to be so rigid and conventional when we may be killed at any time."

The sense of excitement which had taken possession of him as soon as he came into the room was mounting. He looked at her with an intentness which equaled her own. "Perhaps you're right. I haven't thought about it. I've been too busy to think about anything."

She was pouring wine into the one glass. He noticed that her hand was not steady. "We'll have to share this glass, I'm afraid. Do you mind?" She touched her lips to the edge and then drew back her head. "I think we should drink a toast. To us, Francis. Two such very proper and sensible people. Who"—she dropped her eyes again—"will not continue to be so sensible, I hope, for whatever time we have left."

He took a sip in turn. "I was going to propose the same toast."

Her voice was eager. "I want to have one short spell in my life when I'm not sensible at all. I want to be gay, reckless, happy for once. Can one be happy that way? I don't know. Perhaps not. But I should like very much to find out. It's worth a test, isn't it?"

"Yes, it's worth a test, Laura."

She leaned across the table and smiled at him. It was the first time she had smiled. "You said I was lovely tonight. I know I'm not that. But you did mean it a little?"

"Of course I meant it."

Looking across the small table, he realized how desirable she was. He was finding it hard to remember that his devotion was pledged elsewhere. He thought, "She's right, we may have only a short time to live, so why not make the most of it?" It would be nothing more than an episode but—she was really quite lovely; her eyes full of a new light, her cheeks flushed, a little breathless. Why not, indeed!

"Francis!" Her voice had taken on a reckless note. "I have one beauty that I've always had to hide, to cover up. I've worn the plainest dresses always. They've never even fitted me right. But—I've a very good figure, I think. It's dreadful of me to say that, isn't it? I don't think I care. A good figure is a gift you don't want hidden always."

She was fumbling at the top button of the red wrap with fingers which trembled visibly. When it came undone she stood up and it slipped from her shoulders to the floor. If Frank had felt surprise on first seeing her in such unexpected finery, it was multiplied many times over now. The gown was cut low. Her neck and shoulders, fully exposed to view, had the sloping line which is the very essence of beauty; slender and yet well rounded, and with a whiteness that had a slight touch of ivory. Her arms were molded perfectly. The tight fit of the gown accentuated the line of her breasts and the smallness of her waist before flaring out in a cascade of black lace.

"Do you like me?"

He had risen and moved around to her side of the table. "To disguise such beauty with ugly dresses," he said, "is—well, the only word that occurs to me is sacrilegious. You must never do it again, Laura."

She curtsied, laughing with a nervous catch in her voice. "Thank you, sir. I'm glad you find me worth looking at. You *are* looking at me now. You never did before. Oh, I don't blame you! I knew if you ever did it would be because I made you. That's why I dressed up like this tonight."

"Why did you wait so long?"

She raised one foot off the floor and her fingers caught the folds of the lacy *vacquinha* just above the knee, gathering it up until a few inches of a very slender ankle showed. "I might as well be completely shameless," she whispered, "now that I've gone so far. I'm going to feel mortified and ashamed of myself tomorrow, I suppose, but I'm not now. I'm glad, Francis, glad!"

Frank placed a hand on each of her shoulders. "I can't get over it. You look like a young girl dressed up for her first party."

"I'm only twenty-two."

"You don't look nearly that."

"Perhaps there's still time for me to catch up and enjoy some of the things I've missed."

"There will be plenty of time for that."

They were standing so close together that she had to tilt her head back to look up at him. His hands tightened their grip on her slim shoulders.

"Laura!"

A voice said from the window, "Well, what's going on in here?"

They stepped apart hurriedly. Laura's eyes opened wide with distress and alarm. "Oh dear! Who can it be?" she whispered. Frank saw a long leg swing through the window, then a head with tousled black hair and a broad pair of shoulders in a scarlet coat.

It was Leonard Cardyce. He seated himself on the sill and grinned at them, knowingly and maliciously.

"What am I interrupting? A love scene? Tut, tut, how inconsiderate of me! But this is indeed very revealing. The stern disciplinarian, Mr. Francis Ellery, and the complete model of propriety, Miss Laura Brakespeare!" His eyes took in the clinging black gown and the flush on her cheeks. He whistled. "My dear Laura! What a gratifying surprise. May I present my compliments? As I said once before, I've been very blind where you're concerned, but for the first time I realize the full extent of my blindness."

"It isn't necessary to ask you in, Cardyce, because unfortunately you're in already," said Frank. "We've just finished supper. If you had come sooner, we would have shared with you."

"Supper!" The singer's eyes surveyed the table. "I had no supper myself. Where did you get the food?" He shrugged his shoulders. "That's something to look into later. At this particular moment I'm much more interested in something else. The—the metamorphosis of Laura Brakespeare. It's amazing. I can hardly believe the evidence of my eyes."

Laura had regained her composure. She seated herself on one of the three-legged stools and looked at him coolly.

"You mustn't misunderstand me. My surprise is at my own stupidity, my own abysmal lack of perception. I hasten now to tell you that I think you very lovely. A sentiment"—he turned in Frank's direction—"which the not equally obtuse Mr. Ellery seems to share with me."

"You're quite right," said Frank shortly. "Now that we've agreed on that, let's drop the subject. I'm sure Laura doesn't want us to discuss her any further. I was under the impression, Cardyce, that you were on the night watch."

"I was. I am." The singer waved a hand carelessly. "I shall hasten back to my post in a very few minutes, never fear. I confess I'm growing weary of this perpetual tending of bonfires. You can't have a Guy Fawkes celebration every night and continue to find it exciting. But there won't be any flagging in my efforts because I've dropped in here for a moment of relaxation." He turned away and addressed himself to Laura. "Tomorrow I shall be up at the crack of dawn with a musket under my arm. I'll hope to come back with something worth broiling over one of these blasted fires. If I succeed, may I hope you'll share a supper with me? If our friend Ellery comes breaking in through the window on us with as little ceremony as I've shown"—he looked back over his shoulder and winked—"we'll invite him in with more cordiality than he's showing right now. Of course, we might have less reason for regretting an interruption."

"I won't have you jumping to conclusions, Cardyce——"

"Come, come. Don't be a prig. We're three rational and intelligent people. What if you and Laura have finally come to your senses and decided to be a little more human? I can't help regretting that it was for your benefit, Ellery, that she decided to emerge from her chrysalis, but I'm prepared to forgive you, now that we can all see what a charming little butterfly it is. Such very handsome wings! Should we join hands, Ellery, in a manly resolve that nothing must be allowed to tarnish them?"

"That won't be necessary, Cardyce."

The singer threw back his head and laughed. "But would that be fair to the lady? I'm not a naturalist and know nothing of the habits of butterflies, but I'm quite prepared to believe that, if one of them came to the end of its brief span of life with wings that were as glossy and fine as when it first spread them, it would feel it had been badly cheated. After all, what do they have wings for?"

There was a moment's silence and then Laura said: "I've never been called a butterfly before. Am I supposed to be so pleased with the comparison that I can overlook the implication in what you've said?"

"They're such fine wings. You won't have to flutter them very hard. Ellery here is quite dazzled by them. I can see that."

There was a knock at the door. Frank answered and found that it was Windy Topp in a state of considerable excitement. The servant whispered: "Word from the General, sahib. You're to go at once."

"I'll be right over."

He turned back into the room. "I'm sorry, Laura, but I've received orders to report at once to headquarters. I must leave now."

Cardyce got to his feet. "What confoundedly bad luck, old fellow. First an unwanted third party comes like a burglar through the window, and then orders arrive to drag you away. It's odd it should happen that way to you—on the very first occasion you show signs of knowing that war and romance always go hand in hand. Or is it the first? Well, better luck next time." He looked at Laura. "There will be a next time. I can see that. You mustn't take it too hard. As for me, I'll return now to my role of the humble and damnably overworked hewer of wood. Good night, my dear Laura. Fold the wings away gently. They mustn't be creased or torn, you know. That would be a great tragedy. I'm looking forward to seeing them unfolded again."

He grinned at Frank and walked out into the dark. In a moment they heard him singing as he struck off in the direction of the line of fires, his rich baritone seeming to carry a derisive note as he intoned, "O manly Ben! O manly Ben!"

Laura had walked to the table and was bending over the flowers. She did not look up.

"I'm sorry you must go so soon," she said in a toneless voice. "But we're all subject to orders, aren't we?"

"Yes. I've been expecting this summons. It's very important."

"I'm sure it is. Are you riding?"

"Yes. A long distance. I don't know when we'll get back."

"Is there any danger you won't get back?"

He laughed, trying to make it sound casual. "There's always some danger, of course."

"Good luck, then." She hesitated. "On such a long ride, you'll have plenty of time for thought. Please don't think too badly of me."

"I couldn't have anything but the pleasantest thoughts tonight."

She turned suddenly and almost ran across the room. "Francis," she whispered. "Must you go? Must you really go? It can never be this way again if you do. I won't have the courage, or the lack of shame, a second time. Stay with me!"

There was silence in the room for several moments. Frank was thinking, "Why not? I may be killed tonight. And half an hour here won't make me too late. It might have taken Topp that much longer to find me."

He reached out and extinguished the candle.

5

A FARMHOUSE, hiding in a clump of tall cork-oak trees as though it knew a war was on, served as Wilson's headquarters. It was too small to accommodate all the officers, and so tents had been pitched in the yard. One of the trees had been disemboweled to serve as a fireplace and a blaze was going in it when Frank arrived, like the fiery furnace that Babylonish idolaters kept simmering in the belly of Melkarth. They were cooking some scraps of food.

The heat was still so great that he lifted a wad of fresh leaves, which he kept in his saddlebags, and wiped the perspiration from his face. He must have used up a bushel of them, he figured, during the course of the day.

Wilson was superintending the muffling of the horses' hoofs, and seeing to it that plenty of straw and burlap was wrapped over the cork tips. "Not a scrap of breeze!" he said irritably. "Ten o'clock, and you still feel as though you were sitting in the door of a furnace. A devilish climate, Frank." He straightened up and glanced to the north. "It will be better later. Some of the men swear we'll run into rain up in the hills. You'll be surprised how cold it can get then. Norris! Fetch me one of the bottles hanging from the kitchen rafters. The kind with the long neck and leather strap. Step lively."

When the bottle had been delivered he handed it to Frank with instructions to tie it to his belt. "You'll be soaked to the skin if we run into rain. That stuff will help to keep you warm. Get back into your saddle. I'm ready to start."

"I'm going to see Riding Bobby in action," thought Frank exultantly as he swung himself up.

A brisk canter brought them to the remnants of a stone bridge which had been made passable by stringing planks across the broken piers. The wood swayed and teetered as they passed over but there was not a sound. The silence which enveloped them was uncanny, in fact; complete, save for the occasional snort of a horse and the light jingle of spurs and leather. It was almost as though they rode on air.

They struck off to the north through a clump of stunted trees, emerging on a flat plain over which the road twisted and turned in a seemingly aimless way. Flashes of lightning lighted up the sky at intervals, revealing an occasional tree and the skeletons of burned farmhouses. There was no doubt about it now; they were in for a downpour; but the heat in the meantime remained as oppressive as ever.

Frank found to his surprise that the rider on his right was Daniel Norris. He leaned sideways to say, "So you volunteered for it, Dan."

The ex-footman, who was bouncing inexpertly in the saddle, nodded his head with despondent assent. "The General was looking at me, sir," he answered. "I felt it incumbent on me to step forward. I didn't want to. I didn't indeed, sir."

The Portuguese on the other side muttered, "Con liçenca, senhors, it is not to talk."

The rain began when they reached the hill country. It came down in sheets and in a few minutes they were all soaked to the skin. Frank found to his surprise that he was shivering, although he would have laughed at such a possibility a quarter of an hour before. He became so thoroughly chilled, in fact, that he fumbled at his belt for the long-necked bottle and drew it up to his mouth. He had no idea what it contained but certainly it was potent stuff. It seemed to explode in his throat and strike in both directions at once, to the top of his head and the very ends of his toes. He gasped and strangled, but it did him good. A warm and comfortable glow took possession of him.

They rode for four hours, Wilson and a guide in the lead. The violence went out of the storm but enough rain continued to fall to keep them in a state of chill. The roads had become soft, making it impossible for them to live up to their schedule. In spite of the relief he obtained from the bottle, Frank became stiff and numb and he was delighted to pull in when the order to halt came to them from up front.

They had reached a crossroad between banks of clay which showed reddish when one of the party struck an exploring light. An incessant screeching filled the air. The sound came from the branch leading off to the north. No one who had ever heard it before could be in any doubt. Bullock carts, a great many of them. The provision train was approaching.

Frank had picked up enough Portuguese to understand when Wilson ordered the troop to take cover in a bit of woods ahead. Under no circumstances were they to let any of the French escort escape. Their fire must be withheld until the whole of the train had come within range.

One Frenchman got away, however. The volley of musket shots which shattered the air as soon as the long string of creaking carts had lumbered into the ambush bowled the blue-tunicked cavalrymen over like skittles, but by some chance the officer riding in the lead remained in his saddle. He shouted a frenzied order; then, sensing that no defense was possible, dug spurs into the flanks of his horse and galloped off. Torches had been lighted when the firing began, which enabled them to see him weaving in his saddle and urging his mount on, but none of the shots fired after him had any effect. He vanished down the road with a furious clatter of hoofs.

The escape of the officer made a change of plan necessary. Wilson decided that a small squad would guard the carts and swing well off to the right in the hope of getting to the river. The rest would cut back closer to the French positions than had been intended in order to divert enemy attention.

He was shaking his head when he rode over to where Frank was standing. "One chance in a hundred," he said. "We'll probably be cut to pieces. Ever ride to hounds? Well, you'll know how the fox feels about it now. We'll have the whole pack down on us. Where do you want to go—with the carts or with me? Plenty of danger both ways."

"With you."

The rain had stopped and the stars were out, but the air was raw and cold and Frank found it necessary to have frequent recourse to the bottle. He rode almost thigh to thigh with Sir Robert. He wanted to talk, to ask questions, but the profile of the leader was fixed straight ahead and the only remark he made in half an hour was, "It's going to be Willing-and-Catchit all over again." Talk was almost out of the question in any event, for the muffling had worn through and the beat of the hoofs was like the roll of kettledrums. Wilson finally spurred ahead to the rise of a steep grade for a quick survey, and continued in the lead from that time on.

The first shafts of dawn were lighting up the sky behind them as they rode down the trail. Frank tilted up the bottle and took a full drink, rather proud of his ability to swallow the stuff without strangling. A Legionnaire grinned at him and said, *"Bom! Bom!"*

He was not at all cold now, but he was having some difficulty with his thoughts. They kept wandering off to entirely irrelevant matters, without purpose or pattern. A picture formed in his mind of the foul-smelling prison, a disjointed picture which skipped from one thing to another. "The mosher and the burn-crust," he said aloud, laughing for no reason at all. "Now what is a mosher?"

"I'm sure I don't know, sir," said Norris, who was riding beside him again.

"Neither do I. That's strange because I was in prison for a month. Did you know I was in prison, Dan?"

"No sir, I didn't. I find it hard to believe, sir."

"I printed something His Majesty didn't like. Do you know I publish a newspaper in London?"

"Yes sir."

"It's funny I never found out what a mosher is. He isn't a bulk or a file. And he can't be a zad either. I don't know what any of them are, now that I come to think of it. Do you, Dan?"

"I think, sir, you're a bit bosky. In other words, sir, h'intoxicated."

Frank laughed. That was it, of course. That was why he had no control over his thoughts. The gullet-warming stuff in the bottle had gone to his head. He grasped the glass neck in his hand and shook it. Empty! He laughed again and threw the bottle to one side of the road.

"Three cheers for Riding Bobby and the Loyal Lusitanian Legion!" he shouted.

In half an hour's time they came out over the crest of a hill, and the sun, striking gratefully warm on their shoulders, showed them a broad plain with a small lake far to the left. On the other side of the water they could see tents, a great tangle of them, stretching for a full mile with flags fluttering in the air. "Johnny Craps, sir," said Norris, with a catch in his voice.

This was no phantom camp like the one Frank had been keeping up on the far side of the river. It buzzed with activity, and the faint sound of a bugle came to them from across the lake. Wilson reined in and studied the plain below with great care.

"They're waiting for us," he said. "Down there, on the far edge of the mesa with the palm trees. It looks like a full squadron. Well, we'll give them a tussle. Forward! Trot!"

Frank's mind cleared. The effect of the liquor seemed to have vanished, for he found that his eye was steady enough now to study the terrain ahead and that his thoughts were functioning clearly. He estimated that there were at least fifty cuirassiers waiting to pounce on them beyond the fringe of palms, the sun shining on their burnished breastplates and plumed helmets. It would indeed be a tussle. He looked back at the sun, conscious of the fact that it might be his last glimpse of it. "Gabrielle, Gabrielle," he said to himself, "why didn't I have the courage to tell you how much I love you!"

Wilson was issuing orders in staccato Portuguese. The plain below them was flat and they were to deploy to the right. He did not want to give the French the advantage of the downward slope from the mesa, preferring them out on the open where they could be met on even terms. When they came down, the troop was to swing left into line and charge.

That was how it came about. Frank saw a mass of tossing gray manes and blue tunics come over the crest. It amazed him that he was able at such a moment to observe details; but he picked out an officer in the lead with a sword extended above his head, even noting his *ventre de biche* facings and the trimming of gold and red on his shiny black shoes. He tugged at the bridle. It was not necessary, for his well-trained charger swung into line of its own accord. "My good José," he said, patting its neck.

"Easy, easy!" shouted Wilson in English. Then, realizing his mistake, he gave the order in Portuguese. They were to hold in until the enemy came closer.

A bugle sounded and Frank's knees slipped as the horse under him responded with a bound. "Brave José, brave José!" he cried, grasping tighter on the bridle and swinging the point of his lance to the level.

They were riding now at top speed, the plunging hoofs sounding like the roar of thunder. Norris at his left was tugging desperately at the reins, his face distorted, his lips moving, perhaps in prayer. Frank laughed aloud. He was not afraid. Wilson had been right; it was easy to charge with one's comrades, the bugles sounding, the air whistling past, and the enemy just ahead!

The Legion were shouting and singing as they rode. Frank joined in, although he knew neither the words nor the air. His knees had taken firm hold again on his horse's flanks.

The tossing gray plumes drew closer. Frank was in the front file and it seemed no more than a second before the two waves of screaming horses came together. The *ventre de biche* facings were straight ahead of him, and he caught the gleam of distended eyes in a white face. His lance arm moved and the face seemed to crumple and vanish in a mist of red. The gray horse reared and went down, José plunging forward with a jolt. Frank was conscious of a sickening sound beneath him, a crunch and a wild scream of mortal pain.

"Oh, God!" he thought. "I've killed him!"

There was no time for feelings of remorse. Swords were flashing in the air, faces came and went under steel and plume, horses fell and kicked in wild terror. Then, miraculously, he was in the open.

Norris was still beside him. He had lost both stirrups and was clinging desperately to his horse's neck. Tears were streaming down his face. Frank's momentary mood of exultation left him. He had killed a man back there in a horrible way, perhaps more than one. He could not remember anything clearly after the first clash.

His descent in mood became complete when the ex-footman stammered in a breathless voice, "You—you—you certainly sent that—that officer arsy-varsy, sir!"

It seemed incredible but it was all over. The French had had the worst of it. Frank saw gray horses galloping away in confusion, many of them riderless. Wilson and a few green-coated riders were in hot pursuit. He looked back over his shoulder and then jerked his head back sharply. What had happened at the point of impact was not pleasant to see!

In a very few minutes Wilson came riding back and threw an arm around his shoulder. "Thank God, you're safe," he said. "I saw you out of the corner of my eye. You had to pick on their leader, my bold warrior! Good fellow, good fellow! Old England forever, Frank! We gave them a taste of cold steel and, by Gad, they didn't like it." He was in an excited mood but he quieted down quickly and watched the fleeing Frenchmen with a questioning eye. "God damn it, this has been much too easy. There's a trick in it. They wouldn't depend on such a handful for this business."

It seemed, at first, that he was wrong. The French were definitely through. They vanished over the crest of the mesa, leaving their dead and wounded behind. The steep slope of land on the other side of the Yeltes was in plain view, not more than five miles away; all the victorious Legion had to do was to ride west and they were in the clear.

Wilson continued to shake his head and mutter, "I don't like it, I don't like it at all."

Norris, who had not yet passed the blubbering stage, said suddenly, "Great gripe seed, Mr. Ellery, you—you got a stoter after all!"

Frank became conscious for the first time of a pain in one cheek. The hand he touched to it was smeared with red when he drew it away.

"You—you caught it good, sir," stuttered Norris. "Your cheek's laid right open. A sword cut, sir."

Wilson swung his horse around. "You have, by Jove! A bad cut, Frank. You've lost a lot of blood. Norris, bind it up. There's linen bandaging in your saddlebag, in case you don't know it." He was frowning seriously. "A sharp bit of business while it lasted. I've lost quite a few of my poor fellows."

Now that the first excitement was over, Frank was feeling the pain intensely. He winced as Norris pawed at his face with unsteady fingers, thinking with dismal foreboding that a scar across his face would be another handicap to carry through life. Would it be one of those horrible whitish welts from which people turned in repugnance?

"I've got it!" exclaimed Wilson suddenly. "They expected our whole party would go along with the train. They'll be out in force now, back of us. These fellows were posted to catch any stragglers who might attempt to come straight through. Well, that means I'll have to double back and catch them at it."

"Will there be time?" asked Frank.

"It will depend on our cattle. This stout fellow of mine is good for another hard run, but I'm afraid most of them are winded. The worst of it is that I won't have more than fifteen sabers now."

The fumbling fingers of Norris were winding the bandage around Frank's neck. When he was able to speak, Frank said: "The odds will be pretty stiff, Sir Robert. I hope you're counting on me."

Wilson answered sharply: "I am not. You're going back with the rest of the wounded and there's no use arguing about it. It's an order this time. You too, Norris. You sit a horse with all the grace and skill of a country gammer taking a basket of turnips to market. I shouldn't have brought you, but you volunteered, and you're English, and so I picked you out. Don't think I'm not proud of you, man. I am. It was a sporting thing for you to do. But you're not up to the riding we have ahead of us now." He shook his head. "I wouldn't try it at all, but we need the supplies in the most devilish bad way."

Six of them rode back to camp together, a sorry, white-faced lot with bandaged heads, and arms in hastily adjusted slings. One man, who had received a lance point in the side of his neck, lay across the back of his horse inertly, his breath coming in a retching wheeze. They rode slowly, keeping apprehensive eyes over their shoulders for signs of pursuit. The pain in his face was so great that Frank had to clamp his teeth together to keep from crying out with it. Norris rode beside him and whispered with great gusto: "Did you hear the General say he was proud of me, sir? That's something to remember, that is."

Wilson came in to see Frank late that evening, nearly stumbling over Windy Topp, who had been sitting in the doorway for hours, watching his master with worried eyes. The heat was more intense than ever and the air was stifling under the sloping roof of the farmhouse attic. The single candle did little to light the room, and Wilson tripped a second time over a knapsack on the floor.

"Well, we managed it," he said, dropping into a dilapidated chair with a sigh of complete weariness. He picked a bloodstained towel from the side of the bed and used a corner of it to wipe the beads of perspiration from his forehead. "We caught up with the beggars just in time. They were a surprised lot when we pounded down on them. We shook them up enough to let the carts get safely away. My poor old Nolly was killed and I finished things on a French horse we caught. A mean, black brute. Twenty-four hours in the saddle, Frank! I don't mind confessing that I'm completely knocked out." He drew a hand wearily over his eyes. "Only five of us got back. They fought like paladins, my brave Porties. Still, the carts are coming down now on our side of the river. There will be food in the morning here and none on the other side. I suppose it was worth it."

"I killed a man," mumbled Frank. "My lance drove right into his face! I can't get the thought of it out of my mind. He was very young, I think. And brave too. I keep seeing him as he went down."

"I felt the same way the first time. Get it out of your mind, Frank. He's dead and done for now, and wishing won't bring him back. Perhaps he's better off as it is. It's easier to go that way than nailed to a tree. I've seen what happens to French officers when these peasants catch them."

He looked at the clay crucifix on the whitewashed wall above the bed, and the drops on the figure painted red to simulate blood. "They forget they're Christians when they get their hands on them."

The wound in his cheek was throbbing so fiercely that Frank lost all track of what was being said. The slightest move sent excruciating flashes of pain through every part of his body. His head felt hot. He wanted a drink but could not force his lips to the task of asking for it.

"You've had your baptism of fire," Wilson went on. "The surgeon tells me the cut is a clean one and he doesn't think the scar will be bad. Just a token of valor to carry through life. The finest kind of medal, old boy. The French gal will be proud of you."

Frank caught enough of this to feel a momentary sense of relief. Then his mind began to wander again. He was barely conscious of movement in the room when the General got to his feet and closed the door. He did not hear Wilson come back, his feet dragging heavily on the straw matting.

"I'm sending your lot off in the morning," whispered Wilson. "All the women, at least. There will be carts for them and enough food to see them to the coast. The men will follow on foot a little later." Frank roused at this, realizing that something important had happened. "We took a prisoner who let a few words slip. Lapisse is going to move at last. He'll come smashing through on us now. We'll hold him off as well as we can but—you can figure yourself how little we'll be able to do."

Frank forced his sick and whirling mind to anchor on this startling piece of information. He managed to ask, "Any . . . word . . . yet . . . of Sir Arthur?"

Wilson shook his head soberly. "None yet. I was getting too confident. Sure I could hang on here until he landed, especially after the drubbing we gave them last night. But our bluff seems to have worn thin. Well"— with a deep sigh—"you had better get some sleep now. You must have enough strength to get out of here when the blow comes. It may be any day."

On the way to the door the General turned back with a smile. "You said something about this little scrap being a test. Are you satisfied with yourself now?"

Frank did not hear him. His mind had lost its anchorage completely. He was back in the sham camp on the bluffs. "Butterfly wings," he thought; he hoped they would not be damaged in the packing. Then he seemed to be in the prison, with Harry All-of-a-Sweat talking in a jargon of outlandish words. No, it was Norris, after all. What had he been saying to him? Something . . . something. It was agony to move his jaws but he muttered, "Said the mosher to the burn-crust . . ."

6

FRANK RODE ALONG the crest of a ridge from which he could see, by turning his head, an advancing blue line not more than a mile behind.

"The French are getting close," he called to Topp.

"Yes, sahib. Too close for my fancy. They'll be giving us a good polt in the rear if we don't move faster."

A green-jacketed horseman rode by and shouted something to them. Frank could not make out what it was but judged it an admonition to hurry. A brisk rattle of musketry behind them added weight to the suggestion.

"Sir Robert is handling the retreat beautifully," he said.

Topp nodded. "A neat bit o' work as retreats goes. I've been in several in my day and this un takes the haddock. The trouble is I ain't one as cares much for retreats by way o' pref'rence. It's all running, with nothin' in yer belly, and bullets kicking up the dust under yer heels, and the Old Poger takin' the hindmost. Retreats ain't like a picnic at Vauxhall, sahib."

"As an old soldier, you must admire how well it's being done," persisted his master. "You might think we had five times as many men. I'm sure the French still believe we have."

"Yes, sahib, but I'm a old sojer as has a'quired a liking for comfort and a whole skin."

"They could brush us off like crumbs if they knew how weak we are."

"Crumbs!" It was a bitter point apparently. "I ain't had a bite since this magnif'sent retreat started."

When they caught up with their own party, Frank found everyone still filled with the admirable spirit which had taken hold of them as soon as real danger threatened. The bickering and complaining had stopped immediately. There had been nothing but praise for Wilson when he permitted them to remain longer at the front, and the only difficulty had been in forcing them to drop back in accordance with orders.

Mr. Birdsease called to him briskly: "Haven't we done enough running, Frank? We all have muskets, you know. Why can't we lay by in that clump of trees ahead and take a few shots at 'em when they come up?"

The rattle of musketry behind them seemed much closer. "We have

our orders, Harry. We're to get back to Ciudad Rodrigo as fast as we
can."

"I ain't been within a mile of a Frenchy the whole time," said a protesting voice.

"And lucky ye'll be, my fine *put*, if ye never see one any closer," said
Topp in an undertone.

"Sir Robert doesn't want the French taking any prisoners," declared
Frank. "They might get the truth out of them about our real strength
and then they would smash right on through us. We can't have that
happen." He looked anxiously along the line. "Where's Mr. Green?"

There was silence for a moment and then someone said, "He's gone by
this time."

"Gone! You mean——"

"It was this way, Frank," said the wine merchant. "Poor little Green
was so bad with the rheumatism he knew he could never make it anyway. When we saw the Porties hadn't waited to carry out the General's
orders about blowing up the west bridge, he said he might as well stay
and make himself useful. He carried the charges of powder himself under the bridge."

"You might add, Harry, that you were going to stay with him if the
rest of us hadn't insisted you come along," put in another voice.

"I didn't like to think of him there all by himself. But the rest of you
were right about it. No sense in unnecessary loss of life when every pair
of hands counts."

Frank said in worried tones, "Then he's been captured."

The wine merchant shook his head. "He hasn't been taken. He intended to stay *under* the bridge."

Frank thought with deep contrition of little Tobias Green, of Brighton, the last one he would have thought capable of such a sacrifice, giving his life that the French might be held up for a few hours longer.
Why had he kept his condition a secret until after the carts with the
women had left? A place could have been found for him. He felt bitterly
conscious of the fact that he had been in the saddle all day, although
there could be no possible blame in that. He had been serving as aide-de-
camp, carrying orders along the thin retreating line of the Legion, under
fire a good part of the time. Topp, also mounted, had been set to the
task of expediting the departure of the commissary carts. Neither horse
could have been spared for any other purpose. Frank was certain they
all understood this, and yet he felt in some way responsible for the death
of the little man.

It went deeper than that with him. How self-satisfied he had been

because of his part in the cavalry charge! Courage? All men had courage
when it came to the test. Tobias Green, of Brighton, had proved that.

To relieve the tension the wine merchant said, "You look like a bloody
pirate, Frank, with that black beard and your cheek in a bandage."

Frank dismounted. "If you could see yourself, you wouldn't be making remarks about my appearance. Who's most in need of a lift? Topp
and I have been in the saddle all day and it will be a relief to get on
our feet for a change."

Topp was off his horse also. "Only thing I needs more than a good
meal is a five-mile tramp," he said cheerfully.

There was quite an argument, but finally two of the older men were
helped into the saddles, one of them being Dr. Perkins. The *vihuela*
was still strapped over his shoulder and, on the urging of his comrades,
he struck up:

> *"None of your gammon, this is your job!*
> *So get along, hop along, jog along, Bob!"*

The whole company joined in the chorus, shouting, "Jog along, Bob,"
at the top of their voices, almost drowning out the sound of the guns
from the rear. Frank looked at them in wonder. They were soaked with
perspiration and the dust had stuck to their faces and necks and hands.
They were dirty, tired, hungry, but for the moment none of this showed
in their eyes. Courage, certainly, was not a quality which any one man
need pride himself on possessing!

Sir Robert was surrounded by his staff on the citadel ramparts when
Frank put in an appearance there next morning. He nodded and waved
a gloomy hand toward the east.

"They've gone," he said. "Decamped in the night."

"The French?"

"Johnny Craps himself. Lapisse took a leaf from my book. His drive
on the city was a feint. It's clear enough what he's up to. He still thinks
we're too strong for him here and he came on only to force me into
drawing back my right flank. That left the pass open. Now he's on his
way south. He'll get into Portugal at Alcántara."

It was warm already. The officers, standing about in uneasy groups,
were showing the effects. Some of them had discarded their tunics and
all had packed leaves under their headgear. Without exception they
were in tatters and they looked thoroughly worn out from the incessant
activity of the past three months.

"Gentlemen," said Wilson suddenly, "I'm marching at once. I realize you've been under heavy pressure and that you're pretty well near the end of your powers of endurance. Any of you who prefer to remain behind may do so. Call out your companies and explain the situation to the men. I want none but volunteers."

They came in sight of Alcántara four days later. A noon sun was blazing down on them from a sky without a single fleck of cloud. To Frank it was as though a hammer were beating continuously on the top of his head. Sir Robert Wilson reined up when the town came into full view and shook his head despondently.

"Not a sign of them," he said. "That means they've found out how little strength I have. They haven't thought it necessary to post a rear guard. By this time they're over the border with the valley of the Tagus wide open before them."

His green tunic had been cut from his back the day before in a sharp clash with a French cavalry patrol and he had donned in its place a jacket taken from a prisoner. It was royal blue with the remnants of a lapel which had once sported trimmings of yellow, red, and gold. On his head he was wearing a wide-brimmed peasant's hat with a fusilier's white cord around it. Most of the Legion were attired in similar make-shifts by this time. Some even were naked to the waist, their skins browned by the fierce sun to the shade of ebony. There was not a whole pair of boots in the lot.

Wilson shaded his eyes and gazed at the huddle of red and white roofs ahead. "We've failed," he said sadly. "There's no chance left. Victor will move in and Soult will strike south." Frank was surprised to see that he was blinking his eyes rapidly to keep back the tears. "I did my best. I held them back. Three months. Think of it, Frank. A long time to check three armies on a sheer bluff. But not long enough. They'll have Lisbon now in three weeks." He drew a deep sigh. "If it had worked, it would have been one of the greatest feats in military history. But it didn't work. They'll say at the Horse Guards it was just another of Wilson's wild schemes. I don't care about that; not now, at least. I'm thinking of what Boney will do next. He has the whole Peninsula in his hands."

The march down to Alcántara had been a depressing experience. The French had been in a savage mood and had left a trail of smoking villages behind them. The bodies of hanged peasants had dangled from trees by the side of the road. They had even found one corpse, that of a white-haired old man, nailed to the door of a barn. It was not until they rode into the environs of the town, however, that they sensed the full measure of Napoleonic reprisal. Wilson pointed to black wooden crosses which they found planted in front of houses, at street corners, in gardens and fields.

"The butchers have been at work," he said. "These people always put up crosses to mark the scene of tragedies. Look at them! I can see at least a score from here. The French have killed every man they could lay hands on. The worst of it is that the town seems to have made no attempt at defense. This has been sheer, wanton killing." He leaned from his saddle and gripped Frank's arm. "The people of England must know of this. Tell everything you see. Don't leave out a single detail. They must be made to realize at home what may be in store for them."

The black crosses were everywhere. There were two in one field with a wide ditch between, which had been carelessly spaded over; so carelessly, in fact, that arms and legs stuck out above the earth in places. Here, clearly, a file of prisoners had been lined up and shot; thirty of them, at the lowest reckoning. A huge cross stood in front of a church which had been wrecked by cannon fire. All shops were empty and the streets were deserted. Occasionally a white face gazed fearfully from behind window blinds, but no one ventured out to meet them.

The Legion halted in an open square. Sitting down in whispering groups on the cobbled stones of the square, they munched at the bits of food still left in their saddlebags and looked about at the dismal closed houses. Frank heard them expressing grave fears over the plight of their own people now that three French armies were to be loosed on them. There would be scenes to equal this all the way down the valley.

A fire was lighted in the square and coffee was handed around. In spite of the grief which lay so heavy on the town, people were beginning to gather: men in the inevitable sugar-loaf hats and circular cloaks; women with mantillas wrapped over their heads so that no more than one eye showed; children clamoring to get near the blaze and asking shrill questions. Food had been produced from somewhere and chaffering was going on. One woman came leading by the hand a plump daughter in a lace-fringed *vacquinha*. Life had returned to normal for the moment.

Wilson came out on the balcony of a house overlooking the square and shouted, "Ellery!" As he made his way through the knots of people standing about and staring up at the tall leader of the Legion, Frank heard them whispering excitedly about the great *Don Bobby* and the feats he had been performing. Apparently a Wilson legend was beginning to grow up along the border.

The leader met Frank at the head of the stairs, holding a massive candle above his head. His eyes had a new glow in them.

"Frank!" he exclaimed. "An outrider has just come in from Lisbon. He managed to get around Lapisse's flank and he's brought us the most wonderful news. What do you suppose it is? One guess, my doughty Francis, no more than one. I see by your face you have it right. Yes, Wellesley is in Lisbon! His army has landed!" He tossed the candle in the air and caught it again, causing strange beams of light to flash along the dark walls. "Frank, the day is saved! Portugal is saved! England is saved!"

They walked into the room at the head of the stairs, a long apartment with a monstrous bed and the portrait of a Spanish king on one wall. The French had been using it as their headquarters, quite obviously. A map was spread out on the table, pegged down at the corners and with a multitude of pins stuck in it to mark strategic points. On leaving, the invaders had fired a salvo of pistol shots into the once fine chandelier hanging above the table, and the broken crystal was distributed all over the room. An officer's helmet and a pair of tall boots had been left in one corner.

"I'm so happy I can hardly speak," said Wilson, beginning to pace about the room. "I feel lifted right up to the heights. The turn has come in the tide at last. Boney is toppling on his throne." He waved an exultant hand at the map. "We'll be rolling up the new maps now, my boy. Boney's Europe will soon be a thing of the past and we'll have the old one back. The old maps and the old boundaries. And peace again, peace and prosperity and glory for all of us!" He came over and clapped Frank on the back. "I wanted to tell you first, my fine right-hand man. You're the best soldier I have, my fighting scribbler. And now that you've heard, I must announce it to the rest of them. Now my men will thank their stars and their saints they came along to see the end of it!"

He strode out on the balcony again and shouted the great news to the thronged square. At first there was a moment of silence and then the men of the Legion sent up a lusty cheer. The townspeople joined in, crying, "Viva, Inglez! Bravissimo!" An English voice piped up, "Three of the best for Riding Bobby!" A thunder of cheers followed.

Frank went out and stood behind Wilson, quite unaware that tears were streaming down his face. He saw that the square was jammed with people now, a sea of excited faces straining up at them from the dark, arms waving, hats flying in the air.

Intoxicated with excitement and success, Wilson turned to him and shouted above the din: "A moment for the history book, Frank. Here we are, all that's left of the little brigade that checkmated the armies of Bonaparte!" His gingery hair seemed to be standing on end. He glanced down at his nondescript costume and laughed wildly. "A lot of scarecrows who did a great thing out there along the Yeltes. Tell them about it in England, Frank. Lay it on good and strong. We deserve it, by God, for we made history!"

Wood was being brought in armfuls by the exultant crowd and piled on the fire. The flames were soon shooting up above the level of the balcony. The heat was stifling but no one seemed to notice it. "Liberty! Liberty! Death to the French!" they were shouting. Some of the townspeople began to sing a national anthem, the men removing their wide hats, the women pulling off their mantillas and waving them frantically in the air.

"Take a good look at 'im!" Frank recognized Topp's voice. "He's the one as made it possible. Riding Bobby Wilson!"

After a few minutes the two men went back into the room. Wilson seated himself at the table. His mood had changed and he looked at Frank with a sober face.

"Sit down," he said. "I've something more to tell you."

Frank seated himself, wondering what it could be. He studied his companion's face, noting its gravity and intentness. There was a moment of silence.

"My boy," said Wilson, "the rest of the news is not good. I've been ordered to turn the command over to Colonel Mayne and report to headquarters."

"My God, Sir Robert! What can that mean?"

"Oh, it's not hard to understand. The order comes from Beresford, who's commanding all the Portuguese forces. He never liked me and he insists on running everything his own way. I may be cashiered for staying on against orders." His voice began to rise. "I don't care what they do! No one else would have dared do what I've done here. No one else could have carried it through. They can't take that away from me. Be damned to them!"

7

FRANK'S STAY in Lisbon was a short one. He was standing in Roly-Poly Square when he heard a cool English voice say behind him: "Mr. Ellery! I don't think I can be mistaken, sir. I was going to send for you, and now, by Gad, we can both save ourselves some trouble."

It was Sir Arthur Wellesley. He had emerged from the side entrance of a large marble building, followed by a number of staff officers. The commander of the British forces was in the plainest kind of uniform, but his attendants, many of them conspicuously young, balanced the scale by their befrogged and lacquer-booted and purplish-whiskered splendor.

Frank said, "Good morning, sir," and waited for whatever the gleam in the cold blue eye portended.

"I recall, sir," said Wellesley, "that when I saw you after Vimeiro—which was the first intimation I had of your presence in the country—I gave you instructions to leave at once. It seems, Mr. Ellery, that you saw fit to disregard my order. I'm going to see to it that you obey me this time. There's a ship sailing for England this evening. You will pack up your belongings and sail on her, sir."

Frank began a vigorous protest. "I'm serving the public here, Sir Arthur. I'm keeping people informed of the progress of the campaign. I'm sure there's been nothing in my articles to which objection could be taken from a military standpoint."

The commander indulged in a bleak trace of a smile. "I can see no reason, sir, why the public should be informed of what is happening here. The members of His Majesty's Government will receive reports from me, sir, and will give out such information as they see fit. I deny the need for any other form of enlightenment."

"But other newspapers may be sending correspondents out, Sir Arthur. The London *Times* had a man at Corunna during the whole of the last campaign."

"I am aware of that fact. I read the articles by Mr. Henry Crabb Robinson. I've also read yours, sir. I don't mind telling you I found them —hah—quite interesting and informative. But there's a real danger in this sort of thing and I've no intention of permitting it to continue."

"But, Sir Arthur——"

Wellesley turned his back on him. He looked over the group of staff officers. "Mr. Brinker! Step forward, if you please." There was no response, and he repeated in a sharp tone, "Mr. Brinker, sir, didn't you hear me?"

A small and blond young man, on whom he had fixed his eye, said in a hesitating tone, "If you mean me, sir, my name isn't Brinker."

"Not Brinker? Then what in thunder is it?"

"Gubbins, sir."

"Gubbins! I could have sworn—still, I suppose you *do* know your own name. Now, sir, I want you to give Mr. Ellery the benefit of your company today. You're not to let him out of your sight until the ship sails and you can swear he was safely aboard. Do you understand that, sir?"

"Yes, Sir Arthur."

The commander turned his attention back to Frank. "I'm sorry it's necessary to take such steps, Mr. Ellery. But you gave me the slip once and I've no intention of letting it happen again. I trust you'll have a pleasant voyage home, sir."

When the rest had moved on, the young officer looked at Frank with a scarlet face. "I must say! Actually now! I'm a soldier, not a damned tipstaff. He blawdy well has no right to do this."

Frank was in a mood of indignation to match that of the angry Mr. Gubbins but it was directed at himself. Why had he not stood up to the General and disputed the authority by which he had been ordered to leave? His tendency to knuckle under in such circumstances was a constant gall to his pride.

"I object to this as much as you do," he said.

Gubbins nodded. "I'm not blaming you. It's the—the blasted insolence of it. Gad, sir, I—I—'Mr. Brinker!' Actually now! All the fellows will hear about this, and I wouldn't be surprised if they began calling me that, damn them! How did he ever get such a silly name in his head? I must say!"

"He's a bit arbitrary, I judge."

The officer looked ready to air his opinions on that point in no uncertain terms. He thought better of it for, after a moment's silence, he said in a less aggrieved tone: "Well, there's this to be said for it, by Gad. I won't have to tag at his blasted heels all day long. You wouldn't believe, Mr. Ellery, how many places he can visit in a single day and how many beastly things he can think up for us to do." He mopped his face with a limp handkerchief. "I'm drenched. Gad, what a climate! What a beastly city! Did you ever smell anything like it?"

Frank was turning the matter over in his mind. He was more than half convinced that he could not help himself by lodging a formal protest. On the other hand, he could return to London and send one of the staff back to carry on the work. If proper precautions were taken, the identity of the new correspondent might be kept from Wellesley long enough to secure for the *Tablet* the benefit of news of the whole summer campaign. Much as he disliked the idea of giving in, he could see the good sense of the other course. He was beginning to realize also that it would be pleasant to get home. He had been in the field for the better part of a year and was thoroughly tired out. Above everything else, he wanted to see Gabrielle.

He called to Topp: "Get our things together, Windy. We're sailing tonight."

Topp came forward with mouth hanging open. "Going home, sahib? To Frog-and-Toe? This calls for a bit o' gig,* this does! I'll have the packing done and be back, sahib, in less than no time at all."

They spent the rest of the day on a balcony of the hotel with a bottle in front of them.

Gubbins smacked his lips over the wine. "*Vinho de termo*," he said. "Tuppence a bottle. Actually, tuppence. One thing we can say for the beggars. They have wines." His small, inquisitive eyes squinted at Frank with sudden interest. "See here, Ellery, don't tell me you were with Riding Bobby all through this business?"

"I saw the last month of it."

"Gad, now, really! Get that tidy gash there? Lucky dog, hope I get the same. Proof of service. Your looks not hurt at all. Gad, Ellery, real soldiering that! Whole army's buzzing with it. Even Sir Arthur said it was capital thing. Beresford's sour about it, though. Says Wilson disobeyed orders. Orders be damned, I say."

"An unpleasant fellow, Beresford."

"Soldier, though. Lost an eye and has a face as round as your blind cupid. Snaps at you when you deliver him dispatches. Going to make trouble for Riding Bobby."

"If he does, I'll make trouble for him!" declared Frank heatedly. "I'll see to it that the truth is told in the press at home. Wilson has done a tremendous thing. Only those who were with him can know how great he was through it all. One thing that reconciles me to going home is that I'll have a chance to tell the whole world about it."

*A spree.

BOOK III

England, Again

THE COUNTRYSIDE had never been so green, so abundantly clothed with the flowers of early summer, so satisfying to eye and soul as when Frank rode out to the Towers. He was in a happy mood to begin with. Spending the previous evening in the offices of the *Tablet*, he had been delighted with the bustle which pervaded the place, the racking hum of busy presses, the upward slant to the lines on the circulation charts, the figures which Evans had laid before him. There had been a satisfying hour of talk with Cope. The latter, who had gone country-squirish in dress, had nearly jumped out of his red-tasseled Hessian boots when he first set eyes on his prodigal proprietor. His mild face had beamed as he told of the warm reception now given to the *Tab* newsmen when they tooted their horns in the streets of London.

All the servants were in the great hall and the demonstration was so warm and loud that Mrs. Easty had to say, "Ssh! You'll disturb the mistruss."

"Where is Mrs. Ellery?" asked Frank, after shaking hands all around.

"In her room, Mr. Francis. She hasn't been at all well, sir, but she wants you to go up at once."

In spite of this adverse report, he found his mother looking quite well. She was propped up with pillows and was wearing a bed jacket of a most becoming blue, while her French maid, Paulette, brushed out her hair. A footman was searching under a table for some mislaid article, and a sustained snuffle indicated that the favorite poodle was somewhere in the room.

"Francis!" exclaimed Mrs. Ellery, smiling at him affectionately. "Come here and kiss me, sir. I'm so happy to have my fine son home again."

Wondering a little at this reception, which differed so vastly in mood from their parting scene, Frank walked to the side of the bed and kissed the cool cheek she turned to him. The footman emerged triumphantly with a spool of silk thread and was dismissed with a wave of the hand. Paulette continued her ministrations, however, giving the newcomer a rather sly nod.

"Sit down, my dear. You must tell me the news. I want to hear Everything."

"Well, Mother, I've been the bearer of good news from the Continent. The first to get back with it." He drew a copy of the morning edition from his pocket with an air of pride. "It's all here. No other paper had it, of course. Wilson upset the whole French campaign, and so Wellesley was able to land his army. There will be more good news soon, I'm sure."

Mrs. Ellery clapped her hands lightly. "I'm so glad to hear it. I've been reading all your letters in the paper. They were splendid. I've been so proud of you." She gave a sudden wince and said sharply: "Paulette, you pulled! Be more careful, please. Well, Francis, I'm glad to hear something pleasant, for I'm not at all pleased with what's happening here. The breach has not been healed."

"You mean——"

"Between Caradoc and poor Mary. She hasn't returned home, and I'm sure I haven't any idea where she is. I'm very much afraid she's unhappy."

"Do you think we should discuss it now?"

"Do you mean because of Paulette? Dear Francis, Paulette's a perfect model of discretion. And can't you see she hasn't finished with my hair?" There was a pause. "Caradoc has made up his mind to marry someone else."

The silence which fell was so intense that it could almost be felt. Frank's mood of elation oozed away with the fear her words had inspired. He did not dare ask for further information.

"I can't talk him out of it, the foolish boy."

It had to be asked finally. "Who—who is it, Mother?"

Mrs. Ellery's face took on the set expression he knew so well. "Run along, Paulette. Put on the list for Mrs. Easty a bolt of blue sarsenet, dittany powders, and she's to speak to Mr. Jonas Punt in the village about the recommendations for the new maid. And, Paulette, remind me later to ask Dr. Trenchett for dinner Tuesday a week but *not* his old witch of a sister." When they were alone, she said bitterly: "It's Gabrielle de Salle. She's very highly connected, of course, but I don't approve. I've done everything I can to make him change his mind but he's proving most determined and provoking."

Another silence fell on the room. Frank was staring straight ahead of him, no longer conscious of the warm glow of the sun, the blue of the sky. Everything had suddenly become dull and overcast. The poodle wriggled out from under the counterpane and glared at him, chewing its ribbon petulantly. He turned to look at his mother finally, his eyes moving slowly as though the movement pained them.

"I was more than half expecting this, Mother."

"The girl is really quite lovely. And, of course, there's some satisfaction in them being one of the *very* oldest families in France. If only they had better prospects! Now that the Emperor's going to divorce his old wife, the situation's quite hopeless. He'll marry a young woman—the Emperor, I mean—and have Progeny. The De Salles will never get their estates back now. What kind of a wife will she make for my Caradoc? It won't do, Francis, and I've told him so a dozen times. Blue blood is all very well but he must marry money as well. I said just that to the old Comte and her brother when they came down a month back to talk it over."

"I heard in town," said Frank slowly, "that the Comte died a few days ago."

Mrs. Ellery's manner showed some indication of relaxation. "Yes. I take some comfort from that. Of course," she added hastily, "I'm sorry about the Comte. What I meant was that her brother is as much opposed to the match as I am. He wants Gabrielle to find a wealthier husband than my poor Caradoc can ever hope to be. He's certain to put his foot down."

Frank had not been listening very closely, his mind being filled with unhappy speculations. "Mother, is Carr very much in love with her?" he asked.

Mrs. Ellery pursed up her lips as she considered the point. "I suppose he is. But not so much that he couldn't get over it."

"And Mlle. de Salle, is she in love with him?"

A satisfied nod accompanied the answer this time. "Naturally. She's quite infatuated with him. I do wish their financial position was less desperate. It would be such a good match then. I must say, they seem very well suited."

Frank said in a low tone, "It doesn't seem to me there's anything you can do to prevent it if they both feel that way."

"Perhaps there is. You forget the brother. He seemed to me a very selfish and domineering man. I had a long talk with him and I'm sure we understood each other. He said quite positively that something substantial would have to be settled on her so that she can help support the family. If it isn't done, he'll refuse his consent."

"Perhaps Gab—Mlle. de Salle will disregard his wishes in the matter."

"It's not at all likely. She's French, and you know how they are about matters of marriage. We talked over the possibility of getting the French King to refuse his consent."

Frank sighed involuntarily. "If their hearts are set on it, should anything be allowed to interfere?"

His mother changed the subject abruptly, saying in an affectionate tone: "Francis, I want you to know I'm sorry we had our differences. I think both of us were in the wrong. You must have thought I was unfair to you. I want to make it up to you in some way."

He turned back and looked at her intently. Did she really mean it? She was smiling warmly, and his heart began to feel a little less heavy. He had always wanted to have a larger share in her affections and thoughts.

"I thought I was acting for the best," she went on. "It did seem that it was for the good of the whole family. Perhaps I saw Caradoc's side of it more than I did yours. If so, I'm very sorry. From now on, my dear son, it will be different."

"It's all over and done with," said Frank. "The paper is doing well again so we won't have financial worries. I'll be only too happy to forget everything that happened."

"I'm *so* glad to hear you say that, Francis. You've always been generous and kind. And now that old Mr. Clayhorn is dead, you can buy in his share as the will provided. That will be fine for you, won't it?"

"I was talking to some bankers yesterday about a loan to carry the purchase. It can be arranged, I think."

"Splendid, Francis! That will give you three full shares."

"Yes. It puts control pretty well in my hands, and I think you'll agree now that it's better for the business that way."

She hesitated. "I'm afraid that Caradoc hasn't enough to buy in his second share for you."

"I hardly expected he would be in a position to do it yet. I'll have to wait until the profits begin to roll in again. It will be easier for him then."

"Have you any thought of demanding the property back if he doesn't live up to the agreement in the time set?"

"No, Mother. I don't intend to be arbitrary about it."

"If he marries Gabrielle, he won't be able to do anything about it. He will have to settle so much on her that he won't have anything left. I've been thinking about it a very great deal. That would be unfair to you."

Frank left the window and began to pace about the room. He saw now that she had been leading up to this point, that she wanted him to realize he had it in his power to prevent the marriage. Had her contrition been nothing more, then, than a means to an end? He wanted to believe that her change of heart was genuine, but doubts were beginning to creep in. She had made no reference to the scar on his cheek. Was her concern for him so small that she had failed to notice it?

He could not dismiss immediately the thought that it was possible for him to stop the marriage. Why shouldn't he refuse to let Caradoc break the agreement? It would be quixotic in the extreme to allow his brother to rob him of the property as well as of the girl he loved.

"Mother, I don't know what to say." He stopped in front of her and gave his head a shake. "If Carr married and did not arrange to transfer the share to me, I could take the property back. It would make a breach in the family that time would never heal but—why should I give up everything? I must give it careful thought before deciding."

Mrs. Ellery shook her head with decision. "For once, Francis, you must think of yourself and be Firm."

2

IT WAS EVIDENT at once that a funeral had been held recently. When Frank arrived at the De Salle home, a cadaverous individual with a "weeper" attached to the crown of his hat and hanging down over his shoulders was removing the hatchment from beside the door. Several spectators were watching the operation with open mouths, wondering, no doubt, what the curious figures meant on the diamond-shaped sable shield, heraldic devices being something new in this part of town. Further evidences greeted his eye when Antoine, smiling glumly, admitted him to the drawing room. There was a funereal air about the somber hangings. A carboy, containing presumably the heart of the deceased, still stood on the marble mantel over the fireplace. Poor Comte Robert, thought Frank, he would no longer rouse to look for the sun and speculate on the likelihood of a speedy return to his beloved France.

He felt his own heart give a bound when Gabrielle entered. She looked slender and subdued in her high-waisted black gown, her face pale against its tall upright collar. As soon as she recognized him, she cried, "Frank!" and almost ran to greet him. It was the first time she had ever called him that.

"Gabrielle!" He found it hard to relinquish her hand after kissing it. "It's been such a long time."

"Nearly a year. Much too long, Frank." She noticed the scar at once. "Why, you've been wounded! We didn't hear about that."

"A small wound luckily."

"It's quite becoming. All you need now, sir, is a slight touch of gray around the temples and you'll be positively irresistible."

"I'm sorry to find you in so much trouble. You know how deeply I sympathize with you in your loss."

Her dark eyes showed a trace of tears. "Poor Father, he wanted so much to live long enough to see the end of things! The news you sent from Spain excited him so much. He was sure it meant the Emperor was going to be beaten." She drew out a small handkerchief and dabbed at her eyes. "I would have to translate all your articles for him and he got so impatient with my slowness that he even threatened to learn English, after all, so he wouldn't have to depend on me! He didn't want to miss a word." The handkerchief was frankly busy now. "Antoine found him in the morning."

"He would have had a long wait for the end of things, I'm afraid." Frank looked about him. "You've had many changes since I went away. I've been told you're no longer at the dress shop."

"Not for several months. Sosthène became very set against it and so I had to give in. It was just as well, for I was able to be with Father all the time. Was it—was it Caradoc who told you?"

She pronounced the name with some hesitation, watching him as though to test the effect of its use. Frank shook his head. No, he had not yet seen Caradoc. He had just returned from the Towers and such news as he had heard had been given him by his mother.

"You knew then that we visited the Towers? Father and Sosthène and I."

"I was told about it. And about other things as well."

"You mean about—about Caradoc and me?"

"Yes."

He had been keeping his face turned away, but at this point she laid a hand on his arm and forced him to meet her eyes. "Frank," she said, "I want to know how you feel about it. And I can't, if you won't look at me. There, that's better. And you've smiled too. Now you must tell me what you think."

His smile had been a poor pretense. Her nearness was making it harder than ever to accept the fact that she was lost to him irrevocably.

"If you want me to tell the truth, I'm very unhappy about it. You see, I had been presumptuous enough to think—but it's too late to say anything about that now."

She said slowly: "I thought you felt that way about me. Sometimes I hoped it would turn out as you wanted it." There was a pause before she went on. "But we must always be the best of friends. Especially as we're to see so much of each other. Or am I jumping to conclusions? I know that nothing has been settled yet."

"It's settled as far as I am concerned. I'm going to do everything I can to bring it about. There's only one thing I want, Gabrielle, and that's to see you happy."

She pressed his hand gratefully. "I knew I could count on you. I knew it the very first time I saw you. Dear Frank!" There was a pause. "But it's much more difficult than you think. Your mother is against me. She's let me see that very clearly."

"It's only because of money, Gabrielle. She admires you very much, and I know that the prominence of your family rather dazzles her. But Carr has very little, as you know. Taking over the Towers has put him in pretty deep and he must manage to improve his financial prospects somehow. Mother feels he must do it by marriage."

"Let's sit down and talk it over." She led the way to a sofa under the front window. Frank followed, glancing about him with an uneasiness which had nothing to do with the question of her marriage. He had been noticing signs of still greater prosperity about the room; some new and expensive pieces of furniture, an opera sheet beside a lorgnette on one of the tables, fresh-cut flowers in a vase. Where was the money for all this coming from? He remembered with alarm what Wilson had told him.

Gabrielle sat down and drew her skirts together to make room for him.

"Frank, we must face the facts. Your mother is set against the marriage. She's going to do everything she can against us. And, in spite of what you say, I'm quite sure she dislikes me."

"It needn't matter."

"And I—I don't like her! I can be honest with *you*, and it's such a relief."

"Yes, you can be honest with me. I'm completely on your side."

"She's been so unkind to you. Oh, I know all about it, my dear!"

"I'm sure you're exaggerating in your mind the things that have happened."

"No, I'm not. Caradoc has told me about the agreement. He's not very discerning about some things and inclined to be—as we're being honest about everything, Frank, I might as well say it—he's inclined to be very selfish in such matters. I can see that clearly."

"Our differences have been forgotten. Don't let's talk about them."

"But we must. It's very important. To me, I mean. Caradoc sees only his side of things. I understand him thoroughly, Frank. He's still a willful boy. He really believes you saw some advantage for yourself in making the agreement. I haven't been able to make him understand why you did it."

"Why did I do it, Gabrielle?"

"So you could have a free hand to print those articles in the newspaper. That's so very evident, I can't understand why Caradoc feels the way he does."

"*You* are discerning, at any rate." He leaned over and took her hand so she would not be able to see how affected he was by this proof of her understanding.

"Well, we must talk about the agreement and what's to be done now. I'm so glad you've come to me before seeing Caradoc. It will prevent misunderstandings, I'm sure. He tells me he can't live up to his part of it yet and it doesn't seem to worry him in the least. He sees things the way he wants them to be and so he thinks it quite right and proper to keep the Towers himself and leave the settlement with you until sometime in the future."

"I'm agreeable to that. I'll get the share in the business in time and I'm not worried about it at all."

"But I am. Frank, what do you intend to say to Caradoc?"

"That he may use such funds as he has to make the settlement your brother is demanding. It's the only way out of the difficulty."

"You're being much too generous! You say you want me to be happy. Do you think I could be happy that way? No, I've thought it all out and I see what must be done. You're going to do what I say, both of you. If Caradoc will give the property back to you, I'm prepared to defy Sosthène about the settlement. I'll tell him, selfish lump that he is, that we're living in England and not in France, and that he has no right to dictate to me what I'm to do with my life."

"But I don't see how you could get along that way. You'll have a position to live up to. There's Carr's career to be considered."

"Leave his career to me! I think I can take care of that without robbing you for it. We can settle down here in London on what he has left and the income he gets from the paper. Thanks to you, it seems to be quite good again. We can get along very nicely. I don't suppose we'll be able to afford a carriage or a box at the opera, but we'll have a very nice place where we can entertain his political friends. I can be of great help there. What is a wife for?" She drew herself up determinedly. "That's the way I want it, Frank, and no other way will suit me at all."

"But suppose Carr doesn't agree?"

"He must be willing to do what I want."

"He's very headstrong, you know."

"I can make him see it's the only fair way." For the first time, however, the dark eyes showed some signs of wavering. "I've made up my mind to tell him that I won't marry him unless he agrees. I'm—I'm going to try to be very firm about it."

They were interrupted at this point by the opening of a door at the rear. A familiar voice said, "I'm afraid, Gabrielle—why, M'sieur Frank! I'm so glad to see you!"

It was Margot. She came into the room after closing the door carefully behind her. He would not have known who it was if it had not been for her voice. The year had made a great change in her appearance. She was taller and very much grown up in every way. Her face seemed to have filled out, and he realized for the first time that her eyes, still startlingly large under her wide brow, were of the deepest pansy blue. She was getting to be quite attractive, he thought; not to be compared with Gabrielle, of course, but still with the promise of a beauty all her own.

"A pleasant surprise, Margot," said Gabrielle.

The girl smiled warmly as they shook hands. "Indeed, yes! We've been hoping so much you would return, M'sieur Frank. Jean Baptiste Achille has asked for you so often."

"Is that the only reason? I've been flattering myself you would be glad to see me on your own account."

"I am. Very glad."

"That's better. And speaking of Jean Baptiste Achille, how is my canny little creditor? I'm sure he will have some new investment to propose."

Margot regarded him with sober eyes. "No, m'sieur. He's very ill. The doctor doesn't seem to be able to do anything for him."

Frank frowned anxiously. "You don't mean that the little fellow's in any danger?"

"Yes, very great danger. We're afraid—that he isn't going to get well."

Frank looked first at one and then the other, unwilling to believe in the gravity of the situation. "Surely something can be done for him! Could other doctors be tried? I can't bear to think of anything happening to my stout little Jean."

"Would you care to see him?" Margot's face remained grave and composed. "He's asked for you so often."

"Of course." He turned to Gabrielle. "There are many things I want to talk about, but perhaps you'll pardon me if I go in to see him now?"

Gabrielle nodded silently and turned away. She began, listlessly, to arrange some flowers in a marble vase. Even with the new anxiety he was feeling, Frank noticed how gracefully her hands moved among the tall-stemmed roses and larkspur.

"I'll see that the room is presentable first," said Margot. She closed the door behind her.

"Everything seems to happen to you at once," said Frank.

Gabrielle nodded without looking around. "We have other troubles that you know nothing about."

"Perhaps I do know about them. That's what I want to discuss with you."

"You can't possibly know what I mean. I shouldn't have said anything." She stepped back from the flowers and smiled at him; not a very happy smile, however. "Margot is inclined to disapprove of me. She's your warmest champion, you know."

"I'm happy to hear it. If only the same favor could have been felt in—in other quarters! Do you mean she doesn't approve of Caradoc?"

"Her disapproval is chiefly for me. As for Caradoc, she says that he's too handsome, and that handsome men never make good husbands."

"If that's true, I should be a matrimonial prize."

"I'm sure Margot would never subscribe to that. At least, not for that reason. She's a very observant young person, and with opinions of her own. Now that my father's gone, she'll be the real head of the household."

Margot opened the door. "You may come now. He's awake. And very anxious to see you, M'sieur Frank."

As he followed her from the room, she whispered, "Don't be shocked at how he looks."

"Has he been ill long?"

"For several months. He had a fall. That started it, the doctor says."

Jean Baptiste Achille was lying in a small bed beside a larger one in a room opening off the kitchen. The windows were closed tight and a dilapidated screen had been placed between the two beds, depriving the little patient of any benefit from the sun. There was a table against the wall with a cupping glass, a bottle of medicine and a spoon across the top, a rind of orange.

A pair of feverish eyes in a thin face looked up at Frank with an attempt at a smile. "We're all so—very glad you are home, m'sieur," said the boy. He tried to raise a hand but the strength was lacking.

"I'll leave you," whispered Margot. "He wants to see you alone."

Frank was so disturbed at the emaciated appearance of the patient that he found it hard to speak. "This won't do, you know," he managed finally. "It won't do at all. We must have you up and about again, young fellow. You can't win any marbles from the English boys this way."

"I haven't been to school"—the boy paused for strength to go on—"for such a long time. I don't think—m'sieur—that I am going to get better."

"Come now, that isn't the right spirit. I'm going to have a talk with the doctor and see that he gets you out of bed in no time at all."

"I'm—I'm very sick." The voice was so low it could hardly be heard. "I can't see you—very well."

"You mustn't give in, my brave Jean. You won't let a little sickness get the better of you. Why, I've been turning over in my mind another financial deal we could go into together. A real moneymaker this time."

There was a faint flicker of interest in the boy's eyes. "Indeed, m'sieur. I would—like that—if——"

"You and I, Jean Baptiste Achille, we're going to make a lot of money. I've got it all worked out, but we'll have to talk about it when you're a little better. When you're strong enough to sit up, we'll draw an agreement. We'll be partners." As he said this, Frank was noticing how thin the arm of the sick boy had become. It seemed to have lost all strength. "Poor little chap!" he thought. "What a sorry kind of life he's had!"

"I—wanted—to ask—about a will." Frank had to lean over to hear what was said. "I've saved—quite a lot of money—m'sieur. One pound—four shillings—sixpence."

"That *is* a lot of money. I don't see how you did it, my stout Jean. I can see you're going to be the right kind of a partner."

A faint trace of a smile showed on the wasted features. "We—could do so much—m'sieur. But it's too late now."

There was a long pause. Then the thin lips began to move again. "I had to save. My father has been drinking—quite heavy, m'sieur. As much as Mick Finnerty's father. You see, he's had his wages regular." A further proof of the improved financial position of the household! "I must—leave my money for him—so it will be safe."

Frank drew a chair up beside the bed and sat down. "Listen to me, Jean Baptiste Achille. We're going to get you well again. The doctor can do it. Why, I'm going to tell him he must, that we can't have you sick like this any longer." He paused. "But if you're really worried about your father——"

"I am, m'sieur. Oh yes."

"Then we'll talk things over now." Frank was finding it hard to keep his voice steady. "I'm sure it will take a load off your mind to have it settled. Then it will be easier for you to get well."

"Yes, m'sieur. We must settle it now or—we'll never do it." So much talk had exhausted him, and for several moments he made no further effort to speak. His eyes had closed.

"That's right, take a rest now. There's plenty of time. I'll stay right here."

While he waited, Frank looked at the wasted form, convinced that there was no hope, yet wondering if there was anything that could be done. He had always intended to do something for the boy when he grew old enough. A place could have been made for him in the counting-house of the newspaper. He realized that he had often thought of Jean Baptiste Achille seated on a high stool, his head deep in figures, planning things out with that shrewd young brain of his. "The brave little shaver!" he thought. "Trying so hard to protect his drunken father!" He became aware that his cheeks were moist and reached hastily for a handkerchief, not wanting the boy to see.

"I want the money left—in your hands."

"Of course. I'll be glad to handle it. I appreciate your confidence."

"At the—the same rate of interest, perhaps?"

"Certainly. At the same rate of interest."

Jean Baptiste Achille achieved a wan smile. "Thank you, m'sieur. I was so afraid it might not be—be convenient. That—that will always bring my father something to—to depend on, won't it?"

"Yes, Jean. If the newspaper continues to prosper, the rate might even be raised."

"Is it possible!" The sunken eyes studied Frank's face for a moment and then closed again. "I won't—worry about him so much now. He must call to collect himself. At your office. And please, m'sieur, he is never to be paid if he—if he's bosky at the time."

"Of course not. I'll keep an eye on him."

"He must only have parts of the principal in case of—sickness, m'sieur. I leave all that to you."

"Yes, I'll act as administrator. And now"—trying hard to sound brisk and businesslike—"we must have this made shipshape and proper. We must have a witness."

"Yes, a witness. Margot, m'sieur?"

Frank called the girl in and said: "Mademoiselle, Jean and I have been talking about the matter of a will. He's going to get well, of course, but as we're both men of business we've agreed that it's sensible to look ahead. He's told me about his property and what he wants done with it." He went on to explain, the sick boy nodding his head weakly at each point.

"That's what we've settled between us. We felt it should be made legal and binding by having a witness."

"Yes, M'sieur Frank. I understand."

"I'll put it down on paper later and then you can sign it."

Margot leaned over and laid a hand on the boy's forehead. "You may be certain, Jean Baptiste Achille, that M'sieur Ellery will attend to things exactly as you want them. Your father will be looked after."

With this matter settled, the boy's attention wandered to something else. With a smile that had a trace of pride in it, he announced, "Mick Finnerty came to see me last week."

"He did? That was very nice of Mick."

"We had a fine long visit with Mick, didn't we?" Margot took his hand and tucked it back under the covers. "He was so well behaved. And he was very clean and he had gone to such pains to brush his hair. I hardly knew him at first. He said all the boys wanted you to get well soon."

"He said they missed me at school."

"Of course they do. And now you must rest. You've had such a long talk. M'sieur Ellery will come to see you again soon."

"I'll come often. Good-by, Jean."

A look of fear settled on the boy's face. "M'sieur," he whispered, "I can't—see you—at all."

A stout woman came bustling into the room, fumbling with the strings of her bonnet and regarding them with an accusing eye.

"How is my poor little sufferer, my little tippybobbin?" she demanded.

"We're going now, Mrs. Blodgett," said Margot hastily. "M'sieur is an old friend and he wanted to see Jean Baptiste Achille very much."

"Dear, dear, I'm sure you've let him talk more than he should. You must be more careful, you must indeed, miss. I don't dare leave him a minute, not even to get freshened up and have a bite with Blodgett, but you're up to something. Poger's polish, miss, this won't do. I can't have such things."

When they had left the room, Margot explained, "That's the squire. We hired her to attend him nights, but she's so fond of him she stays all the time. She gets very short with me."

"Poor little fellow! He can't last long, Margot."

"No, m'sieur. I know it. He's just like one of the family, and we'll all miss him terribly, even Sosthène. He gave him a shilling last week. And that's most unusual for Sossy."

Frank sighed. "This is a very unhappy time for all of us, Margot."

She gave him a quick look and then glanced away. "Yes, M'sieur Frank. I'm very sorry about it."

"You gave me no warning in your letters."

"I should have told you. But I didn't have the courage to do it. I knew how unhappy it would make you."

He sank his voice to an even lower pitch. "Gabrielle is very much in love with my brother, isn't she?"

She nodded slowly. "I'm afraid she is, M'sieur Frank."

"I wanted to be sure. Thanks for telling me the truth." He straightened up. "I'll come in tomorrow to see him. Will Mrs. Blodgett be very short with me, if I do?"

"Please come as often as you can. We have no visitors at all now."

"Why is that?"

"I—I can't explain."

"Is there anything I can do for Jean? Is there any need for money to buy him things?"

"No, no. We're doing very well now." She looked up at him with a smile that carried the faintest suggestion of pique. "You haven't noticed me at all. This is a silk dress. A very good one. It was quite expensive, M'sieur Frank. See the embroidery! And I've grown more than an inch."

"I noticed, of course. In fact, I hardly knew you when you first came in. You're becoming a young lady very fast. And a very pretty one."

"What are you two whispering about?" demanded Gabrielle, from the other end of the room.

"I was telling your cousin," said Frank, walking toward her at once, "that in another year or two she'll be providing competition for the beautiful Gabrielle de Salle."

"Yes, I realize it." Gabrielle's tone was listless. She got up and walked beside him to the door. "I'm too tired to talk about—those other matters now. I've been thinking, Frank, and it has made me very sad. I don't believe Caradoc will be ready to do what I want. And in a way it's your fault."

"My fault?"

"You've been much too generous with him. It wasn't good for him when you let him have the property. He likes to—well, to strut. Perhaps he'll want the Towers more than he'll want me."

Frank began in a bitter voice, "If Carr does anything to make you un-happy——"

"Now! I won't have you speaking of him in that tone because of a mere assumption on my part. Perhaps I'm being unfair to him in imagining such things." To change the subject, she went on: "And I'm worried about Margot. She's been working so hard. First it was Father and now our poor little Jean."

They were at the door. "Come and see us often. Please! I'm going to need you."

He was looking at her steadily, thinking how different things might have been if he had not made possible that meeting at the Towers. "I'll come as often as you'll let me, Gabrielle. Please don't change your mind about needing me."

3

NATHAN COPE came into the corner room with a self-conscious swagger. He was wearing his Hessian boots and the upper part of his legs were tightly encased in cream-colored woolen smalls with crowns embroidered in scarlet on each thigh.

"The very latest!" he exulted, slapping a hand on one close-fitted knee. "The absolute supreme twig. Straight from Germany. How do you like my *strumpfhosen?*"

Frank dropped the sheet of weekly salary payments which he had been studying. The totals were going up. He was glad of this, and yet it worried him. He knew the prompt action his father would have taken.

"Copey," he said, ignoring his assistant's sartorial experiment, "have you made any progress in our campaign for prison reform?"

"None at all." Cope sat down, crossing one leg over the other, a move which threatened to split his Germanic importations. "It's impossible to get people interested in anything but the war. I did manage to smuggle in a deputation of earnest citizens to see our honorable Home Sec'try, but he cut them off in royal style. 'Prison reform?' he said. 'Don't you know we're allowing certain grades of criminals the right to enlist in the army? What other reform is necessary?'" Cope shook his head with puzzled exasperation. "How can an intelligent man think that way? And what can we expect to accomplish against a policy of that kind?"

"We'll have to wait for peace and then we'll start in earnest." Frank's mind hopped to another problem. "Have we a check on the people coming back from the Peninsula?"

"Of course. We get the lists as soon as a ship docks."

"Let me know when a Miss Laura Brakespeare arrives. She was one of my party at the Yeltes. I'm—I'm very much worried about her."

"Wasn't that the one you praised so highly?" Cope grinned slyly. "I'll see that you know the instant she lands. Is she pretty, Don Francis?"

"Yes, I think she is. Someday I'll tell you about her. Part of the story, at any rate. Any word of a singer named Leonard Cardyce?"

"He's back. He appears at Covent Garden tonight. There's been a lot of talk about him, so I suppose people will flock to hear him."

Frank said shortly: "Praise his singing if he deserves it. But tell our man to go light on the hero stuff. Cardyce was far from heroic."

Cope got to his feet and strolled to the window. The trees on Dacre Square were out in full leaf, and it was no longer possible to see much of the houses on the opposite side. "Even London can be beautiful at this time of year," he commented. "It's worth living through a winter of fog and snow and a raw spring to have one day of an English June." He broke off and then said in tones of surprise: "Now what's got into Sir Caradoc?"

Frank sprang up and joined him at the window. It was easy to see that something had disturbed the young baronet. He was striding across the square at a pace that fell little short of a run, his arms swinging vigorously, his tall beaver hat bent forward. It was one of Caradoc's most often expressed beliefs that, if you never idled, you never had to hurry; yet here he was, hurrying as he had never done before.

Cope said, "I'll be back later," and vanished from the room. A few minutes later Caradoc came in with a loud "Frank! Something has happened. It's a blasted filthy business too!"

Frank had returned to his chair. One glimpse of the flashing blue eyes and finely chiseled features of his brother had sent such a wave of anger over him that everything seemed to go black. He sat still, waiting for the spell to pass. It would never do, he was thinking, to let himself go like this. He must not hate his brother, no matter what might happen between them.

Caradoc strode to the desk and pointed a finger at him. "Did you hear me? Something unbelievable has happened."

"What is it, Carr?"

There was no pretense of a salutation between them, nothing to suggest that a year had passed since they had parted in bad blood. Caradoc straddled a chair and said: "There have been rumors for a long time that some of these mangy Frenchmen were sending information to General Bonaparte." He was following the official practice of allowing the French ruler no higher title. "The Home Office has the proofs now. And De Salle's mixed up in it. Damme, Frank, if Gaby's brother hasn't been selling us out!"

Frank had been expecting this, but he was surprised nevertheless at the effect the news had on him. The events of the past two days had been submerging him in ever deeper gloom, and it needed only this to make him feel that the whole world had gone awry.

"Are there proofs of his guilt?"

Caradoc scowled. "Plenty. The scoundrel has been in the Corsican's pay for a year. He got away, fortunately. I shouldn't say that, but it's a great relief, by Gad, that he did. They just missed him at White's. He must have been nimble, for it's reported he got aboard a cutter down the river at an early hour this morning." His frown deepened into an expression of lordly wrath. "That confounded fellow De Vitrelle is in it too. They got away together."

Frank was thinking, "How can he sit here and talk? Why hasn't he gone to her when she'll need him so much?" Aloud he asked, "Have you seen—Gabrielle?"

"Gad, no! Do you think I can afford to get myself involved in a mess like this?"

"If he's only concerned about himself," Frank thought, "he can't have any real love for her. Poor Gabrielle!"

"A blasted mess, I must say!" went on the younger brother. "It isn't going to do me any good. Lots of people know I intended to marry her."

"Carr!" Frank had risen. He was finding it hard to keep his voice under control. "We must get her out of the country. She mustn't be allowed to suffer for what her brother has done."

Caradoc removed his hat and tossed it on the table. There was a ridge of red across his high white brow. "What an insane idea!" he cried. It was clear from his tone that he had never thought of such a course. "Do you realize we would be breaking the law?"

"There can be no question of lawbreaking until a charge has been lodged against her. We must see to it that they have no chance to do that."

"It comes to the same thing."

Frank broke out passionately: "You don't suppose that I'm any more pleased than you are at the possibility of running foul of the law? You may recall that I went to jail because I was concerned enough over the safety of the country to print the truth. Winning the war still comes ahead of everything with me. If I thought she had taken any part in her brother's dirty plot, I wouldn't make a move to help her. But she's completely innocent! I'm so sure of it that I'm willing to do anything to help her. I know what it's like in prison."

Caradoc regarded him uncomfortably over his starched Brummell stock. "You needn't think, Frank, that it's because of any lack of devotion that I'm unwilling to get myself mixed up in this. A man in public life has to look at things in a different way. I have a higher duty to consider. I don't mind saying I've become a valuable man." He nodded his head with renewed composure, with an almost majestic certainty of the soundness of his position. "It's all very well to talk of rushing in like a knight-errant. I must have the common sense and—yes, the courage—to take the long view of this."

"You mean you're going to do nothing? That you won't try to help her?"

"I can't see that anything I can do would help her."

"Very well. Do nothing if your common sense and your higher courage tell you to stay out. As for me, I'm not going to waste any more time in talk."

"See here, now. What do you propose to do?"

Suddenly Frank began to laugh in deep exasperation. "Don't you see you're in this, whether you like it or not? I've been led to believe you're in the confidence of men high in the government. Isn't it natural for the authorities to believe you've been the source of De Salle's information? They'll suspect you first of all."

The startled look which spread over the younger brother's face was almost comic. "They can't suspect *me!*" he cried. "Why, damme, I've hardly exchanged a dozen words with the poisonous fellow. No one in his right senses would think I helped him."

"For your own sake I hope you're right. But look at the situation coolly. De Salle has been getting valuable information somewhere. He may have picked it up at the clubs where he gambles. On the other hand, his sister has been at a great many assemblies and routs. Army officers and members of the diplomatic corps have swarmed around her. It will be assumed he used her as a decoy, even that she was a full partner in the conspiracy. Where does that leave you? It's known you intended to marry her. They can't fail to suspect you."

"You don't suppose, Frank, she actually has been helping him?"

Frank experienced another black wave of rage. "You can stand there and express a doubt of her! I thought you loved her! Why, you poltroon, I don't want your help. I'll do what's possible to be done by myself."

"Come, old fellow. You said yourself we must consider the situation coolly. Every possibility must be thought of."

"Not that! Not that! You know—or you ought to know—that she's incapable of treachery."

Caradoc groaned. "What a mess! What a blasted mess to find myself in!"

Frank indulged in a moment's thought. Finally he said: "I'll have to attend to the London end of it. If you were caught helping her get away, it would look like a confession of complicity. I grant you that. Cope will help me. He's an ingenious beggar and he'll work out the details. If we get them clear of the city, will you take it up from there and get them to the coast? I'm willing to do it all, but I'm thinking how Gabrielle would feel if you took no part at all. It's your duty, Carr." He paused. "And your privilege."

The younger brother nodded with some reluctance. "It will be a risky thing for me. Still, I can't let you do it all. Yes, I'll go with her."

Another sound could now be heard above the boom of the presses: the beat of a horse's hoofs crossing the square. They looked at each other in consternation.

"I'm very much afraid this is going to be bad news," said Frank.

But the dusty messenger who came pounding up the stairs and into the room a few minutes later had been riding a long distance. He was carrying under his arm a wicker-covered bottle with a small red flag attached to the cork. This he thrust into Frank's hands with a hoarse, "Orders, sir, to deliver into your hands and none other."

Frank took it eagerly. "Where was it picked up?"

"Off the coast, a few miles east of Worthing. Early this morning, sir. I've used up two horses getting it here."

"News from the Continent," said Frank, fingering the bottle with jubilant fingers. "It must be from Vienna. Perhaps the Austrians have followed up their victory at Aspern by wiping out Napoleon's army." He went to the door and shouted at the top of his voice, "Cope! Cope!"

The latter arrived on the run and his face lighted up when he saw the bottle. "So it's here!" he exclaimed. "I was beginning to think Lestrange had been picked up by the revenue cutters and that nothing would get through to us. Something tells me, Frank, we have the best of news here. Boney's been beaten again."

Frank took the messenger out into the corridor. "Tell me how you managed to find it," he whispered.

"The revenuers were atter him and he didn't dare come in very close. We spotted him and, when he started to haul away, we went out. Sure enough, there she be, bobbing on top of the water. We hid it under a mess of fish when the gov'ment cutter overhauled us. They was mad as Georgie-be-damned when they found nothing on us."

"Well, off to bed with you now and get a good sleep. Not a word to anyone, mind!"

Back in his office, Frank said: "Turn this over to one of your men, Copey. Unfortunately we're both going to be too busy on something else to do anything about it. That is, if you're prepared to accept a share in a very dangerous business." He looked at his assistant with a half-apologetic smile. "I need your help the worst way. But I'm reluctant to ask it of you, Copey. We might find ourselves back in prison if things went wrong."

Cope looked at Caradoc and then back at Frank. "I know what you mean. The De Salle affair. I got word of it a few minutes ago and was coming in to tell you about it." He grinned cheerfully. "Well, I lived through one jail term. I could survive another if necessary."

"I knew I could count on you," declared Frank. "You won't need to figure personally in what we've got to do. I'm counting on you to handle the arrangements. We haven't a moment to lose."

The three men drew together in a corner to discuss ways and means. By the time they were through, the writer to whom the bottle had been entrusted put his head through the door with confirmation that the news was good.

"They've got him surrounded on the island of Lobau," he announced. "Bridges destroyed, no way for him to get off. All the Austrians have to do is sit tight and starve him out. Boney's cornered this time!"

"I knew it!" cried Cope. "We've got him at last! Great Barnaby, we've got him at last!"

"And now," said Frank, when the writer had left the room, "we must get to work. I'm going to see Gabrielle at once. I'll depend on you, Copey, to get all the details worked out. Carr, we'll get word to you as soon as possible where you're to meet the coach."

4

A MAN who managed to appear damp and steamy in spite of the dry weather looked Frank over with surly thoroughness. He reeked of surveillance from the crown of his napless hat to the soles of his rough shoes.

"They've lost no time about it," said Frank to himself as he plied the knocker.

Margot answered the summons. Her eyes were red and heavy.

"Oh, M'sieur Frank!" she whispered, looking fearfully at the man in the street, who had taken to twirling a cudgel as he paced by. She motioned the visitor in and closed the door after him quickly. "He's still there. I hoped he had gone. We're in trouble. Very great trouble, m'sieur. And"—she seemed reluctant to go on—"Jean Baptiste Achille is gone! He died during the night. Mrs. Blodgett stepped out of the room and, when she went back, he—it was all over."

"Poor little fellow!" Frank placed a hand on her shoulder. "It's for the best, Margot. He couldn't have lasted very long."

They walked from the vestibule into the hall. It was in complete darkness, a black sheet having been draped over the one window. "I know about the other trouble. That's why I came. Where's Gabrielle?"

"In the drawing room. The Abbé Force is with her." The agitation she was feeling was manifest in her voice. "Two rough-looking men came this morning and asked her questions for over an hour. They left that one out there when they went away."

He let his voice sink to a whisper. "I'm making plans to get you both out of London tonight."

She whispered back: "I started out to find you this morning but the man stopped me. He said no one was to leave the house."

"Some way will have to be found to get rid of him. I think I'll entrust that part to Topp."

There was a moment's silence and then she said: "Antoine is sitting at the back door, looking at the sky. He doesn't hear when you speak to him." Her hand touched his arm with an urgent pressure. "We can't go away and leave Jean Baptiste Achille. We can't, M'sieur Frank!"

"You must, Margot. I'll attend to everything here. May I see Gabrielle now?"

"Yes. Go right in, please."

He was gratified to see how quickly and eagerly Gabrielle rose and came to meet him. Her face looked pale and drawn. "So soon!" she said. "I'll always think of you after this as Frank-in-need. Have you heard? About Sosthène?"

He nodded gravely. "Yes, Gabrielle. I understand he got away safely."

A look of intense relief flashed across her face. "Oh! How wonderful! All we've heard is what the men told us when they came this morning. They said he had been taken. Why would they say that?"

"The usual trick. They thought it would frighten you."

She was holding desperately to one of his arms. "But I've known this was coming. I begged Sosthène so often to give it up! He always denied there was any truth in it. Frank, what am I to do?"

"You mustn't worry. Carr and I will get you away tonight."

Her eyes lighted up. "Then he knows too! Will he be coming to see me soon?"

"Not today. It wouldn't do. You see, he's been put in a very difficult position. Some suspicion is bound to attach to him and he mustn't do anything to add to it."

She nodded her head slowly. "Of course, they would think . . ." Her grip on his arm tightened. "Frank! They won't do anything to him, will they? I would never forgive myself if he got into trouble because of us."

"It won't be hard for him to prove he had no hand in it. And he has powerful friends in the government."

"You do believe, don't you, that I had no hand in it either?"

"I've never doubted you for a moment. Do you think I would be here if I believed otherwise?"

"Caradoc knows I'm innocent, doesn't he?" Her tone was anxious.

"Of course. I've just left him." He lowered his voice. "How much does the Abbé know?"

"He came as soon as he heard of our trouble. For a long time he's been our only visitor. You see, Frank, many of our people suspected what Sosthène and Jules were doing. None of them came to see us. I'm sure your police got their information from them."

"Are you sure the Abbé hasn't been concerned in it?"

"Yes, I'm certain of that. He tried to make them give it up. What has happened to Jules?"

"They got away together. Would it be safe then to let the Abbé know what we're planning? He could be very useful."

"Yes, it would be quite safe. I've come to depend on him a great deal lately."

"Then I'll have a talk with him." His voice fell to a whisper nevertheless. "A carriage will arrive at ten o'clock tonight. You must be packed and ready to leave then. Take as little as you can, Gabrielle. I haven't any idea what kind of accommodation there will be for you on the boat. I'm afraid it will be pretty rough; so the less luggage, the better it will be. Antoine must stay here for the time being. We can arrange to get him over later. You must be ready to leave the instant the carriage stops in front of the door."

She whispered back: "We'll be ready. I'll go and talk to Margot now."

The Abbé Force was sitting in a chair at the other end of the room with a very dismal face. He seemed to flow out in all directions like a discomfited devilfish which had allowed its tentacles to droop.

"This is a serious matter, M'sieur l'Abbé," said Frank.

The churchman nodded. "I've had some knowledge of it for several months back. I entreated the young men to stop but they wouldn't heed me. Not that they can be blamed entirely. They've lived in poverty so long. It is difficult for young minds to remain closed to the glory of Napoleon! And we must consider the cavalier manner in which they've been treated by the court at Hartwell. I can understand how they felt. I have suffered in equal degree."

"You surprise me. I was under the impression there was complete accord since the King moved there from Gosfield."

The Abbé snorted indignantly. "You can have no idea what we've had to endure. The pride and stupidity of those who surround His Majesty is beyond belief. What do they know, the sycophants, of what we've suffered?" His jowls trembled with agitation. "They ignore us, m'sieur. They laugh at our advice. They, in their ease and security! They issue orders, court edicts, for our guidance. We may do this, we may not do that. We may say this, we may not say that. And we, m'sieur, we are starving! I have not as much as a single franc in my pocket. For months I have subsisted—and very badly—on the charity of strangers. At Mittau I was high in the favor and confidence of the King. Here I am nothing." His sense of injury began to run away with his discretion. "Is it any wonder that some of the younger people are losing faith in the cause?"

Frank sat down beside the voluble churchman. "I'm planning to get the two ladies out of the country. But I'm very much concerned over what may happen to them when they land in France. They'll have no friends to meet them, no recollections of the country to help. It will be extremely difficult for them alone." He leaned forward. "M'sieur l'Abbé, would you consider going with them?"

The massive form underwent such a convulsion that it was clear the suggestion had taken the Abbé completely by surprise. After a moment, however, he looked at Frank with a shrewd gleam in his triangular eyes. "It is an idea, monsieur. Will you believe me when I say I have never, until this moment, given thought to such a possibility? I'm still completely loyal to our rightful King and to holy church. I could never bow the knee to the tyrant. But—it is an idea."

"France is full of people with no loyalty for Napoleon."

"That is true, monsieur. I might even be useful at home. Yes, it is a thought to be considered." He shifted his bulk uneasily, and a jingling sound came from his pockets. Frank looked at the silver dish on the mantel. It had been swept clean. "I've lost all confidence in the court at Hartwell. They are incompetents, cowards, leeches!"

"It appears you can't be of any use to the cause here. But loyal Frenchmen can help in France today. Opinion is rising against the butcher."

The Abbé's hands were fumbling with the crucifix suspended around his neck. "The young ladies will be in need of help. I could be very useful to them." He sighed deeply. "Ah, the sunny skies of France! What a joy to see them again! I am tempted, M. Ellery. And I'm almost convinced you are right."

ENGLAND, AGAIN 235

"You would soon find a useful niche for yourself there. I'm sure it wouldn't be necessary to make any compromise with your beliefs."

"You are right." The Abbé got ponderously to his feet. His eyes were blinking with excitement, with new mental alacrity. He settled his skirts with a trembling hand. Beside him was a small table containing what was left of the averil, cakes iced with chocolate on mats edged with black paper. He scooped them all up and found places for them in his many pockets. "My mind is made up. And you may rest assured that I'll see the young ladies safely to their destination."

Frank nodded with deep satisfaction. "Will you be good enough, then, to tell them what has been decided? I must leave at once. I know they'll be happy you're going with them. The matter of the—the necessary funds will be taken care of later."

He walked out to the kitchen. Mrs. Blodgett was sitting in a chair and rocking herself to and fro in an excess of grief. Long weepers, which had been pinned to her bonnet, swayed with the movement of the chair.

"The poor lamb, the patient wee sufferer! The Lord has took him to His buzzom." She sniffed loudly but kept a shrewd eye nevertheless on the visitor. "I done all as a body could for him. Never a closed eye for a blink o' sleep, never a taint o' drink on my lips. I watched over him like he wur one o' my own."

"I'm sure you were very kind to him, Squire." Frank was fumbling in his pocket. He drew out a crown. "Here. From what I'm told, you've earned it."

She grasped it in a moist hand and flipped up her skirt to find a pocket in one of her many petticoats. "Thank'ee, sir. Yes, I wur good to him. A squire's work is hard, sir. There's narsty things one has to do. But when they lays him in his little coffing, I'll be free to look at him with a easy conshunts. That I will, sir."

"May I see him, Mrs. Blodgett?"

The small room was lighted by a single candle at the head of the bed, and the window was draped tightly with black curtains. Frank waited for his eyes to become accustomed to the gloom. When he finally looked down, he could not believe at first it was Jean Baptiste Achille lying there. It was incredible how many years seemed to have been shorn away in the transition; the body was tiny and wasted, the face like that of an infant in its waxen purity. As he looked further, however, he saw that death had left nothing that was not essentially a part of the fine spirit of the dead boy. Intelligence could still be read in the broad brow, resolution in every line of the face, courage in the sensitive lips. The hands, crossed in the habitual position of death, were so fragile that it was hard to remember they had been used for carrying wood and coals, for polishing silver and scrubbing plates, for helping an inebriated father into bed.

"You had a stanch heart, Jean Baptiste Achille," he said aloud. "I'm going to miss you."

Margot, with eyes redder than ever, met him as he made his way to the hall. She caught one of his hands and said in a tense undertone: "M'sieur Frank, I don't want to go! I've been thinking about it and I'm frightened. Why can't I stay here?"

"For a great many reasons, Margot. Where would you live?"

"I don't know. Perhaps I could keep house for you. Or I could be a servant somewhere. I don't care as long as I stay. I'm still loyal to the King. My father and mother were driven out of France and they starved. All our properties were taken. I'll never forget as long as I live. I'm afraid of Paris, m'sieur! I can't think of anything but the guillotine and the terrible carts. I don't want to go there." Her voice was full of passion. "My mind will never change about it. This is my home. I want to stay."

Frank put an arm around her tense shoulders. "But what would the others do without you? Have you thought of that? They'll need you very much, Margot. Yesterday Gabrielle told me you would be the real head of the family from now on. Why, they would be completely lost without you to manage things for them."

"I've thought of that. But—I can't give in! I'll never swear an oath of allegiance to Napoleon! Will they put me in prison?"

"Of course not. They won't pay any attention at all to a young girl like you. You're a minor and your estates would have to be handled by trustees. You needn't have any fear."

"I wouldn't take them if I had to swear the oath. I would starve first. You may not believe me, M'sieur Frank, but nothing will ever make me change my mind about that."

He could feel how taut she had become. "You must be more careful what you say when you get to France. Keep such opinions to yourself, my dear. And you need have no fears of Paris. It's a beautiful city, much finer in many ways than our poor dirty old London. You'll like it from the very first."

Margot sighed rebelliously. "Must I go? Isn't there any other way?"

"I'm afraid not."

"This is home to me. I'll miss it. I'll miss you, M'sieur Frank."

"You must take good care of Gabrielle. She's going to need you."

Another sigh, slightly more resigned. "I suppose I must go then. It would be so much better if you were coming with us."

Windy Topp, who had secured, immediately on reaching London, a full blood brother of the long yellow coat he had always worn before, had been successful in luring the steamy individual away for a few minutes. They had gone to a near-by tavern where the famous Mr. Spicer Crouch occupied the chair and sang nightly his best songs, *O Fie on the Cheating Cries of London* and *Boney and Jarge, Me Lads*. The street was empty when the carriage drew up in front of the door, and in no time at all the luggage had been stowed away in the boot and three muffled figures had climbed inside. Gabrielle and Margot had a moment's argument about the determination of the latter to take along a canary in a wicker cage. Margot won. The coachman swished his whip and called, "Git, Barney! Hup, Will'um!" and the wheels began to grind on the cobblestones. It was music to Frank's ears. He leaned back in his seat beside the Abbé with a sigh of intense relief.

"We've made it!" he said.

The curtains had been drawn close and they were in complete darkness. Frank began to explain the various devices he and Cope had worked out to conceal their identities in case of need. They were to pass as an American family. The Abbé was a French-Canadian priest from Three Rivers, a Father Latour. He, Frank, was to pose as their brother and the family name was Stebbens. Tobias, Miranda, and Mercy Stebbens. How did they like their new names?

Gabrielle laughed. "I insist on being Miranda. I rather like it. *Miranda*. You mustn't forget to call me that."

"I won't. And you must all remember to call me Tobias. We mustn't make any slips."

"Brother Tobias! It's a very solemn kind of name, isn't it?"

"Carr will have to take it over when he joins us and I leave."

"It won't suit him at all. He has quite a sense of dignity, you know. I don't think he'll like being Mr. Tobias Stebbens."

He went on with other explanations. Letters had been prepared for them to carry, addressed from supposed acquaintances in Philadelphia, their home town. These were to be produced if any questions were raised. If it proved necessary to remain at the port for any length of time, the letters were to be left about where they could be seen by casual eyes. There were labels with the family initials to be pasted on the bags at the first stop. He began to recite facts about Philadelphia so that they could show a sufficient knowledge of the place in the course of conversation—Independence Hall, the Liberty Bell, Benjamin Franklin, Pine Street, Broad Street.

"You've thought of everything, dear brother," said Gabrielle. "I'm beginning to think you've had lots of experience at rescuing damsels in distress."

"The ideas were Cope's for the most part. He worked for hours getting everything ready. By the way, if we're questioned we must be very vague about things here. We must make mistakes which will seem funny. And we must claim that George Washington was a greater man than Napoleon." He thought for a moment and then added: "Remember that we're in mourning for an uncle in Glasgow. A Mr. Allister McAllister. A wool merchant. I must remember to take these bands off my sleeves and give them to Carr when he comes."

"This is going to be an adventure." Gabrielle's voice had become animated. "I'm beginning to enjoy it. And I'm very hungry. We've been so anxious all day that we've had no food. Has our very thoughtful brother done anything about that?"

"Of course. There's a hamper on the box. We'll have it down as soon as we get out of the city."

"Frank, Frank, you're wonderful! It's a pity you're not coming with us. I don't see how we'll ever get along without you."

Agreeing inwardly that it was a pity, he said: "We're well out of the neighborhood. I think we can open the curtains now."

He drew his tinder pistol from a pocket and flashed on the light. Gabrielle was opposite him, looking so lovely in her black bonnet and veil that he had to restrain himself from saying, "If you wanted me, I would go to the ends of the earth with you!" She smiled at him. The Abbé was already sound asleep, his head sunk down between his massive shoulders, his face in repose resembling more than ever a moist treacle pudding. Margot sat beside her cousin, regarding Frank with unhappy eyes over the top of the wicker cage. It was clear she was not enjoying the adventure at all.

5

THE ANVIL AND TORCH was in complete darkness. It had been raining heavily for an hour, the depressing kind of rain which seems to be reserved for the special benefit of travelers in a great need of hurry. The wheels sent water splashing in waves as the carriage swerved in under the arch of the inn yard. Frank warned his companions to keep the curtains drawn before he alighted. His feet sank into mud up to his ankles.

Caradoc had not arrived. The landlord, aroused from his slumbers after fifteen minutes of loud and angry rapping, grumbled the information from an upper window that no one had come down from London during the night. If they wanted rooms, they could be obliged. Food, no; he wouldn't put himself out to get food at any such blasted hour as this. As for the horses, both grooms were away for the night and he wouldn't walet a team of prads for old Nobs hisself.

Frank returned to the carriage in such an uneasy frame of mind that he did not notice how wet he was getting. It was a full hour past the time his brother had agreed to meet them. Had something happened which they had not foreseen, or had Caradoc's sense of discretion triumphed over his devotion? He lighted a bougie no thicker than his thumb and stuck it in a sconce on the inside of one of the doors.

"We'll have to wait here for a time," he said, avoiding Gabrielle's eye. "Apparently Carr has been delayed. How would it be if we have the hamper down now?"

The Abbé Force, awake for the first time since the journey began, concurred in this suggestion with a hungry grunt. Frank tapped on the roof with the head of his cane, and the driver, sliding open a panel, peered in at them.

"Time for food, Carberry. Just hand it down. We'll open the wine ourselves."

"Thought ye'd forgot there was sich a thing as stummicks," grumbled the man. "Mine's as hollow as a bowlded owl. If you don't mind, gov'nor, I'll take a bite wi' me to the stables. I'm soakit as it is."

The Abbé, grasping the leg of a capon and a huge round bun, proceeded to eat with an energy which threatened the adequacy of the supply. Frank found that he had a good appetite also, but neither of the girls displayed any desire for food. Margot, who had not spoken since the ride began, pretended to nibble at a slice of chicken, but an involuntary sigh which escaped her proved that her thoughts were still back in the gloomy house they had left. Gabrielle, in spite of her earlier interest in the subject, contented herself with a glass of the wine.

"Caradoc's not coming," she said, after an unbroken silence of several minutes.

Frank answered in as casual a tone as he could assume. "It's possible he won't join us until later. He knows the route we're following and can overtake us on the way. I think, however, we'll wait here an hour to be sure. The horses need a rest in any event."

"I don't believe he's coming at all."

"Of course he is. He warned me there might be some delay. The House is sitting, you know."

"It seems to be a most faithful House. It sits all the time." After a moment she added: "Please don't think me unappreciative of the advantages of having you with us instead. I'm sure we're in the best possible hands. Where are you taking us?"

"To a small port directly south of this. We may have to stay there for some time. Until the ship puts in, at any rate. Carr is certain to join us there."

There was another silence, broken only by the brisk mastication of the churchman. "I'm afraid you'll find yourself in trouble when you return to London," said Gabrielle.

He brushed this aside. "I won't be suspected. No one saw us leave. In any case the unfailing Mr. Cope has already provided me with a perfect alibi. An aunt of ours lives not far from the port. She's in poor health and I'm supposed to be paying her a visit."

"Your aunt Francilea?"

"Yes. She really is quite ill and I intend to see her before returning to London."

"She was at the Towers when we were there." Gabrielle spoke in a thoughtful tone. "I had a long talk with her. She told me some things which I'm now beginning to believe."

The Abbé fell asleep when they started out again and filled the coach with the violence of his snores. Gabrielle also dozed off after a time, with one arm bent under her cheek as a pillow. Margot spent the time whispering to the canary and staring out at the darkness and the rain.

Frank thought how lucky he was that Caradoc had decided not to come. He would have one full day at least without the presence of his successful rival to dim his pleasure. A whole day of Gabrielle's company!

He never took his eyes from the face of the sleeping girl, delighting in the way her dark brown hair clustered in crisp curls above her forehead, in the soft flush of her cheeks, in the deep shadows cast by her long eyelashes. Her other arm had fallen to the seat beside her and the hand lay with the palm curled upward; like the opening bud of a white flower, he said to himself.

"She's in danger and yet that selfish dolt can stay away!" he reflected bitterly. How could anyone, blessed with the love of this divine being, absent himself at a time like this? He himself was drawn to her as though by a magnet.

"You love her very much, I think," said Margot in a low voice.

Frank became aware that the young cousin was observing him over the arched bars of the bird cage. He nodded to her and sighed.

"Yes, Margot. I love her so much that all the light will go out of the world when she boards the ship for France. I don't dare think what life is going to be without her." He turned his eyes back to the graceful figure curled up in the opposite corner. "Is it any wonder? Have you ever seen anyone so completely lovely? I wish there was to be no end to this ride. Look, Margot, at the line of her brow! It's sheer beauty!"

Gabrielle stirred and opened her eyes. "You were talking about me," she charged.

"I was telling Margot some of the things I've never had the courage to tell you."

"That sounds as though you were being very severe about me."

"I don't believe you would have minded what I said. At any rate there was pleasure for me in saying it."

She patted the folds of her skirt into position and adjusted the black lace of her collar. Rummaging in the bag on her lap, she produced a powder puff with a small mirror in the handle. After studying herself in this with a critical eye, she said with a frown: "My eyes are red. I suspect that was what you two were talking about."

"No, it was not that."

"Well, Brother Tobias, you must see to it that I don't fall asleep again. You must be more entertaining."

"I can at least give you some interesting news." Frank proceeded to tell of the turn military affairs had taken in Austria. Gabrielle listened intently, a suggestion of a frown between her eyes. "It looks," he concluded, "as though Napoleon had fallen into a trap."

"If he's defeated, we'll be in a very difficult position. After what Sosthène has done, we can expect nothing if the King gets back on the throne." She seemed very much disturbed. "I've been afraid this would happen. I feel like a deserter, Frank."

"You needn't have any fears yet. Napoleon is still much too strong. A single defeat won't bring about his fall."

Margot was listening with shining eyes. "If only Uncle Robert had lived to hear this!" she said.

"You must remember," he went on, "that all Europe is allied with him. All but Austria and the Peninsula. No, Gabrielle, your brother can look forward to several profitable years with Napoleon at the very worst."

Something in his tone prompted her to say: "Don't think too badly of us, Frank. After all, we're French. I've heard the Duc de Berri exulting over the defeat of an English ship even though it meant his chance of becoming King of France suffered because of it. Only the older people are completely against Napoleon."

"I am!" declared Margot vehemently.

"And Margot," amended Gabrielle with a smile. "I don't know what we're going to do with her, she's such a firebrand. She'll get us all in trouble."

"No, Margot's too sensible for that."

"I'm finding it hard enough to get myself reconciled to what's ahead of us. All my life I've been taught to hate Napoleon. It's going to be very difficult."

"I won't go to his court," asserted the younger girl. "I would rather stay here in England."

They broke an axle on a stony incline near the southern border of Surrey, which caused several hours' delay, and so it was not until early morning of the second day that they reached the *Elephant's Head*. It proved to be a very unpretentious inn with no sign visible to identify it. The landlord, whose hook nose was flattened down on a sharply acquisitive face, welcomed them effusively, as though guests had been a rarity with him.

After breakfast had been served in a low-raftered sitting room on the first floor, the ladies retired to their rooms. The Abbé followed suit, leaving Frank the task of persuading their incredulous host that baths were desired immediately.

"No more'n one biddy," said the latter, unwilling to believe that Americans could have such an exaggerated liking for cleanliness. "Have to take turns. Matter o' hours, sir."

"Very well. We'll want hot water. Plenty of it."

"Hot? That'll make it worse. Never keeps more'n enough hot water to fill a teakettle."

The baths, and the desire for sleep they created, served to use up all the mid-hours of the day. Dinner was served at five, a most satisfying affair of roast beef and a huge raisin pudding. Frank got to his feet when the meal was over and announced that he proposed to learn what he could in the town of the movements of the French lugger. Gabrielle jumped up immediately and said that she would go with him.

"It's clear now," she declared when they were on the street, her hand tucked under his arm, a black shawl covering her head, "that Caradoc thinks so little of me that he's decided not to come. He can't be very much concerned over the danger I'm in. There's no use trying to defend him. As I've said before, I understand him perfectly. Before we leave"—with a sigh—"I want to tell you all about it. In the meantime, please, don't feel too sorry for me. I'm beginning to see it's all for the best. I don't deny that my pride has suffered a blow."

They had reached the top of a hill on the outskirts of the little fishing town, and her fingers closed suddenly on his arm. "Frank, the sea! It's the first time I've seen it!"

He looked down with surprise into her excited face. "Really? I had no idea you had traveled so little, Gabrielle."

"We've been so terribly poor," she said in a whisper. "You can have no idea how hard it's been. Why, I've never been outside of London except for my visits to the Towers."

She stood and watched the dull gray of the channel water with fascinated eyes. A belated fishing smack was tacking in toward the harbor as though weary after a day of struggle with swift and contrary currents.

"Is France directly across from here?"

"Yes. I think Dieppe must be the nearest point."

"How far is it?"

"Seventy miles. A little more perhaps. You can see France from Dover on a clear day."

"France!" There was a catch in her voice. "I've dreamed so much about it. Does it matter who rules there now? Does it matter what Sosthène has done? No, no, nothing matters at all except that it's home and that I'm going there at last."

"I can understand how you feel. England looked good after being away less than a year."

"Home!" Her voice had risen to an ecstatic pitch. "It must be so lovely! So bright and sunny and—yes, so happy, even if the rightful King isn't on the throne. I'm beginning to wonder if *that* is important after all. I'll always love England, of course, and I'll miss my friends here but—I'm going home, I'm going home at last!"

"Your friends—and one at least who feels more than friendship for you, Gaby—will miss you terribly."

She squeezed his arm as they paced slowly along together. "It isn't going to be good-by forever, my dear Frank. We'll meet again. I feel it. I *know* it. When, and where, who can tell?" She looked up at him. "Why, I would feel completely lost without you. I've come to depend on you so much."

They visited the establishment of a ship's chandler, and he left her in the front of the shop while he went back to talk with the proprietor. She looked about curiously at the coils of tarry rope, the nets and canvas, the pots of paint and tallow and beeswax, the crimson-sealed containers of gamboge from the East, the curious instruments and ancient brass lanterns; her nose curling fastidiously as the combined odors of tar and seaweed and rosin assailed it. Frank was back in a very few minutes, wearing a smile of satisfaction.

"We're in great luck," he whispered. "The lugger's due in tonight. The cargo will be unloaded at a cove a mile or so to the east of the inn. They expect to be through and off again before dawn. Our man back there will arrange with the captain to take you with him. He's been doing a lively business in that line recently."

"It has one drawback, hasn't it? We'll have to leave you so soon."

"I may never see you again, Gaby. Have you any idea what that means to me?"

They walked some distance in silence. "Now I must talk about Caradoc," she said. "I want to tell you all about it. When I first saw him, he was standing at the east end of the hall and the light was pouring down on him from the stained-glass windows. I was sure he was wearing armor. It was like seeing in real life a knight of old times." She paused. "It seems to have been love at first sight with us."

When Frank made no response, she went on: "It was perfect at first. We seemed to have the same tastes. He was always gay, and he danced so well, and he always said the things I wanted to hear. I, who had always exacted devotion—I was glad to give all my devotion to him. Father was very much against it, but I soon talked him over. I could have done the same with Sossy." She sighed. "It couldn't last, of course. Things began to go wrong. He was in the House so much and so busy with his career. I began to see how selfish he was. He expected everything to be done for him. I resented his attitude to you, Frank, the things he said about you. Oh, he was in love with me. I had no reason to doubt that. But he had other loves. Most especially his career." Her voice became a little sharp. "That great, that *stupid* career! I tried hard to believe in it. But down in my heart I began to doubt it. I began to see that he would advance by reason of what others did for him. That, I didn't mind. I didn't want him too clever. And I felt capable of giving him all the help he needed. A great deal can be accomplished in politics over a dinner table." Her voice dwindled off. "And now I know the truth. He puts his career above everything. Above me. For all I can tell, he may be secretly glad it has happened this way."

"No, I don't believe that."

"You needn't stand up for him, Frank. I know him better than you do. You may not believe me, but I'm glad he hasn't come." She raised her head proudly. "I mean it. Things will be easier for me now. If he had come to me at once, if he had done all the things you've done, I would have been very unhappy at leaving. I still feel hurt and—and very much humbled. But what he's done to me will help me forget." She quickened her steps. "I don't believe it will take very long."

"I hope not. I want your happiness above everything."

"Soon I'll be sensible enough to see that it's you I'm really going to miss."

He stopped and swung her around to face him. "You *will* think of me then? You won't forget me entirely?"

"Never. I'll never forget you, Frank."

He said in a voice shaken with emotion: "I'll love you, Gabrielle, as long as I live. I've only one thing in life to hold to—the hope that someday you'll need me and that it will be possible for me to go to you at once."

6

FRANK RETURNED to London in a depressed frame of mind. Gabrielle had gone out of his life and nothing else seemed to matter. By this time she would be well on her way to Paris, excited and, no doubt, delighted at being on French soil. Even the relief of finding the authorities not disposed to take any steps in the matter of the escape had done little to improve his state of mind.

To make matters worse, the Austrians had been premature in their claims of victory. Napoleon had burst out of the trap at Lobau and had given them their customary thrashing in the bloody battle of Wagram. It was now certain that he would force humiliating terms on them, and that Britain again would stand alone in his path. The only cheering factor was the wave of horror which had swept over France when the total of casualties had become known. Wagram had been a costly triumph, and it was certain now that any move to invade the islands would meet with bitter opposition from the French people themselves.

An eventless fortnight passed. Trutnall had been sent out to the Peninsula in the guise of a wine commission merchant, but it would be weeks before any dispatches could be expected from him. In the meantime men were stationed in all ports to meet the ships which came in. The news picked up in this way proved, in the main, unimportant.

Frank began to haunt the water front himself, and it was his good fortune finally to come into contact with his Lisbon acquaintance, Lieutenant Gubbins. That disgruntled member of the Wellesley staff came limping through the gangboard of a brig from the Tagus, followed by a servant staggering under a load of luggage including a mattress and a set of steel springs.

"Mr. Gubbins!" cried Frank, elbowing his way to his side. "I didn't expect to see you home so soon. You've been wounded, I fear."

Recognition grew slowly in the subaltern's mind. "You're the publisher," he said finally. "Well, we're in the same boat. I got *my* walking papers too, by Gad! A horse stepped on my foot and the Beau was only too glad of an excuse to pack me off home. I was furious about it, but it's a relief to be free of him. There's no pleasing him, I tell you. But I'm going back, I am indeed. I am going to arrange a transfer into the line, by Gad. It'll be worth the price just to see his expression when he sets eyes on me again!"

"Have there been any developments?"

"When I left, the Beau was getting ready to move north against Soult." Bitterness welled up strongly in the Gubbins breast. "There'll be a hot tussle and, Gad, I'll miss all of it! I've an uncle in the Peers and I'm of a mind to have him do something about it."

"What news of Sir Robert Wilson?"

"He's been given command of a division. From things I heard dropped around headquarters, the Beau has rather taken a fancy to Riding Bobby."

Immensely relieved at this news, Frank proceeded to ply the subaltern with questions. He got little good of it, however; Mr. Gubbins was either uncommunicative or had been singularly unobservant during his last days in Lisbon. He had little of value to tell about the opening moves of the campaign.

In the meantime other passengers had been making their way down from the side of the ship. Frank kept an eye on them as he talked and, when a rather demure poke bonnet appeared in the gangboard, he was quick to recognize under it the attractively tanned features of Laura Brakespeare. She was plainly dressed, but he was surprised to see that she had brought a maidservant with her, a plump Portuguese woman in a poodle-white hat, whose black eyes darted apprehensively over the crowded dock as though she found her translation a terrifying experience.

Laura had engaged a hackney coach and was on the point of stepping into it when he reached her. She turned when he called, "Laura!" and it was clear from her expression that she was both pleased and disturbed by this chance meeting.

"I'm happy to see you again, Francis," she said as they shook hands. "So here we are, safely home in England. There were times when we hardly expected this would happen."

"It did seem a remote chance when we were camped back of the

Yeltes and expected the French to come over any day. You missed the last stages of it, thank heavens."

She noticed the scar on his cheek and instinctively placed a hand on his arm. "Francis!" she exclaimed. "You were wounded! Now I understand why you returned home so suddenly."

"The wound had nothing to do with my return. It was a minor cut, as you can see, but I'll always have it to remind me of my one short spell of soldiering."

"Did it happen to you—that night?"

He nodded. "At the very last minute. We had nearly reached the river on our return and hadn't seen anything of the Frenchies at all. Then a squad of cavalry came down on us. It was a sharp brush while it lasted. I was lucky to get off with no more than this to show for it."

There was deep concern in the steady gaze with which she was favoring him. "I didn't hear anything about it. Just before we left, we were told that your party had returned and that there had been losses. It wasn't until I reached Lisbon that I heard you were safe. I can't tell you how relieved I was." She achieved a rather weak smile. "How fortunate that it was no worse! I think, Francis, that it really adds to your appearance."

"Speaking of good fortune, it was lucky I decided to come down today. I've been expecting daily to hear of your return; although lately I've been more than half convinced you had decided to stay in Portugal for the duration of the campaign."

"It has been difficult for civilians to get places on the boats coming back."

This was a reasonable explanation, and yet Frank was not completely satisfied. Every ship from the Tagus had seemed to carry its full quota of civilian passengers. He said, "I hope you intended to let me know of your arrival."

"Yes," she said finally. "At least—I was going to think it over. I haven't been sure you would want to hear from me."

"Laura! You haven't seriously believed that, I'm sure. I've had men meet every ship in the hope of getting some word of you."

She avoided any direct rejoinder by saying: "I missed you in Lisbon. You must have been there a very short time."

"One day only." Frank indulged in a wry smile. "Sir Arthur saw to that. I was unlucky enough to meet him the first morning and he gave orders I was to leave the country that night."

The maid was already ensconced in the coach, and Laura stepped in beside her. "I expect to be in London for several days," she said with a smile which seemed to him rather strained. "You will come and see me, then?"

"Of course. I must see you at once. We have much to talk about."

She regarded him steadily through the door of the coach. "Yes, we have much to talk about. Unless we should decide it would be wiser to forget everything that happened."

"Would you prefer it that way?"

"I don't know. . . ." She hesitated and then asked, "You are surprised to see me traveling this way?"

"Do you mean, with the maid?"

"Yes. I have no definite plans for the future yet but I—I have no intention of becoming a governess again. That is the only thing of which I am sure." She gave an order to the driver, and the coach began to move. "Good-by, Francis. I hope to see you soon."

He waited expectantly for several days but no message reached him. It became clear then that the omission had been deliberate. Laura had no intention of seeing him again. He realized, as the days passed, that he was relieved at this. Certainly he had entertained no thoughts of resuming their relationship at the point where it had been interrupted, and now she was making it apparent that she shared his disinclination. In spite of this tacit agreement, or perhaps because of it, there would have been embarrassment for both of them in a further meeting.

The satisfaction he felt at her decision not to renew their acquaintance on any basis was tinged, nevertheless, with regret as well as a sense of shame. He was extremely fond of her and he realized also that he should not be glad to escape all responsibility in this way. There was cause for worry in the course she seemed to be charting for herself. Was there anything he could do for her now? Obviously not; she was making it certain that it was not her purpose to let him interfere with her plans. The best thing he could do would be to dismiss her from his mind.

He found, however, that this was not easy to do. He was too deeply concerned over what the future might hold for her.

The news from the Continent continued disturbing. An English expeditionary force which had been sent to divert the French drive against Austria ("Too late! Too late!" the *Tablet* had declared, and some of the other newspapers had echoed the cry) had landed in Flanders a fortnight after the armistice had been signed. Napoleon, having sheared the title of Emperor from the ineffectual Hapsburg, was reported to be dashing back across Europe in his berlin at a rate of speed never before achieved. Would he pause to smash the poorly armed British force in

Walcheren, or would he go on to take command in person of his armies in the Peninsula? He could afford to do whatever suited his purpose. Prussia, never ready to help at the right time, had decided not to help at all. Alexander of Russia, his war with Britain having developed into a stalemate and his liking for Napoleon having cooled, had withdrawn into an inscrutable Muscovite silence which masked his intentions.

The French Emperor, as it happened, did neither. The British Army in Walcheren, rotting from lack of food and medical supplies, was beneath the imperial notice and was allowed to totter home as best it could. For some reason Napoleon seemed reluctant to take the peninsular campaign in hand; perhaps Fate had already spun into the pattern of future events the thread which postponed the meeting with Wellington until a far distant day on the field of Waterloo. The berlin, with its green-covered couch and its ingenious files and pigeonholes, swayed and rattled at breakneck speed all the way to Paris through crowds which gathered on the roads for a peep at the dread conqueror. The British Army, what was left of it, arrived back in due course and was dispersed in shamefaced haste to regimental barracks. Little attention was paid at first to stories seeping out of Paris that Napoleon was really going to get a divorce at last. It had been a matrimonial and not a military urge which had sent him posting across Europe at such speed. He was going to be rid of Josephine and marry instead a peach-complexioned and stupid little Austrian Archduchess. Thus he would bring Austria at last into the chain of alliances he had forged on the Continent.

The nation of shopkeepers would really stand alone now. The people, still grumbling, still bitterly aware of the bungling methods of their government, never gave a thought to the possibility of surrender. Somehow they would go on fighting and in the end they would be on top. They were sure of that.

Napoleon would not have found things to his liking if he had continued on to the Peninsula. The story of what was happening there reached the offices of the *Tablet* one day in August in the form of a dispatch from Trutnall. Frank opened it with doubtful fingers but, after perusing the first lines, he dropped the crumpled sheets on his desk and shouted, "Cope! Cope! Cope!" When his assistant arrived, he was again deep in the dispatch, his eyes devouring the closely written pages.

"Two victories!" he cried. "Sir Arthur made a surprise crossing of the Douro and sent Soult reeling back into the hills. Then he struck south and gave Victor a thorough drubbing at Talavera. Glorious news, Copey!"

Cope's face twitched with an expression of delight in which there was an unwilling tincture of doubt.

"Trutnall saw both operations," exulted Frank. "All the details are here. He's given us a grand story on it. Clear the decks, Copey, we have tidings of good cheer at last for the people of England."

The news of the battle of Talavera reverberated in London like the bursting of a bomb. Parliament could hardly wait to vote Sir Arthur a bonus of two thousand pounds a year for three years. His Majesty gazetted him at once Baron Douro of Wellesley and Viscount Wellington of Talavera. The name "Wellesley" seemed to dissolve into disuse immediately, and people began to speak of the victor as Wellington. Brave Wellington, wily Wellington, sure Wellington! He's the one for our brass! They couldn't talk about him enough.

"Do you suppose anything will be done for the man who made all this possible?" asked Frank, as he and Cope watched a cheering crowd in Dacre Square.

Cope, the complete realist, dismissed the suggestion with a shake of the hand. "Wilson is forgotten already. Talavera has eclipsed the Yeltes."

"I think, then, we must publish a reminder."

This was done, but it had no apparent effect. Even the wounded men, who began to arrive in close-packed ships from the Tagus, spoke only of Wellington and the trouncing he had given Victor, Napoleon's onetime drummer boy.

Frank paid a visit to one of the hospitals when he saw on the list of patients the name of Private Benjamin Fuller. It proved to be a dreary building of greenish stone and could have been nothing but what it was, unless perhaps a prison. It exhibited inside and out the neglect which is the one sure characteristic of all such state institutions. Water was leaking dismally from defective eaves. Breaks in the windows had been repaired with bundles of rags, which made very little difference actually, for the glass was too dirty to admit much in the way of light. Even the angel carved over the main entrance had a sly expression on its weather-beaten face, as though well aware that the stone slab beneath would more fairly state the case if it carried the word "Inferno" instead of "Infirmary." A sentinel was pacing up and down in soggy gloom.

A fetid odor assailed the nostrils as soon as the door was opened. It was as busy as an anthill inside. People of mean station, judging from the condition of their clothes, were milling about, their faces set in the formalized expression of sorrow. There was a constant cry of "Squire!" and the women attendants were scurrying about as though their own lives depended on it. Even the lint scrapers had been pressed into service to wait on the patients, who were overflowing into the corridors.

Benjie Fuller was in a ward which contained at least a score of beds and seemed to excel all others in the rankness of its smell. Frank paused on the threshold with eyes which tried at first to disbelieve what they saw. Each bed in this Temple of Mercy had three occupants: men with bandaged heads and arms; men whose eyes were glazed with suffering, who cursed at their fellows and demanded more room or begged pitiously for the attention of the distracted squires. Some of the pillows and sheets were splotched with red, and the tables between the beds displayed some of the unsightly tools of surgery in addition to well-used towels and sponges and grisly-looking cupping glasses. All the windows were closed up tight, air being the only commodity strictly prohibited. Visitors swarmed about the beds.

"Fuller?" said one of the women, in answer to Frank's inquiry. "He's a legger. Left un off clean at the knee. Four beds down, center man. All leggers in that un. Lucky for them; on'y three legs to use up space 'stead o' six."

It was hard to find a basis for agreement with the statement that Benjie Fuller was in luck. He was wedged in between his two bed-fellows, both of whom were aggressively large. One of them had an arm in a sling for good measure and was jealous, clearly, of his full share of the space. The other seemed to be verging on dementia.

"I hoped you would come, Mr. Ellery, sir," said Benjie. His face was gaunt and pale. "Have to get along on one leg now, sir. It'll mean a different job when I get out of here. Can't be a sojer with one leg. Nor a foots, sir."

"I'll find something for you, Benjie." Frank continued to look about him as though still unable to believe that such things could be.

The third man in the bed, who was called Turk, began to howl dismally, throwing back his head and tensing the muscles of his neck as though in the throes of great pain.

"He's allus a bit worse on banyan days. They make him angry. He's liable to howl when he's angry."

"What are banyan days?"

"No meat, sir. We has two days a week of it."

"Great God, Benjie! Do you mean to say they don't even give you enough to eat! What *do* you get?"

"On banyans we gets soup and bread and gen'rally a bit of cheese. We makes do, sir."

"Could I send out and get some food for you?"

Benjie smiled. "I should say *so*, sir."

"Then I would like to get enough for the whole ward. Is he"—nodding at the vociferous Turk—"well enough to eat anything yet?"

"That he is, sir. Turk's a great eater. That is, when he gets the chance."

Frank moved closer to the bed and said to Fuller, "Have you any news of Sir Robert Wilson?"

"There was plenty of talk about him in the ranks, sir. Riding Bobby's pop'lar with us."

"What part did he have in the Talavera campaign?"

"He commanded the vanguard, sir. There wur talk at first that Beresford wanted him sent back, but the Beau said he'd done a good thing at the Yeltes and so he got his command. The ranks liked that, sir. There wur talk that Sir Robert pulled Victor out o' position by making a dash for Madrid and that it helped us give Johnny Craps his beating."

Frank nodded his head with deep satisfaction at this piece of news. "That sounds like him, Benjie. He's a daring soldier and he'll take a risk whenever he sees a chance to gain by it. Do you mean that Victor had to drop back to cover Madrid and so Wellington caught him on the move?"

"It wur something like that, sir. We did hear, sir, that Sir Robert went further than he wur supposed to. The Beau sent him orders to come back. We heard the Beau said some very sharp things to him. He can be very sharp, sir, when he has a mind to it; which is often, sir."

Frank laughed. "That's exactly what Wilson would do. And it worked, Benjie! That's the great thing about Wilson; he knows when to take the risks. So Victor was misled and Wellington won a great victory!" After a moment's reflection he began to view the matter in a more serious light. "Was Wellington very angry?"

"I 'spects so, sir. He's a hard un, the Beau."

"I must go now," said Frank, getting to his feet. "I intend to see what can be done about getting you out of here at once, Benjie."

"Never mind me, Mr. Ellery, sir." Fuller's tone was quite cheerful. "We has to put up with things. I'm ready to see it through, sir. We must do what we can"—he had quite apparently been hearing speeches of the usual patriotic order—"for England, home, and beauty, sir."

Cope was engaged with a complicated set of steel rules and springs, in which two pens were gripped, when Frank walked into his cubicle. He looked up with an absent-minded smile.

"Someday I'll make it work," he said. "Your father was pretty keen about it, you know."

Frank remembered how hard Joseph Ellery had labored over his idea of using polygraphs in the business so that copies could be made of all letters which went out of the house. He had even hoped to see the day when press copy would be prepared in duplicate.

"I'm afraid it's lost effort, Copey. If the pater couldn't find the answer, I'm sure we won't. It's too slow. We wouldn't get a thing done if we used them regularly."

"I suppose so." Cope lowered the glass cover of the instrument with reluctance. "Still, it's a great idea. It takes almost as long to have copies made of all the letters. Your father was a remarkable man, Frank."

"I wish more people realized how remarkable he was." Frank sighed. "He really believed the time would come when every form of work would be done by mechanical means. Do you suppose he was right?"

"I'm certain he was. When you see power presses at work in this plant, Francis Ellery, you'll have the first proof of it. And it won't be long now."

"You never let up about those presses, do you?" Frank paused. "Who is the best writer we have on the staff?"

Cope sniffed indignantly. "That would seem to indicate you never read the flash articles and the occasional leaders written by one Nathan Cope."

"Good. That was exactly what I wanted to hear you say. Well, you laid yourself wide open. The pen of Nathan Cope will be devoted at once to a series of very special articles."

Cope blinked at him suspiciously. "What about?"

"I want you to visit all the military and naval hospitals."

"Another crusade. I rather thought so."

"Yes. One we can begin without any delay. We mustn't lose a single hour on this one."

"I'm your man, then. Are things pretty bad?"

"Unbelievably bad! The poor devils would be better off under the care of witch doctors in African kraals than in these pestholes we call hospitals. They're worse than the prisons, if such a thing is possible."

Cope said happily, "I'll get to work on them tomorrow."

"No, on second thoughts, you had better wait until Thursday. That will be a banyan day."

7

WILSON ANNOUNCED his arrival home in a letter to Frank, inviting him to dinner at Brook's at four o'clock, and adding, "I hope you'll fetch our friend, Charlie Present." They put in an appearance several minutes ahead of the hour. A few guests only were eating in the Subscription Room, but the smaller tables for play were already well occupied. The air was filled with eager voices and the sound of rolling dice. The members would not get down to serious gambling until later in the day, but in the meantime they were occupying their splendid minds with the making of small bets. "I'll lay ye four to one, Bertie, I can take a grip on my timber-club and whang the poll more'n seventy-five yards," they heard one youth declare. "But it's got to be a brand-new poll, mind ye." "I'll lay any odds"—from another quarter—"the Butcher's new wife'll present him with a blasted heir to the throne inside the year."

Wilson came in, looking in the best of condition and the worst of spirits. His face, burned red from exposure to the sun of the Spanish plains and the sharp Biscayan winds, wore an air of discontent which increased as he gazed about the rooms. "Glad to see you, Frank. And you, Cope. What do you say to a brandy before we settle down to our grilled bone? I seem to feel the need of one. Perhaps I haven't got my shore legs back yet. Or"—with a disparaging glance about him—"it may be the sight of all these fine, bird-witted gentlemen. A cozy lot of Ralph Spooners, aren't they? Sitting here at their ease, betting on golf games and pickling themselves in their damned port while the world goes to pieces."

His somber mood stayed with him through the early part of the meal. "We're never going to do it with a small enlisted army," he declared. "Every able-bodied man should be pressed into the service. I'm for conscription, Frank—absolute conscription, with no favors for blue blood or full pockets. But, of course, our blasted, addled, weak-kneed government won't have the courage to try it out." He speared savagely at the capon thigh on his plate. "I would like to see a press gang turned loose in this place. How these fine bucks would scramble to get under tables or to hide behind the coattails of the waiters!"

"We'll never live to see *that* day."

"I suppose not. Still, it would be a great thing for the country." The thought of loud-voiced sergeants with drawn cutlasses in the Subscription Room seemed to have brought Wilson back to a better humor. "Perhaps Russia will do the trick for us instead. Mark my words, Boney and the Tsar will break one of these days. The Tsar distrusts Boney thoroughly by this time. My wager is that the puffed-up pride of the Corsican will take him soon into the damnedest gamble of all history. He'll march his armies against Russia. And, when he does, he'll find himself in bloody chancery."

Cope squinted up from his plate. "Do you think the Russians can beat him?"

"Beat him?" Wilson laughed so loudly that the rattle of dice at neighboring tables was suspended in shocked surprise. "If he hooks his line into them, he'll find he's caught a fish he can't land. Mind you, Alexander hasn't a general worth his salt. They're a scurvy lot with not an ounce of real military brains. But the climate and the dogged courage of the Rusky-muskies will be something new for the great Bonaparte. He'll beat them soundly if they come out to fight him but, if he invades the country, it will be a different matter."

It was not until the pudding was on the table, a rich one with browned lumps of suet sticking out of its sides, that Wilson got around to the events in the Peninsula. "I found a chance to do something after all," he said, twirling a wineglass in his hand. "You knew, of course, I was given command of the van. Well, I had the most definite orders from Wellington, all cut and dried and apple-pied to the last cartouche. I was to do this and that." He smiled at Frank. "I'm sure you remember the general lay of the country. We had pushed up the valley of the Tagus, and Wellington was getting more apprehensive by the minute. Victor was ahead of us, and there was always the chance that Soult would yank his regimentals up again from around his boot tops and come down on us from the north. It was a chancy spot we were in. You see, we were pretty well away from our base and we knew our Spanish allies would be of damned little help. Their bloated ole mule of a General, Cuesta, wasn't disposed to take any orders from us. Now then." He began to draw lines on the tablecloth with his fork. "Here is Talavera. Here, forty miles to the east, is Escalona; it's on the Alberche. Here, forty miles east of that, we have Madrid. Fat King Joey was in Madrid, teetering and chattering and mewling like a dropsical, muffin-stuffing dancing master. Back of Talavera, Victor was waiting for us, with a larger force than ours. He was keeping one eye on us and one on Madrid. He had his orders from Jumping Joseph that under no circumstances were we to get into Madrid. French prestige would suffer a terrible blow if that ever happened." He paused before adding, "I had the most positive orders not to move beyond Escalona."

Wilson leaned back and began to sip his wine. After a moment he winked at Frank and continued with his recital. "There you have the situation as plain as a blasted packstaff. What would anyone with even an elementary knowledge of strategy do under such circumstances? I put it to you, Frank, and to you, my good Charlie Present. You can see what a magnificent chance it was. 'Well,' I said to myself, 'if the Beau were here he would certainly take advantage of this chance to scare our Joey into an earth bath.' All we needed was to have Joey bleating for help and Victor dropping back from his very advantageous position to cover Madrid." He gestured eloquently with his free hand. "I disregarded my orders. I left Escalona to scorch under its own blistering share of the sun and marched on for Madrid. Oh, I realized the chance I was taking. Sir Gimlet Eye wants his orders carried out to the letter. Go where I say and do what I say, no more and no less. I knew he would be furious with me. But—we needed a victory so badly! Drummer Boy Victor is no genius at best and, if we could get him out of position, he would be ripe for a trouncing."

There was a moment's silence. "It worked out as I expected. Victor began to slew around. Sir Gimlet Eye saw his chance and pounced on him. He gave the drummer boy a good, sound licking. We had our victory."

"And now he's Viscount Wellington of Talavera," commented Frank.

"You think I did the right thing, then?"

"I've always agreed with you that we can beat the French only by being as daring in our methods as they are."

"Boney is the most egotistical leader the world has ever seen, but even he is willing to allow his marshals the right to act on their own initiative. He judges by results." There was a moment's pause. "Don't make any mistake about Wellington. He's a damned good soldier. I'm inclined to think he can fight along conventional lines better than any other general alive today. He hooked into Victor like a good un." This burst of generosity ended up in another spell of grumbling. "But you needn't make the other mistake and think Wellington is a genius. He has his weaknesses. He never takes a chance. He must be so damned sure before he makes a move. It's all careful planning with him—working out schedules, and looking over the mule teams, and inspecting the ammunition carts. He's not another Napoleon, and don't think it for a minute."

"What happened," asked Frank, "when you met him after the—the episode at Escalona?"

Wilson burst into a hearty laugh. "Very little was said, as a matter of fact. Just one sentence. A dozen officers were standing about when I walked in to report. Staff creepers, watching both of us, waiting for the explosion, hoping to see me blasted into outer darkness. Well, he looked at me with that cold eye of his and said, 'I was under the impression, sir, that Escalona was forty miles this side of Madrid.' No more than that, not a word. But he knew, and I knew, that I wouldn't be under his command much longer." He pounded on the table with sudden energy. "Damme, Frank, we won't win this war if all initiative is to be barred. Our army wouldn't be in the Peninsula today if I had knuckled under to Craddock and obeyed his order to leave Ciudad Rodrigo. You know that. I'm not the kind of soldier to go out with forty mule teams and come back to the minute with forty teams. I must come back with forty captured standards!"

"What did Wellington say in his dispatches? They haven't been given out yet in full."

"I understand he treated me handsomely enough. Gave me credit for contributing to the victory. I'll say this for him: he's fair. But I hear he's fallen into the habit of twitching his eyebrows whenever my name is mentioned." Wilson laughed again, grimly this time. "Well, they can't take Ciudad Rodrigo away from me. I'm waiting to see what Parliament will do about it."

There was a moment's silence and then Wilson's pent-up feelings exploded in a burst of words. "Gentlemen, it's all wrong. Here I am, eating dinner in a room filled with gawping, jingle-pocketed nocky boys while an English army is at grips with the French. I should be out there. I'm needed, I tell you. I have the daring and the initiative to meet Johnny Craps on his own terms, but because I have enemies at the Horse Guards they may keep me kicking my heels in London. It's always the way. Will our governments never learn?"

Topp reached down into one of the many pockets of his baggy coat and produced two letters. "I hopes they won't rashun mail from Contynent, sahib," he added, with a broad grin.

Both letters were from France and had been sent to Holland in an embassy pouch, reaching England from there by way of Heligoland. He recognized Margot's handwriting on one. The other was addressed in an easy, flowing hand and he opened it first with an exultant beating of the heart. It was, as he had hoped, from Gabrielle.

Here at 10 Place Lorient there are ten of us [she wrote]. Sosthène, Margot, and I, and seven servants. Actually, Frank, seven! It is like a dream, and such a lovely and exciting dream. Every time I ring for Hortense, my maid, I say to myself, "You might be in a prison cell this minute, and not sending for a maid to do your hair and rub lotions on your face, if it had not been for a very brave Englishman who incurred great danger to get you free." I hope you have not been in any trouble because of what you did for us. I shall never live long enough to thank you for your many great services.

It was apparent in every line that she was already captivated with her native land and most particularly with Paris. *"My wonderful Paris,"* she called it repeatedly.

I am finding how lovely the sun can be. It beats on my shuttered windows and my balcony all day long and I curl up in it like a cat. I have become so lazy, so fond of all this new and strange luxury. I spend long hours at my dressmaker's and watch pretty girls wear clothes for *my* inspection, and how I love it! I fee them handsomely, you may be sure, remembering the long and tedious hours when I did the same. The evenings are so exciting; balls and receptions and state dinners, and, of course, the theater and the opera. I am very popular (is it bad taste to boast, my very sober Englishman?) and it makes me happy. I love to dance with famous generals and to receive extravagant compliments from great diplomats.

I have changed my mind about the Emperor. He is the most fascinating person in the world. A little *fattish* perhaps, but, oh, what a compelling eye! How different he is from that funny old man at Hartwell, although poor Father would never forgive me if he could know I have said such a thing. He singles me out (and how proud it makes me!) and pats my hand and even on a few occasions has called me Gaby. In whispers, of course. He told me once I was the prettiest girl at his court, and that is a very high compliment, for some of the ladies here are really very beautiful. He even said he had given Sosthène such a good post as a reward for bringing me back to France.

I never think of a *certain great parliamentarian.* I am heart-free again.

He read it over three times before opening the other, finding some solace in it, although her last sentence rang in his mind like the finale of all his hopes. If she were heart-free now, it would never be his great happiness to change that condition. He was disturbed also by the rapidity of her conversion to the Bonapartist idea. It was inevitable, perhaps, that she would be caught up in the splendor that surrounded the Man of Destiny, but it disappointed him that she had shown so little resolution. Finally he began to see her position, saying to himself, "If I were French I would probably feel about him as she does now; so it's not fair to blame her for becoming a partisan so quickly."

Margot's letter, written in a correct and neat hand, was much more informative, giving him a detailed picture of the new life of the De Salle household. Sosthène was in the Post, which was a very fine place for him as it took little of his time and paid him handsomely, but most particularly because Comte Lavalette was at the head of it. The Comte was married to a niece of Josephine's and so was very close to the Emperor, in spite of the impending divorce. He, the Comte, had dined with them several times and was a plump and pleasant little man. The Comtesse, who had been Emilie Louise Beauharnais, was a pretty woman and very devoted to her husband, which was unusual in Paris.

Gabrielle was already quite the rage at court, reported Margot. The salon at 10 Place Lorient was always crowded with men, young and old, soldiers and civilians, married and single. Gabrielle flirted with them all ("But that seems to be the rule here, Monsieur Frank") and seemed to be maintaining a strict impartiality. She was getting more beautiful every day and she wore the most exquisite clothes. Jules de Vitrelle, who was going into the diplomatic corps and would be sent abroad soon, was very unhappy about her popularity.

She, Margot, was growing fond enough of Paris but had not changed her point of view in any respect. The De Salle estates were being restored but no application had yet been made about her properties because she still refused to take the oath.

I am a serious problem for them [she wrote, with evident pride in the fact]. Sossy thinks it wise not to let anyone know who I am, because he is sure the Emperor (I must call him that although I still think of him as plain Napoleon Bonaparte) would be very angry about me. I am seldom present when there is company. When I *must* be presented, which is not often, they simply say, "And this is Margot," which makes people think I am a poor relation (I am, of course), although I heard one dreadful old man ask if I were "an indiscretion." I was not *quite* sure what was meant until Gaby laughed and said, "Surely you don't suspect Sossy." I am quite happy to have no attention paid to me. I don't have to bow and scrape to anyone.

The old De Salle house in Paris was being used as headquarters for some army department and so could not be restored to them, but they were most comfortable—in fact, quite grand—at 10 Place Lorient. The housekeeping instinct came out in her strongly when she dwelt on the difficulties they had encountered in settling. There had not been a bell, for instance, in the place. Bells, it seemed, had fallen into evil repute during the Terror, as they suggested servitude. They had been ripped out of all the great houses, and even now workmen got very sulky when they were asked to replace them. It was the same with carriages. There were still very few available in the city, and most of them had broken

springs and needed paint badly. Gentlemen were a little nervous of
carrying canes in the city, and no one dared suggest that servants wear
liveries. A difficulty which had nothing to do with the survival of re-
publican ideas was in the use to which the *coffre-forts* had to be put.
There were three of them at Place Lorient, but only one could be used
for the safekeeping of the family jewels and papers. The others were
used to store sugar! There was so little to be had in Paris because of the
blockade of the British fleet.

She had a charming room to herself with a small iron balcony all her
own. It looked down on a pretty green court with aloes and lemon trees.
She had a fine greedy cat, and her canary seemed to like Paris better
than London, for he sang all the time.

Please tell me about the grave of my poor Jean Baptiste Achille [she con-
cluded]. I hope it is where the sun can reach it and not too crowded. I still
feel guilty about running away from him as we did. And I am always thinking how nice it would be if you could come to see us. Perhaps you will care
to know Gaby and I talk about you a great deal.

8

AUNT FRANCILEA DIED in late fall, when there was a gray haze over the
waters of the channel and the frosts had blackened the grape leaves
covering the stone wall of her Sussex cottage; the ideal time to die, she
had said. It happened on one of Frank's frequent visits with her.

He thought she looked a little better when he went up to see her after
her midday sleep. At any rate her mind, which had been showing a
tendency to wander, had come back into clear focus again.

"There's something I've got to say to you, Frank." There was the usual
touch of vinegar in her voice, but the look she gave him was full of
affection. "Something for your own good. You're a bit of a fool, you
know. You make me terribly angry at times, the way you give in to them.
Still, you're an Ellery through and through. There's one Ellery mistake I
want to save you from. My poor Joseph loved that baby-faced mother of
yours to the very end, and no one can tell me he didn't die of a broken
heart. It's a fault in the family character, and a virtue perhaps, to love
one person that way. It's caused a lot of suffering. That's what I want
to warn you about." She was studying him intently with her sharp eyes.
"You're still hankering after that French gal. I can see that you are
plainly enough. It won't do you any good. There's the channel between
you now and a war for good measure. One of these days you're going to

hear that she's married to some man of her own race. There can be nothing but unhappiness for you if you don't put her right out of your mind."

Frank was thinking, as she spoke, of the time when he and Gabrielle were returning from the ship chandler's shop. She had looked up at him with her warm and eloquent eyes and she had clung tightly to his arm. It was then she had said, "I'll never forget you, Frank."

Put her out of his mind? She would stay in his mind, and in his heart, to the end of his days!

"Find yourself a nice English gal," went on the old lady. "One with some common sense in her head. I wish I could be here when you *do* find her so I could look her over first. I don't want you marrying an Amy Lawcey! If you picked a gal of that stamp, I'd send her packing fast! You must have a family, my boy. You must have a son; and, when you get him, name him Joseph after your father. I want your solemn promise on that now." When he had given it, she said with a deep sigh: "Well, I think I'll have the squire up now to bathe my head and give me something cooling for my throat. Go out for a long walk, Frank, but come back to me before you go to bed. I have some more advice to give you."

He walked along the cliffs until he had seen the sun sink beneath the western rim of the channel. He never did receive the additional advice, for when he returned she was dead.

The will left him her share in the *Tablet*, and there was a handsome sum of money to be divided between Caradoc and Humphrey. All she left Mrs. Ellery was a sealed letter which was duly delivered; and no one but the recipient ever learned what it had contained.

With his fourth share, Frank found himself in complete control of the paper and no longer under the necessity of relying on his proxies. As a result he became more decided in his control of editorial policy, particularly in parliamentary affairs. He even fell into the habit of attending the House debates, squeezing himself into the back row of seats in the gallery, which was generously reserved for the labors of the gentlemen of the press. From here he caught an occasional glimpse of the great men on the floor below. Twice he heard his brother deliver booming addresses and noted that he received loud applause. It was quite clear that Sir Caradoc was winning a following of his own, chiefly among the younger members. He had been right, then; a career could be achieved by playing politics in the usual and safe way.

One of Frank's visits to the House was precipitated by a letter from Mary. It came to him from Westlake, the town residence of the Murreys family, asking that he call on her there as soon after receiving it as he could.

Mary was dressed to go out when he arrived. She greeted him with an almost shamefaced smile and he was struck at once with the fact that she was very thin. He studied her as they shook hands, seeing that in spite of her determination to seem casual she was both nervous and unhappy. Being sure that Caradoc's defection was the cause, he felt unhappy himself. She had made a brave effort to look her best; her hat was small and trim and of the very latest shade known as London Smoke, and she had been careful to catch the fashionable idea by wearing York tan gloves with red morocco shoes. The general effect was, however, rather pathetic.

"Frank," she said in a breathless voice, "I—I was going out so I would be sure to miss you."

"But I thought you wanted to see me. I gathered from your note——"

"I—I lost my courage. I decided I shouldn't tell you after all what I had made up my mind to say."

"Now that I'm here," said Frank, "I think you had better say it."

"Yes, I will. I'm glad you came so promptly. It takes the decision out of my hands, doesn't it?" She allowed her eyes to drop. "It's hard, Frank. I'm throwing my pride to the winds. I want to see Caradoc. I *must* see him. I've been so unhappy! I'm afraid I'll always be unhappy unless I do see him now. But, Frank, I can't ask him to come myself. I can't sacrifice my pride that far. Could you do it for me? Perhaps you could say you happened to meet me and that you were sure I would see him if he came here. Something like that—*anything*, Frank, as long as you persuade him to come."

He nodded reassuringly. "That will be an easy matter, Mary. I'll be quite casual about it. In fact, I'll make him believe it was his own idea. And I guarantee to get him here in the next couple of hours. Keep your hat on so he'll think you're ready to go out."

"Yes"—eagerly—"I think that would be wise. I'll have to be quite casual too, won't I?" She was trying hard to blink back tears. "I'm humbling myself terribly, you know. Do you think I'm doing wrong?"

"No, Mary. I think it would be very foolish to let a matter of pride stand in the way of a possible understanding. You see, Carr can't make any advance himself; not after the beastly way he behaved." He smiled at her. "This is a little conspiracy between the two of us which neither of us will ever mention again as long as we live. We'll forget about it, won't we?" He consulted his watch. "I imagine he's at the House now. I'll go there at once."

She grasped one of his hands. Her own were trembling violently. "Yes, we'll forget all about it. Especially if he—if he doesn't want to come."

"I'm certain, Mary, that he'll want to come."

He found his brother in Bellamy's, indulging in sandwiches with a group of his fellow members. The drone of a dull voice reached the room at intervals when the doors into the chamber opened. Caradoc looked surprised but got up at once and came over to greet him.

"Well," he said in a hearty voice. "I've heard that the stormy petrel of the newspaper world has fallen into the habit of visiting us but this is the first time I've caught him at it. What's on your mind at the moment, old fellow?"

"Nothing at all, Carr. I've heard you a couple of times and you seem to have more than a bit of the Billy Pitt facility with words. By the way, I hear that our most distinguished neighbor is in worse health."

Caradoc registered immediate interest. "The old Duke? I've known, of course, that he's failing. Have things taken a turn for the worse?"

"They're worried about him. As a matter of fact, I dropped in at West-lake House on my way over, hoping to get some definite word."

"I don't suppose any of the family are in town."

"Mary was there." Frank's tone was casual enough to satisfy the most exacting requirements of diplomacy. "I saw her for a minute. She seemed rather upset, I'm sorry to say."

"She did?" Caradoc seemed a little self-conscious at this mention of her name. "Not a bad old boy in spite of everything. I hope he'll manage to fend it off this time. Er—how was Mary?"

"Very busy about one thing and another. She ran up to town to attend to some errands and expects to post back to Bilber this afternoon."

There was a moment's silence. "A fine gal, Mary." Caradoc had fallen into his most forthright manner of speech. "A fine gal in every way. I suppose people say I behaved badly to her."

"That seems to be the general impression. I've never expressed myself on the subject before, but I'm telling you now that I subscribe to it fully."

"Confound it, I—I was too hasty, Frank." The handsome eyes of the younger brother had a troubled look, quite different from their usual serene confidence. "I can't understand now why I ever did such a thing. I'm not only sorry about it for Mary's sake but because it shakes my faith in my own judgment. It was a mistake, and I don't like to make mistakes."

"If that's the way you feel, why aren't you man enough to go to Mary and tell her?"

Caradoc regarded him with doubtful eyes. "But would she see me? I wouldn't want to go there and have the door slammed in my face, you know."

"That's not important. The one thing that matters is that you treated her badly and that you want to make amends."

After some reflection Caradoc nodded his head. "I suppose I've got to face it. I can't very well expect her to come to me."

"You would wait until Doomsday before that happened. If there's anything to be done, you've got to do it."

They had wandered out into the corridor. Caradoc said as they paced along together: "Yes, it was a stupid mistake on my part. I was—well, I suppose you could say I was infatuated. I believe in acknowledging my mistakes, Frank."

"I'm glad you feel that way."

"You're a damned silent fellow, Frank. We don't see much of each other, of course, but I've been expecting to have you come at me for not helping to get Gaby out of the country."

"There's no sense going into that now."

"No, I don't agree with you there. I always believe in bringing things right out into the open. Well, there's something I want to say on that subject. I thought it over very carefully after we parted that day. I considered the problem from every standpoint and decided that I had been right at first. It was too great a risk to take, for a man in my position. And"—he made a gesture with his hand which could only be described as royal—"it's clear now I was right. They're safe in France; and nothing has been done about either of us. It worked out perfectly."

"How do you suppose Gabrielle felt about it?"

"I'm glad you brought that up." Caradoc bobbed his head with emphasis. "I don't care how she felt. That may sound hard, but I've been hearing things, Frank. About the Duc de Berri and now about Bonaparte himself. You've heard the stories, haven't you? Damme, I don't like it! I'm beginning to wonder about her. At the best reckoning, she's a coquette. I don't mind telling you now I always felt pretty sure I could have given her petticoats a flip if I had wanted to— Here! Great God, Frank, what's got into you? Are you crazy, man? Listen to me—"

In the grip of one of his sudden rages, Frank had charged at his brother and was striving to get his hands on the other's throat. They struggled fiercely, but in a very few seconds Caradoc's superior strength asserted itself. He succeeded in pinioning Frank's arms to his sides.

"This isn't allowed," he panted. "We'll cause a scandal. Easy, man, easy!"

"You're a rotten, filthy liar, Carr!"

Frank, raging impotently at his inability to break free, had been backed against the wall. Suddenly Caradoc began to laugh.

"Why, blast you, I believe you're in love with her yourself. You are! I can read it in your face. This is really comic." Caradoc threw back his head and let his laughter boom out. "Frank, Frank! And I never even suspected it. I wouldn't have said what I did if I had known. I would have spared your feelings, Frankie. But you'll have to forgive me for laughing, old boy. It's the best thing I've heard in a long time."

Frank managed to wrench himself free. "It's true," he said. His first blind fury of rage was subsiding. "I do love her. I don't mind saying it, even to you. And I'm going to tell you now that you behaved all through like a coward. I'm ashamed to think you're my brother."

"Come, come, don't lay it on too strong." Caradoc was still enjoying the dregs of his laugh. "I'm not going to let myself take offense under the circumstances, but there's a limit, you know. So you're in love with Gaby. I didn't realize I had competition right in the family, damme if I did. And Mary before that. We seem fated to set ourselves for the same girls, don't we?"

"I was never in love with Mary. I was always fond of her. I still am."

"And you're still sweet on Gaby? Take my word on that, Frank, and forget about her. She's gone out of our lives for good and it's just as well."

Frank straightened his collar, which had become disarranged. The fact that Caradoc had emerged without a single hair on his head out of place made him so furious that he found it hard to restrain himself from renewing the struggle. "I'll get along without any advice, Carr," he said finally. "May I suggest that you—that you take yourself out of my sight before I break the House rules again? The sight of you makes my gorge rise."

Caradoc's eyes narrowed. "I'll take just so much of this abuse," he said. "You've spilled out the poison you've been bottling up inside yourself. I'll thank you to say nothing more."

"If you want to see Mary," said Frank, "you had better get along about it. She'll be leaving soon."

When Caradoc had been handed his beaver hat and helped into his cloak by an obsequious attendant and had taken his departure, shaking his head with an air of unsatisfied mirth, Frank began to wonder if he had done the right thing after all. Mary was too fine to throw herself away like this. What kind of life could she expect, if it came to a reconciliation between them? Perhaps it would have been wiser if he had ignored her plea. He walked slowly from the sacred precincts of Parliament and into the sunshine of Old Palace Yard, still debating the point in his mind. It was a crisp and cold day, He shivered and buttoned his coat up tightly around his neck with fingers which trembled.

"If he were not my brother," he said to himself, "I would call him out for this!"

He heard nothing more for five days. He was preparing to leave his rooms for dinner on the evening of the fifth day when a knock sounded on the door. Mr. Patcher came in, wearing an air of considerable excitement.

"Your brother, Sir Caradoc Ellery, is below," he announced. "There's a ledy with him."

Caradoc walked into the room a moment later, smiling self-consciously, with Mary on his arm. The pair of them stood on the threshold and beamed at him.

"You don't need to explain," said Frank. "You've been to Gretna Green and you're married."

"That's so!" boomed Caradoc. "We've been to Gretna Green and we're married. Sir Caradoc and Lady Ellery. What do you think of that, Frank?"

"And, oh, we're so happy!" Mary was looking quite pretty in a fur-collared pelisse and a red hat with bobbing plumes. Her eyes were sparkling with the happiness she so proudly declared. Frank felt a lump come into his throat. "It may be for the best after all," he thought. "I'm sure now I did the right thing."

He shook hands with his brother, saying rather shortly: "Congratulations, Carr. I hope you realize how lucky you are."

"Of course I do. I'm the luckiest man in the world."

Frank then took Mary in his arms and kissed her. "You know how much happiness I wish you," he said.

"Ours is going to be a perfect marriage, Brother Frank. And, oh, we have other good news. Caradoc has a chance to make some money, and so we'll be able to buy in that share in the newspaper for you."

Caradoc nodded in rather reluctant confirmation. "I'm in a pool with some of the other men in the House. We're going to buy up some food supplies. We happen to know—well, something that's in the cards. We can't fail to make money on it." He cleared his throat and added impressively: "I had a letter from Perceval today. I'm being put on a commission to investigate trade conditions. How to beat Boney's decrees and that sort of thing. It's quite an important step for me, old fellow."

Frank's doubts showed in his tone. "I'm glad, of course, that they're singling you out this way. But are you well qualified for this particular kind of service? Do you know much about world trade?"

"Not a thing. Not a damned thing, Frank. But I'll mug up on it. I'm always ready to work my hardest. I'll make a good showing, never fear."

"I was thinking about what the country's to get out of this. I hope the other members of the commission are better qualified."

"I doubt it. Is it necessary to be blasted experts to handle a thing like this? We're to go around and ask questions and study figures. We'll come out of it with something worth while."

"It's to be hoped you do, if the House is to act on your findings."

Mary interrupted by saying: "And now, Brother Frank, we have a great favor to ask. We're going to Bilber in the morning, and—you know how poorly Father has been. We think the news should be broken to him gently. It would be better if someone spoke to him before we got there. *You*, Frank."

"Don't you think, Mary, it would be better if someone else did it? Why not Hughie?"

"No, not Hughie. Hughie's sweet but he has no tact, none at all. He would be sure to say all the wrong things. We want you to do it, Frank, because we know you would say all the right things. We're depending on you."

"I'll do it then, since you prefer it. I'll ride down early."

When Frank arrived at Bilber Castle he knew at once that the Duke's condition had become a matter of serious concern. The servants seemed to move with stealthy care, and no one spoke above a whisper. Dr. Kilrain, who had been the old peer's physician for as long as anyone could remember, was pacing up and down the great hall, his broad-brimmed hat stuck on his ancient head at a belligerent angle and his yellow-buttoned coat appearing ready to burst with the indignation seething under it. He was indulging in a muttered monologue which made it clear that other medical advice had been sought in the case.

"Ophthalmiater to His Majesty, is it?" he was saying, cracking the handle of his silver-mounted whip against the side of his riding boots. "Aurist, oculist, master of all knowledge since Hippocrates! Pah! Quackist, I say! For nearly half a century I've kept that stubborn lummox in banging good health and now they send posting to Lunnon for a spectacled owl who thinks anything but Latin words are beneath him. I wouldn't trust the feller to treat a buttery boy for the swine pox!" He nodded to Frank. "Good morning, Mr. Ellery. You can't cure old age with long words, Mr. Ellery. By Gad, you can't!"

"Is His Grace in a bad way, Dr. Kilrain?"

"What would you expect after sixty years of overexerting his body? Not to mention gluttony, by Gad! Of course he's in a bad way, my poor old friend." The doctor glanced about him and then sank his voice to a whisper. "The practice of medicine, Mr. Ellery, is full of sham and hocus-pocus. Griping and purging and bleeding and leeching! Snail water for this, nanny berries for that! Drink nettles in March and eat mugwort in May! It makes me ashamed of my calling. I believe, sir, in doctoring by common sense and not hiding my ignorance under a lot of Latin stuff and nonsense."

The butler whispered to the newcomer: "His Grace is in the chapel, Mr. Ellery. He spends a great deal of his time there now. Do you consider it a bad sign, sir? As though he was setting his mind on eternity, sir?"

"Could I go in and see him now, Bilson?"

"Yes sir. I'll take you right in. He may not notice you. His Grace has become very—very *absent*, sir, in his ways."

Little light gained entrance through the stained-glass windows of the chapel. Frank had never visited this part of the castle before, and he looked about him with curiosity and some awe. The walls were lined with black marble monuments. Six notable men of the Murreys line lay on each side, their armored arms folded and the garter on each right leg. It was, he knew, the oldest part of the house; the battlemented cornice on the chimney arch went back unmistakably to the earliest days of the Plantagenets, the diapering on the wall surfaces was wearing thin, the hammer beams in the roof were black with the passage of time.

The Duke was sitting at a table which had been moved in for him and placed in front of the chancel. His head was sunk forward and he paid no attention until the butler had repeated twice, "Mr. Ellery, Your Grace."

"Ellery? Oh yes, Ellery. Mr. Ellery." The old man sat up suddenly and demanded in angry tones, "Not Mr. Joseph Ellery!"

"No, Your Grace. Mr. Francis Ellery."

"A plaguy fellow, Joseph Ellery! Always getting me on a legal hip. Send him away, Bilson." A gleam of understanding began to show finally in the wintry eyes. "It's you, is it, Frank? Glad to see you."

"I'm very sorry, Your Grace, to find you in such poor health."

"Poor health! Ha, that's *one* way of putting it. I'm damned sick, if you must know. Getting very close to the last jump on the course. Playing out the last innings, Frank." He let himself sink back into his former mood of abstraction and muttered to the footman stationed behind his chair: "Wine, William. Where in blazes is the wine?"

"The doctor says no wine, Your Grice."

"Damn the doctor! Damn all doctors. What do they know about what I need? The busybodies, the purgesmiths!"

"I have a message, Your Grace," said Frank hurriedly, fearing he would never regain his host's attention if it escaped him now. "From Lady Mary. She's coming home this morning."

"Mary? I want her here. Why does she go away? She knows how much I need her."

"She's arriving soon. In fact, I expect she'll be here within the next hour."

"Good. She mustn't go away again." The old man added with fresh asperity: "Then why does she send messages? Couldn't she wait and tell me herself?"

Frank hesitated. "Your Grace," he said, "Mary is married. That's what she wanted me to tell you. She's married to my brother."

"Married? My Mary! Come, come, young feller, you're trying to pull my leg. Mary, *my* Mary, is just a child."

"She was married three days ago."

It was apparent from the puzzled frown with which the old man regarded his visitor that he had not grasped fully the meaning of what he had heard. "Married?" he repeated. "Married, you say? Three days ago. That's strange. That's very strange. Married."

"To my brother, sir. To Caradoc."

"Caradoc? Ah, yes, Caradoc. Handsome feller, isn't he? Regular Viking." His voice trailed off. "Caradoc says, Caradoc says—now where have I heard that?"

"Mary hopes you'll approve, sir. She'll be here soon and tell you all about it."

"Good! All girls should marry. That's good. Caradoc, did you say?"

"Yes, Your Grace."

Unexpectedly the slump went out of the ancient back. The Duke sat up straight and regarded Frank with eyes from which all vagueness had departed. "Frank, what have you been telling me? Was it something about Mary? That she's married?"

"Yes, Your Grace. She and Caradoc went to Gretna Green. They are on their way here now."

A look half of rage, half of misery, took possession of the Duke's face.

"I remember now. He threw her over, that infernal scoundrel! Has she gone mad? Why did she do it, why did she do it!"

"She loves him, Your Grace. I'm sure you'll feel different about it when you see how happy she is."

"Frank, this will finish me. I—I can't believe it yet. Here I am, a useless hulk. I'm old and sick and I can't do anything about it! She'll be made unhappy by that fellow, I know she will. God, why did I have to live to see this day!"

"I'm sure, Your Grace, it's going to work out well. Caradoc has recovered his senses and he'll make her a good husband. He's the one she wanted. I saw her before they were married and it was certain she could never be happy as long as they stayed apart. Everything is different now. You'll see that for yourself when she comes."

The old man said savagely: "If I had the strength, I would horsewhip that young whelp! I would damned well see to it that he never laid eyes on her again, married or not married! I would call him out." His voice began to lose its coherence again. "I'm old and sick. Married! My Mary, married!"

"And completely happy, sir."

There was a box on the table beside the old man. He took it up with fumbling fingers and spilled out the contents. Frank saw that it had contained a once prized collection of watches. The Duke took one of them and struck it against the edge, breaking open the case. "William, William," he cackled, his hands playing uncertainly with the broken springs, coils, and stackfreed. "That settles 'em, William. That's the way to stop the silly ticking!"

"I think you had better leave, sir," said the butler. He added with a sigh, "That's the third of them he's broken in as many days, sir."

The footman winked at Frank. "His Grice's axle has begun to wabble bad, sir," he said.

9

IT WAS in the spring of the following year, 1812, that the letter arrived from Margot which completed the destruction of his hopes. He needed to read no more than the first phrase to know the message it contained. Laying it down with an unsteady hand, he walked to a window. Here he stood and stared with unseeing eyes at the busy, noisy life of Prater Street. It was fully a quarter of an hour before he was able to summon up resolution to continue reading.

DEAR MONSIEUR FRANK:

Is it wise to convey unpleasant news by tactful evasions and gradual hints, or is it kinder to break it at once? I don't know. All I am sure of is that I am very unhappy I must be the one to write you this letter.

Gabrielle was married yesterday to Jules. It was a quiet ceremony and they left at once for Russia.

There! I have told you. All I can hope is that it won't make you as unhappy as I know it would have done at one time. There has been nothing in your letters to let me believe there has been any change in your sentiments, and yet it is possible that time has been having some effect. How I pray that it has! If it is any consolation, I am sure she does not love Jules and that she decided to take him only as a means of escape from an alliance which would have been more distasteful. Perhaps I should not have told you that. Now that I have set it down I realize the danger that it may only serve to make you even less reconciled to what has happened.

I can't decide what I should tell you and what I should leave unsaid. I am certain you would like to know that she looked lovely. She was so lovely that I cried for an hour after the ceremony. Her dress was white satin (perhaps such details are completely out of place in a letter like this), trimmed with swansdown, and cut square and very low in the neck. I was allowed to attend—and I had eighteen forget-me-nots in my hair!

The Emperor was furious when he heard of the marriage, but he relented the next day and sent a handsome necklace as a present. Gabrielle whispered to me as she was leaving, "Please, my kitten, write to Frank. I won't have a chance until later." I know you would have preferred to hear of it from her, but truly, Monsieur Frank, the carriage was waiting and she had only a few moments to get ready. Jules is very jealous and is liable to pounce on anything she writes, for a time at least; so it has to be by my hand or not at all. She will write you, I know, as soon as she can.

With much affection, I remain,

Your very lonely and unhappy,

MARGOT

The promised letter never came from Gabrielle. Perhaps it went astray, which was a common occurrence with all European mails under the surveillance of the French police. Perhaps Jules pounced to good effect. On the other hand, it may never have been written.

For a long time Frank felt as though he were living in a mist. The irrevocability of it colored everything, making the business of living wearisome and useless. All the glow had gone out of the world for him, and he was sure it would never come back. He performed his duties at the office in a perfunctory way, finding it hard to force his mind to the making of decisions. He left as much as he could to Cope. Nothing seemed to matter.

The months rolled by. No letter came from Gabrielle, but Frank was kept advised of what was happening by Margot, who wrote him with commendable regularity. Gabrielle, he learned, was already playing quite a part in the functions of the embassy in Russia. The French party among the Russians had been falling rapidly into eclipse and she was striving to gain adherents for it. She never missed a state function, and all the men flocked around her. A certain great nobleman, who was close to the Tsar and had been anti-French heretofore, had gone over to the other side and was now working to keep peace between the two countries. She had received a personal letter from Napoleon, commending her for what she was accomplishing. There was little other news. She, Margot, was living alone at Place Lorient now, Sossy having taken his vinegar-faced wife into more pretentious quarters. The Abbé Force had accepted a post under Talleyrand, where he hoped to be in a position to work for the Royalist cause.

In early summer it was reported that Napoleon was having bitter exchanges with Alexander and was concentrating troops in Poland. Wilson received a note from Palmerston at the War Office to the effect that he had been appointed military adviser to the British Minister in Turkey; where, as everyone knew, there were no military problems on which advice would be needed. At first he decided not to accept, realizing that he was being shelved. When it became clearer, however, that war between the two emperors was in the air, he made up his mind to go.

"You'll be on the edge of the cockpit only," said Frank doubtfully.

Wilson's smile, when he answered, had all the significance of a wink. "It's better than kicking my heels around here and rusting out like an old ale pot," he declared. "And there are certain possibilities they don't realize yet. Once before, as you may remember, I started out for one place and wound up somewhere else. It can be done again. The War Office thinks I'll be safely tucked away in a musty pigeonhole when they have me in Constantinople. But take a look at the map, Frank. The boundaries of Turkey and Russia touch."

"You'll be storing up trouble for yourself."

"As you may also recall, I've disregarded orders on occasions and done rather well as a result. You had better come with me, my boy."

Frank's heart bounded. For the first time in months he found himself considering the future with lively interest. He might see Gabrielle if he could get into Russia in time. It was an enticing prospect, but a moment's reflection convinced him that it was out of the question. He was needed at home to cope with the ever-increasing problems of supply. It was certain also that he would have no more than a meager chance of smuggling dispatches through.

"Not this time, Sir Robert," he said regretfully.

The news which reached them from Paris during the early part of the summer was highly contradictory. The relations between the two emperors were growing more strained, but out of a blue sky Napoleon ordered his Admiralty to begin the construction of two new fleets and then arbitrarily annexed all parts of Germany around the mouths of her important rivers. Was he planning again to throw his armies across the channel? On the other hand, he was granting licenses for the import of some English goods into France, the luxury articles which the people had been so long without because of the blockade of the British fleet.

There was no puzzle in it for Wilson. When he took ship at Portsmouth for his new post, he said to Frank, who had ridden down with him: "Don't pay any attention to what the Butcher does for the next few months. None of the bottoms for the new ships have been laid down yet. That order was all williwash. He's setting himself to strike at Russia. I hear he's organizing an army of eight hundred thousand men. And it's being concentrated in the east, mind you. There isn't a single division back of Boulogne. Don't let yourself be blinded by all this dust he's kicking up so carefully. I know the truth. When the invasion of Russia begins, I'll be there."

It was not until the berlin of the forty-three-year-old conqueror had deposited him on the banks of the Memel that everyone else in Europe knew the truth. The word was carried back across the Continent in record time that he had immediately reconnoitered on the east of the river, remaining there for hours, gazing with brooding eyes at the lands where a rival emperor reigned; and that on his return he had called feverishly for maps. Orders began to fly then, north, south, and west. The world knew that the die had been cast.

Frank's worry over Gabrielle's situation came to a head when he received a letter from Margot, postmarked, to his intense surprise, from Brussels. It was quite brief.

DEAR MONSIEUR FRANK:

We have just received word that Jules has left Russia but that Gabrielle is still there. They had quarreled and she had gone to visit Russian friends when the order to leave came. It is hard to believe that Jules would leave, but he must have acted under positive orders from his superiors.

Sosthène obtained a passport for me and I am on my way east. It is very unlikely that I can do any good, but I have been frantic with anxiety and cannot bear to stay at home. There is a mere chance that I may be able to get some information. At any rate I will be closer to her.

Sosthène could not come with me as his wife has hopes of presenting him with an heir. The Abbé Force is with me.

I cannot write anything more. I feel on the verge of going mad, for everyone says this war will be conducted with extreme ferocity. My poor Gabrielle!

MARGOT

The letter had been delivered at the office. Frank summoned Cope and Evans for an immediate consultation.

"Gentlemen," he said, "I'm fully aware of the inadvisability of leaving at a time like this. Nevertheless I'm placing the conduct of the *Tablet* in your hands for the next few months."

Cope looked at him and smiled. "You're going to Russia," he said.

"Yes, I'm going to Russia. I hope to get dispatches through on the progress of the fighting, but it's only fair to add that I'm not going exclusively in the capacity of war correspondent and that you mustn't expect too much from me. A personal matter makes it necessary for me to get to Russia as soon as possible."

"That," said Cope, "was what I expected."

BOOK IV

Russia

THE GUNS OF BORODINO were still roaring in Frank's ears as he urged his horse across the "living bridge" on the Moskva River. The rafts tipped and swayed, making a firm rein and a watchful eye necessary, and so he had small chance to observe the vivid play of colors on the sky line of the city. What little he saw fascinated him. "Barbaric but lovely," he thought. It was a relief to feel that Moscow was safe after all. The frightful losses sustained in the battle would deter Napoleon from pushing any further forward; that much seemed reasonably clear.

It had not been difficult after all to get into Russia. The letters he carried from Mr. Canning had speeded him on his way from Riga to St. Petersburg, where he had been granted a brief interview by the Tsar. Here he had learned that Sir Robert Wilson was at Russian headquarters and already high in favor, quite obviously, with the ruler. Frank had been granted permission to go to headquarters himself, a rather extraordinary concession, and there Wilson had taken him in hand, making it possible for him to observe at firsthand the early stages of the campaign. His dispatches had been forwarded to St. Petersburg together with Wilson's own reports to the Tsar, and the fact that they had been carried by imperial couriers made it certain they would reach England well ahead of any other reports on the progress of this momentous struggle. This should have been a matter for deep satisfaction, but Frank had achieved little content because of it. He was too disturbed over his lack of success in finding any trace of Gabrielle.

His companion said now in French, with a nod of immense pride: "If we hadn't stood up to him, m'sieur, he would soon have held the heart of Russia, Moscow itself, in his greedy hands. It was a bloody business. Our splendid fellows, *Bogh's Tobeyu*, fought like demons, as M'sieur saw for himself. It was an inspiring thing to watch."

Frank thought, "I'm sure you did nothing but watch." His guide's light blue facings, which identified him as an officer of the Seminovski Guards, were immaculate. There was not a trace of powder stain on him, no hint of fatigue on his handsome face. Aloud Frank said: "Your army behaved magnificently, Captain Bukeran, but it was in spite of very bad generalship. Can you see any reason why Kutuzov chose that particular spot to make his stand? It wasn't a strong position in any sense. No wonder your losses were so heavy. And the troop dispositions were faulty, if Sir Robert Wilson is to be believed."

The young Russian laughed easily. "I'm willing to accept *Boatt* Wilson's opinion of them. What else could you expect from Father Fumble? He's so old he can't stay awake long enough to get anything through his head. Still, he's better than the German.* The old bear had the courage, at any rate, to stand and fight." He patted the rich collar of his tunic with a gloved hand. "M'sieur has been in Moscow before?"

"Never." Frank's eyes were fixed eagerly on a dense cluster of towers and domes which loomed ahead and which, he knew, must be the Kremlin. "I've always thought of it as the most fabulous city in the civilized world."

As soon as they entered the city they found themselves engulfed in a wave of excitement. The streets were filled with people who had turned out to celebrate the news from the front. The first sight of Bukeran's uniform brought them swarming about the newcomers, shouting benedictions. The great bells in all the churches were swinging jubilantly on their beams. The windows of the houses were filled with feminine heads in holiday headdress, and there was much excited waving of hands to them as they rode by. Their horses trod on the flowers with which the streets were strewn.

Bukeran accepted the role of conquering hero with obvious delight. He grinned at Frank and shouted in his ear: "How do you like this, my English friend? The city is ours for the taking."

"I'm afraid the celebration is premature," Frank called back to him. "They seem to think a victory has been won. It was a drawn battle at best, as you know. How will they take it if Boney marches in on the city after all?"

"Old Koot will stand and fight again if he tries it. No, m'sieur, the *varvar* will never see as much as the spires of Holy Moscow."

"I suppose the French people who lived in Moscow have all left by this time," said Frank as soon as they had pressed through to a side street

* Barclay de Tolly, who had been replaced by Kutuzov as supreme commander of the Russian forces. Of mixed descent, De Tolly had been much criticized because of his leaning toward German methods.

and were out of the worst of the hubbub. His object in coming to the
city had never left his mind for an instant.

"Where would they go?" asked his companion. "They're safer here
than anywhere else, considering the temper the country's in. I saw six of
them swinging from trees on one mile of the Kalouga Road. No, it's a
safe wager they are still here, hiding behind closed shutters and praying
for the war to be over before *they* are strung up. That is, if the *varvar*
ever pray, which I am inclined to doubt."

The urgency of his mission was in Frank's voice as he said, "If you
don't mind, Captain Bukeran, I should like to be taken to Prince
Poloff's at once."

The guardsman caught a bouquet tossed down by a smiling woman
on the upper balcony of one of the houses and kissed his hand to her in
return. "We're on our way there, my scribbling friend. Do you know the
Prince well?"

"No. Not at all."

"I'm glad to hear it. Prince Poloff is not a good one to know at this
moment. Let me tell you about him." The officer stuck the bouquet in the
bridle of his horse and inclined his head sideways to view the effect.
"In the first place he's the handsomest man in Russia—after the Tsar,
of course; that goes without saying. He was a leader in the party which
favored the alliance with the French and that, as you can see, was a very
great mistake. He continued in his belief even after it became certain the
Corsican was bent on war. He's a man of stubborn mind, Prince Poloff."

Frank said to himself with satisfaction: "That explains why I've been
sent to him. He'll know where Gabrielle is—if anyone does."

Bukeran continued to sketch in his verbal picture with a hint of
malicious enjoyment in his voice. "The Tsar has never liked him. No one
likes him. I'm referring to men, as I think you will understand; his success with the ladies has always been remarkable. It is easy to understand.
He is six foot four and has eyes the color of the sea on a day of sunshine.
His manners are very bad. His wealth is beyond calculation. It's said he
could match rubies with the richest of the Indian princes. The Tsar
rides out with no more than four horses but the great Prince Poloff must
have six or even eight. Two serfs sleep outside his door at night. There
was a time when he seated one hundred guests at dinner every day, but
the number has dwindled since he persisted in his French folly." The
officer paused and nodded his head with satisfaction over the merit of
the picture he had achieved before adding a final item. "It's doubted if
he knows himself how many bastards he has brought into the world."

The palace of this magnificent nobleman was large but not impressive from the outside. It was built of wood, as were most of the buildings in Moscow. Looking up at its high painted walls and narrow slits of windows, Frank thought it resembled a prison. His anxiety had been augmented by the picture his companion had supplied of the man to whom he must turn in his search.

The immense entrance hall struck a more barbaric note than anything the Englishman had yet seen in this land of sharp contrasts. The stairway was ornamented with wooden figures as grotesque as jinns from an *Arabian Nights* dream, and the walls were covered with paintings in vivid reds, yellows, and purples. A heavy copper bell was suspended on a beam from the ceiling, and the tips of candles, appearing above intricately wrought brass sconces, were almost beyond computation. What attracted his attention first, however, was the presence in one corner of a number of small beds and of handsomely embroidered bags stuffed with straw.

"The Prince must be preparing to leave," he said.

Bukeran shook his head. "New guests have arrived. He always has guests, even now when his political mistakes have brought him a decline in influence. Naturally, they have brought their beds with them."

"Is that a Russian custom?"

The question puzzled the Russian officer. "Is it not done in England?" he asked in turn.

"When we pay a visit, we know our host will have a bed for us."

"But surely you must feel as we do that a bed is a personal matter. One must sleep in one's own. It is the most natural thing to take it with you. What are servants for?"

"Do the servants carry theirs also?"

Bukeran's manner showed that he suspected his companion to be feigning ignorance of such primary matters. "Servants don't expect to sleep in beds," he said gruffly. "Your England must be a strange place indeed, m'sieur."

The household intendant, whose obsequious manners contrasted curiously with the wolf-like sharpness of his features, led them up the stairs to the entrance of a large dining room on the floor above. "His Highness dines, as you see," he said in perfect French. "If he cares to be disturbed it will be for a few moments only."

Bukeran said in a whisper, when the intendant had left them: "He brought us up so the Prince can see us for himself. It's a lucky thing I'm in uniform. It may get you an audience."

Frank was observing the scale of the Poloff hospitality with astonished eyes. Although there were not more than forty guests, the tables had been set for at least twice that number and the supply of food was in accordance. Some of the diners were standing at a side table, heaping their plates with *zakuska*. A hasty glance convinced him that most of the items of food provided were new to him. He had tasted several varieties of caviar but could only guess at the nature of the innumerable fish dishes, the concoctions of cheese and pastry, the vegetable sallets, the savory patties, spread out so invitingly on platters of gold. After a month at army headquarters it was hard to believe that food could still be served in such profusion. People were starving no more than an hour's ride away.

"Well," said Bukeran with a satisfied smirk, "it seems we've passed muster. His Highness is going to see us."

Frank watched the tall figure of the Prince as he walked with an impatient stride toward them. He appeared strange rather than handsome with his high bent shoulders, his pointed blond beard and his blazing blue eyes under a narrow brow. The fact that he still elected to dress in the French fashion, with satin knee breeches, a black frock coat, and a white stock, added to the note of incongruity.

"His Highness, Prince Poloff," said the intendant, who had followed on his master's heels.

The Prince bowed stiffly. His gaze went from Bukeran to Frank, to remain fixed on the Englishman as though he sensed that the purpose of the visit rested with him.

"If you will be kind enough to state your business," insinuated the household official, folding his arms and nodding over them encouragingly.

"I hoped," said Frank, "for a few words with His Highness. In private."

Prince Poloff considered the request in silence, his eyes still intent on the stranger. Then he nodded in acquiescence. "The library, Ivan," he said. He bowed carelessly to Bukeran. "If the Captain of guards cares for refreshment, my table is at his disposal."

In the library, a dank mausoleum of a room distinguished for the antiquity rather than the number of the books and manuscripts it contained, the Prince motioned his guest to a chair but remained standing himself, perhaps as a hint that the visit must be brief. Frank, who found that a dislike for his host was mounting in him, elected to stand also.

"I've been led to believe, Your Highness," he said, "that you may be able to give me information as to the present whereabouts of the Comtesse de Vitrelle. I'm in a position to assist the Comtesse in leaving the country."

The Prince regarded him with an intent look which verged on a scowl. "Your name again, m'sieur?" he demanded.

"Francis Ellery. I publish a newspaper in London."

"Ah, yes. I have heard of you."

Frank's hopes began to rise. If his host had heard of him, it had been from Gabrielle. "I don't need to point out that the Comtesse is in grave danger as long as she remains in your country," he said. "I've been searching for her nearly two months. A few days ago I heard your name mentioned as one who might be of assistance."

Prince Poloff said sharply: "You will be more explicit, if you please. I don't relish the use of my name in such a discussion. Who was your informant?"

"Sir Robert Wilson. I don't know the source of his information."

The noble began to say as though to himself, "It's possible that——" then checked himself. In a moment he added, as though dismissing the matter finally: "There's nothing I can tell you, M. Publisher. The Comtesse, no doubt, has already left Russia."

Frank shook his head determinedly. "I'm sure that she hasn't, Your Highness."

"I have told you," said the Prince with a shrug of his shoulders, "that I know nothing of the movements of the Comtesse de Vitrelle."

Refusing to be dismissed so easily, Frank said: "This is a great disappointment. Her safety depends on her leaving the country at once. You are aware, I'm sure, of what's happening to all French people unfortunate enough to be still here. High rank is no protection; nor sex for that matter."

"I'm well aware of the situation." The Prince made a move as though to ring for the intendant. He thought better of it, however, and turned back to face his guest, saying impatiently: "You assume too much and, what is more, you seem to demand that I match your assumption. What reason is there for me to believe the Comtesse would want you to know where she is? By what right do you propose to interfere in her affairs?"

"I have no such right. However, I knew her when she lived in London and I assure you she would want to know that I'm here."

The Prince waved his arms with growing impatience. "I dislike the English. I dislike the necessity of discussing a matter of such delicacy with one of you, if the truth must be told. His Majesty refuses to deal with spies, but our country nevertheless is full of them. For all I know, you may be one of that breed yourself. How can I tell?"

"Do you care to see my credentials?"

"Your credentials, I am sure, would stand any scrutiny." The nobleman began to pace about the room, running his fingers through his stiff blond beard with an air of perplexity. He finally came to a halt in front of his visitor. "I'm compelled to admit that the Comtesse mentioned you to me on one occasion. She told me of the circumstances under which she escaped from your country."

"I was of some assistance to her then. I can be of equal help now."

The Prince suddenly threw out both hands in a gesture of compliance. "I can't send you away, monsieur. She must judge this matter herself." Still frowning with reluctance, he added: "She's a guest in my household. No one knows it but the members of my family and a few of the servants."

The intensity of Frank's relief manifested itself in an involuntary "Thank God!" He accepted a chair now and sank down into it with a deep sigh. "I was beginning to fear, Prince, that I would never find any trace of her. In fact, I was almost disposed to give up hope that she was still alive."

The set expression of the tall noble did not change. "Your position in the matter is still far from clear to me," he said. "However, I shall tell the Comtesse you are here and learn her pleasure in the matter. Is it necessary," he added, "to remind you that I have placed myself in some danger by this admission?"

"There's a code of honor in England, Prince, as well as in Russia."

"Well"—grudgingly—"I presume there is."

The room was small and round and flooded with sunlight, its shape accounted for by its being part of a tower. Gabrielle was standing in one of the windows with her back to them. She turned and cried, "Frank!" and came running across the room to greet him. Frank was conscious of nothing but the light in her eyes. They seemed larger and more alive than ever and filled with an intense delight at seeing him. That she could be so pleased made him happier than he had ever been before in her presence.

"Thank God, you're safe!" he said in English; correcting himself at once, however, and repeating it in French.

"It's clear," said the Prince in a dry and not too pleased tone, "that you were right, monsieur. Mme. la Comtesse *did* want to see you."

"I'm too happy for words!" Gabrielle laughed breathlessly, as she always did when excited. She drew Frank's arm through hers so that they stood closely together. "M. Ellery and I are the oldest and the very best of friends. We have been through adventures together, haven't we, Frank?" Sensing then that her host was not enjoying this open show of her pleasure, she added in a more casual tone: "You recall what I told you of my escape from England? You will realize, then, how much I owe to M. Ellery."

"I recall the story clearly. As you are such old friends, you will have much to talk about, and the presence of a third party cannot fail to put a damper on the flow of—of your nostalgic memories." The Prince bowed and turned on his heel. The tone in which he continued was distinctly grudging. "I shall leave you then. It seems that M. Ellery has plans to propose which will bear a very careful consideration. I think it will be necessary for me to join your discussion a little later." At the door he paused and added with a touch of malice for Gabrielle's special benefit, "The latest intelligence from the front confirms the fact that the battle went badly for the French."

As soon as the door closed she said in a beseeching voice: "Frank, tell me quickly. It isn't true! I know it can't be. Napoleon has *not* been defeated! Tell me it isn't true!"

He noticed now, to his surprise, that she was dressed in native costume and wondered if it had been necessary to do so as a measure of disguise. Certainly it became her amazingly. The tinge of bronze in her hair and the warm brown of her eyes went well with the oriental note of the dress: a green bodice which fitted so snugly that the line of her breasts was accentuated, and a skirt which flared out in rustling folds of green and white. It was a gay dress, with a sash across one shoulder glittering with beads, and full sleeves with bells at the wrists. A headdress which obviously belonged to it was lying on the table, a jaunty one with beads and bells and bright colors.

He wanted to say, "You become lovelier every day, and so I can't help loving you more all the time," but contented himself instead with an answer to her urgent questioning. "No. It's not true. I don't know how they got such an exaggerated report, but they're due for an awakening soon. It wasn't a clear-cut victory for either side, as a matter of fact, but the Russians withdrew from the field during the night. The honors rest with the French forces."

"I knew it!" Her eyes were sparkling with delight again. "He can't be beaten, my great little Emperor! They kept telling me he had lost but I wouldn't let myself believe it."

"You must be prepared to believe it was a costly victory. It won't do Napoleon any good." Frank shook his head, thinking of the grim picture he had carried away of the field of battle after the last shot had been fired. He could not repress a shudder. "The losses were incredible. Perhaps as many as seventy thousand men were slaughtered! And nearly half of them French. It will be called a victory for Napoleon, but in the end it will be as costly for him as a defeat."

"But he won! He always wins. He's invincible." She had no thought, apparently, for the thousands of common men who had died, only an excited joy in the glory it would bring one man. Still, he reflected, that was natural enough. The victims to her were nameless, unknown, the victor a glamorous figure whose greatness colored her existence.

"Gabrielle," he said earnestly, "your Emperor is losing this war in spite of the territory he has won. His great army has shrunk to little more than a hundred thousand men. He's without supplies. He has almost no cavalry left. I've sent off a dispatch in which I predict he will either withdraw to the Polish border at once or be driven back finally in a complete rout."

"You're wrong, Frank. Wrong, and blind, and very foolish." There was a trace of impatience in her voice. "Napoleon always wins. He will come in and take Moscow now, and the Tsar will have to make peace. It has always been that way."

"But it won't be that way this time, Gaby. This is a different kind of war. The Russians are a different kind of people. I know he can take Moscow if he wants to risk it, but I think he's too wise to try. He'll see that he must retire now while he has the chance to do it without further losses. Before the Russians get organized again."

Gabrielle laughed. "And I say again you're wrong, my Frank. You don't know anything about the Emperor. You have never seen him. If you knew him as I do—oh, Frank, you can't imagine how really great he is! He carries you away. You see at once that he's a man of destiny."

"But, Gaby, the point to be considered is not the greatness of Napoleon. I grant you that. The thing that counts is that the Tsar won't give in as the others have always done. He has no intention of making peace, none at all. He sent Sir Robert Wilson to army headquarters with instructions for Kutuzov to that effect. The loss of Moscow wouldn't change him. His armies will draw back still further. Winter will come and your army will have no supplies at all and no way of keeping up lines of communication. Napoleon will be completely cut off. What will he do then?"

"I'll tell you." She laughed again with an air of unshaken confidence. "My Emperor will find some way of winning. He has his plans made already, you'll find. No, no, Frank, the Tsar will have to give in." She took a chair and motioned him to draw one up beside her. "We mustn't quarrel. Haven't we other things to talk about? I haven't seen you for—

why, it's three years, isn't it? Such a long time and so much has happened! What have you been doing since I saw you last?"

"I've been working very hard. And I haven't been able to reconcile myself to one thing that has happened."

"You mean my marriage?" She considered him with affectionate eyes. "You are still faithful, then, to—to a memory, Frank?"

"Still faithful, Gaby."

"Dear Frank! It makes me happy, and proud, to hear you say it. But you aren't being very sensible. Don't you think you ought to get rid of those memories?"

"They are all I have. I intend to keep them. To cherish them." He looked away, finding her nearness too disturbing. "But we have serious matters to discuss now. You're in the greatest danger, as you must know. I can get you safely out of the country if you'll come at once. But I want to hear first how you came to be left behind. How, in God's name, did it happen?"

Her mood changed at once. "I could see what was happening. Some of the men the Emperor had sent to represent him in Russia were working against him. They were urging him to attack, believing he would be beaten and that it would lead to his downfall."

"They were agents of Talleyrand?"

"I'm sure they were acting with him. There was treachery behind everything they did. I had seen a great deal of the members of the French party here, men like Prince Poloff who wanted the peace kept between the two countries. I wanted peace too. A meeting was called at the Prince's country estates to discuss last-minute plans for preventing the war. I believed I could be of some use, so I went."

"It was a rash thing to do."

"I didn't care. I had quarreled with Jules, so I went alone. I quarrel with him a great deal. He's so set, so sure of things; and always the wrong things. He's very trying, Frank. The meeting came to nothing, of course. Napoleon had made up his mind and the war had started before I could return."

"What did your husband do?"

"I don't know. What could he do? He left with the embassy, no doubt. I haven't heard of him, or from him, since."

"Where have you been all this time?"

"With the Prince's family. They've been wonderfully kind to me. We came to Moscow a month ago because the Prince thought I would be safer here. He knew how much feeling had been stirred up in the country against us. Not only against French people but against him and the men who had stood out for the French alliance. They call him a traitor now, and few people dare to see him openly. His table used to be the largest in the country. Scores and scores of people dined with him every day."

"Every day?"

"Of course. Once you start dining at one of the great houses in this country it's considered almost disloyal to go anywhere else. The Prince was very proud of his following. Now it has sunk to almost nothing."

"It seemed to me pretty large." Frank looked at her with sudden gravity. "Gabrielle, you must leave at once. Everything is ready. Wilson has made the necessary arrangements and the passports will be issued for you. You will have to take an English name, of course. The peasants are completely out of hand and we mustn't take any chances."

She smiled at him. "Frank-in-need! You've planned to run away with me again, have you, sir?"

"I'm going to leave at the same time, but it might be wiser for me not to accompany you. A guard will be provided to take you to the border. I think the safest plan will be to go north and sail from Riga." He hesitated. "Naturally I'll plan to take the same route and I'll never be far away."

"I'm a married woman, so my knight-errant must consider my reputation as well as my safety. But I have a very much better plan. I'll stay right here and wait for Napoleon to march in."

"And if he doesn't?"

"He will. I have no doubts on that score."

"It will be too late for you to get away if he doesn't. Gaby, have you any idea of the danger? I don't dare tell you the things I've heard and seen. And it will be impossible to travel when winter sets in. Do you know what a Russian winter can be like?"

She laughed lightly. "I know what it will be like in Moscow *this* winter. It will be very gay. After peace is declared, I shall stay here. I think it almost certain that the Emperor will remain for the balance of the season."

"Gaby, Gaby, you don't know what you're saying!"

"I know my Emperor. He'll be in Moscow in a week. And then you'll see the Tsar come off his high horse! He'll be only too glad to accept terms." She touched his hand lightly in an effort to reassure him. "Don't draw such a long face. The danger is over now. It's your safety we should be worrying about, Frank. It wouldn't do for you to fall into Napoleon's hands. I know he considers you a dangerous man."

"How can I make you realize what the situation is!"

There was a tap on the door and one of the serving maids entered. She was very young, with the rosy cheeks and turned-up nose of a Fanny Royds doll. Smiling diffidently at Gabrielle, she touched her breast and said something in Russian. The latter smiled and nodded.

"The Prince asks permission to rejoin us," she explained when the girl had retired. "And did you notice what she did? I feel greatly honored. To touch the breast is a sign of everlasting fidelity, and they reserve it usually for the members of the family they serve. They're really slaves, but it's quite amazing how loyal they can be. There are sixty servants in this house and yet not a whisper of my being here has reached the outside. That couldn't happen in any country but Russia."

The Prince returned in a very few minutes, wearing a long face. He glanced at Gabrielle and said with some reluctance: "The news, it seems, was premature. We've just had fresh reports from the front. Kutuzov is retreating and it's said he'll make no further efforts to save the city."

Gabrielle's eyes were glowing, but she made no comment, out of consideration, no doubt, for her host's feelings.

"It will be a crime!" The Prince waved his arms with furious emphasis. "They say nothing can be done with him. The other generals are in favor of making a stand, but all he does is shake his head. He must be insane!"

"Kutuzov is in no shape to give battle again," said Frank. "On the other hand, if Napoleon gives any consideration to his own losses, he'll realize he's in no position to advance."

"But he will advance," declared Gabrielle. After a moment she added, "I've made up my mind to wait here."

The Russian gazed at her intently. Gabrielle made no effort to withdraw her eyes from his but drew herself up with an air of defiance. Frank, watching them both, felt the tension in the atmosphere.

"Mme. la Comtesse," declared the Prince, "that is something I cannot permit. I am responsible for your safety. I am moving my household from the city in the morning. You must go with us."

"No, Prince!" She shook her head. "I must stay."

"You will be in the gravest danger if you do. There's no telling what will happen in the city when the word gets out that no defense is to be made."

"I'm not afraid."

"But I am afraid. For you." A trace of anger showed in his face. "I think, Gaby, I must insist. I think, moreover, I have a right to insist. You will leave Moscow with us in the morning."

Gabrielle flushed. "I shall stay, Alexei, if I have to take my chances in the streets!"

The Prince's face was a study in conflicting emotions. That of anger was uppermost, and it looked for a moment as though he would reach out and shake her. Then he allowed his stiffly held body to relax. Regarding her with a depth of feeling in his deep blue eyes which the bystander had no possibility of fathoming, he bowed his head.

"Very well. I shall arrange to have some of my most trustworthy men remain in the house as a guard. You understand, I'm sure, that I am very much disturbed by the action you're taking?"

The tension in the air was unmistakable now. "I understand, Alexei, and I'm very sorry."

2

ALTHOUGH HE WAS well muffled up in sheepskins, Windy Topp's teeth were chattering so hard he found it difficult to speak. Reining in his small *karabakh* horse, he said to his master: "Courier to the Tsar got off at Elnia, sahib. I put the dispatch in his saddlebags myself. He's to ride north by way o' Dorogobuzh. No *varvar* to stop him that way."

"There are no Frenchmen left east of Smolensk," said Frank. "And very few this side of the grave. Sir Robert estimates that Boney has forty thousand men at best. All that's left out of six hundred thousand! What a mistake he made going into Moscow!"

"All we needs now is to get our mawleys on Boney and the war's over." With a hand in bearskin glove, Topp drew his collar up around his face until only his eyes were showing. His eyebrows were frosted white. "Stands to reason, sahib, he can't do a snivy in *this* kind o' weather. When we does catch up with 'em, they'll all be images like Lop's wife, but they'll be ice 'stead o' salt and we'll have to wait till spring to thaw 'em out and see which one on 'em is Boney hisself."

Frank, who found the severe weather to his liking, stared into the western sky where the sun was sinking over the white horizon. It cast a curious red glow which suggested to him somehow the still and bitter cold of space between the worlds.

"Tomorrow will be the seventeenth," he thought. "November 17, 1812. Perhaps it will be one of the memorable dates of history."

The Russian Army had already lighted their bivouac fires. Jogging up beside a Cossack esaul who had ridden down the road ahead of them, Frank asked: "Is Wilson still with General Bennigsen?"

"I believe so. They're at Chilowa, straight ahead of us."

"Has Napoleon retreated across the Dnieper?"

The Cossack stretched out both his fur-gloved hands and curled the fingers up triumphantly. He leaned across his horse's mane and gazed into the Englishman's face with eyes which sparkled. "He has made the great mistake of remaining on this side. We have him, m'sieur! There he lies at Krasnoi. Thirty thousand men. No more. With few guns. Imagine, Napoleon without guns! It seems too good to be true. We have eighty thousand men and six hundred pieces of cannon. He can't get away! Our General has announced he will no longer play the part of Fabius but will draw the sword of Marcellus."

"General Kutuzov has said that!"

The esaul's eyes gleamed still more fiercely. "Old Koot. None other, m'sieur. He has been won over. Your Wilson helped talk him into it. He will permit us now to go in and finish it tomorrow."

"But why wasn't it done today?"

The Cossack shook his head in a puzzled way. "He always has to be sure. So very sure! Fortunately for us, Napoleon has taken the bold course of waiting for Ney to join him with the rear guard from Smolensk. And so we'll have our chance after all."

The village of Chilowa was so packed with troops that they found it necessary to enter at a walk. Frank was amazed at the confidence he read in every bearded face. These were not the dogged troops he had seen on the long retreat before the advancing French and, later, at the abortive battles of Malo-Jaroslavets and Vyazma. They were laughing like schoolboys and indulging in all kinds of rude horseplay. The houses blazed with lights and officers stood in the doorways, chatting with animation. This was indeed a new army.

In the square a battery of guns on sleds had been drawn up. This being his first chance to see this new and much vaunted winter weapon, Frank dismounted and went over to inspect the black-muzzled monsters. He knew enough about ordnance to suspect, after a quick glance, that the trunnions would be hard to operate on such an insecure base. Turning to express this opinion to his companion, he was interrupted by the sudden appearance of a grotesque figure of a man in odds and ends of equipment, some Russian, some French. Lank hair falling in greasy wisps to his shoulders, and eyes blazing in a face of unhealthy pallor, gave the newcomer a decidedly unhuman look.

"What!" cried the man, who stood nearly half a head over either of them. "These guns are not ready! A fine lot of case-shot experts! Look to the tangent scales here, men. Look to them, I say!"

He spoke French in a cultured accent which consorted strangely with the wildness of his appearance. A gunner poked his head over the muzzle of a gun and began to laugh.

"Well, here he is," chuckled the esaul. "Still with us, Yermak Timovieff himself. I see he keeps things well in hand."

Frank understood now the curious feeling the tall man had aroused in him. On evacuating Moscow, the governor of the burned city had ordered the prisons and asylums thrown open, releasing the inmates. Some of the insane had attached themselves to the forces, trudging with hopeless apathy in the rear and begging piteously for food. One of them, obsessed with the belief that he was in command of the army, had outlived the rest. He was always to be found in the heat of things, hurrying from post to post, inspecting the cavalry dispositions and the gun emplacements, issuing a gabble of orders in his thin, wild voice. It was evident that at one time he had been well versed in military matters. The troops, accepting him with their usual good nature, had nicknamed him Yermak after that almost legendary captain who led a handful of men to the conquest of Siberia in the days of Ivan the Terrible. Even the officers tolerated him, believing that he brought good luck. Frank had mentioned him in one of his dispatches, but this was the first time he had succeeded in laying eyes on him.

The insane man left the battery to gaze up at the standard flying in front of headquarters, gesturing to indicate some dissatisfaction with the set of it. Then he cupped his hands at one of the windows and called a question to the officers within. The sentry grinned and brought his musket up to the salute. Yermak seemed to swell with self-importance. He began a tour of the village, peering in at every light and calling out orders.

"Only in the Russian Army would this be allowed," thought Frank. It seemed to him to reflect credit on the race that this was so. He smiled as he speculated on what would have happened if Wellington had been behind the window at headquarters.

Frank turned in at headquarters himself. The place was filled with gesticulating men, the air gray and heavy with smoke. Wilson sat in a corner, surrounded by a circle of officers, all of high rank to judge from the richness of their facings. He saw Frank in the doorway and came over to greet him.

"You got back," he said with satisfaction. "And just in time, my boy. Tomorrow will see history made."

He was in uniform and his eyes were dancing with excitement. As they shook hands Frank said in a low tone, "The chance you've always expected has come, then."

"Yes. The great chance. Boney will eat dinner in this room tomorrow night after signing papers of capitulation. He's caught, Frank. And I don't mind saying I've had a hand in it."

They found chairs in a corner where they could be alone. Frank's position with the army being decidedly irregular, he had seen very little of headquarters at close range. On one occasion he had stood just inside the door and had watched General Kutuzov, with white cap and red band pulled down over an eyeless socket, argue in sad desperation with eager members of his staff. Now he looked about him with intense interest. Bearded officers were drinking kvass (counted a common drink in polite drawing rooms but a great favorite with the army) and talking loudly. One tall fellow in the uniform of a commander of Malta was debating furiously with a sallow little man in plain blue who might be Bennigsen himself. The small tuft of hair on the shaved poll of a Tartar nodded in agreement with the views of a young officer of the guards. A candle dripped wax on the edge of a map spread out on the table. The place reeked with the grease of riding boots.

The month just passed, during which Napoleon had occupied Moscow and then had begun a belated retreat, had seen Sir Robert Wilson achieve the highest point in his spectacular and uneven career. It had become generally recognized that he was present as an unofficial representative of the Tsar himself. Couriers rode back and forth between them. It was Wilson, clearly, who had now won the promise that at last the sword of Marcellus would be drawn.

"I had no success at Moscow," Frank said. "The city was burned to the ground in some quarters. The people are pouring back—the common people, that is—and they're finding it necessary to burrow in cellars and to put up tents and rough huts. There isn't a Frenchman left in the place."

"I told you it was useless to go back. Your Comtesse came out with the army, of course. They all did. I'm having the prisoners questioned as they're brought in, but so far there's been no report of her at all."

"I'm sure now that you're right. But—I had to convince myself."

Wilson sensed what he was thinking, for he said in a confident tone: "The capture or death of a lady of high rank would have been bruited about. I'm sure Napoleon had the sense to send her on ahead of the army. She may be safely on her way to Warsaw by this time."

"I wish I could believe you. I have dreams every night in which I see her in the hands of these cruel devils. It's impossible to get it out of my head."

"We'll soon know, Frank. By this time tomorrow we'll have our hands on all that's left of them, from the Emperor on down." Wilson's face began to beam with enthusiasm. He whispered: "There's a bit of a conspiracy under way. The old boy has issued orders for a late attack tomorrow; but I'm afraid—I'm very much afraid—there has been a slight mistake in transmitting them. Tormazov on our right will start to move as soon as it's dark enough, and by daybreak he'll be between the French and the Dnieper River. He has thirty thousand men and one hundred and fifty pieces of cannon. Boney will be surrounded." He laughed cautiously. "Can it be helped if Tormazov reads P.M. on his orders instead of A.M.? A simple little error. It will make all the difference between ending the war now and letting it drag along for many more years. If Boney gets away this time, he'll be back in the spring with another army and we'll have it all to do over again."

Frank dragged his thoughts out of the gloomy cul-de-sac in which they had been trapped so long. He even managed to catch some of his companion's enthusiasm. "I count myself lucky to be here at such a time," he said. "There's something quite familiar about the situation, quite Wilsonian, in fact. But can you be sure Kutuzov will be ready to take advantage of things?"

"He can't fail us this time. We have his solemn promise to fight tomorrow, no matter what befalls. He'll shake the lead out of his boots when he finds we really have the lion trapped. You can be sure of that."

"I hope so. It's terrifying to think that the greatest coup in military history can depend on the whims of a fuddled old man."

"I'm not concerned this time. Do you remember what I said to you just before I sailed? It's coming true. I've always been sure it would, even when Father Fumble was letting chance after chance slip through his fingers. I could see Fate at work, weaving the pattern of victory for us. I've dipped my fingers into the web this time just to be sure."

"The plan, then, is yours?"

Wilson got to his feet with no hint of fatigue, although it was certain he had been in the saddle all day. "The plan," he whispered, "is mine. Have you noticed that all of them here are in full uniform again?"*

3

AN OFFICER of the Cuirassiers of the Empress rode by at six o'clock, shouting something in a husky voice. Frank wakened. He crawled stiffly

* In protest at the supine policy of the supreme command, some officers had taken to leaving off their full regimentals and wearing cloaks only.

and painfully out of his sleeping bag into one of the coldest days he had ever encountered.

Wilson, in a light gray overcoat and carrying a pair of field glasses, came striding toward him from the direction of headquarters. He called out exultantly, "They're still there!" Coming closer, he insisted on shaking hands. "We had reports all night of troop movements on the Liady Road, and I was desperately afraid Boney was hopping the twig. But he's waiting still. And that's not the best of it. I've just seen well off there to our right a black smudge on the line of the snow. Tormazov is in position already! He has the French outflanked and his guns are bearing on the Liady Road. Boney's in our net, that usually bold and sagacious bird! All we have to do is send our columns forward."

Other officers emerged from headquarters to hear the news, rubbing the sleep from their eyes and buttoning up their tunics with nervous fingers. One carried a map which he held up in front of him while he fumbled to produce a lorgnette from the sleeve of his other arm. "Great donkey!" whispered Wilson in Frank's ear. "He does that because he knows it's a habit of the Tsar's. These staff fellows are almost as bad as ours, by Gad!"

The man with the lorgnette seemed to sense that something of a critical nature had been said, for he turned and scowled at Wilson. "This will be our decisive victory," he declared. "And without much help from the English, General Wilson. If your government had landed an army in Flanders, Napoleon would never have dared to throw in all the troops he could raise against us."

Wilson smiled easily. "I'm getting weary of listening to that statement, Lubanov," he said. "You seem to forget that we've kept over two hundred thousand of his seasoned troops busy in the Peninsula for the last four years. Is that nothing? Is it possible you haven't heard of Wellington's great victory at Salamanca? That was bad news for Boney, almost as bad as the *billet-doux* he'll receive from Tormazov's guns in a very few minutes."

The whole camp had come to life. Bugles were sounding on a piercing note like the *"Hourra! Hourra!"* with which Russian soldiers went into battle. There was a clamor of shouting, stamping, neighing from the horse lines. A spiral of reluctant smoke rose from the kitchens which had been set up in the village, as though the cooks saw little sense to providing food for men who were going to die soon anyway. A battery of guns sprayed snow in all directions as it went jolting and creaking down the road.

"Au revoir, Frank!" Wilson called. "I'm keeping my appointment with Destiny this morning."

An hour rolled by. It was apparent from the continuous rattle of musketry and the occasional thunder of heavy guns that the action had begun. It was impossible to see anything that was happening. Frank kept up a nervous patrol, each discharge of cannon making him wonder what the target had been. He kept thinking: "Is Gabrielle in the range of fire? Will her carriage have to pass on the Liady Road while it's being shelled?"

He was amazed at the complete inactivity which prevailed in the village. From what Wilson had told him of the plan for the day's operation he knew that the general attack should now be under way. He watched with increasing alarm for signs of a forward movement. The fields around Chilowa were black with troops, standing patiently to attention in the teeth of the wind. Two batteries were drawn up and ready, and he could hear the jingle of harness on the stamping, rearing horses. What were they waiting for? Where was Marshal Kutuzov?

Another hour passed. Certain now that something had gone wrong, Frank's pacing took on an impatient tempo. Would Wilson know that the attack was being held up? Should some way be found of getting word to him? The appointment with Destiny would not be kept if the delay here lasted much longer.

Yermak came striding up through the snow and halted beside Frank's horse. He had found a French shako and was wearing it with an air of immense pride. Muttering to himself, he ran a fumbling hand across the horse's mane.

Seeing him thus at close range, Frank realized that the demented man showed unmistakable signs of decayed culture. His brow was broad, his nose well molded and quite fine in contour, his mouth sensitive. Only the unhealthy pallor of the skin and the fitful gleam of the eyes gave him away.

He began to pat the fine leather of the harness, talking to himself in a low tone. The horse whinnied and nuzzled his arm.

Windy Topp, blue of face as usual, came up behind the lackwit. "He's nobbed about horses, sahib," he said. "I hears they has to drive him away from the lines all the time. My way o' thinking is he feels he should have a prad of his own, being first man in the army."

Keeping hold of the scarlet-stenciled hames with one grotesquely gnarled hand, Yermak began speaking in French in a clear voice. Frank listened in amazement. "Young gentlemen, it is essential that the utmost energy and resource be displayed in pursuit, if the enemy is to be destroyed. You must remember that the beaten army, having no purpose left but to escape, will jettison everything in the interest of speed. It has always been my contention that the Persians should have been little concerned with what Xenophon was doing but should have struck straight ahead for the Euxine themselves. If they had done so, young sirs, the *Anabasis* would never have been written."

Here, then, was the answer to the riddle of his identity. Frank realized that he must have been at one time an instructor at a military academy; which accounted for the turn his obsession had taken. Topp quite apparently had reached the same conclusion, for, in answer to a query as to what was known about the man, he said: "Looks to me like he might be a purfesser gone all to pot. But don't be taken in by his mild spells, sahib. He can get real ugly when he has a mind to it. Keep an eye to him or he may stote ye clean out o' yer saddle."

The lecture had come to an end. Yermak's short spell of coherence trailed off into a brabble of words. His eyes began to roll and he was off with jerky strides to supervise the movements of a company of infantry which had debouched from a side road.

After another hour of agitated pacing Frank saw Wilson galloping up the road, his horse's breath blowing out in clouds on each side. At the same time a droshky came down the road from the other direction with a troop of cavalry jingling along in attendance. Marshal Kutuzov sat in the rear seat, so bundled up in furs that he looked like an irritable grizzly bear. Frank watched him with a sharp sense of resentment, realizing that the stubbornness of this one old man might withhold from the world the boon of peace for many more years.

It was because of the coincidence of their joint arrival that he was within hearing distance when Wilson met the commander of the Russian armies. The droshky stopped and Wilson reined up his horse beside it, saluting in an almost perfunctory way before plunging into an impassioned argument. Frank heard an occasional sentence only. "I implore your consent to the advance immediately. . . . Napoleon, his guards, and what remains of his army are now in your power. . . . I pledge myself, from my own observations, that by the single word '*March*' the war will be won within an hour. . . . Consider, my General, the greatness of the opportunity. You hold peace for the world in your hands."

Kutuzov moved his great bulk impatiently, his one eye fixed on the Englishman with a suggestion almost of malevolence. He grunted a few words in Russian which Frank learned later were, "You had my answer at Malo-Jaroslavets."

Wilson continued to protest. Frank could see that his face was red and his eyes burning with indignation. Kutuzov did not seem to be listening.

He twisted about in his seat, keeping his one eye fixed on some distant object. Officers in all manner of picturesque uniforms had appeared and were watching the conference with eager interest. A regimental band back of headquarters had started to play.

When Kutuzov straightened himself up under the hill of fur covers in the droshky and looked squarely at Wilson for the first time, it was clear that he had made up his mind finally. He snorted and said in a voice loud enough to be heard by all the officers in the background:

"You think the old man is a fool. That he is timid and without energy. You are young and don't understand. If Napoleon turned back, none of us would dare meet him. He is still terrible! If I bring him back to the Beresina, ruined and without an army, I shall have accomplished my task."

An angry murmur rose among the waiting officers. Wilson's face had gone white. For several moments he made no response, then he said in tense tones: "We ask nothing better than to face him! If you let him get away now, he will be back next year with another army; and then he *will* be terrible. You want to hold back, to save the lives of a few men today. A hundred thousand will die in the battles we'll have to fight later because of this."

"I must not risk a battle," persisted the commander.

"You mean that you don't intend to attack at all?"

"That is what I mean. I shall send instructions at once to Tormazov that he's to do no more than harry the flanks of the enemy. If he closes in, he will be beaten."

"He has guns enough to cut the French to pieces!" cried Wilson.

Kutuzov grunted an order to his driver to go on. "You think the old man a fool," he repeated, shrugging his shoulders.

Wilson wheeled his horse about. He was laughing bitterly. "The sword of Marcellus!" he exclaimed.

The crunch of the droshky's runners on the snow and the jingle of harness bells dwindled off into the distance. Angry voices filled the air as the Russian officers clustered around Wilson. He did not seem to be listening, and his face was still white when Frank rode up beside him.

"I'm a coward!" he cried passionately. "I should have shot him where he sat! Then Bennigsen would have succeeded to the command and the plans would have been carried out. My hand was on my pistol and I had all the will in the world to do it; but something held me back."

"Thank God for that," said Frank.

"They would have hanged me at Lobnoe Place. But what if they did? Two of us would have died, but think of the lives of countless English-

men and Russians and Germans and French who would have been
saved!"

"Can't something still be done?" demanded a tall Cossack, fingering
the hilt of his saber.

One of the others answered with a well-known Russian proverb,
"Heaven is high and the Tsar is far away!"

The tension was broken by a sudden burst of laughter down the road,
followed by the staccato beat of a horse's hoofs. Yermak had at last succeeded in stealing a mount from the horse lines and was coming up at a
furious gallop. It was clear that he had had no experience as a rider, for
one foot had lost the stirrup and he was gripping the reins with one
hand and the mane with the other. It seemed certain that he would not
get very far without being dislodged but he was exultantly happy, shouting at the top of his voice. Discipline broke down in the ranks all along
the road. The soldiers cheered the rider on, calling to him: "Bravo, Yermak! He has done it at last, our great General!"

Wilson's lips parted in an angry smile. "Look at him, gentlemen. We
would be better off today if he *were* in command of the army."

It was late in the afternoon before Frank saw his friend again. In the
meantime Kutuzov had been prevailed upon to make one concession:
a grudging order for Tormazov to close in on the retreating French. By
four in the afternoon the disappointed troops had reached the road near
Krasnoi; but by that time, of course, the bulk of the French Army had
succeeded in getting away. Napoleon, it was reported, was already safely
across the Dnieper. The trap had not been sprung!

Nor had the appointment with Destiny been kept.

Wilson was sitting by himself at headquarters in a stony silence, paying
no attention to the clamor of angry debate which filled the room. When
Frank appeared, he motioned him to sit down. For several moments nothing was said.

"I begin to understand," said Sir Robert finally. "It's not just the nincompoops at the Horse Guards and the noddies at the Foreign Office
who are determined to balk me at every turn. It goes deeper than that.
It's—it's in the stars! It's my fate. I'm sure of it now. I upset the Butcher's
grand schemes in the Peninsula but circumstances combined to rob me
of the credit. I saw the chance to catch him here and so end the war,
and I laid plans to accomplish it; and a feeble old man, who happens to
represent the adverse influences at the moment, steps in and refuses to
let me go on with it. Boney will be beaten, of course, and before very
long; and I may still play a part in his final downfall. But nothing that
I've done, or will still do, will be recognized. When histories are written

of the Napoleonic wars, the name of Robert Thomas Wilson will never be mentioned!"

When Frank made no response, he went on: "Well, I suppose I must reconcile myself to it. It's a bitter pill to swallow. It's my nature to crave recognition and applause. Perhaps that's why the gods conspire to withhold the bays from me." He straightened up suddenly and added in a determinedly brisk tone: "Let's share a bottle of wine, Frank. I've done enough crying over this sorry spilling of pure victory cream. And I've news for you; a bit of good news I should have told you at once instead of brooding over my own misfortunes. A prisoner who was brought in an hour ago, a junior staff officer, said the Comtesse de Vitrelle was still with the French forces. She's alive, my boy. All the news in one day can't be bad. I'm delighted for your sake, Frank."

Napoleon had escaped and the war would go on. But did that matter now? Not to one man in the room. Outside it was beginning to snow, a sodden downfall which promised to block the roads and further hamper the movements of both pursuers and pursued. To Frank it seemed as though the sun had suddenly come out.

4

THE SNOW had stopped falling during the last hour, a small and grudging boon from the malignant fates which had seemed to hover on the screeching wind. The sky had cleared sufficiently for them to see an unfriendly sun sinking slowly in the west. Did the hollow eyes of the sullenly plodding Frenchmen detect in its descent a symbol of what had happened to their war-mad leader?

No one paid any attention to the two Englishmen, no one asked any questions. In the French clothes and boots they had secured from the loot at Russian headquarters, Frank and his faithful servant looked no different from the hordes of stragglers and hangers-on who still struggled along with the retreating Grand Army, "like specters walking away from their graves," as Wilson had described them. There was one difference which they tried to conceal: their saddlebags were stuffed with food, a sufficient amount for several days, while the faces of the refugees were tallow-gray with hunger. Topp wore a bandage around his head which covered part of his mouth as an excuse for not speaking and thereby betraying himself. Frank said to himself often, with inner smiles, that his man must be finding this inability to talk the worst hardship of all.

It was the only reason for smiling which he encountered during the course of his long search. The retreat stretched for many miles, the grimmest spectacle surely that the world had ever seen. Beaten, hopeless, hungry, taut with a fear which caused them to shrink and mutter when the dread word "Cossacks!" was heard; a different lot of men, these, from the confident veterans who had stalked into Moscow with eyes avid for plunder. Just before the loss of the vagrant sun a weary voice somewhere in the ranks had struck up the oldest of the Napoleonic marching songs, and a few of the others had chimed in apathetically.

"Au pas, camarades!
Au pas, au pas, au pas!"

In step, in step, in step! But they were not in step. Their knees shook, their feet dragged, their shoulders sagged even under the weight of empty knapsacks. Many of them had thrown away their muskets and were limping along with the help of sticks. Their sunken eyes were on the icy road underfoot, and very few of them had looked up long enough to catch that brief glimpse of the sun. If they were in step, it was with the harsh dictates of hovering death, not with the occasional orders of officers as shaken and weak as themselves!

Frank had failed to secure any reliable information whatever. The Comtesse de Vitrelle? She had been sent on ahead, she was already dead, she had been seen in a *calèche* with fine fat horses (how the eyes of his hungry informants glistened at the suggestion of the fatness of the horses!), she was with the Emperor, she had been captured by the Russians; he heard all these conflicting rumors in the course of one half hour. Where was the Emperor? No one knew. Some guessed he was on ahead, some were sure he had dropped back to be with the rear guard. There was one coherent thought only in these thousands of tortured minds: an intense longing for the rest and warmth and food they hoped to find on the other side of the Beresina.

Their first night with the shrunken army was spent on the edge of a deserted hamlet which had yielded not one morsel of food. In accordance with the orders of the Emperor, wherever he was, the troops camped in large squares and the refugees crowded around bivouac fires in the center, ravenously devouring the meager scraps of horseflesh which were handed around. The two Englishmen settled down beside their horses and Frank whispered to Topp that they would take turns at sleeping. He knew what would happen if they were unwise enough to drop off into welcome oblivion together. Their saddlebags would promptly disappear. Also he had observed the interest that cavalry officers had taken in the horses, envious of the three-calkin shoes which made it easier for the poor beasts to negotiate the solid ice of the roads. No, they could take no chances of that kind.

"You first, Windy," he whispered.

Topp seemed prepared to protest, then turned on his side and began to snore almost at once.

The two Englishmen, having the advantage of good mounts, gained steadily on the piteous procession the next morning. Frank stopped frequently to make inquiries. Had anyone seen the Comtesse de Vitrelle or could they give information as to where she was? Blank stares or sullen headshakes were the usual response. Such officers as he accosted tried to be helpful, assuming no doubt from the richness of his purple and white coat that he was of sufficient importance to merit polite attention. None of them had anything to tell him save a surmise that the Comtesse was with the imperial staff.

"If I can once become convinced of that," whispered Frank to his companion, "I'll feel that we can give up, and leave before any suspicions of us are aroused."

Topp's reply reflected his gloomy state of mind on the score of this mad undertaking. "It's lucky for us as none on 'em thinks of anything but their own skins, or they'd twigged us by this time. My ideas on retreats ain't been changed any by this." He sighed and added: "It 'ud be pleasant, sahib, to be in Lunnon this very minute. I'd be strolling down Whitechapel way with a lot o' pearl buttons on my coat and nothing on my mind at all. What I'd give for a steak and kidney pie!"

Early in the afternoon they overtook a particularly pathetic-looking group of refugees who shivered and bent their heads in the teeth of the rising wind, some of them sobbing with the bitterness that hostile elements can arouse. They were clothed in odds and ends of raiment, some of the men having feminine bonnets tied down over their heads, the women (there were several woebegone specimens in the lot) wearing in return castoff regimental overcoats. Frank was amazed, and very much concerned, to see the tall figure of Yermak in this group.

"How could this have happened?" he whispered to Topp. "He'll get short shrift if they find he's a Russian; as they're bound to do sooner or later."

"This is the kind o' army he *could* command," answered Topp out of one corner of his mouth.

Frank reined in his horse a short distance in the rear and asked one of the others, "Who is that tall fellow ahead of us with the shako?"

The man accosted gave a short and humorless laugh. "Does it matter, m'sieur? He'll soon be dead with the rest of us. He's been driven mad, like hundreds of others I've seen in the last few days."

"When did he join us?"

The other man, who had wrapped bands of charpie around his head until only his eyes were showing, displayed exasperation at being questioned on points of such complete unimportance. "When?" he demanded. "An eternity of suffering ago. Two hours, perhaps three. He came charging in from a side road on a horse which hadn't a single mile left in it. What a stroke of luck that was! It provided many of us with the first meat we had eaten in days. I promise you, m'sieur, the poor animal wasn't dead when we were cutting our slices out of his hide."

Realizing that a single outburst in Russian would rob Yermak of the immunity he had enjoyed so far, Frank decided that he must find some way of getting the demented man out of his dangerous predicament. He slowed his horse to a walk and waited for a chance to speak with him.

The wind was getting sharper all the time. It did little good to bend the head, for it whipped about with apparent malice, coming first from one direction and then from another, sometimes ricocheting across the hard surface of the snow and attacking them with volleys of icy particles like frozen spindrift. Frank shrank back into his cap and muffler but found that he could not escape the spiteful lash of the elements. His face was beginning to feel raw from the continuous bite of the wind and he had to keep rubbing his nose to prevent it from freezing. For the first time in his life he came close to the point of weeping with rage and despair over the antic persecution of the storm.

A leather-hooded carriage came at a fast pace from the west, forcing the stumbling refugees to clear a path. It ground to a stop and its occupant leaned from the window to speak with an officer on foot. He wore a look of extreme gravity and, as his plain uniform carried no indication of his rank, Frank jumped to the conclusion that he was one of the famous Napoleonic marshals. Whether this were true or not, he clearly had authority and was giving some urgent instructions. The officer was nodding his head with equal gravity and with every evidence of respect. When Frank came abreast, he heard the occupant of the carriage say: "There's no sense in underestimating it. The Emperor has ordered the state secretariat burned. Every scrap of paper is to be destroyed."

It was evident from this that the imperial staff could not be much further ahead. Frank's hopes rose.

"And that means, my General," the officer said, "it is not expected that the Old Dowager* will hold the Cossacks back any longer."

* The French nickname for General Kutuzov.

The man in the carriage answered with a serious mien, "They'll be down on us now from all directions."

Sharp orders set the troops to a faster marching pace, and the refugees also responded as well as they could, sensing some additional urgency. Inevitably, however, the unhappy men and women (it was amazing how many of the latter still remained alive on this terrible march) slowed down and came to a halt, allowing the troops to pass them. Frank took advantage of this wait to approach Yermak. Touching him on the shoulder, he asked in guarded tones, "Do you remember me?"

The demented man turned and looked at him with eyes which had been robbed of their wildness by sheer physical weariness. After a moment he nodded his head.

"Yes, m'sieur. I have seen you."

"Then listen carefully. You mustn't say another word. Take hold of my bridle. We must get along at once."

He would gladly have changed places with the tired wanderer but knew that such a move would attract attention to them, the one thing they must avoid. As they made their way past the resting files he leaned down and whispered, "Do you know where you are?"

Yermak's shoulders straightened. "I am with my troops."

"Of course. But listen, please. You're needed further up the line, but no one is to know it yet. Keep closely with me and, remember, don't say a word to anyone else."

"Not a word, m'sieur." Yermak seemed to be striving to sort things out in his poor addled brain. Should he be taking orders, he who commanded the full army? Finally he nodded with an air of pride. "It is enough. I am needed."

They found Gabrielle at noon on the following day.

The snow had fallen most of the previous twenty-four hours, performing one merciful function in covering the dead bodies along the road but more than offsetting this by making it almost impossible for wheeled vehicles to get through. The French, having had no conception of the difficulties of a Russian winter (Napoleon in council had scoffed at the suggestion that it would hamper *his* soldiers), had neglected to provide themselves with runners. The results of this sorry miscalculation were now apparent. All morning the anxious trio (for Yermak still plodded along with them, his delusion manifesting itself at times in gruff orders to do this or that) had been passing carriages stalled in the deep snow. Many of them were quite regal, the French residents of Moscow having been people of considerable substance: low-wheeled *calèches* with rich curtains in their folding tops; elaborate britskas with plate-glass panels and crests embossed in gold and silver on their finely curved sides; two-wheeled vehicles much too light for the racking uses to which they had been put; lumbering affairs of wood and steel with seats on top; even a mourning coach which someone in the laystall trade had used, apparently, to convey his household effects, with damp snow hanging from its funereal carvings. Some were badly damaged, some still in good condition. The snow was covering them fast, being already well over the level of the springs.

Frank had not eaten anything for twenty-four hours but had been doling out morsels of food all morning to the poor wretches who had given up their floundering and raised supplicating hands as he passed. He was looking ruefully in his empty saddlebag and saying to Topp, "Windy, I'm relying on you to remain hardhearted," when the latter reined in his horse and stared at a carriage by the side of the road.

"Sahib," he said, "there's someone in that un. A woman, I think."

It was a fine carriage with the imperial N on the panels. Frank sprang from his saddle, throwing the reins to Topp, and ran over to investigate. There was a woman inside, and he needed one glance only to know that his quest had been successful at last.

Gabrielle was wrapped up in a fur cloak and was crouching uncomfortably in one corner, a position made necessary by the fact that half of the space in the carriage was occupied by a couch; in which, quite obviously, she had spent the night. She was very pale, also very frightened, as her startled "Oh!" attested when he looked in through the door.

He stood and smiled at her for a moment. "There was an understanding between us, I believe, that I would manage to be on hand if you should ever need me. This seems to be an occasion when you need some help; so here I am."

Her eyes opened wide and she gave an incredulous gasp. "Yes," she said breathlessly. "That was understood, wasn't it? You were to come——" She broke off and gave a hysterical laugh. "I can't believe it! I can't believe it!"

"It was a promise I intended to keep, Gaby." He was still smiling.

"Am I dreaming? I know it can't be you, even though I'm beginning to recognize you under that hideous black beard."

Frank ran a hand over his stubbly chin and smiled in apology. "There's been no chance to shave for the past week. I've been moving too fast. But I didn't realize it altered my appearance so much."

"But how . . . ?" She stopped and shook her head, still finding it hard to accept the fact of his presence. Then the look of fear she had been wearing, when he first appeared, returned. "Frank! Are you a prisoner? How else——"

"No, I'm not a prisoner. Your army is too concerned about other matters to pay any attention to me at all. This is the third day, and so far no one has challenged me or thought it necessary to ask me who I am or what I'm doing. That," he added soberly, "is because the retreat is reaching its final tragic stage."

She frowned at that. "I saw the Emperor for a few minutes last night and he didn't seem very disturbed. He said there would be reinforcements waiting at the Beresina and that we could defeat the Russians then."

"He must have said it to keep up your spirits. The situation is desperate."

"No, Frank, he meant it. He was quite cheerful. Several members of the staff were with him."

"How did it happen you were left behind?"

"I don't know. My bed was made up and I went right to sleep. Hortense, my maid, was sitting here beside me. When I wakened, I was alone. The carriage was standing still and then I saw that the horses were gone."

"I can guess what happened, then. The maid and driver decided to look out for their own skins. During the night they took the horses and rode on. Perhaps the carriage had become stuck in the snow and they saw it couldn't be started again."

"But where is the Emperor and his staff?"

"Thirty miles away by this time. More, perhaps. They won't stop until they've crossed the river."

She became sunk in uneasy thought and for several moments did not say anything more. "Yes, that must be it. At first I was sure there had been some accident and that Georges and Hortense would soon be back. I waited so long, and nothing happened! Then I became frightened. I dressed myself. I watched the troops marching past. Frank, I couldn't understand it. They looked so pale, so weak! And there were so few of them!"

"It's becoming clear your staff hasn't realized the gravity of the plight the army is in."

"I kept calling to them, thinking someone would be able to explain what had occurred and would know what was to be done for me. No one paid any attention, not even the officers. For a long time before you came I had been just sitting here, doing nothing. I—I was becoming very frightened, Frank!"

"You had every reason to be frightened." He took one of her cold hands and held it between both of his. Then he bent and kissed it. "Poor Gabrielle! You've been seeing for the first time what war is really like. Well, we must get you out of this at once. There's an abandoned droshky on runners just back of us. Perhaps we can make an exchange, putting the body of your carriage on the sleigh. If not, I have a good horse for you. Do you feel equal to riding?"

"Of course! But if I ride, must you walk? I'm not forgetting about that stiff knee of yours."

"There are two horses, as a matter of fact. Topp is with me. We'll be able to get along easily enough."

She caught his arm. "Don't leave me yet. I'm still a little frightened, I guess. And I'm not clear in my mind yet about everything. I can't yet believe it of Hortense. She's always been so considerate, and I'm sure, too, that she was fond of me. How could she have left me like this!"

"You mustn't blame her too much. People think only of themselves when death stares them in the face."

"And Georges too! Didn't they care what would happen to me at all?"

"It seems not." He stared at the couch with a puzzled air. "This will have to be put out of the way before we can do anything about the coach. What is done with it?"

"This carriage has most of the same appointments as the Emperor's. The couch folds up and fits into the back. I've seen Georges do it, and it seemed simple enough. There's a spring underneath."

Frank continued to look doubtful. "I haven't any idea how it should be done, but Topp will be able to manage it. It's curious I have so little mechanical sense. I can't drive a nail straight. And yet my father was quite a genius with his hands. He was always inventing something."

Gabrielle reached forward suddenly and touched a spring in the space above the front seat. A small panel in the rich green embroidery opened. She looked into the compartment behind it and gave an exclamation of anger and dismay. "A thief too! She's taken all the food and wine. There was some cold meat and bread and a bottle of *yerapheitch* the Emperor gave me himself. It's a Russian brandy he discovered in Moscow." Her voice raised to a still higher pitch of resentment. "And my jewel case! Fortunately there wasn't a great deal in it. Just some trinkets and keepsakes. All my valuables were at the embassy, and I suppose Jules took them with him." She turned to Frank with a furious air. "I can almost wish they come to some unpleasant end, that precious pair!"

"It's very likely they will. The loss of the jewels won't matter, I judge.

But the food! That's a tragedy. We may find it hard to keep ourselves alive during the next week."

"Is food so very scarce?"

"Scarce! They're starving, those poor devils you see marching by. Horseflesh is about all they've had. Sometimes they've had to eat dogs and even the flesh of rats. Raw, mind you." He looked as indignant as she had been on discovering her losses. "Gabrielle, has the staff been well provided with food all this time?"

"I don't know. I suppose so. There has always been food enough. The Emperor never eats very much at any time. He's had meat and some vegetables. And of course there's always been his favorite chambertin."

There was silence for a moment. "I know how you feel about him," said Frank finally. "So I'll have to keep my thoughts about your Emperor and his staff bottled up inside me."

"It hasn't been his fault. It's been this terrible weather!"

"Whatever the cause, it's the beginning of the end, Gaby. You must see that now."

"No! No!" Defiantly she began to sing *Ça Ira*. "All *will* go well. *Will* go well! *Will* go well!" She paused. "You see now how much I've changed. I can even sing the song of the Revolution. I'm a Bonapartist! I can't tell you how strongly I feel."

Frank smiled grimly. "We had better say nothing more or we'll be quarreling. And that wouldn't do. There's a struggle for survival ahead of us."

A trace of color showed in her pale cheeks. "There's one thing more I must say. They're all saying it still, even those men out there. They may be as badly off as you say, but they don't think him wrong." She looked at Frank squarely and cried:

"*Vive l'Empereur!*"

5

IT WAS Frank's turn on the box, and Gabrielle had elected to sit with him. Her face, which had grown a little thin from lack of food, took on color at once and it was apparent that the air was doing her good. It was bitterly cold, however, and she had to keep her chin well down in the collar of her fur coat.

They had been traveling in a southwesterly direction for three days and thus had been getting well away from the line of the French retreat. The roads were piled high with snow. As the marriage of the cumbersome carriage body to the light runners had been so sketchily arranged that a divorce was a momentary possibility, they made slow progress.

"Snow, snow, snow!" said Gabrielle in an awed voice. "I believe the storm is getting worse. Does it seem to you that there's something cruel and unnatural about it? As though we were in another world where we don't belong, and the elements know it and are showing their displeasure?"

"It does seem that way."

"Russia is so aloof and cruel and—and unrelenting. And the people are the same, so strange and hard. They never stop, never give up." With a deep sigh she added, "These dreadful storms have ruined all the Emperor's plans."

Frank said to himself, "They're helping to free the world," but he made no comment aloud. She had become such a militant partisan that a word might lead to an argument, and he did not want to waste the precious time in that way. She continued after a moment: "Now it will have to be done all over again. Russia must be beaten if there's to be peace in Europe. Everyone will see that Napoleon was right in making war on her."

He had heard this curious line of reasoning from men he had spoken to on the retreat. "Clearly," thought Frank, "Napoleon has gone to some pains to impress it on those around him; the next step will be to force his vassal states into accepting it."

"I heard Sir Robert Wilson say the same thing: that it would all have to be done over again," he declared. "But he was speaking from the Russian standpoint."

They had reached a turn in the road, and the drifts ahead looked dangerously high. Frank applied himself with complete absorption to the task of driving, knowing how serious it would be for them if the top-heavy conveyance should turn over. The wind was bombarding them with more furious enmity than ever. The discouraged horses fell to a walk.

"We'll have to take whatever shelter we can find at once," he said finally.

"I'm hungry." It was the first time she had made such a confession.

"Perhaps we'll be lucky enough to find a village or a private house where they'll take us in. It seems unlikely, though. Your army swept close along here on their advance and they burned everything." He added in an anxious voice: "I don't like the looks of the weather at all. Don't you think you should go inside?"

"No, I'm warm enough." Gabrielle raised the toe of a fur-lined boot and said proudly, "The Emperor sent these to me the night before we reached Krasnoi."

He looked about him, protecting his eyes with his hand. Off to the north he caught a glimpse of a clump of buildings against the line of the snow. Reining in the horses, he studied the country which lay between. "We can make it that far, I think. There's a road cutting north just ahead of us. Say a prayer, Gaby, that we'll find some kind of a welcome there."

The side road he had sighted had not been used since winter set in. Traversing it, as a result, was slow work. Gabrielle insisted on remaining with him, and he decided to take advantage of the chance to ask her a question which had been constantly in his mind since his visit to the Poloff household in Moscow.

"Was the Prince in love with you?"

"Yes." She had no hesitation in answering. "It wouldn't have lasted long with him, of course. It never seems to with Russians, at least with men like Alexei who have so much power and wealth."

"And you? How did you feel about him?"

"He fascinated me. He was so handsome and in such a strange way." She seemed to be striving to arrive at a correct delineation of her feeling for the tall Russian noble. "But I'm not sure I even liked him. I do know there were times when I was afraid of him."

"It must have been very difficult for you then."

"Very difficult. His wife knew how he felt. She didn't dare say anything, but I was sure she hated me. She was quite beautiful. Her eyes were the bluest I've ever seen but as cold as sheets of ice. I heard that she killed a serf once with a riding whip. I was more afraid of her than I was of Alexei."

"You were lucky, then, to get clear of that family."

"I never want to see them again."

Frank was studying the buildings ahead with an uneasy frown. They consisted of a large stone house with an impressive spread of wings and a cluster of wooden outbuildings. Clearly it was the home of someone of importance. What disturbed him was that none of the chimneys showed a trace of smoke.

"This place must have been in the path of the French advance," he said. "It's fortunate they didn't burn it, but I wouldn't give a single ruble-assignat for our chance of finding anyone here."

"I don't care. We'll have shelter at any rate. And beds and a good fire. I can even have a bath. I think I look forward to a bath more than anything."

"The fire I can guarantee. The others are much less certain."

The front door, a massive affair of copper-studded oak, was not locked. After hammering on it repeatedly without any response, they went inside. The main hall was large and lofty, with a staircase which wound up into a gloom their eyes could not penetrate. Frank cried "Hallo!" and the word echoed through the place with a hollow sound.

"Empty as Moll Thompson," said Topp. "Suits me, sahib. The less I see of the Ruskies, the better I likes it. I'll tend to stabling the prads."

"The French were here," said Frank when he and Gabrielle had turned into a large apartment to the right of the hall. It was the library, and the books had been flung down from the shelves and were lying in broken-backed confusion on the floor. The room had been completely wrecked, in fact. "They were looking for hidden valuables, I suppose."

Gabrielle attempted no defense of her countrymen. She shivered and said, "At any rate they left a fire ready for us." The huge stone fireplace, which towered to the ceiling with elaborate carvings of mythological figures, was laid with logs at least eight feet long; a most welcome sight.

Frank's fingers were so cold that it took him a long time to achieve a spark from his tinder plate. When the fire began to crackle, they stood in front of it, holding numbed hands to the blaze. The chairs had all been smashed ruthlessly, but a long couch in one corner had managed somehow to escape the destructive notice of the invaders. Frank shoved it in front of the fire and ensconced his companion on it. "We can use the broken furniture if necessary to keep the fire going," he said.

Topp returned in a more cheerful frame of mind. "Everything's bob, sahib," he declared. "Things couldn't be better, 'cept, in course, if this was Caster Towers and the snow was good healthy English snow. The fambly cleared out afore the French came, but one faithful old re-tainer without a zub in his face stayed ahind to look atter things. He was out in the stables and he come at me with a pitchfork, thinking I was a *varvar*. I got that out o' his head fin'lly, and when I hands him a couple o' chervonets he went into a exstay o' nods and smiles. They's a few hens in the stables, and the old square-face perduced a ham from under a pile o' manure. Not my idee of a place to keep food, but it'll be better than whistling on empty stummicks. And how 'bout this?"

He produced a bottle of kvass with an air of triumph. Frank accepted it with a heartfelt, "You're a magician, Windy." They drank from the bottle, as the prospect of finding glasses seemed decidedly remote. Gabrielle shuddered when the potent stuff touched her throat, but it was clear at once that it had done her good. Frank felt a warm glow take possession of him when his turn came.

"Shelter, fire, and food; all arranged," he said, handing the bottle to Topp, who took a long and thorough pull before wiping his mouth with the back of his hand. "You said something about a bath. Windy and I will now see if anything can be done about that."

Gabrielle's eyes lighted up with enthusiasm. "Oh, how I hope so! All last night I dreamed of sitting in a tub of hot water with soap bubbling up around me. It was wonderful, even in a dream."

The two men proceeded then on a search of the house, finding to their dismay that the whole place had been wrecked as thoroughly as the front rooms. Luckily, however, they found an old wooden tub in the kitchen, a damp vault of a room with three fireplaces, in one of which a small fire blazed. The tub was in a dark corner and had either been overlooked or deemed unworthy of the attentions of a French ax. This they carried into the library, where by this time the fire had created a zone of warmth.

When they returned half an hour later she was sitting in front of the fire, well muffled up in her furs and fairly purring with content.

"Frank," she cried rapturously. "I'm clean, clean, clean! Oh, what a lovely feeling! No, that's much too poor a word. It's heavenly! I feel so relaxed. It was dreadful before. I wanted to fly away from myself."

There were slices of ham, sizzling hot, a round loaf of hard rye bread, and even a platter of eggs. Topp left them alone in front of the fire, and they made a ravenous meal. They talked and laughed a great deal in sheer relief from the tension and the hardships in which they had been so long involved, keeping the conversation consciously from the war and never letting it come to the subject of what lay ahead of them. Gabrielle insisted on hearing all about the marriage of Caradoc and seemed to be entirely casual about it. She even said she hoped he would be happy; but it was true, was it not, that the bride was horsy and a little plain?

"And now," said Frank finally, "Topp and I will go on a foraging expedition to see what we can find in the way of covers."

They were returning with their arms full of torn blankets when they heard Gabrielle call in a tone of deep alarm, "Frank! Frank!" She met him at the door of the library with the frightened explanation that there had been someone at the window. "A terrible-looking man," she said breathlessly. "He was looking in at me. He had great staring eyes."

Topp shoved the end of a stick of wood in the fire. When it ignited he carried it to the window she had indicated, which faced north, and looked out.

"No un here, sahib," he reported. "The Cumpess must've fell asleep and dreamt it."

"No! No!" Gabrielle was quite positive. "I was *not* asleep. I sat up to arrange one of the cushions as a pillow and I saw him. Just his face. It was a dreadful-looking face."

Topp began to be disturbed in turn. "D'ye suppose it wur a sperrit? Ye can't tell what to expect in these heathen countries."

Frank took the brand himself and went to all the windows in the room. The snow was slatting hard against the panes. The drifts on the sills were so high that he could see very little.

"It's snowing so heavy that you may not even find any tracks," he said, returning the torch to his man. "I think it would be a good plan, nevertheless, if you and your ancient friend made the rounds of the house. It may be some poor devil looking for shelter." A thought occurred to him. "Do you suppose it could be Yermak?"

Topp shook his head. "It's three days since the nobber gave us the slip," he said. "Stands to reason he couldn't get this far on foot. The idee o' sperrits has kind o' got fixed in my head, sahib, but if you say so I'll have a look outside."

"It wasn't imagination," declared Gabrielle when he had left. "I saw him. I couldn't be mistaken."

"Well, we'll have it cleared up in a few minutes." He smiled at her reassuringly. "Lie down again. I'll stay right here."

She settled back on the couch. "I'm not the nervous kind. And I wasn't asleep, so it couldn't have been a nightmare. Someone was looking in."

"Don't worry about it any more."

"You'll stay right here, won't you? I can't bear the thought of being left alone."

Topp came back in a few minutes and said from the door: "No trace of anyone outside, sahib. We looked all around. D'ye suppose it cud be a sperrit atter all?"

Frank laughed. "Even ghosts would be sensible enough to stay in on a night like this."

"But I hears they got speshull uns here, sahib. Snow sperrits and ghosts with wings as big as ship sails what rides on the wind." Topp shook his head dolefully. "It's a odd country. When we gets back to Lunnon I'll be through with travels, sahib. I've seen more o' the world right now than I cares to see."

"Well, go along and get some sleep. You had better build a fire in the kitchen. I'm going to stay here awhile and keep the Comtesse company."

Topp looked doubtful. "I won't be good for much sleep tonight.

Not atter what's happened. Perhaps Peter the Turrible will keep *me* company."

When they were alone, Gabrielle said in a hesitant tone: "You'll think I'm being very silly, I'm afraid. But—I don't want to be left alone tonight. This is a strange house. I'm frightened. Your man may be right about the spirits."

"I had already decided to curl up here by the fire. We can disregard the proprieties for one night."

"Yes." She gave a nervous laugh. "It will be a great comfort to know you're near. But you'll be so uncomfortable."

"Less here than anywhere else. I'll keep warm, at any rate, which is more than I've done for a long time."

He arranged some of the blankets on the floor close to the fire and stretched himself out at full length. He began to realize how tired he was. Gabrielle had settled herself on the couch with her furs pulled up around her and some of the blankets on top of that. She watched him in silence for several minutes.

"Frank," she said finally, "you should have fallen in love with someone else by this time. Your devotion is very gratifying to me, but I'm sure it's not at all sensible. I always thought you might marry that English girl."

"Which English girl?"

"The one Caradoc married."

"Mary? She was so much in love with him she was in danger of pining away. That seems to be what happens whenever he appears on the scene."

"*Touché!*" She spoke in a light tone. "What a silly little fool I was! Still, it was a *very* temporary derangement of the heart, and my recovery was a quick one. With the first sound of French voices and all the excitement of the journey to Paris, I seemed to forget about him. It was a complete cure by the time I reached Paris."

"I'm glad to hear it. I was worried about you when you left."

"You didn't need to be. I'm afraid I'm a rather changeable person. But we were talking about you. Have you ever thought of Margot?"

"Great heavens, no! She's a mere child."

"Not much of a child any more. She's grown up into a very tall young lady. And a very lovely one. Wait until you see her!"

"We may both see her much sooner than you expect. She's in Warsaw, according to the last word I had."

Gabrielle's eyes opened wide with surprise. "Margot in Warsaw! I can't believe it! What is she doing there?"

"That's the closest she could get to the front. She left Paris as soon as she heard you had failed to get out of the country. She was frantic with anxiety."

For a moment nothing more was said. When Gabrielle spoke, it was in a tone of thoughtful surprise. "I had no idea she would be as much concerned about me as that. Margot and I have been rather at cross-purposes. I was beginning to think she disapproved of me most completely."

The desire for sleep seemed to have left her. She sat up on the couch, drawing the fur up around her shoulders.

"You must realize by this time what an ardent Bonapartist I've become. Margot is still a Royalist. She's quite as set in her views as I am in mine. We had bitter arguments all the time."

"But she's completely devoted to you."

"I can't tell you how happy I am to hear it. I was afraid my little Margot and I had drifted far apart." She was studying him intently. "Frank, I'm quite serious about this. You should marry Margot. Perhaps it's unfair to the poor child to say this, but I really believe she would pack up and return to England the instant you said the word."

Frank shook his head with embarrassment. "I'm certain you're wrong. Why, she hasn't seen me for years. Even if you were right, I would be much too old for her. From what you say, she will be a great beauty; and, when she gets her estates back, as she's bound to soon, a great catch as well. The idea is nothing short of absurd."

"Not at all absurd. I know what I'm saying, Frank."

"Are you determined to get rid of me, then?"

"No, I'm afraid I would feel very sad if anything of the kind should happen. I'm selfish enough not to want to lose you, my dear. But—I'm thinking of you. And of Margot. It might be the perfect thing for both of you."

"Not the perfect thing for me, Gaby. That has always been out of my reach. And now it's further out of reach than ever."

Her glance had strayed in the direction of the north window. Watching her closely, as he never failed to do when they were together, he saw her face become suddenly pale.

"Frank! It's there again! That same terrible face!"

He sprang to his feet. As far as he could see, there was no one at the window. Gabrielle had drawn the fur over her head and was crying in a muffled voice, "Don't let it near me! Don't let it near me!" He ran to the window, stumbling over a pile of books on the way. Darkness had fallen and there was nothing to be seen outside save the snow driving against the glass and the branches of a tree tossing in the wind. He was convinced now that her imagination was playing her tricks.

She was weeping when he returned. He sat down on the couch beside her and took one of her hands.

"There was no one there, Gaby. I'm sure of it."

"But I saw it! The same face, the same wild eyes! Either I saw it, Frank, or I—I'm losing my mind!"

"You're overtired. The long strain is beginning to tell. You've stood everything wonderfully so far and I'm not surprised at all that your nerves are beginning to get a little out of hand."

She turned toward him and almost unconsciously his arm went around her shoulders. It was what she wanted, for she drew herself closer to him and her hand gripped his tightly.

"Perhaps. But I saw it." Her sobs became less frequent. "Frank," she whispered, "I'm still frightened. Stay right here. Hold me close."

"Of course. I won't move until you get to sleep. That's what you need now: a long sleep to quiet your nerves."

Some of the symptoms of panic returned. "No, no! I won't be able to get to sleep if I know you're going to leave me. I want you between me and—it!"

"Then I won't leave you. I'll stay right here."

Her cheek against his arm was damp with tears. With a catch in her voice that was half sob and half hysterical laugh, she whispered: "But you can't stay all night in the cold. Please, Frank! You must share the covers with me."

"But, Gaby——"

"Oh, I know. It would be quite scandalous. But I don't care. I don't care about anything!"

"It's not the laws of propriety I'm thinking about——"

"All I can think of is this dark, terrible place! It's making me see things. Does anything need to matter? Must I shiver in terror all night because of some silly rules? Frank, the people who insist on them are a thousand miles away. They'll never know."

He was no longer capable of thinking clearly. One forearm still encircled her shoulders, but he kept far to the side, with only the outer edges of the tattered blankets over him. He kept saying to himself, "Here she is, in my arms at last, but I must manage to control myself." He wanted to draw her to him, to tell her how desperately he loved her.

"I feel so safe now," she said with a sigh. It was a sigh of tired relief, of almost complete relaxation.

For several moments there was silence. Fear had left her, quite apparently, for she sighed again; and this time, he realized, it was with the deep content and surrender which follows an emotional upheaval.

She whispered: "You said you were afraid. Because you didn't have a sword to place between us, Frank?" Her sense of humor had returned, for she laughed then and added: "But you *have* a pistol. Wouldn't it serve the same purpose?"

He began in a desperate voice, "Gaby, you can't realize how much I love you or you wouldn't——"

"I think you must love me a very great deal. You must, because you put up with so much for me. You're even willing to freeze to death for my sake, aren't you? Come, be sensible, Frank. If we're going to share this couch, it must be on a fairer basis. You must have some real benefit from the covers, my dear."

Her foot touched his. She said, "Oh!" and drew it away quickly. But the damage had been done; his control left him and he found himself lying close beside her in the warm niche beneath her furs, clasping her so closely that he could feel her heart beating through the thin garment she wore. The dampness of her cheek was against his face now.

She said suddenly: "No, no! Please, Frank, please!"

"I'm sorry, Gaby. But—but I love you so much!"

She struggled against him, briefly, and then subsided. After a few moments she murmured breathlessly, "You needn't be sorry, my dear."

6

THE FIRE was burning briskly when Frank wakened, the flames doing much more to illuminate the room than the faint gray light which managed to enter through the snow-covered panes. He sat up with a start, realizing that it had been recently replenished. Gabrielle was still asleep beside him, her head resting on one arm. He sat still and watched her for several minutes, delighting in her beauty, wondering at the length of her eyelashes, which rested so still on her cheeks.

"She's mine at last!" he thought exultantly. Five long years of devotion had brought their reward. She now belonged to him; he was so sure of this that his mind was filled with plans.

He would take her back to England and start at once the legal steps to obtain her divorce. There should be no difficulty on that score. Frank's mind leaped still further ahead. The profits from the *Tablet* were now so substantial that he would be able to buy a country place for his bride. It would be much less ambitious than the Towers but nevertheless a home worthy of the lovely chatelaine he would bring to it. Perhaps in time he would secure a title to compensate her for the one she would be giving up. He leaned over and kissed her lightly, marveling at the greatness of his luck.

"This would never have happened," he thought, "if Napoleon hadn't taken his mad gamble!" With a smile he said under his breath, *"Vive l'Empereur!"*

He dressed hurriedly and made his way back to the kitchen through a labyrinth of dark and tomblike halls. He found Topp there, feeding into a blazing fire the gilt leg of what had been a valuable French chair.

"Morning, sahib," said the latter with elaborate cheerfulness.

"Good morning," said Frank. "What can we get the Comtesse for breakfast?"

Did he imagine a finer shade of respect in his servant's manner toward him or was it actually there? Certainly there was a suggestion of a wink in Topp's voice as he said: "We'll have something tasty for the mem sahib. Peter has baked a loaf of bread and it's piping hot. And what d'ye think o' this?" He lifted a pot with a broken spout from the stone ledge where it had rested inside the fireplace. "Coffee! Peter had a bit o' it hidden away. It took a peck o' perswading to make him perduce it."

Frank sniffed the delicious odor. "I can't imagine anything that would please her more. I'll take it in at once."

Topp found a cup and saucer and a spoon which had escaped the systematic devastation. "Ought to be a boo-kay too by rights, but we don't run to *that*, sahib," he commented. He added in a casual tone as though the matter might be considered of minor importance on this particular morning: "It wur the old nobber atter all. We found him at one o' the back doors."

"Yermak?"

"The cummander o' all the armies o' bedlam hisself. He wur as near to froze solid as a jack-barrel in Jan'ry."

Frank shook his head in amazement. "How do you suppose the poor old fellow ever got this far?"

"No telling 'bout that. Peter has him tucked up in his own blankets. But"—with a doubtful frown—"he's in a bad way, the nobber is."

"I'll go with you to see him in a few minutes."

Gabrielle was sitting up when Frank returned to the library, her coat drawn snugly around her chin. The portmanteau with her clothes, which had been deposited at the foot of the couch, had fallen open, revealing a gay assortment of colors in rather considerable confusion.

"Good morning," he said.

"Good morning."

With one hand she smoothed the edge of the blankets, as though finding in that an excuse for keeping her eyes lowered. Having expected a different greeting, he stood still and gazed down at her with surprise and alarm.

"I have some breakfast for you."

Suddenly he saw a twitch in the delicate curve of her nostrils. "Coffee!" she cried in a delighted voice. "I don't believe it! It's too good to be true."

"It's true nevertheless. And bread, warm from the oven. A breakfast fit for—for Gabrielle de Salle."

Holding the fur around her neck with one hand, she reached out eagerly for the cup with the other. "I should have put on a dressing gown," she said apologetically. "But it's so cold! I lacked the courage to move. Will you forgive me?"

"You look very lovely just as you are."

She took a grateful sip. "Wonderful!" she exclaimed. "It's weeks since I've tasted coffee. Did you wave the magician's wand which produced it?"

"No. But I'm willing to accept whatever reward may be offered."

She turned her face away quickly and so he had to be content with kissing her cheek. Slipping an arm around her shoulders, he drew her tightly to him.

"Frank!" she protested. "This won't do. I expected to find you in a properly contrite mood this morning."

"I'm not contrite at all," he declared, refusing to release her. "I'm so happy there's no room for any other feeling at all."

"But you should be."

"Are you?"

She sighed. "I'm horrified with myself. Didn't you expect me to be?"

Frank's exalted mood was slowly oozing away. "No. I—well——"

She raised her eyes for the first time. They were very grave as she studied him over the rim of the cup. "Well, it happened," she said finally. "I haven't been able to—to think clearly. I realize I should feel too humiliated to look you in the face."

"But why?" He was studying her with equal concern. "You know how much I love you. And I thought—I believed that you——"

"Don't let's discuss it any more now," she said. "Later we'll have to talk about it, of course. But, please, not yet. I must have time to think first."

He said to himself: "I'm a stupid, blundering fool! I should have realized how she would feel." Aloud he said: "Of course. Forgive me, Gaby."

Her obvious distress of mind did not prevent her from enjoying the food he had brought. Frank seated himself on the edge of the couch and watched her as she drank the coffee and munched the crusty bread with real appetite.

"It's still storming," he said. "The snow is so deep now that the roads will be blocked for days."

"And that means we shall have to stay here?"

"Yes. We can consider ourselves very lucky."

When she finished the coffee he remembered that he had not yet set her mind at rest about the apparition at the window. "You did see some-one last night. It was Yermak, our poor old runaway. How he ever man-aged to get this far is a mystery."

"That makes me feel very much better. I didn't like to believe I was losing my mind. But"—with a suggestion of a shudder—"I dread having to see him after the fright he gave me. What can be done with him?"

"From what my man says, that problem will be taken out of our hands."

She looked concerned at once. "Oh, Frank! Is he in serious danger?"

"I'm afraid so. He's an old man and I don't think he can survive what he's been through." In spite of her reluctance to discuss the previous evening, he added, "I shall feel eternally in his debt!"

She remained in thoughtful silence for several moments, staring into the empty cup in her hands. Then she sighed and said: "I feel equal to facing the cold now. If you'll be kind enough to leave me, sir, I shall get myself dressed."

Frank returned to the kitchen, where he took his share of the bread and drank the cup of coffee which Topp had kept warm for him over the fire.

"Did the mem sahib enjoy her breakfast?" asked the latter.

"Very much, Windy. She'll thank you later herself."

Topp said cheerfully, "Wars has their good side atter all."

Frank did not answer, but he thought, "I wish I could be sure, I wish I could be sure."

They found Yermak in a cold rear bedroom. He was wrapped up like a mummy in moldy blankets, and it was clear at first glance that his condition was serious. His eyes stared weakly from a flushed face and his breath was coming with a thin, whistling unsteadiness.

"Well, my General," said Frank. "You gave us quite a surprise last night."

There was a hint of sanity in the gaze that the old man turned up to him. "Yes!" His voice was very weak. "Yes, a surprise. The essence of successful warfare. But"—in a low whisper—"it's the end of the cam-paign. The last battle! A battle that—that can't be won."

Frank watched him as he tossed about feebly under the covers. "Pneumonia," he whispered to Topp. "I haven't any idea what we should try. Have you heard what doctors do in such cases?"

Topp shook his head. "The sawbones seem to depend entire on bleeding and leeching. Why is that, sahib? Is it so the patient will get weak and the disease can get such a good hold that the sawbones can tell then what it is? That's the only sense I can see to it."

"I don't know. Perhaps you've hit on the reason."

Topp looked anxiously at the sick man. "I don't like the looks of him, sahib," he said.

"I think he should be kept warm. It would be a good idea, Windy, to heat stones and keep them beside him wrapped up in blankets."

"Just as you say, but it seems to me he's too hot as 'tis for his own comfort."

Frank shivered as he retraced his steps through the dark corridors of the rambling house. It seemed to be getting colder all the time. It was with relief that he found himself again in the comparative snugness of the library.

Gabrielle was kneeling in front of the fire and washing clothes in the bathtub. She had donned a Russian dress, a tight-bodiced and flouncy-skirted affair of red and white, and had wrapped a red shawl around her head. She was humming *Tante Urlurette.*

The mood of the early morning seemed to have left her. She looked up at him when he entered and smiled. "Perhaps you can help me. How am I to dry these clothes now that they're washed?"

"That seems quite simple. We'll hang them on a line in front of the fire."

"It's not as simple as that. I know very little Russian, but I'm sure I made it clear to the old man that what I needed was a line. All he did was shrug his shoulders and say, 'No, no.' Apparently there's nothing of the kind left in the place."

"I'll cut up the remnants of the hangings and make a line out of them. That ought to serve the purpose."

"Of course! Now why didn't I think of that? The truth of the matter is that I've become completely spoiled and useless. I've had maids to do everything for me."

"A pleasant difference from the days at Brinsley Place."

The room became distinctly reminiscent of the first London home of the De Salle family when he had tied together strips of the mutilated hangings and had strung them up in front of the fire. As Gabrielle draped the wet clothing on this improvised line, she said: "You've no idea how this takes me back. Margot and I slept in a corner of the kitchen and I never went to bed at night or wakened up in the morning without seeing clothes hanging all around me. I can't see a pair of stockings drying without thinking of those dear departed days. And being ah, so thankful that they're gone forever!"

He was devouring her with his eyes. "You look very lovely in that native dress. If your eyes were not so dark, you might pass for a Russian girl."

"Thank you, monsieur."

"I'm inclined to think," he said, smiling down at her, "that you're a little easier in your mind."

She glanced at him quickly, then looked away with a reluctant smile. "Perhaps, a little. It must be that I'm a woman of weak character. I can't remain properly remorseful for long at a time."

She looked disconsolately at her hands, remarking that they would soon be ruined at this rate. Frank dried them with his handkerchief, being very slow and painstaking about it and doing each finger separately.

"Please, may I have them back now?" she asked with a laugh. "After all, they're just a pair of hands."

"No, they're not just a pair of hands. I'm sorry that I haven't the powers of description to tell you what they are. They're exquisite Dresden china, or ivory carved by a Hindu with magic in his finger tips, or perhaps something quite fragile made out of rose leaves and moonbeams. That may give you some impression of what they seem like to me."

He wanted to talk, to tell her of the plans he was weaving for the future. Gabrielle was in a restless mood, however. She wandered about the room, never getting far from the fire, for it was cold and damp a very few feet off. She picked up a book but dropped it at once when she found it was covered with dust.

"I must take an interest in reading soon," she said. "I'm ashamed to say that my education has been very much neglected. The Emperor said once I was as ignorant as a *gamine*. But I don't feel at all like reading today. Would you like to hear more about Margot?"

"By all means."

"Margot has been quite a problem. Sosthène was determined to find a husband for her and he wrote me that he had three eligible candidates. Margot wouldn't even meet them. It must have been that she had ideas of her own on the subject."

"The candidates, I'm sure, knew of her fine prospects."

"But of course. The dowry is the most important consideration in

France, as it should be. One of the three was even young and reasonably good-looking. Not that they wouldn't have been all the more eager if they had seen her. Margot has developed an unusual beauty; like an intelligent, gentle, stay-at-home Joan of Arc."

"I can believe your description is quite apt."

"I sometimes think the life in London put an indelible mark on her. She actually likes housework. It's foolish of her to insist on being so domestic, because someday soon she'll be one of the richest women in France. Do you know anything of her affairs?"

"Nothing at all."

"Her father had very extensive interests in America."

"She told me a little about that once. It was when I was in jail, and she and Jean Baptiste Achille paid me a visit."

"Her father's business was in New Orleans. That's a French city at the mouth of a great river in America."

"The Mississippi."

She repeated the name with some difficulty and then asked, "How did you happen to know?"

Frank laughed. "I studied up on America once. Don't you remember the Stebbens family?"

"But of course! Miranda and Mercy and Brother Tobias. We made a curious family, didn't we?"

"A very pleasant one, I thought. But we parted company too soon."

"Margot should think well of America because it made her father a very rich man. He had a trading house which dealt in furs and rice and tobacco. The profits were quite enormous. Then there's a château at Trémille in Tours and a house in Paris, both of which are held by the government, fortunately. If they had been sold, as so many of the properties have been, there might be a great deal of difficulty in getting them back. When the estate is settled, the rest of us will be quite poor in comparison."

"But will she ever agree to swear allegiance to Napoleon?"

"Sossy swears that he'll make her do it. He has been furious with her because of it. Yes, I'm sure she'll come to it in time." She turned and looked in the direction of one of the windows. "I believe it's still snowing. Doesn't it ever stop, Frank?"

He walked to the window. The outer sections of the room were bitterly cold. The wall, against which he leaned to look out, felt like ice. He found that the storm had not stopped, that the snow was still coming down soddenly and piling up in desolate drifts. There was no wind and not a sound, just that ghostly fall of white from a dull gray sky.

Gabrielle joined him, taking hold of his arm so that she could balance herself on tiptoe to see over the high sill.

"How dreadful!" she said in an awed whisper. "I feel more than ever that we're in a different world. Perhaps this is what the other planets are like. Does it mean we'll be here for some time?"

"Certainly we can't venture out as long as the storm continues. I think we'll have to stay for a number of days."

There was a long silence, and then she said in a low tone: "Now I feel I must say something about—what happened last night. Perhaps you've heard stories—about the Emperor. I'm sure you have. They're told all over Paris, and people believe that—well, that I've been his mistress. Frank"—with fierce intentness—"it's not true! You must never believe it!"

"You know I could never believe that," he protested.

She had thrown her coat over her shoulders before leaving the fire, and he noticed that her face looked pale against the dark frame of the fur. "The Emperor," she went on, "has paid marked attention to me. He finds me amusing and I suppose he admires my looks. Is there anything wrong in that? Should I run away from the court because he seems to prefer my company? I'm proud to be singled out by him." Her voice was rising. "He's the greatest man in the world and I'm happy to think I find favor in his eyes. It's been nothing more than that. It's all lies that the Empress is jealous and refuses to speak to me!"

"I'm sure, Gaby, that no one could blame you."

"But they do. There have been such scenes! Jules, of course, and Margot. They've been furious with me."

"I'm certain Margot doesn't believe there has been anything wrong about it."

"No, no. She doesn't doubt me, I know. But she thought I shouldn't put myself in a position to be talked about. She's very strait-laced."

They were still standing by the window and keeping their eyes on the fall of the snow. Gabrielle shivered and drew the fur more closely about her shoulders.

"You will never let yourself believe them?" she demanded. "No matter what you may hear?"

He smiled and drew her arm through his. "No matter what I may hear."

"Not even after—after last night?"

"Because of last night. Don't you see? You belong to me now. I love you. And I'm proud to believe that you love me."

"Yes, Frank . . ." Her voice trailed off and she looked up at him with troubled eyes. After a moment she looked away again. "I was so tired and so frightened. It seemed that nothing mattered but to be safe in your arms."

"Nothing else did matter. Nothing else ever will."

"I've realized what's in your mind and—I've done nothing but think about it, even when we were talking about other things. We mustn't let ourselves be carried away."

"Why not?"

She hesitated. "We'll talk about it later. This isn't the time. I'm still—well, I can't seem to think clearly at all today."

"Of course, Gaby. I think I understand how you feel."

She repeated: "We'll be together all the time. And so we—we must promise each other not to yield to any more impulses."

"I pledge solemnly that you have nothing to fear."

"No, no!" she protested. "You mustn't put it that way. I can't let you take all the blame. We—well, it's an agreement, then, is it not?"

He nodded, although there was a question in his mind she had left unanswered, the most important one of all, and he felt very uncertain and unhappy about it. "Yes, it's an agreement."

Later in the afternoon she decided to make a tour of the house with him. He insisted that she must be dressed as warmly as though they were going to venture outside, even to the extent of putting on her fur-lined boots. Only one of them could be found. She gave up after a brief search and said that she would wear the one anyway and that a second pair of stockings would do for the other foot. She put it on with a rather gay casualness, allowing him a brief glimpse of her ankle in the process. "The Emperor wouldn't like it," she said, "if he knew I had been so careless of his gift."

After dinner Frank paid a visit to the sickroom. Yermak's fever had mounted. His face was flushed and he rolled about in delirium. Topp had followed instructions, for a warm bundle was wedged against his side. Wishing earnestly that he knew what more should be done, Frank stood and watched the suffering man for a long time.

"Perhaps it's for the best," he thought. From what he had seen of the public institutions of England he was sure the future could hold nothing but misery for Yermak. The insane might be treated better in Russia but he doubted it.

Gabrielle was in bed, and asleep, when he returned. She had not put on a nightcap, and her dark hair lay in fluffy disorder on the pillow of blankets. After pausing to enjoy this glimpse of her, he retreated behind the couch and proceeded to disrobe. It was so cold that he worked with hurried fingers. Stepping on tiptoe, for the floor was icy to the feet, he reached the nondescript pile he had arranged beside the fire, made up of the remnants of blankets and the wadding from chairs and couches.

Lying there, he indulged in troubled thought. Had he been hasty in assuming a new relationship between them which would give her into his care for the rest of their lives? He thought of the closeness with which she had clung to him, the things she had whispered; surely he had the right to believe that she cared for him enough to break all ties and come to him now! And yet their talk at the window had been disturbing. Was her disposition to forget, to put behind her the indiscretion into which they had been swept?

He said to himself with almost frantic insistence that it was nothing more than he should have expected. It was natural for her to feel as she did. Not until later would she come to see that their lives could no longer be lived apart.

"Frank!"

He sat up with a start. She had wakened and was watching him intently with her dark-fringed eyes.

"You look so unhappy, my dear," she said.

"I'm afraid I was indulging in some uneasy thoughts."

"And you're so uncomfortable!"

"Not at all. I'm warm, for one thing. And any time I turn my head I can see you there. What more could I ask?"

She shook her head at him, smiling as she did so. "I have only one thought left in my mind in connection with that lordly brother of yours: a dislike because of the way he acted to you. I can get angry whenever I think of it. Frank, you've really had a great deal to contend with, haven't you? There are times when I feel very sorry for you."

"It isn't pity for me that I want in your heart, Gaby."

She struggled with an English quotation. "But isn't it pity that's akin to——"

"Akin!" The vehemence of his tone was a surprise even to himself. "It was a fear that it was no more than akin that was in my mind just now."

She continued to smile. Their eyes held during the brief silence that ensued. The expression in her eyes was quite new; and he could not understand it. She seemed to be studying him, closely, even broodingly.

"It's not all clear yet," she said. "But perhaps . . . We made an agreement this afternoon. A very sensible one."

"Yes, it was sensible."

"Then I must insist that we use the same good sense about our arrangements. I shall have this couch for half the night and you must take it for the other half."

"I'll do nothing of the kind."

"Don't you see," she said indignantly, "that you're going to make me feel very selfish?"

"How do you think I would feel if I allowed you to sleep here?"

"Don't you see," she repeated, "that you're making it hard for me to insist that our agreement be kept?"

He sat up suddenly. "Gaby! Please put me out of my misery! Tell me——"

One hand disturbed the coverings of the bed. "Quick!" she exclaimed with a flash of mood which bordered on anger. "Before I change my mind!"

7

THEY CAME CLOSE to disagreement only once during the course of the four additional days they remained in the devastated Russian mansion. It grew out of a sweeping criticism of the British blockade in which Gabrielle indulged. She disagreed with him about other matters, of course, but they were always minor differences. She would say with affectionate scorn, "But you are absurd." After many repetitions of this, he never failed to conclude any expression of opinion with, "But, of course, I am absurd." She would nod her head and say, "Certainly, for there is always something of absurdity about the English point of view."

At every other moment of the first three of those all too short days she was in the happiest of moods, radiating gaiety and charm. It amazed him that she could maintain her high spirits so continuously and he was delighted with her open display of feeling for him. Having surrendered, she gave herself wholeheartedly to their brief moment of felicity, bringing to every detail of their days a complete content, a lightness of disposition, and a battery of little traits which kept him in a haze of happiness.

She would steal up behind him and brush the nape of his neck or the lobe of his ear with her lips, saying: "You're very dark and very thin and not at all handsome. And you're so extremely English! I suspect that secretly you disapprove of me. We really shouldn't get along together at all. And yet . . . and yet . . ."

Sometimes he detected a puzzled look in her eyes when their glances met. Once, when this happened, he said, "You look at me as though—well, as though there's something about me that's different and you can't understand it."

She shook her head quickly. "No, no, that's not it. It's myself that I don't understand. I was so sure about you before, Frank. You were a friend, my very best and most dependable friend. Will you be hurt if I say I was certain it would always be that way? That you would remain a friend, and nothing more?"

"No, I won't be hurt. You're speaking of the past. You feel differently about me now."

"Yes," she said, with one of the flashing smiles which brought the dimples in her cheeks into play. "Quite different. I think it began the moment I saw you back there in the retreat and knew that the worst of my troubles were over. It was so much more than gratitude. I knew then that my feeling for you had changed."

"I'm not disposed to inquire into the reason," declared Frank. "That it is so is enough for me."

She liked to dress up for him. She would disappear and he would discover later that she had been upstairs, rummaging through the clothing which had been left in disordered heaps in the bedrooms; for suddenly he would hear "Observe" from the doorway and she would come strutting into the room in some fanciful combination of things; and she would parade up and down the room, swishing skirts of barbaric color and jingling the bracelets which covered her arms. She was particularly fond of bizarre headdresses and, if nothing new of the kind were available, she would put oriental plumes or feathers in her hair.

Once she said, "I think I must resemble Catherine the Great." She was wearing something typically Slavic at the time, with a wide green skirt and a cap with four rows of pearls.

"No, you don't look like her at all," answered Frank. Observing how disappointed she was, he added: "You see, the great Catherine had a round face and high cheekbones. And her *sternum obsquatulum*" (their talk took on a slightly Rabelaisian tinge at times) "was as broad as the back of your Emperor's coach. You, my dear, have an oval face; and viewed from behind, you bear no resemblance to a coach at all. In fact, you're as slender as a silver reed, and much lovelier than any empress that ever lived."

She particularly enjoyed the invention of costumes with a military suggestion, for this gave her a chance to sing the Napoleonic marching songs. Her voice was good, in spite of a tendency to grow thin on the top notes. She would march up and down the room, trilling *Urlurette* or stamping her heels with true regimental emphasis to *Le Joli Sergent*:

> *D'une ardeur martiale*
> *En volant combat,*
> *La Gloire te signale,*
> *Comme un brave soldat!*

She found all manner of names for him, seldom calling him by the same one twice. He became in turn My Ardent One, M'sieur Kvass (because, as she confessed, he had somewhat the same effect on her), George the First, George the Last, Brother Tobias, Mon Petit Chou, and (for no reason whatsoever) My Brave Joseph.

The days necessarily fell into a pattern. They had long and animated conversations about everything but the war and the future as it concerned themselves. Gabrielle had brought an embroidery frame in the carriage and she did a little work on it; a very little, for she would quickly throw it aside and say it was really no use, she was not an industrious person. She found French books and tried to read them with no success at all, her comment on each of them being always the same in effect: "*Must* writers be so dull?" They helped Topp forage for meals and took a great interest in the preparation of them. They salvaged a set of chessmen from some broken pieces in the library and she showed great skill at the game, beating him every time.

The condition of Yermak was the one circumstance which put a dampening note on the happiness of those first three days. Frank paid continuous visits to the bedside, heating the stones afresh, bathing his head, performing any service he thought might aid the sick man or ameliorate his sufferings. Yermak was delirious the whole time now. Only Russian words were on his tongue as he tossed and moaned. It was clear even to lay eyes that the last bivouac was close at hand.

Gabrielle went to see him once but came away quickly. "The poor old man!" she said. "I think he hasn't a terrible face after all. It's a very sad face!"

On the morning of the fourth day Frank wakened early. Having warned Topp that the library was not to be visited in the mornings, it had become necessary for him to see to the replenishing of the fire. After attending to this task he dressed quickly and then hurried with chattering teeth to the comparative warmth of the kitchen. He helped Topp prepare the coffee and took a cup back with him at once, not wanting to miss the miracle of Gabrielle's wakening.

She wakened as usual with no heaviness or reluctance whatever, no rubbing of sleep-blurred eyes or shining dampness of feature. Her eyes opened full and she sat up quickly, her skin clear and healthy, her mood cheerful and alert. There was no transition stage with her, no struggle to take up again the living of a new day.

"Good morning, my sobersides," she said. "Another bright, lovely morning, I see. Ah, this blessed Russian sunshine! I suppose the birds are singing outside?"

The cup of coffee occupied the next few minutes. Then she said with a shiver: "My wrap, please. Will you be kind enough to put it over my shoulders? And no demonstrations!"

He managed to obey this injunction, although it cost him an effort. Gabrielle then dangled a foot over the edge of the couch and, when he made no move to leave, she said: "Come, come, monsieur! It is the signal, is it not? You must absent yourself so that I can bathe and dress."

"Will you be quick about it for once? We mention absurdities frequently, as you will recall. It seems to me that the greatest absurdity of all is to waste so much of our precious time in the simple matter of putting on a few clothes."

"A few? You would be surprised if you knew how many things a lady wears. Still, I shall hurry. One half hour at most, my impatient one."

It was much more than half an hour, however, before the beating of a gong, which he had found in semiusable condition, summoned him back. Even then he found that she had not quite finished her task. There were buttons to be attended to, in which he helped with willing but far from expert fingers, and an endless number of minor adjustments which seemed to him to consist of ineffectual pats and pullings repeated over and over again. And, as usual, one shoe was missing.

"I begin to suspect," she declared, "that you hide them. Do you believe that all my shoes were gifts from the Emperor?"

He was the one to find it, as usual, receiving for his pains: "There! You knew where it was all the time. You were jealous."

The ritual of the toilet followed, a long and very complicated business indeed. The furnishings of the carriage had included a square box, covered in green leather to match the upholstery of that regal conveyance. She now proceeded to take from it a seemingly endless variety of objects.

"Ah"—running a comb through her hair, which never seemed in reality to require any attention at all—"how I miss Antoine, my clever little Paris friseur!"

Salves and lotions and powders and pomatums contributed their part in what followed. She patted and rubbed her cheeks with meticulous fingers, keeping a fragment of mirror (the largest he had been able to find among the many shattered bits) propped up in front of her. She maintained a steady stream of conversation while it went on.

"It's a great nuisance but very necessary. You agree, do you not, that I must make myself as attractive as possible, even in a tomb like this?"

"Of course. Company might drop in for dinner. One can never tell. The Emperor himself might come by."

"I miss that little beast of a Hortense!"

"I fear Hortense has had reason to regret her desertion long before this."

"I hope not. I no longer feel angry about her." More patting and rubbing and impatient twisting of her head to get some use from the inadequate mirror. "I have a good skin luckily. Most women have to sleep in a mask. Do you suppose I'll come to it also?"

"It seems very unlikely."

"But I'm afraid I shall. It's said to be wonderful for the complexion."

He did not mind the time consumed in this way, for it was pleasant to sit and watch her. At intervals she would stop and smile at him. Once she laid everything aside and held out both hands to him, saying: "My very patient cavalier! You should be very annoyed because you are so quick about everything yourself."

He smiled back at her. "I'll never forget a single detail. In fact, I'm storing up a wealth of pleasant memories."

"This is all very *intime*, isn't it? How the tongues in Paris would wag!"

She went back to her tasks. "I'm compelled to say, however, that you must be very untidy. It stands to reason that you are. You can dress— and undress, for that matter—in the time it takes me to powder my nose, so it must be that you don't take enough pains."

She was now reaching the final stages. Taking up a silver utensil about the size and shape of a pepper shaker, she held it above each eye in turn, squeezing a bulb at the bottom and squirming at the first impact of the liquid it contained.

"Orange juice," she explained. "It smarts."

"Aren't you afraid it will injure your sight? I've been worried every time you've applied it."

"Certainly not. Spanish women have been using it for years; and you must acknowledge they have very fine eyes. They should know about such things. They spend three quarters of their time in making themselves beautiful."

"Do they differ much from the women of France in that respect?"

She suspended operations to look at him critically. "Of course. We give only half of our time to it. And I may say your horsy Englishwomen would look a little less like frumps if they knew enough to do the same."

The last stage of all was to color her eyebrows with the tip of a feather (with a silver handle, of course, beautifully carved) which she dipped first in a lotion. He protested vigorously when she said that the mixture consisted of gum arabic and a solution of vitriol. Paying no attention to what he said, she continued to use the feather with a sure hand, even applying the smallest touch to the tips of her eyelashes as well.

A sigh of regret. "I'm running short of so many things. No more Eau de Carmes. No more pimpernel water. I'll be very glad to see Paris again."

"Paris?" said Frank in immediate alarm.

"Where else? It's only in Paris that such things can be obtained."

The better part of an hour had been consumed when she replaced the various articles in the box and locked it with a gratified smile.

"Voilà! Has it been a success?"

"A complete success."

She turned the broken segment of mirror in all directions, frowning intently at her reflection from the various angles thus afforded. "Margot is very pretty," she said. "But I don't think—I really don't think—come, Sir Tongue-tied, must I finish it myself?"

He responded with a smile. "She isn't as beautiful as you, Gaby. No one could be. It would be unfair to your young cousin to make any comparison between you."

She laid the mirror aside. Folding both hands in her lap, she leaned forward with an air of gravity. "I don't want you to think I'm jealous in any way of Margot or that I'm not glad to see her turn out so well. But—it is natural, is it not, that I should wish not to be surpassed?"

"The most natural thing in the world. But I don't see why you give the matter a thought. Does Napoleon feel concerned over the exploits of his young generals?"

"But Margot is even more pretty than I've led you to suppose."

"She can never be more than a minor luminary in a sky where one sun reigns supreme."

"Your metaphor is just a little mixed, I think, but I wanted the very finest compliment you could pay me. Do you think badly of me because I feel this way?"

"Nothing you could ever do or say could make me think badly of you."

"Not even"—she was smiling again, but there was a suggestion of grave doubt in her eyes at the same time—"not even when I've responded so shamefully to—to a most demanding Englishman? Frank, Frank, I wonder all the time what you really think of me now!"

"I worship you!" He gathered her closely to him, kissing her on the hair, the eyes, the tip of her nose. She stayed quiescent in his arms and he folded back the lace at her neck to kiss her throat and the dimple on her shoulder. "I love you to distraction! Nothing else means anything to me at all."

"But afterwards, my ardent one? How will you feel about me when you've had time for the sober reflection that all you English are so addicted to?"

He said brusquely: "There will be no afterwards! Do you suppose I'm going to let you leave me?"

She sighed. "I'm the absurd one now, I think. I shouldn't have brought up the future. We must let ourselves live in the present."

"I'm glad you've brought it up. For the last four days I've been trying to make you listen to the plans I've worked out in my mind."

"Please, not yet." Her tone was urgent. "I don't want to talk about them now. Isn't it enough that we have this time together? We'll face the future when it comes to us. But not now. Please, my dear."

She began hurriedly to talk of other things. He listened, reluctant to let the question drop but realizing she was determined not to go on with it at the moment. He was deeply disturbed. Did it mean she saw nothing ahead but to return to their respective roles in life? Would he be able to persuade her to the bolder course? He had no doubt now that she loved him. Their moments of tenderness and passion were never one-sided; and out of the complete camaraderie of their days together had grown a deep and satisfying understanding. Yes, she loved him; but was that going to be enough?

She had drifted from talk of her life in Paris into the subject she seemed to find most enthralling: Napoleon, the greatness of the man, the glamour of his court, her own contacts with him.

"Think of it, Frank," she was saying. "He had sent for me. He wanted advice, he said. The great Napoleon wanted advice from *me!* It was about the Empress; Marie Louise, of course, not Josephine. It was before the King of Rome was born and he was afraid she was homesick. He wondered what he should do to make her more content."

"What advice did you give?" The question was a perfunctory one, his thoughts being far away from her conversation with the Emperor.

"I was very tactful, I think. I said, 'Sire, isn't it rather that the Empress is dazzled by the greatness of her position and her new responsibilities?' He nodded but I could see he was not entirely convinced. I added, 'When your son arrives, sire'—we all knew he was terribly worried it would not be a son—'the Empress will forget everything else.' He smiled then and said, 'You're right, my little Gabrielle.' He had been with his barber and was in an old purple dressing gown. There was a long rent in the tail of it."

Frank smiled. "That will be something for your memoirs. I hear that all French people who have ever spoken with him are intending to write it down."

"Perhaps I shall too. Tremble, Don Juan Ellery, if I do! What a scandalous chapter I'll have to write about *us!*" After a moment she went on:

"Before I left he pointed to a sheaf of papers and maps on the desk and said, 'My dear Gabrielle, these have to do with that despicable country where you wasted so many years of your life.' Could they have been plans for an invasion?"

"Probably. We know he has his designs worked out to the last detail." Frank's interest centered, however, in the other part of the Emperor's remark. He asked, "Were they wasted years, Gaby?"

She pressed his arm. "No, *mon petit chou.* You must never take seriously the things I say about England. I know how much I owe your country. And, of course, if I had never lived there, I wouldn't have met you. That counts for *something.*"

"Does it count for much?"

"Well—a little." She smiled and then backed away. "For a very, very great deal."

Topp came early in the afternoon and motioned his master to the door. "The General's gone, sahib," he whispered. "I went up just now and found as he had changed coaches while none on us was there."

"What can we do about it?" asked Frank in an equally low tone.

"I can make something in the way o' a 'ternity box. We can't dig a grave for him. Over six feet o' snow now."

"Then we'll bury him in the snow. In the spring they can make a permanent grave for him. Our poor General! He seemed like an old friend."

Topp nodded. "Being buried in the snow won't be bad for a Russian. They thinks of it as a friend. Atter all, it's saved 'em from Boney."

"I saw a Russian uniform somewhere in the house. I'll find it. Don't you think it would be fitting to dress him as a soldier?"

"I'm sure he 'ud want it that way, sahib." Topp's expression took on a lighter note. "Storm's over at last. No snow for more than an hour. Won't be supprised if we gets a look at the sun afore night."

Frank turned to look out the nearest window. Sure enough, there was a faint suggestion of sun behind the banked gray clouds.

"Do you think it will be safe to start on again?"

"In the morning. The main roads'll be open if we can get ourselves that far."

Gabrielle was sad over the news of Yermak's death but she looked up with immediate interest when Frank told her of the better weather conditions.

"We'll start in the morning, I think," he said, watching her closely.

She made no comment for a moment. "Then it's over, Frank?"

"It seems so."

She said in a musing tone: "I suppose it would be unwise to stay longer than we have to. But—I'm sorry it's over. I'm very sorry, Frank."

8

THE COACH jolted to a stop and the panel back of the driver's box slid open. The red face of Windy Topp stared down at them.

"Inn, sahib," he said. "Biggish inn, biggish town. French and Polish flags a-flying in the breeze. Church with a top like a Kurpie cap."

"Stop here until we decide what we're to do," instructed Frank. "Keep well muffled up and don't answer if anyone speaks to you."

For two days they had been inside the Polish border and free from the fear of Russian vengeance. Now, it was clear, they would face other difficulties.

"A staff officer!" cried Gabrielle, looking through the glass in the door. "Frank, Frank, we're back in our own world again! How wonderful it makes you feel."

"It makes me feel wonderfully unsafe, sweeting," he answered. "If your Polish allies suspect Topp and me of being English, they'll clap us into a military jail."

Gabrielle turned away from the glass with a sigh. "The sight of those beautiful uniforms made me forget for a moment. I felt almost as though I were back in Paris again." She was wearing a tricorne hat of mink, tied beneath her chin with brown velvet straps. He forgot the difficulties of their position long enough to say to himself that he had never seen her look lovelier. Drawing her against the back of the carriage, he kissed her on both cool cheeks.

"I'm going to risk making some inquiries," he announced then. "After these months of constant use, my French should pass muster."

"You must be very provincial. Say if necessary that you've never been in Paris."

"The role will fit me like a glove."

He returned in fifteen minutes. "The town is full of French," he reported. "Some of them were in the retreat. I hear the hospitals are overflowing." He was studying her with a grave look. "Parties are being organized to continue on to Warsaw. That settles the problem as far as you're concerned. Topp and I must turn back."

She returned his look with equal gravity. "The future has come to us," she said.

"Yes. We must make our plans now." He plunged ahead briskly. "Margot will be waiting for you in Warsaw. I think it would be wise for you to stay there the rest of the winter. Early in the spring you must get to some neutral country. Sweden, perhaps. You mustn't be caught on any part of the Continent when the fighting begins again. You don't believe it yet, but all the German countries are going to turn against Napoleon."

"Frank," she said after a moment's pause. "It's clear to you, isn't it, that I love you?"

"I've been living in a glow of happiness because I believe so."

"I do, *mon petit chou*. Otherwise . . ." She paused. "You must never believe anything else. No matter what may happen. No matter how angry you may be with me." Another pause. "Frank, I must return to Paris at once."

"To Paris!" The significance of this was so clear that for a moment he was stunned. "No, no! You mustn't go back to France. I've been sure you would come to England as soon as it could be done safely. A divorce can be obtained quickly——"

"Frank, we must face the facts." Her tone was firm in spite of an obvious reluctance to go on. "I can't live in England. Could you live in France? We're at war, my dear. We are enemies. The war is a gulf we can't cross."

"The war needn't make any difference." The bitter alarm he was feeling gave an angry edge to his voice. "It will soon be over and the world will then return to normal. Gaby, it won't be an obstacle for more than a year or two. You'll be perfectly safe in England in the meantime."

"Safe! Do you suppose I'm concerned about my safety? It's not that at all. I'm French and I'm heart and soul with the Emperor!"

"You've made that very clear. But need it change our plans? There is more intermarrying between races during a war than at any other time. Thousands of Frenchmen have married German and Italian wives."

"But there's a difference. Those Frenchmen will take their wives home with them when the fighting is ended. If I married you, I would have to go to England now."

"But, Gaby, you've lived in England nearly all your life."

"What I'm trying to make you understand is that I'm a Frenchwoman and that I glory in it. I can't be anything else! Nothing will suit me but to see the Emperor carry out his glorious plans for a new order in Europe. I want to play a part in it. I can't become an Englishwoman. I can't! In spite of my feeling for you, I can't!"

He tried to reason with her, realizing with inner desperation that every word he used had to be carefully considered. "The war will soon be over. Two years, perhaps three. The French and English people will soon find themselves on a friendly footing again. They always have in the past. Will it matter so much then? Win or lose, the glory that Napoleon has brought to France will remain hers. The English will very soon begin to think of him as a great historical character. That's their way. Listen carefully, darling. We could afford to have a house in Paris as well, and we could live there some part of the time. We could do a great deal of traveling. You wouldn't have to settle down permanently in London. I'm willing, Gaby, to do anything at all to make you happy."

But Gabrielle shook her head. "Why do you say that the war will soon be over? Will the English give in?"

"No. We'll never give in."

"Then you think my Emperor will be the one to ask for peace? That he can be beaten? That *is* absurd, Frank. Napoleon is supreme. He's a giant, and the pygmies, no matter how many of them there may be, will never pull him down! If you English won't give in, then the war will go on and on. Until you *are* beaten. It may be the Hundred Years' War all over again."

He said patiently: "We'll soon know. The next year will be decisive. It may not end the war, but it will be the beginning of the end. All Europe will be combined against him."

"All Europe," she declared, her eyes beginning to show that embattled tinge of red, "will combine against the unspeakable Russians! They see the danger now."

"What they see is the chance to rid themselves of the French yoke."

Gabrielle seemed prepared at first to combat this statement violently. She kept her feelings under control, however, and said instead in a subdued tone: "Frank, that isn't the issue between *us*. Can you conceive what living in England would mean to me? I would be under suspicion all the time. People would say I had turned my coat twice. Even the French *émigrés* would have nothing to do with me. I would hear nothing but the English side of things, the wrong side. I would have to listen to horrible lies about the Emperor. I would hear the planning for his defeat. I would see newspapers (even yours, Frank) which printed nothing but stories I wouldn't believe. I would be living among the real enemies of France. Suspicion, hatred, criticism! I couldn't stand it. I would go crazy. But long before I did, I would hate everyone; even you, perhaps. No, no, it wouldn't do. The war *is* a gulf between us. There is no sense in trying to believe anything else."

"Can't love rise above such things?"

She shook her head. "I don't pretend to be wise but I know this: it's the daily things that love can't survive. A violent crisis, yes, but not continuous irritations. Love couldn't live in an atmosphere of hate."

He had observed almost mechanically that the small clock built into the green upholstery of the front needed adjusting. As though trying to find something to divert him from the reality of her purpose, he began to work with it. For a full minute there was silence in the carriage.

"Is it your intention, then," he asked finally, in a restrained tone, "to return to your husband?"

Gabrielle made a gesture which implied that this was a matter of small importance. "That poor Jules! It makes no difference. My marriage has been very close to farcical, and it can never be anything now but an alliance in name. He's such a vain and futile and stupid man! He seems to love me in his own way, but I really believe a point of court etiquette is more important to him than I am. You needn't be concerned about that."

In a sudden burst of anger Frank's fingers whirled the hands of the clock in the wrong direction. Something clicked and one of the hands broke off.

"You can't go back to him!" he cried. "You can't belong to him, even in name. You belong to me! You're my wife now, in every way that counts." He took her roughly by the wrists. "How long have you been thinking this way?"

"Please, Frank, you're hurting me!"

"Then answer me."

"I've been turning it over and over in my mind for days. I've thought of nothing else. Please, my dear, you must believe that I've tried to convince myself the war would make no difference. But I can't! I can't escape the —the logic of it."

"Logic!" he exclaimed bitterly. "That's the whole trouble, Gaby. You are content to let your mind rule. You won't listen to your heart."

"It's well that one of us can see things in a proper light. We French are a logical people. But you English, although you seem so cold, are really nothing but sentimentalists."

"When did you reach your decision?"

His manner was so abrupt and his voice so harsh that she looked at him appealingly. "Must you speak in such an angry tone?" she asked.

"I'm sorry if I seem impolite. But it happens that I'm in an angry mood." He looked at her silently for a moment and then repeated his demand. "Tell me when you made up your mind."

"Not until a few minutes ago. When I caught sight of the French uniforms. The instant I saw them I wanted to jump up and shout. I knew then that I couldn't leave my own country, not while she's at war. I knew that I would have to forget everything else. I knew if I tried to do what you wanted it would turn out to be a tragic failure."

Frank said bitterly, "But the doubt was in your mind when you—when you let me take you in my arms."

Gabrielle looked away. "No, not then," she whispered. "I was certain then that nothing mattered but love. Surely you believe that."

"I try to believe it. But it's proving hard."

A bugle sounded somewhere in the distance. Gabrielle clutched his arm with tense fingers. "Listen!" she said. Color was mounting in her cheeks. "I've heard that in French camps. I've heard the bugles blowing when Napoleon has ridden out to lead his armies. A thrill goes through me every time." She turned to him with shining eyes. "France! Napoleon! Can you wonder that I feel this way? Don't you feel the same when you hear English bugles?"

There was silence for several moments. Gabrielle kept her eyes on her hands, which were clasped in her lap. Finally she said with a sigh, "Well, it seems to be settled."

"Yes. It seems to be settled."

"I hope you won't be in any danger. I shudder to think of you going back to face the Russian storms."

"We won't be in any danger. The retreat is over now, and the Russian forces will be dropping back to winter quarters. On this side of the Polish border we can pass as French and on the Russian side my papers will see us through. I plan to strike north for Riga as soon as we get back on Russian territory."

"But the dreadful cold! It's the real danger, Frank."

"It won't be an easy ride, but we'll get through somehow. I don't mind the cold myself, but poor Topp will suffer."

A silence fell between them for several moments. Finally she said, "You're very angry with me."

Frank kept his eyes averted. "Yes, I'm angry," he said. "It's the first time in all these years I've felt this way."

"You've been so patient. I've given you reason to be angry with me many times."

"No. Never before. But now—you don't think enough of me to hold out any hope for the future. It wouldn't be so hard if you hadn't given me reason to believe you thought differently."

"Frank," she said with a sigh, "you don't seem to think that this is hard for me as well. Can't you see how I feel? I've tried so hard to believe we could do as you want. As for the future, how can we tell what will happen? All we can be sure is that another separation faces us—a long separation."

"I felt so sure . . ." He shook his head hopelessly. "Well, there doesn't seem to be any use talking about it further. You're convinced the war will be a perpetual bar between us."

"It will be a bar for years. And after that"—she gestured hopelessly—"who knows? You may change your mind about me."

"You mean that you may change your mind."

"That also is possible. We must look at this with open eyes, Frank. We're not children. I'm twenty-five now. How old will I be when the war is over? You must think of your own future. It wouldn't be fair of me to expect constancy from you under these circumstances. I think—I know—that we must let the future take care of itself."

"You can make your own terms," he said bitterly. "Very well, then, we must let the future take care of itself."

A ship was ready to sail when they reached Riga, and they put out for Stockholm in the teeth of a gale. Windy Topp became desperately seasick and remained so for the whole trip. Frank's indisposition, while equally acute, was purely of the spirit. Lashing himself with a belt to the rail, he spent long hours looking out over the tumultuous waters, not caring whether they went to the bottom or not.

"But should I complain?" he kept repeating to himself. "Why can't I accept my bad fortune with as much philosophy as Wilson? He has seen reward after reward snatched away from him. I'm sure he's not brooding over what has happened. I should be content to think that a few years will make no difference; that I'll go to France as soon as peace is made and carry her off with me."

But deep in his mind was the conviction that all was over between them. What reason had he to suppose that she would continue to feel the same devotion to him that she had shown in the ecstatic days they had spent together? He had seen proof that she could change her mind quickly in the abrupt termination of her infatuation for Caradoc. That had been quite overwhelming with her while it lasted. What right had he to hope for better fortune?

He was in a mood of anger with himself most of the time. Why had he given in so easily? Why had he so tamely allowed her to leave him? Caradoc had already supplied the answer to that; he, Frank, was a fellow of poor spirit. He had had his chance and had failed to take it.

There were moments when his anger turned again against Gabrielle but these were never more than quick flashes of mood which he promptly dismissed. He had to acknowledge to himself that she could not have existed in London as long as the war continued. It was not hard to picture what would happen. A dinner party: the usual vapid conversation, coming back to the war continuously; the taunts at Bonaparte in every sentence, the sneers at the Frogs; Gabrielle's eyes becoming sultry with resentment; the inevitable outburst. And that was only part of it. How would she feel going into shops where the windows were filled with anti-French cartoons, listening to bands which blared patriotic airs in the streets, reading leaders in the *Tablet* which predicted the downfall of the country she loved with such burning zeal? No, she had been right about it.

But why had she been so unwilling to believe that the future could hold something better? Even though she was sure the war was due to continue many more years, she must realize that inevitably it would come to an end. If she loved him enough she would have agreed to wait until then, even though sure in her mind that the separation would be a long one. That was the point to which his thoughts always came back; she did not love him enough to feel that time was unimportant.

He said to himself that he must become reconciled to the truth. She could never have been his for very long. She would never belong to any one man for long. She was one of those radiant and lovely creatures who win the love of many men and give to each in return some share of her devotion. She was too rare a prize for one man to win and hold for all time. What presumption it had been to think he could keep her to himself! He, an undistinguished scribbler, the least important of all contenders!

The others kept flocking through his mind, the Duc de Berri, Jules, Caradoc, Prince Poloff, even Napoleon himself. In his imagination he saw endless rows of admirers, bowing and smiling around her, seeking her attention and favor, his own figure always in the background, the most insignificant of the lot. Sometimes he would think with a burst of bitter satisfaction that he had been the most favored of all.

But had he? Of course! He put that doubt ruthlessly aside every time it protruded itself.

He thought of nothing else. The officers of the fast packet which took him from Stockholm to Newcastle must have considered him a morose fellow. He had little to say to them even at meals. Their eager questions about the war in Russia elicited short and unsatisfactory answers from him. He spent most of the time in his cabin, going up on deck at rare intervals only, and even then to indulge in solitary tramps about the decks, his hands in his pockets, his head bent forward, the same thoughts going back and forward through his mind, over and over again, an endless and futile procession.

He returned to a London jubilant over the news from Russia, a London which stood in long lines outside the offices of the *Tablet*, waiting for copies of the issue in which appeared the full reports he had brought back with him, a London which discussed little else but what Francis Ellery thought and said. The past seemed completely forgotten. An official of the Foreign Office called on him, questioning him for hours about the situation and listening with grave attention to the conclusions he had reached.

To Frank the only thing that counted about his arrival home was the fact that a letter from Gabrielle awaited him there. It was postmarked Warsaw and had reached the city several days ahead of him. His hands trembled with eagerness as he broke the seal.

It was full of anxiety as to what had happened to him. Did he suffer much on the way to Riga through the dreadful snow? She would have no peace of mind until she knew he was safely back in England. As for herself, she was, at the moment, suffering one of her *sniffling* afflictions and was being kept in bed. Her nose was very red and she was very miserable and very unhappy and quite unable to think of anything but the grim look in his eyes when they parted. Was he still thinking so very badly of her?

Margot was with her. Their reunion had been an affectionate one, although she had been annoyed to find that the obstinate child, who seemed to insist on dramatizing her financial dependence, had been living in the home of a poor Polish family to save expense. She had whisked her out of there, and now they were living in suitable quarters. They had no money, but a loan was being arranged for them with a Polish banking house.

Warsaw was not a gay city. The Poles seemed to think that the Russian mishap ("How could the campaign have ended otherwise with such a dreadful winter against us!") had destroyed their chance for independence. "I am disturbed," she wrote, "at the talk I have heard, and almost convinced you were *not* absurd (my absurd Frank!) about the attitude of the German countries. Are they going to be ungrateful enough to turn against the Emperor when he has risked so much, and lost so much, fighting their battles against the Russians? I am quite sick in my mind about it. Everyone advises most earnestly that we return to Paris as soon as the weather permits. We shall do so, of course."

There was no hint, however, that she had lost any faith in the ultimate triumph of Napoleon, and it was clear she saw no prospect of an early reunion. He read eagerly through to the last of the closely written pages, hoping to find something to give him a basis for hope. If there was anything of the kind, it was in the concluding sentence, "You must believe, *mon petit chou*, that I wish with all my heart that things could be different. Your loving Gabrielle."

He wrote several letters in reply and then tore them up, realizing how unwise it would be to send them. He had no way of knowing when she would arrive in Paris, and it was almost certain that any letters addressed to her there would fall into other hands. It was maddening that he could do nothing to urge his cause, that he could not put down on paper all the things he should have said to her that day when they parted in the Polish border town.

9

"SIR ROBERT WILSON," announced Lord Ellery of Caster from the head of the table, with a suggestion of relish in his voice, "is due to receive a setback. I happen to know of a letter which will be sent to him soon."

Caradoc's title was so newly acquired (purchased would be a more accurate term, for some of Mary's ample inheritance had figured in the ennoblement) that the servants stumbled still when they addressed him as "M'lord" and Frank also found it hard to accustom himself to the sudden grandeur. This was one of the latter's rare visits to the Towers, and he realized that the remark had been leveled at him. From the fill-in position he occupied near the center of the board, he took up the challenge.

"Having told us that much, Carr, I think you should explain what's in the letter."

"It's official." Caradoc turned the matter over in his mind while all conversation was suspended, and then decided to risk a divulgement. "Oh well, it will soon be out anyway. Wilson is being transferred from his post as observer with the Austrian Army."

Frank stared at him for a moment in amazement. "But, Carr, you must be mistaken," he said. "Sir Robert has been high in the councils of the allied commanders. Don't you recall that the Tsar took the Order of St. George from his own breast and pinned it on Wilson's after the battle of Bautzen? It occurred on the field. It was at the request of Prince Schwarzenberg that he was transferred from the Russian to the Austrian forces."

Purdy brought the roast mutton around again and the host helped himself to a thick slice, disregarding Mary's plaintive look, which said as plain as words, "Caradoc, your weight!" She had provided her guests with a very fine dinner. There were partridges as well as beef and mutton, the sole had been dressed in a French sauce, and the sillery was so exceptional that a footman was kept busy refilling the glasses. Caradoc's head was down over his plate, but he continued to aim his remarks unmistakably at his brother. "I read Trutnall's dispatch from Leipsic today and, frankly, I'm not disposed to put any stock in it. To report that Prince Schwarzenberg depends on the fellow and takes his advice on everything, as Trutnall would have us believe, is—well, it's absurd."

Frank never heard that word without thinking of Gabrielle. As usual in all such cases, he relapsed immediately into a mood of abstraction and heard nothing more of the pontifical pronouncements his brother proceeded to make. He was thinking, "Is she still in Paris? Is there any truth in the rumor that she has gone to Frankfort to be that much nearer the Emperor?" He had received no further letters from her during the six months which had elapsed, and none from Margot, and so had been compelled to depend for news of her on the stories which filtered across the channel. She was more than ever, it was clear, the reigning belle of the French court. It was being said openly that Napoleon was growing more partial to her company all the time. Her husband had been advanced in the diplomatic corps and this was a proof of her influence, for Jules de Vitrelle could never have advanced a step on his own merits. Everything Frank heard, in fact, was like salt rubbed in an open wound.

"Frank," said Mary's voice, "aren't you feeling well? You look pale."

He realized that his brow was damp. With an effort at a smile, he replied: "I'm quite all right, Mary. The air is a little close tonight. That's all."

"Close?" boomed Caradoc. "It's a fine cool evening. I'm afraid, old fellow, that I've been making things a bit warm for you."

Caradoc drew him aside after dinner. "All this gossip now," began the new peer. "Do you put any stock in it, old fellow? Is she Napoleon's mistress?"

"No!" bitterly. "You know her well enough to realize it couldn't be the truth."

"That's all very well; but I'm beginning to wonder. They say she's taken to see him by a private staircase. Some even go so far as to say he has set up a retreat for them just out of Paris. I've been willing to give her the benefit of the doubt but, Gad, where there's so damned much smoke, there may be a blaze after all."

"I tell you it's all malicious gossip. Gabrielle's become an ardent admirer of the Emperor and that's as far as it goes."

"Ah! She writes you, then?"

"No. I saw her in Russia."

"You did?" Caradoc considered him with very much increased interest. "You saw her in Russia, eh? Well. You never mentioned it before. As I've said on other occasions, you're a close-mouthed fellow, Frank. Damned secretive, in fact."

"We've had few chances to talk, Carr."

"How was she looking when you saw her?"

"Quite lovely."

"Did she—happen to mention me?"

"She asked about you. I told her you were married and she said she hoped you would be happy."

"She hadn't heard before, then." The younger brother nodded his head with a satisfied air. "I was first choice with her. It doesn't hurt my pride any to see an Emperor seeking her favor now." He added hastily, "Of course, I wouldn't want Mary to know I feel that way."

"I would strongly advise," said Frank shortly, "that you keep your feeling of satisfaction on that score strictly to yourself."

Frank's responses through the balance of the conversation were almost entirely perfunctory. As soon as he could get away he went back to the gardens and paced about in a mood of the most intense perturbation. "They say she's taken to see him by a private staircase." A vicious lie, of course, one that had been told about many ladies of the French court. "Some even go so far as to say he has set up a retreat for them just out of Paris." Another lie, even more vicious than the first. He stamped about angrily, telling himself that Caradoc had invented the stories for the sole purpose of upsetting him. No matter how stoutly he repelled it, however, a picture kept forming in his mind of Gabrielle walking in another garden, one with high stone walls to keep the prying world out, a stout and masterful figure pacing beside her.

"It's not true!" he said aloud. "It's all a damnable fabrication. I won't be cowardly enough to give it another thought."

But the doubts kept coming back and, when he finally retired to his own old room, he found that he could not sleep.

The news from the Continent suddenly became better. Napoleon was defeated in a three-day battle at Leipsic, and much of the credit was given publicly to Sir Robert Wilson, by Schwarzenberg, the generalissimo in command of the allied forces. The *Tablet*, having experimented with a system of carrier pigeons for the transmitting of dispatches, was the first to publish the glorious news of Leipsic, an advantage it continued to hold as the shattered armies of Napoleon were thrown back to the borders of France. A wave of optimism such as England had never known before swept over the country.

Frank's reaction to this confirmation of the prediction he had made a year before was tempered by the fact that Caradoc proved right in his story of Foreign Office intentions with reference to Wilson. Immediately after the battle of Leipsic the latter was transferred to the Austrian Army in Italy, to act as observer there, the notice reaching him in the form of a terse note from a subordinate in the Foreign Office. The letter he sent to Frank on receipt of this unexpected communication contained for the first time a note of despair. What, he asked, was the purpose of the transfer? There was nothing for him to observe in Italy, nothing for him to do there. "I won't even hear the sound of the guns," he wrote, "when Napoleon is forced back on Paris and our victorious friend Wellington comes over the Pyrenees into France. The climax is at hand and I won't be there to share in it. The heavy hand of official enmity has fallen on my shoulder this time with a touch of finality. I'm beaten, Friend Ellery, beaten and weary and without hope."

No more letters came from him after that. Frank knew that the blow had been too much for even the ebullient Wilson spirits. The most unusual soldier that England had produced in many generations had become thoroughly subdued and disheartened, no longer a believer in his own particular star. The eclipse of his high hopes had coincided with the decline of the great adventurer in whose defeat he had played such a spectacular and unrewarded part.

There was cause for worry also in the conduct of the hitherto amenable Benjie Fuller. Benjie had taken heavily to drink. He had become an unsatisfactory employee, morose and disobedient.

"Fuller's head is full o' stuff and nonsense," the foreman reported. "I think, Mr. Ell'ry, he's going to these Jack-bin clubs in the city. He talks all the time 'bout rights and priv'leges, and he drops hints o' bludy rev'lushun and sich foolishness. I don't like the looks of it."

Frank did not like the looks of it either after a talk with Benjie.

"I've nothing but respeck for you, Mr. Ellery," said the latter with a sullenness his employer had never seen in him before. "But you stand for a class what's going to be dealt with sooner or later. It stands to reason I shouldn't be limping on one leg while young Lord Ellery rides in a carriage with two rainbows on the box. I've fought for King and country and what's he done? He's married a duke's daughter; and me, I can't get *my* girl away from the man what stole her from me."

Frank could see it was the loss of Becky which was driving him into these new ways of thought. "Benjie, I agree with you that things are not fairly distributed in this world," he said. "We'll get that corrected in time, but what can be done about it right now? I wish I knew. What measures are advocated by the orators you listen to in that cellar under Ponderby's pub near Fleet Street?"

Fuller looked startled for a moment. "I'm not telling, Mr. Ellery," he said. "We knows what we're to do when the time comes. But"—darkly— "there's one thing I'll be taking on myself before then. Men that's cruel to their wives has to be 'tended to; and I'm going to see that mangy John-a-Nokes get what he deserves if I goes back where you got me out of, Mr. Ellery."

Frank became thoroughly alarmed at this. "Let me arrange to get some land at the Towers for you to farm. Life in the open will be better for you, I'm sure. You weren't intended for this kind of thing."

"A farmer with one leg!" Fuller's tone was full of scorn. "I like to work with prads but that's over and done with now. You tosses muck with a fork, not a crutch. No, Mr. Ellery, I'll stay where I am so I can keep an eye on Becky. If you don't like it, just say the word and I'll do a cat-in-a-pan and you'll be rid of me."

"No, Benjie, I want you right here. I want to keep an eye on *you.*"

Eight more months passed. Through the spring and early summer of 1814 the campaign in France netted Napoleon many small victories, but the vast forces of allied Europe gradually wore him down. Marshal Marmont, who had received from his master the dukedom of Ragusa, put a new word, *to raguse,* into the French language by handing Paris over to the invaders. Soon thereafter the Corsican conqueror set his hand and seal to a document which vacated the throne he had built for himself on the Revolution.

It was over at last, the Napoleonic domination of Europe. No longer would it be necessary for Englishmen in scratch wigs to drill with broomsticks. Napoleon was to be sent to the isle of Elba and would disturb the peace of the world no more.

Papers ran short in England, and crowds stormed the offices of the *Tablet* for copies of the issue in which appeared the magic announcement. Lord Ellery of Caster delivered an oration before the aldermen and merchants of London in which he said that "by never deviating from the straight line of duty and fighting on in the good old English way, we have brought the tyrant to the dust."

Benjie Fuller disappeared after committing a murderous assault on the butler of Sir James Jenks. The hue and cry that the police set up was not sufficient to bring a one-legged fugitive to justice; perhaps because the war had created so many one-legged men, most of whom were falling foul of the law. Frank had wind of him near Willars Bend but lost all trace thereafter.

Sir Robert Wilson came back from Italy, looking unhappy and with no trace left of his one-time optimism. They had dinner together but it was not until the second bottle of sillery that Wilson achieved a flash of his former spirit. "They won't keep him in Elba," he predicted. "The eagle will break loose and the whole thing will have to be done over again. Perhaps they'll condescend to give me a chance then. In the meantime, Frank, I'm thinking seriously of standing for Parliament." His eyes began to light up. "If I could ever manage to get in, I would rake them over the coals."

Frank received a letter from Gabrielle on Christmas Day, but there was nothing festive about the appearance of the envelope. It had come all the way across the Continent from Leghorn and had been thumbed by many postmasters and scrutinized perhaps by censors. Leghorn was the nearest seaport to the island of Elba where Napoleon had been set up with a toy kingdom and a mock court; quite free and independent, of course, although British ships of war patrolled the waters around the island night and day.

It was a brave letter, but not exactly a cheerful one. She was living in three rooms of a very old house on "a scrofulous canal" and was not able to decide which was responsible for the musty odor, the house or the water. Jules and Sosthène were with her and they were a gloomy pair indeed, not relishing their second taste of exile. Sosthène's wife ("that vinegary vixen") was talking of a divorce and refusing to send him any money. Jules could not reconcile himself to having no part in the restoration of the Bourbon King. "He actually blames me for taking him over to the Napoleonic side," she wrote. "That is a fair sample of how the mind of my esteemed husband works. He refuses to wear a violet." Later on Frank was to learn what this reference meant, but at the time he could no more than guess. Through the letter ran references to many French people of prominence who, as it happened, were also in Leghorn and all of whom, it seemed, were bitterly concerned over the plight of "Papa Violet."

His interest centered in a few paragraphs which he read over and over again.

> I am very sad because I realize fully that a real gulf has opened between us now. Perhaps you will shake your head when you read this but I am sure of it. You have been doing a great deal of serious thinking since we parted, my once ardent one, and you have been very angry with me. It is natural that you should be, even though I was right. I had to do it, Frank; there was no other course open to us. But can you still be magnanimous enough to believe I did not want it that way?
>
> You have thought this all over many times and, as I know you so well, I am sure you have tried hard not to let it make a difference. But you are only human and so doubts have crept in. You have wondered about other men. I am very sure that those doubts have now become a habit from which you cannot escape.
>
> I have no illusions. The place I have in your mind, and your heart, is different. Soon, perhaps, it will be a very small place. I cannot even be sure that you have not fallen in love already with someone else.

"She's wrong, completely wrong," he said to himself. "My love hasn't diminished at all. It would be much easier for me if it had. She's right about the doubts, but could any man be free from them under the circumstances?"

10

IT WAS the morning of June 19, 1815. A feeling of unrest had taken possession of the *Tablet* offices. Men lounged about in the corridors, talking in uneasy undertones. The scratch of pens went on in the tiny offices of the writers but there was a fitfulness to the sound, as though their minds were not on their work. The news vendors, having exhausted their supplies early, had gathered at the rear of the establishment and were noisily discussing the rumors sweeping over London.

The same unrest had taken possession of the four men in the corner office. Sir Robert Wilson was sitting at Frank's desk, his head bent over a map. Lord Ellery was standing gloomily at a window, hands in pockets, feet wide apart, like a Colossus making a pretense at straddling something and not clear just what it was. Cope, his stock rumpled, a sure sign that he was disturbed, was walking up and down the room, cracking the joints of his fingers and giving vent at intervals to scraps of opinion. Frank was straddling a chair beside his desk.

"I said all along it was a mistake," declared Cope.

"What was a mistake?" demanded Caradoc. He seemed to anticipate a charge of error against that blameless institution, the British Government, and was ready to combat it.

"Napoleon should never have been sent to Elba. It was certain he would break loose and start the war all over again."

"What else was there to do with him?"

Cope stopped pacing and blinked at Caradoc with his mild and slightly myopic eyes. "He could have been hanged," he said. "Or sent to St. Helena. He wouldn't get away from there."

Caradoc looked prepared to express an opinion on this but remarked instead in envious tones on the fine sheen of Cope's boots. "Tinker never gets mine like that," he grumbled. "I've a notion to do what George Brummell advises—have 'em rubbed with froth of champagne."

Cope looked properly scornful. "That fellow!" he said. "Only way to get a good shine is polish and plenty of elbow grease."

Wilson was paying no attention to their talk. Without looking up from the map, he said in an abstracted tone: "He's managed to shove in between the armies of Wellington and Blücher. They left a wide gap, and I'm pretty well convinced these rumors from the Continent are correct. Blücher has taken a sound licking. He's a great old fighter but a damned blundering general."

Frank was watching him with concern. He knew what a blow it had been to his pride when Wellington did not take him for the struggle brought on by Bonaparte's surprise bolt from Elba. Wilson had made a determined effort to secure a post at the front, and his failure to do so had left him with a still more hopeless look in his eyes.

Frank himself had been in a state of tension for the last twenty-four hours. The sense of anticipation, which sometimes warned him of the imminence of important events, had been at work. He was certain that the decisive battle had already been fought and that word of the result was on its way to them.

"I'm very much afraid that Wellington hasn't been able to hold him," he said.

Cope nodded in agreement. "He has a miserable army. What a hideous error it was to send his peninsular veterans out to America!"

The Colossus rallied to the defense of constituted authority. "You're wrong, Cope. The damned Americans had to be attended to."

Wilson surprised them all by voicing a hope that things had gone well at the front. "If the battle *has* been fought, Wellington may have won."

He nodded his head over the map. "Boney seems to have his seven-league shoes on again and he has come storming up between them like the old God of Battles he used to be. But there's this about it. Wellington found a formula for beating French armies in the Peninsula. He always waited until he had ground to his liking; a field which sloped upward, not too steep to dissuade them from attacking but just enough to take the edge off their cavalry charges. He would have his squares waiting back of the crest, holding their fire to give Johnny Craps a blast as soon as he came over. It worked every time. Now!" He stabbed a finger at the map. "In front of the Soignes woods and the village of Waterloo, there's just such a field. It's cut to the very measure of Wellington. I consider it perfect because, in addition to everything else, the sunken Ohain Road cuts across it. If Wellington has twigged it, and has stationed himself there, he'll have a chance to beat Boney. I'm pinning my hopes on that."

Caradoc was nodding his head in agreement with the views of Wilson. "Just what I've thought all along," he said heartily. "We'll win. Wellington will give the beggar a thorough trouncing. It stands to reason."

Brushing the crown of his high hat with an apple-green sleeve, my Lord Ellery stamped importantly to the door. Here he paused and turned back. "I don't put any stock in this pigeon idea of yours, Frank. But if the bird *should* arrive——"

"I will be home within an hour."

"In that case send me along whatever news it brings." Caradoc hesitated. "Don't forget now. It's damned important. Well, I must get along. Good morning, gentlemen."

"I'll send a runner with the news," promised Frank.

Half an hour later a runner arrived with the expected tube of waxed paper. Frank took it and looked with a set face at his two companions. His hand, he found, was trembling.

"Here it is!" he whispered. "The future of the world depends on what's written inside of this."

Cope was breathing hard. "It's bad news," he said. "I feel it in my bones. God help us, we've been beaten!"

"Don't keep us waiting, Frank," said Wilson in a matter-of-fact tone. "Nothing can change what's written there."

"I'm almost afraid to look."

With an unsteady hand Frank opened the cylinder and spread out the single sheet of thin paper it contained on his palm. At first he was too tense to make out the words. Then, as the impact of the message struck home, he gasped and sank down into his chair.

"Is it as bad as that?" cried Cope.

"Gentlemen," said Frank in a faint voice, "it says, '*Wellington has beaten Napoleon decisively on the field of Waterloo'!*"

For several moments there was not a sound in the room. The stillness was so complete that they could hear the rustle of trees in the square below. Then a distant rumble of thunder came through the windows, and two of the occupants of the room started involuntarily, as though the sound had been an echo of the fateful guns at Waterloo. Wilson seemed entirely composed, but tears were streaming down Cope's face and he was fumbling in his pocket for a handkerchief.

"Are you sure?" whispered Cope. "There's no mistake about it?"

"Read us what it says," suggested Wilson with a touch of impatience.

Frank was still finding it hard to focus his eyes on the momentous message. "There's just one more sentence. '*The French are in full retreat with Prussian cavalry pursuing but Bonaparte's whereabouts unknown.*'"

Wilson's calm began to show the first sign of cracking. "Your man," he said with gusto, "must have ridden all night to get the news to the coast. Stout fellow! Well, gentlemen, we've won."

Cope sprang to his feet. "Are we made of stone?" he demanded. "Why aren't we out on the streets, shouting this glorious news to the skies so that all England may share it with us?" He subsided with a sheepish grin. "I forgot for a moment that we're running a newspaper. What are we going to do about this, Frank?"

A sudden thought had occurred to the young editor. He glanced up at the astronomical clock on the wall.

"I've an idea, Copey," he said. "We could reprint yesterday's edition with the exception of the front page. That we could use for the announcement of the victory. It's never been done before, but this seems an occasion when we'll be justified in trying something new. We could be selling copies on the streets in a couple of hours."

"We'll call it a special!" cried Cope, taking fire at once. "A radical move, Frank. But we've done plenty of radical things in our time. Let's get to work!"

"It will use up all our thin reserve of paper."

"What of it! There will only be one battle of Waterloo in the whole history of the world. Feed the sheets into the presses as long as there's a whole arm among us to turn the cranks!"

Wilson had not risen. He said now in a reflective tone: "Wellington seems to be made of iron. It's a good thing for England that he was in command at this crisis. Destiny," he added with a sigh, "has a way, after all, of picking the right man!"

"There's a headline for us!" cried Cope. "THE IRON DUKE WINS."

They decided to move a case of type into a separate room and set one printer to work there, Topp to stand guard at the door until everything was in type and could be rushed to the press; in that way the secret could be kept until the first copies were ready for sale.

It was not until all the arrangements had been made that Frank was able to sit back and think. Victory at last! Nearly twenty years of disaster and defeat, of fears and continuous uncertainty, of ceaseless preparation and privation; and now at the finish a complete victory! He looked up and smiled. "This was worth going to the pillory for, Copey," he said.

The story of the victory had been put into type when they visited the pressroom. A few printers were standing about, whispering excitedly to one another. Windy Topp had broken instructions by chalking on the wall:

> *Boney has gone*
> *Arsy-varsy!*

"No one is to leave this room until the copies begin to roll off," ordered Frank. He was in too happy a mood to reprimand his exuberant follower. "We must all be patient for another quarter of an hour. Then we'll shake London with the greatest news England has ever had!"

Tears streamed down Cope's face as he watched the pressman start to clamp the form into place. "I can hardly believe it, Frank," he whispered. "A fine dish of Corsican *mouflon* will be served at the next peace conference! Think of it, victory at last!"

"We must be on the streets when the horns begin to sound," said Frank, realizing that his own cheeks were wet.

The streets of London were filled with delirious mobs. Bonfires were being lighted everywhere. Copies of the *Tablet* were being fought for and the vendors were receiving fabulous prices for the few they had left. Frank and Cope exchanged glances of complete content. It seemed at the moment as though the victory was as much theirs as the Duke of Wellington's.

The once invincible Corsican had met England's Iron Duke and had gone down to defeat. Frank could think of nothing else. It was hours later when it occurred to him that this news, which had made him so happy, would be a tragic matter for Gabrielle. He realized that this was his first thought of her since the arrival of the dispatch announcing the victory.

Never before in the years he had known her had she been absent from his mind for such a long time.

BOOK V

France

THE DUKE OF WELLINGTON was giving a ball. It was an elaborate affair, and guests of all nations filled to overflowing the house of General Junot, which had been secured for the purpose. It may have seemed fitting that the great Duke, who began his victorious career by beating the incompetent Junot at Vimeiro, should celebrate the climax of his efforts in the Paris home of the Bonapartist General.

His Grace, as usual, was not concerning himself too seriously with his duties as host, having ensconced himself for supper in a secluded nook with a pretty and vivacious lady on each side. This also was typical of the Duke of Wellington; being so much in the public eye, he was careful to satisfy his liking for the company of lovely ladies with more than one at a time.

"I'm surprised to see the Comtesse Lavalette here, Your Grace," one of his companions was saying. "Isn't it true that her husband is on the proscribed list?"

"My dear Daphne," grumbled the Duke, "I've no official knowledge of the names on this list you mention. In fact, I've not been informed that such a list exists. Then—ha—it's my privilege, I think, to invite anyone I see fit." He threw back his head and gave out one of his high laughs. "To tell you the truth, my dears, I was so dashed busy I didn't have time to check my own list as carefully as I should."

"I'm surprised she came," volunteered his other companion. "She must know how everyone feels."

"These Beauharnais women are *very* bold," declared the first. "They don't care what people say or think. But they *are* lovely, don't you think, Augusta?"

"Well"—grudgingly—"Hortense is attractive. But so *frail*, my dear. I hear the Comtesse Lavalette is different from her cousin in one respect. She's quite devoted to her husband."

"It's clear then that I invited the wrong one." The Duke indulged in another of his laughs. He stopped short when his eye fell on a man in plain black broadcloth crossing the floor at close range. He called out: "Ah, Mr. Ellery! You received my card, then."

Frank paused and bowed. "Yes, Your Grace. It was very kind of you to ask me."

"I owed it to you, Mr. Ellery. You may recall that I gave you a different kind of invitation once. Perhaps this will help even the score. How are you, sir?"

"I'm quite well, Your Grace."

"I'm very glad to see you, Mr. Ellery. They tell me your newspaper printed a sound report of the battle. Quite different from all this balderdash that's being written about it. I would like to see it."

"I have copies here and will send one to your headquarters, sir."

"Thank you." The Duke nodded his head and proceeded to indulge in what was for him an unusual display of loquacity. "I would do some things differently if the campaign was to be fought over again. But none of these scribbling fellows sees what I had to contend with. I had an abominable army, most of my best men being off in America. It was necessary to keep the line to the coast open and to cover Brussels as well. They say I was floundering around and not keeping in close enough touch with old Blücher. I'm glad you don't subscribe to such nonsense, Mr. Ellery."

"No, Your Grace. It's my opinion that Napoleon was outgeneraled in the decisive phase."

"I'm happy to hear someone say that. I think perhaps my plan will repay study on the part of those who fight the battles of the future."

"You don't agree, then, with the popular belief that the victory at Waterloo has ended wars for all time? In London everyone's saying that the world has learned its lesson at last. They think we'll have permanent peace now."

"Stuff and nonsense!" declared Wellington. "There will be wars, young man, till the end of time. I only hope, by Gad, that I don't have to fight any more of them."

Frank wandered about for several minutes, his mind occupied with the two purposes which had brought him to Paris. His ostensible aim was to report what was happening, but he wanted desperately to see Gabrielle and determine once and for all how matters stood between them. He had received a letter from her a fortnight before which had reflected the conflict of moods and intentions in which she was involved; despair over the fall of the Empire, courage in facing what clearly was the bleakest of futures, a deep degree of feeling for him (much deeper, in fact, than he had ever allowed himself to believe), and at the same time the conviction that her letter was a final farewell. It had left him in a completely unsettled state of mind. It should have been clear to her that she could now live in England with less mental discomfort than in France, even if she would be permitted to remain in Paris, which was more than doubtful, but the thought of doing so did not seem to have entered into her consideration of the future. Did she feel she had become *déclassée* because of the scandal which had connected her with Napoleon? Was she concerned over deserting her husband now that his fortunes were at so low an ebb? Was she too upset over the final pricking of the bubble of Bonapartist glory to be capable of coherent planning? There had been a suggestion of all these things in what she had written.

Her feelings for Margot had been more clearly defined.

We have quarreled again [she wrote]. Bitterly and, I am afraid, irrevocably. I shall never see her again. Her estates are being restored, and she has a rosy and brilliant future ahead of her. I am glad of that. But she's so inflexible and I am going to find it hard to forget some of the things she said to me. As it is certain our paths will never cross again, yours and mine, dear Frank—unless someday you chance to meet three unhappy exiles at some dull German spa—I am trying to be broad-minded enough to repeat the advice I gave you on a certain happy, but not to be more specifically mentioned, evening a long time ago. Are you planning to visit Paris? If you do, you must see my lovely young cousin, determined Bourbon though she is.

The letter had been postmarked Paris, although it had contained no address. Had the omission been intentional, a final proof that she considered everything at an end between them? Or had she felt it necessary to keep her whereabouts a secret, fearing the letter might fall into the hands of Fouché's agents?

Whatever the reason, he felt too deeply concerned to take any interest in the Duke of Wellington's party or in the jumble of famous personages it had brought together. He walked about aimlessly, scarcely noticing the great soldiers and diplomats, the bearers of illustrious titles, the very lovely ladies, who filled the crowded rooms. He could get the list for his dispatch later on.

Supper was over. The orchestra was playing *Dunois le Troubadour* with an abandon which said, At last after twenty years we can play something beside Napoleonic airs. The guests were flocking back to the dancing floor. The Duke stalked by with a lady on each arm, his keen blue eyes sparkling with pleasure. Both ladies were in white. The whole country, as Frank had already noted, had taken to the Royalist color with a sort of determined frenzy. White towels or handkerchiefs fluttered on poles from all the windows of Paris. Bourbon cockades were worn in hats everywhere. It was even being said that women of fashion were carrying the idea to the extreme of absurdity by trying to appear wan and pale, and were drinking quantities of vinegar each day for the purpose.

Sir Robert Wilson, his breast blazing with orders, was talking in a corner to a Russian and a tall Austrian who belonged, apparently, to Metternich's diplomatic corps. Wilson smiled at Frank and waved him to join them.

"Did you chance to come by the field of Waterloo?" The Austrian diplomat helped himself to snuff with a fastidious shudder. "The sight of so many bodies almost turned my well-seasoned stomach. And the stench! They tell me it was quite as bad at Borodino, but I find that hard to believe." He added with a trace of reluctance: "It was a fortunate thing the great English Duke didn't have a nerve in his body. He lacked the imagination to fear the tricky magnificence of Napoleon and stood up boldly to the hardest of his pounding; and so it's over at last. An amazing fellow, this hook-nosed Duke. So cold, so very English, and so right about so many things."

Wilson shook his head with an air of gravity. "I didn't dare visit the field," he said. "I would have felt responsible for every poor fellow left there to rot."

The Austrian looked startled, but the Russian nodded. "You mean about Krasnoi?" asked the latter. "I was sure you referred to that serious slip on the part of our stubborn old bear. Everyone in my country has heard that you said publicly you should have shot Kutuzov so that the plan to capture Bonaparte could have been carried out."

The Austrian looked still more startled when Wilson went on with a further explanation. "Yes, we had him trapped. If Kutuzov could have been eliminated, the war would have ended there. But we all lacked the resolution to save the world from three more years of useless slaughter."

"They would have shot you in turn, *Boatt* Wilson," declared the Russian.

"I understand your point now," said the Austrian. "How lucky for the Duke that you did nothing of the kind. He would have lost his chance to become a world hero." His interest became fixed on an entirely different matter and he laid a hand with thickly corded veins on the Russian's arm. "That pretty lady with the white ermine, my dear Baron. Surely I must be mistaken! It can't be the Comtesse Lavalette."

"It's the Comtesse nevertheless."

Frank, who had already secured the list of the proscribed prepared by the new government of France and knew that the Comte Lavalette was near the top, looked at the lady in question with considerable interest. Why, he wondered, had she appeared so publicly under the circumstances? Was it in the hope of making friends among the allied leaders, who alone could save her husband from the firing squad or the guillotine? The Comtesse was tall and slender, quite pretty, and wearing an air of resolution that suggested she might have some such purpose.

"Lavalette will be arrested and shot," declared the Austrian. "His position gave him the opportunity to be of assistance to *Papa* during the Elba days, and it's assumed he was a leader of the group who wore the violet. He won't be forgiven."

The group who wore the violet! Frank recalled the letter he had received from Gabrielle when she was in Leghorn. So that was what she had meant! She, clearly, had been one of those who assisted in Napoleon's escape. She was not on the list, but a feeling of alarm took possession of him. Was she still in Paris? He must find out at once. She would not be safe as long as she remained in the city, that was certain.

"The Duke," said the Austrian dryly, "was not well advised in sending the lady an invitation. He seems to have asked everyone. Even"—with a smile—"our good friend Sir Robert Wilson."

"The Duke," said the Russian, "is a law unto himself these days. Will he use his power to help Ney? You know, of course, that he was placed under arrest today?"

Wilson, whose interest had been wandering, turned around sharply at this and stared at them. "Ney?" he cried. "Great God, I can't believe it! The royal party is out for blood, I know; they've made their purpose quite clear. But Ney! The bravest soldier the country has produced! They won't dare touch him."

"He's at the very top of the list," said Frank.

"He'll face a firing squad," declared the Russian confidently. "No doubt about that. The people of the court, particularly the ladies, are swarming around *le roi nickard* like angry hornets. They'll be satisfied with nothing but the death of the brave Ney. I think it altogether likely they'll insist on the heads of all the society of the violet."

Wilson's indignation seemed on the point of boiling over. "No one was more determined than I that Napoleon should be unseated, but I can't stomach the idea of these dressed-up monkeys screaming for the blood of soldiers," he exclaimed. "What were they doing when Boney's men were winning glory for France? Living on the bounty of England and making silly little plans which never included any fighting for themselves! It was Englishmen and Germans and Hollanders who died at Waterloo to restore these perfumed dandies!"

The Austrian dismissed that phase of the matter with an indifferent gesture. "Well, it's no concern of ours. Do you know Lavalette, by the way? An amusing little fellow, a very good fellow indeed. He was Napoleon's aide-de-camp in the early days. When Louis Bonaparte wanted to marry Emilie Louise, Josephine's niece, the great man took Lavalette to Mme. Campan's school, where she was being taught, and said to her, 'Here, my girl, is the husband for *you*.' They were married right away, the girl not having the courage to say no. As it happened they fell in love with each other, so it turned out well. Louis Bonaparte got Hortense instead and didn't want her, the blind idiot."

Leaving the other two to continue their discussion, Wilson drew Frank toward the ballroom. "If the Duke is in circulation again, I shall pay my respects and leave," he said. "This news about Ney has upset me. I had a brush with him once. It was in the retreat to avoid the French pincers after Talavera. Ney caught my division before we could get back into Portugal and gave us a bad mauling. I've always had the greatest respect for Le Rougeaud."*

The ballroom presented a brilliant appearance, the Duke having spared no expense. Seven hundred candles gleamed on the walls and in the chandeliers. The band of the guards had been augmented by an orchestra hired from La Belle Limonadière's at the Palais-Royal, and the music rolled through the long rooms with inspiring volume. A minuet was in progress with as many as a hundred couples taking part. Finding little in it to interest him, however, Frank decided to leave with Wilson.

And then he saw Margot. She was dancing opposite a middle-aged Frenchman who wore a satisfied air of sallow dignity. Her movements were light and graceful, her cheeks slightly flushed. Gabrielle had not exaggerated the change in her young cousin. Margot had become a beauty.

How was it that Gabrielle had described her? A gentle, stay-at-home Joan of Arc. Apt enough, as far as it went, he decided; for Margot's brow had a suggestion of nobility about it, and there was a fineness to her features which rose above mere beauty. But the phrase took no account of the vivacity she had acquired since he had seen her last. It was a revelation to observe her in a gay mood. The minuet is a sedate dance, but she was smiling as though she found it a pleasant and even exciting diversion. Her velvety blue eyes were shining.

* Ney's nickname in the French Army because of his flaming red hair.

She was dressed in white, of course. The snowy plumes in her hair, *à la Henri Quatre,* were no different in reality from those which tossed and bobbed on the heads of most of the other ladies on the floor, but they seemed to symbolize with her virginity and grace. Her bodice was of the canezou variety, as worn by unmarried women, with a band of lace to conceal the lines of the breast, but the sleeves, which were wide enough to suggest a Tudor ruff, raised no more than a transparent mist of muslin about her neck, leaving the slender outline of her shoulders fully exposed. The skirt was Empire, a billowing mass of patent net over a base of white satin, embroidered with flowers in red and black, which fell away from the breasts in a straight line and swayed freely in the movements of the dance. It was, Frank concluded, a very youthful and completely charming dress.

Yes, Margot was a beauty. He stood and watched her with a sense of pleasure mingled with incredulity. Could this be the thin little slavey who had labored so industriously at household tasks in London? Even the slender girl who had been so reluctant to leave England had given no promise of such a startling metamorphosis. It was nothing short of a miracle. He was so absorbed in watching her, he did not realize that Sir Robert had left him. He had not moved when the dance came to an end and the participants left the floor in sedate pairs. Margot, on the arm of her plump partner, passed within a few feet of him. She saw him and stopped.

"M'sieur Frank!" she cried. "What a surprise! I didn't know you were in Paris."

"I arrived this afternoon."

"Then you're forgiven. I would have felt very hurt if you had been here long and hadn't been to see me."

"It was my hope to pay my respects tomorrow."

"I'm so glad to see you!" She introduced her partner, and the two men exchanged perfunctory bows. The middle-aged man was a Comte Something-or-other.

"At four o'clock, then? I'm still at Place Lorient." Margot smiled with so much warmth that Frank felt surprised and a little elated as well. He had never subscribed to Gabrielle's belief as to the state of her cousin's interest in him, but it was gratifying to be remembered with so much friendliness. "It will be nice to talk about the days in London. They seem a long time ago, but I remember everything. I have a thousand questions to ask you."

"And I have as many to ask you, Margot."

Her partner, whose face was beginning to seem familiar (Could he have been one of the visitors at Caster Towers?), seemed impatient to get away. He tugged at Margot's arm, but she paid no attention.

"I must see London again soon. I want to visit all the places where we lived. I even want to see that funny little inn where we stayed before we left England. Not that I have pleasant recollections of it at all."

"I," declared her partner, "never want to see London again."

Frank was certain now that this middle-aged Comte had been one of the group which met the King at the Towers. The two men stared at each other with no suggestion of friendliness whatever.

"London hasn't changed in any respect," said Frank. "It's a very dingy city compared to Paris."

"You overpraise London when you call it dingy, monsieur," declared the Comte.

"Did you live there long?"

"Eight years. Eight cold, damp, uncomfortable years. Under no circumstance could I be induced to return to that thoroughly horrible place."

"Unless," said Frank, "you had another revolution in France and needed a friendly asylum. I think, monsieur, you would return with great willingness then."

The Frenchman glared at him. "There will never be another revolution in France," he stated.

"I agree that it's unlikely. The Englishmen who died at Waterloo have insured peace in your country for many years to come."

The Comte began to splutter and Margot said hurriedly, "The music is starting again." They turned to leave. Unwilling, however, to part on a hostile note, she looked back over her shoulder and asked, "Is it possible that Gabrielle is in London?"

"No, I'm quite certain she isn't. The last word I heard of her she was here in Paris."

"How long ago was that?"

"Two weeks."

"I haven't seen her for more than a month. Do you think it likely that she's still here?"

"I hope not."

"If the Comtesse de Vitrelle is still in Paris," declared the Frenchman, "she is very ill advised. Mademoiselle, I shall escort you to your next partner."

Frank bowed and said, "Tomorrow at four, mademoiselle."

Margot's eyes smiled back at him as she permitted herself to be led away. "How extraordinary," he thought, watching her until she was lost in the press, "that one family could produce two such beauties of such completely different types."

Feeling disturbed and depressed by the breach between the two cousins, he resisted an impulse to linger for another glimpse of Margot. He decided to look for Caradoc, who was in Paris on a parliamentary mission and would be present, without a doubt. But Caradoc was nowhere in sight. Giving up the search after a very few minutes, he concluded that he might as well leave.

Wilson, with a light cape over his uniform, was standing in the porte-cochere, looking out at the brilliantly illuminated city. "So you've decided to come after all," he said. "Do you feel like walking? I recommend it. As this is your first night in Paris, you'll enjoy a closer look at the place. I promise you'll get a surprise or two."

They walked down the Rue de Rivoli to the square in front of the Palais-Royal. Here the throng was so dense that they had difficulty in making their way through. Frank's amazement had been mounting with every step he took. Paris, after all, was a conquered city, and he had been expecting to find shuttered windows and barred doors, with the streets given over to the men of the occupying armies. Foreign soldiers were as much in evidence as he had anticipated, even at this late hour of the evening: Austrian officers with laurel wreaths in their hats, Prussians insisting on the center of the sidewalks, Englishmen in scarlet regimentals, Highlanders in kilts who seemed quite oblivious to the intense curiosity aroused by their costume. The astonishing part was that all Paris seemed to be out as well and in a holiday mood. Women, swishing their bell skirts coquettishly and wearing, out of compliment to the victors, scarves of Scottish plaid and hats à l'anglais (quite ugly, most of them) or Russian caps with diminutive peaks, were everywhere, many of them unescorted. They seemed quite gay and more than willing to be friendly, even accommodating.

"One would think they were celebrating a victory," said Frank, who had just had a fan flaunted in his face by a plump lady in a terre d'Egypte shawl.

"A strange race in adversity, the French," declared Wilson, halting to light a cigar. "Of course, a part of them are celebrating victory. Just how large a part is hard to decide; I think sometimes the number who welcome the return of the monarchy is relatively small. However, all this tendency to make a carnival out of what has happened is on the surface. Underneath Paris is seething with hate."

"I felt it when I arrived this afternoon," said Frank. "A squad of Highlanders were standing sentry at the barriers of Saint-Martin, and there was a sullen mob watching them as though waiting a chance to stab them in the back. My landlord is a surly fellow, and I suspected there would be poison in the bowl of soup he brought me. I was quartered on him, and it's easy to see he resents it."

"The Royalists and Bonapartists despise each other, and the old Jacobin element, the men of the Terror, hate both. All three classes, which means the whole of Paris, unite in hating us with an intensity hard to believe when you observe this sort of thing tonight.

"By the way, did you follow what Comte Hallwitz said about that little business of the violet? The whole story is beginning to come out now. Boney's bolt from Elba was a very clever scheme, and quite a number of them had a hand in it. They all wore a violet as a mark of identification."

"Napoleon, then, was *Papa Violet?*"

"Yes. They're always coining names for him, you know. *Jean L'Epée* and now *M'sieur Absent*. The violet is still being worn by the bolder sort. You'll even see 'em tucked away in ladies' hats. But it's getting risky."

"Gabrielle was one of them," said Frank in a whisper. "I'm beginning to worry about her."

"She had better not be found in Paris then. The court is determined to wipe out the whole brood of violet-wearers."

"I suppose the Bonapartists are hatching plots already for his escape."

Wilson nodded. "In the Faubourg St. Honoré—that's the Bonapartist quarter of the town—they get their heads together every night and talk of plans. A lot of good it will do them! He's caged properly this time."

Frank shook off his anxiety to ask, "How do you feel about him, now that it's all over?"

"If you must have it, I confess to a stirring of sympathy. It's completely without sense or justification, of course. I realize he must be kept under lock and key from now on but—well, if I can feel that way, how do you suppose the world will react once people forget the years of blood and trouble he's caused us? They'll think of him rotting on that hot island and they'll blame Britain. Acting as his jailer is going to be a thankless task."

Wilson looked at his watch. "We'll get a calash and I'll drop you off wherever you're going. I think I'll stop in at Galignani's and look over the English newspapers. You know, of course, that I've decided to settle down here? Lady Wilson's with me and we're going to take a house. Poor girl, she's not in very good health. The soft air of Paris will be good for her."

Reaching his dingy and hostile pension, Frank spent some time in uneasy speculation. Was Gabrielle still in Paris? If so, how could he get in touch with her? He was disturbed also by the place that Margot held in his thoughts. The picture of her stayed with a persistence and vividness that was not warranted by the natural pleasure he had taken in seeing her again. He had never seen anything more lovely, he kept thinking, than her wide, tranquil brow, or harder to dismiss than her clear eyes.

He thought: "This is because I'm flattered by what Gaby said. I'm being naïve enough to take an interest in the possibility that it's true. It's not true, of course." The trouble was that he no longer was convinced that it was not true. This, he told himself, was sheer masculine pride and must be suppressed promptly.

"It won't do at all," he said to himself determinedly.

2

FINDING HIMSELF next morning in the neighborhood where Caradoc had engaged rooms, Frank decided to pay his brother a call. Caradoc had a way of picking up information. As he had been in Paris for the better part of a month, it was quite possible he would know something of Gabrielle's whereabouts.

Lord Ellery had just stepped out of his *gummi* portable tub when Tinker admitted the visitor. He dropped the towel he had been applying vigorously to his shoulders and said: "Ha, old fellow! I'd just made up my mind to pay *you* a call. There's something you can do for me."

The rooms Caradoc had been assigned were almost regal in size and furnishings. The spacious bedroom contained a four-poster bed and an assortment of Louis Quatorze pieces, with somber hangings of velvet over the windows. Through an open door Frank caught a glimpse of a table piled high with papers which dripped official seals.

The younger brother made no effort to dress himself but proceeded to stride up and down, flexing his muscles proudly. Frank was rather amazed at the weight he had taken on. His torso had thickened and his handsome legs had assumed heroic proportions. In spite of this, he was still a picture of physical symmetry, and his skin was as white as a woman's.

"I never put on clothes until I have to," he explained. "Free movement is the best possible thing for the body. Matter of fact, we wear too damned many clothes for our own good." He waved an arm to his man.

"Hop it, Tinker. See that I get a real breakfast today. None of their blasted rolls and coffee, mind you. An English breakfast, Tinker."

When the servant had left, Caradoc turned to Frank with the quizzical frown he always put on when he had a confession to make. "Frank," he boomed, "I'm in a bit of a difficulty. I want you to know first I've been an exemplary husband to Mary. Why, I've only been in Harriette Wilson's place once in the last two years, and then it was strictly in the role of onlooker. I went along with George Brummell." This last was thrown out with an air of pride. "But, damme, Mary's expecting in a month, and you can see what that's meant to me. Well, it comes down to this. I brought a little lady along with me. We had a quarrel yesterday and I'm afraid she's disposed to be troublesome."

"She wants money, I take it."

"Yes, that's the size of it. She's made up her mind to hook it back to London."

"Is she making threats?"

"No, it hasn't come to that. But I feel under obligations to her and, of course, I can't take any chances at all of a hint getting to Mary's ears."

"There doesn't seem to be any problem, then. Pay her something and pack her off home."

Caradoc frowned. "Damme, I don't want to see her again. She has a sharp tongue and she got under my skin yesterday. If I go back, we'll have a row and then there'll be no telling what she'll do. Besides, I'm likely to empty my pockets and say, 'Here, take everything I've got and leave me alone.' That's how I am." He reached reluctantly for his shirt and proceeded to struggle into it. "When I got your note, saying you had arrived, I said to myself, 'Frank's the one to do this business.'"

"No, thanks, Carr. This seems to me a strictly private matter. I'm afraid you'll have to attend to it yourself."

"Come, come, old fellow." Caradoc was pulling on his trousers and fumbling with the inside snaps which held the braces. Frank wondered what influence had brought him finally to wearing trousers. Perhaps the great Beau had issued a ukase. "You *must* help me out. Truth of the matter is, she won't let me in if I try to see her again. She made that clear yesterday, the damned hussy! I can't afford to let her go back to London in that frame of mind. God knows what she might do or say."

Frank resigned himself to the task with a feeling of inner resentment. "I don't want Mary hurt," he said. "If it's certain your mistress won't see you, I suppose I'll have to act as your intermediary."

Before Frank could disclaim any intention of acting on this suggestion, Tinker returned carrying a tray heaped up with a substantial breakfast.

The man assisted his master in the completion of his toilet and then stood over him as he set to work on the food.

"Frank," said Caradoc, raising a forkful of fish, "did you know that Gaby's cousin has become rather considerable of an heiress?"

"Yes. I saw her for a moment last night. The Duke sent me a ticket."

"He did? Odd, that, considering." The younger brother seemed a little puzzled over the magnanimity of the Duke, and not too pleased. He munched aggressively on a slice of toast. "Well, then, you've seen her. A pretty little chick, eh? I could hardly believe my eyes."

"Margot has become quite a beauty."

"We're in thorough agreement on a subject for the first time in our lives, old fellow. A beautifully paced little filly. If I were you, Frank, I'd see what could be done about it. I danced with her and she talked about you the whole time, damned if she didn't. You might have a chance." He winked again. "I'm over here on trade matters and I happen to know a company's being formed to take over her American holdings. Biggest bankers in Paris are back of it and some English capital may be allowed in. The plan is to build up a big shipping line as well. The gal will be fairly rolling in pelinpinpin."

"I've heard her prospects are bright."

"Bright! Listen to this, Frank. The French and American governments can be persuaded to wink at a little blackbirding on the side. It's proposed to work the Middle Passage. Deals can be made with King Damel and Mungo Cattee to keep the barracoons filled with black ivory." He whistled. "The profits will be enormous."

Frank was both startled and shocked. "The slave trade? Does Margot know of this?"

"Certainly not. Good God, no!" Caradoc was starting in on a slice of broiled ham. "Be sensible for once in your life, Frank. Think over what I've said. Go in and win the little lady. It can be done."

"I'm much more interested in what you may know about Gabrielle. Is she in Paris?"

Caradoc answered casually. "I've heard she's here but I haven't seen her. No one seems to know anything about her for sure." He paused and then added with emphasis: "Get that chuckleheaded little idiot out of your mind! She's involved herself hopelessly this time. No sense in her sticking by a cause as soundly lost as Bonaparte's. All it's done for her is to confirm the general belief she was his bedfellow. Everything she owns will be taken away from her, of course. Her husband and brother will be in the same fix; and all through her pigheadedness. I hear the pair of them are in Brussels and in a pretty lather over the way she's acted."

"How has she acted?"

"Gad, haven't you heard? All Paris has been talking about her. She went to see him—Bonaparte, I mean—even after it was certain he was done for. Can you imagine anything so utterly insane? Then she had to go and quarrel right and left with the old nobility. Turned her back on Talleyrand. Said sharp things publicly about the king and the Duchesse d'Angoulême. In fact, she's behaved so damned badly the court crowd are angry enough to plump her into jail with Ney and the others."

Frank's spirits were showing a tendency to rise. "Everything you say confirms my belief that she's a lady of high and gallant spirit. Margot was just as outspoken and determined in her allegiance to the Bourbons when things were going the other way."

Caradoc frowned as though unable to see the point of this comparison.

"But, confound it, Margot was for the right side," he said. "Now that's *real* loyalty. I don't understand how you can admire Gaby for the flighty way she's been behaving."

"Don't try too hard, then, Carr."

The landlady at the address Caradoc had supplied informed Frank that the young person was getting ready to leave but that he need not worry about it. There were plenty more of the same kind in the world. Most of them, she was sure, right here in Paris.

When he knocked on the door of the first floor front, an English voice said, "Come in." Obeying the injunction, he found himself in a dark sitting room with chenille curtains everywhere, over the one window, the table, the fireplace, even on the back of a double seat in one corner. It was a very dismal room. A slender figure was bending over a portmanteau on the table.

"Miss Summers, I believe?"

She straightened up and turned. Frank exclaimed, "Good God!" It was Laura Brakespeare.

She smiled at him with complete self-possession. "I recognized your step, Francis," she declared. "And I said to myself, 'Caradoc has sent his brother to deal with me.' For reasons which you'll understand, I'm sure, I almost decided not to let you in."

"Then you *are* the Miss Summers he brought from London?"

"Yes, I'm the highly immoral and disreputable Jean Summers brought from London by Lord Ellery to break the monotony of his official duties." She went to the window and threw back the curtains so that a little light began to get in through the dusty panes. "Sit down, Francis. As you *are* here, there are many things I must tell you."

They sat down in chairs facing each other. He saw that she was looking very smart in a dark traveling dress (of the shade called *frightened
mouse* by dressmakers) and a small feathered hat. She regarded him
closely with grave eyes.

"For the past three years," she said, "I've been living what is called a
sinful life. But, as I see it, I've been following the only sensible and
logical course."

"I—I can't get myself accustomed to the idea yet."

She went on in a suddenly impassioned tone. "It's sensible and logical
because men have so arranged things in this world that I couldn't hope
to win comfort and peace and happiness in any other way! Francis, you
must understand! I went through those exciting days in the Peninsula. I
saw life for the first time without any conventions. Could I go back to
the silly, stifling life I lived before—teaching stupid children, never hearing anything that went on outside the walls of a nursery? Snubbed, held
down, forced to suppress all my natural instincts? Could I go on being
the genteel slave of a heartless social order?" She paused and then added
in a more rational voice: "I made up my mind I wouldn't go back to it.
I saw a way to escape and I decided to take it, no matter what the cost
might be."

"But isn't the cost too high?"

"Why?" she demanded. "What have I lost? The respect of other people?
I never had it really; I never was given more than a kind of offhanded
pity. My own self-respect, my peace of mind? Not a mite!" She paused
suddenly and considered him with understanding eyes. "There's no call,
Francis, for you to look so conscience-stricken. Have you been thinking
that you started me on the road to ruin? We disagree about the nature of
the road; and I—well, I think it only fair to say that I threw myself at
your head that night. What has happened since has been entirely a matter
of my own deliberate decision. I've had the courage to follow the only
course which gives me a chance for freedom in the future."

"Can you be sure of that future?"

"I can now." She said this with an air of defiant confidence. "I might
as well make my confession complete. I have had six—shall we call them
protectors? I've been completely realistic with them. Each of them has
made me a settlement when the time came for us to part. The parting,
incidentally, has been in each case a matter of my own decision and contrivance." The note of defiance in her voice had become more apparent.
"I'm independent now. Does that offend you as much as I expected it
would? I don't care. I've accomplished what I set out to do. I won't have
to be a humble governess now for the rest of my life. I won't have to

marry some weak excuse of a man like the Rev. George Leesby. I saw him, and he *has* a weak chin and a perpetual cold in his head! Just as I said he would. I can now carry out the other part of my plan." She was watching him closely. "You look properly shocked. Perhaps I had better not tell you about it."

"I want to hear, of course. I'm in sympathy with your determination to have a fuller life. But did you have to adopt this method of escape?"

"Can you suggest another? Without some kind of influence—and I had none—there was nothing else for me to do. Rather than remain as I was, I chose what they call the primrose path. I've managed to walk it safely—and here I am. Starting from the time I get back to London, Jean Summers ceases to exist. I step then into a new life. Oh, I've prepared for it with the greatest care! Every single detail has been thought out. I'll have a new name, which I mustn't tell even you, a new and completely fictitious background. I shall be a widow from America and I'll arrive in a certain small town, already selected, with letters of introduction, honest ones too—I've been quite clever, Francis—to a few people: the clergyman, a lawyer to help me with my investments, a married woman of some substance. I'll buy a small place and settle down with one maid, a garden, just enough income to live nicely and with complete independence. Francis, what a good prospect, what a great, great relief!"

"Do you intend to marry?"

"No!" with almost furious emphasis. "The clergyman, the lawyer, the gardener—they'll be the only men in my life from now on! I'm going to try my hand at writing. I think—and please don't laugh at me—I shall try my hand at a novel. A different kind of novel, not the sentimental romance which goes under that name. It probably won't come to anything, but I'll have the satisfaction of trying, at any rate."

There was a long pause. "I can't say I think you've done the right thing, Laura," said Frank finally. "But I'm delighted to know that the—the first phase of your plan is all over with now. I hope you'll be happy and that your novel will set the literary world on fire. We need honesty in our literature."

"Thanks, Francis. I'm glad to have that much of your approval, at any rate. I know you well enough to be sure you mean it. I hope you may even come to see that I haven't been completely at fault."

Frank hesitated. "What are we going to do about this brother of mine?"

"You may tell your brother I want nothing from him at all." She looked at him reproachfully. "Do you suppose I would consider anything else now that we've met again and I've told you all about myself? No, Francis, I meant it when I said Jean Summers has ceased to exist.

I—I intended to treat your brother like the rest but—I seem to have lost my mercenary instinct. Perhaps I think it will help me to retain these small shreds of your respect. I was sure I was going to lose it all when I heard your step on the stairs. Not a shilling from my Lord Ellery. He'll be pleased to hear it, no doubt."

Frank smiled. "Pleased, and very much relieved. He was a rather frightened young man when I talked to him."

She got to her feet and stood at the window, looking down at the crowded street below. "I've heard a great deal about you, Francis. About your devotion for a certain French lady. She's beautiful, Caradoc says."

"Yes, she's very lovely."

"I hope you're not going to go on being unhappy about it."

"That is something over which I'll have no control. I've lost track of Gabrielle for the moment. Things are in such a troubled state here that I'm very much concerned about her."

"She seems to have a great deal of courage."

"Courage, unfortunately, is a quality which seems to be falling into disrepute. I judge that Carr has been telling you many things."

"He has been quite loquacious. I'm afraid I've been urging him to tell me everything. I know a great deal about your relations with him and the rest of your family. Things haven't been very pleasant for you, have they?"

"My family troubles are well in hand at last. Carr and I don't see eye to eye and I doubt if the relation between us will ever get any better. At the moment we're on a basis of neutrality."

"Your brother——" she began. After a pause she shook her head. "It will be better to leave my opinion unsaid. Please tell him he needn't have any fears. No word of his indiscretion will ever get out."

Frank bowed. "Thanks, Laura. You are returning today?"

"Yes. I've booked a place in the afternoon diligence. In my new name. Laura Brakespeare and Jean Summers will never be heard of again. I've even written to my sister, preparing her for the fact that I'm taking up a new life in which she'll have no part. It will be a relief to her, I'm sure."

"Then there's nothing more for us to say."

Frank walked to the door and she followed him slowly. "Don't think too harshly of the wicked Jean Summers," she said.

He stopped with his hand on the knob and smiled back at her. "Her three personalities are beginning to merge into one in my mind. You know how much I like her. I hope she'll be happy in her new life."

"I think she'll be content," she said in a low tone, "if not completely happy. Good-by, Francis."

Margot met him at the entrance to the salon at Place Lorient with an apologetic smile.

"I have company," she whispered. "I'm very sorry. I hoped we could have a long uninterrupted talk. As soon as I can, I'll get rid of them."

"One of the penalties, Margot, of your enviable position."

There were three old ladies in the drawing room. Two of them belonged to the upper reaches of the nobility, and there was an unmistakable note of deference in Margot's voice as she introduced him to them. The third was a relative who lived at Place Lorient in the role of chaperon and was known as Tante Blanchefleur, a curious wisp of ancient womanhood, so thin and faded that she looked as though she had fallen out from between the pages of a very old book. All three were diligently embroidering altar cloths. The Abbé Force was squatting inertly on a couch in a far corner. He nodded to Frank but did not get up. A bowl of fruit and a platter of cakes (actually iced with sugar!) seemed to be holding his attention.

"Mr. Ellery is from England," said Margot. "He was one of our very best friends there. You will remember, dear Comtesse"—turning to one of the visitors—"that the meeting with His Majesty was at Mr. Ellery's home in the country."

"Ah, yes." A flicker of interest showed in all three pairs of eyes at this. "I was not there and so did not meet Monsieur. I seem to recall that he has a handsome brother of whom it was said——" The Comtesse stopped, as though unwilling to put into words anything that concerned the erring Gabrielle.

"I saw your brother at the Duke of Wellington's ball," said Margot, to cover up the lapse.

"He's here on a parliamentary mission. I believe he's returning to London in a very few days."

"It will be a happy day for our poor France when all our visitors leave," declared the Comtesse.

Frank made no comment. He found a chair and watched Margot as she stitched with quick fingers on the embroidery panel she had immediately taken up. She was dressed in white, and the tip of a very small merino shoe, laced at the sides, showed under the hem of her skirts. Her dark hair was done with complete simplicity, being drawn back from a part in the center and braided together at the back, a style most becoming to her. It made her look very little older than when she left England six years before. Those six years, the most memorable in history, had been very kind to her, he said to himself.

He looked about the room with interest. It was a bright apartment, the sun flooding in from two sides. Its appointments achieved perfection in both arrangement and color combination. It was like a painting, carefully composed and meticulously carried out, without a single flaw. If it had ever reflected the personality of Gabrielle, all traces of her had been lost. It was now completely Margot's.

He was conscious of the fact that all of the elderly women were watching him covertly as they talked and stitched. They regarded him, it was clear, as an interloper, and their interest in him had an unfriendly wariness about it. No word or look that he exchanged with Margot went unnoted. "They are keeping an eye on their heiress," he said to himself.

The monotony of the conversation was interrupted when the Comtesse asked suddenly: "What does Monsieur think will be the feeling abroad on the arrest of Marshal Ney?"

"I can speak only of the English viewpoint," answered Frank. "I'm sure our opinion will be against any drastic action in the case of so brave a soldier."

"He must die!" exclaimed the Comtesse in a voice which contrasted strangely with the placidity of her wrinkled old face. "An example must be made of the man."

The other ancient visitor took it up with equal venom. "I had a cousin in the Abbaye," she said. "Poor René! He was go gentle, so fine. They refused to give him a hearing and he was killed by the mob as soon as he stepped outside the grating. Why should any more mercy be shown this soldier? A firing squad will be too merciful a death for him!"

"The excesses during the Terror can hardly be laid at the door of the Bonapartists," Frank pointed out. "I know nothing of Ney's political views. But I saw something of the Moscow retreat and it was only because of the personal gallantry of Ney that any of the French Army escaped."

The Comtesse regarded him coldly. "It was not important," she declared, "for any of *that* army to be saved."

"It must be considered also that the terms of capitulation provided for full amnesty. All Europe undoubtedly will be surprised at the news of the Marshal's arrest under the circumstances."

"It's a matter that concerns us only!" exclaimed the Comtesse. "No interference from the outside will be tolerated."

He had been watching Margot to see how she reacted to this violent talk. Her fingers continued steadily at work and her expression did not change. If she disagreed with them, and he felt sure she must, she made no effort to express a dissenting opinion.

"I have Antoine with me," she said finally, when the talk of reprisals showed signs of slackening. "I shall always keep him, of course."

"I hope he has reformed."

Margot frowned and tightened her lips slightly. "Very little. I have to keep an eye on him all the time." She looked up from her work and sighed. "My poor Jean Baptiste Achille! How I miss him. It's very sad to think he didn't live to share in these better days. I think I would have made an attorney of him. What a fine, sharp attorney he would have been!"

"A perfect financial watchdog, certainly. I have a settlement to make with Antoine. The funds entrusted to me have increased quite as much as our stout Jean hoped."

"You were always so generous with him, M'sieur Frank. He thought you were quite wonderful. But we must have a talk about the funds. Perhaps you had better place them in my hands now. Antoine isn't to be trusted with money."

Just before five the grandson of the Comtesse arrived to escort her home. The tone of the conversation changed at once.

"Henri!" cried the old lady in an animated voice which contained the merest note of reproach. "You are late! I'm sure our dear Margot would have preferred your company to that of three dull old ladies. Where have you been, naughty boy?"

The newcomer, who had been introduced to Frank as Henri Lestange and had acknowledged it with a jerk of the head which might pass for a bow, was a pale youth with a copy of *Quotidienne*, the Royalist paper, protruding from a pocket of his long embroidered coat. He continued to stare at Frank with an intentness which was far from friendly.

"I'm sure Henri had good reasons for not arriving sooner," said Tante Blanchefleur, speaking for the first time.

"I was at the Maison d'Or," said the youth in an indifferent voice. "I thought there might be some talk worth hearing. There wasn't." He continued to stare at Frank. "It was very dull. And annoying. I'll stop going there, 'egad, if foreign officers are allowed in any longer. The place was full of them. One might as well go to the Café Lemblin and mix with Bonapartist scum."

"Was there any talk of the Ney case?"

"Yes. Oh yes. Even the foreigners were discussing it." He said this with a note of definite grievance.

"What was being said?"

The youth replied in a bored voice: "Nothing. Nothing worth repeating."

"There must have been, Henri!" exclaimed his grandmother. "Anything they said would be interesting. I want to hear all about it."

Her persistence seemed to annoy her grandson. "I've told you. It was very dull." In a grudging tone he added, "Of course, there was talk of Lavalette. He's to be arrested."

Margot's head came up from her work at this. "Lavalette!" she said in a shocked voice.

"There!" cried the Comtesse. "I knew there would be something. What did you hear, Henri?"

Henri sighed with a suggestion of annoyance. "Well, it seems the papers are being signed."

"I'm delighted! That vulgar, intriguing nobody! Ah, this will be a blow to the Bonapartists."

Knowing that Comte Lavalette had been on the friendliest terms with the family, Frank looked at Margot to see how she was taking it. Her cheeks showed a touch of additional color but she continued at her embroidery with steady fingers.

"The whole Bonaparte family, and all its connections, should be wiped out," asserted the vindictive old lady. "This will show them what we mean! Henri, what was said about it?"

Henri frowned in concentration. "Nothing much," he said. "I don't think I was listening." He added with more animation, "Two Englishmen were killed in duels this morning."

A metal figure in the guise of a Tyrolean peasant popped out from the smallest of the many clocks in the room and struck an ax across the head of a goose. The goose flapped its wings and squawked five times.

The Comtesse began to roll up her work, saying to Margot: "I know, my dear, that you always drive at five o'clock. We won't detain you a minute. Henri is to take me to the De Chauls'."

Henri said in a stricken voice: "The De Chauls'! You know I don't like them, Grandmother."

"If you hadn't gone to the Maison d'Or," said the Comtesse significantly, "I might have let you off, young man. As it is, you go."

Margot finished wrapping her panel in the strands of silk and got to her feet. Frank realized for the first time that she was quite tall, at least an inch taller than Gabrielle.

"I shall drive Mr. Ellery to his lodgings," she announced. "We've so many things to talk about."

The two old ladies departed with the reluctant Henri in a dilapidated carriage with two footmen in gorgeous livery on the box. Margot's carriage, which rolled up to the door a few minutes later, presented a marked contrast. It was new and shiny and handsomely accoutered, driven by a team of lively roans. The top being down, it could be seen that the inside was upholstered in white leather and that the most luxurious of down squabs were piled up on the seats. By way of further contrast, the two footmen in attendance were in a quiet maroon.

Tante Blanchefleur appeared in a fringed shawl and a mood which said, I am going and I shall be on guard. Frank was already conscious of an antagonism toward him on the part of the ancient kinswoman, as though she saw in him a danger to plans of her own for Margot. The latter had thrown a lace shawl over her shoulders and had donned a hat shaped like that of the French *voltigeurs* with white plumes curling down over the front. It was exceedingly becoming. She stepped into the carriage and motioned to Frank to sit beside her. Tante Blanchefleur frowned with disapproval as she ensconced herself opposite them. Margot raised a frivolous parasol with tiny balls of white ivory dangling around its edges and called an order to the driver.

"I love to drive," she said as they started off. "It's the best time of the day always."

"I was under the impression," said Frank, "that it was still a little dangerous to own a carriage in Paris. Didn't you mention it in one of your letters?"

"All that is changed already. Oh, things are going to be so very different now."

"I hear talk to that effect. But I can't feel sure about it. There have been twenty years in which people have become confirmed in certain ideas and ways of living. It may prove impossible to restore the old order completely."

"Perhaps it shouldn't be restored completely; although I wouldn't have dared to say that in the hearing of my two old friends." She reached out with the tip of one foot for the satin-covered squab on the floor of the carriage. "As I told you, I was very sorry there had to be company today. They came unexpectedly, and there was nothing I could do about it. You needn't look at me like that, Tante Blanchefleur; I mean it."

He was thinking he had never seen anything to compare with the purity of her profile. He was driven back to the oldest of similes in the matter of her brow: it was literally as white as snow, and no other term would suffice to describe it. Feeling the intentness of his gaze, she turned her head and smiled at him from under the rim of the diminutive parasol.

"You look at me as though I were a stranger," she said.

"You *are* a stranger. And a very lovely one."

Their chaperon said in a determined tone: "Margot, I think Henri is improving. He is taking more of an interest in affairs."

"Is he? I hadn't noticed." Margot tilted the parasol so that Tante Blanchefleur's view of them was seriously obstructed. "And now, Frank, I'm going to start on my thousand questions."

3

FRANK STAYED in Paris for two weeks. He heard nothing from Gabrielle and he saw Margot every day.

Margot made it clear that she wanted him to spend as much of his time in her company as he could spare from his work. She seemed happy when he was with her, chattering with animation over her endless embroidering (it was almost a rule of the court, which had swung back to clerical influences, that ladies should work on altar cloths) and during their almost daily drives. When the time came for him to depart, she would say:

"You will lunch with us tomorrow?"

"I'm afraid it will be impossible. I've many calls to make and a long dispatch to get off."

"You'll come in the afternoon, then. And you must stay with us for dinner. I'll have a very special dinner. Jacquart is at last learning to make some English dishes—most unwillingly, it's true—and there will be beef and a batter pudding. Peaches are coming in from Provence now—there's nothing in the world to equal them, as you'll find—and I'll have Jacquart make a peach fool for your special benefit."

With such urging he dined frequently, and well, at Place Lorient. On days when that was impossible he would call during the evening. Several times he escorted the two ladies to the opera, which in his case was a real test of friendship, for he found it hard to sit through the endless trilling of the soprano and the deep puffing of the baritone and could never get any amusement out of the absurd clowning of the buffo. He enjoyed their visits to the theater much more. Talma was a brilliant actor and Mlle. Georges as lovely as reports made her out to be. The plays were more provocative than any he had seen in London. He found it hard, however, to accept the jibes at his own country which punctuated all of them. A comedian, imitating an Englishman by saying, "God damn!" could always convulse the audience.

The household ran smoothly under Margot's precise management. It consisted of Tante Blanchefleur, the Abbé Force, who seemingly had settled down into the role of pensioner, and a staff of six servants, all capable in the extreme with the exception of Antoine. Margot was an exacting mistress, with a keen eye for dust and a quick reprimand for any slackness in service. The pansy blue of her eye could become hard in an instant at any slight break in the routine perfection. The rooms were always fresh and cool, the meals beyond compare.

Frank found it a pleasant harbor after a busy day in the departments and clubs of the city. The balcony back of his favorite chair was so well shaded that even in late evening the blue of large morning glories still showed over the wrought iron of the railings. Margot kept cut flowers in every room, arranged with a flair for artistic effect. The striking and bonging of the many clocks proved a soothing interruption to the hush of the salon.

The only flaw was the popularity of the young chatelaine herself. People were always dropping in: old ladies of the court who came to gossip and watch; elderly gentlemen who ogled her and paid florid compliments in the manner of the old school; young bucks of the stamp of Henri who sat about in insolent silence and made no effort, other than the mere fact of their presence, to achieve the success with this most desirable of heiresses which had been their object in calling. Henri himself was continually in attendance, spurred on, no doubt, by the new fear of competition. He paid no attention to Frank other than to give him an abrupt jerk of the head by way of greeting and an even less perceptible nod on leaving. Tante Blanchefleur put herself out to show the young Frenchman every attention, and it was obvious that she had selected him as her entry in the matrimonial sweepstakes; just as it was manifest that she regarded Frank as a rank, though dangerous, outsider. Frank she strove to make uncomfortable in every way in her power, seldom speaking to him, pretending an inability to remember his name, simulating surprise whenever he put in an appearance, and acting always on the assumption that he was due to leave.

"Your household dragon doesn't like me," he said to Margot on one occasion. "Is there anything I can do to improve my standing with her? I must confess that I find the role of pariah dog rather trying."

Margot shook her head with annoyance. "She makes me very angry," she said. "Pay no attention to her, please. Tante Blanchefleur is a stupid old woman and very trying in every way. I can't do anything with her. I tell her she must mend her habits and she always promises; but then she goes right on doing as she pleases. If she weren't so old I would shake her."

"I can bear up under her very apparent disapproval of me if I can be sure she isn't influencing you."

"She has no influence with me whatever." Margot's tone left no doubt that she meant what she said. "I never stay alone in a room with her if I can help it. Her talk is so dull and petty that I can't listen to her. I must have someone here with me and she happens to be the only relative available. If I could find anyone else to take her place I would send her back at once to her brother, my uncle Pippin, in Nîmes."

"I was wondering if a judicious present would tend to sweeten the old lady's attitude toward me."

Margot's frugal sense took alarm at once. "Please, you mustn't spend a sou on her. It would do no good at all. I give her an ample allowance which she hides away at once in the toe of a stocking in her trunk. The trunk has three locks and she hides the keys in different places." The eccentricities of her ancient kinswoman won a reluctant smile from her. "Really, she's just like a raven, always taking little things on the sly and concealing them in her room—bottles, needles, sugar tongs, lumps of coal, anything she thinks I won't miss. Her room is quite dreadful."

"She seems to think highly of Henri."

"Yes, she's convinced I ought to marry him. Henri belongs to one of the oldest families in France, and that impresses poor Tante Blanchefleur very much."

"What do you think of him, Margot?"

"Oh, I like Henri. He's a little dull, perhaps, but he's really very nice."

"He also seems to find my presence irksome."

"Then," said Margot, "I must find some way to discourage him from coming so often."

As a matter of fact, she showed considerable skill in managing her continuous stream of visitors, speeding their departure without letting them perceive the delicacy of the pressure she applied. "We have so little time to talk," she would complain to Frank, "that I think it would be nice if you could manage to come early." She was always on hand to greet him when he arrived, looking neat and cool in tablier robes of sprigged muslin and with smiles which evidenced the pleasure she found in seeing him. Once, when he came unusually early, she was in a white silk douillette, a wadded gown which swept the floor and made her seem absurdly young to be the head of such a large household. "I'm not properly dressed!" she said in a dismayed voice. "You'll have to be patient while I correct this very great error. A few minutes only, M'sieur Frank."

She was back in five minutes exactly in misty India muslin of the shade called graine de réséda and looking as perfectly groomed as though she had spent hours at her toilet. She was doing her hair in a different way now, with curls massed on her forehead. It was quite charming, but he sometimes regretted the youthful simplicity of the earlier arrangement.

Margot had an almost juvenile desire to see anything that was new, and as a result their afternoon drives took them on occasions into curious sections of Paris. They even drove to the end of the Champs Élysées to see the unfinished Arc de Triomphe; and Margot, who seldom allowed anything to ruffle her calmness of mood, became quite indignant over the folly of Napoleon in building it.

"Observe!" she said. "Nothing but truck gardens and farms! Did he think he could create a new Paris out in this wilderness as a scene for his boastfulness?"

Frank, who was experiencing a sudden feeling of awe as he realized for the first time the full splendor of the conqueror's military exploits, shook his head in dissent. "The city will grow well beyond this in time," he predicted. "I feel sure also that someday the arch will be finished, and that it will stand then to the end of time."

Association of ideas, perhaps, led her to speak of Gabrielle and the reason for their final quarrel. "It was after he had been defeated at Waterloo and everyone knew it was the end. He was hiding at Malmaison—surely the memory of his poor wife must have haunted him there!—and Gabrielle was determined to see him. I tried to stop her. It would cause so much talk, especially after all the gossip there had been." She paused for the briefest moment, and her dark-lashed eyes studied the expression of his face. "Gabrielle became very angry and she said things—much as I loved her, I knew I would never be able to forgive some of the things she said. I was equally at fault, of course. I told her how foolish she had been acting all along. It was quite a scene, Frank. But she went."

After some hesitation Frank asked, "Did she go alone?"

"Tante Blanchefleur went with her. I insisted on that. They stayed at Malmaison for several hours. She and the Emperor walked together in the garden and people saw them. There were always crowds outside the walls, trying to get a glimpse of him. The court talked of nothing else for days. His Majesty, who had always been fond of Gaby, was furious." She sighed. "I haven't seen her since."

"I can't understand why she doesn't let anyone know where she is."

"She knows she's in danger. You should hear how they talk at court! They want to see her punished. She may still be in Paris. At any rate, she hadn't joined Jules in Brussels, the last time I heard." She was clearly very unhappy over the plight in which the other members of her family found themselves. "Both Jules and Sosthène wore the violet, and so they had to leave Paris. It's going to be very hard for them. All their property will be confiscated and they may never be able to return."

"They brought it on themselves."

"Poor Sossy! I feel very sorry for him. He's had so much trouble with his wife as well."

"I heard the gossip about Gabrielle," said Frank after a moment. "It was distressing to me to see how the other papers in London took advantage of it. Anything to throw discredit on Napoleon! They even printed a story that he had set up a—a sort of establishment for her. How can such malicious lies be invented!"

Margot sat in thought for a moment. "Everyone believed it here, or pretended to," she said finally. "He bought a place not very far from here. It was said he invited other women there as well. That made it so much worse." She leaned forward and gave some instructions to the driver. "Gaby didn't seem to mind it at all. She would laugh when I spoke about it and say, 'Let the old cats talk if it gives them any satisfaction.' I believe she was so proud to be singled out by him that nothing else mattered. He had a curious power over her."

"There's no doubt about that. He was a god in her eyes. Nothing he did could be wrong."

"Poor Gaby! She ruined her life because of it. People will never forget or forgive."

The carriage had turned on to a road leading to the north and east. Well out in the direction of Neuilly, the driver reined up in front of a rather pretentious house standing back behind a stone wall.

"That is the place," said Margot. If he had not been so intensely interested in the house itself, he might have sensed that she had brought him here as a test. She was watching him closely. Her manner suggested that she was in conflict with herself for going to such a length.

It was a beautiful house, as far as could be seen, with graceful lines and a steep old roof of slate. Frank found himself resenting the unnecessary height of the surrounding wall and the suggestion of furtiveness with which the windows peered out from the thick covering of ivy on the front. The garden was completely hidden and there was not another house within close range; a perfect setting, certainly, for the purpose with which rumor associated the place.

"This is proof of the absurdity of the story," he declared finally. "If it had been anyone else but Napoleon! He wouldn't need to go to such pains. All he had to do was issue a command. You'll have to pardon me, Margot. I know I shouldn't be talking so frankly about such things."

She did not seem entirely satisfied with the results of the experiment, if that had been what she had in mind in bringing him here. Instructing the driver to turn about, she leaned back in her seat and toyed dispiritedly with the handle of her parasol. "There was no truth in the story," she said. "What a pity Gaby had to be involved in it!"

"You're right, of course, that it will never be forgotten. People believe all such stories without any hesitation. Even that brother of mine. He actually took a sort of vicarious pride in it."

Margot said in a low tone: "Both Jules and Sosthène were sure it was true. Can you see what a terrible situation it has been? Jules would get into rages about it, but she paid no attention to him."

"The marriage was a great mistake. That's clear now."

"I'm not sure of that. Only a man like Jules would have put up with the way she was acting. We had terrible scenes all the time." She burst out with sudden vehemence: "I can't see that I did wrong! Something had to be done about it. It was one long quarrel."

"Will they get a divorce now?"

Margot shook her head. "Jules will never consent to it. No, they'll have to get along together as best they can. Gaby refused to leave with them when they went to Brussels."

"Then why did her husband go? He showed very poor spirit."

"It was too dangerous to stay."

Frank gave a scornful laugh. "But Gabrielle stayed."

"I think," said Margot after a moment, "it would be better not to talk about it any more."

He was continuously impressed with the many ways in which Margot resembled her cousin. If she were wearing something new, a *fichu d'Angoulême*, a shawl of florentine bronze, or an Ipsiboe bracelet, she liked him to notice it at once. If he made no comment, she would preen herself in an unobtrusive way to call attention to it. Frequently she sang as she came into a room and her voice was better than Gabrielle's, fuller, less prone to quaver or break on a high note. There was similarity in their walk, in the tilt of their heads, in all gestures.

He was as often impressed, however, with the many ways in which they differed. Margot seldom argued any point with him, even when it was clear that their views were far apart. Her prevailing mood was one of thoughtfulness, and she seldom fell into the gaiety which came so easily and naturally to Gabrielle. She read a great deal. On one occasion he found her absorbed in a thin leather volume and saw to his very great surprise that it was Baour-Lormian's *Ossian*; his surprise deepening when she discussed it with him in a highly intelligent vein. There was never the faintest trace of the *gamine* in Margot; and, of course, she was thorough and tidy in the extreme.

He took advantage of her thoughtful mood, after their discussion of *Ossian*, to speak of the hint Caradoc had dropped. "I understand there's some likelihood of your American interests being taken over and combined with a new shipping line."

Margot looked up quickly, laying the book aside. "Men don't seem to keep secrets very well," she said. "It's not supposed to be known."

"Perhaps I shouldn't have said anything about it then."

"Oh, I'm not blaming you. But I wonder where you heard it."

"Caradoc told me. I haven't any idea of his source of information."

"Nothing has been decided. As a matter of fact, my properties are still in the hands of the court. The idea has been discussed, of course."

He decided to proceed cautiously. "Do you know what a barracoon is, Margot?"

"No. I don't believe I've ever heard the word before."

"Well, it has to do with a trade called blackbirding. African natives are captured by raiding parties, or are sold by their rulers, and then they're held in pens along the coast until slave ships come to take them off. These pens are called barracoons, and I've heard that the world has never seen anything to equal the cruelty of them. But the profits in the trade are amazingly large." He paused. "Shipping companies, even the most respectable of them, are always tempted to engage in it."

"Are you warning me of something, Frank?"

"Yes. Carr dropped a hint that the proposed line would engage in black cargoes as well as more legitimate lines of trade. He would be furious if he knew I had told you."

There was a moment's silence. "I'm glad you told me. I don't think I need say that it would never be done with my consent. Were you afraid I might sign away my rights and so be unable to interfere?"

"Yes. You've had no experience of business."

"It's quite true that I haven't. For that reason I had already made up my mind to proceed with the greatest caution. I'll be doubly on my guard now; but there was never any danger, Frank, that such a thing could happen. I've no intention whatever of letting any of my father's interests fall into other hands."

He looked at her with surprise. "You mean that you intend to manage everything yourself?"

"Not quite that. But I intend to keep full control."

"A Catherine the Great of commerce! Well, it will be a surprise, and I imagine an unpleasant one, for certain smart gentlemen."

"I'm quite in earnest."

He studied her face for a moment. It was evident that she meant exactly what she had said. "I'm glad to hear it, Margot. A conviction is taking hold of me that you'll be very successful too."

"I didn't try to regain the estates as long as it meant taking an oath of allegiance to the Empire. I couldn't have done that, not for all the money in the world. But now they're mine. *Mine!*" She looked up at him with serious eyes. "You see, I found many of my father's letters and I've read them all, over and over again. He was very ambitious. He wanted to make himself another Jacques Coeur, to found a trade empire. Perhaps it can still be done."

"There are greater chances now than ever before. There will be steamships on the ocean soon. And railroads—carriages that run by steam on iron rails. I've seen models of them."

A rapt look had come into her eyes. "I owe it to his memory to try, Frank. I may be very presumptuous. But, with the right help, I don't see why I can't do some of the things my father was planning. I've thought about it a great deal." She nodded her head. "Besides, I can't bear to think of anyone else deciding what's to be done with my estates. They're mine, and they must remain mine."

He had noticed before that her sense of possessiveness was quite pronounced. She liked to go shopping and was a keen hand at a bargain; and when once an article became hers she exercised a care over it which was almost fanatical. This was another respect in which she differed from Gabrielle. A complete madcap, Gabrielle, never knowing or caring what she possessed, quite unperturbed by losses, willing to give away almost anything she possessed. Even willing, it seemed, to lose his devotion.

"Why am I always comparing them?" he thought. "Why can't I take them as they are? There's no balance to be struck, no choice to be made."

But perhaps there was a choice to be made, in his own mind at least. It had become quite evident that Margot preferred his company, that she was unhappy when his work kept him away for any length of time. She was not subject to sudden fancies. Could it be that Gabrielle had been right about her, after all? He was almost convinced of it.

The time had come, he knew, to put Gabrielle out of his mind. Where was she now? What did she plan to do with her life in the unsettled years ahead? Having helped to involve her husband in the final ruination of all his prospects, was she not obligated to remain with him? He had no way of finding the answers to any of these questions, and it was becoming clear that he must settle his own problems without any thought of her.

But could he do that? Gabrielle was a habit, both in his heart and in his mind. She had pre-empted all his considerations of the future for so long that it seemed impossible to think of any plans except in relation to her.

Margot had picked up her embroidery and was stitching at it with diligent fingers, her fine white brow bent over the frame. The animation she had shown a few minutes before had already subsided. There was something infinitely appealing and restful about her ease of manner; the promise, certainly, of pleasant companionship.

"Margot," he said suddenly, "you're planning a busy life for yourself. Have you any idea of the amount of attention and work which will be involved in this for you? Business is exacting. I've found that out myself. You can't do it halfway."

"I realize that. But it doesn't frighten me at all. I'm looking forward to it."

"It will mean that you must live in Paris, of course."

Her fingers paused for the merest fraction of a second and then went on with their work. "I suppose so." A short silence followed. "At least, I must live here part of the time."

Had she meant this as a loophole for him? It must be clear to her that his own work anchored him in London.

"Make up your mind," he said to himself. "Put it to the test now; ask her! It's the sensible thing to do; perhaps it's what you really want. She's everything you could desire: lovely, companionable, intelligent, fine. And she likes you. That is clear now!"

He got up and walked to the fireplace. A silvery sentry on one of the miniature clocks presented arms and a thin bugle sounded nine notes. He knew that Margot was watching him but, when he glanced back, her head went down again over the frame. It was a scarf she was working on, not an altar cloth. Was it intended for him?

"No," he said to himself after further reflection, "I must wait. I can't make any decision as long as I'm in the dark as to the fate of Gabrielle. I owe that much to her, at least. Once I hear from her, I will be free to consider my own future."

"I must return to London the end of this week," he said aloud.

Margot looked up in dismay. "Oh no!" she exclaimed. "So soon? I thought——"

"Things are settling down here. And I'm needed in the office. Cope writes me that conditions are very upset in England. Of course I'll come back when Ney goes on trial."

"But that won't be for months."

"Much sooner than that. I hear they intend to get it through with as quickly as possible."

Margot's face showed that she was both hurt and perplexed. "But I thought you were going to make such a nice long visit! You told me so. I—I've been counting on it."

"If they delay the trial, I'll find another reason for coming back soon."

She had gone back to her work. "I hope it won't be too hard to find another reason," she said.

It was Saturday morning, and Frank was sorting out his papers before packing them away in a dispatch case. The work was being done in a purely mechanical way, for his mind was full of a piece of news contained in a note handed in to him an hour before from Sir Robert Wilson.

A certain lady's husband and brother have arrived in the city. It's said they intend to sue for pardon and reinstatement, but in view of something I happened to hear I believe there may be another reason. See me before you leave. I'll be at Galignani's.

What did Wilson mean? Had he news of Gabrielle? It seemed almost certain to Frank that this was what he meant. Snapping the case shut, he walked to the window and looked out. It would be an enormous relief to know something definite about Gabrielle before he left. Perhaps, he reflected, it would be necessary to delay his departure. It was a beautiful morning, with a warm sun gilding the spires and towers of the city. He realized that he did not want to leave so soon.

He thought of what had happened the previous evening. He had called to bid Margot farewell, still very uncertain in mind as to the state of his feelings. She had dressed for the occasion, with obvious intent to please, in an evening gown of pale lavender which touched the floor in a bewildering mass of dainty puckered muslin and edged her shoulders and wrists with lace and Amadis embroidery. They had stepped out on a balcony and, as the evening had turned chilly, she had thrown a Wellington jacket of twilled material about her. Frank had thought, "They hate the Duke and yet everyone praises him and they even name clothes after him."

Margot said in a pensive voice: "We were so terribly poor in London and it was always a struggle to pay the rent and buy food. But I haven't grown out of the habit entirely of thinking about it as home."

There was a pause. "Would you ever consider going back?"

After a much longer pause Margot said: "I've been thinking a great

deal about the future. Of course, I belong here. It will always be necessary for me to appear at court. But it seems possible that I can arrange my
affairs so that I'll have no need to remain always in Paris. The offices of
the shipping line will be Marseille and London. In time London may
be the real center."

When Frank made no comment, she went on: "Father had planned to
bring over cotton from New Orleans and have his own factories to manu-
facture it. I've been thinking it might be better to have the work done
in England. You have a new kind of machine I've read about."

"The Radcliffe power loom?"

"Yes. I don't understand much about it, of course, but it's clear England will be making cotton materials much better and cheaper than we
can make them here in France. Won't it be wiser, then, to send my cotton
direct to your country and have it made up there?"

"You would have to pay duty on the finished article before you could
import it back for sale on the Continent. Still, the lower cost of manu-
facture might more than make up for that." Having raised this point in
complete seriousness, he suddenly squared around and regarded her with
an amused smile. "You must pardon me, Margot, but doesn't all this
seem to you a little—well, incongruous? Here you are, young, lovely, all
Paris at your feet—I've been keeping my eyes open and I've counted no
less than fourteen young bucks with a determined air of conquest about
them, who come here as often as you'll let them—and yet you seem much
more interested in ports of entry and power looms than in romance."

"But, Frank," she protested, "I have the future to think of. I'm going to
have such heavy responsibilities! Do you think it unmaidenly?"

He hastened to correct that impression. "I spoke in wonder, not in
criticism. I think you're sheer perfection, Margot. A view, by the way,
that is shared most unmistakably by the most persistent of the fourteen."

"Do you mean Henri?"

"I mean Henri. The most eligible of the lot, no doubt. The good Tante
Blanchefleur, who hovers vaguely in the background like a family ghost
at all other times, gives a convincing suggestion of a matchmaking
mother whenever Henri appears."

"I like him better than any of the others, I think. He's rather sweet
when you really know him. But what would he do if I mentioned power
looms to him?"

Frank laughed. "I think he would dash away to the Maison d'Or and
call for a brandy quick."

"Perhaps he would," said Margot, joining in the laugh. "Still, he's shrewd in some ways. His grandmother keeps him on a very small allowance, and yet he never gets into debt."

Frank was watching her with an amused but deeply affectionate eye. "He seems cut to the perfect measure of a prince consort."

Margot took alarm at once. "Frank, I didn't intend to talk this way tonight! I can see I'm giving you the wrong impression. I'm not more interested in business than in—other things. You mustn't think that about me! It makes me much happier to have you say I'm beautiful than to have you think well of me because I know a little about cotton machines."

Perhaps he should have declared himself there and then. He was quite certain she had expected him to. But one phrase he had used became lodged in his mind. Did he want to be a prince consort? It might come to that. She had spoken so determinedly of her intention to keep all the reins in her own hands. "*Mine!*" she had said. This needed thinking about. And so he had said nothing, even though the soft moonlight of a Paris evening, slanting down over the roof of the nearest house, had lent a glamour to her beauty which should have precluded all such sober speculations.

Sir Robert was in the reading room at Galignani's, poring over a newspaper; the *Tablet,* Frank was quick to note.

"The *Northumberland* has sailed for St. Helena with Napoleon on board," he announced.

Frank burst out impatiently: "But, Sir Robert, your news! Does it concern Gabrielle?"

"Yes, of course——"

"Do you know where she is?" eagerly.

"I know she's staying with friends not far from Paris but that's as far as it goes. No one seems to know her exact whereabouts. But that isn't what I have to tell you. Since I sent you the note, something quite strange has happened. Some men broke into the lodgings where her husband and brother were staying, and the police just managed to get there in time to save their lives."

"Royalists?"

"No. That's the strange part of it. According to police reports, they were Bonapartists; which confirms the information I had earlier about them and which I wanted to tell you. The husband didn't get off as easily as the brother, by the way. In the melee he was tossed over the balustrade and had a long drop to the floor below."

"Was he badly hurt?"

"Probably not. They've taken him to a hospital, and the report I hear is that he has some broken bones but will pull through. The brother wasn't even bruised. He was shaking rum over an omelet when the mob broke in, and all he suffered was the loss of a good breakfast. The police have whisked him away to protect him from further attacks."

"I don't understand this at all," said Frank. "Why should Bonapartists try to kill them?"

"They intended to go over to the other side," said Wilson. "That much is clear. Fouché is having some difficulty in building up a case against Lavalette. The brother, having been in the Post, may have information that will help convict him. At any rate, he could be used effectively for the prosecution. I had it straight that he's promised to go on the stand. Apparently the word got out and this morning's excitement was an effort to close his mouth."

"I can believe it. They turned their coats once before."

"As the French say, *sauve qui peut*. They've undoubtedly been promised the restoration of some part of their property."

"This will be the final blow for Gabrielle," said Frank after a moment of troubled thought. "She will never hold her head up again if they turn state's evidence."

"I'm sure that's the way it is."

Wilson folded up the *Tablet* and laid it aside. "Boney is accusing the British Government of broken promises. Some idiots at home are saying he's right. That's the way it will go. Pretty soon the whole world will be saying the same thing."

Frank was too concerned about the other matter to take any interest in the fate of Napoleon. "I intended to leave today," he said, "but now I think I should stay."

"Why? You can't do any good here."

"I must find Gabrielle."

"I wish I could help you there but I haven't a single clue. You may be sure she'll keep even more closely under cover after what's happened. No, Frank, you'll simply waste your time here. I don't advise you to stay."

"Haven't the police any information as to where she is?"

"It's certain they haven't. If they knew, they would have had her in for questioning long before this."

"But she'll come if her husband's life is in danger."

"It's not as serious as that. What's a broken bone or two to a thick-skulled fellow like this Comte de Vitrelle? It's certain, in any event, that the Bonaparte crowd will take good care she doesn't show herself. Some of them must know where she is. They won't let Fouché get his hands on her. She could be very useful to him. Oh, I'm not saying she would ever willingly help him; but the police have little ways of their own of making people talk."

Frank got up and began to pace about the room. He was reluctant to leave, and yet it was clear he could not accomplish anything by staying. If he could only see Gabrielle before leaving!

"The best thing you can do," said Wilson, "is to get back to London and start preaching against the proscription. World opinion must be aroused. It's the only way I can see to save Ney's life. The British Government can protect him if it decides to step in. You must force their hand."

"I suppose you're right." Frank gave in with the greatest unwillingness. "Well, then, I'll go. I have places booked on the afternoon diligence."

Windy Topp finished the packing in the most cheerful of spirits. He had, as usual, been picking up information by ways and means of his own and was well content to be returning. "Things are going to be in a pretty mess here," he said. "Lavalette's been took. *His* goose is cooked and so's Ney's. These Frenchies just can't seem to agree among theirselves."

"And there's nothing we can do about it."

"Not a thing, sahib. I hears as how mem sahib's husband got a real shaking up. They says the odds is about even." He looked on the point of saying something more but thought better of it. "There we is, all packed and ready to go."

When they reached London, Cope came in at once to Frank's office with a grave face and laid a dispatch on the desk. "News," he said. "You heard about the attack on the Comte de Vitrelle? He died twenty-four hours after they got him to the hospital."

4

THE EVENING was not proving a success. There was tension in the air, a note of impatience in voices. Undoubtedly the fact that the Chamber of Peers was still debating the case of Marshal Ney and would reach a verdict before the night was out had something to do with it.

Supper was now being served. Small tables had been brought in by the servants and set up around the salon. The guests, agreeable to this hint that the strict rules of court etiquette might be disregarded, had seated themselves as they saw fit. Margot herself had become a bone of contention between a suddenly determined Henri Lestange, in full court dress of blue and silver, and a handsome young Englishman in black broad-cloth who was a stranger to Frank. The result had been that the hostess now shared a table with the two of them and a decrepit lady in rusty black lace. Frank caught Margot's eye occasionally and each time was rewarded with a smile which expressed her regret that the full length of the room separated them.

He had arrived back in Paris the day before. Alighting from the dili-gence, he had been met by two footmen in new and immaculate white livery with amaranth trimmings and escorted to a waiting room where the ravages of travel could be repaired immediately. A basket had been handed him containing sponges, scented towels and soap, almond paste, powder, everything necessary for the toilet of even a Beau Brummell. There had been biscuits and a bottle of superior wine. Then he had been taken to rooms which had been reserved for him in a most luxurious pension. Cut flowers everywhere, a lunch set out and ready, a charming little note of welcome from Margot—the reception had carried enough suggestion of regal magnificence, in fact, to bring back into his mind those two disturbing words, "prince consort."

As a result of several months of serious consideration, however, the words had lost much of their power to distress him. He had become convinced that the situation would work itself out. Margot was reason-able and intelligent; she could be depended upon not to let the power she was soon to wield interfere with the normal relationships of her life.

He had not declared himself yet. When he had met Margot the pre-vious afternoon, he had taken both of her hands in his, saying, "It has been longer than I intended."

She had answered, "Longer than I—than I hoped it would be. They kept postponing the trial."

"It's not that I lacked another reason for coming back, Margot. Will you let me tell you what that reason is?"

Her eyes had made it clear that she was ready to hear, but Tante Blanchefleur had come into the room at that moment. Her discomfiture at seeing him had been so apparent that he had laughed and said, "I'm afraid it will have to wait."

It did not matter that he had found no opportunity since to complete his declaration. Margot knew what he was going to say and she left him in no doubt as to what her answer would be. She let him see every time their glances met, in spite of the fact that there were always others in the room with them.

He had found less to be content with in the city itself. Paris was in a state of unhealthy excitement. Lavalette had been tried and found guilty and was now confined in the Conciergerie, awaiting the day of execution. Little hope was felt that Ney would escape the same fate. The city seemed as a result of this, more disturbed, more unhappy, harder to fathom in its sudden political shifts, than immediately following Waterloo.

The atmosphere at Place Lorient did not reflect any of this. Margot seemed completely happy, so much so that Frank had said to himself a dozen times: "I can't understand it. She has scores of suitors, all of them more eligible than I am on every count. She could have a title, wealth to match her own, an assured position at court. Why then should she prefer me?"

Sir Robert Wilson, who was sitting beside him, said in English: "A suspicion is growing in my mind about you, Frank. Well, if it's so, you're probably a very lucky fellow. Certainly she's a lovely little lady. Reminds me of my Jemima when I whisked her off from under the very nose of the old Chancellor." He lowered his voice. "But if I were you, I wouldn't let Michael Bruce have too free a hand."

"So that's Michael Bruce with her! I haven't met him." Frank looked over at the handsome Englishman as he asked, "What do you think of him?"

"I like him. We see eye to eye on many things." Wilson's voice dropped to a whisper. "He agreed with me that a demonstration in force might have saved Ney. Of course, it's too late now. The government is taking every precaution. All officers on half pay have been rounded up and sent out of Paris. Six thousand of them."

"I'm glad you didn't get into anything as foolish as that, Sir Robert."

"I find it hard to sit back and see my gallant old enemy face a firing squad. They've been treating him most abominably. You must print all the details so the world can judge. For months they've kept him in a single room with no ventilation. When they saw he found pleasure in playing a flute, they took it away from him. Mark my words, if he's brought in guilty they'll lead him out and shoot him inside the hour."

Any discussion of the kind always took Frank's mind back to the uncertainty of Gabrielle's position. He asked now: "Have you heard any word of her—of Gabrielle?"

"Not a word. A lady of high spirit, your Comtesse. I'm surprised that she hasn't been heard from."

Frank let his own voice drop. "Would you care to give me the benefit of your advice?"

"You mean . . ." Wilson's eyes went to the other end of the room, where Margot was engaged in close conversation with Michael Bruce. "No! I refuse to give advice of the kind. I know no surer way of losing a friendship."

"But I feel in need of it."

"I don't mind saying this much—that my Jemima has a very decided opinion. She's taken an interest in you, young man, ever since that morning when you paid us your first visit. It probably isn't necessary to tell you how she feels about it. My Jemima, bless her, has lived a secluded life and she—well, she believes in rumors and, of course, she feels strongly on the subject of the marriage vow. She seems to have made it her business to find out as much as she can about your little heiress. Mlle. Margot stands very high in her esteem."

"Having told me that much, is it fair to withhold your own opinion?"

Wilson squirmed in his chair. "Well, if you must have it, you must. In the first place, I don't believe any of the stories about your Comtesse and Napoleon. They don't fit with anything I know of her. He won her over to his cause and she has remained true to it through everything. A very brave and very rare kind of lady. For all I know, the little cousin may be just as fine. But here's what I have to say: if I had tied the fair Gabrielle's favor on my visor, I would keep it there in spite of everything until my dying day."

Frank said after a moment, "I thought you felt that way."

"For all I know," grumbled Wilson, "you've made up your mind in the other direction. And if you have, you're probably thinking ugly thoughts about me already." To change the subject, he went back to the plight of the unfortunate Ney. "I can't get him out of my head. I suppose he's pacing up and down his cell this very minute, waiting for the verdict. He has faced death a thousand times on the battlefield, but this is different. This time it's not danger he faces with all of his men; it's a grim certainty which he must meet alone. I wonder how brave I would be under the circumstances?"

The tone of the party had improved with the appearance of the fine supper Margot had provided. There was a clear soup, cold roast capon, hothouse asparagus with an appetizing chilled sauce, and a novelty in the way of a frozen dessert called Nesselrode, after its inventor, an Austrian general, who apparently had been, like so many continental generals of the day, a more discerning gourmet than soldier. The wines were exceptional: a superior burgundy, iced champagne, pacaret. Everything was served with great care, even the carafes being lined with a shell of ice. The guests were now enjoying themselves, and the conversation became animated in all parts of the room.

It was not until supper was over, and Wilson had paid his respects to his hostess and left, that Frank was able to get a word alone with Margot. The smile with which she greeted him had no coquetry in it at all. She was happy to be with him and quite content that he should know it.

"You shouldn't have deserted me," she whispered.

"It was through no choice of my own. I allowed myself to be out-generaled. You seemed to be having a good time."

"Mr. Bruce is quite charming and witty. I like him. But Henri behaved badly. He became as jealous of Mr. Bruce as he has always been of you."

"He never makes any secret of his feelings about me. He turned a positive green when he saw me enter this room yesterday."

Margot smiled and said something which he did not hear. He was thinking, . . . *in spite of everything until my dying day!* He could not get Wilson's words out of his mind. For eight years he had loved Gabrielle with such a depth of devotion that no other personal element in his life had been of any importance whatever; and now he had made up his mind to marry Margot. Was he incapable of the unswerving adherence to an ideal which Wilson had always displayed? He felt uncertain, depressed, completely dissatisfied with himself.

"But," he thought, "Gabrielle has given me no option. She refused to marry me. She held out no hope at all for the future. She put her love of country ahead of everything. Now she has vanished. She has deliberately shut me out of her life."

He was realizing how deeply he had felt this exclusion. It had always been to him she had turned in need. No matter what reasons she had, it was quite clear that now she did not intend to let him play any part in the tangled skein she had made of her affairs. Was he not justified, then, in accepting her decision that everything was over between them?

There was a deep sting, nevertheless, in what Wilson had said: . . . *in spite of everything until my dying day!*

"You're very quiet tonight," said Margot.

Frank rallied from the mood of abstraction into which he had fallen. "What do you think the verdict will be?" he asked.

"I was sure you were thinking of that. You seem to take it very hard. But why should you? You're an Englishman; it's no concern of yours really. I suppose it does you credit that you can feel so much sympathy for him. I think he'll be found guilty, of course. Is any other verdict possible?"

"It will be a great tragedy if he is."

She had taken up her embroidery. Every feminine pair of hands in the

room were now back at the customary task. Stitching carefully, she said:
"But, Frank, he was a traitor. He was entrusted with the command of
troops against Napoleon and he went over to him instead. I don't see how
anyone should feel sorry for him."

"You don't yourself, then?"

She looked up at him calmly. "No. He went against his rightful King.
That is what I always remember."

There was silence between them for several moments. "Margot, where
is your cousin Sosthène?" he asked finally.

She hesitated. "He's in Naples. At least, he set out for there a very short
time after the death of Jules. I haven't had word from him since."

"Then he wasn't a witness at the trial of Comte Lavalette?"

"Of course not." Her tone implied that she considered such a suggestion absurd.

"I heard before I left that he might be. I'm glad it wasn't true and
that he's now safely out of the country."

"I don't believe poor Sossy will ever come back."

Margot went on with her work. She was wearing a silver dress with a
tracery of oak leaves on the skirt and the puffed mancherons on her
sleeves. Once, when she shifted her position, he caught the merest
glimpse of a silver stocking embroidered with the same pattern. She
looked more mature and, he thought, lovelier than ever.

He sat and watched her in silence, marveling at her calmness in the
face of the situation which had set all France into two bitterly opposed
camps. Life would never be a complicated matter for Margot. Her beliefs, her loyalties, were all clearly defined in her mind. It was both easy
and natural for her to adhere to them.

One of the white-and-amaranth footmen came in and said something
to her in a low tone. Frank saw that her composure seemed to desert her.
She looked blankly at the servant and then turned her head and gazed
into space. It was several moments before she made any response, but by
that time she seemed to have regained her composure.

"Some of the candles are getting low, Jacques," she said. "Replace
them, if you please."

Frank saw that she still looked pale. "Have you received bad news?"

She nodded her head, almost on the point of tears. "Frank," she whispered, "the verdict is in. They found him guilty. I'm just beginning to
realize what it means. I've been so—callous about it that now I feel
guilty myself."

He made no response at once. It seemed unbelievable that the peers of
France had allowed themselves to be influenced to such a decision by the

pressure of the court. Michel Ney, bravest of the brave, the beloved Rougeaud of the Napoleonic armies, the man who had saved the remnants of the phantom forces retreating from Moscow! He remembered dimly that he had felt the same horror when the news reached England of the executions of King Louis and Queen Marie Antoinette. There had been some alleviation then in the conviction that the enormity of the crime would cause the people of France to rise up against the Revolutionary leaders. But they had done nothing then and they would do nothing now.

"Shall I tell the others?" he asked, realizing that she dreaded the necessity of doing so.

Margot agreed with evident relief. "Please," she said. "I don't want them to see how I feel. I'm afraid, very much afraid, that they are all going to be glad."

5

FRANK AND WILSON decided to walk to the Odéon despite the fact that a flaw of rain and wind had descended on the city. They had very little to say to each other. Finally Wilson remarked: "The play's by Scribe. He's a milk-and-water dramatist, so there won't be any politics in the piece. Did you hear the King's going to attend?"

"That explains why Margot was so set on going. Do you suppose there will be a demonstration?"

"I doubt it. After twenty years of continuous trouble, the people of Paris seem to have lost their appetite for it. I was at the Café Lemblin this afternoon. It was filled with grognards, but all they did was complain."

"Grognards?"

"Old campaigners. They all get irritable and crotchety, you know. Some of them were weeping over Ney's death. They loved the brave redhead. But all their talk will come to nothing."

"I tried to reach the Duke of Wellington for a statement but didn't get beyond the front door. Fouché talked to me but in a most guarded and unfriendly way. They have a poor opinion of the press in this country."

There was a mob in front of the theater, attracted by the fact that the King would attend. It was an orderly one. The two Englishmen had been late in arriving, and they found the lobby almost deserted except for a file of soldiers standing indolently along one wall. "Look at them!"

said Wilson in a whisper of intense exasperation. "No discipline at all. One of Napoleon's sergeants would bring them to attention fast."

An attendant ran forward and put out a hand for their canes, offering slips of paper in exchange. "*Echec, messieurs*," he said.

"What's this?" demanded Frank.

Wilson smiled. "A new custom the theaters have been compelled to adopt lately. There have been so many brawls at political plays that the managers now insist on all patrons parting with their swords, canes, and umbrellas before going in. The only way, apparently, to keep them from breaking each other's heads. As a matter of fact," he added, "it's a very convenient plan. I always find it a nuisance to keep a cane by my seat. I think we might surrender our hats as well."

"It does sound sensible. I'm going to suggest in the *Tab* that the London theaters take it up."

The attendant said, "*Merci!*" in an astonished tone when Frank dropped a small coin in his palm. He then scribbled on their slips a note of the articles they had confided to his care.

They were the last of Margot's guests to arrive, but she had reserved two chairs beside her for them. "You're late," she whispered reproachfully to Frank. He made some apology as he took his seat. Henri Lestange was in the party and seemed very dissatisfied over his banishment to a chair in the second row. He did not look in their direction.

The royal party had not yet arrived, and the special chair installed for the use of His Majesty looked enormous in the empty box. All the boxes were filled, with one other exception, and the pit was buzzing with an overflow attendance. An orchestra, from an unseen position in the rear, was already tuning up.

Frank got his courage to the point of asking the question which had been in his mind ever since he had arrived. "Margot," he whispered, "you haven't mentioned Gabrielle. Have you heard from her since the death of her husband?"

Margot nodded; with some reluctance, he thought. "She took it very hard and seemed to feel she was to blame. I agreed with that."

"Where is she now?"

"I believe she's with Sosthène in Naples."

He waited for her to go on, but her manner suggested that she resented his interest in Gabrielle. She picked up her lorgnette and gazed at the people in the pit. It was clear she did not intend to give him any further news of her erring cousin. Wilson, on his other side, whispered: "An orderly lot. There'll be no demonstration tonight."

The orchestra was playing O *Richard*, the most popular of Bourbon airs, but the hum of talk throughout the house was almost drowning out the music. Every woman in view was wearing white and the men had Royalist cockades on their shoulders. A restless stamping of feet in the gallery above seemed to suggest, however, that in one part of the house the people were not in an entirely happy frame of mind.

Wilson leaned forward suddenly. "Frank," he whispered, "we've judged too soon perhaps. Look at that lady who has just taken the empty box."

Frank turned his head in that direction and his surprise was so great that for a moment he sat perfectly still. His heart seemed to have stopped beating.

It was Gabrielle. She was alone and had taken a chair in the front where she could be seen from all parts of the house. Frank realized with one glance that he was still held in the spell under which he had lived for so many years. He was still in love with her. Why, he asked himself, had he ever doubted it? Nothing, he realized now, could ever change him. He was so happy to see her, to know that he loved her, that he sat in a glow, reveling in this glimpse of her after such a long separation. She looked pale and a little thin but, in his eyes, at least, she was as beautiful as ever. It was always the way: he carried in his mind a picture of her which seemed real and satisfying, and then he would see her and realize how completely she transcended his recollection. This time, with such a long lapse to dull his mental visualization, the contrast between memory and reality was greater than ever before. The sight of her took him by the throat and made him almost breathless.

Gabrielle was dressed in black velvet and her hair was drawn up high on her head with no ornamentation of any kind, in sharp contrast to the elaborate plumed coiffures which seemed to fill the house beneath them. She was wearing a corsage on one shoulder.

"It's Gabrielle!" he whispered to Wilson.

"So it is." The soldier suddenly dug an excited elbow into his companion's ribs. "The flowers, man! I believe she's wearing violets!"

One glance confirmed the fact for Frank that she had indeed achieved the supreme audacity of wearing in public the lavender Parma violets so closely associated now with the Napoleonic cause. The house was becoming aware of it and an excited hum of comment was rising on every side. As they watched, an usher carried in a large basket filled with bunches of the same flower and placed it in full view on a chair beside her. There was a black mourning bow tied conspicuously to the handle.

Wilson said in an awed tone, "The only person in all Paris with the courage to show how she feels!"

Frank's mind was in a turmoil. "Gabrielle, Gabrielle! How proud I am of you!" he thought. At the same time he was filled with intense concern over the outcome of her bold venture into the public gaze. The court, he knew, was in no mood to forgive such an open display of her sympathies. Should he go and warn her to leave at once?

Margot, becoming aware that something unusual was happening, turned at this moment and her eyes fell on Gabrielle. The lorgnette dropped from her hand. "Oh!" she exclaimed. She looked at her cousin with an air of amazement which turned almost at once to anger. "How could she do this! How could she dare!" After a tense moment she turned to Frank, her eyes blazing. "This is incredible! This is too much." She seemed to be demanding of him that he agree with her.

If a dramatist had arranged it, the sequence of events could not have moved with more telling effect, for at this moment the orchestra crashed into the opening bars of an anthem and the court party began to file into the royal box. Frank's feeling of alarm mounted. "It's too late now," he thought, turning to look at King Louis XVIII and his attendant train.

It needed the urgent pressure of Margot's hand on his arm to arouse him to the fact that he must stand up. The whole house had risen and a storm of applause was being tendered the aging monarch. The first glance he took at His Majesty caused Frank a curious sense of consternation. Surely this mountain of flesh, moving with uncertain steps to the huge chair in the front of the box, could not be the King of France! It was so incongruous that, in spite of the other emotions gripping him, he found it hard to stifle a laugh. A king should never look like this! It was absurd. He watched until the royal bulk had subsided into the chair and then gave a quick glance at the ladies and gentlemen accompanying their ruler. They seemed like gnomes by contrast, whispering among themselves in a state of nervous tension. In spite of their fine raiment and their glittering diamonds, they seemed to Frank like a bevy of monkeys in the cage of a great polar bear.

"Twenty-five stone on the hoof," said Wilson in Frank's ear.

Gabrielle was the only one in the theater who had not risen. She sat in her chair without a single movement, her eyes fixed ahead of her on the lowered curtain. How small she looked, Frank thought, barely to be seen through the wall of standing people. Then, watching her over Wilson's shoulder, he saw one of her hands go to her breast and begin to detach the corsage. His feeling of alarm mounted at once. What was she going to do?

"Magnificent!" he heard Wilson say. "She might just as well have walked into the royal box and slapped the King in the face!"

The eyes of the royal party had been attracted by this time to the lone sitting figure. They stared at her as though turned to stone, some with faces that mirrored incredulity, some with an immediate appearance of anger. One functionary tapped on the King's shoulder and whispered in his ear. His Majesty did not look around. His own eyes were fixed on the curtain with a passivity remarkable under the circumstances.

Margot's fingers had curled around Frank's arm with a convulsive clutch. He saw that there were tears in her eyes. "This is the end!" she said. "It can't be forgiven. I hope I never see her again. Never!"

The anthem came to a finish. The members of the royal party took their seats, their eyes still glued furiously on the still figure of the daring sitter. The people in the other boxes followed suit, but in the pit they continued to stand, staring up at the unexpected tableau with avid eyes.

Gabrielle rose, holding the violets in her hand. She buried her face in them for a moment with a manner suggesting reverence, then with a sudden gesture tossed them over the railing. Her voice could be heard all over the house.

"A reminder of a very brave man, now dead, who won great glory for France!"

The flowers, bound together with a black ribbon, floated out over the pit and then fell. Hands reached up and there was a sound of scuffling below. Suddenly a voice from the high gallery cried out, "*Vive Papa Violet!*" Other voices, gaining in daring, cried, "Ney! Ney!" Gabrielle turned, looked once in the direction of the royal party, and walked slowly from the box.

The whole theater was in a turmoil. Everyone, with the sole exception of the obese monarch, had risen again. People were surging into the aisles, shouting, gesturing, waving angry fists in the air. Some were cheering. The sharp division of thought and loyalty had been dragged into the open. There was so much noise that few heard Sir Robert call, "Bravo!" as he forced his way through the chairs behind him on his way to the exit. Frank, unaware that he had wrenched his arm clear from Margot's fingers, was close on his heels. Frank was thinking, "I must get her out! She'll be mobbed when she tries to leave!"

In spite of his fears, a mood of high exultation had taken possession of him. What a magnificent gesture of defiance it had been! The world would now see Gabrielle in the proper light.

In the lobby Wilson said, "Steady, now, steady." It was deserted save for the lounging guards in their blue and silver uniforms, but in less than a minute it was filled with people. The carpet, covered with orange peel and the ash of careless smokers, deadened all sound of movement, but the air became filled with angry disputation.

"Here she comes," said Wilson.

The crowd parted to make an aisle for her as she stepped from the dark stairway into the lobby. Her skirts swayed gently as she came forward, holding another bunch of the violets in both hands. She was smiling and seemed completely at ease. Frank's heart bounded with love and pride.

Then one man reached out to take the flowers from her, and in an instant a scuffling mass hid her from view. With flailing arms Frank fought his way to her side. Wilson had reached her other side, and the pair of them struggled furiously for several moments to clear a space about her. Gabrielle, still unperturbed, smiled up at Frank and her lips moved. He thought what she said was, "So you're here."

Foot by foot, they forced their way forward. It was a hard struggle, but after what seemed an eternity of buffeting and shoving they reached the front doors. Even then Gabrielle seemed unwilling to go, protesting in a breathless voice, "But I don't want to run away!"

"We must get clear of this as soon as we can," panted Wilson.

They were on the steps leading down to the street and a file of the guards stood at the bottom, watching the sudden eruption from the theater with uncomprehending eyes. Knowing that they would soon spring into action, the two Englishmen urged their unwilling companion down to the pavement.

"We must get over to the Rue de Vaugirard," said Wilson. "There we may find a carriage or a chair for the Comtesse."

The drizzle had changed to a cold rain which carried a threat of hail. Frank took the cloak Gabrielle was carrying over one arm and wrapped it around her shoulders. "You'll get wet," he said, "but it won't do to wait for a carriage here."

Gabrielle turned and looked back. She laughed triumphantly and called out:

"Vive l'Empereur!"

Wilson seized one of her arms and urged her forward. "You've made your point, dear lady. Now we must run for it."

She was not yet ready to leave. Drawing an arm clear, she extracted a purse from a pocket of the cloak. "There's another reason beside the political one for not wearing violets this season," she said, looking inside the purse. "They're hard to get and extremely expensive. My little gesture tonight has cost me my last franc." She laughed suddenly and tossed the purse into the street. "I've no regrets. It was worth it."

Frank ran after the purse and rescued it from a street urchin who had pounced at the same time. "I want this," he said, catching up with them after recovering it, "as a souvenir of an evening that all France will remember."

An officer had emerged from the theater and was shouting orders to the squad of guards. "We may be too late," said Wilson. Gabrielle picked up her skirts and began to run between her two companions. She said breathlessly, "A very undignified way to end it."

They were lucky enough to find a carriage at the first cross street. "Where to?" asked the driver, giving his whip a preliminary flourish. Gabrielle answered, "Drive us to the Faubourg St. Honoré." She sank back on the seat between them and said, "I would like it very much if you would both come with me to meet—to meet some friends."

"We're at your service," said Wilson.

She settled down with a sigh of relief. "I'm glad we managed to get away. I didn't want to have you involved in whatever might have happened to me." She paused for breath. "I'm sure you feel I behaved very foolishly."

"You had the courage," said Wilson, "to do what everyone who deplores the proscription has wanted to do. It was foolish, undoubtedly. But very brave, and I want to say you've won my deepest admiration."

"I think perhaps, Gaby, that you've already guessed that it's to Sir Robert Wilson you owe your escape."

Gabrielle looked up at the tall soldier. "I was sure it was your famous Sir Robert. You've made it very clear, Frank, that he's always on hand at times like these. How very lucky for me that you were both there tonight!"

"Let's hope the luck will hold." Wilson leaned out of the window and looked back in the direction of the theater. "They're buzzing around like angry hornets. I rather think they'll be coming after us."

The carriage, in response to his urgent order, rattled furiously over the cobbled streets. No sounds of pursuit followed them. Gabrielle drew the cloak about her neck as though conscious for the first time that her dress was wet. "You were surprised, no doubt, to see me back in Paris, Frank. I arrived yesterday. I didn't want to come. I dreaded seeing the city in the hands of the enemies of the Emperor."

"Your visit is going to be a short one," asserted Frank.

"Yes." She gave a shudder. "It's like a strange city. The people are different; they're so hard and bitter and unhappy. I feel as though Paris has lost its soul. I shall leave at once—and never come back!"

"Making it possible for you to leave, dear lady, may prove quite a problem," declared Wilson. "But I'm sure I speak for my friend Ellery when I say that we're happy to put ourselves at your disposal in the matter."

Frank drew her arm through his and pressed it warmly. He was thinking with a deep sense of happiness, . . . *in spite of everything, until my dying day.*

6

THERE WAS a brooding, withdrawn look already about the Faubourg St. Honoré where the Bonapartist aristocracy had settled. Few of the houses showed any lights at all, and the wind drew creaking sounds from the chains which stretched across many of the front gates. Streets which once had rattled with arrogant carriages were silent now, and such pedestrians as were to be seen walked quickly and furtively. Wealth and power had been taken away from the unlettered and vainglorious men who had built these high-windowed houses and laid out the pretentious gardens. The taking had been so sudden that there was hardly time yet for material decay. Nevertheless the suggestion of disintegration hung over the district and could be ascribed perhaps to the mental attitude of the owners themselves, who were living in fear and a new humility.

They stopped before the front door of a dark house rising up four stories from the edge of the pavement, and Gabrielle gave proof that the mood of the neighborhood had already gripped her by saying in a whisper: "The owner went to America after the first abdication and was lucky enough not to come back. It's rented now by an Englishman. You will know him, perhaps? A Mr. Michael Bruce?"

"I know him," said Sir Robert, looking up doubtfully at the tightly shuttered windows. "Rather roomy for a bachelor; but Bruce has always been quite a hand for entertaining. It doesn't look as though he's at home."

"There will be company here tonight," asserted Gabrielle. "I wanted you to come with me for the express purpose of meeting one of them. A lady."

"Bruce's guests are generally ladies."

"I should warn you," continued Gabrielle, "that everyone here tonight will be from the wrong side of the political fence."

"I'll feel completely at home, then," declared Wilson. "I've a positive gift for finding myself on the wrong side of political fences. It has one advantage: the company is more entertaining."

The door was opened in response to their double knock by a major-domo with a wooden leg and an armless sleeve tucked into the pocket of a threadbare coat. He nodded briskly and smiled in response to a whispered message from Gabrielle. A hum of voices came from a room to the right of the hall and the major-domo led them there, stumping along with brisk energy. Three men, all in uniform and wearing the tricolor cockade of Napoleon pinned to their shoulders, rose to their feet. One of them bowed elaborately to Gabrielle and said, "Your servant, madame!"

"This is a great pleasure, my dear Colonel. It's a long time since I have seen you."

She did not introduce her companions but led them to a corner of the room where they ensconced themselves on a deep couch. "Colonel Patronne," she whispered, "is one of the very few who have fought in every campaign since Italy. It makes him quite arrogant."

"Fouché was less thorough than he thought in his roundup," said Wilson, looking at the trio of officers.

It was a curiously jumbled room. There was a grand piano, piled high with hats, cloaks, and swords, a harp beside it, one table covered with maps and another laid for supper. The walls were covered with war paintings: Napoleon at the Arcola bridge, Napoleon at the Pyramids, Napoleon on the raft at Tilsit. The furnishings were the result, clearly, of years of looting; a cupboard of Spanish design, an Austrian console, a Dutch ambry with doors open to display an assortment of *objets d'art* from all parts of Europe. A Russian icon, studded with precious stones, hung on the wall above the piano.

The three soldiers returned to the argument which had been engrossing them when the new company arrived.

Frank looked down at Gabrielle and asked, "Why have you hidden yourself away from me all these months?"

She answered in a low tone without looking up. "Pride, perhaps. Or it may have been a sense of fair play. I thought you should have a chance to—to make up your mind about certain things."

"But you've been in trouble. Our agreement was that you would always let me know."

She glanced up at him now and smiled. "Well, my Knight of the Rueful Countenance, you may find you have me back on your hands after all. I may prove a troublesome charge this time."

"Gaby!" he whispered tensely. "I can't tell you how happy I am now that I've found you again."

"Even . . . ?" she began, raising her eyebrows. "You know I've been hearing reports of you."

The door opened again and a very pretty woman came into the room, flanked by two men in uniform. Her hair was almost silver in its extreme blondness, and her eyes, under startlingly dark brows, were large and of an unusual liveliness. It seemed impossible that she had been attending a party on this particular evening, yet she was wearing a tinsel fool's cap on her head and carrying a silver cage with two white mice.

"I believe it's La Bellilote," said Gabrielle in a whisper.

Frank looked at the blond woman with immediate interest. Pauline Faures, generally known as La Bellilote, had figured notoriously in the Egyptian campaign. Going out, against orders, with her husband, who was a minor officer, she had caught Napoleon's eye. He had been so enamored of her that he had promptly sent the husband back to France with dispatches. A dinner party was then arranged, in the course of which the great man contrived to spill a cup of coffee over her dress. This necessitated a trip upstairs for repairs, with Napoleon playing lady's maid. The affair had followed the usual lines after that, except that he had brushed her aside on his return to France; and she, most unexpectedly, had continued in love with him ever since.

La Bellilote stood in the doorway for several moments, staring at Gabrielle. Then she crossed the room and sat down in a chair facing her. She was dressed in black crepe with no relieving color save a minute tucker of white in the triple-fluted flounce of her skirt and in the sleeve jockeys. Crossing one knee over the other with a careless display of a slim ankle, she said in a throaty voice: "The Comtesse de Vitrelle! And both of us in black. For the same reason, I wonder, Mme. la Comtesse?"

Colonel Patronne called out in an anxious voice: "Come over here, Pauline. I must have a talk with you."

"Later, Jacques." The discarded mistress of the Emperor, who had now gone into the discard himself, refused to be diverted. "I want to talk with the Comtesse first. I've never had that great honor."

"I'm glad to meet you, Mme. Faures," said Gabrielle. "I've heard a great deal about you."

"Yes?" with a rising inflection. "And I've heard a great deal about *you!* I think it's time I made the acquaintance of—of my successor."

Someone said, "Ssh!" and Patronne walked over to La Bellilote, taking her firmly by the arm. "This won't do," he said. "You've been drinking, Pauline. I'm going to put you in a corner by yourself and I don't want you to say another word."

"I'll say what I like." Nevertheless she got to her feet unsteadily. "You're beautiful," she said to Gabrielle. "But no more than I was. You should have heard what the Emperor said——"

La Bellilote stood quietly for several moments, staring at Gabrielle, her forehead puckered with concentration. She seemed to be striving for some conclusion. Finally she shook her head slowly from side to side.

"Everyone has heard the stories about you," she said in a low tone. "And everyone has believed them. I believed them. There have been so many of us, and it seemed natural enough that his fancy might be taken by one who was said to be so beautiful and a member of the old nobility as well. But now that I've seen you, Mme. la Comtesse, I've changed my mind. I know the stories are not true."

"Come, Pauline," said Patronne, tugging insistently at her arm.

She shook him off. "What an honor to have missed! I have been more fortunate than you. An ordinary mortal could not hope to enjoy the favor of the god for very long but to have had his love for a few months is enough. I have that to remember." She swayed unsteadily on her feet. "Ah, Mme. la Comtesse, I am sorry for you!"

"If you say anything more," declared the Colonel, "you'll find yourself out in the rain again, you and your silly mice."

La Bellilote's mood veered instantly. She began to giggle. "I call them Joseph and Lucien. Two such timid little mice! They—his two brothers —turned him against me. I've never forgotten it."

She teetered across the room, pausing beside the harp to run a finger over the strings. "*She* used to play the harp," she said with a throatily contemptuous laugh. Everyone understood she referred to the Empress Josephine, who had made a pretense of culture. "They praised her playing and said she looked so beautiful bending over the strings. Pah! She knew only one tune!"

Patronne urged her away from the harp and into a corner chair. He then helped her to a glass of wine and a plate of Algerian grapes. She began to eat the grapes and to toss the skins casually under the piano.

"You see now how generally the story has been believed," said Gabrielle in a whisper. "I knew I could count on you not to believe it, Frank. But I'm afraid there are few who agree with you."

"Margot doesn't believe the story."

"Are you sure?" Her voice took a questioning lift. "Well, perhaps not. Margot is always fair. She tries to be so fair and just. But the last time I saw her she talked as though she had no doubt at all of my guilt." Gabrielle sighed. "The truth will never be known now. It doesn't matter much."

"It doesn't matter at all," said Frank, looking at her steadily.

She returned his gaze for several moments with equal steadiness. Then she smiled. "*Mon petit chou!*" she whispered.

Over in her solitary corner La Bellilote was weeping into her wineglass. "It's so hot on that dreadful island!" she whimpered. "He'll die there. I know he will!"

"Poor woman!" said Gabrielle. "He treated her very badly, I'm afraid." Her smile had vanished and was replaced by a look of concern. "I feel as badly about that island as she does. My poor Emperor won't be able to stand the climate."

"Gaby," said Frank, "haven't you a great deal to tell me? Where have you been? Why do you come back to Paris now?"

Wilson, sensing that they had much to discuss, had gone over to join the French officers and they were already deep in some military dispute. Gabrielle said, after a moment's hesitation: "You thought I was completely mad tonight, I'm sure. Frank, I had the best of reasons for what I did." She indulged in a longer hesitation. "It's humiliating to tell you this. You see, Comte Lavalette was convicted through evidence that—I can hardly bear to tell you!—that Sosthène supplied to the police. He didn't appear in court but he gave them the necessary information. He and Jules had been offered some restitution of property if they would tell what they knew. That was what brought them to Paris. I didn't know it then, not even when poor Jules died. I still didn't know it when Margot arranged with us to go to Naples."

"You saw Margot then?"

"Of course. I came to Paris as soon as I heard about Jules and I went to see Margot first." She stopped and looked at him questioningly. "You didn't know anything about this at all?"

"I heard a rumor about your brother. That was all."

"Margot said nothing about it?"

"She told me your brother had gone to Naples. She didn't say he came to Paris."

"One can't blame her for keeping it from you. You least of all, Frank."

"I don't understand it at all."

"Think, Frank, think!" She shook her head with a trace of exasperation. "She was afraid—don't you see? She was quite right not to say anything about it. She offered Sossy an allowance if we would both leave France. He took it because it was clear by then that Fouché, having what he wanted, was not going to live up to his promises." Alarmed by his set expression, she added vehemently: "Frank, please! You mustn't blame Margot. She was very fair and generous about it."

"I'm wondering why she kept the whole matter from me. She allowed me to think she hadn't seen you. That she didn't know where you were."

"That was natural. I would have done the same if I had been in her place."

"No. I'm sure you wouldn't."

"But I would! Any woman would. You had been so—so very constant. It was her only chance. You should feel complimented that she felt as she did about it. You mustn't let what I've said influence you. I wouldn't have told you this if it hadn't been part of the reason for what I did tonight. You must be fair to Margot."

"It doesn't matter now, Gaby." He added in a repressed voice: "But I'm still in the dark. What has this to do with tonight?"

"Everything. Sossy said something when we were on our way south which opened my eyes. I was horrified! I knew then that Lavalette's blood would be on our hands. I had to do what I could to save him."

"And you thought you might help him by stirring up feeling over the shooting of Ney?"

"Yes, it seemed the only way. I had no plan in my mind when I came back. But today, when the whole city took his execution so quietly, I saw that something must be done at once to make the King see how the people of France felt about it down in their hearts. I hoped to start a demonstration which would make them all see it."

"I understand now. You realize that you've put yourself in almost as much danger as Lavalette himself?"

"What does it matter?" she cried passionately. "I must do what I can to save him after the terrible part my brother has played!"

The major-domo had come in with a tray of glasses. He paused beside Gabrielle and stooped down to whisper something to her. She nodded and stood up, saying, "Thanks, Guillaume, I'll go in."

At this point their host arrived in a handsome lavender coat and a contrite hurry. "My apologies!" he called from the door, throwing the coat on the back of a chair. "Have you all heard what happened tonight? I stayed to find if there was any further news about it. The fair Gabrielle——"

He saw her then and came striding across the room with both hands stretched out. "My dear Comtesse! I'm delighted you got here after all. I was worried about you. My sincerest congratulations! All Paris is talking about it this very minute."

Frank's first impression of him the night before had not been entirely favorable, but now he found himself liking Michael Bruce. There was an infectious quality about his easy good nature, and he was almost as handsome in his dark, sleek way as Caradoc.

"Delighted to see you, Sir Robert. And you, Ellery. It was a happy thought to bring them, Comtesse." He looked about him. "What, no supper yet? Come, come, this won't do at all. Guillaume, bring it in at once." He leaned over to Gabrielle and whispered, "Has she come?"

"Just a minute ago."

Patronne asked what had happened to throw their host into such an exuberant mood and Bruce proceeded to tell the story, adding certain graphic details which were new to the three participants; the report, obviously, had been growing as it made the rounds. He concluded: "They say the ladies of the court are in a state of mind. The Duchesse d'Angoulême went straight to bed, refusing to touch a bite of supper. *How* upset she must have been! There's talk"—he hesitated—"of an immediate arrest. We must see that nothing comes of *that*."

The story was received with the greatest enthusiasm, the company crowding around and demanding more details. One of them went to the piano and began to drum out with heavy fists the rousing air of *Mironton, Mironton, Mirontaine!* The officers sang the words with gusto, one of them dragging a sheet of music from the ambry and wrapping it into the form of a trumpet to supplement the music. The din was so great that Frank wondered what passers-by would think of it.

La Bellilote came over to Gabrielle and said in a tremulous voice, "Please forgive me, Comtesse."

"You have shown them that the soul of France is not dead," declared Patronne pompously. "We were boasting of our battles. Ah, Comtesse, you are braver than all of us!"

Servants were now carrying in platters of food, and a thoroughly happy mood took possession of the guests. They would sup on bounteous fare and it added salt to the viands that the hated Royalists would have this open affront to digest as their supper seasoning. Bruce took advantage of their good nature to say: "I've something important to discuss with my three friends here. It won't bear delay, so please don't wait supper for us. We'll rejoin you later."

The hungry Bonapartists needed no further urging to begin their meal, and Patronne waved a reassuring drumstick at them as they walked out into the hall. Bruce led them to a small room behind the stairs.

It was not empty. A lady with a pale and tragic face was sitting in front of the fireplace. Despite the heat of the coal blazing briskly on the hearth, she had a cloak muffled up closely around her neck, and an occasional shiver testified that something more than artificial warmth was needed to give her bodily comfort.

"I apologize, dear lady, for keeping you waiting," said Bruce. "Permit me to introduce two gentlemen from England. Sir Robert Wilson and Mr. Francis Ellery. This is the Comtesse Lavalette."

Frank looked with sharpened interest at the wife of the unfortunate Bonapartist. She had a gentle face, slightly pitted by smallpox, but comely in spite of that; and she wore an air of resolution which rose above the obviously delicate state of her health. She was plainly dressed in black merino under the heavy cloak. It was clear that she had once been a beauty.

She inclined her head to each of them in turn and then smiled warmly at Gabrielle. "I have heard what you did, my dear," she said. "It was very brave of you. Pray God it will bring us help."

Bruce drew up chairs around the fire for his other guests. When they were seated, he asked, "Have you any good word for us, Comtesse?"

The wife of the condemned man shook her head sadly. "None," she said, dabbing at her eyes with a handkerchief. "I saw His Majesty. He holds out no hope of pardon. I have tried many times to speak to the Duke of Wellington and the Tsar. They decline to see me. I fear there's nothing more I can do."

There was a long pause. "The Comtesse," said Bruce, "is sadly in need of advice in this desperate pass. And help. Have you any suggestions to make, Sir Robert?"

Wilson had been watching the Comtesse with an air of deepest sympathy. On being thus appealed to, he said slowly: "I'm afraid that I'm not familiar enough with the heads of the French Government to give advice that would be helpful. It clearly is a matter of bringing influence to bear in the right quarter."

"I have seen everyone!" exclaimed the Comtesse in a desperate tone. "The Duchesse d'Angoulême, Richelieu, Talleyrand, even Fouché. It does no good. They won't listen. Their minds are made up."

"I regret," said Wilson, "that I have no influence with the Duke of Wellington. He's the one whose word would count. He could save your husband if he cared to interfere, but it's too much to hope that he'll do such an unprecedented thing."

"My husband," said the Comtesse with a catch in her voice, "is reconciled to his fate. He begs me to do nothing more."

"But you are not content to do that?"

"No, no! I must go on trying. I mustn't give up."

Gabrielle said with sudden fire: "The hand of the King must be forced! If meetings are held all over France to demand a pardon, he will have to give in."

"It's my impression that the people of France want nothing so much as peace," declared Wilson. "I'm very much afraid it would be impossible to fan their ardor to such an extent. It's possible also that the government would seize on demonstrations as proof that vigorous steps are necessary."

"Then must we sit back and do nothing?" demanded Gabrielle.

Frank was watching Sir Robert Wilson. That unpredictable soldier twisted uneasily in his chair and seemed reluctant to add anything further to the discussion.

"Must we let the royal family have their way again?" asked Gabrielle.

"There's always the possibility of arranging an escape," said Wilson suddenly. "It would depend on how far the Comte himself is prepared to go. And, more particularly still,"—turning about to face the Comtesse—"how resolute his wife may be."

"I would do anything!" declared that lady eagerly.

"I understand there has never been an escape from the Conciergerie," went on Wilson. "Not, at least, of recent years. Is it as hard a nut to crack as the Tower of London? What's your opinion, Bruce?"

"Of course not," said Bruce positively. "It goes without saying. The Tower—well, there's nothing like it in the world."

Wilson smiled. "How short memories are! I wonder if there are a score of people in England today who recall that a prisoner *did* escape from the Tower? It wasn't so very long ago; just an even hundred years, in fact. It was quite a remarkable business, Bruce; and it was planned and carried out by the man's wife."

Gabrielle said quickly, "Tell us about it, Sir Robert."

"It happened in 1715, after the Old Pretender's effort to get back his throne. A number of Scottish noblemen were captured and sentenced to the block. The wife of one of them wasn't content to sit back and see her lord die. She was a delicate and lovely lady. The redheaded Countess, they called her afterward. Winifred, Countess of Nithisdale. It's not very gallant of us to have forgotten that very gallant woman."

"Please, tell us *all* about it."

"It's a long story. Briefly, she smuggled clothes into his cell in the Tower and dressed him up as a woman. Several servants were in it—all of the gentler sex, mark you, not a bungling male concerned in it at all —and they managed to distract attention while my lord of Nithisdale walked calmly out of the Tower. It was very neatly contrived. They never caught him."

"What happened to his wife?" demanded Gabrielle.

"She walked out an hour or so later. They didn't catch her either. The pair of them got away from England and joined the court of that ineffective and misanthropic gentleman, the Old Pretender, on the Continent. I'm compelled to add that they lived unhappily ever after. They existed in extreme poverty for many years and finally died in Italy."

Gabrielle's eyes were shining. "A sad story but an inspiring one," she said. "Did you have a purpose in telling us about it, Sir Robert?"

Wilson took again to an uneasy shifting about in his chair. He frowned in an abstracted way. "Perhaps. It could be tried, at any rate. I believe the Comtesse is the only one permitted to see him, so it would depend on her. I'm *not* recommending that she attempt anything of the kind, mind you. I want you to understand that."

"She would need a great deal of help," said Gabrielle.

Wilson nodded. "A great deal of help. And every single detail would have to be worked out carefully in advance. A carriage at the prison gate; or, better still, a chair first and a carriage a block or two away. A chair would look less urgent. A relay of carriages might be necessary in case of an immediate pursuit, to throw them off the scent. A diversion would have to be created at the entrance to distract the attention of the guards. Yes, it would take a lot of planning."

"And," said Gabrielle, "it would call for the help of what you have called bungling males, Sir Robert."

The Comtesse had listened intently while Gabrielle persisted in her obvious effort to enlist support. Now she said with an air of great resolution: "I'm not clever at all and I'm afraid I wouldn't prove adept at the plan you have in mind. But I'm of a will to do anything to save my husband's life. Tell me what I would have to do."

The eyes of both women, full of the most earnest appeal, were fixed on Wilson. He looked away hastily. "You have many friends," he said. "If you decide to try the plan—and I want to repeat that I don't advise you to; it might not succeed a second time—you should select your aides with the greatest care. They should be men of spirit and very considerable discretion."

"I asked the Comtesse here tonight," said Gabrielle, "in the hope that some of Mr. Bruce's usual guests would find a way to lend her aid. But" —she hesitated a moment—"it seemed to me wiser to state the problem first to one with more resourcefulness and a cooler head."

Bruce spoke up. "As you know, my dear lady, you can count on me. I hoped to have Hely-Hutcheson here but he was assigned to duty at the last moment. He was furious over the execution of Ney and he might take a hand. 'Pon my word, I believe he would."

Wilson looked up at that. "A fine fellow, the young squire of Knock-lofty. You may remember I served a year under his uncle back in '08. Old Hutch was a crotchety fellow but we got along famously."

Bruce drew his chair up closer to Wilson's. "It's a diverting idea. 'Pon my soul, I think we could do it. You and Hely-Hutcheson and perhaps Ellery as well."

"*Wilson et Compagnie!*" cried Gabrielle with sudden enthusiasm. "A close corporation, formed to save an innocent man's life. And to administer a rebuke to a stupid and vengeful government."

Frank spoke for the first time since the discussion had begun. "I've been a member of Wilson and Company for a great many years."

Gabrielle looked at him with shining eyes. "I knew, Frank," she said softly, "that we could count on you."

Wilson shrugged his shoulders helplessly. "I had a presentiment this evening, when I first saw you sitting in that box and fairly smothered with violets, that no good would come of it." He sighed. "You must see my difficulty. I don't mind the risks myself. I've spent my life taking risks, many of them more foolhardy than this. But these three young men, if Hely-Hutcheson should elect to come in, are English. It's no concern of theirs. Why should Englishmen be involved in it?"

In spite of his words, it was clear to them now that he had made up his mind. Comtesse Lavalette smiled for the first time. Gabrielle made a gesture as though she would have liked to clasp all of them in her arms at once. "But," she cried, "you are most exceptional Englishmen!"

7

ANTOINE was cleaning windows, sulkily but efficiently, when Frank arrived at Place Lorient the next morning. A sense of bustle pervaded the inside of the house, and from somewhere in the rear he could hear Margot's voice raised in cool but decided insistence. The Abbé Force greeted him in the salon, which already was as immaculate as a freshly laundered muslin dress.

"You arrive early," said the churchman. "This is *nettoyage* day. It comes twice a week. The dust flies. Everyone steps to a livelier tune than any that the Revolution produced."

Frank had previously noted the remarkable change which had come about in the Abbé's appearance but he had never speculated on the cause. His clerical gowns were always fresh and unrumpled, his shoes were shined, his face and hands as clean as though a currycomb had been applied to them. What little hair he had left lay flat and tidy on his knobby dome of a head. Frank realized now that Margot had been responsible for the improvement.

He had come on a double errand: to apologize for leaving the party the previous evening in such a cavalier way and to tell her what he had come to know of the state of his heart. It was not going to be easy and he was not looking forward to it. He realized now that he had chosen the worst possible time.

"We are dedicated to cleanliness as well as godliness," went on the churchman but without any of the zeal which should have accompanied the statement. "We are very systematic. Has M'sieur seen our *Livre Journal?* I keep it myself. Each day I enter up all the facts of our well-ordered existence: the visitors who came, the items of food served at each meal, the amounts laid out, the prayers said, the tasks performed by each servant, their sins of omission. Before retiring our young mistress reads it over and, if I have been accurate and painstaking, she writes an approving M.M. at the bottom of the page. And there it is," the Abbé concluded with a suggestion of a wink, "for the benefit and edification of posterity."

"System is an excellent thing," commented Frank.

"You mustn't think, m'sieur, that I speak in a spirit of criticism. She is an admirable young woman. She attains, in fact, to the peak of human perfection. She is kind of heart and infinitely just. I am tenderly devoted to her."

Tante Blanchefleur put her head in the door for a hurried moment and cried in an urgent voice, "Abbé, Abbé, the *inventaire!*"

The churchman got to his feet in great haste. "I had forgotten. This morning also we make our lists of all supplies in the kitchen, and I'm needed to act as clerk." He started to walk across the room, pausing at the door to bend a shrewd eye on the visitor. "Have you seen today's *Quotidienne?* There are two references in it of considerable interest. I would suggest that M'sieur read them with the utmost attention."

Frank identified the two items without any difficulty. The first recorded the incident at the Odéon in the acrimonious spirit which characterized so much of French journalism, concluding with the fact that the Comtesse de Vitrelle had left the theater in the company of two Englishmen, one believed to be Sir Robert Wilson, the other "an unknown man who limped conspicuously." The second was a brief note to the effect that the final decisions in the settlement of the March estates would be handed down in a few days. There was some speculation as to the amounts involved. They were certain, in the opinion of the writer, to prove colossal.

He had read and digested these references by the time Margot came.

She smiled gravely, and he thought reluctantly, in response to his greeting.

"I didn't expect you so early. You find me in my working clothes and, I'm afraid, rather untidy."

She looked, as a matter of fact, both neat and trim in a white tablier robe with a thin ruche at the neck to match the color of her eyes. Taking a chair near a window, she gazed steadily out at the bare framework of the balcony as though unwilling to meet his gaze.

"I came at this hour because there would be no one here. I wanted to have a serious talk with you."

"Yes. We have much to talk about." She paused and then burst out vehemently, "Why did you do it!"

"I'm very sorry I left you so abruptly. But—the circumstances hardly allowed time for politeness. We were just in time as it was."

She said in a low but intense tone: "Can you think how I felt at being left that way? It was as though—as though it had become a choice between us. And you had chosen Gabrielle."

He hastened to explain. "It came close to being a riot in the lobby and then outside in the street. She would never have gotten away safely if we hadn't been there to help."

"I had a note of apology from Sir Robert Wilson this morning. He said the same thing."

"You can't mean, Margot, that you think we shouldn't have gone to her assistance? That we should have stayed in the theater and left her to face it alone?"

There was a brief pause before she answered. "No. No, you had to do it. I'm glad you were able to get her away safely. But"—the tense note had come back into her voice—"you didn't even speak to me before you went. You tore yourself away as though you didn't know I was there! I felt—have you any idea at all of how I felt?"

"I can see that I behaved badly. But the alarm I felt for her safety must be my justification. You must realize that I felt in complete sympathy with her attitude."

"I don't understand why you do. You went to prison for criticizing your own government when you thought it was lax in conducting the war. You said so often that Bonaparte was a menace to the whole world. Don't you see that the time has come for examples to be made?"

"What you don't seem to see is that the people of Europe, who have suffered most at the hands of Napoleon, had no desire for the death of Ney. He was shot to satisfy the French aristocracy. A gallant soldier executed to please a vicious court circle! No one outside of the court wants Lavalette to suffer the same way. He's an amiable and decent man who happens to have married into the Bonaparte family and so must be sacrificed to the petty spite of the royal ladies."

"I can't understand you at all. And as for Gabrielle, it was inexcusable. So cheap, so theatrical!"

He looked at her steadily. "Margot, I don't believe you realize just what Gabrielle's reason was. You wouldn't say that if you did."

"Nothing you can say will excuse her! She insulted her King publicly. It was an incredible way to act."

After a moment's reflection he said: "I regret the necessity of saying this because it must have hurt you as much as her. Gabrielle was trying to do what she could to make up for her brother's treachery."

She turned to him at this with a startled look in her eyes. "I don't understand. What has Gaby told you?"

"She told me of the part he played in the conviction of Lavalette. She didn't know it herself until they were on their way to Naples. As soon as she heard he had turned state's evidence, she left him; and came back to Paris with the intention of doing whatever she could to make up for his terrible mistake. Her purpose last evening was to rouse people against the policy of the court. She hopes that Lavalette may still be saved."

"She has only made it worse!" Margot's voice had risen to an almost hysterical note. "How can you defend her when you must know that I feel the opposite way?"

"I think it was a brave thing she did. I have every sympathy with her desire to do whatever she can to save him."

"Even if you believed she was right, did you have to take her side so publicly? Against me? You're English and it's no concern of yours. Everyone there saw what you did. Can't you see the position in which I've been placed? They knew that we——" She stopped suddenly, her eyes full of tears. With one hand she fumbled blindly for her handkerchief. "What can I do now? What *can* I do?"

He was beginning to feel very sorry for her. In a humble voice he said, "I know this makes it very difficult for you."

"If you—if you had cared for me at all, you would have thought of that before everything."

"Will this have any effect on the ruling of the courts?"

"I hope not. I'm going to do everything to make sure it doesn't. It wouldn't be fair for me to pay for the things she's done." She wiped away the tears with a manner which said she did not intend to yield to such weakness again. "It wasn't *that* I was thinking about. You know it wasn't."

"You have no reason to fear what people say or think."

"But I do. I value the opinion of people of my own class."

"Everyone knows how loyal you've been. Nothing that can happen now will affect that."

She said in a very low voice: "I know that I have nothing to fear if I do what I should now. If I never see you again."

He was realizing how hard it was going to be to put into words what he had come to say. Before he could make the effort, she looked up suddenly and asked, "What else did Gaby tell you?"

"That she had seen you. That you knew she had left with her brother. I was surprised at that because you hadn't said anything about it."

"I intended to tell you. We've had no chance to talk at all. Did you think that I had purposely said nothing to you?"

"No. I was sure you intended to tell me later."

Margot spent several moments folding and refolding her handkerchief. She did not look at him while doing this, and he sensed that she was struggling to reach some decision. Finally she asked, "Are you going to see her again?"

The time had come when he must tell her of his decision. He hesitated, wondering how best it could be worded. "Of course I shall see her. In the first place, I must do what I can to get her safely out of Paris."

"Must it always be you? Have you no pride at all? Will you always run to her if she as much as crooks a finger?" The questions poured out with sudden violence. Her eyes were stormy and rebellious. In all the time he had known her he had never seen her give way to her feelings so completely.

"Margot, I must tell you——"

She got to her feet. "I want to think. We mustn't talk any further until I've had a chance to consider my position carefully."

Aware that he was losing his best opportunity for telling her what was in his mind, he watched her walk to the other end of the room. She sat down in a dispirited manner. In the position she took it was not possible for him to see her face, but the tense lines of her figure told him that she was fighting a battle with herself. "Tell her before it's too late," he thought. But he made no move to do so.

She sat there a long time. Finally she stood up, paused in a mechanical way to straighten a *nappe* on a table beside her, and then walked back to face him. Her manner had regained its usual composure.

"Before you came," she said, "I had made up my mind not to see you again. This is the kind of life I want. I want it, I think, more than anything else; and that may be impossible if I forgive you for taking sides so openly with Gabrielle." She was speaking in even tones. "But when I heard you were here I thought—never mind what I thought! I see now that I was wrong. You've said none of the things I expected you to say, that I wanted you to say. It's clear you haven't changed, Frank. That you never will."

The thought ran through his mind: "She's saying the things I intended to say myself. It will be much better this way. Let her have the satisfaction of thinking it has been her own decision."

"I'm quite sure now that I was right in the first place. Please, let us consider it settled without saying anything more." She smiled with almost complete composure. "So this must be good-by, Frank."

He bowed silently. Margot turned and walked toward the other end of the room. At the door she paused.

"It will make no difference in—in any other respect. The allowance will still be paid to them. Will you tell Gabrielle, please?"

"I'm certain she has no intention of seeing her brother again. It's not likely that she will want anything done for her."

"This is a family matter. We have our own ways of attending to such matters. I refuse to see her again but I'll send the Abbé to her to make the necessary arrangements. Will you be kind enough to tell her so that she can plan to meet him?"

"I'll tell her what you've said."

She reached for a bellpull on the wall. When one of the maids answered the summons, she said, "M'sieur Ellery is leaving, Mathilde."

In spite of the relief he felt that it had been settled, Frank was in a depressed mood as he followed the maid to the door. He had not loved Margot (he knew that now), but he had always been deeply fond of her. He always would be fond of her. It was sad that they must part on such terms. As he took up his hat he heard her footsteps crossing the parquetry floor toward him.

"You may go, Mathilde. I have something to discuss with M'sieur Ellery."

When the girl had gone Margot said impulsively, "We must part as friends, Frank."

"I'm glad you feel that way too. I was hoping——"

"We've been such good friends, haven't we? And for so long! I'll never forget how kind you always were to me—and to all of us."

She held out both her hands. Frank took them eagerly and they stood silent for several moments, looking steadily into each other's eyes. "There will be so many memories," she said then. "Jean Baptiste Achille and his savings. And his concern over his marbles!"

"And the feud with Mick Finnerty."

"And those sad days when poor Jean died. And the long ride when we were running away from London. I'll never forget how you looked in the prison when Jean and I paid you our visit."

"And your letters as well. I always looked forward to receiving them."

She smiled slowly and withdrew her hands. "It's so much better this way. Good-by, Frank."

"Good-by, Margot."

As he walked through the door he heard the Abbé return and ask in a hopeful tone, "It is hardly necessary to make out the list in duplicate, do you think?" and heard her answer, "But isn't it always wise to make lists in duplicate?"

Topp was waiting outside, his face and hands blue with the cold. Frank looked at him in surprise.

"Why didn't you go in?"

The man smiled knowingly. "I knew better'n that, sahib. No sense in two argyments going on at oncet."

"You mean the servants there knew——"

"In course, sahib. They allus knows everything what's going on. How that Romaine in kitchen wud a pitched into me!" He began to thresh his arms about in an effort to restore his circulation. "I sees beyond the end o' my nose too, sahib, even if I keeps my manchester quiet."

"We won't be coming back here, Windy."

"I knowed *that* afore ye went in." Topp's manner was cheerful. "If I might venture a 'pinion, it's all for the best. She's growed into a handsome ledy and from what I hears she'll have plenty o' the dimmock. But, sahib, she's got so she likes to do all the driving. And what a tight rein!" He shook his head emphatically. "She'll marry t'other un now. The young mouser with the Totterin' Bob face and I thinks we better be getting back afore we gets into a cod o' trouble here."

"Trouble? What do you mean?"

Topp looked up at his master and winked. "Vi'lets," he said. "Mighty expensible things, vi'lets. They'll cost some of us our heads if the Cumpess goes on wearing 'em. No sense to it, sahib. Can't she be perswaded to wear roses or orkshers for a change? Or"—with a sly wink—"to settle down and get hitched insted?"

"Would you favor the latter course?"

Topp grinned. "I allus liked the Cumpess," he said.

8

THE PLAN had been worked out with meticulous care. A single slip might ruin everything, so Frank was keeping an observant eye on the entrance wicket in the tall dark walls of the Conciergerie. The test would come in one minute and forty-five seconds exactly. If the Comtesse Lavalette had succeeded in changing clothes with her husband, and the latter had then passed the scrutiny of the inner guards, he would arrive before the last barrier at that precise instant. The gatekeeper would be more on the alert than the rest, that being his sole responsibility; and so the plan that Wilson had contrived to distract him must be timed perfectly.

It had been snowing moistly all day, and now ribbons of white were twined through the tracery of stone moldings, lending to the sooty buildings an even more mottled look, although it disappeared under the feet of pedestrians as soon as it settled. The slow-falling flakes were threatening to turn into rain, which, of course, would favor the plan; for then people would be in an even greater hurry and would have no eyes for what was happening in the streets. In spite of the comfort it brought him, Frank was sorry he had worn his long Polish overcoat. The double rows of round buttons down the front were nothing more than a sartorial sham and it was the hooks and eyes underneath which kept the garment fastened about him. He was very much afraid these would delay him in reaching in for his pistol if the need for it should arise. He considered transferring the firearm to an outer pocket but decided the action might attract attention.

"This is a completely absurd situation," he thought. "Why am I risking my liberty, and perhaps my life, on the slim chance of saving from the guillotine a man I've never even seen? Margot was right. I'm English and this is in no way my concern."

It was no more absurd, however, than breaking the laws of England to assist two suspects out of the country nor risking entry into the French lines during the Moscow retreat. It had been his devotion to Gabrielle which had led him into those past adventures, and now it was because of her he was lurking outside the great Paris prison to help cheat the knife of its Bonapartist victim. It was true that this time there was less excuse for his participation. Gabrielle's own safety was not in question. Why had he and Sir Robert Wilson allowed themselves to be talked into anything as thoroughly quixotic as this?

He was aware of a dark figure lurking in the shadows some paces back of him. This would be Michael Bruce. A sedan chair had appeared from a side street, and its two carriers had set it down on the pavement in front of the prison entrance. They were blowing on their fingers as an excuse for loitering there. So far, so good; everything was in readiness. He was disturbed, however, to find that a woman had stopped at the entrance and was talking to the outside guard. This could upset the plan, for two pairs of eyes might see more than one.

His lagging steps fell into a more purposeful stride as the last seconds ticked away. He heard Bruce walking briskly behind him—it must be Bruce, although no signal of recognition had passed between them—and his nerves tightened. As he came abreast of the entrance the man behind was right on his heels. He heard a sound of grating metal and saw that the doors were slowly swinging open. To the very second!

He turned sharply. Yes, it was Bruce. "Keep your distance!" he ordered. "Have you designs on my purse?"

"I'm no thief!" declared Bruce in angry French. "And I allow no be-damned Englishman to question my honesty!"

They could see that the altercation had won the attention of the guard and that so far the man was paying no attention to the opening of the doors behind him. Frank laid a hand on the shoulder of his fellow conspirator and the latter shook it off roughly, exclaiming: "If you're seeking trouble, Englishman, I'll be happy to oblige. My seconds shall call on you."

"Move on!" ordered the guard. "Take yourselves off, messieurs, and find another place for your quarrel."

"I appeal to you, m'sieur!" cried Bruce. "You've seen and heard. Am I to swallow such an affront?"

The woman spoke up at this point. "These English!" she said in tones of bitter scorn. "One would think the city belonged to them. They have no manners, these foreign pigs!"

Frank was taken completely by surprise. Since the night when Wilson and Company had been formed, Gabrielle had remained in strict seclusion and she had not been given a part in the operation of the plan. Nevertheless the voice was hers. He looked at the overdressed figure and received a quick glance of greeting from the one eye not concealed by the long drooping ostrich plume.

The guard came down the stone steps, motioning them to leave. Behind him the gate had swung open. A woman emerged wearing a long black cloak and leaning on the arm of a girl in her early teens. She was holding a handkerchief to her eyes and her shoulders were shaking in the intensity of her grief. Frank's heart gave a bound, for he knew it was not the Comtesse Lavalette. That distressed lady was a shade taller and much more slender than the figure in the black cloak. The Comte, he had been told, was a full inch shorter than his wife and inclined to be pudgy in build. The exchange had been accomplished, then, and all that remained was to keep the custodian of the gate from suspecting anything. Exultantly he went into action.

"I tell you the fellow had his hand in my pocket!" he cried, grappling with Bruce.

They wrestled with an angry exchange of insults, bumping into the guard and nearly throwing him off balance. The departing visitors had reached the pavement before the guard was able to extricate himself. Things were happening so fast that he had become completely upset.

"You must return the admittance card, madame," he said, at the same time endeavoring to shove the disputants aside.

The girl handed him the official slip, saying in a quavering voice, "My mother is not very well, m'sieur."

"It's not to be wondered at." The guard glanced at the card and folded it away in a pocket. He took a step forward as though to look them over more carefully. Everything depended now on what might happen in the next few moments. Would he insist on the removal of the handkerchief?

"I'll report to the Duke of Wellington that Englishmen are being robbed in the streets!" shouted Frank. He laid an arm on the guard's sleeve. "You saw it. You'll be a witness."

Gabrielle contributed a scornful, "We care nothing for your *Villainton!*"

The guard apparently had not heard this recent stage witticism, which had become very popular in Paris, for he looked at Gabrielle approvingly and laughed. "That's very good, mam'selle. No, we care nothing for *Villainton.*"

"You'll have reason to care when I've made my report," said Frank with increased heat.

One of the carriers had opened the door of the chair. The figure in black stepped in, the young girl following with nervous haste. The chairmen took their places between the shafts and began to move off, the vehicle swaying and creaking as though the fears of the conspirators had been communicated to it.

Frank found it hard to restrain an impulse to shout: "Not too fast! Don't let him suspect anything! Not too fast! Not too fast!"

The pace of the carriers steadied down. The guard said to Gabrielle in an important tone: "That was the little Lavalette! Her last visit to him, poor lady."

Gabrielle answered excitedly, "Really, m'sieur? You must tell me about her."

Bruce had already moved on. After waiting a few breathless moments, Frank also began to walk away. He was now repeating the mental warning for his own benefit. "Go slowly. No haste. He mustn't suspect anything now." He was trying desperately to conceal his limp.

He could see over his shoulder that Gabrielle had taken the guard by the arm and was talking to him in an animated way. The guard threw back his head and laughed. He was so interested in her that he did not look once in their direction. Frank thought exultantly: "The plan has worked! We've saved him."

The escape of so important a prisoner could not fail to be discovered quickly. Perhaps the attendants inside the forbidding stone walls had already found that the figure crouching behind a screen in the cell of the condemned man was the Comtesse. Frank expected momentarily to hear the loud hue and cry which would follow this discovery. He fumbled with nervous fingers for his pistol, ripping off several pairs of hooks and eyes in his haste. He had succeeded in transferring the pistol to an outer pocket when a hand touched his arm and Gabrielle said in a breathless voice: "Oh, Frank! He's free! Isn't it wonderful? He's free!"

Bruce, a dozen paces ahead, turned and said, "Ssh! Not so loud." He stopped for them to catch up. The flawing wind was wet with rain now, and the side street into which they turned was deserted save for themselves and the swaying chair. Bruce patted Gabrielle's arm and said, "Well played, my dear lady," in a highly approving tone. She accepted an arm of each and almost skipped along between them, saying in awed tones, "He's really free!" and then, "Isn't it exciting?"

"A bit too exciting for my taste," confessed Bruce. "'Pon my word, I thought for a moment back there my heart would stop."

Two cabriolets were waiting where the Quai des Orfèvres faced the Rue d'Hurlay. The chair came to a stop and one of the carriers said in a cultivated voice, "Here we are, my dear Comte."

A figure in a dicky greatcoat and a round silver-laced hat emerged from inside and looked uneasily about. Lavalette had changed clothes in such frantic haste that he had forgotten one shoe, and he gave a gasp of dismay as his stockinged foot sank into the slush on the cobbled road.

"Quick! The first carriage, Comte!" admonished the carrier.

The escaped prisoner said, "Is that you, Georges, old friend?" and then plunged hurriedly into the first of the cabriolets. The driver whipped up his horses and was off with a grind of wheels and a clatter of hoofs. In a very few moments the carriage had disappeared on the Pont St. Michel.

"Well," said Bruce, "that seems to settle matters rather nicely. Did you notice the driver of the carriage? That was our doughty Sir Robert."

The house in the Faubourg St. Honoré was in darkness when they arrived. Guillaume took the precaution of inspecting them through the judas in the door before opening it.

"I'm at home to no one for the rest of the evening except Sir Robert Wilson," said Bruce cheerfully. "And now I really think we're entitled to a comfortable bite of supper. We won't wait for Sir Robert. There's no telling when he'll put in an appearance."

A table had been laid in the same small room back of the stairs. The host, after ensconcing Gabrielle in a chair before the fire, busied himself over the selection of the wines. She sank back and closed her eyes with a sigh which she tried to stifle. Frank drew a chair up beside her.

"Are you very tired?"

She opened her eyes and smiled at him. "A little." Her hand rested on his for a moment and then was withdrawn. "Frank, I've balanced the account!"

"Yes, he owes his escape to you."

"I feel free in my mind for the first time since I found what Sosthène had done. I feel very happy." Her eyes began to smile. "You didn't recognize me at first, did you?"

"Not immediately. Your disguise was most effective. Of course I knew your voice as soon as you spoke."

"That poor guard was quite taken in. He thought I was—what you thought at first. I had to make up an address to give him. Will Sir Robert be angry with me?"

"Not when he finds how helpful you were. I don't believe we would have managed it without you."

She closed her eyes again. After a moment she asked, "What news have you for me of Margot?"

"I haven't seen her for several days. Not since the morning after the excitement at the Odéon." He hesitated. "I'm not going to see her again."

Gabrielle sat up straight in her chair at that. "Have you quarreled?"

"No. But we found we held different views on many things."

She was watching him intently. "Everyone said you were going to marry her. I've seen very few people but I've made a point of finding out all about you. It seems they've been very much upset at court because an Englishman was to carry off their richest heiress. Was it true? Were you going to marry her?"

He found explanations difficult. "I—I realized you had put me completely out of your life. I had been very unhappy about it, and finally I decided I would have to plan something else for myself."

"You needn't be so apologetic about it. I *have* treated you badly. It was the natural thing for you to do."

"But it wasn't. Not for me. The natural thing would have been to go on exactly as I was. To go on hoping." He was finding it increasingly difficult. "I did the unnatural thing. I tried to fall in love with Margot; and there were times when I thought I was succeeding. But . . ." He looked around cautiously. Bruce was bending over a side table, deep in consideration of the relative suitability of two wines. "When I saw you at the theater I knew I could never love anyone else. I knew in the very first instant that I was as much in love with you as ever."

"I don't think you should tell me this."

"Why not?" His voice was emphatic and eager again. "I'm back now where I was before. Where I've always been, if I had known my own mind. I can still go on loving you. I can still hope perhaps."

She sighed deeply. "But, my constant one, it's more hopeless than ever. You must see that. I've succeeded so thoroughly in ruining my life! I have no reputation left, no prospects. I have no regrets for the course I've taken, but also I have no illusions. You heard what that foolish La Bellilote said. Everyone believes I was Napoleon's mistress." She turned her head on the back of the chair to look at him directly. "And I can't help feeling sorry for Margot."

"I'm sure you don't need to. I went there that morning with the intention of telling her what I've just told you. But she took the decision into her own hands. I came away with the conviction that she values her secure way of living above everything else."

Gabrielle shook her head thoughtfully. "I'm not sure of that. It's true she wouldn't want to disturb things. She likes her way of living. *Her* way. But she wanted you also. Which was the stronger?"

"She made that quite clear."

"You're forgetting, Frank, that you had offended her bitterly. And you didn't try to make your peace with her. *That* was what drove her to making up her mind. If you really wanted her, she might have braved all the consequences of standing by you."

"But she would have regretted it later. I've thought about it a great deal since and I'm sure of that. I don't need to tell you how completely set she is in all her beliefs and ideas."

"But she's unhappy about it now. And that makes me unhappy for her."

"My man—a consistent admirer of yours, by the way——"

Gabrielle smiled. "Like master, like man?"

"It seems so. He took the liberty the other day of saying she would always have to do the driving; and with the tightest kind of rein."

The smile grew into a light laugh. "He's very shrewd, that Topp. Our little Margot is the masterful kind. She always was, even back in the London days. Now that she's in the driver's seat, she'll never give it up. And with *such* a tight rein! The gait will always be the same. Steady and sure. No mad cantering, no going off at full gallop just for the joy of it."

"Not even when a full gallop is the only way to get there on time?"

"Margot will always get there on time without any need for hurrying." She subsided again with a sigh. "How different we are! I'm such a rattle-brain. Never on time. Always in trouble."

"If you didn't get yourself into trouble, I would never have any part in your life." He raised one of her hands from the arm of the chair and kissed it. "Well, here we are, exactly as we started. I'm at your feet and you're doing your best to create an obstacle between us. A new one, this time."

"A very real one, *mon petit chou*. I have no wish to ruin your life. You must see how completely *déclassée* I've made myself."

"As to that, we shall see. I'll have something to say about it at a more suitable time. And before we drop the subject of your cousin, she wants you to see the Abbé Force."

"The poor old Abbé! What is it about?"

"The matter of an allowance."

Gabrielle shook her head with fierce determination. "No, no, I won't have that. I'll get along somehow. Sossy will take money from her but I prefer my independence. My pride is all I have left."

"I'm sure you'll get along somehow. In fact, I have an idea how it can be done."

Bruce, who had left the room on some errand relating to food, returned with a cheerful announcement that supper was ready. "There's a splendid allspice soufflé, my fellow conspirators," he said, rubbing his hands. "And a most meritorious sole with lobster sauce. There's even a cold round of sirloin for any of us who still hold by *Jean Bool* tastes. We shall do very well. A glass of wine, Comtesse?"

"Thank you. I think that's all I shall want. Excitement robs me of my appetite."

"It stimulates mine. Well, then, a toast. To the Comtesse Lavalette, who has earned a place in history with that brave Englishwoman we were told about and whose name has already escaped me."

Frank raised his glass. "The next toast must be to another gallant and still more lovely lady."

It was a full hour before Wilson arrived, accompanied by a tall young Irishman who was introduced as Captain Hely-Hutcheson. The pair of them were in the highest spirits. Wilson was so completely on top of the world, in fact, that he had reverted to the tumultuous manner of speech which Frank had noticed in him during the early days of their acquaintance.

"I hear you were out with us after all, my dear Gabrielle," he said, setting to work briskly on his supper. "Well, we may all feel we did a neat job of it. A remarkably successful little coup. Everything went like clockwork. And a remarkably fine bit of beef, Bruce. That's the worst of living in Paris. You get such damned bad beef and mutton. I get tired of kickshaws dressed up in nauseous sauces. Give me a cut off the joint every time." He looked up from his plate with a broad smile. "The city's buzzing with excitement. People are mad with joy over the escape. Positively mad. In the theaters they stood up and cheered, Royalists as well as Bonapartists. That should teach old Twenty-stone something. In spite of the rain there's still a mob outside the prison, booing the police. We dropped in at the Lemblin and found it full of grognards, swigging brandy in a positive delirium of enthusiasm."

"Has a safe place been found for him?" asked Bruce.

Wilson's eyes lighted up. "We've done a rather smart thing there. A damned smart thing. The Comte at the moment is"—he looked around the board with an air of self-congratulation—"in the Department of Foreign Affairs!"

"Do you mean it?" Bruce looked properly aghast.

"I mean it. The very last place they would look for him, barring the Tuileries and police headquarters. A friend of his has rooms in the Office and was willing to take him in for a few days. They may be holding a conference there this very instant to discuss what's to be done about it; and their man sleeping like a baby on the floor above them. Rather amusing, eh?" He was attacking his sirloin with an exuberant appetite. "We'll get him out of there as soon as the first excitement dies down. I thought, Bruce, you might take him in here until we can risk getting him clear of the city."

"Of course," said Bruce, as though the matter were of no more consequence than an addition to a week-end list.

"My stout fellow! I knew I could depend on you. And now that we've put our shoulders to the wheel or, to be more accurate, now that we have our fingers deep in the French political pie, there's going to be more work for us. The story we hear is that the gentle court ladies are more determined than ever to find victims. They're fairly shrieking for the heads of some of the others on the list—Lallemand, Chartrain, Mouton-Duvernet, Drouet d'Erlon, just to mention a few. Under these circumstances"—he smiled at the expectant company over the rim of his wineglass—"we shall have to take steps to see that they don't succeed."

Bruce raised his glass. "To Wilson and Company!" he cried. "And the continuation of our efforts."

"You want to go on with it, then?"

"Count on me," said Hely-Hutcheson.

Frank noticed that Gabrielle did not seem in accord with the idea of further meddling in political matters. She was watching Wilson with a worried frown.

"Wilson and Company will lose at least one of its members tomorrow," said Sir Robert, turning in her direction. "It comes down to this, my dear lady: the court party is alarmed over the feeling shown in the city and they're disposed to blame you for starting it. The talk at the Lemblin was that they would insist on your arrest. They want to make an example of you. That won't do at all. I've already made arrangements to get you out of Paris."

Gabrielle looked both surprised and disappointed. "I think, if you don't mind, I would rather stay. I started this. I talked you into taking this serious risk. I can't run away now and leave you."

Wilson shook his head emphatically. "Suppose they got their hands on you? We can't allow them that very great satisfaction. No, no, our very next step will be to see you safely on your way. You're to leave with the family of a very fine South American tomorrow morning."

"So soon! Please, Sir Robert——"

"There won't be a better chance. Quick action, that's the ticket. We must have you out of here before they stop gnashing their teeth over tonight's little success. I've made all the arrangements. You're to go along as the family governess, with a black hood over your lovely and very well-known face."

Gabrielle asked in a humble voice, "At what time do we leave?"

"Seven o'clock sharp. You'll find yourself in rather extraordinary company and the trip will be interesting; and you'll be as safe as a new pupil in a girls' seminary." Wilson turned to Frank. "I anticipate no difficulty over this, but we must think of every contingency. If anything slipped, the South American would be powerless. The best he could do would be to say that he hired his governess with no knowledge of who she was. I think, my militant publisher, you had better be on hand to help."

"I was on the point of suggesting it," said Frank.

"Your papers are in order?"

"Yes. I'm at liberty to travel about the country and to cross the border at any time or at any point."

"Good. In the police reports an Englishman who limps is associated with the Comtesse de Vitrelle. You must never be seen with the party. Some nosy official might put two and two together. The plan, then, will be to follow the same road, to be in the offing whenever stops are made, and to put up at nights in the same towns. You and the Comtesse can devise some method of keeping in regular communication. The weather's going to be nasty. I hope"—with a smile—"you won't mind the hardships of the journey?"

Frank smiled back. "I'm willing to face them."

"Now that we have all that settled, I think I'll have another slice of beef, Bruce."

A cobwebbed bottle of port was produced. Gabrielle whispered to Frank when the other three men drew together to discuss it, "I've something to say to you." No attention was paid to them when they rose and left the room.

They walked down the hall to the room in front, which was in darkness. Frank lighted a candle in one of the wall sconces with a hand which had become suddenly nervous. He was thinking, "This will be my chance to win her over." There had been company in the room earlier, for the atmosphere was heavy with tobacco fumes and a map was spread out on the table with a forest of pins sticking in it.

Gabrielle chose a chair beside the piano. "Frank, I'm frightened," she whispered. "Something came over me as I listened to Sir Robert. A premonition, if you like. There's going to be trouble. Serious trouble. I'm sure of it."

"We knew the danger when we went into this."

"I was the one who persuaded you. That's why I'm worried now. We must see they do nothing more. Sir Robert has a cool head but he loves risks. The others will follow him blindly. We must stop them from going on."

"I'm afraid he has the bit in his teeth. I've seen him in difficult places before. The greater the danger, the better he likes it."

"You must all leave the country at once. There shouldn't be any difficulty about it now. Later—I tremble to think what may happen. Your

Sir Robert is impulsive and I think he's inclined to talk more than he should. Something is sure to get out. You're all Englishmen and this isn't your quarrel. What you did tonight was wonderful; but, please, it should be the end."

"I think you're right. I'm devoted to Wilson, as you know, and I don't want to see him in trouble."

"And I don't want to see you in trouble." Her worried air gave place to a smile. "I think we might say that I'm devoted to *you*. Enough to give you some advice as well. You're not to come with me, Frank. I'll be perfectly safe. You must leave France as quickly as you can. But before you go"—she hesitated a moment—"you should see Margot and make your peace with her. I mean it from the bottom of my heart."

"We parted on the best of terms. We're friends now and, I think, we always will be. But nothing more, Gaby."

"It's not too late to repair the breach I've caused between you."

Frank leaned down and tried to capture her hands. She drew back, shaking her head.

"Gaby, understand this. I'm in love with you. I'm never going to change, no matter how many obstacles you find."

Gabrielle shook her head with almost fierce determination. "I'm trying to be unselfish for once. Do you realize, Frank, how utterly selfish and unfair I've been to you? I've thought of myself always and never of you." There were tears in her eyes. "I was willing even to involve you, and your friends, in this conspiracy in order to repair a wrong my brother had committed. To give myself peace of mind, I persuaded you to risk your lives and your freedom for a man you had never seen." A wisp of handkerchief was applied to her eyes with sudden energy. "From now on there shall be nothing more of the kind! I'm going to think of you, of others, and not of myself. I'm going to do what I know will be best for you. And I know—oh, how well I know it!—that you should put me right out of your mind and marry Margot."

"Wouldn't it make you unhappy at all if I did?"

"That's something we won't discuss. If I were unhappy, it would be nothing more than justice."

Frank smiled. "But we must discuss it. It's the only point that counts. But first I must dispose of these obstacles you are raising."

"I'm not raising them. They already exist. It's not only that you couldn't marry a woman with my reputation. I'm dreadfully poor. I haven't anything left. I've sold most of my jewelry and even some of my laces and linens."

"Your poverty is a heaven-sent opportunity. I'm prepared to take full advantage of it."

"Frank, I know your situation at home. It will be a long time before you own the paper, and you need a wife with money to help you. Margot is the perfect match for you. If you won't look at your position sensibly, I must do it for you."

He smiled again. "When have you been inclined to look at things from the sensible viewpoint?"

"I'm not sensible about anything concerning myself but I'm going to be about you. The sooner you're quit of me, the better it will be for you. And that's not all."

"What! Still another obstacle?"

"One more. The most serious one, perhaps. I'm not a constant person at all. Men seem to like me and—well, you've seen for yourself. I've always been a flirt and I'm afraid I always shall be. My poor weak Jules suffered a great deal because of it, and now that he's dead I realize how badly I treated him. If I should marry again, my husband would suffer even more because my flightiness would keep that dreadful story alive. There's no use my saying I will reform. I would make you perfectly miserable."

"You would make me perfectly happy. I understand you thoroughly. Your flirtations wouldn't mean a thing and I would never be unhappy about them."

"You may believe that now. You would change your mind about it later. No, no, Frank, we *must* be sensible. Nothing you say can make me change my mind."

"You're overlooking a fundamental truth. All people are divided into two classes. There are those who get happiness through having the love of others. They are the ones who show jealousy. And then there are the more fortunate ones who achieve content and happiness through loving. It happens I belong to the second class. I can be happy just loving you. I would never be jealous. You could flirt as much as you liked. No! I would draw the line, after all. I could never condone flirtation with Caradoc."

She laughed unwillingly. "How stubborn you are! How can I make you see I'm right about this?"

"You belong to me, Gabrielle, and I'm going to go on asserting my claim until I force you to give in." He was watching her intently. "Were you unhappy with me in Russia?"

She still refused to look at him. "No," she said in a low tone. "On the contrary . . ." She got to her feet. "It was a mistake to talk about this now. I should never have started it. We have something to settle before we can begin to think about the future. We must see to it that Wilson and Company is dissolved."

He snuffed out the single candle and then, as the room reverted to darkness, he gathered her into his arms. She yielded, willingly enough, as he held her fiercely, possessively.

"Gabrielle?"

"Yes, my brave Englishman?"

"You do love me a little?"

"A very great deal. Enough to know I must protect you from future unhappiness."

He kissed her then and she returned the embrace with a breathlessness that equaled his own. It was several moments before she drew herself free.

"The last time, my Frank," she said. "I'm sorry, but it's the very last time. This must be our real farewell. I mean it. Oh yes, I do. I mean it."

He laughed confidently. "We'll see about that. And now we must go back. I hope you're more successful in convincing Sir Robert."

9

WILSON HAD ADVISED Frank to make contact with the South American party at La Chapelle. When he arrived there, however, he found that no carriages answering the description of the quite extraordinary train of the Mendoza family had been seen.

"Must have missed 'em, sahib," said Windy Topp with considerable satisfaction. He was not enjoying the ride at all, and it was clear he expected the mishap would result in a change of plan.

"No, we haven't missed them," declared his employer. "I think we've been deliberately misled. Now we shall have to find what road they *did* take."

He was wondering if Gabrielle had persuaded Señor Mendoza to travel by another route. Her determination to have him follow what she believed was his only sensible course had been so clearly expressed the previous evening that it was quite possible she had taken this precaution. He smiled and said to himself, "You can't make me change my mind as easily as that, Gabrielle."

It was not until they reached Senlis that they overtook the five carriages making up the Mendoza cortege. Wilson had said that Gabrielle would travel in bizarre company and it was now clear that this was not an exaggeration. The leading carriage, a cumbersome and gilded affair with silver mountings on the panels, looked a little like a royal conveyance but also very much like a funeral coach. Cantering up and down the line, with muskets hooked to their saddles, were half a dozen outriders. On each box sat a footman in a blue cloak and an absurdly wide hat. If the party had some of the magnificence of a regal processional, it completely lacked the dignity. The outriders sang with true gaucho abandon, the drivers cracked their whips at dogs, all of them swore loudly and continuously. Children poked their heads out of the windows and screamed at each other, causing a pompous gentleman, who undoubtedly was *el papá*, to put his head out in turn from the white and silver monstrosity in front and shout admonishingly: "Joaquín! Eufemia! Rafael! Angela!"

It was growing dusk and the carriages, with more shouting than ever and a great deal of whip-cracking, turned for the night into the courtyard of an inn. Frank and his man reined in at the far side of the road to watch. Don Lope Sancho María Miguel Mendoza emerged at once to take charge of the disembarkation. He was a porpoise of a man with a kindly face not at all in keeping with the truculent upward twist of his immense mustaches. Taking on himself the superintendence of everything, he rushed about, waved his pudgy arms and bawled orders like an excited quartermaster. Doña Mendoza seemed well content to let her clucking spouse carry this burden; she was small and reserved in wide black bombazine skirts and with a gentle face conspicuously marked by the dread *bexigas*. The children, carrying food and confections in bags, swarmed out after her. Frank counted them until he gave up in wonder.

"Fourteen!" he said to Topp. "Do you suppose they all belong to the one family, Windy?"

"In course, sahib. These Spanish wimmen don't perduce one scrawny brat and then quit. They perduces twenty scrawny brats."

The children seemed to have the full responsibility for a great variety of pets: parrots and lovebirds in cages, a pair of fat poodles, a kinkajou on a brass chain which they called Potto and seemed especially concerned about, a number of disobedient cats. It was not until they had disappeared into the inn, pets and all, that Gabrielle stepped down from the second carriage. She was bundled up in a black coat and a lace-trimmed fur hood. As it was quite cold, she hurried inside at once.

"The mem sahib 'ull be glad o' a little peace and quiet atter a day o' *that*," said Windy Topp.

Following dinner in the inn they found for themselves, Frank wrote a

note to Gabrielle and dispatched it in care of his man. Topp returned
with a brief reply.

I thought I had been so clever about changing our route! Frank, Frank,
will you never be wise where your own interests are concerned? I meant
it when I begged you to forget me and to make your peace with Margot
before leaving for England.

But now that you *are* here, I must confess that I am weak enough to be
glad. I purposely did not look about when I left the coach this evening because I could not bear to think I would not see you. How inconsistent I
am! And how incurably selfish! I am living with a traveling circus. All we
lack is a striped tiger and a troupe of tumblers. But they are all very sweet
to me. I don't like to think of you riding so forlornly in the cold behind us,
but there is comfort in the thought that you are well away from Paris. I
fear that our impulsive R.W., who laughed at our advice, may be headed
for trouble. *Adios.*

G.

The next day was stormy and they did not travel far as a result. When
night came Frank indited a note into which he poured all his devotion
and his desire to take her on with him to England; where, he assured her,
she could be happier than in any part of France under the existing circumstances. Her reply was disappointing, for it lacked the unreserved
tone of her first. He must forget her, she protested. All the reasons she
had given him still held good. She was planning to continue on to Brussels with the Mendoza family, and it would save them both much unhappiness if he did not follow them beyond the border.

Had she really meant it, then? Must he reconcile himself to the fact
that the fleeting glimpses he would be able to obtain of her during the
course of this journey would be the end? He sat for a long time in front
of his meager fire and thought gloomily of this sad prospect. It was not
even certain that he would have an opportunity to talk to her again, to
make one final and desperate effort to change her mind.

Well, there would be plenty of work for him to do. The war was over
and the influence of the paper could be turned at last to the many matters
which needed attention at home. He might be able to forget his unhappiness in the struggles for reform which stretched ahead. It was not peace
he was going back to, he reflected soberly, but war of an even bitterer
kind than the one from which the world had just emerged. There was a
letter in his pocket from Cope in which that ardent crusader demanded
his immediate return, that the work might begin.

The journey proved a slow one. Frank and his man rode at a discreet
distance and never put up at the same inn. There was snow on the

ground, and a penetrating wind blew continually from the north. There was ample reward for trying hours in the saddle when he would see her alight at the end of the day; but Topp, lacking this, was disposed to grumble at the cold and to dilate on the comfort of the government diligences. Frank wrote a note to Gabrielle each evening and received brief but cheerful replies, sometimes by way of Topp, sometimes delivered by one of the swarthy servants in the inevitable broad hat and enveloping cloak, like the villain in a melodrama. He began to acquire through her comments an acquaintance with the amazing Mendoza household. "We live in turmoil," she wrote once. "We carry our own linens, and all the beds have to be made over as soon as we arrive. We have our own cook, who must be installed at once in the kitchen. One of the carriages is packed with special foods, even fruit sent on from Spain (*packed in ice*, actually!) but which they call by their own curious names: manoons, grumaxims, custard apples. In spite of the profits, the innkeepers are always relieved to see us go!" The small Josefa, her favorite among the children, had acquired a touch of colic and was requiring a great deal of attention. She insisted on the presence of Potto, which was the first real hardship Gabrielle had encountered. Don Lope, knowing who she was and aware also of the hovering escort, was becoming very curious about her invisible cavalier. She had told him that he, Frank, was an Englishman of great wealth and mysterious influence.

In one note she gave him the reason for the presence in France of the Mendoza family. Don Lope, who was unbelievably rich, was filled with the belief that the world had gone through the greatest period in history and he wanted *los niños* to see as much of it as possible with their own eyes. So here they were and they were missing nothing. They had gone over Paris from top to bottom and had paid visits to Malmaison and even to Morefontaine, where Joseph Bonaparte had lived. Don Lope had been quite upset on finding three billiard tables at Morefontaine while he had only two at home, and special tables for biribi and macao, of which he had never even heard. Now they were on their way to spend the winter at a watering place, and in the spring they would begin a tour of the battlefields. They planned to go even as far as that dreadful Russia. Don Lope was gathering souvenirs with a lavish hand and one of the carriages was already filled with them. He spent his evenings writing down his impressions and she was proving of great help to him in the matter. He had begun to call her his *chica* Gabrielle. "They are the most affectionate family in the whole world, I think," she wrote, "and they have taken me right in as one of them. They insist I must spend the rest of the time with them."

"I shall have something to say about that," thought Frank, folding the note away among *his* souvenirs.

At Courtrai, with the ordeal of the border inspection behind them, he felt justified in intruding himself on the party. After allowing them time for dinner and for the children to be packed off to bed, he called at the inn where the Mendoza entourage was installed. The place was in an uproar, with the visiting servants everywhere, and as a result there was some delay in announcing him.

He was shown, finally, into an upstairs parlor. Don Lope had been engaged on his notes, for the table was littered with papers, but he had given up the work and retired to a seat beside his wife in front of the fire. A *vihuela* lay across his knee, and he was thrumming on it in a desultory way. Gabrielle was not in the room.

Don Lope bounced to his feet and came forward to greet the visitor. "Ha, the mysterious stranger!" he intoned in very bad French. "At last we set eyes on our hovering guardian angel! We've been much interested in you, señor, and in all that the Comtesse has told us about you. Rachel, I present the Señor Allaire."

Frank bowed. "It did not seem wise to pay my respects until we had crossed the frontier. As you know, there was reason to fear the Comtesse might encounter some difficulty there. That's behind us now, thanks to your very great kindness."

"Phut! It was nothing. Nothing at all. We've enjoyed the slight seasoning of suspense the Comtesse's presence has lent to our journey. Take a seat, señor, if you please." Don Lope fell back into his own chair, causing it to creak alarmingly. "As I said, we've been hearing a great deal about you, and all most favorable. It is our hope you will continue with us for as much of the journey as now remains."

Doña Mendoza, who had suspended work on her stitching, smiled compliance with this. She had been a beauty in her day, Frank decided, but such share of her once good looks as remained to her was confined to a pair of fine dark eyes, expressing the utmost kindliness and warmth. She was wearing a great deal of jewelry, including a cabochon emerald of remarkable size at her throat.

"I'm afraid I can't have that pleasure," said Frank, taking a chair. "You are on your way to Brussels, are you not? I must return to England at once and I'm hoping the Comtesse will also go to England."

"No, no!" cried Don Lope with so much agitation that the round gold buttons on his purple coat, each with a cluster of diamonds in the center, shook visibly. "She has promised to continue with us. We couldn't think of parting with her."

They seemed so genuine and so friendly that Frank decided to take them into his confidence. They might, he thought, be won over to his support. "I'm hoping to persuade her to become my wife," he said. "I've been in love with her for eight years, and this will be my last chance to win her consent. If she leaves me now, I may never see her again."

Doña Mendoza's eyes lighted up with immediate understanding and sympathy. "Then we must put no obstacles in your way," she declared.

Don Lope's fingers swept excitedly across the strings of the *vihuela*. "The fact of your devotion has been very clear to us. But eight years! It's an eternity!" He leaned forward to address his wife. "Rachel, the one for whom you are named, compelled Jacob to wait seven years for her. You were less cruel and exacting. Our courtship was a matter, rather, of seven weeks."

"Seven months, I think, my heart." She smiled at him and then turned to Frank. "I'm sure you have met with very special difficulties, señor, to cause such a very long wait."

"There have always been difficulties. Gabrielle's family left England to return to France and she was married shortly after. You may know, perhaps, that it wasn't a successful marriage. There's a rather more subtle difficulty now. Gabrielle feels——" He paused, uncertain as to whether he should continue with any further explanations. "This is something I have no right to discuss, but you are being very kind and understanding; and I feel desperately in need of advice. The truth of the matter is that she feels it would be against my own interests for us to be married now."

An outburst of sound reached them from the floor above—childish voices raised in expostulation and much stamping of feet. The head of the family ran to the door and shouted: "Julian! Xavier! Cristina! María Rosa!" The noise stopped at once and he returned to his chair, raising his hands in a despairing gesture.

"*Los niños!*" he exclaimed. "They are blessed with such spirits! If they knew the English señor was here, they would not hesitate to invade us in a body. They talk about you, señor, a very great deal." He picked up the instrument and drew a few chords from it in an absent-minded manner. "It's a good thing our *chica* Gabrielle retired early this evening. It gives us an opportunity to talk with full freedom."

"It's clear," said his wife, "that such a reason is hard for you to combat, señor. Has Gabrielle made it clear that she has a—a preference for you?"

"As to that," cried Don Lope, "there can be no doubt at all! I tell you that I have been watching her. She carries a pensive air all the time. How impatiently she waits for the notes which come every evening! How disappointed she was when none came this time. It was clear she wasn't expecting you, señor. No, Rachel, we need no assurances on that score, none at all."

"I can't tell you how happy it has made me to hear that," said Frank. "But—I must be a very poor advocate. So far I've failed to shake her resolution."

"When words won't prevail," cried Don Lope, "it's time to resort to action! Señor, you must take matters into your own hands. She must be swept off her feet."

"And how, my heart, would you advise doing that?" asked his wife. The head of the family opened his mouth to supplement his advice but the practical application she had demanded seemed to elude him. He said finally: "There must be a way. There's always a way."

His wife took up the burden herself. "I think there may be a way. But the señor must be very sure there is no other reason for her to refuse her consent."

"I know of no other reason," declared Frank.

"There is none," affirmed Don Lope with a wave of his pudgy hand which swept all doubts aside, as far as he was concerned at least. "I know the signs. Our Gabrielle is waiting for him to make up her mind for her. It's the way with all women. They can never be coaxed or wheedled. They must be carried away in spite of all their doubts and fears. Haven't I good reason to know that, my Rachel?"

His wife nodded her head and smiled. "I think there's some truth in what you say. But it would be very difficult if we should follow the plan I have in mind, only to find that she had reservations of which we knew nothing."

"It must be risked. The señor must have his opportunity." Don Lope dropped the *vihuela* to the floor in the intensity of his interest. "Santa María, what is your precious plan, then? Must there be so much mystery about it!"

Frank was thinking, "They have taken the matter completely out of my hands." Certainly they paid little attention to him as they threshed out between them the conduct of his matrimonial campaign.

"Must you be so impatient?" Having thus admonished her spouse, the good lady went on in even tones. "It's very simple. We must have Father Iniguez ready and this room prepared for the ceremony. I may not be able to obtain flowers in this cold country—it would be so simple at home! —but perhaps it will be possible to find holly and evergreen branches. The altar must be set up, the candles lighted. The señor will then bring Gabrielle to the door——"

"Yes, yes! That's it!" exclaimed Don Lope, fairly bouncing in his seat.

"The element of surprise! She mustn't know a thing about it until she enters the room——"

"Not a thing. Not a hint. She must be entirely unprepared."

"The very idea I had in my mind! It's the only way to bring her to her senses. I swear it will succeed where any attempts at persuasion might fail."

Doña Mendoza nodded her head several times. "But it will all depend on the señor himself. When she sees what has been done, and stands there at the door, he must know exactly the right words to say to her."

"Words!" cried Don Lope with deep scorn. "Not words, my Rachel. He must take her firmly by the arm and walk her to the altar before she has any chance to think at all. I swear again it is action which will carry the day for us."

"Perhaps. But I think we must leave that to the señor. I'm sure he will know then the right thing to be done."

Frank was finding it impossible to think clearly. This extraordinary course they were planning might bring him the supreme happiness he sought; but, on the other hand, it might alienate Gabrielle so completely that his hopes would be quenched for all time. While he hesitated the worthy couple continued to discuss details in self-congratulatory tones.

"It is clearly the only way, Rachel."

"Yes, my heart, I agree. We must get right to work, then." There was the light of battle in her eyes. "There are only a few hours to do so many things. I'm disturbed about the material for the pall——"

"A few hours!" Her husband looked suddenly doubtful. "Are you thinking it can be done tomorrow?"

"And why not? Do you see any objections? You, the impatient one, the preacher of action!"

The discussion continued at a still more staccato pace, with Frank taking little or no part. Eufemia, the oldest of the girls, was summoned from above and inducted into the secret, after first being pledged solemnly to secrecy. She was a lovely child of about ten years with enormous black-fringed eyes.

"Now, my Eufemia, you must help me," said her mother. "You must see to it that the rest are very tidy and very well behaved. But there must be no hint to any of them. That small Josefa would run to Gabrielle the very first thing and tell her."

"But I think Gabrielle would like to know," protested the child.

"It would be fatal!" cried her mother. "No, Eufemia, she must be kept away from this room all morning. Perhaps she would take them all out for a walk. Are there not churches to be seen? Or shops to be visited? I leave it to you, Eufemia."

"Yes, Mother."

The girl sat down in front of Frank and stared at him seriously for a matter of several minutes. He squirmed under her steady regard and was very much relieved when she turned to her mother to engage in a discussion of the suitability of the match.

"Does it seem to you, *madre mía*, that he is perhaps a little young?"

"No, no, Eufemia. Not too young, not too young at all."

"But *el papá* is much older than you are. Shouldn't a husband always be quite old? See, he has no beard."

"But in England, where the señor comes from, they may not wear beards."

"I thought husbands always had beards."

The child turned back and renewed her steady scrutiny. "The English señor is very rich, Mother?"

"I don't know. That's not a question for us. Perhaps the señor and *el papá* will have a talk about it."

"Gabrielle is *very* poor. She must marry someone who is rich to make up for it. I have heard Teresa say so."

"Teresa has too much to say for a servant. I shall speak to her sharply about it."

Eufemia finally gave Frank the delayed accolade of a smile. "I think perhaps I like him well enough. To be a proper husband for Gabrielle, one must be liked a very great deal."

"Thank you, Eufemia," said Frank.

When he arrived at the appointed hour next day, Frank found a spirit of anticipation pervading the inn. The Mendoza servants stood about in groups, whispering and smiling with a holiday air. By way of contrast, Don Lope, in sky-blue coat and breeches and white satin stockings, was in an unmistakably nervous state. He informed Frank that Gabrielle had just returned with the children from their walk and had retired to her room. The weather being very cold, none of them had enjoyed the walk and the children had seemed in no mood for the dressing up which Eufemia was now enforcing, as far as the younger ones were concerned, with much admonitory slapping.

"How did Gabrielle seem?" asked Frank in an anxious whisper.

Don Lope poised a hand in front of him with thumb and middle finger joined to dramatize his search for the correct word. "Suspicious," he said finally. "Perhaps a little resentful too. I didn't dare speak to her for fear she would sense something in my manner." His manner showed clearly that he shared Frank's trepidation in at least equal degree. "How do *you* feel?"

"I didn't sleep a wink all night, Don Lope. I'm afraid we're making a great mistake."

The South American shook his head doubtfully. "I share the same fear. We shall all look ridiculous and the result will be that our *chica* Gabrielle will never forgive us. If it were not that I hesitate to show my doubts to Rachel, I would think it wise to call a halt while there's still time."

"Great cowards!" hissed Doña Mendoza, who had come up behind them. "You, my heart, the brave demander of action! Have you lost all your courage or did you use it all up in bold words last evening? And Señor Allery! Has your courage deserted you also?"

"Can a prospective bridegroom have courage?" demanded her husband testily. "It's not to be expected."

"I'm concerned about Gabrielle," sighed Frank. "Is it fair to subject her to such an ordeal?"

"Come, come, young man." She patted him consolingly on the arm. "It can't be as bad as you fear. Didn't you say you had given up hope? Even if we fail, you'll be no worse off." She smiled at him warmly and added in a whisper, "But we're not going to fail."

"Why are you so sure, señora?"

"Call it intuition. I talked to her about you this morning and—she is *very* fond of you. I had to be sure of it first. Now I must go and see if the children are ready. Eufemia, I'm sure, is having a time with them. They were *so* cross when they came in. Then I shall go to Gabrielle."

"Rachel has told her we're to have important guests," explained Don Lope in a voice still packed with foreboding.

Frank went to the door of the parlor and looked in. The altar which accompanied the family on all their travels had been set up at the end of the room. The curtains had been drawn and candles by the score had already been lighted. The fireplace was a mass of evergreens and there were sprigs of green on the walls. The festive air thus created had a depressing effect on him, for it made the ultimate failure of the plan harder to bear.

The children had been marshaled into the room under the sharp supervision of Eufemia, and the servants had filed in after them, before Doña Mendoza returned with Gabrielle on her arm. The latter had been persuaded to adorn herself in a manner befitting the role for which she was cast and, despite the sinking of the heart that Frank experienced at the near approach of his humiliation, he was more conscious than ever before of her loveliness. She was dressed in white (that much he saw, but the other details he was to learn later) and her slender sleeves were rounded out at the shoulders with puckered muslin. The skirt was long enough to touch the floor and so wide at the base that it swayed as she walked. Frank watched her approach with tremulous absorption, sure that this was the last time he would ever see her and, on that account, desperately determined that no detail slip his memory.

She gave him a reproachful look. "You've been a long time in coming to see me," she said.

"I came last evening but you had retired," he managed to get out.

"You did?" She glanced with a puzzled air at the older woman. "No one mentioned it. And we were talking about you this morning." She looked up at him with sudden alarm. "You look very glum, Frank. Has there been bad news?"

"No. No news at all."

"Then why the gloomy air? You don't seem glad at all to see me. And I'm wearing my very most becoming dress. Has your gallantry deserted you, sir?"

Doña Mendoza had gone ahead into the parlor. Frank extended his arm and they followed slowly. His feet felt like lead.

"What's it all about?" she asked in a whisper. "Is it a surprise? Has Comte Lavalette arrived already? Tell me what it is."

At the door she stopped and gave a gasp. He could feel her hand tighten on his arm.

"What is this?" she demanded in a tense whisper.

He could find no words to answer her, and the silence which fell had for him all the certainty of doom. He tried to catch her eyes but she was looking straight ahead. Her hand had fallen from his arm.

"Gabrielle," he said in a low tone at last, "I intended for once to play a masterful part. But I find that I can't. All I can say to you is this: If you will walk to the altar with me, I will give you for all the years of my life the same adoration I feel for you now, that I've felt from the first moment I saw you. And all I'll ever ask in return is as much of your love as you can spare for me."

Her eyes raised to his with an expression he had never seen in them before: bewilderment, wonder, even submission. She dropped them quickly. Side by side they stood for several moments, and in the complete silence of the room he could hear his heart beating.

Then her hand touched his arm again very lightly. She took a step forward.

10

THE WEATHER took a turn for the worse, and the newly wedded couple elected regretfully to remain in Courtrai until travel became less difficult. This had one disadvantage because of the possessive sense the Mendoza family began to display. Urged insistently to take meals with them, they seldom had the strength of will to stand out. *El papá* loved his game of lansquenet, and Frank found himself pitted against the worthy don for long hours at a stretch. Doña Rachel had the insatiable curiosity of the truly good woman and subjected Gabrielle to frequent cross-examinations of an embarrassing nature. The most trying manifestation of the family interest was the regularity with which the children dropped in. They came singly, in pairs, and *en masse*, with servants in attendance and with all or most of the pets. Doña Rachel had presented her spouse with four sons before the arrival of Eufemia—Frank had counted them up to four but was not quite certain of his accuracy—and all of them came daily to ask questions about the war or to sit around and stare with the solemn concentration of young Indians. The most frequent visitor was Eufemia herself, leading the small Josefa by the hand, both of them wrapped up to the eyes in grotesque furs. When Eufemia came, it was an all-day visit. Her curiosity about everything exceeded that of her mother, if such were possible. The small Josefa's passion was to climb on chairs and meddle with the bellpulls.

On the fifth day Frank learned to his intense relief that Comte Lavalette had arrived in Courtrai. He repaired at once to the small inn where the escaped prisoner had taken up his quarters.

Lavalette proved to be singularly commonplace in appearance for one whose case had set all Europe talking. He was short and plump with a round face which expressed the utmost amiability. He welcomed Frank with the greatest cordiality.

"My dear M'sieur Ellery," he said, coming forward in a quilted dressing gown which had been cut to the measure of a much taller man and threatened to trip him up at every step, "this is indeed most fortunate. I am happy at this opportunity to thank you. I shall never get over my wonder at the generosity of four Englishmen, all strangers to me, who risked so much on my behalf. The Comtesse de Vitrelle is safely across the border, I trust?"

"She's here with me." Frank's face flushed with the self-conscious air of the very new bridegroom. "She's now my wife."

"Indeed!" Lavalette looked blank for a moment and seemed to be fumbling for words. "This *is* surprising news. I—I had no idea. Congratulations, my most hearty congratulations! You're a lucky man, m'sieur. Gabrielle is so very lovely, so very brave, so very fine!"

"I realize that I'm the luckiest man in the world."

The Comte shook his head in dissent. "I think I have that honor, m'sieur. My heroic wife and my amazing friends have made me free again. There are times when I can't believe it's true and am sure that it's all a dream."

"What word is there of Comtesse Lavalette?"

"She was still in prison when I left Paris." The plump face had lost its air of content. "They're treating her with great severity. The court ladies say she must be made to suffer in my stead. That's only talk, of course, and I'm not allowing myself to take it seriously. But it's clear enough, my dear M'sieur Ellery, they intend to keep her in prison for a long time." He added in a melancholy tone, "She's in very bad health."

He proceeded to tell of the means by which his escape from Paris had been effected. He had been taken to Bruce's house, as Wilson had planned, and a suit of English regimentals had been tailored for him. Hely-Hutcheson had applied at the British Embassy for passports in the name of Colonel Losack. The officials there had never heard of Colonel Losack, but the young Irishman had said in an offhand way, "Why, he's the brother of the Admiral, of course." There happened to be an admiral of that name on the retired list and, as Hely-Hutcheson was heir to the Irish earldom of Donoughmore, which counted for something, the secretary had submitted apologetically and drawn up the papers without further question. Armed with these credentials, Wilson had driven Lavalette out of Paris in broad daylight and in an open carriage, Hely-Hutcheson cantering on horseback beside them. The sheer audacity of it had enabled them to pass the city barriers without any difficulty at all.

"We had one narrow escape," concluded Lavalette, rubbing a hand over his nearly bald dome. "I've little hair left except this one lock in front. It's so stubborn my friends have always called it the Indomitable. I was wearing a wig. When we reached Compiègne, it slipped out of position and there was the Indomitable standing up in full view. I wondered why Wilson looked so tense all of a sudden. He had observed what had happened and he knew that my one remaining lock had been mentioned most particularly in the descriptions which had been sent out. Fortunately the guards didn't notice it. When we were well on our way again, Sir Robert produced a pair of shears and lopped it off."

"Where is Sir Robert now?"

"He has gone back to Paris. I believe it's his purpose to do what he can for other Frenchmen threatened with the fate which so nearly overtook me. What a stanch spirit he has! A truly great man, M'sieur Ellery! It is he who should be called the Indomitable."

When Frank rose to go, the Comte accompanied him to the door with further protestations of his eternal gratitude. "All I can ever give you, alas, is my thanks," he said. "For the rest of my life I shall be an exile. A hard fate for a Frenchman, m'sieur. To us there is no place to live but our own beloved country. I shudder at the thought of subsisting in Germany or Italy; or even in your own generous country."

"The French Government will recover from its present fit of spleen in course of time. I'm sure you may expect a pardon, Comte, when that happens."

"It may be." Lavalette gave an unconvinced sigh. "But I'm not counting on any such good fortune. The enmity of the court cuts very deep. They will never forget the Terror or the long years of exile."

At the door he said: "It will interest the Comtesse—your pardon, m'sieur, I should say your wife—that her cousin is to be married soon. The announcement was made before I left Paris. To Henri Lestange. A good match, it seems. Her estates have been fully restored. Do you happen to know her?"

Frank bowed. "I was acquainted with both cousins in England."

"Of course. It was because of your friendship that Gabrielle interested you and Sir Robert in my behalf. How fortunate for me, m'sieur! Margot is a splendid little person in spite of her intense Royalist sympathies. And a great catch! This young man is very lucky."

Filled with the good news of Lavalette's arrival, Frank raced up to their rooms as soon as he reached the inn. Gabrielle, who had seemed in the best of spirits when he left earlier in the morning, had taken to her bed. He found her with her hair down over her shoulders, a bedwarmer smoking hot on the counterpane beside her, and with a rueful smile by way of welcome. As was to be expected, Eufemia and the small Josefa were seated in the room, Potto crouching on the knee of the latter and tugging at his chain.

"Another of my beastly snifflings!" said Gabrielle. "I feel dreadful. I shall be sick for days now and I'll look so badly I may have to refuse to let you see me. My nose is red already."

"Nonsense. Your nose isn't red in the least. You look as lovely as usual, sweeting. But I'm sorry you're not feeling well."

"The nose is a *little* red," commented Eufemia.

"Perhaps the great news I bring will make you feel better. Lavalette is here in Courtrai. I've just had a long talk with him."

Gabrielle sat up at once, her face beaming with delight. "Hurrah!" she cried. "I'm so glad! That brave little Lavalette! Frank, I do feel a little better already."

Eufemia rose dutifully, but reluctantly, to her feet. "It is perhaps best for us to go now," she said.

"Yes, Eufemia, I think it is best. My husband and I have many things to talk about. You will tell your mother that I'm ill and that we can't have *comida* with you today. Please give her my love and say I hope to see her very soon."

"Josefa! Get up at once and come with me. Bring Potto."

But Josefa did not want to go. She continued to sit in silence, watching Gabrielle with adoring eyes.

"Wicked child!" cried Eufemia. "Have you no obedience? Must you be reported again to *el papá* for the stubbornness? Must the giant Cabrackan be told about you?"

The threat of the giant Cabrackan, most dreaded of Latin bogeymen, was too much for Josefa's resolution. She rose at once. Eufemia rang for the maid who had accompanied them and then led her sister to the door. Here an interesting possibility occurred to her.

"When our mama is ill, it means there will be a new baby in the morning. Perhaps"—hopefully—"it will be the same here?"

When the pair had departed Frank endeavored to take his wife in his arms but she drew herself back under the covers with a determined shake of the head. "You will get sick too," she protested.

"I won't catch your snifflings. I'm much too healthy for that."

"You must sit at a safe distance. If you won't be sensible, my great goose, I won't allow you in the room at all."

When he obeyed she picked up a mirror from the table beside her and studied herself in it. A grim shake of the head evidenced that she was not pleased. "The little vixen was right. The redness shows already. I'll be a fright by morning. You'll have such an ugly wife that you'll wish you had married——" She stopped there as though unwilling to finish what she had started to say.

Reminded of the other news he brought, Frank told her of Margot's announcement. Gabrielle regarded him silently for a moment.

"I'm very glad," she said finally. "She'll make Henri into a model husband; and Henri, stupid fellow, will never want to be anything else. I'm very glad she's been so prompt about it." Her tone was quite different from any she had employed before in discussing their relationship with the cousin in Paris. It was cool and matter-of-fact. Had matrimony changed her viewpoint already? he wondered. She asked after a moment, "Would I dare write her?"

"I think you should. She'll be anxious to know what has happened to you."

Gabrielle pondered the matter and then shook her head. "No, not yet. I would have to tell her about us. It will be better for her not to know until she has married her Henri. I'm sure it will be better to wait." Her face suddenly took on an expression of mock dismay. "Frank! You heard what that child said. Do you suppose——"

"You mean? That——" He sat up straight in his chair, his face a study in conflicting emotions.

"Of course I don't mean it. After all, I'm not completely ignorant of such matters. Must you take everything I say with such deadly English seriousness?"

"We've never discussed the possibility. Do you want to have children, Gaby?"

"Naturally we'll have children. Do you think I'll have any chance not to?" She laughed lightly. "Your brother has a son and we must at least keep up with *them*. Two, perhaps? Even three. But you mustn't get it into your head that I'm going to enter into any kind of a competition with Doña Rachel."

"I'm under a solemn promise to name my first son after my father," declared Frank doubtfully. "Joseph. I don't like it very much but my father's memory means a great deal to me."

She pretended to shudder. "I like it much less. Still, I suppose I could call him Jo-Jo. That's rather nice."

Frank sat back to consider the vistas opened up by this promise she had made. Gabrielle's mood had changed, however. She lay back on the pillow and regarded him with anxious eyes.

"I wish that all of them had come with Lavalette," she said. "I've a premonition that something really tragic is going to happen in Paris. The secret will get out; and then our friends will have to pay for it."

"Wilson is too shrewd to be caught."

"He may be shrewd but he likes to talk. He's too bold a man to be good at secrets." She sighed and turned so that she could study his face more closely. "Frank, are you going back?"

"I must rejoin them, of course. After I have you safely located."

There was a long silence. "I suppose you must. But I—I'm terribly frightened that something will happen. Why wouldn't they listen to us!"

"I can return with complete safety. I'm a newspaperman and I can come and go as I please. I'll make you one promise—that Wilson and Company will be wound up as soon as I get there."

"Now that you've forced me to marry you—and I'm becoming rather content that you did!—what do you propose to do with me while you're away?"

"We'll go on to Ostend and I'll put you on the tender for London. I'm afraid you'll have to stay with Mother. It won't be for very long, I hope."

There was a long pause. "I'm beginning now to pay the price of my selfishness," she said finally. "I was so set on saving the Comte by any means that I allowed myself to involve you in it. I can't remember that I gave a single thought to the consequences. Now you must go back to face whatever may happen. I can't even beg you to stay, although I wish with all my heart that you would. Well, I can share the danger with you at any rate. I shall go too."

"No, Gaby. I won't allow that."

"You can't stop me. I must go."

Frank looked at her with a full heart. She returned his gaze with such determination that he saw she meant to go with him in spite of anything he might do. Fearful as he was of the consequences of such a rash step, a sense of elation began to grow in his mind. This was the surest proof he had yet had that she really loved him.

"Gaby, it's my turn to insist on the sensible course. I must return, of course. I think I can do so with safety. But for you to go back now would be to put yourself into their hands. What possible good could that do us? It makes me happy to think that you want to go with me but—it won't do. You must stay on this side of the border."

"No! I must go with you. I'll never be at peace with myself if I don't."

"You keep insisting that you have been selfish. I can't see that you have. And I can't allow you to go on believing that you must pay some form of penance."

"But I have been, hopelessly so, Frank. You are blind to my faults or you would see it."

"I'm blind to your faults—if you have any. I can see your perfections so clearly, Gaby, that there's no chance to observe anything else. I know that you have courage, and it's impossible to be really selfish and brave at the same time. I know also that you are never ill-natured or spiteful. In all the years I have known you, I've never heard you speak ill of anyone or show any jealousy or meanness. It can't be such a serious matter if you have been a little selfish as you are so determined to prove. I wouldn't want you to be perfect. I love you just as you are and wouldn't have you different in any single respect." After a moment of eloquent silence he added, "And so, if you please, we will have no more raking up of the past and no more talk of penances."

There was a grateful warmth in her eyes but she shook her head, nevertheless, with unabated purpose. "I'm very happy that my husband has such a favorable opinion of me," she said. "When do you think we shall be able to start for Paris?"

She became no better, and the weather became much worse, so they were compelled to remain for several more days in Courtrai. Lavalette, reluctant to get far from the borders of his beloved France, was glad of the excuse to postpone the continuation of his flight. Realizing that he was in a despondent frame of mind, Frank devoted as much time to him as he could, listening to his gloomy speculations as to the plight of his wife and child and trying to comfort him.

It was on the fourth day after Lavalette's arrival that he came to the inn where Frank and his bride were staying with a serious look on his face and a letter crumpled tightly in his ungloved hand. Gabrielle was up and about for the first time, and insisted on seeing him.

Lavalette faced them for a tense moment in silence. "Gabrielle, Gabrielle," he said at last, "I owe so much to you that I'm doubly distressed to be the bearer of bad news! The very worst has happened. They have been arrested, Sir Robert Wilson and our other two friends! The word has just reached me."

Gabrielle's face became white. She said in a tense whisper: "I knew it! I knew it!"

Frank walked over to his wife and placed his arm around her shoulder. "You mustn't be alarmed. Nothing can happen to them."

"I was sure it would end this way!" she cried. "My meddling has borne bitter fruit!"

For several moments the three stared at each other in an unhappy and bitter silence. Then Frank asked, "How did they find out?"

"Sir Robert wrote a letter," explained Lavalette with a doleful shake of the head. "It was to a friend in England, an Earl Grey. In it he told everything. The letter was put into the British Embassy pouch and should have been free from scrutiny. No rules of international decency are observed by Fouché. His agents rifled the pouch and found the letter—and the truth was out! My dear friends, it would have been better if I had been left to suffer my fate! What will be done to them? What will be done to my poor Emilie now?"

Although he felt no conviction of hope himself, Frank tried to comfort the others by saying, "The Duke of Wellington will have to intervene this time."

"He will do nothing," declared Lavalette. "Did he lift a finger to save Ney?"

"It's different now. They are English."

"Your Duke will do nothing," repeated the Comte. "You will see! Nor will the Tsar act to help them. He's interested only in the séances of the Baroness von Krudener. He's trying to find divine guidance in the settlement of the affairs of the world. He refuses to see anyone."

"What will be done with them?" asked Gabrielle in a stricken voice. "Is it possible they will be shot?"

"That is quite possible," answered Lavalette. "The bitterness of our new government is beyond belief."

After a long silence he went on. "It's all my fault. I should not have gone through with the plan. You must believe, my friends, that I was most unwilling to try it. I knew the dangers. I stood out against it for a whole evening. I predicted that, even in the event of success, it would come to some such pass as this. I should have remained firm!"

"No," said Gabrielle in a low voice. "The blame is all mine!"

"No one is to blame," declared Frank. "There's only one question before us now. What can we do to help them?"

The answer to that was found in the blank looks they exchanged. There was nothing they could do.

"My advice to you, M'sieur Ellery," said Lavalette after a moment, "is to return at once to England and to take Gabrielle. You own a powerful newspaper. Perhaps you can stir up your own government to take steps in their behalf. That is the only way you can be of help."

"But will there be time?"

"I think so. They can't be tried immediately."

"It's maddening to think we must sit by and make no other effort than that!" exclaimed Frank. "I would feel as though I had run away."

"How do you suppose I feel?" demanded Lavalette bitterly. "My wife is in their hands and I can do nothing to help her! I could go back and give myself up, but could I be sure it would make any difference in the punishments prepared for her? My poor wife would then have gone through all her suffering in vain. Would it help the case of your three friends at all if you allowed yourself to be taken and stood beside them in the dock?"

"I can see it wouldn't," said Frank. "You're quite right, Comte."

11

MRS. ELLERY was in her private sitting room on the ground floor with a damp towel across her forehead. A new maid—her maids always seemed to be new—was preparing to replace it with another, freshly dipped in Eau de Cologne.

"Francis! I didn't know you had returned. I think you might have notified me."

"I arrived this morning, Mother. I'm sorry you aren't feeling well and I wouldn't intrude myself on you if it weren't that I have an important matter to discuss. Mother, I'm married."

"Married!" Mrs. Ellery sat up so abruptly that the towel fell unnoticed to the floor. "You may leave, Esther. Don't forget any of the commissions I've given you." The girl dropped a curtsy and left the room. "This means you were married in France. May I ask why such haste? And why I wasn't consulted?"

"There was no possible way of consulting you, Mother. It's—Gabrielle."

"Gabrielle!" The look she gave him indicated that at first she was incredulous. Then a deep furrow, which showed only when she was angry, appeared between her eyes. "That—that wanton! I can't believe you would do such a thing! I won't believe it!"

"There's no use going into a tantrum about it."

She stood up to face him. When she became really angry, her good looks deserted her entirely. Her eyes became hot and seemed to draw in together; spots of red showed above her cheekbones.

"Tantrum! I must say! You marry a notorious woman, the mistress of that Bonaparte—one of his many mistresses, I should say—and then you talk of tantrums when I speak my mind as a mother has a right to do!"

Frank held himself in control and managed to say in even tones: "She has been the victim of scandalous gossip. She wasn't Napoleon's mistress. No one could believe it if they knew her——"

"Everyone believes it. You may be fool enough to think her innocent, young man, but you'll be the only one who does." She shook her head furiously. "You seem determined to drag our name in the gutter. First you get yourself sent to prison and now—this! Have you no sense of shame? We'll never live this down, never!"

"If you please, we'll not discuss Gabrielle any more."

"I'll discuss her as much as I like. I never liked her, never trusted her.

First she tried to get Caradoc and now she's taken you as second best. After what she did that night at the theater—everyone knows about that, you may be sure—she can't go back to France. That's the only reason she had for marrying you, my son."

"I love her and she loves me. That's all that counts and I'm not going to let myself get angry, Mother. What I came to discuss with you was this. I must take over this house now. Gabrielle is in my rooms at present but I intend to bring her here tonight."

His mother switched to the defensive so suddenly that he wondered if her tumult of resentment had been partially assumed. She picked up the towel and placed it on her forehead, moaning slightly as she patted it into place.

"My poor head! It's throbbing as though it would burst. Do you see what you've done to me, Francis? You seem to have no regard for me at all. You've never had any, never as long as I can remember. You're exactly like your father."

"That's the only compliment you ever pay me, Mother. I'm sorry if your head is worse. I would gladly have postponed this discussion until later but it must be clear to you that an understanding should be reached at once. I must get Gabrielle comfortably settled."

"You think of no one but her. What about me?" She put both hands to her head and moaned again. "Oh, my head! I don't think I can stand it. It's driving me Frantic."

"You had better go to bed. We'll continue our talk tomorrow if you're feeling better then."

"And you'll bring that woman here? I won't stay under the same roof with her!"

"That's something you must decide for yourself. This is my home and I intend to bring my wife here without delay."

"You gave the house to me. It was part of the bargain."

"I gave you a five-year lease. It was up three years ago."

She sat down and reached under the satin curtains of a console table for a bottle of pills. She put one in her mouth, regarding him accusingly as she did so.

"I'm going to be quite ill and it's all your doing, Francis."

"Then we won't talk any more today."

"But we must." She closed her eyes for several moments. "Your rights, young man, may not be as clear as you think. We'll see about that, you may be sure. And there's Caradoc to be considered. He has been using the house to entertain his friends. Now that he's being so well thought of——"

"Carr will have to look after himself. I want you to understand, Mother, that you are to make your home here if you want to. You'll always be welcome. But surely you must see we can't go on unless you change your attitude to Gabrielle. If you're going to stay here, I won't permit you to show any of this feeling you've displayed to me. That must be thoroughly understood."

"Oh, why did you have to come back now! This terrible mistake of yours will make things difficult for Caradoc and Mary. I know it will!"

"We all have our own lives to live."

"It's clear, then, you're going to think of nothing but your own convenience."

"Put it that way if you must."

Mrs. Ellery burst out with even greater vehemence, "I won't stay in this house if you bring that woman here!"

"As I said before, that's for you to decide."

"You would put your own mother out of her home for an adventuress? Is that what I'm to believe?"

He repeated with as much patience as he could summon: "If you go, it will be of your own free will. I've nothing more to say."

"You can stand there, Francis Ellery, and speak to your own mother that way?"

He said in a tone of finality: "You must realize, Mother, that under the circumstances I'm not speaking as a son. I'm speaking as a husband. As the husband of the finest and loveliest of women, whose happiness I place above everything else in the world."

The house was in darkness when Frank brought his wife there late in the evening. Receiving no response to his ring, he opened the front door with his latchkey. He called several times but there was no answer.

"Doesn't seem to be anyone here," he said.

Gabrielle held tightly to his arm in the dark. "I'm rather relieved," she whispered. "It puts off the—the dreadful moment a little longer."

"You may never have to see her, darling. The way I feel at the moment, I hope it will be that way."

"You said so very little, my quiet one, that I knew the talk with your mother hadn't been easy." She sighed. "I was sure it would be like this. I warned you."

He took her in his arms and kissed her several times. "Do you think I care? I'm not concerned about their attitude in the least. No matter what happens, you must always believe that."

"I won't care either if it isn't going to make you unhappy."

He kissed her again before releasing her. "I must light up. Fortunately I have my tinder pistol with me."

The spark caught and he held it up in front of him. There was a candle sconce on the wall and he lighted the taper.

"I've never been here before," said Gabrielle, looking about her. "My new home! It looks most impressive."

It became apparent, as they passed from room to room, lighting candles as they went, that his mother had packed and gone away in a very great hurry, taking all the servants with her. None of the fireplaces had been laid and the dinner table had not been cleared. Topp, it developed later, had witnessed the departure. His report of it to cronies at the office was to the effect that "the widdy went away as sour as a mess o' early honey-blobs and I could see the smoke a-coming out o' her ears."

Gabrielle had recovered her spirits and was in almost a gay mood. Holding on to his arm, and at times fairly skipping with eagerness, she insisted on going over the house at once from top to bottom. Her comments delighted him. "It's much the largest house I've ever lived in. Except, of course, when I was in Russia. A little on the gloomy side, perhaps, but I'll soon attend to that. We'll have a wonderful time, shopping for all the things I'll need."

"You're to have everything you want, Gaby."

Gabrielle stifled a yawn when they returned to the drawing room. "I'm very tired," she confessed. "You said you would visit the office but I can't let you go now. I don't want to be left alone. Besides, some of them might come back and have the unpleasant surprise of finding the scarlet woman sleeping in one of the family beds. They might turn me out on the streets in my shift."

"I've no intention of leaving you. There's no news yet. Topp brought me that word."

"Then I'll go to bed at once."

"We had better use my room tonight." He considered the problem further with a trace of doubt. "Coming to think of it, I'm not sure it would do. It's small and at the back of the house."

"Has it a bed large enough for two, and a fireplace?"

"A large bed and a small fireplace. The flue draws like sixty and I could make a roaring good fire."

"I think it would be nice to spend our first night at home in your old room. Did you ever think the time would come when I would sleep there?"

He looked down at her and shook his head slowly. "My sweet," he said, "I've lived for eight long years without any real hope at all that such a thing would ever come about."

When he reached the bedroom with an armful of wood, she was already undressed and snuggled down under the covers. She sat up and drew his worn old coverlet up around her chin to protect herself from the cold and damp of the room. Her hair was falling in tight ringlets over her shoulders.

"I forgot where I had packed the nightcaps. Do you mind?"

"You know very well," he said, kneeling before the grate and piling on wood, "that you nearly always forget where they are and have to sleep without one."

"That's true. I'm very untidy."

"We'll find a maid for you tomorrow. A French girl, if possible. One who will know all about such absurdities as pomatoms and lotions and pimpernel water."

The fire began to blaze briskly. There was only one chair in the room and it was beside the bed with Gabrielle's clothes heaped upon it. He turned about on the floor and sat watching her with arms clasped around his good knee. He felt completely at home and completely happy. Nothing had been changed in the room. All his oldest books were heaped about, on the window sill, in piles against the walls, on top of the sad-looking brown wardrobe. His prized old prints of the three English paladins of the Hundred Years' War, Chandos, Manny, and Knowles, were still tacked on the wall and beginning to look quite faded.

For a long time nothing was said.

"Does this remind you of a somewhat similar occasion?" she asked finally. "When we were alone and having to make the best of things? You built a fire that time too and then sat and watched me. I tried to forget about it. But I find that I remember everything."

"I was thinking about it too."

"Did we make the best of it? Or the worst? And do you remember how concerned I was about your comfort and how hard it was to convince you that you needn't sleep on the floor?"

"I didn't need any convincing."

She snuffed out the single candle on the window sill. "Are you going to need any convincing now?"

He made no reply. It was a wonderful thing to see her there, with her dark hair spread out on his old pillow, the coverlet turned back just enough to allow him a glimpse of one white shoulder. He dreaded to make a move for fear it would break the spell. He was afraid she might vanish and that he would then find it had been another of the dreams

with which he had consoled himself so very many times in this small,
bare room.

"What are you thinking about?"

"That this may be all my imagination. That you aren't here in reality
and that soon you'll fade away and I'll find that I'm alone after all."

"It seems very real to me. I'm lying here in a very cold bed and thinking
how unfair it is of you to wait until I've made it warm and cozy for you!"
She started a sigh which changed into a yawn. "Have you any—any
doubts or reservations about that other time?"

He smiled and got to his feet. "None," he said. It was the first time
they had spoken directly of that particular phase of their sojourn together
in Russia.

It was a sign of the changing times that Nathan Cope was wearing
trousers when Frank met him at the office the next morning. They were
very full trousers, as of course they would be with Cope, and they were
fastened so tightly over his varnished boots that it seemed certain no
cloth made would be capable of standing the strain. The collar of his
shirt rose up stiffly on each side of his face, reaching within an inch of his
cheekbones. He looked very much in tune with the latest fashion and also
very uncomfortable.

He shook his head soberly. "Word has just come by carrier pigeon. The
trial's over. They were convicted."

Frank collapsed into a chair and regarded his assistant with unhappy
eyes. Cope nodded twice between the sharp shields which confined his
head.

"All three were convicted. I must say, I expected nothing else."

"Nor I," said Frank in a hollow voice. "The case was complete with
that letter of Wilson's as evidence."

"In all my acquaintance with that remarkable man," declared Cope
impatiently, beginning to stride about the room, "I've never known him
to commit such a complete folly. Why did he write that outrageously
indiscreet letter? What got into him? Did he feel that he needed
applause?"

"But, Cope, Cope, what was the sentence?"

"Light enough." The assistant editor nodded in reassurance. "I fancy
the Duke had something to say about it after all. Or the Tsar. Someone
brought influence to bear, certainly. They were sentenced to three
months' imprisonment."

Frank's breath exploded in relief. "Thank God! I was afraid it would be much more severe. I even had a fear it might be the guillotine or a firing squad."

Cope waved that aside. "There was never any question of a death sentence. After all, France is a conquered nation and the city of Paris is still under the control of our very stern but very just Duke. He wouldn't let them go that far. But I expected a much longer term." He grinned at Frank. "Old hands like us know that three months in prison isn't such a serious matter."

Frank hesitated. "Copey, was my name mentioned in connection with the escape? Or my wife's?"

Cope paused in his nervous pacing. "Your name! Were you in it too? Great Barnaby, the idea never entered my head; although, now you tell me, I see I should have expected it." His smile drew into a more serious pattern. "He protected you, then. Your name wasn't in that absurd letter. Bruce and Hely-Hutcheson were named and have to suffer with him."

"I feel guilty to be getting off scot-free."

"Huh, don't let that bother you. It means you lose your share of the hero worship. London has been seething with it ever since word came of the arrests. I swear the three of them could organize a new party when they return and sweep our present government out of office. I tell you, the city will explode with rage when we publish the news of the conviction. I'm thinking of a special, by the way."

"No, not a special, Copey. I don't want to capitalize on the misfortunes of my friends."

Cope protested, "Riding Bobby won't thank you for not giving the case every possible bit of notice." He came and leaned across the desk, his right hand stretched out. "I heard of your marriage last evening. Congratulations, Frank, dear boy. I jumped out of my chair in sheer delight when Topp told me. The happy culmination of a long dream, eh?"

"A very long dream and a very happy culmination." They shook hands. Cope seated himself on a corner of the desk, taking pains first about the proper set of his trousers. "I'll tell you the whole story. Of my wedding and of the part we played in the escape. But not now. I want to know first what punishment Sir Robert will face when he returns to London."

"The rumor is that he'll be cashiered. If they do that, and damme if I don't think they will, it means he loses his pension and every penny he invested in his commissions. It's even being said that he'll be stripped of all his decorations. That would cut deep with him. He puts great store in those proofs of what they think of him abroad. How he loved to appear with his breast blazing with them!"

The relief Frank had felt over the lightness of the sentence was swal-

FRANCE

lowed up at once by a feeling of the deepest depression. "And that's to
be his reward for all he's done!" he said bitterly. "The maddening part
of it is that he'll have no further chance to show what a fine soldier he is.
The Horse Guards have beaten him finally."

"To my notion," declared Cope, "this is the best thing that could have
happened. Didn't you hear what I said about the feeling in the country?
I tell you the public has really wakened up at last to the fact that we've
had another hero in this war besides the Iron Duke. Stories about Wilson
are being told in every drawing room in England as well as in every tip-
pling shop. It needed this to set the legends flying. Damme, he's coming
into his own at last."

"Then you don't think this is the end for him?"

"The end? It's the beginning. It would be interesting if the pair of
them came home the same day, Riding Bobby and the Duke. I wonder
which one the crowds would cheer the loudest for?"

Cope began to fidget about, to look at his watch, paying scant attention
to the matters of business on which Frank questioned him. He seemed
to be waiting, with very little patience, for something to happen. Several
times he walked to the door of the office and put his head out to listen.

Finally it came. A rumbling sound rose from the cellar of the building.
It started and stopped, began again, gained in volume. In a very few
moments a sustained roar filled the whole plant. A look of triumph
lighted up Cope's face. He fairly skipped across the room and leaned
over the desk to look squarely into Frank's face.

"Hear that? What do you suppose it is?"

Frank was worried. "It sounds as though another riot had broken out.
What in God's name has happened? Why are you looking so smug?"

"It's the first power press!" cried Cope, his eyes blazing with a zeal that
approached the fanatical. "Koenig completed it two weeks ago. I persuaded Evans we should take matters into our own hands and install it."

The roar had risen in volume. The air seemed filled with a jarring
vibration.

"Listen to it, the great beauty!" exclaimed Cope. "Running them off
by the thousands! There's the answer, Frank, to all our troubles. Soon
we'll be flooding the city with copies of the *Tab*—ten, twenty, fifty thousand a day. I tell you we'll be turning them out so fast and so cheap that
every living soul in London will have a copy."

"I've just enough of my father in me," said Frank, "to be worried about
the cost."

"The cost?" Cope raised a prophetic forefinger. "Does it matter? It's
the cost of preaching our crusades in a way to make the whole country

listen. Now we'll be able to get after these boggling, miggling, muddling political cart horses at Westminster. Now we'll be able to insist on better prisons, decent hospitals, better wages for working people, better laws." He paused dramatically. "A newspaper with the power supplied by that rumbling giant can no longer be throttled. We'll have a free press at last, Frank."

Frank got to his feet, his eyes lighted up with the same fire. "I haven't been as unmindful of all this as you've thought, Copey. I've been looking forward to this opportunity as much as you have. I even remember what you said the first time we discussed power presses, and I can repeat it word for word. 'You'll hear a sound all through this building like the distant rumble of cannon. And it will be music to my ears, a symphony of human progress, the promise in booming chords of a free press and a free world.' That's what you said, Copey, and I stored it away in my mind. And now it's here."

"And now it's here!"

"We'll start tomorrow. There's so much to be done! We won't let anything stand in our way—profits or trouble or danger. We must show them what a free press can do!"

Postscript

THE MIRROR set into the breakfast-room hatch—Gabrielle was forever installing such things in the town house and even at Gravely, their country place in the Wiltshire Downs—brought home to Frank that his hair was now completely silvered. He did not mind this in the least. Gabrielle declared that it made him almost handsome, so he considered that time (fifteen years of married life!) had done him a good turn. He sat down to his pot of chocolate, a bad habit which stemmed from his peninsular days, and his grilled trout with a lack of interest which had something to do with the early summer sun beating on as much of the window as it could reach, and the song of a bird in the silver-green foliage of their one poplar tree. It would be so much more pleasant at Gravely. There he would be able to look down on a moat lined with marish mosses and water lilies nearly ready to burst into bloom. From his bedroom he would be able to see the dark line of the rolling hills and catch the distant bay of the Brinsleyfold hounds. There was much to be done at Gravely this summer, and he begrudged every hour he had to be away from it. But his duties at the office were increasingly pressing; so here he was, waiting for Windy Topp to deliver his mail and facing a day of irksome dispute over new press equipment and the attitude of the paper on the latest phases of the bitter struggle for the Reform Bill.

He always felt a glow steal over him when he thought of Gravely. It had taken hold of him at the very first glimpse he had of it: a warm red house with high-pitched gables and tall chimneys with miniature buttresses, and a suggestion of calm which hinted at an earlier origin than could actually be claimed for it. Now that it was his, he had come to love it passionately. He loved its mullioned windows, the smoky black of its old beams, the dark embrasures of the library where he was voraciously gathering a treasure of books.

Gabrielle came briskly into the room with a penitent, "Am I late as usual?" and sat down beside him. She was wearing a chintz dress and a lace cap. It was a pity, he thought, that fashion would not permit women to appear at any time of day without a head covering of some sort, for she had adopted a new way of doing her hair which he thought most becoming. As always, he marveled at the small impression time had made on her. As slender as ever—well, almost as slender—she was still without a line in her face and she looked so much younger than he did that occasionally he knew a twinge of worry. No wonder she had made so many friends. The conquest of fashionable London had been partially accomplished; but, alas, she had not yet carried the stern redoubts of King Billy's respectable if somewhat stuffy court.

"No mail yet? That lazy Topp! He gets later with it every morning."

"He's getting old, Gaby."

"Old? You should hear him talking in the kitchen with the maids!"

Barklamb, a younger and much more dignified edition of Purdy, brought in the letters and laid them on the table in two neat piles. Gabrielle riffled through hers as she sipped her coffee and selected a few for immediate perusal. Frank shoved his aside. He would take them to the office, where attention to mail had become an easier habit.

"Jo-Jo will be home a day sooner than he expected," she said. "Isn't that nice? In the meantime would his kind mamma broach the subject of a little more pocket money to see him through? I would send it to him myself but I'm running very, very low."

"Are you ever anything but low?"

"No," she conceded cheerfully. "I seem a little careless about my allowance. So, Old Moneybags, I turn the problem of Jo-Jo's needs over to you. . . . Mary writes that your mother will be ready to come on to us as soon as we go to Gravely."

"You won't mind it too much, I hope. You have quite a way with her."

"I make her toe the line when necessary, if that's what you mean. No, I don't mind too much. And, actually, here's a note from Margot."

She fell into absorbed silence as she perused the closely written pages from her cousin in Paris. They had not seen Margot since their flight from France, and probably never would, but letters passed back and forth at long intervals.

"She's such a good letter writer," said Gabrielle enviously, turning a page. "The very best I know."

"Is there any news?"

Gabrielle looked up. "I thought your interest would be aroused. Yes, a great deal seems to be happening. Margot is frightened about the look of things in France. She's buying an estate in Louisiana in case there's another revolution."

"It's coming, and very soon. Margot doesn't need to worry about it from a financial standpoint. She's transferred a great part of her investments to this country and America."

"It's absurd," declared Gabrielle, "for anyone to be as wealthy as Margot. . . . Emilie hasn't fully recovered her reason yet, and Comte Lavalette is afraid she never will. They're settled in Paris now. . . . It seems Henri has something wrong with him. Margot skirts the symptoms with her usual reticence, but I get the impression it is what's known as a sour stomach. Would you care"—with a lift of eyelashes which dared him to say yes—"to read her letter yourself?"

"No," he answered promptly.

She went into a long silence as she proceeded with her breakfast. "Frank," she said suddenly, "it seems to me that Jo-Jo grows to look more like his uncle Caradoc every day. I would be simply frantic if I thought he was going to take after him in any other way. Fortunately he seems to resemble you in everything else."

"Not a bad combination, perhaps?"

"I only hope he doesn't grow fat early like our great orator and statesman. I almost laughed when Caradoc got up to speak at that *deadly* Corn Law dinner. He looked like two melons, a small one on top of a very large one. I wouldn't have been surprised if seeds had dropped out of his mouth when he opened it instead of those pearls of wisdom Mary is always quoting. *Caradoc says, Caradoc thinks!* I want to shake her!"

"He told me the other day to watch for the next list of birthday honors. Do you suppose——?"

Gabrielle looked up at him compassionately. "My poor, dear Frank! You mustn't expect anything, you really mustn't. I'm afraid your name will never appear on the honor list. You've earned a title a hundred times over but—you married the wrong kind of wife, you know. You'll never be knighted, because then I would have to be received. No, no, my husband, put the thought right out of your head."

"I want a title only because of you. Do you think I enjoy seeing you go in to dinner near the end of the line? I can't stand having you always sit with secretaries and aldermen and the wives of nobodies. You, the loveliest woman in London!"

Gabrielle laughed and leaned over to pat his hand. "But what happens after dinner? Don't I have my revenge then?"

"All the men flock around you. Is that sufficient compensation? I sometimes think that official memories would have been less persistent if you had been less beautiful."

"Would you want me received at that price?"

"No! For my part, I'm satisfied with things as they are."

But that was not true. He was thinking: "My poor Gaby! She's been so brave through all these years. Her head has always been held high. I wonder—has she minded the rebuffs very much? If I could only manage to have her presented at court! It would make all the difference."

She was speaking in a light tone of the previous evening's entertainment. He caught a reference to the Duke of Wellington.

"That reminds me," he said. "I'm dining with Sir Robert Wilson tonight and we're going on later to see the Duke. It's really amazing what close friends they're getting to be. Wilson goes to see him all the time."

"The Duke has become a regular old darling. Yes, it's nice to see those two enemies become such cronies. I wish something could be done for Sir Robert. He looked positively threadbare the last time I saw him."

"No one can do anything for him. He's as proud as Lucifer. I offer him good prices for articles but he suspects my motives and so he never accepts. There should be a salary for members of Parliament. The worst of it is that he's always in opposition and will never have a chance to get into a paying office."

"And he's always elected by such handsome majorities!" Gabrielle indulged herself in a reflective smile. "Even if you made such a scene about it, I *did* win him a lot of votes."

"I think I've always been broad-minded but I draw the line at my wife offering a kiss for each vote. There will be no more electioneering for you."

"The Duchess of Devonshire did the same for Fox and no one thought anything of it. Does it make a difference if you're a Duchess? Well, I'll try not to be too disconsolate over my solitary dinner tonight. Have a good time with Sir Robert and my nice old lamb of a Duke."

Frank went out to the kitchen, where he knew he would find Windy Topp. The presence of the latter was manifest before the door was opened, for he was imitating the master of ceremonies at the popular *Three Spinsters* for the benefit of the domestic staff, singing in a nasal voice:

> *"With a tiddy e rumsy bum*
> *And a taddy e rumsy bay."*

He stopped short and grinned at his employer, revealing by so doing that the Topp supply of teeth was becoming very scarce.

"Morning, sahib," he said. "I hear the teapot's a-b'iling over in France again. Seems there's no doing anything for Johnny Craps. We gets him all tucked up nice and snug and then he goes and kicks the covers off again."

"We may have to go over and straighten things out for him, Windy."

Topp shook his head emphatically. "Nuh, nuh, sahib. What I says is, let 'em stew in their own sauces from now on. I've got a crick in my back and a crick in my legs and a crick in each o' my arms. Seems like I'm just a mask o' cricks."

"And with no taste left for campaigning?"

"Sahib, it's the retreats I ain't any stummick left for. We'd get into one. There's always a retreat, seems to me. And Johnny Craps 'ud catch up on us this time. Nuh, sahib, I says let's go fishing insted."

Returning to the front hall for his hat and cane, Frank heard Gabrielle on the floor above, whistling to her parrot Dudgeon and then admonishing him in indignant tones, "Come, Old Stupid, won't you sing for your mistress?" She came running to the balustrade and looked down over at him.

"You must not forget," she called, "to convey my respects to the Duke."

Frank stood in silence for several moments, looking up at her and thinking. One whole day and then a long evening ahead of him, without a single glimpse of her! It was a bleak prospect. They were always together when they went down to Gravely. Perhaps that was the real reason why he enjoyed it so much there.

"Gaby," he said with mock severity, "did you flirt last evening with His Grace?"

She leaned her elbows on the upper newel post and nodded her head. "Outrageously!" she said.

The *Tablet* had grown so much that it seemed now like a circus giant in clothes designed for a man of average height. The space in front of the old building was filled with carriages and drays and the air was filled with the noisy arguments of the drivers. Inside, the place thrummed with activity. As Frank walked down the dark passage to his office, he saw a continuous succession of employees, with papers under their arms and pens behind their ears, scuttling in and out of a maze of rooms like so many rabbit hutches.

Nathan Cope, elevated many years before to the editorship, had a corner office of his own now. Frank turned in there for a chat. That ardent looker to the future had fallen into reactionary ways as far as clothes were concerned. In a world which was running to sober hues for men, he still flaunted himself in a bottle-green waistcoat and a coat of red, tan, and black.

"I hope the damned French don't get started before we can really wake the public up to the need for prison reform," he grumbled, striking a match on a sheet of glass paper. It flared for a moment and then fizzled out. "These newfangled congreves are no good. I think I'll go back to spunks. They're more of a bother but you can always be sure of a light. As I was saying, the fickle mind of the public can't be pinned down to anything else when a drum begins to beat anywhere."

"I thought," said Frank mildly, "that you regarded international troubles as good for circulation."

"We can't afford more circulation," barked Cope, "not until we have that new double platen press in. They're having a bit of trouble with it. The platen is showing a damnable tendency to hitch out of line as it revolves——"

Frank stopped him with a raised hand. "You know I don't understand a word about such things. Have you been able to run down the anonymous author of that novel of prison life yet?"

"*Peine Forte*? It's a woman." Cope seemed a little disgusted at the necessity of making the admission. "I was amazed. There was a vigor about the writing which didn't prepare me for such a discovery. The name is Mrs. Ralph Isbister. It seems she visited prisons all over England to get her material. She poked her nose in everywhere and, from all reports, had a rather bad time of it with some of the wardens. She's fairly burning up with zeal. A regular Joan of the Clink."

"We must get her to write for the paper. Where does she live?"

"I don't know. But it doesn't matter. She's here now; in your office and waiting to talk with you."

Laura Brakespeare was seated in a chair by one of the windows. She rose and held out a gloved hand to him, smiling in response to his startled exclamation of recognition.

"I did it, you see," she said. "I told you I would write novels that were different."

"I should have known it was you. Now that I come to think of it, this last book was published as by the author of *Slave of Gentility* and that was a story of a much abused governess. How stupid I was not to put two and two together at once."

"Confess, Francis, that you had forgotten all about me."

She was thin and apparently not in the best of health. However, her eyes were as alive as ever, retaining for her a share of her former attractiveness. They began to glow as the talk turned to the work she had done.

"I think I managed to see everything," she said. "I even visited the cell in which you were kept, and the grated door where the prisoners were shot that day. Francis, the conditions are almost as bad still as they were then. We don't seem to learn or to care."

"In spite of the way we've kept hammering at it in the *Tablet*. Sometimes I get discouraged and wonder if there's any use going on."

"You mustn't give up! I think we're on the point of getting results at last." Her mood relaxed sufficiently to allow a smile. "You can judge how deeply I feel from the fact that I've dared come and see you. I've placed my security in your hands. You're the only one who knows that Mrs. Ralph Isbister was once Jean Summers. Do you realize what a power I've given you over me?"

Frank smiled in return. "I've seen you now in four phases, all of them startlingly different. What will the next one be? As a feminine Lord Gordon, leading mobs to Westminster to force the hand of the government?"

"Perhaps even that. Or I might blossom out as advocate of the most unheard-of demand in the whole political history of the world—the right of women to vote."

"The idea may not be as farfetched as it sounds. I won't be surprised after this at anything you do, Laura. The last time we met, by the way, you were quite certain you would never marry."

"Not only did I go back on that resolution but I married a clergyman. A widower, moreover, with five children. You may well laugh at me, Francis Ellery."

"It seems to have worked out very well."

"Oh yes, it has! I've been very happy. My husband comes as close to being a saint as any human being can in these days. And I'm fond of all my stepchildren."

"You've done well with your novels. I haven't heard the figures but I know they've sold enormously. I hope you stood out with your publishers for good terms."

She nodded her head. "I've been quite exacting. We have so much money now that I don't know what to do with it all. It's pleasant to think that the two girls in the family, both of whom are rather plain, poor little things, won't have to become governesses. I'm seeing to *that*. I'm in a position even to subscribe to the prison funds."

"What we need most from you is the help of your pen, Laura. What a vigorous and trenchant pen it is! You'll be recognized someday as a genius."

When he escorted her to the door an hour later, she paused to ask, "And you, Francis, have you been happy?"

"Completely. I've been lucky in everything—my family, my home, and my work."

"Your life has been rather less exciting of late years. For a time you were playing quite a part in the making of history. You see, I follow everything you do."

"I've played a very minor part, Laura. I've never been more than one of the sceneshifters, working in the flies."

Her eyes were warm with sympathetic interest. "Your wife is very lovely, Francis. I've seen her several times. At the opera and the theater. You see, I sometimes slip up to London and indulge in what my husband would consider the most sinful pleasures."

"Now that we're joining hands for the cause, we'll see a lot of each other," said Frank. "It will be like the old days on the Yeltes, won't it?"

"Yes. But in a much better cause." She added after a moment, "Still, those days are my most treasured memory. I've been foolish enough even to keep my scarlet coat as a memento."

After dinner Sir Robert Wilson and Frank cut across Hyde Park in the direction of Apsley House. In spite of Cope's glowing predictions so many years before, the former had not been enjoying a prosperous time. He was gray and thin and quite threadbare. He had been silent during the meal, but the excellent bottle of wine they had shared after their grilled capon began now to loosen his tongue.

"Ever since '23 when I got that bullet in my thigh in Spain," he declared, "I've been nothing but a useless hulk. Sometimes, when I'm sitting there in the House and listening to a lot of windy gabble about nothing at all, I say to myself, 'This be none of I.' I'm a soldier, not a blasted, vote-pulling politician. I've no more right to be in that company than the Duke. Of course, he's in the Lords, where they're more polite even if they're a lot duller. Well"—with a sigh—"he's too old and too important for service and I've got this bit of steel in my leg. All we're good for is what we're doing."

To bring the talk to a more agreeable basis, Frank said: "I've been glad to see how friendly you've become with the Duke."

Wilson laughed. "The good old Duke! I've grown to love him, Frank. It's positively amazing how mellow he's become. He hasn't changed a single idea, of course. If liberalism should swamp the world like another flood, the Duke would build an Ark of his own and fill it according to his own beliefs: a team of horses, male and female, a pair of hunting dogs, a brace of foxes, and the rest of the space for purple Tories and pretty women. He might take a few old soldiers along. Apart from all that, he has developed a strain of kindliness that passes belief. Have you seen much of him?"

"I haven't spoken to him since the night of his ball in Paris."

"Well, then, you're due for the surprise of your life."

The ugly dark contours of Apsley House, with its high pillars, loomed up in front of them. There were no stars out and a flash of lightning off to the east warned that a storm was brewing.

"Soldiering is never anything but a messy, bloody business," said Wilson as they stood on the pavement and stared up at the iron-shuttered windows of the house where Britain's great warrior lived. "But it does something to a man. Your grognard never has any of the meanness of your solid citizen who has slept in sour comfort all his life and grown fat on the fruits of ease."

The streets of London seemed to be growing noisier with each passing year. Even at this hour of the evening a continuous roar came from the direction of the City, rising and falling like the sound of the sea at a distance. This was due largely to the increase in wheeled traffic, for the streets were filled with overloaded hackney coaches and private conveyances of all kinds—curricles and tilburies and cabriolets, rattling and grinding and screeching, with the coattails of handsomely attired "tigers" swaying to the motion, and obadiahs with their single seats so high up in the air that one might suppose the builders had experienced a rush of Euclid to the head and had equipped right-angled triangles with wheels. The din was so great that even the "Come, nah, get yer fine crusty muffings!" of the tray vendors seemed less raucous than before. This latter manifestation, however, may have been attributable in part to a falling off in the muffin trade; for, although some of the people of London were living more sumptuously than had been possible in the restricted days of the Napoleonic wars, most of them were now eating a great deal less.

A hoarse voice from behind them in the shadows asked: "Would ye be kind enough to help an old soldier, gentlemen? I ain't had a bite to eat for two days."

Frank's hand went to his pocket at once, although it was too dark to see anything of the supplicant. He remembered the old dragoon who had begged from him the night before his first meeting with Riding Bobby Wilson. The latter touched his arm with a restraining gesture.

"Come up closer, my man," ordered Wilson. "We must have a look at you. London's full of beggars who claim to be soldiers but never had a scarlet coat on their backs."

The man moved nearer with the clump-clump of a wooden leg. He said in a defiant voice: "I've done my share of fighting. Make no mistake about that, gentlemen. I lost my leg at Talavera."

There was the whine of the professional beggar in the voice but to Frank there was something familiar about it. His hand trembling with eagerness, he struck a congreve and held it up in front of him. The man was bent over and his face was partly covered by a cap drawn down tightly over his forehead. Frank recognized him at once, however.

"Benjie!" he cried. "I've found you at last. Benjie, man, where have you been all these years?"

After a moment's silence Fuller said, "Yes, Mr. Ellery, it's me. I wouldn't have come up if I'd known it was you."

"Why not? Why haven't you let me know where you were? I could have cleared up that scrape for you." The match had gone out and Frank took hold of Fuller's arm to be sure he could not get away in the darkness. "Well, thank God, here you are at last! There's a comfortable berth waiting for you at my place in the country as soon as I can settle things for you."

Fuller tried to pull himself away. "I'm looking for no favors," he mumbled. "I've got along without favors from the likes of you for all these years. I'll get along without 'em now."

"Come, Benjie, that's no way to talk. You were one of the Duke's men and we're going to see that the government does the right thing by you."

"The guv'ment!" Fuller spat the words out with the accumulated bitterness of fifteen years of beggary. "The guv'ment leaves me and my likes to starve. Someday we'll have a guv'ment of our own. Someday—and it's not so far off—we'll rip up those iron shutters and show your bloody Duke what we think of *him*. And all the rest of yer kind at the same time!"

"My man," said Wilson sharply, "this sort of talk won't do at all. You've had a hard time of it, as we can easily see, but you must drop all this if we're to do anything for you."

"I don't want you to do anything for me. I've said that already and I mean it."

"We're going to take you in hand whether you want it or not. I'm an old soldier too, a much older one than you. Do you know who I am?"

"I knowed ye as soon as ye spoke. Ye're Riding Bobby Wilson." The old soldier gave a scornful snort. "People has forgot to sing about ye any more. '"Ride with me," said Bobby.' Where are the poor fellows now what did ride with ye? Dead, or begging on the streets like me with legs and arms gone or their backs doubled up on 'em. And what has yer precious guv'ment done for you, Sir Robert, if I makes so bold as to ask?"

"Not very much. It doesn't seem to be the way of governments to do anything for the men who win their wars for them. But that isn't the point. You're in need of help and Mr. Ellery wants to look after you. Drop all this wild talk and listen to what he has to say."

"I'll call a cab and take you to my home now," said Frank eagerly. "Come, Benjie, we've always been the best of friends. Give me a chance to make things up to you."

"Give me a bit of money and let me go!" cried Fuller. "If the craving wasn't on me, I wouldn't take a thing. But it is. I need a drink so bad I'll take yer money and thank ye for that much. But nothing more!"

"He's not in his right mind," declared Wilson. "Frank, we'll have to handle this in our own way."

"No, ye don't! Ye don't go calling the police!" Fuller pulled himself free with furious energy, and they heard the clump of his wooden leg as he stumped off in the darkness. "I'll do without the drink. I'll see ye both in hell, and all yer kind, before I'll be beholden to ye. Ye mean well, Mr. Ellery, but ye're quality and I'm against everything ye stand for. The upper class'll go down someday and I won't be able to do anything for you then, just as you can't do anything for me now. That's the way it is and I wouldn't have it any different. My day's coming, and make no mistake about that."

They heard the thump of his leg diminish in the distance.

"He's as mad as a coot," said Wilson. "I'm afraid there's nothing you can do now for the poor devil."

"I'm going to try," declared Frank. "Tomorrow I'll have my staff comb the city for him. We'll find him. I'm sure he can be brought around."

"It's my belief that if you do find him it will be at the bottom of the river."

They stood for several moments in silence. "It's a curious coincidence, Sir Robert," said Frank, "but this is the second ghost from the past that I've met today."

Apsley House was imposing in a rather grim and heavy way. With all its trophies, it looked much more like a museum than a private home. The small study to which they were shown was quite different, however. It was a bare and soldierly room, with a few chairs and a desk and very little else.

"Ha, Wilson, you rascal!" cried the Duke, getting up from his chair back of the desk. "I'm glad to see you. And you too, Mr. Ellery. I was very happy when Wilson said he would bring you. It's a long time since I've laid eyes on you, sir."

"Fifteen years, Your Grace. It was at a ball you gave in Paris after Waterloo."

"Gad, as far back as that? I'm getting old, gentlemen." He shook hands vigorously with each of them in turn. "I realize it when I look at a pair of giddy young sprigginses like you. Sit down, sit down. We'll have in a bottle of wine."

The Duke was right; he was growing old. His head was rimed with a silver thatch and his shoulders showed a tendency to stoop. But time was dealing leniently with him, nevertheless. He looked completely content. His blue eye, which had been once as clear and as cold as ice, had become as mild as a schoolboy's. His high-pitched laugh, which burst out at any provocation, came straight from a heart and mind at peace with the world. He was still very much the dandy: a purple waistcoat and a glossy black stock, a well-tailored coat and black trousers strapped down over trim shoes; no change at all in that respect from the Beau of peninsular days.

"And now, gentlemen," said the victor of Waterloo, settling back happily into his chair, "we'll talk of the old days. The good old days, when we fought our battles with muskets and swords and not with long speeches and silly motions and amendments. What a pity we haven't Boney here himself, sitting over there between you. Ha, it would be interesting to hear what *he* had to say about things."

The talk flowed on for an hour. Frank took small part, for this was soldier's talk and the views of a civilian could carry no weight. Wilson's spirits had soared again to their usual high pitch and he kept himself abreast of Wellington's conversational canter, agreeing at times but disputing many points with an energy that set the great man back on his haunches. The Duke argued and spluttered, sometimes glowering darkly, sometimes throwing his head back and neighing in delighted reminiscence.

At one point the Duke's eyes took on again the frosty light that men who had served under him would never forget. "Wilson, you disobeyed orders," he said. "It worked out well but I should have sent you packing, there and then. I thought of doing it, by Gad!"

"Well," said Wilson, falling suddenly into a quieter mood, "they did send me packing finally."

"Ha, so they did. I think you deserved it, Wilson. What a damned, go-it-your-own-way, troublesome dog you've always been! You were a thorn in the flesh to the Horse Guards, just as you are today to His Majesty's Government."

"I always do what I think should be done. And I always say what I think should be said."

"There have been plenty of times when I wanted you shoved behind bars and kept there." The Duke's eyes began to twinkle. "But in spite of everything, you were a damned fine soldier, Riding Bobby. I always knew it. And now I'm beginning to have a downright liking for you, you rascal."

"Time works miracles, Your Grace," said Wilson with a smile.

"Sometimes," said Wellington, who had become completely mild and benevolent again. "And sometimes the hand of Time must be given a jog. I've been saying to myself, 'Something's got to be done about Wilson.' I get an uneasy feeling whenever I think of you being fobbed off into a mean little parliamentary corner. You shouldn't be in the House, damme; you're no more of a politician than I am. You should be back in the army where you belong. And so I decided to do the jogging myself." He reached down and drew a paper from a drawer of the desk. "You've been reinstated, Sir Robert. Here's the order. You're to be gazetted as lieutenant general, and you deserve it, by Gad. His Majesty was happy to confirm it this afternoon."

Wilson took the paper with a hand that trembled in spite of his efforts to remain calm.

"Lieutenant general!" he said. "That's a step up, Your Grace."

"A bit of back pay goes with it. You can find a use for it, no doubt."

Wilson's head was still bent over the paper. "Yes, I can find a use for it. I—I've been a little hard up, as a matter of fact." After a moment he added, "I wish Jemima had lived long enough to see this. She would have been very happy."

Wellington cleared his throat and turned to Frank. "I'm glad you're here, Mr. Ellery. It gives me a chance to express before a third party my admiration and respect for Sir Robert Wilson and the pleasure I feel in seeing him brought back into the service. I grant you it should have been done long ago. We've been forgetful of the remarkable things he did for the country. But—better late than never, eh?"

"I can't find words to thank you," said Wilson. He was blinking his eyes to keep back the tears. "This is one of the happiest moments of my life. I've always been at odds with authority but I've never had any other desire than to serve my country the best way I could."

"I don't know what post we'll have for you, General Wilson." The Duke looked over at Frank with an air that said he still had something up his sleeve. "Have you anything in mind yourself?"

"No. But I might be more useful in a post where I'm not likely to come head on with those above me."

"Exactly. A spot where you can do things your own way more or less. I'm in favor of that. I don't want these armchair fellows pestering me with notes that General Wilson is doing this or General Wilson won't do that. Much better to have a bit of water between you and our masterly exponents of peacetime strategy. Much better. What would you say to Gibraltar?"

"Gibraltar!" Wilson sat up with a startled air. "The prize plum, Your Grace. I won't expect that."

"I promise it shall be yours. A nice spot for an old campaigner with a bit of steel still in his hide. Not too exacting in times of peace. But important, damned important." The Duke exploded into one of his laughs. "You'll have to promise not to let the monkeys die out. There's a belief, you know, that we'll lose the Rock when there's no more of them. Perhaps from the top you may be able to see the ghosts of your green-coated rascals riding the Andalusian plains."

"Yes," said Wilson slowly, "I think it likely that I would."

The Duke coughed with an air of embarrassment. "Now there's another matter. Your orders." He swept a huge blotter from the top of the desk. "Here they are, every damned one of them. They had no right to take them from you. Typical foreign impertinence. I said so at the time. It's been on my mind ever since to do something about it. Well, I took it on myself to write each government that the time had come to make amends. They've all come back. Here, put 'em on."

Wilson got to his feet and walked to the desk like a man in a dream. He looked over the glittering array of jeweled orders spread out there. He touched one of them with an unsteady hand.

"They were wrong about these trinkets," said the Duke gruffly, "and I told 'em so in no uncertain terms. I'm afraid I was a bit on the acid side with them." He turned to Frank with a chuckle. "He's a vain dog, this young friend of ours. 'Pon my word, I think he would rather have these bits of ribbon than be appointed Master of Ordnance."

Wilson proceeded to pin the orders on the front of his coat. They made a striking display: the gold-bordered cross of the Russian St. George with its orange and black ribbon, which he had received from the hands of the Tsar himself on the battlefield of Bautzen; the red medallion and white *fesse* of the Austrian order of Maria Theresa; the Red Eagle of Prussia with its motto *Sincere et Constanter*; the ornate cross and wreath of the Portuguese Tower and Sword on its rich blue background of ribbon; the glittering gold sun of the Turkish Crescent; the Russian Order of St. Anne and the Moscow Medal. He stood up very straight and saluted.

"Lieutenant General Wilson reporting, sir," he said.

Wellington chuckled again. "Didn't I say he was a vain dog? Ha,

Sir Robert, you did me a shrewd turn twenty years ago. I haven't forgotten your stand at Ciudad Rodrigo and what it meant. We're not quits yet, but perhaps I've balanced the scales a little. Sit down, my boy, and we'll have a bite of supper before I toddle off to bed."

When a footman began to lay out a frugal meal of cold mutton and toast, the Duke was reminded of something else. He said to Frank, "And I have some news for you, Mr. Ellery."

Frank's mind went back at once to his talk with Gabrielle that morning. The honor list! Could it be . . . ?

"That brother of yours. A reliable man; you always know where he is, what you can depend on him to do. The birthday list will be out in a few days and he's due for a very great honor. An earldom, in fact."

Frank's hopes had risen for a moment only, because he knew it was too much to expect that anything would be done for him. But he had not been prepared for this. Caradoc an earl! For a moment he thought the Duke was joking. What had Carr done to merit such a monumental reward? It verged on the absurd, allowing even for the way things happened in the world of politics. Yes, they always knew where he was, what he could be depended on to do; but was that enough? He knew at once that it had been influence which had done it, the powerful forces which can be massed behind a move for individual preferment.

He met Wilson's eyes and for several moments they stared somberly at each other. He could read the silent message his friend was trying to convey to him. You must not take this hard, Wilson's eyes were saying; you have played your part, an unselfish and important part, without any thought of recognition or reward; let the rewards go to those who seek them and who don't care what the price may be.

The serious look on Wilson's face turned into a smile, an affectionate and understanding smile. Frank's spell of resentment gradually died away. He found that he was able to smile back.

Wilson was beginning to laugh. Well, why not? This was the kind of wry jest that had sent the ancient gods into peals of ironic laughter. Caradoc an earl! There was something comic about it, and it was worth a laugh even though it was an indictment of a political system. Good for Carr; he had won what he had set out so determinedly to achieve. He, Frank, had memories more precious than any title: his campaign for the freedom of the press and its climax in the pillory; the part he had played in the great bluff at the Yeltes; his silent participation in the operations of Wilson and Company. What was much more important, he had what he really wanted in life—Gabrielle, his fine young son, important work still to do in rousing the country to the need for change, a warm circle of friends, Gravely. Let Caradoc have his empty title!

He found himself laughing with Wilson. Once started, they could not stop. They laughed until tears came into their eyes. Their enjoyment of the jest grew until it equaled in volume the homeric mirth which, if the annals of mythology are to be believed, had so often echoed down the slopes of Mt. Olympus.

The Iron Duke had been buttering a slice of toast. He looked up and grumbled, "What are you two blasted young idiots laughing at?"